THE SWORD AND THE DRAGON

THE WARDSTONE TRILOGY BOOK ONE

(Hardcover Edition)

M.R. Mathias

ISBN: 978-1-946187-08-6

2016 Modernized Format Edition
Created in the United States of America
Worldwide Rights

I'd like to thank Kristi, who took the time to ferret out what all of us missed in the earlier versions. And a special thanks to Tim at Dominion Editorial for polishing it off.

Jack Hoyle is responsible for these amazing 2016 Modernized Edition covers
Find him at www.t-rexstudios.com

Thank you JT, for the formatting help. It was timely.

If you enjoy this read, please tell a friend or write a review. Enjoy, M.R. Mathias

This is for my mother and father.

To hear about new releases, sales and giveaways, follow M. R. Mathias here:
www.mrmathias.com or @DahgMahn on Facebook, Twitter, and Instagram

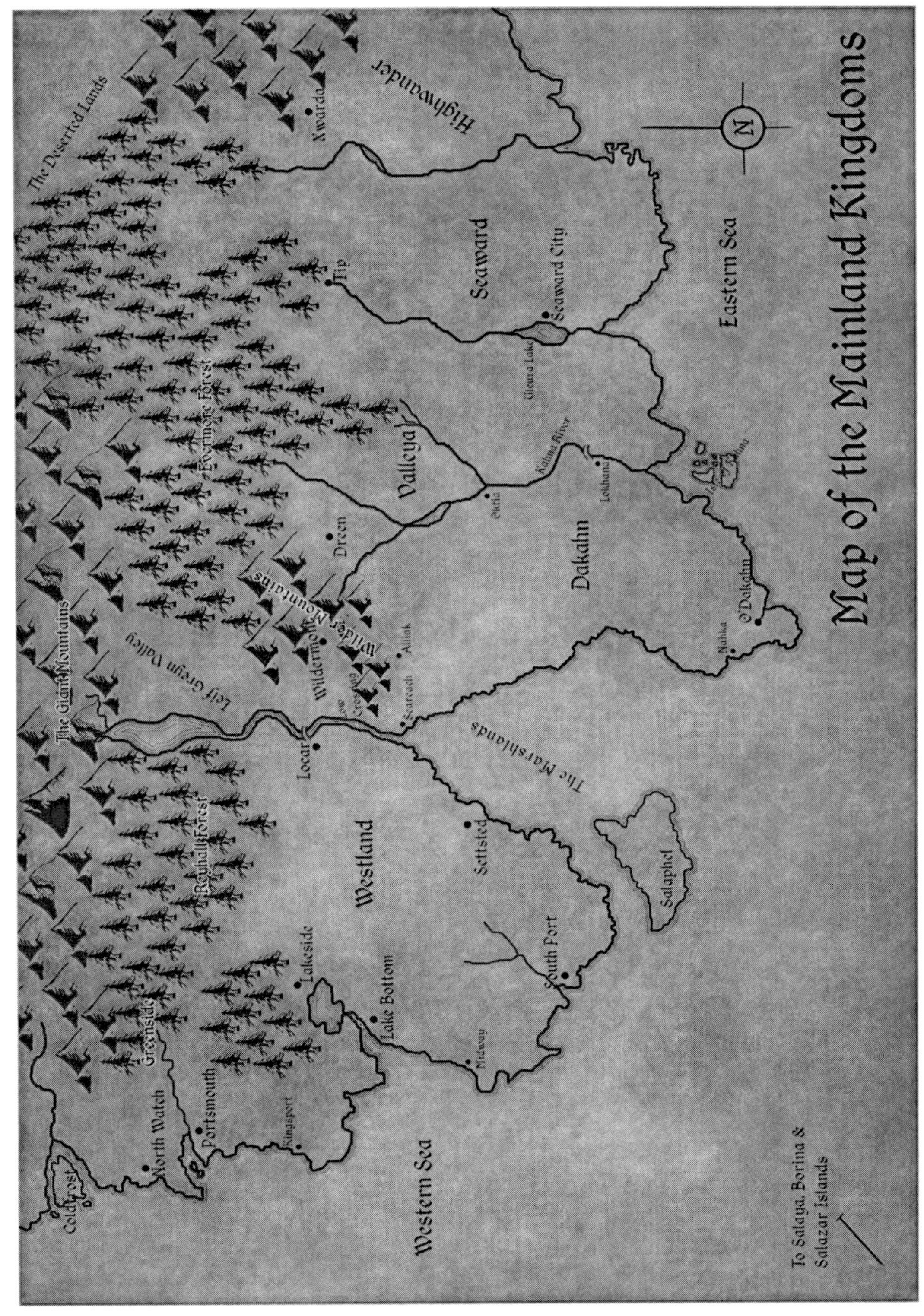
Map of the Mainland Kingdoms
N
The Deserted Lands
Highwander
Xwarda
Tip
Seaward
Seaward City
Eastern Sea
Evermore Forest
Valleya
Dreen
Dakahn
O'Dakahn
Nahka
Wilder Mountains
Leif Greyn Valley
The Giant Mountains
Locar
The Marshlands
Westland
Settsted
Salaphel
South Port
Midway
Lake Bottom
Lakeside
Greenside
Portsmouth
North Watch
Kingsport
Coldfrost
Western Sea
To Salaya, Borina &
Salazar Islands

THE SWORD AND THE DRAGON

Chapter One

Gerard Skyler used his free arm to wipe the sweat from his brow before it had a chance to drip into his eyes. Scaling the towering, nesting cliff for the second time was far harder than he expected it to be. No one had attempted the climb two days in a row before. His body was still sore and raw from yesterday's climb, but he could not afford to stop and rest. He was more than three hundred feet above a rocky canyon floor. A fall would undoubtedly be fatal. The last thing he needed at the moment was burning eyes and blurred vision.

A few dozen feet above him was the wide, flat shelf they called the Lip. Once he was there he could lie down, stretch out his aching body, and relax his muscles before continuing into the nesting shelves to gather the precious hawkling eggs he sought.

Why the blasted birds nested so high on the cliff, and so late in the spring, he could never determine. All of the other avian species he knew had hatched their young and headed north already. Why he was foolishly climbing the cliff a second time was another question he kept asking himself. He already knew the answer though. He was doing it for his older brother, Hyden.

Gerard's free hand reached up and slid snugly into a small gap above him. As he pulled his weight up, the hold suddenly crumbled. Dust and scree rained down on his upturned face. Luckily, his mouth was closed and he hadn't moved his feet from their points of purchase yet. He didn't slip, but he had to contend with his racing heart and the sandy grit that was collecting on his face.

"Damn it all, Hyden! You owe me a dozen pairs of boots now," he muttered.

He shook his head, trying to face downward so that some of the crud might fall away. Then he stuck out his bottom lip and blew up at his eyes, shaking his head awkwardly. The thought of how silly he looked at that moment almost made him laugh. He fought to contain it.

Having mixed with his sweat, most of the grainy dirt had turned to mud. He finally used the thumb and index finger of his free hand to rub his eyelids. Eventually, he cleared his vision and then reached up for a different handhold. This one held his weight.

Far below, Hyden Skyler paced the canyon floor, looking up nervously at his younger brother's progress. He was supposed to be the one making this climb. Gerard had already made his own. Their father and uncles decided that Hyden should stay on the ground this year. He was the Skyler clan's best hope to win the coveted Summer's Day archery competition, their best hope to come along in a generation.

Hyden had argued vehemently against not being allowed to claim a rightful share of the hawkling eggs. His Uncle Condlin had to physically restrain him when they told him this year's climb wasn't going to happen. Hyden had called them all to the settling circle in his anger, even the Elders.

"Why can't I do both?" he'd argued.

The Elders explained that it was because the archery competition and the egg harvest this year were too close together. Not even the most experienced climber could finish his grueling harvest without a tear or strain. The Elders, who consisted of Hyden's grandfather, his father, and five of his uncles, wanted nothing to happen to him that might affect his ability to aim. Nothing.

Like most young men who feel like they've been wronged, Hyden had been caught up in the moment. The Elders' arguments made sense to him now that the heat of his frustration had cooled, but it had taken a while. Only after long hours of soothing and explaining did he finally relent. The fact that the prize money from the archery competition was equal to the value of more than a dozen hawkling eggs helped him put things in perspective. The idea of having his name etched permanently into the Summer's Day Spire had its own appeal. Eventually, he decided to comply with the Elders' wishes and stay on the ground. If he managed to win the competition, the honor and respect he would gain, not only in his clan, but also among the men of the kingdoms, would far exceed the satisfaction of making his egg harvest.

At one hundred paces, Hyden could put three out of five arrows in the Wizard's Eye. The other two arrows would be in the King's Ring, only because the center of the target wasn't big enough to hold them all. Only on rare occasions did an arrow from Hyden's bow venture out into the Queen's Circle, but it did so only because the wind was blowing, or for some other extreme reason. Even on the windiest of days, his arrows strayed no further away from the middle than that. He was as accurate as a target would allow a human to be. To put four arrows in the Wizard's Eye was nearly impossible. The elven archers who had won the competition for the last four years running had done it, though. If Hyden wanted to win this year, he would have to do it, too.

Hyden's stubborn arguing over being kept on the ground had paid off in a sense. He contested that the financial loss of not being allowed to harvest his rightful share of hawkling eggs would be ruinous to his home and family. He pointed out that the Elders could give him no guarantee that he would win the archery competition. He was only eighteen winters old, with no family of his own yet, but he would have one soon enough, and it was the principle of the matter. By clan law, a large portion of the money generated by the sale of the harvested hawkling eggs went to the individual who harvested them. None of the Elders could deny Hyden, but then Gerard suddenly volunteered to climb in his stead. The Elders reminded the younger of the two headstrong young men that a second climb would be very dangerous, not to mention that all the credit and the yield of the harvest itself, would be Hyden's, not his. The Elders were pleased, though, that Hyden would still be receiving his due without having to climb.

Hyden had never felt a stronger bond with Gerard, nor had he ever felt more love for him. When he saw his little brother finally gain the edge of the Lip, he couldn't help but breathe a sigh of relief. He had never felt this much worry, or concern, over Gerard's safety in his life. Usually, he was trying to kill him for some reason or another.

Little Condlin, or maybe Ryal, helped Gerard up onto the ledge. Hyden couldn't tell which of his many cousins was up there. They all looked the same from where he was standing, with their sun-darkened skin, their thin frames, and the thick mop of dark hair all of the clansmen shared.

Hyden had been out behind Uncle Condlin's hut shooting arrows all week while the other members of the Skyler clan took their turns on the sacred nesting cliff. He wasn't sure which of his cousins had made their climbs yet. All he knew was that Gerard came down yesterday from his harvest with eight unbroken eggs. From what Hyden heard, it was the best single take so far this year. Gerard strutted around with his chest puffed out the whole evening. Uncle Condlin brought down only seven eggs this year. Hyden and Gerard's father, Harrap, would have had seven as well, but an angry hawkling caused Harrap to drop one in order to protect his eyes from its razor-sharp talons.

It was a shameful thing to waste an egg, even when protecting oneself. Their father hadn't been seen since he'd packed his six remaining eggs in a small crate full of keep moss two days ago. He had gone off into the woods seeking absolution. The eggs would be safe until he eventually returned. The keep moss, as the name indicated, would keep the hawkling eggs from hatching for as long as they were packed in it.

Gerard and Hyden knew that their father was off in seclusion somewhere, seeking forgiveness from the clan's goddess. He hoped that the White Lady would give his father a sign soon. Hyden had done the same thing last year, after one of his eggs broke in his pack while he was climbing down.

The hawkling eggs were sacred to the clan and very expensive to the kingdom folk who purchased them each year at the Summer's Day Festival. The location of the nesting cliff was known only to the Skylers, and though they could have made a king's fortune by harvesting all the eggs at once, they didn't. Each clansman able to climb the cliff was allowed one opportunity each year to make his harvest, but only if he spent his share of the days in the off-season attending to the roosts and vacant nesting areas. Loose rock, old nests, and other harmful things such as scorpions and blood ravens, were removed or frightened away so the hawklings would have a safe place to breed and hatch their young each spring.

During the harvest, it was forbidden to leave fewer than two eggs in a nest, so much of the climbing a man did—sometimes his whole harvest—was fruitless. The hawklings were fierce hunters, and their wingspan from tip to tip could be as wide as a man is tall. Sometimes, an angry bird would attack and maim, or even dislodge, a climber. Many a member of the Skyler clan met their death on the rocky canyon floor.

Hyden didn't expect much from Gerard. The lower nests would all be down to two eggs by now, and the climb took such a toll on a man's body that Hyden didn't think Gerard could push himself into the higher reaches today. Two or three eggs would suffice. He told Gerard as much this morning when they broke camp. Hyden would wait until all the other eggs sold, and then would drive up his price. The money from two eggs would sustain him through the winter. Three would provide him not only what he needed, but also what he wanted.

"I'll get you half a dozen at least," Gerard bragged. "You'll win that competition, too. When you do, you owe me a new pair of Valleyan horsehide boots and a wizard's hat."

Hyden laughed, thinking about his brother's simple desires. Gerard's immaturity still showed itself often. He was just a year younger than Hyden. At least the new boots were a reasonable and responsible request. Gerard could buy himself a wagon full of wizard's hats and a dozen pair of boots with what he would earn for his own eight eggs. After the Elders took out the clan's share, Gerard would still have a small fortune.

Hyden found a rock, sat in the shadow thrown by the midmorning sun, and munched on a piece of dried venison. Gerard would rest awhile on the Lip before continuing up into the nesting shelves. The cliff face would be warming quickly now. It would grow as hot as a skillet in the morning sun, but only for a short while. The sun would swiftly put the cliff in its memory and for the better part of the day, its face would be cooling in its own shadow.

Movement from above caught Hyden's eye. A long, green ribbon on a crooked stick poked into the air from the edge of the Lip. There wasn't enough wind to make it do more than flutter lazily. It disappeared as quickly as it had shown itself, and then one of his cousins began the long climb up to make his harvest. Hyden could tell by the bright green color of the climber's headdress that it was one of Uncle Condlin's sons. He knew that Gerard's headdress was red with blue highlights. That was the only headdress he cared to see.

The bright, ornamental hats were worn more to deter the fierce birds than for any other reason, yet each branch of the clan had its own colors and designs. Hyden's was made of light wire and shaped like an open-winged bird, with red and gold ribbons tied about the frame. Gerard's was similar, but with red and blue ribbons fastened to it. The headdresses made it appear that a brightly colored bird was already on the climber's head. They were a distraction at best, and they usually ended up on the canyon floor long before the climber came down. Hyden hated wearing one, especially when the wind was up. He usually threw his off after a while, but one time, an angry hawkling had torn it off his head for him and nearly caused him to fall to his death.

It was rumored his Great Uncle Jachen's fatal fall was caused solely by complications with his headdress, but it was still considered an ill omen to start up from the Lip without one. Two of Hyden's cousins attempted to climb after the wind had blown theirs off the ledge a few years ago. Both boys perished that day, thus reinforcing the ancient superstition.

It wasn't long before Hyden saw his own red and gold headdress starting up the cliff. It made him smile. Gerard must have taken it from his pack earlier at the camp. Hyden didn't expect Gerard to wear his headdress. He was proud that his little brother was honoring him by wearing it for this climb. His heart swelled with emotion, and he decided on the spot that he would buy Gerard a wizard's hat, a wizard's robe, and a magic wand at the fair, even if he didn't win the archery competition. It didn't even bother him when Gerard later let the awkward headgear fall away and tumble down the canyon.

It became clear that the cousin making the climb ahead of Gerard was Little Condlin. Little Con was chubby, slow and deliberate in his moves. He climbed more sideways than upward, as if he was trying to cover the entire width of the cliff. He never extended his reach and he always used caution. Gerard, on the other hand, was quick like a lizard and, before long, he was a few hundred feet above the Lip.

The cliff itself was well over a thousand feet high. It looked to Hyden like Gerard was trying to climb to the very top of it. As far as Hyden knew, that had never been done before. An area not too far above Gerard's current location was so thick with the nesting birds that the gray and brown stone seemed to be striped black with them. It was obvious now Gerard had been completely serious when he'd bragged he would bring back half a dozen eggs. Hyden hoped his brother wouldn't put himself in a bad spot up there while trying to show off for him. At the moment, Gerard was as high up into the nests as Hyden had ever been in his life.

Gerard could see something glinting and shining. It was a few dozen feet to his right, a little below him, and sitting in an old, broken nest on the other side of a wide, vertical fissure. He couldn't tell what it was, but it was metallic and golden. For some reason, there were no hawklings screeching at him or making sweeps at his intrusion in this area. He wasn't paying attention to the hawklings' activities any more, though. Whatever that thing was in the nest, it was commanding his attention and causing him to lose concentration on his climb. He already had five eggs for Hyden nestled in his padded shoulder bag. He was determined to have the sixth he boasted of, but he knew five would please his brother immensely. He also knew he needed to start back down soon so as not to be caught on the wall after sunset. Climbing down in the dark was impossible, but that blasted shiny thing was fiercely calling out to his curiosity.

His mind filled with visions of jeweled riches and praise from his clansmen and Elders. He had to reach it. He wouldn't be climbing here again until late summer, or just before winter set in.

It might not be there then. If he didn't get it now, he might not be able to find it again, even if it stayed exactly where it was.

He cleared his head by shaking it, then tried to spot a way to surpass the open gap between him and the prize. If he just climbed a few dozen feet higher, he could reach across a narrow place in the fissure, and then he could climb back down to the thing. It was risky, but he told himself he could do it.

As he started up toward the niche, the sun passed over the ridge and sent the whole of the cliff face into shadow. It took him longer than he thought it would, but he finally reached the place where he could stretch across the span of open space. He positioned himself on a tiny ledge, and when he leaned into the cliff, he could stand with all his weight on his feet, leaving both of his hands free.

His palms were wet and slimy from the numerous patches of excrement he'd encountered in this higher, more heavily nested area. He shook his arms at his sides, letting the blood flow back into them while waiting for the muck to dry. A warning began to sound in the back of his mind, telling him he should already be headed back down, but he chose to ignore it. He gathered another egg on the way up to the niche, so he now had the full half-dozen he'd promised Hyden. All he needed to do now was reach the little treasure beckoning him. Once he had it, he could start down.

After a few moments, he rubbed his hands on his hips briskly. The crusting stuff on them powdered and fell away. He then took turns scuffing the toes of his old boots on the ledge until they gripped with ample traction. He found a good handhold with his left hand not too far above him and stretched his body out to the right, reaching across the gap as far as he could. He was still at least two feet shy. He harrumphed in frustration and pulled his body weight back over the little ledge.

He repositioned himself so his handhold was lower. This would allow him to reach farther. He tried again but found his right foot was still some inches away from a safe purchase on the other side. As he started to retract himself this time, his left foothold slipped a fraction. His heart fluttered up through his chest like a startled bird. He almost fell, but instinct and common sense took control. After a few deep, calming breaths, he gingerly eased his weight back over.

He would have to give up the prize and make his way down. It was the only sensible thing to do. If he started to hurry down now, he could still reach the canyon floor by nightfall. Hyden would be happy to take the six eggs and the Elders, along with the rest of the clan members, would praise his efforts and his skill as a climber.

A quick glance back over at the object caused him to change his mind. He was here, and he didn't want to waste the chance the Goddess had granted him. He would retrieve it, whatever it was.

Gerard squinted. In the shaded light, the object finally revealed itself to him. It was a ring. Golden and shiny, it had a fat, yellow gem mounted on it, and it looked extremely valuable. He rolled his neck across his shoulders. It would be his, he decided. He could reach it and still get down before dark. If not, he could even sleep on the Lip if need be.

He looked at the other side of the fissure and studied it intently. He took in the subtleties, the nooks, the crannies, and the shape of the stone. Then he sucked in a deep breath, resolved himself, and leapt for it.

Hyden paced nervously. His cousin was almost back down to the Lip, but Gerard was still way up in the heart of the nesting shelves. To Hyden, he seemed to be frozen in place next to a wide vertical split in the rock. As it was, Hyden figured Gerard would have to sleep on the Lip this night. Hyden wasn't sure his brother could even climb that far back down by nightfall. He was about to pull his hair out with worry.

"It's my fault," he told himself aloud. He knew no one had ever made it down the cliff face in the dark, and it looked as if Gerard was running out of time. "I should've never let you climb for me. Damn the bravado, Gerard! Just get yourself down before it's too late."

Hyden stopped pacing and stared up anxiously as his brother stretched across the gap for the second time. He thought his heart stopped beating in his chest, until he saw his brother shudder and slip. Then his heart exploded like a pounding skin drum.

"Oh Gerard, don't fall," Hyden pleaded to no one that could hear him. "Take a breath and steady yourself. That's it! Now quit fooling around and get down here before the darkness takes you!"

Hyden's neck muscles were raw and sore from looking up all day, but he couldn't look away. Gerard seemed to have regained his composure, and Hyden assumed he was about to start back down. A few seconds later, when Gerard leapt into the open air, across the fissure from one side of it to the other, Hyden was certain his heart really exploded. So violent was the thunderclap that went blasting through his chest that even he felt the strange and horrifying sensation of falling.

Chapter Two

Of the two brothers, Gerard had the better landing. His lead foot stuck perfectly into the crevice he intended, and his fingers grabbed true in a little crack on the far side of the fissure. He paused only a moment to catch his breath, as if he hadn't just jumped across a gap of empty space more than seven hundred feet off the ground. Almost casually, he looked down at the little gleaming prize and started after it. It was his.

Hyden didn't fare as well. He had been looking up at Gerard while pacing. At the same moment his brother had leapt, Hyden's feet had found a shin-high boulder and his momentum sent him sprawling. He was so transfixed by Gerard's leap that he didn't even look down as he fell. It was probably for the best, because he didn't have to see the pile of jagged rocks into which his head slammed. When he next opened his eyes, it was almost completely dark outside. Blood leaked from the gash in the side of his head and formed a matted clot in his long, black hair. He wasn't quite sure where he was or what was happening.

"Hyden?" a familiar voice asked sheepishly. "I thought you'd never come around."

Through his pain, Hyden's world came back to him. It was Little Condlin who spoke. His fingers found the split lump over his ear, and a sharp pain shot through him when he touched it. As he caught his breath, Gerard's leap flashed through his mind.

"Gerard!" he croaked in a panic while trying to climb back to his feet. "Where is Ger—?"

"He's nearly down from the Lip," Little Condlin said, not understanding Hyden's worry. He hadn't seen Gerard risk his life like a fool jumping from hold to hold. He took Hyden by the arm and helped him to his feet.

Hyden winced as the world swam back into focus. It took him a few minutes but eventually he steadied himself. In the near darkness, he found the boulder he had eaten lunch on and sat down.

"Gerard's really almost down?" he asked.

"Aye," Little Condlin grinned. "He's as good a climber as you are, maybe even better." He tried to suppress his adolescent mirth, but it was impossible. "What befell you down here?" With that, he burst into laughter.

Hyden snarled menacingly at the fourteen year-old boy's wit. It was enough to make Little Condlin's glee vanish instantly. The boy quickly averted his attention to a dark pile of rocks at his feet.

A few moments passed in silence, but Hyden finally spoke.

"How was your harvest?" he asked.

Little Condlin's eyes lit up. He was bursting to tell someone of his good fortune this year. "Five eggs, Hyden!" He held an excited hand up, all his fingers extended and wiggling. "Five!"

"Great!" Hyden said, a little more flatly than he intended. He was glad for Condlin, but he was still a little bitter at being cheated out of his own climb. Last year, Little Con harvested one egg. This was his second year of harvest and five eggs was an excellent yield for a more experienced climber, much less a novice.

"I did just as father told me to do," Little Condlin rambled excitedly. "I didn't try to go high like Gerard does. I went way out to the sides."

"I saw you," Hyden said with a nod of respect.

Hyden only retrieved three eggs before nearly falling over the edge of the Lip during his second harvest. The memory made him think about Gerard again. It was almost full dark now. He stood up and started toward the base of the cliff to look for his brother.

"What happened to your face, Hyden?" Little Condlin asked. Even though he was at a safe distance, he made sure that his voice carried nothing less than concern in its inflection.

"I was attacked by big, hairy scufflers," Hyden deadpanned. His expression didn't hold though and, thinking about his earlier folly, he broke into a sarcastic grin. "What do you think happened?"

Little Condlin took on a frustrated expression and sighed heavily. He was the fourth of five brothers, so he knew where he stood in the pecking order with Hyden and his other cousins. He had hoped his successful harvest would have gained him a little more respect, Hyden knew. Gauging the distance between him and his older, faster cousin, Little Condlin gathered his courage and prepared to run away.

"I think you fell down and busted your fat head."

"Aye," Hyden laughed at the boy's well-placed caution. "I did. I was looking up, watching Gerard act like a fool, and I wasn't watching where my feet were leading me." He made a silly face, and his cousin relaxed a little bit.

"Well I have to say, you look quite a bit better than you did before. That bloody knot brings out your eyes."

Hyden burst out laughing at the boy's boldness. He started to say something about it, but was cut off by a welcome voice.

"What's so blasted funny, Hyden?" Gerard said from the darkness, near where the cliff face met the canyon floor.

Hyden felt the wave of relief wash over him. It was followed immediately by a flood of anger. "What's not funny is what you did up there today! You could've gotten yourse—"

His voice stopped cold and Little Condlin gasped loudly. Gerard thrust the ring out of the darkness at them. Even in the starlight, its amber gemstone captured enough illumination to sparkle brightly. It almost appeared as if it were glowing.

"Where did you find that?" Little Condlin asked with a voice full of awe.

"In your sister's pantaloons," Gerard replied sarcastically. He looked sore, tired, and raw in several places. He was clearly in no mood for silly questions. He looked at Hyden, in an obvious attempt to judge his brother's anger. "It was high up in an old broken nest by a fissure. The one I jumped across," he said in a way that let Hyden know he knew the risk he had taken and didn't want to hear any more about it. After a moment, he reluctantly handed the ring to his older brother.

Hyden looked at him oddly. It took him a minute to grasp the meaning of the gesture. Gerard had been climbing for him, not for himself. He was offering him the ring. Hyden refused it with a nod.

"You wanted it bad enough to risk your life for it. It's yours. You earned it."

Gerard cocked his head and studied Hyden some more. Hyden truly did want him to have the ring. Gerard took it back and a broad grin spread across his weary face.

"If you refuse these, I'm going to kick you where it counts." Gerard took off his pack and thrust it out to Hyden proudly. "Half a dozen, just like I promised."

Hyden passed the pack to their cousin and grabbed up Gerard in a big bear hug. Gerard hugged him back. While his hands were close together behind Hyden's back, Gerard slipped the ring onto his finger. After a moment, Hyden held him back by the shoulders and looked him dead in the eyes.

"Don't scare me like that again." He pointed to the gash on his knotted head. "You almost killed me."

It was too dark even to think about starting back to the harvest lodges. They ended up building a fire where Hyden and Gerard camped the night before. The three of them exchanged stories and had a great laugh at the fact that Hyden was the only one who hadn't left the ground, but was the only one who fell.

While Little Con boiled some dried beef into a stew, Hyden inspected the eggs his brother brought him. He was pleased beyond words at what he saw. All six of them were safe, sound, and nestled in a bed of fresh keep moss. He made up his mind to buy Gerard a whole wizard's costume—the robe, the hat, and even a staff, if that was what he wanted. He didn't think it would be, though. Gerard seemed to have matured a great deal since just that morning. The sparkle of the ring in the firelight and the tired, serious look on his face made him look anything but youthful. Hyden saw a man where only this morning, he'd seen a boy. It was a strange sight to see because most of the time he didn't even consider himself an adult yet.

"Wendlin, Jeryn, and Tylen are the only ones left to harvest now," Little Con informed them. "They're camped at the other end of the canyon. They probably think I fell since I didn't come back to camp tonight."

"If they thought you fell, they would be out looking for your carcass," Hyden said matter-of-factly.

"Or dancing a jig," Gerard added with a laugh.

"They probably saw you come down," Hyden reasoned. "Same as I did."

"How could you have seen him, knot-head?" Gerard smirked, "You were busy kissing rocks."

They all laughed heartily at that. Little Condlin dished the stew into Hyden's and Gerard's bowls, then waited for one of them to finish. His bowl was back at his brothers' camp. Hyden ate a healthy meal while Gerard and Little Condlin were busy climbing, so he slurped a few mouthfuls, then passed his bowl to his young cousin. Gerard, on the other hand, attacked his meal like a starving dog.

"Are you going back to the lodges with us in the morning or what?" Hyden asked.

"Back to Tylen's camp," Condlin answered. "Wendlin and Jeryn climb early in the morning. Tylen goes last since he is the oldest in the clan who's not on the council." Little Condlin always spoke of his brothers proudly, but when he spoke of his oldest brother Tylen, his chest swelled bigger than usual. "Tylen's gonna break my pap's record this year."

Hyden knew in his heart that Gerard could have brought back a dozen eggs today if he hadn't been sidetracked at that fissure by the ring. A climb that high up into the thick of the nesting band was rare. Gerard went higher than anyone Hyden had ever seen. The weather had been exceptional and the hawklings themselves were far less aggressive than most years, but he still wasn't sure if even he could have climbed as well as his brother today. He would have never risked that leap, that's for sure. Another thing he knew for certain was Tylen could climb like a lizard, too. If tomorrow was as perfect a day as today had been, then Tylen really might have a chance to break Big Condlin's record. Hyden kept his thoughts to himself though, because Little Condlin's chest and head were already swollen enough.

As soon as he finished eating, Gerard lay back and went to sleep. Little Condlin wasn't far behind him. Hyden took the time after he ate to clean the dried blood from his head. He covered

Condlin with his blanket and lay down close to the fire. It had been a long and eventful day, and sleep found him quickly.

The next morning, Little Condlin was anything but quiet as he gathered up his things in the predawn light. He woke up Hyden and Gerard with eyes full of excitement and pride. With a mouth full of chatter he wasted no time leaving. He was off to his brothers' camp in the hopes of catching them before they started their climbs.

Gerard wanted to throw a rock at him for waking them for no real reason, but he couldn't find one that wouldn't crack his head in half if it hit him.

The day started with much moaning and groaning from both brothers. Hyden said his head hurt badly. It was not so much the actual wound that bothered him, he explained, but a deep, inner ache that felt like a hot rock was loose inside his skull. Every little move he made caused the rock to roll around and scald another part of his brain.

Gerard was no better off. Like burning wires cutting through his muscles, his pain spread throughout his shoulders, back and legs. His movements took great effort and came with audible strain, but he didn't dare voice a complaint. He didn't want to hear Hyden razz him for whining.

Hyden managed to boil some water over the fire. At least Little Condlin built the blaze up before he left. Hyden added chicory root and some gum leaf to the pot and the warm, thick smell of the brew brought Gerard to the fire with his cup in hand. The dark, flavorful liquid put a little energy into their bodies and helped leech out some of the aches and pains. After a few cups, they felt well enough to break camp and start back to the harvest lodges.

While Hyden doused the fire, Gerard was waiting to go. Hyden went to grab the shoulder pack that held the eggs his brother harvested for him, but stopped suddenly. He heard a sound coming from inside the bag.

"Oh no!" he said, thinking that one of the eggs had broken.

"Are they all right?" Gerard asked with concern. He watched Hyden's face from where he stood, trying to gauge his brother's reaction to what he saw as he peered into the bag. He expected to see either relief or anguish spread across Hyden's face, but what he saw was a strange, somewhat confused look. The odd expression slowly morphed into a wide-eyed grin full of wonder and amazement. The curiosity to know what Hyden was looking at overwhelmed Gerard, and he hurried over to his brother's side to see for himself.

Hyden reached into the bag carefully. His cupped hand came out with a squeaking little hawkling chick in it. As Gerard knelt down beside him, Hyden worked a piece of jerked venison from his pack with his free hand. He tore a piece off with his teeth and chewed it vigorously.

"Do you think it's the prophesy bird?" Gerard asked, with a look from the bird to his brother and back. "Or was it just bad keep moss?"

"I—mmm—don't—mmm—know?" Hyden answered as he chewed. Once the venison was softened, he spat a wad of the chewed-up meat into his hand. He dangled the meat over the little gray chick's snapping beak and it gobbled the stuff up greedily. Immediately, it started squawking for more. Hyden bit off another piece of the meat, chewed it up, and fed it to the hungry bird. With Gerard's help, he made a makeshift nest out of his rough-spun shirt. Once the little chick was nestled in, it immediately fell asleep.

By all rights, it was Hyden's egg that hatched, but it was Gerard who harvested it. Hyden turned to his brother with a serious look on his face.

"You brought it down from the cliff, but it hatched after you gave it to me. I don't know if it could be the legend or not, but if it is, who is the chosen one? Me or you?"

"The Elders will know," Gerard said, trying to remember the exact words of the prophetic campfire story. He realized after a moment that it was no use. He had heard the story told a dozen different ways.

The most common version of the legend stated that one day a clansman's harvest would be blessed by the Goddess in the form of a special egg. Even keep moss wouldn't keep this supposedly blessed egg from hatching. The lucky clansman and his hawkling were supposed to bond and go off into the world to do extraordinary things together. They would have adventures far beyond imagining. They would travel beyond the mountains and across the seas, and their lives would be exciting. They would serve the Goddess abroad and possibly earn a place in the heavens at her side.

After Hyden shouldered the pack with the five remaining eggs in it, he carefully picked up the shirt nest with both hands. Gerard led the way out of the canyon and, as they skirted the forest, he took extra care to make sure no branches or footfalls hindered his brother's way. The trail wasn't long, but it was rocky in places and awkward. It was meant to remain hidden, so it took them a while to make the short journey to the harvest lodges.

They made it to the small group of crude huts by midmorning. They tried to make it to their grandfather's hut with as little notice as possible, but it was impossible. Tales of Gerard's leap from the day before had made it back to the lodges already, told by clansmen who watched the cliff face from afar. A handful of younger boys rushed forth to question Gerard about it. Because the clan women weren't allowed at the harvest, the boys who weren't yet old enough to climb were starved for attention and ran wild like a pack of scavengers. They wanted to know how well Gerard's second harvest went, and if Gerard and Hyden knew how well Little Condlin had done. Gerard shooed them away as best he could, but a few of them spied the hawkling chick in Hyden's hands and grew overly excited. It took only moments for the tale of the gift the Goddess had bestowed upon Gerard, or maybe Hyden, to reach every set of ears at the lodges.

Having just heard the news from a group of his grandnephews, Hyden and Gerard's grandfather received them well. He quickly ushered them through the door to his shabby little hut. He gave an angry scowl to the line of boys that followed, which sent them scurrying every direction but forward. With that, he pulled the elk skin door closed and tied it fast.

"On the table, boy," Grandfather said, with an excited grin on his wrinkled, old face.

Hyden set the bundle down gently on the table, while Gerard found their grandfather's food box and pulled out some bread and cheese as if he owned the place. In council and in public, this man was the Eldest of the clan. All of the Skylers treated him with the utmost respect, but here inside his harvest hut, just like in his home, he was simply the grandfather of two excited boys.

He leaned over the table and studied the chick for a moment, then he brushed the long, silver-streaked hair out of his face and sat down. He motioned for the boys to do the same, indicating Gerard could bring the bread and cheese with him.

"This is a wondrous thing," he said in his deep, scratchy voice. "Great things will come of this." He looked to Gerard, then to Hyden, and the smile on his face slowly faded. "But there is the potential for terrible things as well."

Gerard handed Hyden some bread and cut them both some of the cheese as he spoke.

"The story says a man will harvest an egg and it will hatch for him. Then, he and the hawkling will go off and do great things together."

"Aye, Gerard," their grandfather agreed. "That the story does say."

He stood slowly, then walked to the other side of the little hut and began rummaging through a pile of old furs and leather satchels.

"The story though, is just that. It's a story. The true legend is written in the old language—the language of dragons and wizards. It may or may not be a true prophesy. The Elders and I have often argued that."

He stopped speaking suddenly as if something came to him. He dug around some more, then pulled an object out of an old bag made from the skin of some shaggy mountain animal.

"Here it is!" he exclaimed. "My father's translation." He opened the tattered volume and looked at the pages for a while.

A few long moments passed, so long that it began to appear he forgot the two boys sitting at his table.

Hyden looked at his brother with a grin. He was about to clear his throat to politely remind the old man of their presence, but the hawkling chick did the job for him.

The little featherless bird wiggled his body and rose trembling to its tiny, clawed feet. It extended its neck up into the air, opened its beak, and began screeching for food. Gerard immediately pulled some jerky from his pack and gave it to his older brother. Hyden chewed it up just like before. Once the meat was soft, he gave it to the bird.

"Is this the first time you've fed it?" their grandfather asked with a look of childish excitement on his old face. He seemed to have forgotten his book entirely now, and he watched with rapt attention as Hyden took out another piece of chewed meat and fed it to the hungry bird.

"Mmm—no," Hyden answered as he chewed. "I fed it—mmm—once this—mmm—morn."

"Then it will be your familiar," the old man said matter-of-factly. It was the voice of the clan Eldest speaking now, not their grandfather. "It will bond with you alone now, Hyden. You're its mother."

All eyes seemed to fall on Gerard at that moment, searching for some sign of disappointment or other ill reaction to the decision. Gerard wasn't very upset. He had the ring, after all. Besides, he told himself, what respectable clansman wanted to be a mother?

"I and the Elders who are here at harvest will hold a council on this at moonrise," their grandfather informed them as he opened up the old book again. "Stay near the lodges this night. We will want to speak to you about this. Both of you," he added before Gerard could ask the question that was already formed on the tip of his tongue.

Walking with his face in the old book, the Eldest gracefully shouldered his way through the elk skin door and was gone.

Chapter Three

"Where ye headed, Mik?" Ruddy, the nightshift stable master at Lakeside Castle's Royal Stables, asked.

"Can't say," Mikahl replied. Mikahl was the King of Westland's personal squire, and the king had told him with much distress in his voice to prepare for a long journey, and to do so quietly. Mikahl was almost certain that by quietly, the king meant undetected. Mikahl asked if he should prepare the king's mount as well, and the answer was firm. "You'll be going alone, Mik, and the journey will be a long one. No one can suspect you're leaving."

The conversation took place a short while ago when Mikahl and the king were alone, just after the feast for the Summer's Day delegation. The oddness of it was just now starting to sink in. "Just be ready, Mik," King Balton told him. "I'll try to send for you and give you more instruction later this night."

All of this was very cryptic to Mikahl. King Balton, the ruler of all of Westland, seemed afraid. The way he'd cleared the entire dining hall and whispered into Mikahl's ear with wild, darting eyes, was unnerving. To top it off, the king sent Mikahl out through the back of the kitchens so the bulk of the nobility and the castle's staff would not see him depart. King Balton had never acted like this before, at least not around Mikahl. It was all very strange and Mikahl was beginning to worry about the king's health. The man was fairly old, no one could doubt, but this was different. Maybe he'd reached the end of his rope?

"Bah!" Mikahl chided himself for thinking such thoughts. King Balton was a great man; fair and wise beyond measure. He had been terribly kind to Mikahl, and his mother, before she died. There had to be something wrong. The sudden journey must be extremely important for it to be so secret and cause the king such distress.

Mikahl looked at the nosy stable master, thought about it for a second, then pulled a small but fancy silver flask out of his saddlebag.

"They never tell me where I'm going or why," Mikahl lied, "but it doesn't matter at the moment because I've been itching to try this. I filled it from the royal cask at dinner."

"King Balton's own brandy?" Ruddy asked eagerly.

"The very same." Mikahl took a sip and passed it to the man. "Missy, the servant girl, held the table's attention by leaning over and wiggling her arse while I filled my tin."

Mikahl pretended to sip and let the stable master slowly finish off the flask. His story worked like a charm. The size of Missy's breasts was well known to every man on the castle staff. They were so large that even the priests couldn't keep their eyes off them. In truth, Mikahl drank from the king's cask often. Doing so was just one of the many benefits that came with his job as King's Squire.

There wasn't enough liquor in the flask to put Ruddy down, but it was enough to dull his wits. With thoughts of Missy's giant breasts swirling around in his head, his mind wouldn't dwell on Mikahl and his business. At least Mikahl hoped not.

Just as Mikahl finished loading his packhorse, a man peeked through the stable doors. After wrinkling his nose at the fresh, horsey smell, he told Mikahl that King Balton required his presence again, immediately.

As Mikahl followed the scurrying servant through the castle's myriad of torch-lit hallways, it became clear they weren't going to the council chamber, or the throne room, or even back to the dining hall. The ancient castle was a monstrosity of towers, hallways, apartments, and gardens, all added one on top of the other. Mikahl was born in the servants' wing almost twenty years ago. He spent his entire youth running the castle's halls and corridors, but he still hadn't managed to see it all. The fourth flight of stairs they climbed told him exactly where they were going, though. They were going to the king's personal bed chamber. Mikahl had visited the Royal Apartment only once since becoming the king's squire.

As they topped the stairs and turned from the landing to face the Royal Apartment's large oak double doors, Lord Alvin Gregory came out. He was extremely pale and the look of sadness on his face sent a chill through Mikahl's blood.

Lord Gregory was the king's good friend and most trusted adviser. He was also the current Lord of Lake Bottom Stronghold and was known across the entire realm as the Lion Lord, or Lord Lion. This was because he fought with great courage, pride, and skill. He was the epitome of bravery and a famous Summer's Day brawling champion, but he looked nothing like that fierce and brave champion at the moment. His normally bright green eyes were haunted and his expression was dark and grave.

Mikahl was Lord Gregory's squire for three years prior to becoming the king's squire. Lord Gregory taught him the proper etiquette, customs, and everything else he needed to know to serve at King Balton's side. The days Mikahl spent at Lake Bottom learning from the Lion Lord were days he cherished deeply. The man was his mentor and his friend, and he could plainly tell something horrible was afoot.

Lord Gregory walked up to Mikahl and touched him on the cheek. He looked at the young squire long and hard, then forced a smile. He gave Mikahl a nod that seemed to be full of equal parts respect and regret, then vanished down the stairwell without a word. Mikahl watched the empty air at the top of the landing long after Lord Lion disappeared. The next thing he knew, the servant was pulling him by the sleeve toward the king's chambers.

The apartment was hot and silent. A dozen candles and a dim flickering lantern barely illuminated the beautifully furnished room. Mikahl expected to see the king sitting in one of his high-backed chairs or on one of the plush divans, but he was in his bed under piles of thick covers.

"Ah, Mikahl," the king said weakly. A tired smile spread across his slick, gray face. Mikahl almost didn't recognize this man as his king. Balton Collum looked so near to death that it made Mikahl's head spin.

A sharp glance from the king sent the servants and the black-robed priest who was attending him quickly out the door. As soon as they were alone, King Balton motioned for Mikahl to come sit at the edge of the bed.

"We haven't time to parley, Mik," the old man rasped. "The poison has almost run its course."

"Poison?" Mikahl was aghast. Who would do such a thing? The king was loved and respected by all. Mikahl was shocked speechless as he slid off the edge of the bed and knelt before the man who was the closest thing to a father he had ever known. He wondered how long the King knew he was poisoned? King Balton seemed a little too accepting of the situation. Was that what all the secrecy was about? Was he dying? The look in King Balton's eyes said so, but to Mikahl it didn't make any sense.

"Go to the temple by the north road gate," King Balton whispered. "Father Petri has something for you to take with you on your journey. Take what he gives you deep into the Giant Mountains. A giant named Borg will find you and lead you to his king."

As if saying all of that had leeched the life from the poisoned old man, his head lolled to the side. For a long while all that moved were his eyeballs and his heaving chest.

Mikahl wiped a stray tear from his cheek.

"Borg?" he asked. Who in all the hells is Borg?

"—esss. He is the Southern Guardian," the dying king rasped almost inaudibly. "Go deep into the Giant Mountains, Mik. He will find you and lead you. Deliver Father Petri's package to the King of the Giants."

Unable to comprehend anything other than the fact his king was dying before his eyes, Mikahl ran to the door and ushered in the priest and the servants who were attending him before.

He stood there, watching in horror. One of the servants helped King Balton drink from a cup while the priest said a prayer that Mikahl remembered all too well from his mother's funeral a few years past.

Suddenly, the king's arm shot up and he pointed directly at the door. Wide, white eyes full of authority and love locked onto Mikahl's. The king was ordering him to go. After wiping the tears from his face, he went and did his best not to look back. It was the hardest thing he had ever done.

Ruddy, the Stable Master, mumbled something angrily at Mikahl as he reentered the stalls. The man was busy readying two other horses for departure. One was already saddled and the other was waiting patiently for the half-drunken stableman. It was far too late for a jaunt through the woods. Mikahl recognized one of the horses as belonging to Lord Brach and that made him worry.

Lord Brach, the lord of Westland's northern territories, was Prince Glendar's constant companion. Lord Brach and that creepy, bald-headed wizard, Pael, never seemed to leave the side of the heir to the Westland throne. Lord Boot-licker, King Balton had often called Brach in private because the man agreed to everything that Prince Glendar or the wizard suggested. Mikahl was far from a nobleman and he didn't meddle in the games they played, but he knew Prince Glendar was about to assume the throne now, and the rotten fool hadn't been in his father's favor for many years. Prince Glendar would gain the most from King Balton's death. In Mikahl's eyes, Prince Glendar, or one of his men, was most likely the murderer. Why else would they be preparing to ride at this time of the night?

Mikahl realized the very same thing would be said of his departure. As King Balton's personal squire, he had enough access to have easily slipped him some poison. He would be a suspect, but Lord Gregory and his wife, Lady Trella, would vouch for his integrity. Everyone close to King Balton knew Mikahl loved and respected his king dearly. The problem was that soon-to-be King Glendar didn't like Lord Gregory, nor did he know his own father's heart very well. If Glendar had a part in his own father's murder, then Mikahl could easily end up being the scapegoat. It didn't matter at the moment, though. His king had given him orders from the deathbed. He would find this giant named Borg and deliver Father Petri's package to the King of the Giants, or he would die trying to do so.

Mikahl didn't want Lord Brach or his men following him. He had to find a way to slow them down. He walked over to where Ruddy was working and tapped the unsuspecting man on the shoulder. As the Stable Master turned, Mikahl slugged him heavily across the jaw. Ruddy fell into a heap on the stable's dirty floor. Mikahl then led the two other horses to the running pen behind the stable. He sent them galloping off into the darkness with a sharp slap on their rumps.

Wasting no time in preparing for his own departure, he mounted his horse, Windfoot, and led his packhorse out the unattended gate that opened onto the cobbled streets of the inner city. He did exactly as King Balton instructed him to do and went straight to the chapel.

Father Petri was expecting him. The priest seemed both sad and nervous as he led Mikahl and both of his horses up the entry steps and into the chapel.

The chapel's vaulted ceiling was high overhead and row after row of empty wooden pews spread out to each side. Sitting on a horse whose clomping hoof beats echoed loudly and deeply into the huge, and otherwise empty chamber, Mikahl felt very out of place. As they made their way down the center aisle toward the altar, the gods and goddesses all seemed to be scowling at him from their permanent places in the colored glass along the higher reaches of the walls. One of the horses whinnied nervously and the ghastly sound sent a chill snaking up Mikahl's back.

"Come, Mikahl," the priest said. He took the reins of the packhorse from Mikahl and led them out of the worship hall, down a long corridor, through several arched doorways, then into a large, nearly empty room at the back of the church. Mikahl had never seen this room before and it shocked him. It was not the sort of room he would have ever expected to find in a hall of worship. One entire wall was a huge, steel-banded door that resembled a gate. Two of the other three walls were covered with pegs. Hanging from the pegs were hundreds of weapons: swords, crossbows, long bows, and pikes as well as shields, helmets, and miscellaneous pieces of chain and plate armor.

"It's a secret way out of the castle for the king in the event of a siege." Father Petri answered the question in Mikahl's mind. "You follow the briar path to the right, along the wall, until you come to the discharge drains. Then follow the smelly stream away from the castle until you are well into the Northwood. Stay away from the city. People are about in Castleview even in the late hours. If you have to, stay in the woods until you reach Crossington. Once you are that far north, you should be safe to go wherever the king has told you to go."

Mikahl hoped to gain some insight from Father Petri as to whom Borg was and where exactly he was supposed to go, but the priest's last statement indicated he was unaware of Mikahl's destination. Mikahl had at least a dozen questions he wanted to ask, but he held his tongue. He did ask the one question that couldn't wait.

"King Balton said you had something for me. What?" This was all too much for Mikahl to understand, so he tried not to think about it. He knew what he had been told to do. It wasn't his place to question it.

Father Petri gave a short nod, reached into his robes, and produced an ornate leather scroll case.

"This is the message for you to deliver." He bent down, lifting something heavy from the floor, and offered it up to Mikahl. It was a long, black leather sleeve, such as might be used to protect a prized longbow or an expensive two-piece staff. Mikahl carefully secured the scroll case in his saddlebag and took the item.

He knew what it was the moment he felt the weight of it in his hands. The consequences of having it came flooding into his brain and he almost dropped it in fear. He had to search deeply in his heart for courage. It was Ironspike, King Balton's notorious sword. He knew because he had polished it a thousand times as part of his duty as the king's squire. He had seen firsthand the wealth of gold and jewels inlaid into the leather-wrapped hilt and cross guard. He had seen the covetous looks of those who longed to possess it, and he had seen the fear it could inspire. He had watched the magical blade glow red hot as it clipped Lord Clyle's insolent head from his shoulders, and he remembered vividly seeing King Balton dispatch at least a dozen of the feral half-Breed giants with it during the Battle of Coldfrost. Its actual weight was slight compared to his old iron sword, but holding it now made Mikahl want to crumble.

"You are not to use it, unless it is to preserve your life, or to maintain possession of the blade." The priest softened his serious look. "But always remember your life is more important than the sword."

Mikahl looked at the priest with furrowed brows. This was the deadliest of burdens for him to carry and he knew it.

"To use it would attract men to me like carrion to a carcass," he said. "How am I to—?"

"We!" Father Petri snapped, raising a hand to halt Mikahl's protests. His voice was harsh and the man looked distressed to say the least.

"We do not have to understand the tasks we are given, Squire."

The use of Mikahl's meager title, and the reference it implied as to the origin of his orders, permeated the priest's words.

"We have to do as we are told, Mikahl, and do it the best we can."

Mikahl swallowed hard. He felt the need to be on his way. Prince Glendar, soon-to-be King Glendar, would most likely want Ironspike immediately. Once the sword was found to be missing, Glendar's cronies and his wizard, Pael, would be after it. Mikahl could see it now: a dozen lords and all of their men would be hunting him, a huge price on his head; bounty men and trackers, coming from all reaches of the realm to try to claim the reward King Glendar would surely offer. Suddenly, the Giant Mountains seemed like the safest place for him to be and, with each passing moment, he found more and more reasons to reach them quickly.

After a brief goodbye, Father Petri cranked open the great door and Mikahl eased out into the night. A glance up at Lakeside Castle put a twist in Mikahl's guts and a lump in his throat. He had lived there most of his life. His mother had been a kitchen hand, and he himself had been in the service of the kingdom in one way or another since he could walk. At first, he had been a message runner and a candle-snuffer. Then, he was a stable hand, and even a scribe's aide for a while. As he grew older, he began training with the soldiers and had excelled with his skills on the weapons yard to the point of notice. Lord Gregory took him on as a squire, and he spent almost three years down at Lake Bottom Stronghold learning the proper ways to behave while in the service of royalty. Other than the not so distant traveling he'd done with the king as his squire, he had never been away from this place. Now, he was leaving his home, and he doubted he would ever be able to return.

Because his mother died, he didn't have any real family here, but both King Balton and Lord Gregory had become father figures to him. He had never known who his real father was, but he had never really been without guidance until now. Now he was alone.

Knowing his possession of Ironspike was a secret known only to a dying king and his loyal priest, Mikahl realized he would soon be branded a thief of the highest order, or worse, a murderer. Ruddy would tell everyone about Mikahl's late night preparations. Being the king's squire meant he would have had full access to the king's private armory. Not only would he be blamed for poisoning the king, he would most likely be blamed for taking the sword as well. These things were forgotten, though, as he looked back at his home. He was on a journey to meet a giant he didn't know, with an entire kingdom soon to be on his tail. He couldn't imagine being any more alone than he felt at that moment. He took a deep breath and sighed at the sheer enormity of it all.

The castle no longer looked inviting or homey. Its looming, massive gray bulk, with the half-dozen squat towers and the few taller, narrower spires, suddenly seemed like a dark upthrust of teeth. Would he ever be able to come back? He took a few minutes to say goodbye silently to his mother and wiped the tears from his cheeks. King Balton's voice came to him gently and reassuringly. "Think, then act," it said in his mind. It was one of the king's favorite sayings. When indecision halted the progress of a situation or things came to an impasse, he would say, "Think, then act."

Think, then act. Mikahl repeated the mantra to himself.

Reluctantly, he spurred Windfoot away from the stinking discharge stream and went deeper into the Northwood. He rode like that for a while, until he was sure Castleview, the city that grew from the base of Lakeside Castle's outer wall, was far behind him. It was dark and he was surrounded by the thick of the forest, but he thought he knew exactly where he was. Now all he had to do was figure out a way to reach his destination without being caught.

The distant sound of horses' hooves pounding on a hard-packed road caused a nearby owl to burst into flight. Mikahl froze, trying to discern over the pounding of his heart just how close to him those hoof beats were. He realized he was very close—far too close—to the Northroad. He was relieved to hear the rider was racing toward the castle, not away from it. It was probably just a messenger from Portsmouth or Crossington; nothing out of the ordinary.

Mikahl had a choice to make. He could chance the road, make time, and risk being seen, or he could continue through the Northwood and arrive at the Midway Passage road somewhere beyond Crossington. One way he would be able to enter the Reyhall Forest without being seen, but the other way would take him there a full day sooner. He didn't want to be seen in Crossington. It was a fairly large town, but the people were always alert to late night travelers. Many a bandit roamed those roads, searching for easy victims this time of year. The Summer's Day travelers were about and most of them were as careless as they came. If he went through the woods and bypassed the town, there was the chance Glendar, or more likely his wizard would have people looking for him on the Midway Passage before he even reached it.

"Think, then act!" The words sounded audible this time. Before he knew it, he spurred Windfoot toward the road. For the sake of the gods, you're the king's own squire and everybody knows it, he told himself. No one outside of the castle knew the king had been poisoned yet. If anyone tried to stop him, he could talk his way out of it. No one would doubt him. His saddle had the royal seal embroidered into it and Windfoot was a destrier of obvious castle stock. Once Windfoot and the packhorse were on the hard-packed road, he gradually worked both animals into a steady gallop. He doubted anyone would have the courage to question him.

He made the right choice. By dawn, Crossington was a few miles behind him and he didn't think a single soul had noticed his early morning passing. The cutoff road that connected the Northroad to the Midway Passage avoided going through Crossington proper, and it had been deserted. Only a light scattering of cottages and farmhouses were on the eastern side of the crossroads town anyway. The Midway Passage, however, was normally a heavily traveled cross-country trade route, but even so, the whole of the sun was completely in the sky before he saw another person. An old shepherd, who was obviously driving his sheep to the shear-house in town, urged his animals out of Mikahl's way with an apologetic wave. Once the man was out of sight, Mikahl decided to rest the horses.

He let them graze at the roadside while he enjoyed the cool freshness of the late spring morning. He had another choice to make soon, but he was too caught up in the peaceful morning to let it worry him. Over the course of the night, he decided he would take this one day at a time and try to enjoy what he could of it. Summer was ready to take over. Birds soared high overhead and the hum of various insects filled the air. He watched them as they buzzed back and forth between the colorful patches of wildflowers that dotted the gentle, southward rolling hills. Eventually the land in that direction flattened and became a patchwork of golden brown crop fields, but here, it served as grazing ground for the many herd animals on their way to market.

Ahead and to the north, like a great green fog hovering heavy on the surface of the land, was the Reyhall Forest. It extended from the road as far north as the eye could see. Behind Mikahl there was nothing but trouble, which kept him from looking that way. He knew that three days' ride beyond Crossington was the sea and the busy city of Portsmouth. Those places had to be behind him for good. He doubted he would ever see them again.

He rode as far as he could that day, but didn't quite reach the town of Halter. He knew it was for the best he didn't make it that far. The temptation to sleep at an inn and eat a warm meal was stronger than he imagined it would be. The whole last part of the day, he entertained thoughts of pushing on and doing just that. Good sense finally prevailed, however, and as the sun started to set he led the horses a good way into the Reyhall Forest and hobbled them near a patch of lush green grass. He decided against a fire. He had plenty of dried, salted meat, and two whole wheels of cheese. He brushed and watered the horses, then fed himself. Afterward, he leaned back against a tree and stared up through the branches at the star-filled sky. It wasn't long before exhaustion took hold of him and he fell into a deep and dreamless sleep.

Dawn's light had just breached the world and turned the sky a pink, peachy color, when the sound of an unfamiliar horse snorting and the rough, urgent whisper of a man awakened Mikahl with a start. When another nearby voice coldly asked, "Are we gonna kill him?" Mikahl knew he was in serious trouble.

Chapter Four

Normally when the council of Skyler Clan Elders met, there was a great feast accompanied by much festivity and ceremony, but not on this occasion. The women of the clan were four days away in the foothills of the Giant Mountains, at the clan's home village. There was no one here to decorate and prepare the elaborate meals usually served before such an event. The men didn't forego tradition completely, though. A group of boys were sent out to gather enough deadfall to build a bonfire, and another trio of older boys were sent out to hunt up some fresh meat. Others came to clear out the Eldest's hut, which would be used as the meeting hall. Hyden and Gerard were forced to move themselves and the hawkling to their father's smaller hut.

After they had gotten settled, Hyden fed the bird again, then he decided it needed a more permanent nest. He waited until the chick was sleeping, then went out and gathered some sticks and straw. In the bottom of an empty bucket, he built a new nest for the hawkling. Later, when the hawkling woke up, he transferred it from his shirt to its new home. The tiny thing chirped and squawked and hissed its distaste for the bucket. Hyden mistook this display for hunger and fed the chick until it couldn't eat anymore. Still, the hawkling protested. Only after Hyden tore up the shirt he'd first carried the bird in and put the pieces of it in with the little chick did it finally quiet down. By then it was mid-afternoon and Hyden's head was pounding. He cleaned his wounds again. Afterward, he laid down next to the bucket nest and fell fast asleep.

While Hyden built the new nest, Gerard safely packed away Hyden's five eggs with his own and their father's. When that was done, Gerard went to answer all the questions his cousins were dying to know the answers to. He was the center of attention, and he enjoyed it. They asked him about his daring leap and the extreme height of his climb, but mostly they asked about the hawkling chick and Hyden. Gerard tried not to let that bother him. He was sort of glad because he didn't want to tell anyone the real reason for the leap or the extended climb. He told no one about the ring. It was put away in his belt pouch. Something odd had happened earlier, and he was certain that the ring caused it. He hated to admit it to himself, but he was a little frightened over the matter.

His uncle, Pylen, asked him if he held any ill will toward Hyden since the egg had hatched for him. "Of course not," he replied. Unfortunately, the questions kept coming along those lines, and they made Gerard uncomfortable. Finally, while Uncle Pylen was in mid-question, Gerard screamed inside his head, "STOP IT UNCLE PYLEN! GO AWAY! LEAVE ME ALONE!"

The words weren't said aloud, but Pylen didn't finish the question he was asking. He simply stopped speaking, his eyes glazed over with confusion, then he just up and walked away. The ring heated on Gerard's finger and he was filled with a tingling rush of energy. The energy from the ring seemed to swirl up and wrap itself around Uncle Pylen like invisible smoke. Gerard felt it more than saw it, but there was no doubt it was there. The ring was magic and that scared him as much as it thrilled him.

For a long while, Gerard just stood there watching Uncle Pylen walk off as if they never spoke. Finally, he removed the ring and put it away. He did his best to forget the event, but he couldn't. He decided to tell Hyden what happened, but Hyden had fallen asleep. He ended up carrying on with the younger boys long enough that the event faded from his mind almost completely. Every now and then though, he could feel the heat of the ring tickle his finger, even though it was put away. It wasn't until later when he saw his father striding proudly across the lodge grounds that he was able to let go of the memory completely. He raced to his father's side with his chest swelled out, head held high, and a beaming smile stretched across his face.

"I got eight eggs, pap," he bragged, in a voice far higher in pitch than he intended. "And six, no, well, five for Hyden."

"I know, son," his father replied, with a smile as big as Gerard's. "I asked the White Lady to show me a sign when I'd been forgiven for my wastefulness." He stopped walking and spread his arms open wide to embrace his son. "And lo and behold, she gave me so much more than just a simple sign!"

He gave Gerard a squeeze and ruffled his hair as they started walking again. "I'm proud of you, son. You did well."

Gerard's step took on a new cockiness, and if it was possible, his chest swelled out even further than before.

"Where's Hyden?"

"Asleep in your hut," Gerard answered. "He tripped over some rocks yesterday and split his melon."

"Hmmm," his father sounded with a curious expression on his face. "I'd best go check on him."

"Aye," Gerard agreed with mock seriousness in his voice. "You really should. After all, he's a mother now!"

Gerard wasn't sure, but he thought he heard a grunt of laughter come from deep inside his father as he strode away.

Hyden was awake and feeding the squawking chick when his father entered the hut. His father took the oil lamp from the hook by the open entryway and carried it closer. He had to hold it high over the bucket to be able to see the chick in the bottom of it. He stood there a long while, studying the baby bird. Hyden glanced up with a grin on his face. His father returned the smile, only it was the smile of an Elder, not the smile of his father that Hyden saw.

"Much responsibility has been bestowed upon you son. Do not take it lightly. The rearing of this Godsend, and all the choices you make from this very moment, will determine whether your future will be terrible or grand."

Hyden wasn't sure exactly what it all meant, but he nodded as if he understood. He felt his father's demeanor change as he knelt beside him and peered into the bucket for a closer look. The seriousness of the Elder passed, and his father's pride and wonder began to show through again.

"It eats a lot," Hyden said excitedly. "I've already fed it more than I can remember."

"Its mother would be feeding it strips of fresh meat, bugs, mice, squirrels, rabbits and the like," his father informed him. "I don't think the dried salted meat is robust enough to fill its little belly."

It made sense. The jerky, Hyden mused, did little to fill him on the trail. It barely quelled his hunger pangs most of the time. He decided when the chick was asleep again, he would go find some fresh meat. Someone in the camp surely had some.

"The bucket was a clever idea," his father said. "The hawkling can't fall out and you can carry it easily enough without disturbing it."

He shifted his gaze to Hyden and waited until his son met his eyes.

"Is Gerard jealous? It was he who took the egg from the cliff, yes?"

"Aye. He took the egg in my stead, but he found a treasure of his own on the cliff. I think it's more to his liking than this little chick."

"Oh, he didn't mention it earlier when we spoke."

"He offered it to me, too, since he found it on my climb."

Hyden didn't say what it was. He felt he had already said too much. He didn't want to betray Gerard's trust. If Gerard wanted their father to know about the ring, then he would tell him himself.

"I could see that he wanted to keep it, so I refused it without offending him. I hope."

"Aye," came the grunted response. He must have heard the reluctance in his son's voice to speak on the matter, because he didn't press the issue.

"They will be putting the doe that Orvin and his brothers killed on the fire soon." He used Hyden's shoulder as a handhold to help himself get back to his feet and groaned with the effort. "You should try to get a big piece of the liver. It's lean and full of good stuff. Get either that or the loin. Cut thin little strips the size of earth worms."

"Aye," Hyden nodded, trying not to show that he had felt how much age was affecting his father these days. "Thank you for the advice."

"Has the wound on your head affected your aim? Have you been practicing?" his father asked as he returned the lantern to its hook by the doorway.

"I don't think it has," Hyden answered.

The truth was, he had forgotten the archery competition entirely. He was reminded suddenly of how important the upcoming event was to his father and the other Elders.

"I'll resume practice in the morn."

His father smiled and gave an approving nod.

"That is the first of many wise decisions I hope you make, son."

Hyden understood the desire the Elders of his Clan had to win the archery competition, at least in theory. The seriousness and vigor with which they pursued victory year after year, though, was beyond him. For generations, the Skyler Clan's hunters had been the greatest archers in the realm. The Elders spoke of those times often, but it had been before Hyden was born. The elves, who hadn't been heard from for almost a hundred years, returned to the Evermore Forest the same year Hyden was conceived. Where they disappeared to or why they came back, no one really knew. Since their return, though, they had dominated the Summer's Day archery competition. Even stranger was the fact that it was the only competition they ever entered.

The elves insisted, in their haughty way, that the title had always been theirs. They said the only reason the Skyler Clan ever won was because they were tending to a different forest, and hadn't been competing. The Eldest remembered it differently. He spoke of years long ago, when the Skyler Clan's hunters bested even the elven archers.

The Clan respected the elves as a people. In ancient times, they even fought together side by side with the giants and the kingdom men against evil. They just couldn't stand the fact that the elves hadn't been beaten in such a long time, that only a few of the Elders could remember a Skyler Clan victory.

It was said the annual contest had been around longer than the human race. From the time that man began to record history with parchment, quill, and ink, on the first day of Summer every year, in the sacred Leif Greyn Valley, under the shadow of the great, black monolith simply called the Spire, the people of the realm had come together in peace to celebrate the spirit of life and competition. There were sword fighting and jousting competitions, as well as the three stone throw and the great tree pull. Over the last few decades, the biggest event had become the Bare Fisted Brawl. The Brawl drew a crowd as big as any that had ever gathered. Like the elves though, the Skyler Clan had only one competitive interest: the archery competition.

Traders of all sorts came to the Summer's Day Festival and set up wagon stores or pavilion tents to sell and display their wares. Horses and cattle were judged and marketed. Storytellers, bards, and puppeteers, as well as fortune-tellers, magi, and charlatans ran rampant. It was a festive gathering, in a mostly wholesome atmosphere, and it was the highlight of the Skyler Clan's year.

Hyden knew he needed to do well. He was sure anything short of a win would disappoint his people. They had been trading at Summer's Day since the beginnings, since the time they say it all began. The Summer's Day Festival was where the harvested hawkling eggs were always sold, and where the goods and supplies the mountains didn't provide the Clan were purchased, but the archery tournament was all that really mattered. The event became the Elder's passion, and over the last few years, winning it had become an obsession.

The winners of each event each year not only won a small fortune in gold, they also had their name carved in the base of the spire for all to see. Hyden remembered standing at the base last year while his grandfather read the list of names. He pointed out the Clan members as he came to them. For quite a few years in a row, it was only his ancestors who won the archery competition, and his grandfather was one of them. Then, for the last eighteen years straight, there were only elven names; Vagion, Droitter, Pattoom, and Ghanderion, all of them strange sounding and hard to pronounce. Hyden wanted badly to win this year, not for himself, but for his people. He had to admit though, he wouldn't mind having his name etched and immortalized into the spire for all of eternity.

"Don't take all the liver!" an angry, youthful voice barked out at him.

Hyden was jolted from his trance by the words. He had been thinking about what it might be like if he could actually win this year.

"Sorry," he mumbled.

He was unintentionally hoarding the good meat of a kill that wasn't his own. With an apologetic grin, he took a few of the dark strips of liver meat he cut and added them to the bright red strips of loin in his hand. He then made his way back to his father's hut. Hyden's head was still hurting and he felt a little dizzy. He wondered if the daydream he slipped off into was brought about by his head wound. He felt odd. It was a feeling he couldn't quite describe even to himself. A moment later, he found himself staring down at the strips of meat in his hands. How had cutting so little of the stuff gotten his hands so bloody?

Gerard was waiting for him back at the hut. By the way his little brother was fidgeting and squirming in the chair, Hyden could tell something was amiss. He intentionally ignored Gerard for the moment and went about draping the strips of meat over the top edge of the bucket. The little bird woke with a screech, began stretching its neck and reaching up toward the meal. A recognition of instinct washed over Hyden, but he couldn't quite grasp how he understood the feeling. It was like a fond memory of a favorite food. Only this longing was for a taste he was sure he had never savored before. He wanted to eat the raw liver himself. Strange.

"Hyden!" Gerard half yelled, half whispered. "Come here, listen to me."

After making sure that the hawkling could get at all of the strips by itself, he took a seat at the table and gave Gerard his full attention.

Gerard told Hyden, with a voice full of equal parts excitement and fear, how he had sent Uncle Pylen off with the magical ring and a thought. He went on to tell him how the same sort of thing worked on their father only a moment ago by the cook fire. Gerard said their father had eased up to him and asked him if there was anything he wanted to talk about, and said that if there was, he would be willing to listen. Gerard had just mustered enough courage to put the ring back on, and after the incident with Pylen, he didn't want to talk to his father about it yet.

"I told him in my mind to go ask Sharoo the same question," Gerard said with huge eyes and waving hands. "He did! He just up and walked over to Sharoo and started talking to him. I felt the ring tingle through me, Hyden. I felt it make it happen. I swear it."

"Bah," Hyden was doubtful. He could usually tell when Gerard was lying or exaggerating, but strangely enough, his brother seemed to be telling the truth.

"I'll believe you if," he paused for a moment, thinking, and a devilish grin slowly crept across his face. "Come on. Prove it to me."

They both hurried outside. Hyden searched the groups of men and boys milling about for someone in particular. Gerard followed nervously, with one hand covering the ring. Hyden led them to the far side of the lodging grounds.

"There, over by the well," he pointed. "Do you see Tevar and his brother, Darry?"

"Yeah, I see them," Gerard answered, wondering what his brother was up to.

"Make Tevar go tell Sharoo what he did with Sharoo's sister the night before we left the village."

A wide grin spread across Gerard's face. This would be great.

"Call them over here."

Hyden did. When they were all standing close, Hyden struck up a conversation.

"So how was your harvest, Tevar? Darry?"

"I got four eggs," Tevar said proudly.

"Three for me. I could've had two more if I would've started earlier," Darry added.

"I heard you're going to be leaving us, since Gerard got you that hawkling chick," Tevar said. "Where are you going to go first?"

Hyden didn't register the significance of the question at first, and by the time he did, it was too late. When he made to ask Tevar what he meant, the boy was already heading toward the cook fire, blindly obeying Gerard's silent command.

"What's gotten into him?" Darry asked. "Hey, Tev, where are you going?"

"Leave him be," Gerard said through a yawn. He was suddenly very tired. "You got three eggs, huh? That's pretty good." Gerard put his arm around Darry's shoulder and suddenly slumped to his knees.

Just then, a commotion broke out at the big fire. There were shouts and gasps, then a primal battle cry. Several men burst out in laughter. Tevar then went racing past Hyden and Gerard with a terrified look on his young face. The older and much bigger Sharoo was right on his heels, brandishing a flaming chunk of wood as if it were a club. A few of Sharoo's brothers trotted along behind them, making a half-hearted show of trying to stop their enraged older brother.

Laughing, Hyden turned to tell his little brother he believed him about the ring now, but Gerard was curled up at Darry's feet, sound asleep and snoring. With Darry's help, Hyden got his brother back to their father's hut and into the bed.

After everyone partook of the fresh meat, the Council of Elders convened inside Hyden's grandfather's hut. Hyden was told to wait in his father's hut, and to be ready to bring himself and the hawkling chick before the council when called upon. He was also charged with taking care of Gerard. Thankfully, everyone attributed his brother's sudden slumber to the fact he had climbed the nesting cliff two days in a row. Hyden strengthened that idea by suggesting Gerard's exhaustion had finally caught up with him. He knew it was more than just fatigue that caused his brother to suddenly collapse, but he didn't let on to the others.

The giantess Berda, who frequented the clan's village in the mountains when her husband's herd of devil goats was grazing nearby, had told the people of the Skyler Clan many stories.

Hyden remembered one in which a wizard cast a spell on a horse to make it fly. The wizard needed to sleep for several days after casting the spell because magic took its toll on men. Berda told them that using the magic had sapped his strength. Hyden figured something similar happened with Gerard. At least he hoped so.

As Hyden waited, he watched the dying cook fire from the open doorway of his father's hut. The blaze had reduced itself to a pile of embers, visited occasionally by a flicker of flame that danced around fleetingly before it wisped away in a curling stream of smoke. He wished the Elders would hurry and call him. He also wished he had taken a lot more of the stag meat before it had gone on the spit. Already, the hawkling chick was up and squawking, begging for more food. As he fed it the last bit of uncooked meat, his father stepped through the doorway.

"The Elders would like to see the hawkling chick now," he said in his loving, fatherly tone. "We have decided we must consult the White Lady, through the dragon skull back at the gathering chamber before we can give you advice with any measure of confidence."

The aging man walked over to where his younger son lay asleep. He knelt beside him and ran his hand through the boy's hair.

"We all agree that yours and Gerard's destinies are intertwined in some strange way. I only hope it isn't in a bad way. We hope the White Lady will help us guide you true, but consulting her will have to wait until we are home, when the Summer's Day Festival and the archery competition are behind us."

Hyden wasn't sure how he knew it, but he was certain his father was correct. Gerard's strength and love had brought the hawkling chick to him. On the same token, Gerard wouldn't have been up there to find the ring he seemed to be so fond of if he hadn't climbed in Hyden's stead. A strange revelation suddenly unfolded in Hyden's mind, and he realized all the little events of now would someday come to influence greater ones. He had a feeling that some would be grand, and others terrible. It all seemed very strange to him. All he could do was what his father asked of him: try to make good decisions and do what he could to raise the hawkling, which at the moment was squawking loudly for more food.

In his grandfather's crowded hut, the Elders only had a moment to gawk in awe and wonder at the hungry little hawkling chick. Hyden kept the bucket in his hands protectively as he showed it around the room. A commotion from outside seemed to be intruding on the gathering, drawing everyone's attention away from the bird. Then someone outside gasped loudly. Another voice shouted out something that sounded urgent. A moment later, Little Condlin burst into the Eldest's hut. All eyes shot toward the sweat covered, wide eyed boy.

"Wendlin has fallen from the cliff!" He choked as the tears started to pour from his eyes. The room erupted with questions and concern, but the boy held his hand up to stall them.

"That's not all of it," he sobbed. "Jeryn is stuck above the Lip in the darkness."

Chapter Five

"It's just a boy," a rough male voice whispered. "It's easy pickings."

Mikahl cracked an eyelid and could just make out the booted ankle of a man standing a few feet from his head.

"He's got himself an ample load, Jerup," a different voice said from somewhere near the horses.

Mikahl could see by the poor condition of the boot that the man nearest him wasn't from the King's Guard. These were probably bandits. He silently cursed himself for not being more prepared. His sword was tied to Windfoot's saddle and his bow was still in its case on the pack horse's rig. He did have a utility dagger at his hip, but the way he was lying made getting to it without notice next to impossible.

"Waxed cheese, hard bread," the man by the horses called out quietly. "Ah, what's this? A silver flask. Bah! It's empty, but it's real silver."

Mikahl could tell it was the packhorse's saddle the man was pilfering. It wouldn't be long though till he found the king's sword. It was tied to Windfoot's saddle.

Think, then act, Mikahl recited the mantra in his head. He yawned and rolled over sleepily being careful to keep his eyes closed as he did so. He ended up in a near fetal position, with his head facing the horses and his hand on his hip next to his dagger.

"This one's a heavy sleeper, Donniel," Jerup, the man standing over Mikahl said. "Go on and take your time, see what else we got there."

"Must have emptied the flask `fore nodding off," Donniel said a little louder. The bandit apparently relaxed his guard, because he began grunting and chuckling as he continued rummaging through the pack saddle.

Mikahl hated giving his back to the man standing near him, but he had to make a move soon while he could still surprise them. One against two wasn't very good odds, but he found he wasn't afraid at all.

"A fancy longbow, Jerup," Donniel nearly shouted. "Worth its weight in gold I'd bet."

The sun was starting to give color to the world now, and in the new light Donniel eyed the golden lion emblem embroidered on Windfoot's saddle.

"He's the kings man, Jerup!" His voice was suddenly edged with fear. "We should just leave him be."

"Nah. We can just kill him," Jerup said coldly as he stepped one leg over Mikahl's body so that he was straddling him.

Mikahl saw that Jerup's boot was pointing toward Donniel and the packhorse's saddlebags. He chanced a peak up at the man, and the instant he saw that Jerup's attention was set on his partner, Mikahl attacked.

The utility dagger found Jerup's crotch and sank deeply into his inner thigh. Hot blood spurted when the blade came out, and Jerup crumbled on top of Mikahl. The crossbow Jerup had been carrying fell to the ground and the impact caused it to loose its bolt. In an explosion of bark, the razor sharp projectile ricocheted off of a tree and sliced right through Windfoot's tether. As if slapped on the rump by some unseen hand, the startled horse tore away from Donniel and headed at full speed into the deep woods.

"Oh...oh no! Donnie come and help me!" Jerup pleaded through clenched teeth. "Hurry before he gets—"

Mikahl's bloody dagger found Jerup's chin then. He quickly forced the man to roll off him, and Jerup howled as the sudden movement affected his wound.

Donniel looked to be at a loss. He had no idea what to do. He started toward Mikahl, but when Mikahl to his feet, he must have the golden lion on the breast of his tunic, for he froze, staring at it.

"Donnie!" Jerup's voice was weak and full of terror. "Come...c ome help me, man!"

Mikahl started towards Donniel, and Donniel started to untie the reins to the pack horse's bridle.

He wasn't fast enough.

With a hard overhand throw, Mikahl's dagger went spinning across the distance between them. It missed the bandit and buried itself in the tree limb where the leather lines were wrapped. With a yelp, Donniel started to run away, but he was suddenly yanked to a halt. To Mikahl's surprise, the dagger had pinned Donniel's sleeve to the tree. The man's panicked face was full of urgent fear as Mikahl closed in on him, but oddly, his expression calmed when they were finally face to face. He could see over Mikahl's shoulder that Jerup was now on his belly reloading the crossbow, with nothing less than dire determination on his steadily paling face.

"We...uh...I didn't do na...nothing t' you man!" Donniel stammered, trying to buy Jerup some time. "We...uh... didn't get away with anything. So...no harm, right?"

Mikahl untied the packhorse's reins with a blank, doubtful expression on his face. He didn't care about these two fools. He just wanted to find Windfoot and be on his way.

Jerup struggled to aim the crossbow, right at the base of Mikahl's skull. By the time he managed to pull the trigger, the blood-covered boy was turning to lead his packhorse off into the forest. The bolt he'd just fired wasn't wasted though; it found Donniel's neck. The bladed tip nicked both his windpipe and his jugular vein. For most of the morning, while Jerup tried desperately to stop the flow of blood from his inner thigh, Donniel's life leaked from his neck, in a gurgling, pleading hiss.

Windfoot's trail wasn't hard to see. The frightened steed had broken branches, trampled undergrowth, and knocked patches of bark from the trees as he fled. What made the trail hard to follow was that Mikahl had to search out the signs, with eyes brimming over with hot, salty tears. He was sad and afraid. His whole body shook at the thought of taking Jerup's life like he had. He knew beyond the shadow of a doubt his blade had found the fat, vital artery in the man's leg. There was no doubt that he would soon bleed to death. The fact he was a thieving bandit, and was about to kill him, did little to ease the empty feeling he felt inside. He had to stop more than once as terrible sobs racked his body. Only after he cleared his mind and took several deep breaths, could he think straight.

He was now as wanted as a man could be in the Kingdom of Westland. He reminded himself of this fact, over and over, when his emotions threatened to overwhelm him. It helped keep his dire situation in perspective, but didn't make him feel any better about what he had done. Taking a man's life was a monumental thing. Though he had witnessed more than one man's end, Mikahl had never had to kill anyone. He fought through the powerful emotions assailing him and found a way to continue on. He had no choice. Ironspike was strapped to Windfoot's saddle, and the horse was running scared. He had to find him, and quickly.

Mikahl's distraught condition kept him from noticing that the sun had crept high overhead. He was getting deeper than he would've ever intended into the forest. By the time he realized this, the morning had turned into afternoon. Now he would have to spend the night out here in the woods. Even if he found Windfoot soon, it would be dark before he could work his way back out to the road. He took another look around and found he wasn't sure he could even find his way out of the forest again, much less find the trade road.

He cleared his mind of the ill feelings about killing the bandit. The fear of being caught eased now that he had other things to worry about. King Balton's sword, as well as his own weapons, were secured to Windfoot's saddle. He had to catch up to the horse no matter what the cost. Windfoot's trail was leading generally northward, so Mikahl wasn't losing ground, but if the horse was allowed to wander throughout the night, there was no telling what sort of forest creature might get a hold of him. Rumors of dread wolves and saber cats had been spread for as long as he could remember, but he didn't recall ever seeing any such higher predators come out of the Reyhall Forest. There were things out here that would, and could, kill a horse, or a man for that matter. Of that there was no doubt.

"Think, then act," he told himself again.

Mikahl began trying to mimic the distinct whistle he often heard the stable man use to call the Royal Herd in from pasture. He felt a little better now. Knowing that none of Prince Glendar's men would be looking for him way out here in the middle of nowhere went far to that effect. He would find Windfoot and Ironspike and get himself up into the Giant Mountains, even if it killed him. He winced at the thought and bit back a laugh as the weight of it sank in.

After he whistled for the fourth time, he thought he heard the horse in the distance, snorting its disapproval at something. He quickened his pace and noticed the trees were thinning somewhat. The sound came again, and this time he was sure that it was Windfoot.

The forest eventually gave way to a sizable clearing. On the far side of it across the lush, green, flower-filled expanse, was a pond. Not too far from the water was Windfoot. His reins were tangled in a shrub. The poor horse wanted to drink desperately and was fighting the plant with all he had. It seemed to Mikahl the bush was winning. As he approached the disgruntled animal, he saw the king's blade still tied securely to the saddle, and a tidal wave of relief washed over him.

The packhorse whinnied and stomped. It was glad to see its companion again. Windfoot gave a frustrated snort of acknowledgement in return. Soon, Mikahl had them picketed side by side at the pond's edge, where they took to drinking and grazing contentedly.

The glade was full of life. Insects buzzed by busily and the birds sang, calling out to one another. Mikahl saw a rabbit tearing across the tree line as it fled some invisible predator, and by the variety and quantity of tracks pressed in the mud by the water's edge, he knew this was a popular watering hole. It was a beautiful and peaceful place, and Mikahl decided to rest here for a while.

He washed himself in the pond. He was sure that, save for the battles at Coldfrost, he had never seen so much blood in all his life. He was glad to see it all slide away from his clothes and skin. When he was done, he laid his things out to dry in the warm evening sun, then went about getting the dried blood out of his chain mail shirt with an oil cloth. When that task was done, he took his dagger and tore the fancy, embroidered Westland lion from his saddle. It was slow work. The emblem had been carefully sewn with tiny wire threads that had been painted with enamel. The saddle was a gift from King Balton on Mikahl's most recent birthday, and defacing it brought a tear to his eye. Since his tunic also bore the kingdom's lion insignia, he sank it in the pond. He simply tied a fist sized stone to it, and threw it out into the middle of the water. From now on, he would have to try to blend in with the common folk. Anything that connected him to the king or the kingdom would only draw the wrong sort of attention. He stood there a long while, watching the rings that the splashing bundle created in the pond grow larger.

Suddenly, he realized the forest had gone deathly quiet. He looked around, turning a slow circle, but he saw nothing out of the ordinary. He told himself it was only the sound his tunic had made when it splashed into the water, but he knew it wasn't true. Just to be safe, he pulled his damp britches back on and took his sword from Windfoot's saddle. After slipping the chain mail back over his head, he buckled his sword belt around his waist, and began quietly unpacking his longbow. He had just gotten the longbow strung when a loud crash of breaking branches and undergrowth came from out in the forest off to his right. The sound was huge and heavy, like a big tree being torn apart. Whatever caused it must have been enormous.

Mikahl's heart raced. He had heard tales of dragon's, trolls, and bloodthirsty flying swamp dactyls. He had listened to campfire stories about night stalkers, orcs, and giant snakes, but he had never seen any of them. He didn't have to remind himself that he was no longer in the Northwood outside of Lakeside Castle. This was the Reyhall Forest, where the monsters of all those campfire stories originated. What kind of creatures truly dwelt here, he had no idea, and even though the Royal Huntsman once told him all those monster stories were just tales told to keep curious young boys from wandering off, Mikahl found he was more than a little afraid. By the way Windfoot and the packhorse were snorting and stomping around him, he could tell they were afraid, too.

A flash of movement from across the pond caught his eye, but it was fleeting. Another massive crack of timber came from the right. The screeching calls of a thousand angry, unseated birds came with it. Whatever it was, it was getting closer. He took the reins of the horses and began leading them away from the pond, to the side of the clearing opposite the approaching noise. He tried not to look back, but couldn't help himself. The ruckus was becoming a constant, cracking, grinding crush accompanied by a strange hissing sound. He saw nothing at first, but then something happened that staggered him.

A single tree, one a little taller than the others around it, suddenly shook violently, sending loose leaves and birds scattering. It was back in the forest from the clearing, but only a short distance. Above the thrashing treetop, the halo of displaced birds flew in ragged, angry circles, each and every one of them sounding their displeasure. Mikahl couldn't even begin to imagine what could cause a tree to jolt and shake in such a sudden way. The tree shook again, and the ground might have shaken with it, but this time a long, slithery roar accompanied the violence.

Mikahl could look no longer. He and the horses were still in the open clearing. He wanted to get into the forest quickly, so he swung himself up into Windfoot's saddle and heeled his mount into a gallop. The frightened packhorse jumped the other direction, yanking the reins from Mikahl's hand. He would've chased the animal, but the closing sound of crashing trees and a great splash sent Windfoot tearing off into the woods on his own head. Mikahl was nearly flipped backward out of the saddle. Branches ripped at his chest and shoulders and tore at his face as he struggled to right himself. He was almost beheaded by a low hanging limb but somehow he managed to slow, then turn his terrified horse.

The pond's surface was churning. Ripples broke like knee high waves in several directions. Not sure he was seeing properly, Mikahl wiped his eyes and looked again. On the far side of the pond, there was a tree trunk freshly stripped of its limbs. It was sliding across the ground toward the water of its own accord. Clumps of fresh dirt still fell from its root cluster. Brush, debris, and pieces of other smaller trees were tangled in the jagged stubs where its own limbs had just been torn away. When it was just a few paces from the water's edge, the trunk stopped moving completely.

Mikahl patted Windfoot to reassure him, but he wasn't sure of anything himself. He urged the horse forward a little bit so they were still in the trees but could see the majority of the clearing. The pond's surface stilled and the birds were returning to their roosts in the nearby trees. The packhorse trotted aimlessly in an arcing circle. If it weren't so close to the water, Mikahl thought he might try to chance going after it. Instead, he started whistling and calling for the animal from where he was.

His eyes were eventually drawn to the strangest thing. A tree, or log, was slowly breaking the surface of the pond. It was rising up, end-wise, like a pillar. As with the trunk still lying by the water's edge, it was stripped of all its limbs. It was rising up so slowly, that it made no ripples whatsoever on the surface of the pond. It was like some giant prayer totem, slowly thrusting itself up to the gods. Two small branches lifted from its sides. At the end of each branch, was a cluster of smaller limbs that looked like claws. Mikahl rubbed his eyes and blinked. They were claws. The thing was sticking up out of the water nearly twenty feet now. Before Mikahl could discern any more detail, it dove with viper-like speed out into the clearing and at the unsuspecting pack horse as it came back around toward the water.

The tree trunk lying on the shore jerked forward with the huge creature's lurch. Mikahl realized that the monster was somehow leashed to it when, like a dog hitting the end of its tether, its jaws snapped shut just short of its target. A great, pink maw slowly opened up, revealing rows of finger-long pointed teeth. Then, a flickering, forked tongue shot forth, but the pack horse managed to buck and leap out of its way. The creature wasn't finished though. It hissed and lashed its tongue out again. This time, its tongue wrapped around the horse's neck. The packhorse reared, twisted, and tried to get away, but it was no use. The giant lizard-like monster was already pulling it toward its slavering mouth.

Without even stopping to think about what he was doing, Mikahl drew his sword, and spurred Windfoot out into the clearing at a full gallop.

Chapter Six

The wizard, Pael, had been in the service of Westland for twenty-five years, which was exactly how long Prince Glendar had been alive. Pael arrived on the day of Glendar's birth, and with his clever magic, he made his way through Lakeside Castle all the way to the queen's bedchamber. Once there, he snuffed out her life like an old tallow candle while baby Glendar was still suckling at her breast.

Pael began raising Glendar, playing the caring, motherly role in the boy's life. When he was schooled, Pael was there. When he was hurt, Pael was there. When he needed comfort, support, or just a pat on the back, Pael was there. Slowly, and seemingly effortlessly, the wizard molded Glendar to his will.

It wasn't hard. King Balton was busy with the ever-quarreling eastern kingdoms or off hunting with Lord Gregory and Lord Ellrich. None of the kings and queens of the east seemed to remember the wars, or even the generations of hope and peace that followed them. It seemed every kingdom, save for Westland, had grown discontent with its boundaries or the trade agreements that had been long established. Some rulers were bold enough to check the strength of their neighbors. Defenses were tested, weaknesses exploited, and alliances formed. It was that way all of Glendar's life, and that was good for Pael. Pael had a grand plan, and he was patient. Some would say he was as patient as an age.

"But Master Wizard Pael," Glendar said coolly from his recently deceased father's throne, "the sword is the power of the kingdom."

"In symbol only," Pael lied. "It's no matter. Ironspike will soon be recovered, my Prince."

"It's Your Highness!" Glendar corrected, a little more forcefully than he intended to. "I am the king now, Pael."

The wizard had found him sitting on the throne this morning, about to call court. It was ridiculous. Until now, Pael had kept his anger in check, but no longer.

In a flourish of black robes, the wizard flashed from in front of the throne to directly behind it. His chalky white, bald head pressed against the side of the throne, and his hot, chemical breath found Glendar's startled ear.

"You'll be the king when I say you can be king, boy!" His voice was full of malice and power. "On the morrow, you'll bury your father with tears in your eyes. The day after that, I will let you take the crown."

Pael was already moving around the throne and down the three steps in front of it. He appeared to glide, as if under his floor length robes his feet and legs weren't moving at all. At the bottom of the steps, he turned and looked back at the brooding prince.

"After all that is done, Glendar, then you may be my king."

A dismissive wave of Pael's hands kept Glendar from catching the dual meaning in his last statement.

"We have more pressing business, Glendar." Pael's voice grew serious. "Lord Ellrich has men quietly looking for the sword already, and Lord Brach is commissioning the call to arms that will soon be posted in all of the Westland cities. Soon, he and his captains will ride out and round up every able-bodied man and boy who can fight; after you formally make the command, that is. Lastly, Lord Gregory is preparing to ride to the Summer's Day Festival with the group of competitors that will be representing Westland this year."

"Lord Gregory is my father's man," Glendar said. "He will rally against our plans. I don't think he's to be trusted."

"You don't think." It wasn't a question, but a statement of fact. "That is your biggest problem, boy." Pael's tone was mocking. "I know Lord Gregory is not to be trusted. Why do you think he is about to go to Summer's Day, when he really wants to be preparing to bury his king? He was ordered, before your father died, to lead the competitors this year. I had your father sign those orders. Lord Gregory will be brawling and grieving from afar, while we are getting all of our things in order. When he returns…"

Pael paused as an idea came to him. He laughed at the absurdity of the coincidence and the old saying that fit the situation.

"To kill two birds with one arrow," he mumbled the words aloud.

"What?" Glendar asked.

"Nothing!" Pael's gleeful smile faded. "If Lord Gregory returns from Summer's Day, then we shall deal with him."

A sinister grin crept across Glendar's face when he realized Pael had said, "If Lord Gregory returns."

"You should take a symbolic escort of men and visit your mother's grave in the garden yard later today," Pael suggested. "Linger there a while and place flowers upon her stone."

"But Pael–" Glendar started.

"Do as I say!" Pael snapped.

He knew that Glendar was dying to hold court as the new king. It was just too soon.

"There will be time enough to rule, son." Pael's voice became comforting and sensitive. "You will be the King of Westland, and soon the king of all the Eastern lands as well. Mark what I say, you will be the King of Kings, if you will just be patient."

Pael left the throne room. Glendar was still a spoiled child, and having to pander to him even the slightest little bit set the wizard's blood boiling. For a moment, he wondered where he went wrong with the boy, and then he cursed himself for thinking like a doting mother. None of that really mattered now, he told himself. With King Balton gone, the rule of Westland was his, not Glendar's. He would control the boy with magic if it came to that, but he doubted it ever would. Glendar was like putty in his hands.

A servant girl carrying a tray of meat and bread saw Pael in the corridor and froze. Her eyes went to the hem of her apron. When he passed, she was trembling so badly he could hear the silverware rattling on the tray. Her fear disgusted him almost as much as the sight of all of the food. It was probably more slop for that fat pig, Lord Ellrich. The huge Lord of the Marshlands was rooting himself fiercely into the Royal Guest Apartments. No doubt he wanted to gain Glendar's ear and favor. The only thing good that Pael could find about the obese man was his beautiful, budding daughter, Lady Zasha. Later, he would suggest to the girl and her ladies that some fresh air in the garden would help take their minds off of the sad and dreary process of preparing for the king's funeral. He wouldn't tell them Glendar would be there, or that the King-in-Waiting's Queen Mother was buried there. They would just happen upon each other.

Pael could think of a dozen reasons for Glendar to take Zasha as his queen. For one, the people loved her, but the main reason was with Lady Zasha as his bride, there would be no quibbling when her father met his end. That heavy task would be taken care of, just as soon as the marriage was consummated.

"First things first," Pael mumbled to himself as he ducked into a not so well-known passage. To get to his tower, he had to traverse a labyrinth of halls, tunnels, and stairways. Some were bustling with staff and grieving visitors, and some, like this one, were more private and hidden. There were other passageways only he knew about.

The castle's outer walls were laid out in a diamond shape. Each towered corner of the diamond pointed in one of the four cardinal directions. The southwest wall loomed over the huge body of water known as Lion's Lake, thus the name, Lakeside Castle. The bulk of the noble folk and merchants who lived in the castle resided in the smaller towers and apartments that sprung up around the massive King's Spire there. Most of them looked out over the water. The southwest wall was also the only wall without its own gate. There was no need for one there, for it would only open up to the lake.

Pael's personal tower was in the southernmost corner of the grounds. It overlooked a well-used guard barracks. It was so close to the castle's southern turret tower that an agile man could easily leap from the lower landings of the Wizard's tower to the top of the crenellated wall, where they met the southern turret.

Pael knew old King Balton kept spies in the turrets and among the members of the wall patrols, to keep an eye on him. He wondered if they were still there now. He and King Balton started off well enough, but the King of Westland hadn't liked the subtle ways Pael tried to influence him.

Pael always sided with Lord Brach. Both of them constantly wanted to expand the kingdom by use of force and trickery. King Balton, on the other hand, was a man of peace who remembered the lessons of the old wars, even though he hadn't been alive for them. Balton Collum also remembered the stories of peace and hope that filled the years after the demons were defeated and purged. Pael had been loyal enough to him, though. The wizard helped strengthen the kingdom, with his arcane skills and with plenty of hard work as well. But King Balton never fully trusted him, and Pael always knew it.

The crafty Master Mage used the king's spies to his advantage by making sure that any and all of his suspect activities took place well above the eyes of the guard patrols. To do this, he required a means of traversing the heights of his tower quickly and quietly. To meet his need, he created a hidden lift. It was a small, cylindrical cage, just large enough for three men to crowd into. Each floor in Pael's tower, and half a dozen floors below it, all the way down to the dungeon's lowest floor, had a hole bored through it that was in line with the center of the tower. By way of the powerful and naturally enchanted stuff known as Wardstone, the lift would rise up and down at Pael's command, stopping at whatever floor he directed it to. This allowed Pael to work on complex, questionable spells and other dark magics in private, while still being seen every now and then reading in his library, or making charts in his map room.

His contraption kept unwanted eyes out of his true affairs. The lower floors, the ones visible from the castle wall and the turret tower, still had stairs and landings curving around the inside. Pael had masons wall in the lift tube on these lower floors, so it couldn't be seen as it moved up and down through the tower. Of course, he killed the masons when the job was finished. The upper floors were only accessible by his lift. The stairs and landings above the turret tower had all been removed to make more room. Only Pael and his assistant, Inkling, knew how to use the lift and, in all of Westland, only Pael knew that Inkling existed.

Inkling was an imp, a small, minor demon, who could assume the shape of many different living things, though not very large ones. He could change into a human child, a full grown dwarven woman, or a thin, hungry-looking wolf, and nearly any creature smaller than those. He was in the form of a young boy when Pael glided off the lift onto the second highest floor of his tower. This level was one wide, open, circular room with several open windows. Pael called it the Nest.

"Any news?" the wizard asked as he seemingly hovered just above the surface of the thick, plank wood floor.

"Only one bird has returned, Master," Inkling answered in his thin, wispy voice.

He thrust a finger-sized scroll toward Pael. Pael looked at the rows of empty cages that lined the shelved walls. Only two hawklings and a pigeon remained. His gaze shifted to Inkling for a moment. No matter what form the imp took, his eyes were always solid black pools, with no whites at all. It was unsettling even to one such as Pael.

He put the unread scroll down on a table that was crowded with various shaped flasks and jars. He raised one that held a clear blue liquid up to the light of an oil lamp and swirled it around as if he were studying the consistency of its contents. It was thick, like honey. Satisfied with what he saw, he carefully poured a drop of the stuff into another flask that was full of what appeared to be dirty, yellow urine. He swirled that mixture around until it changed into a bright, greenish color, then raised it to his nose and sniffed.

"I've got a task for you, my little friend," he said to the imp, before downing the contents of the flask. Only a minor look of distaste crossed his colorless face as he swallowed.

Inkling scurried closer, shifting into his true form as he did so. The lamp light reflected brightly off his shiny red scales as he shivered his leathery wings with anticipation. As terrible as his devilish visage was, the horns, pointed ears, and needlelike teeth, the imp would have a hard time intimidating anybody as he was the size of a child. He didn't get to leave the tower often, so the idea of a mission for his Master excited him greatly. He was hissing and ringing his little clawed hands together nervously when Pael finally told him what it was he would do.

"At the Summer's Day Festival, you'll find the truest of hawkers. You are to purchase a dozen hawkling eggs from them, no matter how much the price. You'll do this in a mannish form."

Inkling sighed in disappointment. Pael grinned, because he had expected this reaction. He drew out the rest of his instruction, just to taunt the imp.

"Once the eggs are secured, seek out Lord Gregory." Pael sat the empty flask down on the table and paced a few steps across the room. Inkling all but ran into him when he stopped, and Pael had to bite back his laugh. Seeing he'd tormented the little devil long enough, he ended the suspense. "When you find Lord Gregory, kill him."

"Yesss, master!" The imp hissed gleefully. His feet were rising and falling in place, causing him to rock back and forth. It almost looked as if he were dancing. "Can I eat his flesh?"

Pael held out a pouch full of gold coins.

"Once you've secured the eggs, contact me in the ethereal. Then, as far as my concern runs, you can eat everyone at the festival. Now go before the hawker clan heads back up into the hills."

Inkling pranced a step and a half away from his master, then snapped open his leathery wings and took to the air. He changed into the form of a large buzzard, snatched the bag of gold from Pael's hand, and flew out the open window.

A great sigh of relief escaped Pael once the imp was gone. Now he could get something done. He floated over to the lift and rose smoothly up to the uppermost floor of his tower.

It was dark, save for the light of four flickering candles spread evenly around the room at waist level. Every surface of the chamber was blackened so deeply that the walls were nearly invisible. It was as if Pael and four little flames were hovering in empty, black space. Pael spoke a quiet word and his lift lowered out of the room. The light that shown up through the hole in the floor illuminated the space and made the area seem small again.

Pael began turning a wooden crank on the wall that was attached to a chain. A clanking, ratcheting sound filled the silence as a huge crystal sphere began to lower from the ceiling. It was so big around that three men holding hands might have trouble reaching their arms around it. It hung in an iron ring that had three evenly spaced chains leading up and out of it into the darkness. The crystal sphere slowly came down to rest, cradling itself in the hole in the floor where the lift had just been. The top of the globe was now at chin level to Pael and the light from the hole underneath made it glow faintly from the inside.

Pael kept turning the crank, until the chains lay slack across the floor, and then he walked completely around the ancient artifact, examining it. After a moment he stopped, and even though he was alone and the room was dark again, he pulled the hood of his robe up over his bald head. He was careful to make sure the top of it hung down over his eyes. He then raised his arms and began to chant.

The wizard went slowly at first, because it was hard for him to get the inflection and the tone of his voice the way he wanted it. Soon, the chant picked up its tempo and became smooth and rhythmic. Pael began to circle the orb quickly and his strange voicing became even faster and took on a melodic quality.

In the depths of the sphere, a tiny cloud began to swirl. It grew rapidly inside the crystal, spinning, and changing colors. Pastel blue and purple churned, then crimson and a bright golden yellow, until finally inside the sphere there was nothing but a roiling mass of color. The sound of Pael's voice was a constant now. The meager boundaries of the room had long since faded away. There was no roof overhead, no wooden floor below, and no walls around him. Even the slight reverberation of Pael's voice off the chamber's surfaces disappeared. He, the four flickering candle flames, and his spectral orb were no longer in the world – at least not the same world as the tower.

A diminished harmony joined the wizard's voice, letting him know he was no longer alone. The cloud that filled the crystal suddenly pulsed red and stayed that way. The roiling mist faded and a strange, phantasmal face took form inside the orb. The intensity and brightness of the crimson light radiating out from within the sphere made it impossible to make out any certain detail of the face's features. Pael let his voice trail away. He brought his arms down in front of his chest and put his palms together as if he were about to pray.

"What is it you seek, wizard?" the booming voice of the demon called Shokin asked. "Have you opened the Seal yet?"

"I seek the location of the sword you so greatly despise, oh Mighty One," Pael said. "Ironspike has gone missing."

A long silence ensued. So much time passed that Pael started to think the demon had forgotten him. He started to sigh, but remembered himself. It wouldn't do to anger an ally as powerful as this one. Even though the demon had long been banished from the physical world, Shokin went out of his way to aid Pael. To aggravate the spectral demon would be to invite ruin to all of his plans, for enslaving the demon was part of them.

"The sword will not reveal itself to me."

Shokin's voice seemed irritated. It sounded like a thousand ancient trees creaking in a storm.

"Only when the blade is drawn by one with the cursed blood of Pavreal flowing in his veins will I be able to locate it."

Pael almost swore aloud. King Balton only had one son. Prince Glendar was the last who carried the blood of the ancient hero King Pavreal. Shokin wouldn't be able to locate the blade unless Glendar drew it, and if Glendar was in a position to do so, Pael wouldn't need to locate it anymore. Pael thought carefully for a moment, letting his frustrations subside.

"Is there no other way to seek it?" Pael asked. "What about locating the king's squire, or the priest that disappeared? Can you learn where those two are? It is surely one of them who has the sword."

"The priest is in Portsmouth seeking passage to the Isle of Salazar," Shokin's voice grated. "The squire I cannot find, but he will show himself to me sooner or later."

"He may have the sword."

"There is another matter worthier of your concern, little wizard," Shokin boomed coldly. "A boy has found Illdach's old ring. If he is allowed to keep it for a while, then I think he might be able to help us with the Seal. I feel a deep and certain connection to him. The ring itself is unimportant, but the boy is one of the sacred climbing folk from the mountains. He will be at the festival."

Pael started to ask another question, but the tone of the specter's voice caused him to hesitate. By the time the wizard had mastered his thoughts, the demon was gone from the orb. Already the bright crimson glow was fading.

Pael cursed himself for sending Inkling off to Summer's Day so hastily. There was no way he could go himself. Glendar needed supervision far too badly. The fool prince could destroy a lifetime of work and planning with a single thoughtless command. He hated to heap more on Shaella's plate at the moment, but she was the one that was going to dance with the dragon, so to speak. She was also on her way to Summer's Day to handle another matter for Pael. He knew her loyalty was unquestionable and she could handle the young hawker who found the ring. Most all of Pael's planning was for her anyway. If she wanted to be a queen, then she was about to have to get her hands dirty.

He laughed as he started to raise the orb back up so he could go down to the Nest and write out a message for her. He found he truly regretted not being able to be there for the festival this year. This Summer's Day would be a day to be remembered.

Chapter Seven

Hyden considered the mood of his clansmen. Here they were, wandering through a beautiful forest, heading toward a place of peace and fellowship, on the cusp of a great and exciting competition. Very soon they would be seeing their wives and children for the first time in weeks. The Summer's Day Festival lasted for days and days, but on the first day of summer, it was the greatest celebration Hyden had ever known. Yet his people moved lethargically, as if they were dragging an enormous weight behind them and wading in sludge. Heads were down and shoulders were slumped. The exhilaration and bravado that ignited them like a wildfire on their way to harvest the hawkling eggs had been completely extinguished. Wendlin and Jeryn's fall from the nesting cliff sapped the joy completely out of them.

It was like this nearly every year, Hyden reflected. He couldn't remember a harvest where someone hadn't fallen to their death, or somehow left them all disheartened. In the first year he attended the Summer's Day Festival, no one perished. The long walk from the nesting cliffs, through the great forest toward Summer's Day that year, was as hope-filled and exciting as all his trips to harvest combined. But since then, the trip to the festival from the egg harvest was always bittersweet. This year, one set of brothers and a father were mourning, while the rest of the clan tried to get past it so they could enjoy the upcoming festivities. It was the cruelest of clan rituals, or maybe just bad timing on nature's part, that the harvest and the Summer's Day Festival were almost always tainted with sorrow and death.

"It's a reminder from the goddess," Uncle Condlin said after burying Wendlin in the canyon. "We as a people may climb high and reach farther than nature intended, we may reap great strength, and we may profit from these deeds, but we must remain humble, for it's as a gift we are granted to be able to do such things. Every gain has its cost, and every loss is the cost of our gain."

Uncle Condlin looked directly at Hyden as he spoke of gain and loss. Hyden wanted to scream out that he had nothing to do with this year's harvest. He hadn't asked for, or even earned, the God's Gift that found its way to him. But he held his tongue. Condlin already lost one son, and another was lying broken on a travois. Condlin carried one end and refused to let anyone else ease his burden. Hyden's father, Harrap, and a few others took turns carrying the other end. Hyden had a deep respect for the determination and strength his Uncle Condlin showed day in and day out, but he refused to feel guilty for anything. He may have been the recipient of a gift from the gods and his cousins may have paid a price for it, but he had done no wrong.

The somber mood caused Gerard to give up on finding more devious ways to use the ring he had found. He long ago exhausted the fun out of the trick of having someone tell someone else something that got them clobbered. The thrill of that was gone. Instead, he kept to himself and stayed out of the way while trying to do other things through his mind with the ring. One night he spent the whole evening by the campfire trying to levitate a small stone, but it never once moved. He tried to make a stick catch fire and also to extinguish a flame, but it was all for nothing. What he did manage to do was halt a deer in its tracks the previous afternoon. Gerard might have even called the animal to them, but there was no way to be sure. All he knew was he had called out to the forest to send them a fat doe and one actually came.

Gerard, Hyden, and Little Condlin had ranged ahead of the rest of the clan to hunt. They weren't really short on meat, Hyden just wanted to keep sharp with his bow. The boys weren't even quiet. It shocked them all when the deer bounded out of the woods into their path. As soon as it saw them, the doe started to bolt away, but Gerard cried out, "Stop! Wait!" and amazingly, the creature stayed rooted there. Gerard had been about to call the deer to him when Hyden's arrow pierced its heart with a thump! The Doe just stood there, with its eyes locked on Gerard's, until its front legs crumpled underneath it. As soon as the animal fell onto its side, Gerard felt the tingling, burning rush of the ring's magic fill his blood. It was a grand feeling, and it was all the proof he needed to know the ring caused the deer to freeze in place. What else the ring might have caused, he was left to wonder about.

Gerard didn't tell anyone of his part in it. He left Hyden and Little Condlin to guess whether or not his voice had anything to do with stopping the deer in its tracks. He let them tell of the strange encounter at the fire that night and was glad Hyden didn't mention the ring at all. The Elders attributed the weird happenings to Hyden's hawkling. Gerard held the truth inside, and some odd voice from within told him that was the best way.

As the clan walked in a northwesterly direction under the spacious canopy of bird-filled oaks and maples, Gerard couldn't help but try to manipulate every creature he saw. A squirrel had his attention at the moment.

"Are you well?" Hyden asked.

Gerard didn't hear him. Being the older brother, Hyden took the liberty of slugging Gerard on the shoulder. Gerard stumbled to the side, but didn't lose a step.

"Blast you, Hyden!" he cursed. "I was thinking."

"Aye!" Hyden laughed at the stupid expression on his brother's face. "No doubt thinking of how easy it'll be to get into all the girls' small clothes now that you've got your ring!"

That idea hadn't crossed Gerard's mind as of yet and he wasn't mad at Hyden for the suggestion, but he tried to act that way. It wasn't easy. He tried hard to suppress the smile it brought to his face.

"You're looking up into the trees like that bewitched Miller from the story Berda told us."

"Aye, Hyden." Gerard laughed. "But it's no golden acorn I'm seeking."

"Well, watch your step or you'll end up with knots on your head like me." When Gerard didn't offer any explanation, Hyden asked, "What are you looking for up there?"

Gerard glanced at Hyden. He didn't want to answer. He didn't really want to do what he did either, but even though he knew it was a mistake, he did it anyway.

In his mind, he told Hyden to leave him alone and just walk away. Instantly, he felt the tingle of the ring's magic burn into his blood. For a long moment, he stared at his brother, waiting for him to comply.

Hyden felt the command come into his mind, a subtle suggestion that made him want to move away from where he was and walk alone for a while. He didn't do it. Just as suddenly as the idea formed, it drifted away, and just as suddenly, the tiny hawkling nestled in the bucket he was carrying screeched out. Hyden didn't take his eyes off Gerard's. He watched his little brother's eyes widen with panic as he realized Hyden knew what he had just attempted. Gerard sighed and slumped his shoulders. Hyden wasn't sure if it was a slump of disappointment, or a slump of shame. He decided he was so angry at being commanded like that, it didn't matter.

"Don't you ever use your magic on me!" Hyden said through clenched teeth. "Ever!" Then he stormed off and busied himself feeding the ever-hungry hawkling chick.

Gerard was left speechless. He was at a loss. He knew by the way the magic dissipated away from him instead of gathering around Hyden, that his brother wasn't going to obey his mental suggestion. It put a strange feeling in his guts. He began to wonder if the ring had actually been meant for him. For a fleeting moment he was certain it had been meant for Hyden to find. It was his now, though, and he wasn't about to let Hyden have it. No one would get it from him. Reflexively, he covered the ring with his hand and made for the other side of the procession.

Just after midday, the forest began to thin. There were still trees about in small clumps of twos and threes with the occasional copse here and there, but they were no longer in what you could call a forest. Soon, they would angle northward and start down into the gradually sloping valley that the giants called the Leif Greyn. Berda had told them it meant "Life Giver." Hyden had always wondered if Leif Greyn was the name of the huge river that flowed out of the Giant Mountains or the name of the lush valley that embraced it. He wanted to ask the giantess, Berda, that very question, but he could never remember to ask it when she was in the clan village visiting.

Berda was the wife of a herdsman and the very best of storytellers. She loved to tell tales that showed the young clansfolk the ways of nature and life. She was old and wise as well as huge, and Hyden loved her dearly. Hyden couldn't wait to show her the hawkling. He knew she would have a tale for the occasion. She knew everything, and she had a way of teaching through her stories that was very effective. Those who listened learned much as she narrated her captivating tales. Most of the people in the kingdom lands thought of the giants and the mountain clansmen as barbaric and primitive savages, but they were wrong. In many cases, the mountain folk were far more intelligent. She told him this repeatedly, and he smiled outwardly wondering what wisdom she would have to offer about his little bird.

The mood of the rest of the clan began to lighten as they made camp for the night. The morrow would bring many smiles, and a few tears, when the group was reunited with their wives and children under the towering black monolith that marked the festival grounds. The actual festival wouldn't officially begin for a few days yet, but for the Skyler Clan, it would start as soon as the men met up with their families under the Spire.

Hyden sat by himself with the nest bucket in his lap. He had just finished feeding the chick and was using the last of the daylight to look at how much it had grown in the last few days. Its feathers were coming in now and its beak was turning from a soft, gray triangle into a longer, sharper bill. Its eyes were still filmed over, but Hyden could tell that very soon they would clear and the little hawkling would be able to see the world around it. It was walking around the nest now without wobbling or stumbling, and every now and then it would unfold its wings. The wings would shiver as the hawkling stretched out the tiny muscles it would eventually use to fly.

"Someday your wings will open as wide as my outstretched arms," Hyden said gently. "You'll be able to soar through the heavens and hunt rabbits and snakes." The little bird made a warm, cooing sound, as if in reply to Hyden's words. Hyden stroked its head with a finger until it fell asleep.

A murmur of commotion among the Elders caught both Hyden's and Gerard's separate attention. The sun was setting, bathing the world in lavender and gold. Neither brother saw the other as they eased to the edge of the camp to investigate. As they drew nearer to each other though, Gerard, who had stayed away from Hyden all day long, gave his brother an almost apologetic look. Hyden noticed and halfheartedly sneered, letting Gerard know he might be forgiven, but the look in his eyes left no room for doubt that the intrusion into his mind would not be forgotten.

"What is it?" Hyden asked his father.

"Campfires down in the valley by the river's swell," Harrap replied. "Probably a group of traders coming up through the lower Evermore Forest, or maybe an envoy of competitors from one of the Eastern Kingdoms."

"A lot of fires for an envoy," Uncle Condlin said.

The man was not only tired from carrying his injured son all day long, he was exhausted from a deeper sort of weariness, the kind of fatigue no amount of sleep could relieve.

Hyden wondered what his Uncle Condlin would to say to his wife. He wondered what his own father would say to his mother if it were he or Gerard who had fallen. He glanced at his uncle, who was looking right back at him, and a pang of sadness twisted in his guts. Condlin seemed as if he were about to speak, then suddenly his expression went vacant and he turned and stalked away. Hyden looked sharply at Gerard, wondering if his brother had just used the ring to send their uncle to bed. He started to berate him, but caught himself when he realized that bed was exactly where Uncle Condlin needed to be. It turned out Gerard hadn't even been paying attention to Hyden or their uncle. Gerard's eyes were captivated by the tiny orange constellation of the fires down in the valley bottom.

"How far are they from us?" Gerard asked their grandfather.

"Most of a day's walk, I'd guess," the Elder replied. "We might do well to stay up and away from the river as we travel." He turned to one of his older nephews. "At least until we know who they are."

Gerard wanted to ask why, but didn't. Still the question formed in his mind. Without even intending to do so, he used the ring to send out the question and immediately he felt the warm comforting tingle of magic rushing through his blood.

"I have an ill feeling about that lot," the Eldest said quietly. Then, the old man suddenly glanced at Gerard. His thick eyebrows narrowed for a moment. With a quizzical, contemplative look on his face, he walked over to the fire and received a bowl of food.

It felt so good to have the magic flowing through his body, that Gerard nearly forgot the fear he felt the moment his grandfather peered into his eyes. The old man's gaze was intense and penetrating, and Gerard's heart hammered through his chest. It wasn't the fear that his grandfather might know what he had done. It was the fear that if his grandfather found out about the ring, he might use his power as the Eldest to confiscate it. The idea that the old man was up to just that came flooding through Gerard in a tidal wave of paranoia. The curious look he saw on Hyden's face at that moment made him think his brother was in on it as well.

A short while later, when the rush of power had subsided, Gerard moved away from them all. He found a place outside the firelight where he could watch the rest of the clan. He stayed there with his mind racing, watching over every movement his people made until finally, late in the night, sleep crept up and snatched him away.

He ended up dreaming of dark, suspicious places full of crude teeth and wings. Conspiracies hid in every shadow like hungry wolves waiting to chase him tirelessly through his fitful slumber.

Hyden dreamed that night as well. Beneath him, vast stretches of sparkling blue ocean and endless expanses of wavering, emerald grass blurred together as he soared over them. He circled slowly, rising upward on drafts of sun-warmed air until he could touch the clouds with his wing tips and the world below was merely a collage of multicolored smears. Then he pulled his wings back and dove toward it all. The wind rushed through his long, black hair. His wings folded in even more with the speed of his descent. His eyes focused on a darting hare, as if he were right above it. He tilted and slowed on a banking turn to gain position on his prey, then dove again to attack in earnest. The unsuspecting rabbit grew in his eyes as he drew nearer. It sprang forward just as he opened his wings to stall his dive. It was a futile attempt to flee; Hyden's claws already gripped its wriggling body. As he lumbered away with the struggling weight of his dream kill, Hyden had to use all of his strength. He forced his wings downward to keep himself aloft. Each wing beat was fought for as the weight of the carcass threatened to pull him down.

Hyden woke to the hawkling's screeching call for food. The sun had not yet risen, but the sky was already painted in a copperish, pre-dawn glow.

As he fed the chick the last of the fresh meat from the doe he'd killed, he wondered if the bird dreamed the same dream experience. Strangely, the idea that he had just been allowed into one of the hawkling's dreams came to him. Where the thought came from he didn't know, but he didn't doubt the notion.

One of his uncles, Corum, seemingly materialized out of nowhere before him. The man was winded and glazed with sweat, but still managed a smile. Hyden knew where Corum had been, so he positioned himself to eavesdrop as the man told the Eldest what he had seen down by the river swell.

"It's an armed and armored party," Corum said with concern in his voice.

"How many?" asked the Eldest. Harrap and a few of the other Elders were coming awake now.

"What banner do they fly?" One of them asked before Corum could answer the Eldest's question.

"I counted forty men and half again as many horses." Corum took a few deep breaths, then continued. "By the looks of their gear, they are seasoned fighters, and they fly the Blacksword banner of Highwander."

The Eldest sighed audibly. "I wonder what Willa the Witch Queen and her Blacksword soldiers are up to."

"Maybe they're just here to compete at the festival?" Harrap suggested.

"Aye," Uncle Condlin grumbled. "And maybe all my sons will be there as well."

There was nothing any one could say to that.

Chapter Eight

Mikahl heard a shout over the thrashing and splashing sounds the giant lizard-like creature was making in the pond. The sound might have come from the forest beyond the water but it was hard to tell. Mikahl couldn't be sure if it was a human voice or just a strange bellow from the beast. "Hold!" it seemed to say, but if it was a person trying to halt Mikahl's mad charge, they were far too late.

The packhorse was strong enough, or maybe just heavy enough, to keep from being pulled back into the creature's huge mouth by the long, forked tongue that wrapped around it. The struggling steed was going to break a leg, or worse, trying to get away, so Mikahl didn't even think about veering off of his present course. In fact, with his old sword raised high, he spurred Windfoot on faster.

Another shout erupted from the far side of the clearing. This time, the voice was unmistakably an angry man. What he was trying to say though, Mikahl couldn't understand. The words were drowned out by the beast's slobbery, open-mouthed attempt to roar.

A grunting hiss filled the clearing as the creature lowered its upper half flat to the ground. The rest of it still trailed off into the water, thrashing for traction on the pond's muddy bottom. It dug its fore-claws into the ground with such a force that they sank into the soft earth and formed mounds as it pushed itself back toward the pond with all its might. Its long tongue constricted around the packhorse, and wet, ropey strands of saliva dangled from the massive reptile's open mouth. The monster's intended prey began to flounder.

Mikahl was nearly to the packhorse now. He figured if he could cut the lizard's tongue completely through with one swing of his blade, maybe the terrified horse could get away on its own. For whatever reason, the lizard beast was tethered to the limb-stripped tree trunk and couldn't move further out into the clearing to give chase. It was straining mightily and shaking its head violently back and forth, trying to topple the pack horse. The problem with his hastily planned attack, Mikahl realized, was that the lizard's tongue was stretched across his path like a clothesline. If he didn't get his blade all the way through it on the first try, he would undoubtedly be unhorsed. He was only strides away now. It was too late to balk, and Windfoot was too close and charging too swiftly to turn away. The many lessons of swordsmanship Mikahl had taken under Master Aravan and Lord Gregory flooded into his mind. All those days of hacking, slashing, and building his strength gave him confidence. He was sure he could make the swing he needed to make, at least until the packhorse fell over, turning the lizard's tongue from a clothes-line into a tripwire. Mikahl had made a terrible mistake. The creature had finally won its tug of war with the animal. The fallen horse slid right into Windfoot's path and Mikahl didn't know what to do. Being a well trained fighting horse, Windfoot leapt high and hard into the air. Mikahl wasn't expecting the leap from the horse and went sailing out of the saddle. Only his quick thinking got his feet out of the stirrups. The world spun around him, in a swirl of green, then blue, then green again. He saw the ground rushing up at him and let his sword go so that he might use his hands to break his fall. The soft, grassy earth and the strength of his arms did little to cushion his impact. Like a cliff diver going into the sea, he hit the ground coming straight down. The earth didn't part for him as the water would for a diver, though. Mikahl's last sensation before blackness engulfed him was the back of his own hand crunching into his face. After that, there was nothing.

"...yer pack! Get up, man!" An insistent voice pierced through the throbbing blackness. "Come on, man! Get up. Blast it all to the hells!"

Mikahl tried to swallow and found his mouth full of dirt, grass, and blood. He nearly choked on it, and he could barely breathe. His eyes flew open; his body heaved to force the clod out of his airway. The world came back to him like a blow from a war hammer. He rose up onto his hands and knees and heaved again. This time, the mess in his throat came spewing forth in a spray of stinking, crimson vomit.

"By the God's, man!" The voice came from very close behind him, over a rasping, angry reptilian hiss. "Get your arse up, lad! I need ya!"

Mikahl's head was still spinning. He couldn't say where, or even who, he was at the moment. He didn't get up, but did turn to look back behind him to see what the person was yelling about. He saw the wild-looking man thrust up his spear, then jump out of the way of a huge, bloody maw. All of this was transpiring only a few paces behind him. He couldn't help but wonder how long he had been out of it. It took a few seconds for it all to register in his brain. When it did, he stumbled to his feet, and a rush of fear and adrenaline shot through his battered body.

"Get your fargin sword, man!" The man's voice was savage. "Ye better hur—" He jumped out of the way of all those razor sharp teeth as the beast's mouth snapped shut just inches from his face. "Come on then, ye slithery bastard!" he yelled at the creature when he recovered.

The king's sword was the only thing Mikahl cared about at that moment, and he turned a slow circle looking for Windfoot. When he saw the front half of a horse laying a half dozen yards away, panic shot through him. It was the packhorse he realized, and even though the saddle pack that contained most of his supplies looked to be intact, he dismissed the gory sight. Only Windfoot and Ironspike were important. On the far side of the clearing, just inside the tree line, he spotted the horse. The animal was limping badly, but the sword was still plainly visible, strapped to his back in its protective sheath. Another shock of panic came rising through the haze of Mikahl's brain. He would be forced to put his beloved horse down now. After the harrowing jump over the packhorse, one of Windfoot's legs was surely broken. Why else would he be limping? Now Hyden would have to walk all the way to the Giant Mountains.

"It's here man! Here!" The man beside him yelled hysterically. Mikahl was brought back to the moment by the beast's hissing roar. He followed the man's finger. He was pointing down at Mikahl's sword. It was lying in the grass just a few feet away.

The creature roared again. The horrible blast sent bloody, foamy spray out over them in a warm, breathy spew. The whole idea of the situation filled Mikahl with rage. He strode purposely over to his old sword, picked it up, and turned toward the blasted creature that killed his horse. "Think, then act." He heard King Balton's voice speak the words in his mind, but he ignored them.

The giant lizard's skin looked like rough tree bark, but it appeared to be much harder. The blood-drenched man had managed to gouge several deep wounds on the inside of and around the thing's mouth, but his attempts to stab it anywhere else had resulted in mere scratches. Only its neck and breast area looked to be vulnerable to Mikahl. He still didn't understand why the bloody beast was leashed to the fallen tree. He was glad it was, though. It couldn't leave the water to get all the way to them.

Then there was the man. He was bald and huge, almost as big as Lord Gregory. He was covered in blood but didn't seem to be hurt too badly. The giant lizard beast was dripping and spraying blood everywhere. Mikahl decided that was where the blood on the man had come from.

He saw the lizard's tongue wasn't a problem anymore. Only the snapping mouth, which twisted and shook, then lunged and withdrew, had to be avoided.

"Where are you at, man? Are ye daft?" the frustrated man managed to ask, just before the creature snapped down at him again. As the beast withdrew, he stepped forward, and stabbed his spear into the pale, scaly flesh under the creature's jaw.

"Drive it deep, and hold it up!" Mikahl suddenly yelled, as he charged up under the beast's neck. He'd had enough of this. His half-conscious brain was clouded in a scarlet mist. He aimed for what might be the throat and yelled. He used all the strength he had to drive his blade home. The creature brought its head down hard, trying to crush Mikahl under its weight. Mikahl let go of the sword just in time and leapt away, leaving his blade buried halfway into the lizard's neck. The creature's attempt to smash him only forced the sword in deeper. A scrabbling claw managed to hook into Mikahl's chain mail armor, but his momentum somehow won him free.

"Yahhhh!" the blood-covered man yelled in acknowledgment of Mikahl's insane attack. A second later, he was slung away from the grip he had on his spear when the creature raised up from the ground and shook its head like a terrier shaking a rat. The spear went flying from the monster lizard's mouth and the man followed it with his eyes as he urged Mikahl away from the beast.

The creature thrashed, hissed, and thrashed some more, throwing bloody spume and pond water everywhere. Its death throes didn't last long though, and the thing slowly collapsed into a twitching heap. Only its head and front legs were visible at first, then gradually the rest of its long, reptilian body floated to the surface of the pond, jerking occasionally in protest of death.

"Fargin big bastard, eh?" The man was bent over with his hands on his knees, laughing between his gasping breaths.

Mikahl fell to the ground and glared at him. He wanted nothing more than to go to Windfoot, but was too sore to move.

"Why didn't it advance on us?" he asked.

"See that busted up tree over yond?" The man pointed across the pond to the stripped trunk Mikahl had seen sliding across the ground earlier.

"A little while ago that was a healthy tree, still in the ground," the man explained.

He squatted down a little closer to where Mikahl was lying and he continued.

"That fargin Bark Skinner pulled it up roots and all, and drug it through the forest." He laughed at the absurdity of it. "I was sure my chain would snap. I guess it's true, Wildermont steel is the best in the world. That chain proved up to the test today, even when yon tree wedged itself stuck over there."

"Why in all the hells was that thing chained to a tree?" asked Mikahl.

The man's brows narrowed as he looked closely at Mikahl. He reached up with his hand and used his thumb to wipe away some of the blood under Mikahl's busted nose.

"Bah!" The man stood with a wince. "It got caught in my trap, boy." The man belted out a hearty chuckle. "I thought ye had hair on your lip, but it was not but dirt and blood. You're just a pup."

Mikahl felt himself flush. The sensation was partly from embarrassment, but also from indignant anger. Either way, the rush of blood to his face reminded him of how swollen and battered it was.

"I might be a Squire, a boy, but I just saved your hide."

The man looked at him again, taking him in from head to toe. After a moment, a white grin split the man's dirty, bloody face.

"Aye. Exactly so." The man laughed. "And a fat sack o' gold that hide will bring us if we can skin her without a tear."

Mikahl started to his feet, but a spinning sensation stopped him. He wasn't sure what the man meant, but he didn't voice his ignorance. The man offered a hand to Mikahl. He took it and was pulled to his feet with a heave. Mikahl couldn't help but notice the man was incredibly strong.

"They call me Loudin."

"Call me Mik," Mikahl lied. "It's short for Mikken."

"Well met, Mikken." Loudin put one hand on Mikahl's shoulder and extended the other out toward the dead bark-skinned lizard.

"Yer due a share of the take from the skin, lad, but you have to help me skin'r and sell'r. We'll need yer good horse to help tote it as well."

Mikahl laughed. He just now caught the unintentional joke he made when he told the man he'd saved his hide.

"My horse appears to be lame, sir…uh…Loudin. And as much as I thank you for the offer, I must continue north into the mountains. My business there is urgent."

"Well, firstly, my friend, yer horse is limping. But its leg ain't broke. It just lost a shoe. Probably a bit of nail left in the hoof gathering mud and grass as he limps around. Secondly, if yer going into the mountains, even this time of the year, you'll freeze your castle-raised giblets off at night dressed in those clothes. Thirdly, Summer's Day is at the foot of the mountains, and that's where we will most likely have to sell our prize. That's only if we can get the big bastard skinned and get it there before the festival is over and all the traders go home."

The wave of relief that washed over Mikahl when he heard Windfoot was all right was so overpowering that he didn't even wince at Loudin's jab. Mikahl had been having a futilely hard time trying to hide. He wasn't sure what he said that gave him away, but the big trapper had apparently seen right through him. "Castle-raised," Loudin said. Was Mikahl that transparent? He was starting to feel like he was swimming in water that was full of venomous serpents and far too deep to stand in. He wasn't even sure he could find his way out of these woods. He'd never thought he might need warmer clothes. He wasn't sure he could trust this man. His accent was like those of the sailors from the Kingdom of Seaward that often docked in Portsmouth. They were notoriously questionable folk who tended to spend a lot of time whoring and gambling. Not as bad as the Dakaneese Pirates, but bad enough. A long look at the dead barkskin lizard helped make up his mind. There was no telling what other sort of dangerous creatures roamed this forest. Besides, if he got to the Summer's Day Festival, he wouldn't be lost anymore. From the great, black spire, he could go due north and within a day or two he'd be in the Giant Mountains.

"Will my share be enough to outfit me for the mountains?" he asked the trapper.

"Aye! Twice as much and then some, lad," Loudin answered.

It was true. The skin of this huge lizard would bring in a small fortune. Loudin was a fairly honest man, and though he had cheated many a fool at dice, fortune wheel, and card table too, he saw no need to try to cheat this fool boy. The boy's ignorance would allow Loudin to keep nearly all of the gold. He could outfit the boy well and fill his pouch full of silver coins, then send him off to get eaten or to freeze to death in the mountains. The bulk of the profit he would keep for himself. They had to hurry though, or the traders would be gone. He wasn't sure, because he had lost count of the days while tracking the great lizard through the forest, but he felt certain that Summer's Day was upon them. Tomorrow or the next day might be the first day of summer. He thought about asking the boy what day it was, but didn't want the lad thinking he was daft. It didn't matter. He was sure if they got to work quickly, they could get the lizard skinned and the hide to the festival before all the traders were gone.

Loudin was right about Windfoot's hoof. Mikahl couldn't figure how the old hunter knew it, but he did. It only took Mikahl a few moments to clean away the clod caked to the nail and work the nail itself free. Windfoot would have to do without the fourth shoe. Out there in the forest where the ground was relatively soft and free of sharp rocks, the well trained horse could manage. Mikahl would have him re-shod when they got to the festival.

It was near dark by the time they had the huge lizard out of the pond, into the clearing, and rolled onto its back. Even Loudin marveled at how big it was. He said it was the biggest Bark-Skinned Lizard he had ever seen. He paced its length off and found it was six paces longer than the biggest he had ever heard of, thirty-two paces, from nose to tail. Its mouth was big enough to swallow a man whole, and was as pink as a maiden's ribbon inside. Its four legs stuck up from its stiffening body like grotesque tree stumps with wickedly sharp, stunted limbs.

Mikahl learned that Loudin had a horse and a camp not too far away. Together, the horses had done most of the hard labor of moving the big beast, while they used Loudin's ropes to guide and roll the lizard over. It was no easy task even with the horses, but they managed to get the creature ready to skin.

Mikahl did his share of the work without complaint, even though he was horribly sore and bruised from his crash landing. His nose was broken and swollen, and black circles were forming under his eyes. He had seen his reflection in the pond water when he washed away the blood. No one at Summer's Day would recognize him, unless they were looking for a raccoon.

Mikahl let his mind wander while they worked. He had never been to the Summer's Day Festival and found himself more than a little excited. King Balton sent a delegation of competitors each year to represent Westland, and Mikahl had listened raptly to the tales they carried back with them. Lord Gregory once won a fistfight called the Brawl, and his name was engraved into the great spire for the victory. Lord Ellrich also won a prize once for eating more sausage coils than his competitors, but that feat didn't warrant getting your name etched into the Spire for all to see. Elves were said to come out of their hiding places in the Evermore Forest to win the archery tournament every year, and wizards turned stones into snake-birds or fruit trees for coins. Wild men breathed fire and hawkers sold everything imaginable. He couldn't wait to see such things. The prospect of it made it easier to labor through his pains in hopes that they wouldn't arrive too late to witness them.

They stopped working at sunset. Loudin said there was no use trying to skin the beast by torchlight. Mikahl wanted to retrieve his sword from the creature's gullet, but decided it could wait till the morrow. He would also have to find his longbow. He'd thrown it down somewhere in the clearing when he and Windfoot made their hasty retreat into the trees. He would have searched for it earlier, but he was too embarrassed to admit losing it to the hunter.

They cleaned up in the pond again before they made their way to Loudin's camp. Loudin said it would be better to stay away from the clearing for the night. There was no telling what sort of things would come sniffing around the carcass.

"Won't something try to eat the meat and ruin the hide?" Mikahl asked. Loudin held a branch aside until Mikahl took it, so that it wouldn't whip him in the face.

Loudin answered, "The tongue, or what's left of it, and the eyes maybe; the hide's too thick."

While they were washing, Mikahl noticed Loudin was slick bald and had large black tattoos on his scalp and back. This was confirmation of his Seaward heritage. The contrast between skin and ink on the hunter's back made it easy for Mikahl to follow him in the darkness.

"The big scavengers," Loudin was saying, "the ones that could possibly get a tooth or claw through that thick bark hide, won't bother."

Loudin ducked a low hanging branch and turned sharply to make sure Mikahl didn't bash into it. He waited until he saw Mikahl duck and then continued.

"The big'uns will run off the little'ns feeding on the tongue and eyes. They'll keep the little'ns away 'til they get their fill. And they won't bother with the stuff that's hard to get to. Ah! Here we are. Hold tight, Mik, I'll get the fire going so we can see."

Loudin did just what he said he would do: he built up a huge fire. Mikahl was glad for it. He got so close to the fire his battered flesh was nearly singed by the heat, and he knew he would feel better for it later. After Loudin sat down, Mikahl studied him. He gave the hunter a big piece of cheese and some bread he'd retrieved from his pack saddle. Loudin was roasting some of the lizard's tongue meat on a stick, but he took the offer with a nod of thanks.

Mikahl could see the hunter was older than he first guessed. The lines that formed at the corners of the man's eyes when he smiled were deep and worn in. His body was well muscled and darkened from the sun. Mikahl figured he was far more than just a trapper. The tattoos were the strangest thing about him, though. He was tiger striped horizontally from his belt line, up his back, and onto his head. He had big stripes that wrapped around his arms and the tender flesh at his sides. The highest stripe wrapped around his neck, just under his ears, and came to crisp points along either side of his jaw. From between his eyebrows, a point gradually widened into a two-finger-wide stripe that ran back over his forehead and melded with the rest. The effect was such that if you looked at him from the front, you could only see the hint of the mohawk tattoo on his head. But from behind, he looked quite animalistic.

Mikahl wanted to ask him about the tattoos, but was afraid to offend the man. He knew from his studies that warriors from Seaward and some sailors from the Isle of Salazar marked themselves in such ways, but he wasn't sure why.

Loudin gave him a piece of the tongue meat when it was done and put his own piece on the bread Mikahl had given him.

"That there piece of meat would fetch a whole piece of gold in some places I've been." Loudin took a bite and closed his eyes, savoring the rich flavor.

"My people say it's bad fortune to eat meat from a scaled beast, but—" He took another bite.

The expression on his face left no need for him to finish the statement. The look was that of pure bliss.

Mikahl tried to sniff the meat before he took a bite, but his nose was clogged with blood. He finally braved a taste and was rewarded with a thick, powerful flavor that was quite delicious.

Loudin grinned. After he swallowed his bite, he continued speaking.

"The giant folk will give a small fortune for such a delicacy. These bark-skinned lizards don't live up in the frigid mountains. I know a giant that would have filled my fist full of gold for the piece of meat you're eating now. I mean filled it!"

"Giant? Did you just say that you know some of the giants?" Mikahl asked the question, just to be sure he had heard correctly. He had.

Chapter Nine

The black obsidian spike of Summer's Day Spire thrust up out of the Northern Leif Greyn Valley and pointed toward the heavens. It was hundreds of feet tall, yet only twenty-eight paces wide at each of the three faces formed by its base. What purpose it was supposed to serve and who had built it, no one, be they human, giant, or elf could say. It had been standing before history was written. The giants called it the Monolith. The elves simply called it the Spire. Tens of thousands of years' worth of stories and lore from all the races of the realm spoke of it. Religions rose and fell over it, but no one came close to guessing what it was about. Even the oldest of the elves, who heard the tales of their forbearers firsthand, had no clue as to why the thing existed or who might have put it there.

The towering, perfectly formed structure was there, though, and around its base in the Valley of Life, the people of the realm were congregating as they did every year around the first day of summer, in the spirit of peace, fellowship, mercantilism, and competition.

Three crowded lanes led away from the base of the Spire. One extended upriver, north toward the foothills. Another ran downstream, keeping parallel to the river almost all the way to Wildermont. The third road led eastward, away from the river altogether. Between the Spire and the river was an area known simply as the Grounds. This was where the contests took place. Sections were marked off for archery lanes, fighting circles, muddy tug of war pits, and other similar competition areas. An open field, filled with quickly assembled wooden bleachers built around it, held the hammer throwers at the moment. The dwarves once dominated this event, but a few hundred years ago, the little folk went underground and had not returned. Only a few handfuls of dwarves could be found in the realm these days, and they would be in the kingdom of Highwander, in the city called Xwarda, where Willa the Witch Queen held rule over the people with her potent magic and her Blacksword Warriors.

The three roads, or Ways, as they were commonly called, were lined with wagon carts, tents, and makeshift table stands. People from all over the realm sold their wares and services: armor made from boiled and painted leather; the pungent frog weed from the kingdom of Dakahn; farming implements, leather goods, and riding gear, along with the finest horses in the land, from the Kingdom of Valleya. Barrel kegs, sailcloth and rope, and just about anything else to do with the shipping trade, was sold by the merchants from the Isle of Salazar, and in fierce competition with the Seaward vendors who dealt in similar merchandise. There were fantastical potions, healing powders, magical spell scrolls, venomous curses, and personal charms of every fashion to be had at Summer's Day.

One of the larger pavilions had an old, silver-haired man standing out in front. He was wearing wizard's robes and claiming the jeweled items he sold were powerfully enchanted and be-spelled. Daggers that never dulled, rings that made the wearer more attractive, medallions that would keep you from harm, and a longbow that would never miss its target if you could find the strength to draw it were just a few of the items he was trying to sell. He swore he could make anything imaginable, and every so often, he would make a dove go flapping away from his empty hand in a puff of smoke or pull a flower out from behind a passing maiden's ear. The people who saw these feats either scurried off with terrified looks on their faces or hurried inside to spend their coin.

Gerard was intrigued by the man, but didn't scurry away or hurry inside to spend his money. He chose to watch the wizard from across the way. He bought a piece of roasted meat skewered on a wooden stick and a mug of ale to wash it down, then leaned back against the food seller's cart and watched the old man draw in his next group of potential customers.

Gerard was transfixed by the man's commanding tone and strange accent, but he wasn't lured by the charlatan tricks that seemed to amaze the rest of the onlookers. Berda told many a tale that included men like this one, and Gerard knew feats such as these were a trick of the eye and not real magic. What kept Gerard watching was the fact that, when he had tried to use his ring's power to catch the wizard out in his act, the old man only glanced at him without so much as a stutter. Like Hyden, the old man was somehow unaffected by the ring. Gerard might have thought the ring simply lost its magic had he not used it earlier in the afternoon to persuade a castellan from Wildermont to pay him twice the asking price for his last two hawkling eggs. The other six of his eggs he sold with Hyden's six to a strange little black-eyed woman who wanted an even dozen. Gerard's pouch was full and he could have easily afforded any of the old silver-haired wizard's wares, but he wasn't interested in the fancy trinkets, only in the man selling them.

The woman who bought the eggs from him and Hyden gave Gerard the creeps. She acted and spoke more like a distracted boy or a skittish animal, and her eyes had been as black as the Spire itself. She paid well though, and without argument. Actually, she had slapped the heavy pouch full of golden lions down on the table stand the Skylers were using for a countertop and demanded the dozen hawkling eggs. Harrap started to question her, as he always did the strange buyers. He seemed to want to know everything about them, their home kingdom, what type of business they were associated with, and the reason they wanted to buy the eggs. Most people wanted to incubate the birds to carry messages over long distances. Others wanted the yolk for its healing properties. This woman had grown defensive and said an old woman's business is her own. After waving a hand around and chanting a word that caused Gerard and his father both to forget she had even been there, she took her eggs and disappeared. The memory of her came back soon after, and Harrap had grown angry. His cursing and irritable manner drove Gerard out of the selling booth just as soon as he'd sold his other two eggs.

Hyden was in the middle of a preliminary round for the archery competition. Gerard used that as his ruse to go. Gerard knew Hyden would get to the finals, so instead of going to watch his brother, he went off into the Ways exploring and ended up here, in front of the silver-haired wizard's pavilion. It was becoming obvious the goods weren't truly enchanted, so he was starting to lose interest.

Disappointed, he stepped into the flow of the passing crowd. He was curious to see what else he could find. He hadn't taken ten steps when a woman's arm hooked around his. The lady didn't pull him into the gap between the two tents they were passing as he half expected her to do. Instead, she just strode along beside him as if they were long acquainted companions out enjoying the festival together.

He could smell the sweet, flowery scent of her, and from the corner of his eye he could tell she was attractive. He turned to look at her curiously and was pleasantly surprised.

She was close to his height, and other than the long, straight, raven black mane that hid most of her face from him, all he could see was the ample amount of cleavage her studded leather vest revealed. Once he got past that, he saw her entire body was beautifully curvy and clad in tight-fitting protective leather. He also noticed she wore a long sword at her hip.

"You're one of the hawkling sellers, aren't you?" she asked as they walked along.

Gerard knew right away by the way she spoke that her accent was Dakaneese. He had heard the Dakaneese were dangerous and violent people. "Sell swords and slavers, mercenaries and gamblers, all!" Berda said. Dakahn was one of the two great human kingdoms that bordered the southern marshlands. They constantly defended themselves from wild swamp creatures and the like since the kingdom's capital city, O'Dakahn, was located at the mouth of the Leif Greyn River. It was a horribly overpopulated hub of river, land, and sea trade. This, of course, accounted for all the unsavory characters drawn there, and the bad reputations that followed them.

He glanced at her again. This time he stopped in the middle of the Way and roughly turned her to face him. She didn't resist or protest.

Her face was exotically beautiful with huge, dark, doe eyes and a small, slightly upturned nose. From just below one eye, a pink knife scar trailed down her cheek like a permanent teardrop. Her full lips were painted a faint strawberry color, and above her eyes on her eyelids was a sparkling, bluish green powder. Her mouth was set in a determined slant, but her eyes looked to be pleading for something.

"Yes I am," he answered. His eyes had found her cleavage again, and he couldn't seem to pull his gaze away. He could feel himself blushing, but was helpless to do anything about it.

She didn't seem to mind his exploring eyes at all. Her expression didn't change and her eyes never left his. "We need a climber."

Her tone was matter of fact and conflicted strongly with her beauty. "The job should only take a few days. The rest of the time will be spent traveling, a long week at my best guess."

Her lips spread into an inviting smile and suddenly resumed her stride, leaving him gawking at thin air.

He hesitated, but only for a heartbeat. He quickly caught up to her and resumed his place at her side. He noticed her skin-tight leather britches fit her rump perfectly, and her sword's hilt was modestly jeweled. He waited for her arm to hook into his again, but it never did. He found it disappointing. When she had touched him before, he felt as if he were floating. He longed to feel that sensation again.

His mind churned now, searching for reasons to go with this beautiful woman wherever she led him. A dozen reasons he shouldn't go came flooding into his mind with the others. He needed to find out more about this job, and there was no doubt he wanted to find out more about her.

"Where would we be going?"

"Into the Southern Marshlands," she answered as casually as if she went there every day. Gerard began to wonder if the wild stories he heard about the place and the creatures that dwelled there were only exaggerations. This woman wore a thick, armored vest and carried a fancy sword with a jeweled hilt; not the type of things a person would wear if they were afraid of where they were going. She was only a girl really, no bigger than and not much older-looking than he was. If the idea of going into the marshes frightened her, it didn't show at all.

"What in the world would you need a climber in the marshes for?"

The idea of using his ring to have her spill the truth of it all crossed his mind, but he stopped himself. He wanted to see what she told him of her own will first.

"I cannot just blurt out the nature of my campaign." A slight look of frustration crossed her face. She stopped and hugged him to her. He couldn't help but feel the softness of her breasts pressing against him, even through the thick leather vest.

"Some would try to take what we seek before we get it," she whispered into his ear. Her breath was warm and sweet, and made his head swim. "Others would conspire against our efforts. I must be sure you are trustworthy before I share the details with you. The fact you are interested is enough for the moment."

She backed away a step, then hooked her arm in his again. She had to pull him along to get his feet moving.

"To answer your question, though, out in the deep marshes there's a place called the Dragon's Tooth. Oh, don't look so frightened. It's only called that because of its shape. There's a cavern in the side of it, up good and high. What we seek is in the cavern. We need a climber to go up and get it, or at least to make a rope way up for a few others to climb up."

Gerard was satisfied with her answer, but the idea of using the ring was starting to consume him. He wanted to feel its power coursing through his body as much as he wanted the beautiful Dakaneese girl beside him. Without further thought, he used the ring and told her in his mind to kiss him.

It was in that moment, when her warm soft lips met his, that Shaella knew she had him. She wasn't sure where the urge to kiss him came from, but it didn't matter. The kiss sealed his fate. The look of pleasure in his eyes told her he was putty in her hands.

The burn of magic in Gerard's blood accompanied by her hot, wet, probing tongue was a feeling like none he had ever known. It was ecstasy beyond reason; a sensation that from that moment on he wouldn't be able to resist. He was addicted.

Over on the archery lanes, Hyden put three arrows deftly into the Wizard's Eye and the next two into the King's Ring, from both fifty and one hundred paces. Two other men matched the feat. The sole elf participating in the preliminary culling didn't bother to loose his arrows at fifty paces at all. Instead, he put four arrows into the Wizard's Eye at one hundred paces. Then, with a contemptuous scowl at the awed group of human contenders, he backed fifty more paces away and arced his last arrow into the edge of the King's Ring as if it were nothing. It was amazing.

Hyden only put four in the Wizard's Eye twice in his life. It was hard to do and the elf had made it look easy, but he tried not to get discouraged. Since he had done it before, he knew he could do it again. If he wanted to win the competition, he would have to do it on the morrow. He'd have to do it in front of a great crowd of onlookers, too. The few dozen spectators who watched the culling today made him fairly nervous. He would try his hardest, though.

The elves' smug confidence and arrogant attitude toward the other competitors gave Hyden a better understanding of his people's desire to beat them. The yellow-eyed devil thought he was too good to even speak to humans. After the hundred and fifty pace lob into the King's Ring, Hyden complimented the elf. The cocky bastard smirked and walked away, as if annoyed by the respectful words.

The two other elves watched the culling take place and seemed to share this contempt for the other archers. They watched with narrowed brows on their skinny, pointed-eared faces, only to mock and heckle each time a man's arrow missed the center mark. It was no wonder the Elders and most of the giants spoke of the elves return to the land as if they were a plague. At the moment, Hyden didn't want to think of the morrow's competition. He had made it through the culling, which began with more than thirty contenders. The field had been narrowed down to four. He decided to be pleased with that accomplishment and enjoy the night's main event. He was ready for the Brawl.

All day people had been talking about it. The Western Lion Lord, whose name was already carved in the Spire for his victory of a few years ago, was to take on the Seaward Monster. The monster was a tattoo-covered mountain of a man who made his living toting and standing ships' spars and mast poles. Hyden had never seen the sea or a ship, much less a mast pole, but he had seen a riverboat with a sail and knew that the pole on the riverboat would have weighed as much as a shagmar beast or a full grown bull moose. He listened closely to the descriptions of the kind of ships this Seawards man helped build and knew it was no typical occupation. They said the man was a freak of nature; possibly half giant, someone even suggested. Hyden knew the last statement couldn't possibly be true because Berda told him giants and humans couldn't interbreed. She said the offspring came out feral, but nevertheless, he was intrigued about the event.

In every corner of every space, wagers were being made and stories about the two combatants were being told. Hyden saw the Lion Lord win his battle against the Valleyan Stallion a few years ago. It was a long and brutal fight. The Lion had outlasted the Valleyan. He won with a late flourish of hammer blows. Hyden remembered vividly the screams and cheers of the onlookers, and the curses from those who lost their wagers. There were a dozen more fights in the crowd after the Brawl ended. Hyden remembered being afraid he and his father wouldn't get free of the mass of people without being pummeled to death themselves.

Gerard hadn't been old enough to go to harvest that year, and their mother kept him at the selling tent during the Brawl. Hyden would never forget the bond he and his father formed that year. Hyden harvested one lousy egg and was teased to tears on the long walk back from the harvest lodge to the festival. His father held that single egg out until all the others were sold, then he acted like an auctioneer between three potential buyers. When the deal was done, Harrap handed Hyden a fat little sack of gold, patted him on the head and said, "Your single egg was the best egg of the whole harvest, son." That one egg sold for what three eggs sold for earlier in the day. No one in the Skyler Clan dared make fun of Hyden's one egg harvest after that.

When Hyden made it back to the clan's group of tents and pavilions, his pleasant memories were shattered. His father's and Uncle Condlin's moods were still foul over being tricked into selling eggs to a spell worker, and it made Hyden want to hurry away. He only stayed long enough to feed and tend the hawkling chick.

The women of the clan were selling beaded jewelry and woven blankets they made during the year, along with some pelts the men hunted and trapped over the last winter. He asked them if anyone had seen Gerard, and complimented a particular bracelet his mother had made.

No one had seen Gerard for a while. After searching this whole side of the upriver Way where his clan had more or less taken over, Hyden decided to go buy his brother a wizard's hat and a good pair of horsehide boots like he promised. On his way from the clan's area, he was cornered by two of his uncles. They interrogated him about the culling and warned him not to get drunk or injured between now and the competition. They gave advice and though he didn't want to think on the matter, he listened politely and promised he would do his best. Eventually, he broke free of them and went out into the Ways.

Later, he found himself searching for Gerard. He wanted to treat his brother to the special seats he managed to acquire for the Brawl. When that was over, he would give his brother the presents he bought for him.

He looked for Gerard in a few places, then he saw the old, silver-haired wizard's pavilion and decided Gerard would've been tempted by such a display. He was disappointed when he didn't find Gerard there.

On the way out of the fancy tent, he turned toward the Spire and ran face first into a pair of fully armored men. He mumbled an apology and tried to step around them, but they mirrored his sidestep and continued to block his way. Hyden immediately recognized the white, rectangular patch over their breasts. It had a black sword running across it like a stripe. It was the banner of the Blacksword Warriors of Highwander. A shiver of fear ran through him. These were Willa the Witch Queen's men. It was said she fed her enemies to her soldiers in their stew. Others said her men cooked the dead right on the battlefield and ate them on their own. At the moment, Hyden wholly believed it. One of the men was smiling wickedly, showing a mouthful of jagged, half rotted teeth. They looked to be pointed at the ends like fangs, and both of the men smelled of sweat and filth.

Hyden tried to get around them again, but one of them moved to block his way a second time.

"You want to pass?" The man snarled. His breath smelled worse than his clothes. "A pint will get you by." The man chuckled and elbowed his companion.

Hyden was just about to turn and run to his clan's section of the Way when a sharp boot tip came up between the man's legs from behind. It caught him just under the codpiece and doubled him over with a grunt. The other Blacksword soldier drew his sword and whirled to face the attacker. He wasn't fast enough. A raven-haired woman who moved as fast as a mongoose pushed the point of her dagger into the man's throat.

"Go find someone else to bully, Barton!" She commanded. Then she pushed him away as if he were a child.

The wide-eyed soldier grabbed his doubled over companion's shoulder plate and hauled him to his feet. It was obvious he recognized and feared the woman, and the two men took special care to avoid Hyden as they eased into the crowd and disappeared.

"Shaella," Gerard spoke as he stepped out from behind her. "This is my brother, Hyden. Hyden, Shaella Ga'shen from Dakahn."

"Thank you," Hyden said stupidly. He was dumbfounded. He couldn't imagine how Gerard had come upon this beautiful woman, much less how he managed to gain her acquaintance.

"You're most welcome, Dar Hyden," she replied in her heavily accented voice. She threw in a little head bow with her words that made Hyden feel even more out of place than he already did. But what she did next mystified him completely.

Shaella turned and ran her finger lovingly down Gerard's nose, and smiled brightly.

"Think about my offer, Gerard," she told him. Then, in an almost girlish gesture, she tiptoed up to his lips and quickly kissed him before rushing away.

After she left, Gerard grinned at his brother triumphantly.

Hyden started to make a comment, but found he couldn't even manage to speak.

Chapter Ten

The two brothers walked the Ways of the Festival together, taking in the vastness and diversity of the carnival-like atmosphere. The sun left the sky, but it wasn't quite dark yet.

As they weaved through the crowds, Gerard told Hyden about Shaella's offer. Hyden found it made him jealous. Both he and Gerard dreamed of finding fame and fortune somewhere beyond the sheltered little world of their clan. Hyden was about to say something about his feelings to his brother when a great gout of fire erupted up into the air before them. The sound of drums filled the area and a man whirled and jumped, then acrobatically turned a flip before landing perfectly on his feet to blow more fire out of his mouth.

He was bald and painted bright scarlet from head to toe, with wicked symbols painted in black on his arms and chest. He wore only a loincloth made of some wild animal's skin, and he held a fist-sized skull of what looked to be a cougar or a mountain cat in each hand. Every so often, the captivating drumbeat would stop dramatically. The man would arch his back so he was facing painfully skyward, then another streaking blast of flame would shoot forth from his mouth, causing the people around him to scream with terror and delight.

"It's no trick!" Hyden exclaimed. "There are no liquids and no torches. It must be magic – real magic, like your ring."

Gerard shot him a look that started out as anger, but ended up being more annoyed than anything. Instinctually, his left hand moved over the ring on his right protectively. Realizing Hyden was just trying to make conversation, he kept himself from getting riled over the matter by studying the fire breather. After a few moments, the wonder of the wild man wore off and they moved on. They were nearly trampled when a pair of towering stilt walkers dressed like flamboyant knights, one chasing the other with a wooden sword, came stalking by. The crowd cheered the pursuer as he almost, but not quite, cornered his quarry.

A short while later, the boys found themselves at the base of the monolithic Spire. They paced around its three sides until they found the names of the archery champions. They saw several names they recognized from the tales of the Elders, but all the recent names were elven. Hyden tried to look upward to see the top of the towering thing, but couldn't crane his neck far enough. Even when he took a few steps back, the top disappeared into the darkening sky.

The area was far too packed with people, and Gerard saw the pressure of the upcoming competition showing plainly on Hyden's face. He knew the Elders were putting a heavy load on his brother's back. They didn't just want him to win the archery tournament, they expected him to win. Gerard pulled Hyden away and dragged him back into the throng.

Neither of them had been down the Way that led away from the river, so they started off eastward to see what they could find. There was still a good while left before the Brawl started so Hyden felt they had plenty of time to investigate.

It wasn't much different from the rest of the festival: barrel makers, potters, leather-men, and jewelers, all yelling, bartering, and arguing with the passersby. The only thing noticeably different about this part of the gathering was the more frequent groups of armed and armored men moving about. Some were even on armored horses. These men wore polished, steel plate mail armor and had the horse-head shield of Valleya emblazoned over a field of yellow and red checks proudly displayed upon their shields. A few of them wore rich, blue cloaks as well. Hyden assumed this was a sign of authority for it was far too warm to wear something that heavy for any reason other than recognition.

Other men moved about the crowds wearing uniforms of studded leather vests with matching gauntlets and hard boots. These soldiers had bald heads and wild designs inked into their skin. A few of them had breast patches showing the orange on blue rising sun of Seaward, but most wore only black. The most frequently seen standard among the armed and armored men, though, was the Redwolf of Wildermont.

The Leif Greyn Valley was considered sacred ground by all the kingdoms and races of the realm. No one ruled here. It was a place used only for this peaceful celebration. The rest of the year, only travelers venturing to or from the Giant Mountains, or people coming to see the Spire, passed through. Blood was rarely shed here except in the spirit of competition. To kill on these hallowed grounds was a violation of some ancient oath very few people even remembered. A few times, it happened though; business arguments, cheating husbands, and drunken gamblers always managed to leave a corpse or two behind when they gathered.

The small Kingdom of Wildermont was the closest to the Leif Greyn Valley, and they owned the crossing rights to all the bridges that must be traversed to get there by road. Every year they added a small tax to the regular tolls and used the money to police the event. No one seemed to mind, because the ruler of Wildermont, King Jarrek, was notoriously fair and honest, and his men kept a lot of situations from getting ugly.

Wildermont was mainly a kingdom of miners and smiths. Being nestled in the ore-rich Wilder Mountains just south of the Leif Greyn Valley, they brought in their soldiers and did the best they could to keep the unavoidable private quarrels from getting blown out of proportion.

Being that the majority of the weapons and armor made in the realm, along with the iron fittings for most of the shipbuilding, came from Wildermont's forges, no one argued with King Jarrek's assumed Summer's Day authority. Known as the Redwolf Warrior, King Jarrek was as shrewd and honorable as he was intimidating. He had no problem raising the price of Wildermont exports to a kingdom who didn't keep their own folk in line at the Summer's Day Festival, and he personally made sure the men he had policing the event were well trained and highly disciplined. It was a conceded fact that only a fool angered the Redwolves while at Summer's Day.

"Why aren't there any elves about?" Gerard asked.

Hyden noticed this, too. He didn't really know the answer, but the big brother in him caused him to answer anyway.

"I think they're scared," he said matter-of-factly. "There never really have been any elves about, not any of the years I've been here."

Hyden saw an old, gray-haired woman through the crowd. She was standing in the flap of a room-sized tent, calling to them as if she had known them for years.

"Look!" Hyden pointed her out to Gerard. Out of sheer curiosity, they started angling her way.

"Those yellow-eyed devils hate us," Hyden continued speaking about the elves. "They live in the forest like beasts. They don't want or need the goods and services of the kingdom folk, or us clansmen for that matter. The Salazarkian archer who fouled out of the competition today said the only reason they come out of the forest for Summer's Day is to spite us all with their uncanny prowess with the bow."

Satisfied with the answer, Gerard changed the subject.

"Father said we were tricked today by a sorceress. She charmed me and him into selling her a dozen eggs for ill intent."

"If she really was a sorceress, why did she bother to leave the gold behind?" Hyden asked rhetorically. "She could've easily tricked the two of you out of that as well."

"Aye," Gerard nodded, accepting Hyden's reasoning as sound. "I don't know why."

They had made it over to the old crone's tent by then, and she was waiting for them with her palm held out for payment. Her voice was strong and full of authority, but her breath smelled of cheese and her teeth were mostly blackened stumps. "You weren't tricked out o' your gold so you'd have enough left to spare me a bit o' it. For a bit o' your gold, I'll tell you your fortunes true."

Hyden made a face at Gerard that caused them both to giggle like boys half their age. The woman was obviously blind. Her milky white eyes had no pupils or irises at all. They were brightly bloodshot though, the glossy white orbs streaked with tiny crimson veins. That's not what caused them to laugh; the woman's hair was somewhat normal on one side, but on the other, the hair stuck straight up and out, and was tangled with bits of straw and string.

Gerard fumbled a coin out of his pouch and with a roll of his eyes at Hyden, put it in the old woman's bird-claw hand.

"I said gold!" she barked, causing them both to hop back a step. She flipped the silver coin back at Gerard with a sneer.

Hyden was amazed. Even if her eyes were good, she hadn't so much as glanced at the coin before she'd snapped. She must have felt by its weight that the coin was made of silver.

Gerard suddenly felt like they shouldn't be here. The woman scared him deeply. He couldn't admit that to Hyden, though. He would never be able to live down the jabs if he chickened out now.

She put out her open palm again and narrowed her brows.

"A bit o' gold from him, and a bit o' gold from you. Place it in my hand and I'll tell your fortunes true."

She chanted the rhyme as if she'd said it a thousand times. After a heartbeat, she shook her wrinkled hand again for emphasis.

Hyden was about to turn and walk away, but Gerard surprised him by dropping two golden lions into her hand. He turned and looked at his little brother. They shared a look of anticipation and giddy fear that both of them knew well. Many times in the mountains while climbing a risky ledge, or back in the village waiting for the giantess Berda to tell them a tale, they shared the same wide-eyed expression of coming excitement. Gerard's unease was forced away by the anticipation Hyden's gaze instilled in him. It was as if the look alone left no doubt in either of them that something extraordinary was about to take place.

"Come in, come in," the old woman urged.

She stepped to the side and held the tattered tent flap open for them. A single candle flame, wavering from a low table, provided just enough light to see. Off to one side of the space was a sleeping mat, and next to it a small iron pot full of various cooking utensils. Most of the ground was covered by an ancient carpet, making it appear like there was actually a floor. At the center of the carpet sat a plate with several unlit candles melted onto it. In the middle of the plate was a shallow bowl, full of the bones of a small animal – a rabbit or possibly a squirrel. There was a sweet, musty stench in the tent; the smell of meat, just as it's beginning to spoil, mingled with the oniony smell of sweat.

The light from the lanterns and torches outside disappeared when the woman closed the tent's flap. The single candle struggled to illuminate the space. The old crone hurried around the boys and used the candle's flame to light the wicks of those on the floor.

"Sit. Sit," she kindly persuaded.

As they squatted down and sat cross-legged beside each other, Hyden realized she couldn't actually be blind to do all these things so proficiently. Could she? At the moment, she was lifting up her bedroll and pulling out a foot long roll of cloth. She brought it with her when she came and joined them around the plate full of candles. She squatted down across from them with the plate and bowl before her.

Both boys were full of excitement, and more than a little trepidation, but they wiggled themselves comfortable. Hyden ended up at her right hand side, and Gerard, fidgety and grinning, was at her left.

She unrolled the cloth onto the rug, revealing a long, sharp dagger with a big, yellow jewel mounted in its hilt. The candlelight reflected off the well-kept steel and filled the precious gem with sparkling glimmers. Gerard took one look at the blade and grimaced at Hyden fearfully. The old crone hadn't bothered to look up from her lap, but responded to his unease as if she could see his expression.

"Only one drop of blood, little brother," she chuckled. "That's all it'll take."

Gerard's eyes widened. He didn't think he looked any younger than Hyden. Besides, she was supposed to be blind, wasn't she? To anyone who could see, it was obvious they were brothers, but how could she tell which one was the oldest? And how could she see through those dead, bloodshot eyes? The thought was as unsettling to him as it was frightening.

Hyden was no more comfortable than his younger sibling. Since they had been in the tent, he felt the presence of a fourth person amongst them. He searched the little area with his eyes and saw nothing that could validate his suspicions; nevertheless, he felt something there. His thoughts were yanked away as she grabbed his hand, squeezed it, and pricked his finger all in one smooth, powerful motion. He tried to pull away, but with an otherworldly strength, she held his arm fast until several drops of his blood dripped into the bowl. He looked at Gerard with alarm showing plainly on his face.

Gerard grinned with delight at Hyden's expression of absolute terror. It wasn't often he got to see his brother in such a state. Even though the sight ratcheted up his own fear a few dozen notches, he found himself pleased they had come here.

Hyden let out a sigh of relief when the old woman finally let go of his hand. He sat back with a look of grim satisfaction and enjoyed Gerard's terror when he felt the old crone's unnaturally strong grip latch onto him. Hyden almost laughed out loud, but that strange feeling came over him again, and he darted his eyes around in search of its cause.

After letting go of Gerard the woman hawked loudly, drawing both of the boys' full attention to her. She spat a fat, yellow wad of phlegm into the bowl of bloody bones and began to chant as she stirred the mess with the dagger's tip. The chant grew rhythmic and louder as she went on and on, and suddenly, in a shuddering fit, she tumbled the bowl's contents onto the carpet before her. She threw herself forward and down as if pressing her face to the ground to pray. She wheezed and rasped for breath as she studied the throw of bones up close.

Hyden almost shoved her up, as her nest of hair missed being set afire by the flickering candles on the plate by only a finger's breadth. He started to warn her, but she suddenly jerked back upright and stared out into empty space. This caused both boys to jump, but the look on the woman's face caused the color to drain completely from them.

She had eyes now, but they were like no eyes either of the boys had ever seen before. The pupils were deep crimson with tiny white speckles across them, and the irises surrounding them bore a ring of flickering, yellow flame. The depth of the creases in her ancient face had lessened. Her hair now seemed to be flowing in place and was as shiny as spun gold. It was as if she had aged backward half a hundred years in an instant, and taken on the eyes of a demon.

Hyden wanted to look at his brother, but was afraid to pull his eyes away from the woman. Gerard was transfixed as well. Both of them were truly terrified now, but curiosity's grip wouldn't release them. She started speaking in a voice that sounded like falling icicles shattering on rock.

"First born," her head turned slightly toward Hyden as the words came. "You will soar through the sky with your newfound friend. You will save the life of one that despises you, then mourn his death. You will help a king find a king, and you will triumph in a tower. Someday, you will watch helplessly as one you love dearly attempts to destroy what the one that sits beside you is to become." She paused and shook her head back and forth.

"There is more there, so much more, but it is unclear. I see you struggling to survive in the nether regions of hell, your body full of poison, and your heart full of fear. But why or how, I cannot see."

"What about me?" Gerard blurted out, in an angry-sounding and commanding tone.

A long silence ensued. Hyden couldn't imagine mourning the death of someone who despised him, and he couldn't fathom leading a king anywhere. Nor could he see himself watching helplessly as someone tried to kill Gerard. It all seemed so far-fetched that he didn't even want to consider it. He would've dismissed it all as nonsense had the crone not spoken of him soaring with the hawkling. He shared dreams with the bird already. Her tone and the wicked look in her eyes made him feel that at least she believed what she said. Somehow, she had seen these events. He was sure of it, and it scared him no end.

"The second son of Harrap," the woman hissed, and her head whipped toward Gerard.

Hyden let his distracting thoughts slip away so he could better listen to what she had to say about his brother.

"You will journey far and you will learn the truth of love. Often, you will get your way with those around you. You'll climb to the top of the blackest fang, and you may or may not be betrayed there. You will find the power you long for in the depths of those heights, and you will use it to command legions. But that will come later. Sooner, you will want more than you came for and it will cost you your life. You will die Gerard Skyler, but you will live again. You will die and live again!"

The air around them crackled and popped. The old woman's face was wrinkled and withered once more. She gave Hyden a blank look that might have been full of fear, then began coughing and gasping for breath.

Gerard didn't notice. He was in a trance brought on by the woman's strange prophesying and caught up in his own struggling emotions. She started to gag and was turning purple. The veins in her neck and forehead stood out like earthworms. Even though it was happening right in front of him, it wasn't registering in Gerard's mind. He seemed to have his eyes locked onto the empty space where the crone had just been.

Hyden looked around the tent for a skin of water or a flask, but he couldn't find anything. He was starting to panic. The woman was choking to death right there in front of them. The telling of the two fortunes apparently drained the life right out of her.

Wheezing and hacking, she grasped at her throat desperately. She tried to rise to her feet, but ended up falling on Gerard. He pushed her away hard as if she were on fire or contagious. She rolled across the flaming candles and bloody bones on the floor, then coughed out harshly one last time. Her body extinguished the flames, leaving the tent in darkness. Her breathing filled the sudden silence; ragged, wet, and harsh, but steady nonetheless.

"Leave me," she croaked.

Her words were wasted. Gerard was already throwing open the tent flap with Hyden right on his heels. He stopped and looked back to make sure there wasn't a fire, but he wasn't lingering. By the light of the lantern poles along the Way, he saw there were bones, blood, and globs of candle wax stuck to her robes, but she was struggling to rise to her feet. Satisfied, he hurried to catch up to his fleeing brother. He felt guilty leaving her in that condition, but she told them to go. Who was he to argue with a demon witch?

Trying very hard to put what just happened out of his mind, Hyden gained Gerard's side. He saw his brother was just as troubled by the ordeal, but Gerard's expression showed more anger than confusion.

"Are you all right?" Hyden asked.

Gerard started to dismiss the question, but changed his mind. "I felt... No, I saw her...Shaella, betraying me in a cavern." He unconsciously covered his ring with his left hand.

Hyden noticed the protective gesture, but ignored it. He wanted to say the crone said he may or may not be betrayed, but he held his tongue. He could tell Gerard was confused and searching for words.

Gerard was searching for words all right, but not in the way Hyden suspected. He was trying to sort through all the strange visions he had seen in his mind's eye, especially the ones he wouldn't dare tell Hyden about. He envisioned dark and powerful things he would never speak about to anyone; sinister and malignant things he might someday have control over. The idea of it was intoxicating, and he liked it.

"I'll be going with Shaella," Gerard finally said. "When they leave the festival for the marshes, I'm going with them."

The conviction with which he spoke left little room for argument, so Hyden didn't bother. He wasn't sure he wanted to dissuade Gerard from his adventure anyway. The fortune-teller had spoken of great power and of commanding legions. How could Gerard not want to seek out his destiny with the beautiful swordswoman Shaella? As with his own prophetic glimpses, he was sure there were a lot of truths to what had been predicted for Gerard. Some were obvious. He had already begun using the ring to get his way with the people around him, and he was already considering a journey to a black formation that supposedly resembled a fang.

"Do you want to go with me to the Brawl?" Hyden asked, even though the idea of watching two men beat the hell out of each other somehow seemed a little less exciting after hearing the old woman's grand prophecies.

To Hyden's surprise, Gerard lit up at the suggestion. "Yes! Let's go. Bludgeon, the Seaward Monster, is in the group going with Shaella to the marshes!"

Gerard instantly changed back into the little brother Hyden loved so much. His excitement was contagious, and he picked up the pace as he spoke. "He's huge, Hyden! His arms are as big as your waist and his legs are like tree trunks. He's covered in tattoos, like that fire breathing guy we saw earlier, but without all the red paint."

"Lord Gregory, the Westland Lion, is pretty big himself," Hyden said. He'd watched the Lion Lord destroy the Valleyan Stallion a few years ago and knew Bludgeon would have to be good to win against him.

"My money is all on Bludgeon," Gerard said with a devilish grin on his face. "I already wagered most of my profit on him, all but a few golden lions."

"I hope he wins," Hyden said, wondering why his brother would do such a thing with so much money.

Chapter Eleven

Every year, the Brawl drew a massive crowd, and this year was no exception. The fighting ground where the combatants would actually battle was a circle about thirty feet across. Its boundaries were marked with a rope line, and the area was illuminated by dozens of lanterns dangling overhead from poles planted into the ground. It was the largest open space the eye could see. Men crowded its edges, buying and selling betting tickets, gold for the Western Lion Lord and blue for the Seaward Monster. A dozen or more of Wildermont's most intimidating Redwolf guards worked the perimeter of the fighting circle, trying to keep order where there was none. They were extremely busy. The fight was scheduled to start soon, and everyone was jostling and screaming, trying to get a last minute wager put in.

A slight, natural hill rose up and away from the ring, thus creating a sort of riser for some of the spectators. Some enterprising young men built wooden scaffold stands around the rest of the area. They offered tiered seats above the heads of the rest of the crowd. Seats on these platforms sold for three times the cost of a regular spot. It was from one of these structures that Hyden and Gerard were looking down at the fighting circle. The view they had was one of the best available. Hyden paid the handsome bit of coin to treat his brother to this, and both were extremely excited and pleased with their vantage point.

All thoughts of the future and the past were lost for the moment. Hyden had all but forgotten his archery competition and Gerard was thinking about the fight, instead of how he would explain to his father he wasn't going back to the clan's village when the festival was over. Now, it was time for the Brawl.

Trumpets were sounding in the distance, and there was a snakelike procession of torchbearers weaving their way through the darkened crowd toward the lighted ring. As the parade grew closer, it became clear that it was the Westland Lord and his entourage. The banner they were flying was raised so much higher than the torches they carried, that just a hint of its golden field flashed here and there. Every now and again, the triangular pennant would catch the light just right, to reveal the reared and roaring lion silhouetted on it. Men cheered, and reached out to pat the Westland Lord on his huge back as he passed. Some booed and heckled, and some raised their fists and shouted encouragement. By the time he reached the roped fighting circle, a chant was resounding through the crowd, "LI-ON LORD! LI-ON LORD! LI-ON LORD!" The sound and intensity of the voices increased tenfold when the banner man ran around the lighted circle, waving the Westland banner back and forth crazily.

It became obvious to the boys that the number of people from the huge Kingdom of Westland far outnumbered those from the smaller, eastern kingdoms. The boys didn't know it, but Westland by itself was nearly as big as all five of the eastern kingdoms combined. Hyden had already decided he would buy a map of the realm later. He saw a mapmaker hawking maps of the recognized kingdoms while he was searching for Gerard. He wanted to have some idea where Gerard was going and where Shaella's home, the Kingdom of Dakahn, was. He knew both places were far to the south, but that wasn't enough information to satisfy his curiosity. He hoped someday Berda would show him on the map where all the places she'd told him about were.

A loud, groaning crack resounded through the night, silencing all that heard it in an instant. A good portion of the crowd was still obliviously chanting, but those closer to the brightly lit fighting ring were hushed, staring at one of the scaffold stands with wide eyes and open mouths. Another crack, followed by a long series of crunching noises quieted the rest of the crowd.

Fingers pointed at the particular bleacher as it lurched a few degrees to the side, then stopped. Screams filled the night when the bleacher fell a little bit farther. The people sitting on it scrambled down in a mad rush. Some leapt into the throng of people below, while some clung to the splintering wood with all they had. It was total chaos. Both Hyden and Gerard watched the whole scene in utter disbelief. More than once, Hyden shook himself in place to check the sturdiness of the structure on which they were sitting. It felt good and rigid, unlike the one they were watching. Instead of leaning further over to the side, the whole structure suddenly tumbled straight down upon itself. The massive crowd all watched the madness in stunned silence. A handful of people got caught under the platform when it fell. Dozens were injured, and the people calling up said a few were even killed.

Again, Hyden tried to rock the scaffolding they were sitting on. It was sturdy as far as he could tell. Gerard hit him in the arm to get his attention.

"Look!"

A great gout of fire jetted up into the sky in the distance, and suddenly the sound of drums filled the silence. It was a feverish beat, deep and solid, and it was being pounded out over the gasps and screams of the crowd. The fallen structure and the injured people beneath it were seemingly forgotten. The Seaward Monster was coming to the battlegrounds.

As with Lord Gregory's entrance, a long string of torches were weaving toward the circle. Every few moments fire blasted skyward, lighting the huge combatant and the four red-painted fire breathers, who were taking turns exhaling the flames before him. In the bright explosions of light, the rectangular Seaward Kingdom banner, an orange sun rising from a blue sea, reflected clearly and proudly. A new chant began to form to the rhythmic beat of the drummers.

"EAST-ERN BEAST! EAST-ERN BEAST! EAST-ERN BEAST!" This mantra slowly but steadily overtook the Lion Lord's chant, as the other eastern kingdom folk from Valleya, Dakahn, Wildermont, and Highwander all joined in.

The event was turning into an East versus West grudge battle, which brought the intensity level of the crowd up to a fevered pitch. The betting became furious. The eastern kingdoms, well known for their constant squabbling amongst each other over borders, trade tariffs, and river crossing rights, pushed their differences aside for the moment to cheer on the Seaward fighter. Nearly all of the people from the eastern kingdoms wanted to see the overbearing Kingdom of Westland's favorite fighter go down.

By the time Bludgeon stepped into the circle, the chant for him was completely drowning out the voices of the people still cheering for Lord Gregory. Two of the red-and-black painted fire breathers sent up simultaneous pillars of flame for the monster to pass between as he entered the fighting circle. The crowd exploded into screams and cheers. The people that fell with the scaffolding were long forgotten as the two brawlers paced around the fighting circle, flexing and stretching their massive muscles.

Hyden saw that Bludgeon was a bit larger than Lord Gregory, but the Valleyan Stallion had been bigger, too. Hyden had planned to root for the Lion Lord until he learned about Gerard's foolish bet. If Gerard lost his wager, his entire harvest this year and the risk of making it would've been for nothing. The idea of risking that much coin on a gamble disturbed Hyden. He could see betting enough to make the fight more exciting, but the amount Gerard wagered was extreme. He found himself wanting the giant, tattoo-covered Seawardsman to win just so Gerard didn't lose all his money. He glanced at his brother. Gerard was on the edge of his seat, excitement radiating from him like heat from a forge fire. It made Hyden smile despite his concern over Gerard's purse.

"I hope you win!" Hyden yelled, but Gerard didn't hear him.

Hyden looked back to the fighting circle and saw why Gerard wasn't paying any attention to him. Shaella was down there among the fire breathers, wearing a hooded cloak that didn't quite conceal the bulge of her sword hilt, or the swell of her ample bosom. She threw the hood back, and her face was the most beautiful thing visible in the entire crowd. She spoke a few words to Bludgeon, then was pulled out of the roped off area by another tattoo-covered Seawardsman just before the Wildermont Redwolf soldiers began clearing the circle for the Brawl.

As soon as the ring was cleared, the Redwolf guards took up positions spaced evenly around the battleground. Each of them turned their bladed pike to a horizontal position, then passed the tip end of it to the guard on his left. When the synchronized maneuver was finished, each soldier had the butt end of his own spear in his left hand, and the business end of his neighbor's spear in his right. The pike shafts created a waist-high rail that was intended to keep the pressing onlookers out of the fray.

There were very few rules to the Brawl. The main rule was that no weapons were to be used by the brawlers. Other than that, it was a battle to the death unless one of the fighters yielded, or was incapacitated due to unconsciousness or severe injury. Once a fighter yielded, the other man couldn't continue to beat on him. If a fighter went down and lay still for any length of time, he could not be molested until he made it back to his feet. Biting, eye gouging, hair pulling, and blows below the belt were sometimes booed by the crowd, but were all legal maneuvers.

A hush fell over the crowd as the two combatants began to slowly circle each other. When his back was to them, Hyden saw Bludgeon's tattoos formed the skeletal shape of a winged creature, whose skull and beak climbed over the top of the man's head. Its wings and body spread out across his back; the wing tips reached around the back of his arms to his elbows. When Bludgeon's arms were held at his side, the wings looked to be pulled back, as if the creature were in a dive. When he threw out his arms to dart in at the Lion Lord, it looked as if the tattooed skeleton was spreading out its wings to take flight.

Bludgeon attacked first, feigning a grappling hold, then throwing a looping right-handed punch. The Westland Lion leaned back, letting the huge fist pass a hair's breadth in front of his determined face. He ducked under with his head down, throwing a thundering flurry of blows to the bigger man's gut. It sounded like a butcher's tenderizing hammer, smashing into a thick slab of fresh meat. The Seaward Monster roared and flexed his body. He growled at the crowd as he took each and every punch without faltering. Then he brought both his fists down like war hammers into Lord Gregory's spine and sent the Lion Lord to his knees.

Gerard jumped to his feet, shouting his approval with thousands of others. At the moment, Hyden thought his brother might have made a good bet. He only hoped the steadily rocking scaffold they were perched on would hold until the fight was over. Already, it was rumbling and swaying more than he would've liked.

Lord Gregory seemed stunned, but only for a heartbeat. He lunged forward from his lower position into Bludgeon's knees and lifted the big man's feet clear of the ground. The thump of the Seawardsman's body when he slammed flat onto his back into the trampled grass caused an audible gasp from the crowd. The onlooker's collective intake of breath sounded in perfect unison with the whooshing exhale from the Monster. Since Bludgeon was still moving around on the ground, the Lion Lord didn't hesitate to pounce. He leapt to the big man's waist, straddled him, and began throwing violent hammer blows at his opponent's head. Left and right, left and right, over and over he pounded to the cheers of the Westlanders in the crowd. Lord Gregory's shoulders rolled with the force of his blows, and soon his hands were slinging blood.

Just when it began to look hopeless, Bludgeon somehow managed to heave and bring a knee up into the Lion Lord's back. With a scream of fury, he took advantage of the moment of imbalance, twisted, and rolled out from under the Lion, then staggered to his feet.

His face was a bloody mess. One of his eyes was swollen closed. The white of his other eye was as red as the blood pouring out of the gaping gash above his brow. His nose and lips were battered flat, and a tooth was missing from his jaw. A triumphant cheer exploded from the groups of Westland spectators when they saw him.

"Come on Bludgeon!" Gerard yelled down at his fighter. His voice was but one of thousands urging the big man on. He glanced nervously at Hyden, who was already looking at him worriedly. They both cringed in unison and shared that old excited, anything can happen, look. Hyden turned back to the fight and yelled for Bludgeon to "Stomp the Lion!" Gerard joined in the call as the Seawardsman attempted another attack.

Bludgeon stepped in just like he had the first time, throwing the same looping right-handed punch that had missed. This time when Lord Gregory leaned back to slip the blow, the Monster took another step forward and kicked out hard. His heavy boot hit the Lion Lord square in the chest with such force that the Westlander's hands slapped his boot tips in midair as he was launched backward. A cheer and a sympathetic, "Oooh!" swept through the mass of people simultaneously when Lord Gregory crashed into the ground in a heap. He tried to roll to his feet, but ended up clutching his chest and yelling out in anguish. Bludgeon saw his chance and dove in at him.

Momentarily satisfied that his wager was safe, Gerard scanned the edges of the fighting circle for Shaella. If Bludgeon went on to win the fight, there would surely be a celebration. He wanted to be there to see her, to taste her lips again. He wanted to tell her that he was going to go with them to the Dragon's Tooth Spire. In his mind's eye, he had seen her betray him there, while the old crone was telling him his future, but he knew in his heart he could change the outcome. If he could make her love him, there would be no betrayal. If that didn't work, he knew he could always use the ring to keep her from it. The other things he'd seen happen in that black, rocky cavern were dark and grand, far too tempting to resist. He pondered those vexing thoughts while he searched for Shaella. He looked at the faces, but didn't see her again. He did, however, see a face that commanded his full attention.

"There, Hyden! There!" Gerard pointed down at a person standing between the farthest two Redwolf guards that formed the pike rail.

"What are you pointing at?" Hyden was fully focused on the Brawl and glad his brother seemed to be winning his bet. He saw nothing out of the ordinary.

"The witch that bought our eggs!" Gerard yelled, as he shook his finger toward the fighters below. "That woman, over there, with the whistle! She's the one that tricked father and I this morning!"

Hyden looked around and found her at the very edge of the pike rail. His focus zoomed in on her unexpectedly, causing his head to spin. Nothing like that had ever happened to him before. She looked close enough to touch now. The wild visual shift was unnerving, but he didn't let it distract his mind. He wanted to know what this woman was about. It wasn't a whistle she held to her mouth. Was it a flute? A strange kind of smoking pipe maybe? What was it?

Suddenly she paused and looked directly at the boys. It was as if she sensed them staring at her across the great distance that separated them. Hyden swallowed hard when he saw her eyes. There were no whites at all, just jet black orbs that chilled his blood to the bone.

"Charm me will ya?" he heard Gerard say. He knew without even looking what his brother was about to do.

The witch jerked her head up a fraction and locked her eerie gaze on some other part of the crowd for a moment. Hyden realized what the tubular item in her hand was then. Her attention returned to the fight, put the thing to her mouth, and pointed it at the entangled combatants. Hyden watched on helplessly as she took in a deep breath and blew into the tube with a burst of force. A look of shock crossed her face then, and she twisted her black eyes up at Gerard, but Hyden didn't see the gesture. He was looking at the tiny little needle dart protruding out of Lord Gregory's shoulder. His attention was drawn from the dart when Gerard elbowed him excitedly, but not before he saw the Westland Lion swat the thing away into the trampled grass.

A gasping sound as the entire crowd drew in a breath at the exact same moment, resounded again when the little witch ducked under the pike rail and stepped into the fighting circle. One of the Redwolf guards snatched at her robe and spun her, but she screamed out with wide, terrible eyes, causing the guardsmen to take a step back. The whole crowd fell silent. Even the brawlers stopped as the witch started spinning in a blurring circle, howling out with rage in a voice that was far from human. When she stopped spinning, she was no longer a woman. Instead, a child-sized, red-scaled devil stood there. It hissed and snarled, its dead eyes looking at Gerard. It leapt into the air and flew away on thumping, leathery wings.

Both fighters staggered to their feet and looked up at the wild little creature as it disappeared into the darkened sky. After a few moments of bewildered silence, the battle slowly resumed.

By the smug look of satisfaction on Gerard's face, Hyden knew his brother caused the witch to step into the circle and reveal herself. He wondered if Gerard knew the witch put a dart that was most likely poisoned into the Lion Lord. No, he reasoned, Gerard wouldn't have brought attention to the witch had he known she was doing something that would ensure Bludgeon a victory. The idea Shaella had something to do with it crossed Hyden's mind, though. He scanned the crowd for her and noticed his eyes were still focusing extremely sharp for some strange reason. Shaella was nowhere to be seen. He dismissed her as he noticed the Lion Lord faltering. The Westland fighter was stumbling to and fro like a drunkard trying to keep his balance. He wasn't giving up the fight though, even with the bigger man having his way with him. The lion was battered and bloody now, currently taking sledgehammer blows to the neck and side of his head. In the middle of one such flurry, he slumped forward, put his hands on his knees, and heaved for breath.

The giant Seawardsman was breathing as hard as a forge bellows, but he stood alert and ready to continue the pounding he was giving. He spoke a few words to Lord Gregory, asking him if he was ready to surrender yet, but no answer came. The Western Lord only swayed a little to one side, as if he were about to topple over. With a look of regret, tinged with sadness and frustration, the man known as the Seaward Monster took a quick step forward, and kicked up at the Lion Lord's face with all he had. He was going to end it here.

As quick as a flash of lightning, the Lion rose up, letting Bludgeon's foot glance off of his pectoral muscles. He twisted his entire body in place, and came around from the spin with sickening speed and force. The back of his clenched fist cracked into the Seawardsman's temple with a crunch of breaking bones that was heard over the din of the crowd. The Monster was left stumbling and dazed, unconscious on his feet.

Lord Gregory fell; the poison had completely stolen his equilibrium. He went into the ground face first. The Seaward Monster stumbled as well, but caught himself. He reared back his head and let out a brutally primal roar. When the chilling sound subsided, the whole place was deathly quiet. Bludgeon leaned forward and spat out a long, slimy string of thick, crimson muck. When he rose back up, his hands went reflexively to his grossly misshapen head, as if to feel if it was still there. Then he too fell face first toward the ground. It was nothing more than random chance that caused him to land right on top of the Western Lion's poison-saturated body.

Chapter Twelve

After the Brawl, the night's excitement ended abruptly for Hyden. Gerard followed him back to the clan's bonfire, which was relatively deserted at this late hour. A lot of other clansmen attended the Brawl, but they were either still out among the crowds or already retired for the night.

Hyden presented Gerard with the pair of expensive horsehide boots he bought for him earlier in the day. Gerard thanked him and gave him a long hug of appreciation, then begged off, saying he needed to go collect his winnings. Hyden figured he just didn't want to face their father, or any of the Elders, with his decision to leave yet.

Hyden didn't mind Gerard's departure. He was tired and his eyes ached. He still had to compete against that blasted elf in the morning, and he couldn't get to bed until he cared for the hungry hawkling chick he had neglected all evening.

He took the nest bucket from his tent and carried it over to the dying bonfire. The chick ate greedily, and Hyden saw its eyes had finally cleared.

The memory of the old crone's prophecy, and of his eyes zooming in on the tiny dart the little witch-devil shot into Lord Gregory's shoulder came to him. His stomach knotted and churned, and he sat down hard in a cross-legged hunch.

He finished feeding the bird and scooped it out of the bucket gently. He put it in his lap and began stroking its new feathers with his finger.

The feathers were brown with traces of red and silver running through them. In the dim fire glow, they seemed to hold an illumination of their own. The bird's beak and head had taken shape as well, but all in all, the little hawkling was still no bigger than Hyden's hand.

"Are you really a gift from the gods?" Hyden wondered aloud.

As if in response, the young bird fluttered its wings and managed to fly a few feet. It didn't land well. It toppled sideways on a half open wing and made a little shriek of pain, or maybe it was frustration, after righting itself. It turned around and leapt from the trampled ground. With a quick double flap of its wings, it flew back to Hyden and landed almost gracefully on his knee. Hyden had to chuckle, for the bird seemed to be puffing out its chest, proud of the accomplishment.

Hyden stroked the back of the bird's head with one finger, and put the index finger of his other hand out before it. Somehow the bird understood his intent and stepped onto the offered perch. Hyden marveled at how strong its tiny claws gripped him.

"I suppose the gods didn't name you yet, did they?" Hyden whispered. "Your tail feathers haven't lengthened enough for me to tell if you're male or female. We need a name that will suit you either way."

The hawkling cooed at him, then dug its claws into his finger deeply. Instinctively, Hyden yanked his hand away and shook it. The bird flapped and fluttered back to the ground awkwardly.

"Your talons are sharp!" Hyden growled, then sucked a droplet of blood from his finger. The hawkling bobbed its head up and down, and then cooed again. Hyden froze.

"Talon?" he asked the little bird, as if it could understand him. To his surprise, the hawkling bobbed its head again, and leapt back onto his knee. Again, Hyden chuckled in disbelief.

"Talon it is, then. We'll call you Talon."

While Hyden slept, he dreamed the dream of flight again. Distant mountains loomed ahead and field mice scattered in the pastures below him. Around his wing tips, cottony clouds floated on warm, uplifting air. It was a night of glorious dives, wild swooping attacks, and long, slow, spiraling climbs. He slept as well as he ever had, and when he was finally startled awake, he could still feel the wind flowing over his feathers.

Several angry foreign accents and his father's voice barking out harshly from somewhere nearby jerked him from his dreams. He sat up and looked around, slowly forcing the confusion of waking from his mind. He'd fallen asleep outside by the fire pit. The Ways were already crowded with people. He remembered today was Summer's Day: the day of his competition. A wave of nervous excitement washed over him. Talon was perched on the top edge of his nest bucket with part of a grasshopper hanging from his beak. He had eaten most of it and didn't seem to know he had missed the morsel. Hyden laughed and rubbed the sleep from his eyes. From behind him, a small voice spoke.

"Hey, Hyden."

It was Little Condlin. The boy had become distant and reclusive since his two brothers fell at the harvest. Hyden saw him hovering around the women mostly since they'd been at the festival. No one could blame him for wanting to be close to his mother. It was probably a good thing for her and him both.

"How are you?" Hyden asked as the boy squatted down in front of Talon to look at the bird eye to eye.

"I'm all right, I guess," Little Con replied before going into a nonstop series of questions.

"Does he have a name yet? Can I be your squire, or page, or whatever they call them, since Gerard has left us? What do you think it is? Is it a boy or a girl hawkling?"

"Slow down Condlin, slow down." Hyden rose to his feet quickly. "What do you mean Gerard's gone? How do you know?"

"My father sent me to fetch you," the boy said without looking away from Talon. "Gerard left a note last night saying he was leaving. I didn't know he could write."

"Here," Hyden fumbled a silver coin out of his belt pouch and tossed it to his cousin. "Go across the Way to the vendor and buy some raw meat. I'm not sure if the hawkling is a he or a she yet, but its name is Talon."

Hyden ruffled the boy's hair. "Cut the meat into little strips and feed the bird. When I'm finished speaking to our fathers, we will discuss the possibility of you accompanying me to the tournament."

The boy was off before Hyden even finished speaking. Hyden lingered with Talon like a protective parent until he saw Little Condlin returning with the bird's food.

Harrap wasn't the angry, cursing man he was the day before. Today he was quiet and reserved, with eyes full of what might have been regret and more than a little sadness.

"Why wouldn't he have claimed his winnings if he knew he was leaving?" he asked his oldest son.

Hyden didn't have a definite answer. It was a curious thing that Gerard put all his winning blue tickets in with the note he left their father, but Hyden didn't see it as a cause for alarm.

"Maybe he cashed a few of them in. Just what he thought he might need," he suggested, even though it didn't seem like something Gerard would do. Gerard's nature would've been to collect all of his gold and leave just a little bit behind, not the other way around.

"He told me he was going to leave, but I didn't think he would go so soon."

Hyden didn't say he knew of his brother's plans since early yesterday evening, just after they left the fortune-teller's tent. He kept what he told his father about Gerard's destination, and traveling companions, as vague as he possibly could. He didn't want to fill the Elder's head full of unwarranted concern. With the ring at Gerard's disposal, Hyden was sure his brother could take care of himself. Hyden did find it frustrating he couldn't share that bit of knowledge with his father without betraying Gerard's confidence, though.

After a long silence, Harrap sighed and then nodded, as if he was accepting some part of a reality he had no control over. The subject of his concern changed then.

"Are you ready for today, Son?" he asked with a forced smile.

"The elf is terribly good, Father," Hyden said matter-of-factly. He made sure it didn't sound like he was making an excuse. "I will do the best I can."

"Aye," Harrap's smile became genuine and held a great deal of pride in its curve. "If you do your best and lose, there's no shame in it. As men, we sometimes put too much value on trivial things. I wish…I wish that we, as a clan, hadn't put so much pressure on you. It's not fair. You cannot win back the losses of the past. All you can hope to do is compete with pride, honor, and dignity. If you manage to do that, then you've already won."

Harrap put his arm around his oldest son and squeezed him lovingly.

"Honor among men, it seems, has grown scarce these days," he mumbled to no one in particular.

"Thank you, Father," Hyden said.

The weight of the load he'd been carrying on his shoulders seemed to lighten a little bit, but not so much he felt he could relax. The rest of the Elders, including his grandfather, still expected him to win. He didn't want to think about the competition at all yet. It was still a few hours away, and he had other things on his mind.

"What were you and those men arguing about this morning?" he asked, trying to tactfully change the subject.

"One of the men that fought in the Brawl last night, died. Now some of the Dakaneese wager men are trying to dispute the Seaward Monster's victory."

Hyden wasn't surprised.

"Lord Gregory looked to be dead when he fell." Hyden didn't say anything about the witch and the poison dart. "The Monster won, despite the Lion Lord's final blow. What is there to dispute?"

Harrap was shaking his head.

"It wasn't the Westlander that died. The Lion's last blow shattered the Monster's skull. The crowd saw the Lion fall first, so, by all rights, the Seawardsman won, even though he was probably dead before he landed on top of Lord Gregory. The wager men tried to balk on payment of Gerard's tickets, until they saw how large and formidable our clan is. It wasn't easy getting Gerard's prize. I had to threaten to harm them while we had them surrounded. I also reminded them we are not part of the human kingdoms, but from the Giant's lands. Most of the folk who bet last night don't have the numbers we do and aren't getting paid at all. The whole place has turned into a boiling pot. It wouldn't surprise me if the kingdom folk start killing each other over it."

"But today is Summer's Day," Hyden said. "Today is the day all the people are supposed to celebrate peace and friendship."

"Aye it is," Harrap returned. "But the people of the kingdoms have long forgotten the ways of old and the sacred oaths their ancestors swore here. It is sad, but it is not our concern. We are the Skyler Clan, and we are free. Only the king of the giants can command us, and that's only because we live in the mountains they call their own. King Aldar doesn't even presume to rule over our people, even though he has the right. As I said before, the men of the kingdoms have long forgotten what honor is all about."

A short while later, Halden, the Eldest, patted his grandson's back and wished him well. Hyden's uncles, Condlin, Sharoo, Benald, and Pylen, all did the same. His grandfather's brother, Harren, mussed his hair as if he were still a little boy. Uncle Mahr, the clan's spirit leader, said a prayer to the White Lady, their patron goddess. All of the Elders and most of the women would be watching him compete later. What little bit of pressure his father lifted earlier had now been replaced tenfold.

Outside the crowded tent where they were gathered, the younger clansmen waited patiently to add to it, all of them except Gerard. This fact gnawed at Hyden more deeply with each passing hour.

After he spoke with his father, Hyden jogged past the shining black spire, down the southern Way to where Gerard said Shaella and her party were encamped. The day was as perfect as a day could be. The sun was bright and the sky was blue and clear, save for a few puffy white clouds drifting lazily. There was a cool and steady breeze coming from the west, carrying the fresh smell of the river's swell and the blooming foliage along its shoreline.

The people he passed, though, were visibly on edge. Untrusting eyes darted here and there suspiciously. Everyone was traveling in groups and were all armed with some sort of weapon. All of the clumps of people moving about were from the same families or kingdoms and they tended to stick together, as if a stray would be swept away by some unseen magical stream.

The cheer and mirth of the previous day was gone. It was like a rain storm washed away the joy and left a sticky film of worry and fear over everything. Some of the people seemed oblivious to the foul mood. Others scurried from shop, to cart, to tent, buying up things as if it were the last day of the world. Hyden saw a few groups packing up their belongings to leave. Horses were hitched to waiting wagons and pavilions were being rolled and stored for travel.

Hyden felt the tension hanging in the air like the slow, sizzling sound of a knot in a fire log. Sooner or later, it would pop and send a shower of sparks swirling out of the pit. The embers might just burn themselves out, but something as simple as a breeze could cause them just as easily to flare into flame and burn a whole forest to the ground.

As he expected, the Dakaneese woman's camp was empty. Nothing but trampled grass and a few rock-ringed fire pits remained. The trail they left led southward. The nearest camp was far enough away that he didn't even bother asking about the sudden departure of Shaella's party as he passed it on his way back. Gerard was gone, chasing after his dreams. Hyden had to respect his brother's determination, even if he didn't like the fact he had gone.

When he returned to the Skyler Clan's area, he was ushered in before the Elders. The competition would be starting soon, and they too wanted to heap piles of pressure on his shoulders.

Hyden eventually left the crowded tent and emerged into another pack of his clansmen. They patted his back, wished him well, and offered little tidbits of advice and support. These were mostly tinged with the opinions of their parents and the older clansmen. Comments like: "Beat the skinny forest freaks," or, "Show those yellow-eyed devils what it's about!"

Hyden knew that not one of the younger men, or boys, had been as close to an elf as he was yesterday at the culling, yet they hated them just because the Elders did. It didn't matter, Hyden decided. He smiled and thanked them, but his head and heart were somewhere else. Hyden was trying not to let his worry over Gerard, or the pressure from his people, get the better of him. This day was too perfect of a day and win or lose, he was going to try and enjoy it.

Little Condlin parted the group and handed Hyden his bow. To everyone's delight, Talon awkwardly flew from the boy's shoulder to Hyden's. He helped the struggling little chick land

and get a grip on his shoulder, but once Talon was settled he puffed out his chest proudly and let loose a squeaking caw.

A few minutes later, Hyden was walking toward the tournament grounds with Little Condlin a few paces behind him, while Talon was flapping and struggling to maintain his balance beside Hyden's ear.

The archer from Westland looked angry and distracted, like he hadn't slept in a while. He was sharply attired though, in a crisp, white doublet, sporting the golden lion of his kingdom on the front and back. From fifty yards away, he put three arrows into the Wizard's Eye and two just outside it in the King's Ring. Loud boos and jeers came from the crowd gathered behind Hyden, but they were quickly drowned out by the cheers that erupted from the other side of the shooting lanes.

Hyden saw the bleacher scaffolds from last night's Brawl had been rebuilt along the length of the archery tournament grounds. They weren't nearly as tall now. Hyden guessed it was more because the field was long and narrow, than for any sort of safety concern. Unlike the night before, where crowds were happy to be mingled hodgepodge together, today the kingdom folk were segregated into factions bearing their kingdom's colors and sitting separate from the other kingdom folk who were in attendance.

The Redwolf soldiers of Wildermont were present in abundance, and wisely seated the Seawardsmen on one side of the range, with the Westlanders on the other. This left them facing each other, which created an opening for some colorful gestures and crude threats to be thrown across the field, but the arrangement otherwise kept them from getting too close to each other. Hyden also noticed there were plenty of Valleyans and Dakaneese in attendance. They chose to sit on the same side as the Seawardsmen, but stayed amongst themselves just the same.

"A true representation of the politics of fools," the elven contender said, from a few feet away.

His two companions chuckled beside him and directed their wild, yellow eyes at Hyden.

"See," the elf continued, as he pointed toward the people who were booing from behind them. Hyden looked, and saw his clansmen and the womenfolk filing in and taking seats together, yet separate from the people of the kingdoms.

"The weaker kingdoms fight among themselves enough to warrant the slight separation between them, yet they all take the same side against the west." The elven archer looked directly into Hyden's eyes. "The rest of the pathetic humans just hide in the mountains."

Talon let out a loud shriek from Hyden's shoulder. The sound drew the feral gaze of all six yellow elven eyes to him.

"And some people are so afraid, they only crawl out of the forest once a year to the one place where we humans are sworn not to fight," Hyden returned hotly.

He wanted to say more, but held his tongue and fought down his anger. If the elf was trying to unsettle him, the trick worked.

The elves kept their eyes on Talon, but Hyden's sharp words caused all three of them to narrow their brows, and the elves were colored with rage. The elven archer gave Hyden the slightest of looks, then pulled his bow from its leather case and began to string it.

The crowd around the tournament field quieted as the Valleyan archer took the line. He looked resplendent in his ringed leather armor, sporting the yellow and red checked Valleyan shield patch on his breast, and a similar shield-shaped symbol of his kingdom's honor guard on his shoulder in shining silver. It had been rumored, and in fact was true, that the man's mother had been born in Dakahn, so a sort of alliance formed within the crowd. The part of the story where the Valleyan horse trader bought the Dakaneese woman from a slaver for an old mare and some sacks of meal had been conveniently left out.

Hyden watched with respectful understanding as the young man took several deep breaths and squeezed his eyes shut for a quick prayer. No doubt someone piled up a wagonload of pressure on his shoulders, too. The myriad distractions that seemed to come from everywhere probably weighed on him. Only the glittery haired, alien-looking elf seemed oblivious to the tension humming through the air.

The Valleyan man took his time and shot well. He repeated the Westland archer's results to the boos of the greater kingdom's overwhelming numbers.

A large Valleyan man wearing ringed leather armor, probably the archer's father, bolted across the field hurling curses and insults at the whole of the Westlanders' bleachers. Before the Redwolf soldiers could get to him, a pair of green and gold clad men rushed out to rebuke the man's words, and a fight erupted. There was an explosion of screaming and yelling between the two sides across the archery field, and Hyden was a little concerned the whole place would turn into a battleground. Finally, the skirmish ended when the three men involved in the actual fight were put in chains and marched slowly across the field for all to see. Needless to say, the crowd settled down. The place was at a near hush when the combatants were placed in a wagon cage near where the targets were and hauled away.

As soon as the Wildermont soldiers motioned for the event to continue, the elf stole away all of the kingdom men's hope for victory. He loosed five arrows at his target in rapid succession, as smoothly and calmly as if he were merely sipping wine from a cup. All five arrows appeared to be sprouting from the Wizard's Eye, but Hyden could see plainly when he looked down at the target that only four were completely in the center mark. He would have to match the score, or the event was over. Either way, the crowd had been silenced completely. Neither of the kingdom men could win now. It took a few minutes for this to sink into the minds of the spectators and when it did, they all seemed to lose interest and started to filter away from the stands.

Hyden took his place at the line and urged Talon from his shoulder onto his finger. He traded Little Condlin the bird for his bow, then took a deep breath.

It occurred to him that it was more of a distraction to see all those people leaving from out of the corner of his eye than it would have been if they stayed and made some noise. He forced it all out of his mind, took another deep breath, and sought out a place inside him that was both calm and serene. From there, he began to focus.

His eyes seemed to zoom in on the Wizard's Eye, and before he knew it, he had loosed an arrow. Seeing the shaft sprouting out of the dead center of the target helped keep the world around him at bay. In a daze-like state of concentration, he saw the coin sized Wizard's Eye as if it were the size of an apple. He pulled back on another arrow and let it fly. Twice more his arrows struck the Wizard's Eye true. As he put his fourth arrow to the bowstring, he distantly wondered what Shaella and her company was doing at that very moment. It took a moment for him to find the space in the target's center for the fourth arrow, but he saw it between the first three, just a tiny triangle of black that grew in his eyes, like a rabbit did from the sky. He loosed the arrow and knew before it even struck the target that he had hit his mark. He reached for his fifth arrow. If he could fit it into the crowded Wizard's Eye somehow, he could end the tournament right here, but it would be next to impossible to make that happen. The target's center was already full.

Somewhere, outside the world of his focus, he heard the trio of the elves gasping and grumbling. He let the satisfaction the sound gave him fade, and studied the Wizard's Eye. Even if he put his fifth arrow in the center, it would force the edge of one of his previous shafts out into the King's Ring. It was worth a try though, so he raised his bow, drew back on it, and took aim at the center of the target yet again. A flicker of movement he thought was far beyond the target caught his eye, then disappeared again. Maybe it was an insect up close that distracted him. He wasn't sure. No, he could still see it. It was moving through the air, too uniformly to be a bug. Finally, he realized that it was an arrow arcing toward them from a great distance. A glance at where it would've been loosed from revealed a small group of mounted men. A banner wavered in the light breeze among them. It was a white rectangle, with a black sword emblazoned on it horizontally. It was the Blacksword of Highwander, Willa the Witch Queen's men.

Hyden almost loosed his arrow astray when he saw the face of a woman that greatly resembled Shaella peeking out from under a hood amongst them. Was it her? He looked again, but they were too far away for him to tell.

The arrow was coming down toward him now, and it was fast. Hyden could tell that it would miss him, but it would be close. He followed its trajectory with his eyes. It was coming down right at the elven archer. There was no time left to think. He turned swiftly and loosed his arrow at the incoming missile. It was a one in a million shot but he somehow found his mark only a few feet before the shaft pierced through the elf.

All three of the elves shrieked in startled pain as they were showered with wooden splinters. Thinking instinctually that Hyden had attacked, one of them drew out a dagger and charged.

"HOLD!" the elven archer screamed out, so loudly it startled Hyden out of the strange, trance-like state he had fallen into. The knife-bearing elf froze in his tracks. The elven archer was looking up at the sky with his hand held at his brow to shade his eyes from the sun's glare. Several trickles of blood ran down his cheeks like tears. For some reason, Hyden was reminded of the tear drop scar on Shaella's otherwise perfect face. Then the sound of fat, heavy rain drops, and the screams of people from several different directions, filled his ears.

The elf was screaming something Hyden couldn't understand, then Little Condlin made a wheezing, muffled grunt behind him. Hyden whirled around to find the boy had an arrow sticking up out of his shoulder. His cousin was trying to scream, but for some reason couldn't manage it. It wasn't raindrops he was hearing, Hyden realized as tears filled his eyes. He dove to catch the boy as he staggered to his knees. Talon somehow got pinned between them, and was shrieking and flapping madly. Blood dribbled down Little Condlin's chin from his mouth. Arrows were raining down on them, and Hyden had no clue as to why it was happening or what he could do about it.

Without any regard for his own safety, he hovered over Little Condlin and Talon, shielding them with his body while shouts, screams, and the sound of ringing steel filled the air around them. A perfect Summer's Day had just turned into an incomprehensible bloody nightmare.

Chapter Thirteen

Skinning the huge barkskin lizard would've been an easy task if Mikahl hadn't felt like a one-eyed sack of broken bones.

Upon waking, he found one cheek had swollen his eye closed, and his body ached and burned in places he never even knew existed. Loudin, the hunter, seemed to be in a hurry, but he didn't push Mikahl too hard. Mikahl was glad of it because it took most of the morning just to get all his parts moving properly. After that, in spite of the pain, he was able to help get things done in a reasonably expedient fashion.

Once the lizard skin was sliced away from the beast and rolled up like a castle carpet, Mikahl washed the gore from himself in the pond. The cold water eased the pain and swelling in his face. This, in turn, eased the anger he felt when he found out his old sword was badly bent during the creature's death throes. All of that was forgotten though, as a flood of embarrassment washed over him. Loudin had found his abandoned bow and was laughing at his shame.

Loudin rigged the surprisingly lightweight roll of skin between their two horses in a way that allowed him and Mikahl to still ride them. Windfoot had to walk directly behind Loudin's roan, and Mikahl had to keep the distance between them from stretching or shrinking too much. The amount of attention this required kept his mind off of his pain as they traveled. The whole situation was awkward. Having the long, bulky tube of rolled skin tethered alongside the horses caused Mikahl and Loudin both to have to sit with one leg cocked wide and thrown over the roll. Today was right leg day, Loudin had explained. Tomorrow, he would rig the roll on the other side of the saddles, so that their left side would suffer the uncomfortable position. Mikahl didn't complain. In his battered condition, walking would have been far worse than riding.

Most of the Reyhall Forest was openly spaced and easy to traverse, with little undergrowth and plenty of shade, but a few places were extremely dense. The going seemed slow. More than once they had to dismount and cut a path through the underbrush, or maneuver the horses around closely spaced obstacles so that the skin didn't get snagged, torn, or pulled out of its bindings. For the most part though, the spaces between the old tree trunks were wide enough that a small wagon could've probably made it through.

Considering they hadn't gotten underway until early afternoon, they traveled a great distance by nightfall. When they stopped for the night, it was nearly full dark. Mikahl built a small fire while Loudin unrigged the lizard skin from the saddle, and hoisted it up off the ground with ropes he'd thrown over some tree limbs. He explained as he worked that keeping the roll off the ground would keep insects and varmints out of it, but Mikahl was softly snoring before the old hunter had finished speaking.

Mikahl wasn't sure how long he slept. It was still dark and the fire was nothing more than a pile of glowing embers when he woke. Above the natural, chaotic chorus of insects and other nocturnal creatures of the forest, the rhythmic, snorting growl of Loudin's snoring filled the night.

Mikahl's aching body protested as he sat up. He almost cried out from the pain caused by the movement, but he managed to bite it back. As he caught his breath, the faint outline of Windfoot and Loudin's roan jostling on their picket lines caught his eye and startled him.

He spent a few minutes rolling and rubbing his neck and shoulders, then craned his head back. He searched the underside of the forest's thick canopy for any sign of the sky. He wanted to see the moon, or at least a few stars. He found neither. He harrumphed with frustration, went to his saddle bags, and rummaged for some food. Ironspike was there; safe in its leather sleeve, the sight of it caused his curiosity to take hold of him.

He checked to make sure Loudin was sleeping deeply; by the sound of the snoring, Mikahl was confident he wouldn't wake any time soon. Dawn was still a few hours away, so this was about as much privacy as he could expect to ever have. He took a deep breath, shoved the hunk of cheese he was eating into his mouth, and held it between his teeth. With his hands now free, he unstrapped the leather bag that protected and concealed the sword, and carried it back to his bedroll.

He'd seen the sword a thousand times while it hung menacingly from King Balton's hip. He even got to handle it, but only when he was cleaning and polishing it. The blade served as a warning to those who thought to cross the old man, and it gave comfort to those who looked to him for protection. Mikahl remembered cleaning the battle gore from its gleaming surfaces a few years ago after one of the battles up in Coldfrost. More recently, he wiped away a Dakaneese sell-sword's blood from its razor edge after he had been beheaded for robbing and killing a Portsmouth merchant. Mikahl had polished the sword's beautifully etched blade and its jeweled hilt a score of times and could remember every single one of them. All of those memories caused him to think about King Balton. He started to take the sword out of its protective cover but stopped as a flood of warm, salty tears poured over his swollen cheeks.

He missed his king. The old man had been wise and kind. Except for the time Mikahl had gone exploring off into the Northwood without telling anyone where he was going, King Balton never so much as cuffed him on the head. Most young squires got whacked regularly when they messed up or caused problems. When Mikahl did wrong, he usually got a fatherly lecture.

Mikahl missed the castle, too. The room he shared with the king's two Royal Pages was warm and close to the kitchens. He ruled the roost there. He tried to wipe away his tears but found his face hurt too badly to touch. It wouldn't have done any good anyway; already more tears were falling. It was as if a dam had broken inside him. The idea that King Balton was dead, that he could never go back home again, wouldn't leave his mind. It was a long time before sleep found him again but thankfully, it did.

He woke groggily to the smell of cooking meat and was still clutching the covered king's sword as if it were Lissy, the cook's skinny niece, who often snuck into his chamber back in the castle when the nights were cold. The idea he took the sword out of its place on his saddle, and it was semi-exposed, brought him out of his slumber quickly. He didn't begin to relax until the bundle was secured back in its place.

The old hunter watched him curiously out of the corner of his eye but said nothing about the peculiar behavior.

The breakfast meat was tough and stringy, but filling. Mikahl didn't ask what it was, because the animal's innards and its pelts still sat at the edge of the camp. He also didn't want Loudin to know he didn't recognize the remains. He didn't want to be thought of as a fool. He searched his memory for any sort of a creature that had fur such a bright shade of red, but couldn't think of any. This lack of knowledge only served to remind him of how far out of his element he was.

He needed Loudin, he realized. The hunter said he knew a giant, and Mikahl wanted desperately to ask him about it, but hadn't yet. He decided he would offer Loudin his share of the proceeds from the lizard's skin, and the bag full of gold coins he hid deep in Windfoot's saddle bags, as payment to guide him into the mountains. He hoped after he finished his current business at Summer's Day, Loudin would be employable. He was finding he didn't relish the idea of venturing into those infamously treacherous mountains alone.

"You're looking better this morn," Loudin said as he stood and began unlacing his britches.

The old hunter pulled out his manhood and started pissing out the campfire. Mikahl took the action as a sign he needed to get moving. He had no desire to watch the hunter relieve himself, so he put his back to the man, wolfed down his breakfast, and rolled up his blankets. A few minutes later, they were underway. Both had their left legs hung next to their saddles, out and over the roll of lizard's hide.

It was a beautiful day. Birds fluttered about from tree to tree and insects buzzed around, intent on their business. The occasional squirrel or rabbit darted away from the sounds of their passage. The forest's shade was pierced here and there with uniformly angled shafts of sunlight. Flecks of dust and pollen glided through them, sparkling golden in the air. Just before they stopped for an afternoon meal, a brown-and-yellow-striped limb lion growled down at them from above. Loudin yelled at it sharply, and it went bounding away from tree branch to tree branch, like some gigantic squirrel. A slow shower of green leaves floated down to the forest floor behind it. Mikahl was amazed. The cat had been about twice the size of any of the mousers he'd seen roaming the castle back home, but its growl was as deep and intimidating as one of the wild lions that roamed the Westland Plains. Loudin cursed the fact he didn't have his bow ready. Apparently the tree cats tasted extremely good, for the hunter talked about the missed opportunity throughout their whole stop.

They ate the last of Mikahl's bread and some more of his cheese. Loudin shared some salted dried beef he had stashed, made a joke about how much cheese Mikahl ate, and how it had already plugged his bowels completely. Determined to have fresh meat for supper, Loudin strung his bow and indicated Mikahl should do the same. After that, they mounted up and got back under way.

Mikahl got a glimpse of what they ate for breakfast when Loudin's arrow narrowly missed a fox-like creature that had bright red fur splotched with gray. Mikahl laughed as it bounded away through the forest to Loudin's curses.

"What's so funny, boy?" the old man asked.

"It's a wonder you could hit wood in all this forest, as bad as you aim."

"So, you was the jester back in that castle you came from," Loudin snorted at his own wit. "No wonder they sent you away. You're far from funny."

Being called a fool sent a rush of prideful anger through Mikahl, and he blurted his words without thinking.

"I'm the squire to the king himself, and I could best you with the bow any time you—" He let his voice trail off as he realized what his stupid slip of the tongue cost him.

"Aye! The king's own squire!" Loudin laughed. "And I suppose that bundle you're so protective of is old Ironspike herself."

Mikahl's heart stopped in his chest. How could he know? Had he gone through Windfoot's pack while he was asleep? Had he—?

"Maybe on a practice field loosing at targets you could best me, boy," Loudin continued, "but when what you're trying to kill is looking to make you its next meal, then by the gods, lad, it would be dining on the king's own squire."

It took a moment for Mikahl to understand Loudin was mocking him. He wanted to defend himself, but thought better of it. The comment about him carrying Ironspike, he realized now, was only spoken in jest. Loudin knew nothing about his burden. It was a welcome relief, but Mikahl wished he hadn't come off like some spoiled castle-born brat in the verbal exchange.

"It is true that I am out of place," Mikahl said, after a time.

He felt the strong urge to try and gain back any respect he might've lost with his childish boasting. "I just want—"

Loudin laughed. "You've got the balls of a man and the brains of a boy! It's a common enough ailment for young men. Be we castle raised or ship born, we all go through it, lad."

They rode in silence for a long while. Once, Loudin stopped his horse and raised his hand with a hiss of warning. They sat there, as still as stone, and Mikahl tried desperately to hear what it was that had the hunter cupping his hands to his ear.

The pace quickened after that. Mikahl wanted to ask why, but the look of intense concern on the hunter's face kept him from it. He dared not make an unnecessary sound. It was growing dark around them when Mikahl finally mustered the courage to speak.

"Are we going to stop soon?" he asked, as quietly as he could manage.

"Aye," Loudin whispered back to him with the same alarming intensity. "We ain't stoppin' for long, though."

When they did stop, Mikahl learned they weren't going to make a camp. Loudin quickly put away his bow and after rummaging through his saddlebags, produced three iron-jawed snap traps. It took him only a few moments to set them in a row across the path they had been traveling. Then after kicking brush and leaves over them, he went to his packs again. It was so dark that Mikahl couldn't tell what the man was doing.

"Cut me a good sized chunk of your cheese, Mik," the hunter whispered.

When Mikahl handed Loudin what he asked for, he saw the man was holding a silver coin or maybe a button up to see how it reflected in the forest night. Loudin took the object, the cheese, and something else Mikahl couldn't see back to where he set the traps. Curiosity was gnawing at Mikahl's guts like a starving dog. The sensation only worsened when Loudin didn't mount back up, but instead led them cautiously away from the area on foot.

It seemed an eternity before the hunter finally broke the silence.

"Stay on your horse, Mik," he whispered.

Moonlight reflected off of Loudin's shiny, tattoo covered head and caught the whites of his eyes. Mikahl shivered at the sight. The old hunter could have been one of the forest's creatures, or a monster out of some bard's tale. At the moment, he looked anything but human.

"Something's following us," he whispered to Mikahl. "We're not stopping again this night."

"What is it?" Mikahl asked the dark, empty place where the hunter had just been.

"I'm hoping to know soon enough."

Loudin's voice came from somewhere ahead of Mikahl now. Mikahl guessed correctly that Loudin was getting back on his horse.

Windfoot had been following Loudin's roan long enough now that he kept himself the proper distance behind without Mikahl having to worry about it. This made riding through the darkened forest an easy task, but it left Mikahl's mind idle enough to wonder over the hundreds of possibilities of who, or what, could be behind them.

The insects' nocturnal song was constant, but each time a bird fluttered from the trees or leaves rustled in the distance, Mikahl's heart boomed through his chest. He told himself over and over again to relax, but no sooner would he calm himself, then another sound would erupt out of the darkness to startle him. Just when he finally became used to the strange symphony of the night, everything hushed to a dead silence around him.

A horribly chilling scream pierced the air like an ax cleaving flesh. Whatever it was, it almost sounded human.

Windfoot balked, then tried to rear up, causing Loudin's roan to try to bolt. Luckily, the roll of lizard skin was well secured to each of the saddles. Mikahl and Loudin were taken on a short, wild ride through the darkness, but they weren't separated from the horses.

When Loudin finally got them stopped and calmed the animals somewhat, he turned and glared at Mikahl. Even in the darkness, Mikahl could tell that the hunter's expression was anything but kind.

"I don't know who you really are Mik, or what it is that you've done." The words were growled through clenched teeth. "But I can tell you those men who are following us aren't after me!"

Chapter Fourteen

Duke Fairchild of the northern Westland town of Greenside wasn't a child, nor was he fair. He was a tall and lanky hunter with raptor eyes and a hooked nose, and he had ranged the Reyhall Forest since he was in swaddling clothes. He was one of Lord Brach's favorite men, and he was the head of one of the wealthiest, most well-connected families in all of Westland.

The Duke deservedly earned the reputation, not of a stalwart nobleman, but of a ruthless interrogator and a fearless, formidable battlefield warrior. His exploits during the conflict against the half-Breed beasts at Coldfrost earned him the nickname "The Butcher." In the frigid north, he served both Lord Brach and King Balton extremely well. It was the luck of the gods, though, that put the duke in the position he found himself in now. He was about to earn the favor of the new king and elevate his standing with his liege, Lord Brach, as well.

Back before the Summer's Day festival, the day after King Balton died, but before the news was made public, the duke was summoned to a library room deep inside the walls of Lakeside Castle. He came to Lakeside with a small group of his men and a nephew his wife elevated to some sort of godly status in her mind. She could have no children of her own, so she latched onto a select few of her sister's children.

The nephew was an archer. The Duke, at the direction of his wife and her gaggle of honking sisters, went to the castle to ask Lord Gregory if the boy could accompany the group going to the Summer's Day Festival. Of course, there was already an archer of great skill among the Lion Lord's party. This outing to the Festival had been planned for months, which made this an inconvenient last minute request. A fat pouch of golden lions had been passed to Lord Gregory. The Lion Lord declined the bribe politely, but did make a suggestion to the surprised Duke. Duke Fairchild passed a far thinner bag of coin to Lord Gregory's archer, who suddenly decided he needed an assistant. The nephew was pleased to be hired for the position. Duke Fairchild was pleased to be rid of the boy, and was on his way before anyone could change their minds.

Since the boy was out of his hair now, the duke wanted to take care of some other business. He dismissed his men to the tavern near the North Road Gate with simple instructions. They were not to get too drunk, and they were to still be at the tavern when he returned from his engagement.

After sneaking through one of the many back entrances into the castle proper, the duke eased into the secondary dining hall and scanned the crowded room. It was just before midday and most of the castle staff was there, taking a meal before going off to serve the nobility. It didn't take him long to spot who he was after. She was a server in the hall, and he wanted her to serve him privately, just like she served him the last time he was at Lakeside Castle without his wife. It came as a great shock when his brief conversation with her was interrupted by a nervous young pageboy, sporting the king's sigil on his breast.

Disgruntled, but not so much as to disregard a royal summons, the duke followed the boy through the castle, wondering the whole way how his presence was so quickly discovered.

He had met Lord Gregory in the stable yard as the Summer's Day party was about to depart, and he had only just left his men. The midday bell hadn't rung, and he couldn't fathom how anyone could know he was in the city, much less send a pageboy to summon him in a particular room inside the castle.

As the boy led him deeper and deeper into the castle's depths, he began to grow nervous. He wondered if some of the things he had done to his captives after the Battle of Coldfrost were coming back to haunt him. Had he offended one of the Greater Lords? He searched his mind for every single encounter he had ever had with King Balton and the favored courtiers. He couldn't remember ever doing anything that might warrant this strange summons. What made it worse was that all the faces he saw, nobleman and servant alike, looked sullen. He could tell something was dreadfully wrong. He only hoped he wasn't the cause, or the one who would take the blame, for whatever had happened.

The library room was small and crowded. A candelabrum on a polished oak reading table provided insufficient light. The table was pushed against a desk, and the surfaces of both were covered in open maps. There were four, no, five, men in the room, Duke Fairchild was certain. The only faces illuminated in the sparse light were those of his liege, Lord Brach, and the nearly albino-skinned Royal Wizard, Pael. The Duke wondered when he saw the creepy wizard smiling at him if the mage used some sort of devilry to locate him.

The other men in the room were standing out of the candlelight at the back wall. Their faces couldn't be discerned. This was obviously intentional. They were either observing or silently guarding. Duke Fairchild knew they were there whether they wanted him to or not. Their presence only served to put him on the defensive, and his liege, Lord Brach, noticed.

"There's no time for formalities, Vincent. I can sense your concern," Lord Brach said. "I trust you can keep the words spoken here to yourself?"

It wasn't really a question, but the duke answered with a nod. The two men knew each other as well as any two men possibly could. The trust between them was deep and generations old. Brach often used Fairchild's skills to extract information from rogues and road bandits, and Duke Fairchild's stronghold was ideal for housing prisoners who might suddenly need to disappear from the realm altogether. Duke Fairchild was relieved by the expression on Lord Brach's face. From it, he could tell that he was not the focus of this strange meeting.

Pael looked at Duke Fairchild as if he were studying the inside of his skull. Pael's gaze was unnerving, but Vincent Fairchild didn't blanch under the scrutiny. He had committed horrors that were unspeakable. It would take more than the stare of a man so white he could've been carved out of marble, to unsettle him.

"The king is dead," Lord Brach said finally. "Poisoned, or magicked, we're not sure which, but that is not your concern. We're keeping it quiet for now. I only tell you so that you might see the magnitude of the duty we're placing upon you."

"Bring the stableman!" Pael commanded.

The strange wizard had a sinister, giddy quality about him that touched a nerve in the duke.

Two of the men standing against the back wall stepped forward into the light. Fairchild instantly recognized one of Lord Brach's personal guards. He acknowledged the man with a nod.

The other was dressed in what were once probably quality working clothes, but were now stained filthy with sweat, vomit, and more than a little blood. The stableman's face was swollen on one side, as if he held an apple in his cheek. Fairchild saw there was another man still concealed in the shadows. He silently congratulated himself for counting correctly.

"Last night while the king lay dying, the king's squire, a boy called Mikahl Thayne, made ready for a sizable journey and fled the castle," Lord Brach explained.

Thayne, Fairchild knew, was the name given to bastard born children. Thayne was the god of the needy, protector of the lost and alone. The duke filed that bit of information away and continued listening.

"He left sometime in the night after assaulting this man." Lord Brach indicated the stableman with a look of extreme distaste. "We assume he left through the Northroad Gate. It was the only one open throughout the night."

At that point, Duke Fairchild knew what his duty was. He was, after all, a hunter and interrogator. He was glad he brought Tully and Garth with him on this most fortunate of errands. They were both experienced and loyal men, men who understood how to track and kill the sort of prey they would be after. A look of eagerness and longing crept over Duke Fairchild's face. The expression was lustful and predatory, like a hungry beast with the scent of blood finding its nostrils. Pael, who had been silently studying the duke, read the intent in the man's countenance and found he was pleasantly surprised.

"Learn what you can from the stableman, then dismiss him properly."

Fairchild hadn't needed the emphasis on the word dismiss to understand his Lord's meaning, but he nodded for the benefit of the wizard and the hidden spectator. Lord Brach continued.

"We want this squire alive, if at all possible. His manner of departure, and the timing, suggests he was involved and is possibly carrying a message to an unknown party. We would like to know who that someone is, no matter what the cost."

"Bring him alive!" Pael commanded, his eyes conveying an intensity Fairchild understood completely. "No matter what his condition is, if he is alive and can speak, I will be able to leech his mind of the knowledge we seek."

"I understand," Fairchild told them with more than a little eagerness showing in his voice. "If it pleases m'lord, can your man escort the stableman back to the stable? I would do so myself, but it seems time is of the essence here. I have other preparations to make and men to round up and outfit before I get to him."

With a nod, Lord Brach granted the request. Duke Fairchild was turning toward the door to leave when a voice he recognized right away caught him short.

"Your diligence in this matter will be well remembered," Prince Glendar said from the shadows. Duke Fairchild smiled to himself. King Glendar, he corrected his thought, and continued on with his duty with much more fervor.

After he exacted what information he could from the stableman, then cleaned the blood and skin from his dagger, Duke Fairchild met his men at the Northroad Gate. The trio of night watchmen his men cornered seemed annoyed at being rousted this early in the day. They grew quite cooperative and obedient, however, after the duke threw all ten of the stableman's bloody fingers in the dirt at their feet.

No one left through the gate after dark, they all agreed. Only a single wagon, and later a lone post rider entered. Duke Fairchild knew from experience the watchmen were telling the truth so he left them and moved on.

The next morning, on the Northroad just south of Crossington, Duke Fairchild found a farmer who had heard but hadn't seen two horses galloping toward the crossroads two nights previous in the pre-dawn hours. The Duke then split his men and sent them to all of the farmhouses close enough to the road to hear a passerby. By midday, the first man's story was confirmed. Another man claimed he saw a post rider with a packhorse galloping eastward on the cutoff road away from Crossington. It was no post rider Fairchild knew, and for the first time on this new hunt, he felt like he had the true scent of his prey.

Duke Fairchild didn't believe in luck; he believed he was a favorite of the gods, so he credited them as the cause of his recent good fortune. When one of the two extra men he hired in Crossington relieved himself at the side of the Midway Passage Road and heard the distant sound of a man groaning, the duke's faith in his gods was confirmed.

They found a trail leading north into the Reyhall Forest that was as obvious as a cobbled road. They found a dying bandit there, who confirmed it was a king's man who had pig-stuck his inner thigh and left him for dead. After torturing the man for all the information he was worth, Duke Fairchild slit his throat and ordered Garth, Tully, and the two extra men to get rid of the two bodies. He then lit a fire and camped in the same place Mikahl had only nights before.

The Duke grew confident then; the gods had smiled upon him again. They continually led him in the right direction. It was like Coldfrost, he mused, when all those feral half-Breed giants confessed to the things he needed them to. Lord Brach and old Lord Finn had praised him. His victims always told him what he needed them to say when he pressured them properly. It never occurred to him then, or even now, that the tortured almost always ended up saying what the torturer wanted to hear, if only to quicken their own death.

Sitting there in the woods at Mikahl's camp, the duke became so confident that he never even questioned how a lowly squire could've killed two hardened road bandits all by himself. Garth, Tully, and the other two men wondered about that, though. In their mind's eye, their prey suddenly seemed a little more formidable than merely a simple, spoiled castle boy.

The next afternoon, when they came into the clearing where the half-eaten carcass of the giant skinless lizard lay, they were attacked by a greedy pack of wolves. One of the men's horses was dragged down and, while he was pinned beneath it, the wolves set upon him. Tully killed two of them with his well-placed arrows. The duke killed two more with his sword while trying to save the pinned man. He rode into the fray, fearlessly hacking and slashing, with little or no concern for his own safety, but it was wasted bravado. The hungry wolves tore the man to pieces. Garth ran down the other hired man when he tried to flee, but he still managed to trample a wolf under his horse's hooves as he did so. The dozen or so wolves that remained reluctantly scattered and skulked away. One wolf turned and growled at them, as if to rally his pack-mates for another attack, but one of Tully's arrows nipped it, and sent them all darting back into the forest.

Duke Fairchild wiped the blood from his blade and sheathed it. He dismounted his horse, dragged the hired man out of his saddle, and knocked him to his knees with a brutal blow to the temple. He almost killed the man then and there, but to Garth and Tully's disappointment, he made the man gather up all of the arrows from the area around his half-eaten comrade.

Tully went with him to filch the dead man's pockets and pouches. The man's saddle bags were next. Tully stopped pilfering only long enough to waggle one of the corpse's severed hands at the craven man.

Garth and Tully were reminded of their liege lord's strength and fearlessness when he rode into the pack of wolves without a care. They were also reminded quite brutally of his ruthlessness when after the craven man handed Tully back his arrows, the duke ran his sword through his stomach and rode away, leaving him to die slowly in the field. He would still be bleeding out when the wolves returned. Garth and Tully wouldn't have had full confidence in the duke's plan to catch up to and overtake their prey, had they not found the old sword protruding proudly up out of the huge, dead lizard's throat. It shone in the sun like a cross rising out of a sea of reddish brown death. After confirming it was standard Westland issue, they decided the lowly squire they were after might be more of a predator than Duke Fairchild himself.

The three of them made good time, because the trail wasn't hard to follow. That night Garth and Tully took turns leading the horses on foot by lantern light. The next morning they learned just how close they were to catching their quarry, when they came upon a newly deserted camp. They started stalking then, gaining on the squire slowly. The Duke decided to wait until the boy made camp that night. They would take him in his sleep. They learned from the tracks at the camp there were two men. Duke Fairchild hoped it was the squire and the conspirator Lord Brach and King Glendar wanted to learn more about.

Thoughts of praise and grandeur carried the duke through the long day, but he was never distracted from the scent of his prey. He felt certain the gods had led him to this very moment in time. A place where he could do what he loved to do, while raising his standing with his liege lord and gaining the favor of the new King of Westland. He had no doubts that when the boy and his companion finally bedded down for the night, he and his men would overtake them; but as nightfall came and the darkness deepened, he began to wonder.

They dared not light the lantern. They were too close now. The Duke didn't want to spook his quarry. Knowing the squire couldn't move any faster through the darkness than they could, they pressed on. Fairchild had Tully dismount and lead them on foot. The Duke was still reveling in the greatness this capture would bring him, when Tully stopped and bent down to retrieve something shiny he saw on the ground. The horrible, primal yell the man made when the iron jaws of Loudin's trap snapped shut on his arm carried a long way through the forest night.

The bone-chilling scream frightened every living thing to silence, but the sound that threatened to scare the trees up out of their roots was the low, menacing growl of rage, that rose up from deep inside of the Coldfrost Butcher.

Chapter Fifteen

Hyden hovered over Little Condlin's wounded body to shield him from the arrows still raining down on them. As strange as it seemed, the three elves formed a protective ring around them as well. One of the elves voiced his displeasure at the deed, but complied with his peers anyway. Condlin's squirming struggle underneath him let Hyden know his cousin was still alive.

Talon narrowly missed being crushed when Hyden dived on Little Condlin. He was trying to fly away from the mayhem, but his untrained wing muscles weren't cooperating with his will. He was half-flapping, half-hopping his way across the turf. Yells, screams, and the sound of battle could be heard breaking out all around them. The sound of steel clashing on steel and wood was unmistakable even to Hyden, who had never so much as touched a sword, save for one in an armory shop along the Ways.

"The arrows have stopped," the elven archer with the blood-streaked face said as he knelt down to look at Little Condlin's wounds. Hyden would've tried to stop the yellow-eyed creature from touching his cousin, but the elf's tone and the gentleness of his movements, belayed his objection.

Hyden glanced around them. His father and Uncle Condlin were both charging toward him. Anger and fear showed plainly in their eyes. Beyond them, Hyden could see Little Condlin's mother on her knees with her face in her hands. In the last few weeks, she lost one son and had seen another crippled. Hyden couldn't imagine what she must be feeling after seeing another one of her children being struck by an arrow. It appeared as if the Redwolf soldiers were torn between joining the growing battle around them and protecting those few who were still on the tournament grounds unarmed. There were enough of them present on the archery range that the attackers and the other angry people seemed weary, and were staying away from that particular area.

Hyden felt it in his blood like a gritty tingle before he saw the elf's magic working. It was such a sudden and powerful thing that he was drawn to it reflexively. The elf opened the top of Little Condlin's shirt, and was pulling the arrow slowly out of him with one hand. The other hand was making a slow, circular motion over the boy's chest. A place deep inside the child's skin was glowing a reddish-orange color. The glow moved along the arrow's path, out toward where the shaft protruded from his collar. They eventually could see it was the arrow's sharpened, steel tip that was glowing, and it was still glowing when it came free of the flesh.

Harrap and Uncle Condlin shouldered their way into the huddle forcefully. Talon was nearly crushed and went hop-flapping into Hyden's lap for protection. Little Condlin was staring with a wide-eyed, terror-filled grin, looking up at the elf who had just magicked him.

"Thank you," he managed to get out of his mouth before his worried father scooped him up into his arms. Tears of loving relief streamed down the Elder's face as he wordlessly toted his boy back to his mother. Seeing his son was also all right, Harrap went back with the others. His terrified people needed him more than Hyden did at the moment.

Some of the Elders of the Skyler Clan began negotiating with a knot of Redwolf soldiers. The Elders wanted the clansmen to be protected and their possessions guarded while they gathered up their belongings in preparation to depart the festival. They also wanted a safe passage guaranteed, at least until they were in the foothills of the Giant Mountains. The guards wanted to comply. The amount of gold the clan offered them was more than sufficient, but the Wildermont soldiers were far too honorable to shirk their duty for handfuls of coin. They did, however, send a man to find a certain commander, who was greedy enough to agree to such a quasi-noble and profitable undertaking. The Skyler Clan was asked to wait where there was little fighting going on, while a few of the Redwolf guardsmen went with some of the Elders to protect the clan tents and other belongings. The rest of them huddled together on the archery range amid the Wildermont soldiers while around them chaos ran rampant.

Just a few hundred paces away, a sizable battle raged on. Hyden watched as swords, fists, daggers, and even farm tools were used openly to kill and maim. Men were dying right there in the rich, green grass of the sacred Leif Greyn Valley. A lot of the kingdom's folk were involved. Hyden saw the Golden Lion of Westland flying from a flagstaff amid one group of engaged fighters. A small band of Valleyan horsemen displayed their kingdom's shield and stallion on their breasts proudly as they tore into the Westland flank. An organized troop of Seawardsmen, with the rising sun emblem of their kingdom painted on their shields, was tangled in with the rest of the mob. The bulk of the combatants were common folk, though. They were fighting right there among the trained soldiers, and dying in droves. Hyden then realized he didn't see the Blacksword banner of Highwander anywhere anymore. He scanned the area around the tournament field, paying special attention to where those first arrows were fired from. He didn't see the banner anywhere. They started all of this, or at least tendered the spark to flame. Now they were nowhere to be seen. Hyden realized, other than the one time out on the Ways that the two Highwander men harassed him, he hadn't seen any people from that kingdom at the festival at all. He searched his mind for another instance where he saw the Highwander men, but could only come up with the large encampment his Clan spotted south of the festival grounds on their way here from the egg harvest.

It occurred to him that Shaella's group camped very near that area. She was the one who sent the two rude Blacksword soldiers scurrying away in the Ways. Had Willa the Witch Queen started this? He asked himself. Or was it something else? Hyden knew very little about kingdom folk and their strange ways. However, he did know spilling all of this blood on the sacred ground of the Leif Greyn Valley was a violation of some ancient pact all the races of the realm had made with the dragons. At least, that's what Berda the Giantess told him once.

"I am Vaegon," the elven archer said. The elf put his hand out and placed his palm over Hyden's heart.

Hyden recalled the gesture was the elven equivalent of the kingdom men's handshake and mimicked the action.

"Hyden," he said, as he held out his hand. He was confused by the events taking place around him. The elf's strange eyes were yellow where a human's were white, which unnerved him as well. He had never looked into the eyes of an elf from this close before and was surprised by how wild they looked.

"Hyden Hawk!" Vaegon corrected, with what might have been a smile on his fair face.

One of the other elves gently picked up Talon and offered him to Hyden.

"This is my father, Drent." Vaegon nodded toward the elf holding the hawkling. "And this is my brother, Deiter." He indicated the third elf.

Hyden placed Talon on his shoulder, then made the stiff arm greeting gesture to the other two elves in turn. He noticed Drent, the father, looked as young as either of his sons. The only discernible difference Hyden could see was his hair was a silvery blue, the color of deep ice, where the two brothers' hair had a tint of gold to the silver. All three of the elves were a hand span shorter than Hyden was, and though they were a bit on the thin side, they moved with an obvious strength and grace.

"I am honor bound to you now, Hyden Hawk," Vaegon said, as if the words tasted slightly bitter. "You saved my life. I am at your service."

Behind Vaegon, Drent nodded proudly at his son's acceptance of his honor debt. Deiter's expression showed plainly his disgust at the idea, and Hyden couldn't meet the elf's frightening narrowed gaze.

Not sure what was happening, Hyden fumbled for his words. "You...uh...you saved my cousin's life. You...you owe me nothing."

"Your cousin wasn't going to die, Hyden Hawk," the elf said matter-of-factly. "I merely quickened his healing and saved him the pain of having the arrowhead removed with a blade."

A gurgling scream rose above the surrounding clamor and drew all of their attention. The number of people still fighting near that end of the archery field had decreased dramatically, but only because so many now lay dead or dying on the grass. At one end of the battle, a blood-soaked man in merchant's clothes was on his knees. He was clutching what looked like a young girl's broken body. Another man stumbled aimlessly around the carnage, carrying a severed arm in one hand, and a small dagger in the other. His head and face were covered in blood and he appeared to be lost. Some of the Redwolf soldiers waded in, braving the smaller numbers of combatants, to try and separate the fighting groups. The effort seemed futile at best.

"They will not stop until there is no one left to kill," Vaegon said sadly. Hyden could tell the elf was speaking about more than just the skirmish before them. He meant this was only the beginning of something far bigger and more destructive.

"The arrow that almost killed you was loosed by men flying the Blacksword of Highwander," Hyden said.

He wasn't sure why it mattered. He just figured the elf would want to know who tried to kill him. He noticed then all the contempt had faded from the elf's expression.

"You're sure of this?" Vaegon asked, without turning his eyes from the fighting.

"I saw them on the rise, there." Hyden pointed to the place beyond the targets, where he had seen them. He noticed for the first time, several dark plumes of smoke rising up from the Ways beyond.

Vaegon said something to his brother and father in the elven tongue, then listened as his father responded. While they spoke, Hyden looked toward his people. It seemed they and the three elves were the only factions in all of Summer's Day not fighting.

"Fare thee well, Hyden Hawk," Drent said, with a slight bow. "I hope we see each other again in better times."

Dieter didn't say anything to Hyden. He scowled as he gave his brother a quick hug. There was no mistaking the look was for the human his brother now owed his life to. The two elves wasted no time starting off toward where Hyden had pointed out the original attackers. Vaegon gritted his teeth as he watched them go.

Hyden was about to explain to the elf that his people needed him, that he had to help them gather up their belongings, and make the journey back into the mountains, when the sun was abruptly eclipsed. Shadow enveloped them like a shroud. It was as if night had come in the middle of the afternoon.

Talon leapt from Hyden's shoulder. At first, it appeared the little hawkling would flutter straight to the ground, but about halfway down, his wings caught air. A few flaps later, Talon was flying like an arrow toward the target stands.

Fighting to breathe in the thick cloud of smoke that had blown over them, Hyden searched for the bird. He spotted him perched on one of the targets over fifty feet away, and marveled at the distance the little chick had flown. Thinking the bird exhausted itself, he strode off to get it. A light breeze dissipated some of the smoke and allowed a bit of sun to find its way to them. A single ray brighter than the rest spotlighted Talon. Vaegon, with his keen elven sight, pointed this out to Hyden. The illuminating sunshine held on the hawkling while all around it, varying degrees of shadow churned and roiled with the breeze. When Hyden and Vaegon were a few paces away from the target, the bird leapt into the air again and flew even farther away.

Hyden glanced back at his clansmen. His father was holding his mother around the shoulders, comforting her at the edge of the huddle. Hyden was sure she hadn't taken Gerard's departure well and that his own presence would help ease her worry, especially after she witnessed a few hundred people get massacred only a stone's throw away. His people weren't kingdom folk. They didn't understand battle on a large scale. War was something Berda talked about in her tales; a thing as vague and incomprehensible as fairy trees, ocean waves, and sea ships. He wanted to go to them. His people needed him, but Talon was leading him away. Deep inside himself, he felt the pull of the hawkling. He knew without a doubt it was his destiny to follow the bird. The feeling was overwhelming.

Vaegon saw the worried expression on Hyden's face. He also saw the spirit aura of both Hyden and his familiar. The ability to see such things was part of his elven sight. The spirit aura of the bird, the man, and the elf were as intertwined as a vine is to the tree that supports it. To Vaegon, the path for all three of them was clear.

"Come," he urged gently, guiding Hyden toward where Talon had landed. "Your people are protected by the Wolf King's men. They're safe enough without you."

As if Vaegon's comforting words were the words of the White Goddess herself, Hyden turned toward his destiny and set off after the bird.

Lord Alvin Gregory, the Lion Lord of Westland, was sure he was in a living hell. No matter how hard he prayed for death, it would not come to take him. Some blasted insect stung his shoulder, causing it to swell to the size of a melon. His body was so bruised and broken from his Brawl with the Seaward Monster, his piss was a bloody red froth. He could only remain conscious for short periods of time, in which pure madness reigned around him. He found himself waking this time to shouts, screams, and the sounds of distant ringing steel, but he couldn't move to look outside his tent. At one point, a soldier with the Blacksword of Highwander on his shield looked in at him with violent intent, but he was immediately thrown to the side and tackled by another soldier. Now the familiar voice of Gowden, one of his captains, was crying out, "TO ME MEN! TO ME!" as if they were on a battlefield somewhere. The Lion Lord tried to yell out and ask what was happening, but his throat was as dry as the bark on last year's dead fall. He remembered vaguely his father, or was it some other voice, telling him there'd been another fight after the Brawl, a fight between some of his men and the people from Seaward.

That snotty boy that Duke Fairchild insisted they bring along had been beaten half to death, the voice added, and one of the timber jacks had been stabbed in a bad sort of way. Had that been this morning? Or was it two mornings ago? It could've been a week ago, for all Lord Gregory could figure.

He was just about to drift into blackness again when a leather boot came tearing through his tent's wall. The leg that was still attached to it stepped, twisted, then tore the canvas wide open as it pulled free. Lord Gregory was blinded by the brilliance of the sun. The boot stepped closer to him, and it became obvious it was connected to a man who was engaged in serious swordplay. The boot lifted and came down on his swollen shoulder in a stomp. A gush of warm, thick pus that smelled of rot and vomit erupted from the wound. The harsh daylight in his eyes wasn't nearly as blinding as the pain that ripped through him like a jagged blade. He tried to scream, but the effort only served to tear his parched throat open. In his mind he cursed every god and goddess he could think of for leaving him alive to suffer this way.

Gowden's voice shouted out another command, but it was cut short in a way that left no room to wonder why it ended so abruptly. A relative silence followed, where all Lord Gregory could hear was a few footfalls coming from close by and the sound of retreating hooves. He craned his neck to see what he could see, but his shoulder throbbed with the effort. The tattered wall of his tent blocked the view on one side, but on the other, he saw a handful of men fighting in the distance. He couldn't tell if any of them were his. He squinted at the sky and prayed for death again. The bright sun was suddenly blocked out as a face appeared, hovering upside down, over his. He hoped his prayer had been answered, but was disappointed when the person began speaking to him.

"Lord Gregory!" Squire Wyndall said. The boy was breathless, distraught, and covered in gore from the battle. "Milord, we've been routed," his unturned voice squeaked and cracked as he spoke. "First those fargin Seawardsmen came, then the Blacksword."

"What? Who?" the Lion Lord croaked, then managed to say, "Water!"

Wyndall fumbled through the tent looking for a wineskin or a flask as he spoke.

"Fargin Seawardsmen got us at first!"

A pitiful groan from not so far away caused the boy to poke his head out of Lord Gregory's tent and look around. Seeing nothing immediately threatening, he continued.

"Denny, Turl, and half the others ran like curs and left us at a disadvantage. Ah! Here we are."

He poured a sip of water from the skin into his Lord's mouth, then another.

"We all but bested the lot of them, but the blasted Highwander Blacksword warriors came a riding through out of nowhere. It was just a few of them, but they hacked and cleaved everything in their path."

Wyndall paused for breath and poured another dollop of water into Lord Gregory's mouth.

"Why?" Lord Gregory asked after he swallowed. He didn't really expect the boy to know the answer.

"That's not the whole of it, m'lord," the boy continued. "They did the same thing in the Ways. The Blacksword rode down unarmed folks, crafters, and merchants. Women and children, even!"

Wyndall's face contorted at the idea of it all. Anguish was threatening to take hold of him.

"They cut down Westland innocents, Redwolf soldiers, and they killed half a herd of Valleyan horses. They set fire to some of the Dakaneese wagering pavilions, while people were still in them," he sniffled. "Then they came through here. It was only me, Gowden, and Parker who survived it!"

He started to break down. Tears flowed down his dirty cheeks, and the ghastly reality of the horrors he had just seen racked through his young body with a force. He shuddered as he finished.

"A Seawardsman got Gowden and Willem. I fell and I-I didn't get back up. Not until after-after they had moved on." He slumped down into himself and began bawling like a babe.

They know about King Balton's death, Lord Gregory thought to himself. The thick blackness in his skull seemed to be ebbing. Fear of what was to come was like a torch light in the dark, foggy muck. He was sure someone here knew King Balton was dead.

The funeral had been public. Poisoned, King Balton told him, from his own deathbed. Now Prince Glendar, the wizard Pael's little puppet, would have the whole of Westland behind him when he started his war on the east. Gregory couldn't figure out why the kingdoms of the east were playing so perfectly into Glendar's hands, though. Another thought struck him like a hammer blow. Lady Trella, his wife.

"Wyndall," he rasped. The boy was lost in his grief and didn't seem to hear him. "Wyndall, listen to me!"

This time the boy responded by wiping his nose on his forearm, then taking a deep breath.

"Yes, m'lord?" he whimpered.

"Listen very closely, Wyndall."

It was painful to be speaking, but things had to be done and people had to be warned. King Balton gave him orders that still had to be carried out, and now he understood the magnitude of them. The king foresaw his own poisoning and this collapse of order, and prepared for it wisely. Gregory was sorry he wouldn't be able to complete his part of the design. Hopefully Mikahl would be able to get along without him.

"Take my ring. It will be proof of the origin of this message. Take anything else you might need, save for my horse. Ride like the wind to my stronghold at Lakebottom and tell my wife... Tell Lady Trella these things for me..."

When he finished giving his orders, he made Wyndall repeat the messages and swear to deliver them. He also made him swear to protect Lady Trella with his life. The boy foolishly thought he shamed himself when he hadn't gotten back up earlier to be slaughtered by the impossible odds. He was glad for the chance to regain his honor and gave his solemn oath that he would die before he let any harm come to her.

Sometime later, Lord Gregory slipped out from the blackness again. He dreamed that he died, but found now he no longer wished to be dead. He still hurt so badly he couldn't move his body, and he was sure he pissed himself yet again, but his mind seemed clear. He felt, at the moment, like he might somehow survive. He had a duty to King Balton that needed to be fulfilled. Its importance demanded he get up and fight for his life, but no matter how hard he tried to rise, he couldn't.

He was still lying there, half-conscious in his misery, when an eager carrion bird came flapping in and landed on his face. It was a hungry looking, scraggly brown crow. He was sure it would try to eat his eyes out first. They usually did. He had seen it happen dozens of times. He wished he could move his arms to bat it away, but he couldn't. When he rolled his head and yelled, the bird just flapped and hovered, then re-landed, as if his nose were its favorite perch.

Feeling stupid now for cursing the gods and asking them to take his life, he squeezed his eyes closed and waited for the inevitable. He only wished he wasn't letting his beloved king, his wife, and probably the entire realm down by dying. He remembered his mother then, of all people, chiding him for something or another in that matter-of-fact voice that only mothers can muster.

"Be careful what you wish for Alvin, because you just might get a barrel full of it!"

Chapter Sixteen

"Look!" Mikahl whispered.

Loudin turned to see what alarmed Mikahl. The tattoo-covered hunter was leading them due east now, trying to get them to the Leif Greyn River before their pursuers caught up with them. At the very least, he wanted them in the thick, dense strand of forest that ran alongside the riverbank. They could use the cover to make an ambush point, or better yet, just hide until the trouble passed. It was a foolish hope, Loudin knew. If the men tracked them this far, a confrontation was going to be unavoidable. Hiding wouldn't be a viable option. He saw what Mikahl had seen; the lantern light their pursuers were using to care for the man who stuck his arm into Loudin's steel-jawed trap was just extinguished.

"Did you see it go out?" asked Loudin.

"No. I looked back, and it was still way back there where it's been. Then, just now, I looked again, and it was gone."

"Aye." Loudin's voice was grim. "They'll be after us again then. We've gained a turn of the glass or two on them. Not much more than that."

He climbed off his horse and went to his pack.

"You'll be wanting to check that bowstring of yours now. We'll stay on foot until we get a little daylight, but if they want you bad enough to ride through this forest in the darkness, they'll be catching up soon, no matter what we do."

It took a while for the seriousness of the situation to sink in. It made Mikahl nervous to the point of trembling. He was glad to be on foot. In the saddle, especially with the lizard skin making the ride so awkward and uncomfortable, he would've been fidgety and distracted.

Walking briskly behind Loudin, he was at least moving and forced to listen to the hunter's barely audible footfalls. Only every now and again, when the forest's canopy broke overhead, could he see the tattoo covered man. Even then, it was only for a fleeting moment. He was grateful for Loudin's help, even though he was sure the hunter would've abandoned him long ago had he not needed Windfoot to help carry his prize lizard skin.

"Why did they stop so long? Why risk the light?" Mikahl asked.

"It probably took a while to get that leg or arm out of my trap, lad. They know that we know they're after us now."

Mikahl thought he heard a slight chuckle escape the old hunter's mouth as he spoke.

"Then it took a while longer to splint the broken limb."

The mirth suddenly fell from Loudin's voice like a heavy stone.

"After that, they found the other traps, then wisely rested their horses so they'd be fresh enough to run us down in the morning light."

"What will we do?" Mikahl's mind was racing.

"The river is not that far ahead of us. I can smell it."

Loudin's voice held very little confidence and Mikahl found no comfort in it. Mikahl was starting to form an idea of what they should do on his own.

"The forest grows thicker there," Loudin was saying, "more underbrush. The trees are smaller and closer together. We might be able to ambush—"

"But we don't need that cover!" Mikahl cut him off. His idea manifested itself into a plan the moment Loudin spoke the word "ambush."

"Don't need cover?" Loudin responded rather loudly. He stopped in his tracks and cringed at himself for being so careless with his voice. "Are you daft?" he finished in a harsh whisper.

"Why don't you hunt bark lizards with a bow and arrows?"

"Because arrows won't pierce the hide, but—" Loudin looked like he suddenly understood what Mikahl was getting at.

"We'll make a blind then, just as soon as we can see to do it," said Loudin, finally.

If Mikahl could've seen the look of respect on the hunter's face, he would've beamed with pride. As it was, he could barely see Loudin at all.

The length of time that passed between their idea's conception and daybreak seemed like an eternity to Mikahl. Already his old life as King Balton's Squire, living in a warm castle, where the biggest concern of his day was which serving lass he would try to bed that evening, was but a memory. They were the memories of a lifetime ago. In a way, he was glad to be preparing to make a stand. The fear of flight, of being chased and hunted, was wearing off now. He was an excellent swordsman, one of the best on the training yard at Lakeside Castle. He was a fair archer, too. He was trained by Westland's best, and Lord Gregory advised him personally while Mikahl served him at Lakebottom Stronghold. He was ready to stand and fight. At least he told himself these sorts of things while helping Loudin unroll the bark lizard's skin to make their blind.

They sat the roll on the ground between two tree trunks that were spaced about four paces apart. They unrolled only enough of the skin so that the top edge was at chest height, then stretched it between the two trees. To pin it in place, they broke the shafts off two arrowheads, caked them in dirt, and hammered them into the tree with the butt of Loudin's dagger.

Loudin made Mikahl squat behind the blind and went to where they tied the horses. The barkskin was so perfectly blended in color and texture that the hunter was amazed. All they had to do now was cover the rest of the roll with deadfall and leaves.

"Can you stand and loose from there?" Loudin called out to Mikahl.

Mikahl hopped up, and mocked the action of drawing and releasing an arrow. It looked to Loudin as if a head and torso had just popped up from thin air and he nodded his satisfaction.

"With ease," Mikahl responded competently. The hunter couldn't help but notice a smile on the boy's face. He wasn't sure yet if that was a good sign or not.

"All right then, Mik. Come over here and start digging."

"Digging?"

"Aye!" Loudin laughed.

His entire part in the plan hinged on whether Mikahl could hit his target on the very first shot. He hoped the castle-born boy wouldn't throw down his bow and flee the way he did when the lizard attacked his packhorse. Loudin wasn't even sure he wanted to make this stand with Mikahl. What exactly was it he was risking his life for? A lizard skin? He knew he could easily take the boy's horse, elude him, and the other pursuers if he wanted to. He had lived in this forest for the last half dozen years and he knew its ways well. He wasn't doing this just for the lizard skin, he decided. As much as he hated to admit it, he liked the boy. Something deep inside him was compelling him to protect Mikahl. What it was, he wasn't sure, but the compulsion was there and he couldn't ignore it.

"If there are four or five of them, we might be setting a trap for ourselves," Loudin said, in an explanation of his command to dig. "We can't afford to put all of our coins in one pouch."

Duke Fairchild almost killed Tully on the spot for being so ignorant as to stick his arm into a trap. He would have, but Tully's keen tracking skills might still be needed. Something as simple as a silver coin tricked the man. Now his arm was a ruin, and it was his sword arm at that.

Duke Fairchild found himself impressed with the cleverness of his prey. The choice of baits laid in the jaws of the three traps told him a lot about the two men he was after. Setting one of the traps to catch a man was ruthless and smart. They knew they were being followed, and Tully's scream had told them what sort of a predator was stalking them. He was just happy Garth found the other traps. A horse could have easily been crippled there.

The Duke decided it would be better to wait for daylight. There was no telling what other sort of traps the squire and his companion might've left for them. He considered it a pity the lamp light was needed to tend to Tully's arm. Its light would tell his prey he was stopping, which in turn would give them a few more hours distance and the time they might need to set more pitfalls, or maybe even an ambush.

When the sun finally colored the forest an amber gray, they were already up and moving, and had been for a while. Even the horses were eager to resume the pursuit. Tully's arm was splinted and wrapped tightly with pieces of torn canvas. The Duke gave him a dose of his personal elixir. It would dampen the fool's pain and make his mind as sharp as Wildermont steel for a while. Fairchild always kept some of the sweet medicine on hand in case he was ever wounded in the field. An expensive blend of ground flower seeds and Harthgarian herbs, mixed with fine brandy wine and honey. Only the wealthiest of men could afford the luxury of it. Tully would get no more of it after the squire was captured, no matter how badly he was hurting.

They made good time, even though they were being extremely cautious and looking for more traps. The forest was still too spread out for an ambush, the duke figured, so he pushed them on. Tully rode out in front, wincing, as his trotting horse jostled his wounded arm. Garth was next in line. Fairchild would let them find the trap if there was one. His level of awareness was increasing as the morning wore on. His blood was beginning to tingle with the thrill of the hunt, but his patience was wearing thin. He was just beginning to think Tully lost the trail or maybe his dose of elixir had worn off, when the tracker all of a sudden reined up his horse.

"They stopped here," Tully pointed ahead, as Garth, then the duke, gained his side.

Fairchild sensed deception here, and slowly scanned the area. It was still too open for an ambush, he decided. Nevertheless, he drew his sword quickly from its scabbard.

"Ready your bow," he ordered Garth. Something in his guts was telling him to beware. "Tully, go search the surrounding area and tell us what you see."

Mikahl saw there were only three of them with a flood of relief. He would soon have an easy shot on the one with his arm in a sling. The man was off of his horse and moving closer as he inspected Loudin's mocked-up camp.

If Loudin could take out one of the two still on horseback, then Mikahl felt certain he would have time to draw and loose on the other one before he could get too close. Ironspike was leaning against the tree nearest him, but he didn't want to have to draw it from its sheath and use it unless he had to. He was already going to have to explain why he had it to Loudin. The hunter was struck speechless when he'd seen the jeweled hilt, then grew angry thinking he conspired to help a common thief elude the sword's proper owners. Only after Mikahl swore a blood oath the sword wasn't stolen, and promised vehemently he would tell the whole of his situation to Loudin if they survived this encounter, did the old hunter relent.

The fargin bastards are nearly standing on top of me, Loudin thought. He hoped they weren't too close for him to attack. He heard the sound of steel ringing free from its scabbard. There was nothing else that even resembled the ringing hiss of quality steel being freed, and the sound electrified something in his blood. The other had a bow, he heard them say. That's the one he would go after. He wished he knew how many there were. Even though he felt as if the boy betrayed him somehow, he would do his best to keep these people's arrows out of him. Just then, he heard the unmistakable thump of Mikahl's arrow hitting the first man. A heartbeat later, Mikahl yelled, "THREE!"

For an instant, Mikahl felt wrong about putting an arrow into an unarmed and unsuspecting man, but a glance at King Balton's sword steeled him to the task. He stood up as calmly as you please, loosed his arrow at the startled fellow, and then yelled, "THREE!" so that Loudin would know how many they faced. The arrow he'd loosed, he saw, went most of the way through the wounded man's chest.

Loudin burst from his shallow leaf-covered grave, startling the swordsman's horse, so that it charged right at Mikahl. The tattooed hunter's spear drove up at Garth's side, but only grazed him.

Mikahl's heart was exploding in his chest. A wild-eyed destrier was almost on him and its semi-armored rider was, of all people, the infamous Coldfrost Butcher. Mikahl recognized him and panicked. He threw away the bow, grabbed Ironspike, then dropped to the ground behind the lizard skin blind and rolled. It was a foolish gamble of a move made in haste, and Mikahl realized this as soon as he committed to the action. The Duke's horse wouldn't try to leap the blind. It was too high, and the color and texture would confuse the animal. Mikahl could only hope that he rolled to the side opposite of which the horse chose to take around it. If they went the same way, he was sure to be trampled. It was too late to stop when he saw he chose wrong. All he could do was clinch his eyes closed and wait to feel the battle horse's steel shod hooves crush into him.

By some stroke of luck or maybe divine intervention, when Mikahl rolled into its path, the heavy horse leapt completely over him, instead of trampling him. He barely had time to get to his feet and draw Ironspike from its sheath. The terrifying man that King Balton himself nicknamed "The Butcher" was already turned and about to run him down.

Loudin managed to dodge the single arrow Garth loosed at him, but the man had the advantage of being mounted, and quickly spurred his horse out of Loudin's weapon's range. Rather than try to dodge the next arrow that Garth was already nocking, Loudin launched his weapon at the horse and charged. The blade of this spear hit the horse in its rump, and sunk deep enough to make it buck and scream. Garth was thrown from the saddle and landed badly. Before he could get up, Loudin was there to deliver a running boot to his face. The kick had enough force behind it to render Garth unconscious, but Loudin took no chances and pounced on the fallen man. In one fell swoop, Loudin drew his dagger and cut Garth's throat wide open.

Duke Fairchild's eyes gleamed with murderous intent as he casually spurred his horse into a slow trot toward the squire. He would have to wound him, then kill the other man. Lord Brach and the wizard, Pael, wanted the boy alive and at least able to speak. The man on top of Garth would die though. The Duke recognized him as one of the many poachers that plagued the Reyhall Forest. He wasn't the unknown conspirator his lord wanted to find, he was just a hunter the boy came across in the woods. The squire would get to watch the slow death of his companion. It would go far toward deterring any attempts the boy might make to escape. Fairchild would enjoy the slow kill, and watching the boy's will break.

When Mikahl pulled the sword free from its scabbard, he felt its perfectly balanced weight in his hands. He had brandished it before in the privacy of the king's Royal Weapons Closet while he was cleaning it, but he hadn't unsheathed it since King Balton died. Dropping the scabbard, he took the leather-wrapped hilt in both hands and got into the proper stance for fighting a mounted attacker from the ground. For all its familiarity, the sword somehow felt different. A strange vibration was coming from deep inside the blade. He could feel it in the bones of his wrists and arms. It had never done that before. He nearly dropped the weapon as the strange sensation grew into a visible tremor. He tried to ignore it and gripped the hilt even tighter. Was it his own fear causing him to tremble so? He didn't think so, but he was terrified. The duke was almost on him now, and Mikahl couldn't see even the beginnings of fear in the Coldfrost Butcher's eyes. The man was one of the most ruthless killers in the entire realm, and Mikahl knew he was in serious trouble.

When Duke Fairchild saw the terrified boy was holding Ironspike, he hesitated. Surely, Lord Brach and Prince Glendar would've told him the squire had stolen it. Unless they didn't know it was missing. With all the worry over Balton's death, it must have gone unnoticed. The idea that returning it to the new king was far more important than keeping the squire alive flashed into his mind like a whip crack. Convinced now that sparing the boy was no longer a priority and that Ironspike was, he dug his heels into his horse's flanks, and charged.

The moment of indecision Mikahl saw in the Coldfrost Butcher's eyes coincided with the brilliant surge of energy that shot through his entire body. Suddenly his blood felt charged and his skin prickled from head to toe. It was as if he were trapped inside a bolt of lightning. The world around him began to move in slow motion, and he was compelled to step to his right. The duke's sword sliced downward at his left, and realizing it was a committed stroke, Mikahl waited until the last second and spun across the charging horse's path. Deftly, he ducked under the horse's chin, and came twisting up on the duke's unprotected, left hand side. Riding the momentum of his spin as if it were a tidal wave, he continued around again. Ironspike was humming now, the sword's razor sharp blade glowing a pale pastel shade of blue. Mikahl could feel and hear its power coursing through him and electrifying his body, filling his head with an angelic symphony of glorious music. He and the sword, for that moment at least, became one.

As Duke Fairchild's sword went slicing through the air where Mikahl had just been, Mikahl came around swinging with all his might from the other side of him. Ironspike's magical blade cleaved into the duke's back just above the waist, with little or no resistance at all. Plate mail, padded leather, then flesh and spine alike, were sheared through. Mikahl barely had time to push the blade tip in as it came out of the Butcher's belly. If he hadn't, it would've hacked right into the back of the duke's horse's neck.

Chapter Seventeen

Mikahl tried to run away from the top half of Duke Fairchild's body as it tumbled away from the terrified horse. An exposed root caught his boot and he half stumbled, half fell to the ground. He ended up on his knees right in front of Ironspike's scabbard. The rush of power that had just consumed him so completely—the electric tingle, the harmonic symphony, and the sensation of the world around him moving at a snail's pace—was quickly abating. Where the magic of the sword filled him, he was now left with an empty hollowness. He was more than a little afraid. It was all he could do to get Ironspike back in its sheath before he collapsed to the ground in a trembling heap.

It took a few, long moments for Loudin to move from where he was standing. He was in sort of a shocked daze, brought on by awe, fear, and more than a little disgust at what he just saw happen. What held his attention at the moment had his stomach in his throat. The bottom half of the man Mikahl just cleaved was still sitting in the saddle. Booted feet were still in the stirrups, and the horse was walking in a nervous circle, as if the legs and the arse of the dead man were still somehow guiding it. Blood and entrails were everywhere. It took all of Loudin's willpower to keep from vomiting. He knew he had to go after the horse. They needed it too badly to let it go. Even if they didn't need the beast, he would've gone after it. With half of a man's weight of raw meat riding on its back, the horse wouldn't last the night out here in the deep forest. The archer's horse was as good as dead, he knew, and he felt sorry for wounding it to kill its rider. He had done what he needed to do to stay alive, though, and he reminded himself of that fact when the guilt of harming the beast crept up on him.

He couldn't help but think as he motivated himself to go after the bodiless horseman, that the scavengers would eat well this night. Three men and a dead horse would draw a crowd. The crowd, in turn, would probably draw a big lizard. Under normal circumstances, he would've wanted to take advantage of the carnage and try to trap it when it came, but these circumstances were as far from normal as any he could imagine.

When Mikahl finally sat up and looked around, he couldn't see Loudin anywhere. He immediately looked for the blind. It was still there. He took a deep breath, and let out a long sigh of relief. He knew the old hunter wouldn't leave his precious lizard skin behind. There was a horse tethered near the blind. It was the one that belonged to the man who got his arm caught in Loudin's trap; the man Mikahl killed with an arrow in cold blood.

Another horse was snorting and limping badly. It was out in the forest a little ways and obviously scared. When it turned, Mikahl saw that its hind quarters were covered in bright, red blood. He sat Ironspike against one of the trees that formed the blind, and found his bow. He put an arrow to the string and made his way toward the injured animal, talking gently to it as he went. When he had a sure shot, he loosed. The horse bolted deeper into the woods, but fell headlong into a thicket, after only a few dozen strides. Mikahl was glad his arrow struck true. The beast had surely suffered enough already.

On his way back toward the blind, he saw the bottom half of the duke's body lying at the edge of the camp. He was forced to take a knee when the sheer magnitude of what he had done, and the power that he had felt while doing it, came back to him. He made a decision then and there not to use Ironspike again unless he had no other choice. As glorious as it made him feel, the idea he had somehow violated the memory of the king he loved so much was stronger. He felt as if he had taken something that wasn't his. He decided to take the Coldfrost Butcher's sword. If he could manage to get the scabbard unbuckled without vomiting, he could use it. It was obviously quality steel and would do just fine if the need arose again.

He had just gotten the body turned over and was gagging his way through the gore to get at the buckles when Loudin called out his name from the distance. The sound startled him so badly he nearly fell over from his squatted position. The belt had been broken, or more accurately, it had been nearly sheared through. As quickly as he could, he collected the blood-soaked sheath and stumbled away.

Loudin was on his own horse, along with Windfoot and the duke's big destrier in tow. The bald-headed hunter didn't look pleased as he approached. His whole head was as red as an apple, and it made his tattoos all the more menacing.

"Tell me again you're not just a thief of noblemen's swords!" He reined his mount to a stop in front of Mikahl. "Make me believe you, boy, or I'm done with you."

Mikahl looked down at Duke Fairchild's bloody scabbard in his hand, and let out a sigh of frustration. He was a man of his word, and he swore to tell Loudin the whole of it. He would keep his word. He just hoped he wouldn't live to regret doing it. He had to let this good-hearted hunter know what danger the knowledge would put him in though. It was only right to do so.

"I owe you the whole of it, friend," Mikahl spoke seriously, with his eyes looking directly into Loudin's. "It's a tale that comes with more than words though. Your life will be at risk for just knowing it."

"Aye," Loudin nodded.

He was already sure the boy was more than a common thief, and he wasn't so sure he wanted to hear the story behind all this mess. He was a known poacher, and he already helped Mikahl kill a Westland nobleman, he reminded himself. The halved man's rank was as obvious as night or day. If he had a lick of sense to himself, he would just kill the boy and ride away. Nobody could ever tie him into this treachery. He would have enough horses to carry his lizard skin to Summer's Day, too. The animals would blend in there and draw no ill attention at all. He could probably sell them for a bit of coin to a Valleyan Breeder who would know how to cover the mark they bore.

He told himself all of this, but he knew he was just angry. The look in the boy's eyes was something to behold. Mik was no ordinary castle-born pup, and that sword was no stolen weapon. Loudin knew these things instinctually. What had happened though was magical to say the least, and Loudin knew it was the good kind of magic, not the bad. He felt as much in his very bones. So much for having a lick of sense, he told himself, as he decided to keep helping the boy.

"I'll hear your story, Mik, my friend, but there's too much blood here. This is no place to be. I can listen while we ride. By the time we get resituated, we'll still have a good bit of daylight left to us."

They made good time then. The skin was attached to the dead men's horses, allowing Loudin and Mikahl to ride in a normal, comfortable position. Neither had the stomach to eat, so they didn't bother stopping to do so. They were both exhausted, but putting distance between themselves and the feast they left for the forest creatures was reason enough to stay awake and keep moving. Just before dark, they reached the river. They made a camp in the open area between the bank and the forest's edge, where the spring thaw flooded the banks and washed away most of the vegetation.

It was good to see the sky again, Mikahl thought. He was glad to be out in the relative openness, and out of the claustrophobic confines of the forest. It was good to have the weight of his secret off his chest as well. He felt as if he could breathe again after he told Loudin.

Loudin was silent throughout the evening. He listened to Mikahl's story and decided he believed the boy. No one could have made such a thing up. He also decided, but hadn't told the boy yet, that he would lead him into the Giant Mountains to the giant named Borg. Borg would know exactly what to do, and how far into the giants' lands Mik, or Mikahl, he had learned, would be allowed to go. Borg was the guardian of the giant king's southern borders, and he and Loudin had traded before. Loudin doubted Mik would ever see King Aldar or the mysterious castle city called Afdeon, but Borg would relate Mikahl's messages to the giant king, there was no doubt.

He hadn't told Mik he was going to guide him, mainly because he didn't want to commit himself until he got them some good mountain clothes. He no longer wanted to sell the lizard skin at the Summer's Day Festival. Borg would pay thrice what the human hagglers would for so large a single piece of the precious hide, and now they had horses to carry it. It was rare and the giant could use it to make a cloak without having to patchwork smaller pieces together. The humans would just cut it up and parcel it out.

It was a good twist of fate Loudin decided: do a good deed, and receive a just reward for the doing. The biggest problem was the Westlanders were surely looking for Mik at the Festival. There were probably kingdom men all over the realm searching for the king's squire and his parcels. Loudin knew a place where the new King of Westland's men would never think to look for them. It was a place where they could trade for devil deer hide coats, furred boots, and everything they needed to travel into the treacherous heights of the Giant Mountains. Loudin accidentally stumbled upon the place once. He was almost certain he could find it again. At least he hoped he could, because the village of the Skyler Clan was far enough up into the vast foothills that they could possibly freeze to death while looking for it.

"I've healed the damage, but I cannot make the poison leave his blood," Vaegon, the elven archer said to Hyden.

"You speak of me as if I weren't even here," Lord Gregory said from the ground inside his tattered tent, where Wyndall left him hours ago.

He thought he had died and gone to one of the nine Hells when he opened his eyes, to find the yellow-eyed demon looking down at him. It was confusing, because he always thought the angels would have the gold and silver hair, not the devils. For some reason, the fat little crow that wanted to eat his eyes had flown from his face to land on the demon's companion's shoulder. He couldn't feel the pain in his body anymore and they were speaking about him as if he weren't even there, so all he could do was assume he wasn't alive anymore.

"Am I dead?" he finally asked. Before anyone could respond, his body answered for him. Slowly, his shoulder began to burn again from the poison. He felt it oozing through his veins like some thick, nauseating taint.

"You're Lord Gregory, the Lion of the West," the person with the bird on his shoulder said to him.

He wasn't sure if it was a question or not, but he answered anyway. "I am Lord Alvin Gregory. Who are you?"

"I am Hyden, son of Harrap, of the Skyler Clan." He gestured at the elf. "This is Vaegon." As if it wasn't obvious he added: "He's an elf."

"Then I'm not dead?" Lord Gregory tried to sit up and found it wasn't hard to do. It surprised him. He coughed spasmodically when he got a lungful of the acrid smoky air. Looking around as he recovered himself, he realized it was starting to get dark.

"You're not dead yet," Vaegon answered flatly. "But you've still got the poison in you."

"That little black-eyed witch tried to kill you, but she was unlucky," Hyden added.

"Witch? What are you talking about?" Lord Gregory asked.

"It was no witch," Vaegon corrected, with a slightly annoyed smirk at Hyden's ignorance. "It was an imp. A wizard's pet most likely. The little devils aren't good for much else."

"Pael," Gregory groaned, as the horror of the past few days came flooding back to him. The wizard probably poisoned King Balton as well. On his deathbed, the king had told him as much, without actually saying the words.

He hoped Wyndall wouldn't fail him, otherwise his wife and Lord Ellrich would never get his warnings. Pael would probably kill them, too.

"I must find a giant," he blurted out.

If he wasn't speaking to an elf and a mountain clansman with a baby bird on his shoulder, he might've felt foolish for saying such a crazy thing. Rising to his feet, a wave of dizziness swept over him, but Hyden and Vaegon caught his elbows and steadied him.

"What you need is some squat weed," Vaegon said. "The imp's poison is still running through your body."

"Maybe we can find some in one of the herb shops on the Ways." Hyden looked at the cloud of dark smoke roiling around the base of the monolithic spire. "If the whole place hasn't burned to the ground by the time we get there."

"If not, I can swim the river and pick some from the forest you humans call the Reyhall," Vaegon told them. "For some reason, it only grows on the west side of the Leif Greyn flow."

They helped the Lion Lord onto his horse and made their way along a trail of corpses and smoldering debris. The carnage only grew more abundant as they neared the Spire.

A couple of groups of sullen women and teary-eyed children hurried past them as they went. The first group was guarded by Wildermont soldiers, the second, by a handful of poorly armed common folk who had only taken up the weapons they carried to try to get their loved ones home. More groups were preparing to leave. A pair of young boys stood still as stone over a mangled woman, as if they were expecting her to get up at any moment to tend them.

"What madness is this?" Lord Gregory asked gruffly. The fever was on him again. His whole body was growing hot and his mental clarity was fading fast.

"The madness of men," Vaegon answered flatly. He winced at his own coldness. A man, after all, saved his life earlier this day. He decided he would try not to forget that fact again.

A shadowy shape that might have been an iron skillet shot across their path, hurled from a group of Valleyan folk at a pair of bloody, limping men. Curses were thrown after it. The men hurried away, with their heads hung low.

The first of many fires was in front of them now, and they had to skirt the beaten path to get around it. A pair of wagons had wrecked in the middle of the road, and now served as fuel for a bonfire. A bolt of what was once probably fine, white, spider-silk lace was flaming green at the edge of the mess. Beside it laid a charred corpse, whose arms and legs were drawn up into a fetal ball.

The sound of fighting still echoed from the distance. As grim as the fires were, they were drawing people to them. Hyden saw the burning wagons' flickering glow reflected in hundreds of eyes. They were everywhere. The people who survived the day's insanity watched them pass with fear and sorrow on their faces. It was unnerving to say the least.

When the fire was behind them, Vaegon spoke. "I can be across the river and back by morning with the squat weed. It would be foolish and dangerous to be out on the Ways searching for the herb with all the hatred and vengeance that has permeated this place. Among your clansmen, Hyden Hawk, that is where you and the Westland Lord should spend this night."

"It's Gregory, you blasted demon. My name is Gregory. Lord Gregory!" the nobleman said. "I've got to get into the mountains. I cannot delay!"

He was slumped forward over his saddle horn and sweating profusely, even though the breeze coming down off the mountains was relatively cool.

"Lord Gregory," Vaegon corrected, as respectfully as he could manage. "Your Brawl with the tattooed man has caused most of this. I know you did not intend it to happen, just as I never intended to see past my hatred for your race, but here we are, nonetheless. If you truly wish to find a giant, then go with Hyden Hawk. When your mind is not so clouded with the poison's fire, you'll understand."

"Why do you hate us?" Hyden asked Vaegon without any anger in his tone.

"Some wrongs, no matter how ancient they may be, cannot be forgotten. Like a scar remains on the flesh to remind the bearer of the wound and the circumstances that created it."

"Then I hope the scars on your face from the shattered arrow this morning show plainly for all to see," Hyden said with a deep intensity. "Let them remind those who look upon you that it is sometimes better to be scarred than not."

Vaegon considered the words for a long time, then nodded at the wisdom of them. He made a fist, placed it over his heart and made a short bow toward Hyden. The significance of the gesture was lost to Hyden, but he returned it anyway.

The gesture meant several different things, depending on the situation in which it was used: honor, respect, understanding, friendship, and love, to name but a few. In this instance, Vaegon meant most of them.

Chapter Eighteen

Gerard had never ridden a horse before. The Skyler Clan's isolated culture never adopted the practice of using beasts of burden for personal transportation. There was no need for them. The terrain was often too steep and inhospitable, and the winters far too harsh to try to keep animals that couldn't stand to be confined in an underground pen for almost half of the year. To endure the mountain winters, the Skyler Clan's folk lived in underground burrows. It was a necessity of survival.

Outside of the few times Gerard, Hyden and their young cousins tried to ride the big horned Billy goats that Berda's husband herded, Gerard never tried to ride any sort of creature at all. It was an awkward and thrilling feeling. Especially since the group left in the dark of night just after Bludgeon died.

A strange looking man, tall, pale-skinned, and bald as an egg, was the lead rider. His name was Cole and he wore wizard's robes and carried a lantern for them to follow—at least it seemed to be a lantern's light. Gerard wasn't sure the light was natural. They followed the man on a mad dash southward, to the north end of the river's huge, lake-like swell, called the Belly. They stopped there at the water's edge that first night, and made a cook fire as the sun came up on the morning of Summer's Day.

When Gerard dismounted from the horse Shaella provided him, he stumbled along on watery legs and fell to the ground. Laughing at himself with the others of the group, he looked around. In the pink light of dawn, he saw on one side of the makeshift camp was an endless expanse of silvery blue water, while on the other side was a sea of grassy green valley bottom. Both extended as far as the eye could see.

There were six men besides him in the group, and all of them save for Cole and his would-be twin, Flick, were roaring at his folly. The laughter stopped abruptly though, when Shaella crawled on top of him right there where he was sprawled in the dewy grass, and began kissing him deeply. She rubbed and squeezed his inner thighs where the ride had made them sore until he was dazed and breathless.

"There's something a few of us must tend to," she whispered into his ear. Her hot, sweet breath made his head swim. "We won't be long and besides, it will give the potion time to do its work on your back and legs." She kissed him again before he could respond.

"Potion?" he asked dreamily, when she finally pulled away. "What kind of potion? Where did you get such a thing?"

"At the festival, silly," she lied through her brilliant smile.

She pushed herself up off him, then reached down, and pulled him up into a sitting position. As she went to get the potion from her saddlebags, Gerard glanced at the men by the fire.

Three slack-jawed heads quickly turned to study the flames. Cole wasn't at the fire, nor was the man named Flick, who was a slightly rounder and shorter version of him. Both wore black wizard robes and had clean shaven heads, and both of them had skin as pale as milk. Greyber was at the fire with the other three men, but his huge tattoo-covered back was facing Gerard. Greyber had been close friends with Bludgeon. When news of Bludgeon's death reached them, the man roared in anguish. All during the ride, Gerard saw his jaw muscles working, and more than once the big Seawardsman wiped his eyes with the back of his hand. He, unlike the other swordsmen of the group, paid little attention to Gerard and Shaella's open affection.

Trent, Dennly, and the other man—Gerard couldn't recall his name—were all Valleyan outlaws who escaped a wagon cage and turned into sell swords. Shaella called them glorified bandits. Glorified lecherous bandits, Gerard thought, with the way they watched her as she went about her business.

Dennly was ogling her backside that very moment. Gerard's blood burned at the idea of it. It wasn't so much jealousy, as the blatant disrespect it showed. Before he could change his mind, he silently told Dennly through his magical ring to grab one of the pretty red coals out of the fire. Almost instantly, he felt the warm tingle of the ring's power coursing through his veins.

"AAAUUUGGGHHH!" Dennly screamed.

For a long moment, he just stared stupidly at his blistering hand. Then he bolted to the river and thrust it into the cool water.

"Don't do that!" Shaella whispered in Gerard's ear. She'd returned and was watching from behind him. It angered her, and she worked to master the emotion, but she managed it. Disgusting as he was, Dennly's sword was needed. He couldn't wield it properly with a ruined hand. Still, Gerard's gesture was a sweet one, and its intent was not lost to her. She took a breath and masked her emotions completely.

"Why did you make him do that? How?" she asked.

She knew the answer of course; that's why she chose him over the other climbers. She would have rather had the older brother, but Gerard was the one with the ring, the one Pael said could help her with the dragon.

He wasn't bad to look it. He could have been a far worse specimen, she told herself. Gerard would do just fine, if she could keep his jealous reactions from maiming all of her soldiers.

Gerard was at a loss for words. He hadn't thought she knew about his power. The ring's power, he reminded himself, quickly. Did she know? How could she? She just asked him why he had done what he did. He felt a slight wave of embarrassment wash over him. He had used the power on her back at the festival. Was he any better than Dennly? She saved him from his thoughts when she kissed him.

"I...uh...I..." he stammered, as he attempted to answer her question.

"Shhh!" She touched a finger to his lips, then squatted down beside him. "It's all right, my young warlock. Just drink this."

She tipped a small clay vial to his mouth and poured the contents in. He swallowed and smiled back at her. It didn't taste bad like he expected. His ego was swelling out of proportion as he thought about her calling him her warlock. He was so full of himself he didn't realize he was already growing sleepy.

"Greyber will stay here with you," she told him, as she stood back up. Her tone had become commanding again. "Cole, see to the pervert's hand."

Gerard felt disappointed as she seemed to forget all about him.

"Flick!" she called out. "Ready the horses. It's time to ride for the Witch Queen."

Gerard watched through a thickening fog of slumber as the group hurried back up river. He noticed they looked different somehow, but he couldn't quite figure it out. He dismissed the idea, then took a place in the grass next to the fire across from Greyber. He started to make conversation with the big Seawardsman, but his fuddled mind and the saddened look on Greyber's face kept him from it. Instead, he let the potion take hold of him and he slipped into a deep, dreamless sleep.

When he opened his eyes again, Gerard found it was nearly dark. He had slept the daylight hours away. A panicked jolt shot through him, and he jumped to his feet.

Shaella? To his great relief, she was there tending to Trent. He appeared to be horribly wounded. Cole held the man's head up while Shaella worked intently over his bloody midsection. She began chanting something strange and an eerie, yellowish glow filled the space between her palm and the gaping wound.

Flick was opposite her, across Trent's body. He pushed the two sides of the gash together and held them in place while Shaella's magical glow moved slowly across the wound. Gerard watched breathlessly. He was awed by the spectacle. He couldn't decide what impressed him more: the fact he was a witnessing actual magic—real magic like the stuff in Berda's stories—or the fact it was Shaella using it. No wonder she knew he used the ring on Dennly. He smiled at the thought, knowing now she kissed him that first time on her own.

As the light from her palm passed over Trent's gut, the wound grafted itself together. It scabbed quickly under the light and before the glow had left, a fat, pink scar formed there. It was as if a whole season's worth of healing was happening in a brief instant.

Cole must have heard Gerard's breath catch. His long neck craned at an almost impossible angle and his eyes locked on Gerard's briefly. Gerard shuddered. The man's eyes seemed cold and empty.

Cole spoke a few sharp words to Shaella. She continued what she was doing for a moment, then the glow suddenly disappeared. She responded harshly to Cole. Gerard couldn't hear the exchange, but he sensed it was about him.

Her tone softened as she spoke a few words to Flick, then she rose and came toward Gerard with a forced smile on her face.

For a fleeting moment, her eyes seemed as dead and lifeless as Cole's. Gerard dismissed it as his imagination or a trick of the wavering firelight. She looked fine now, save for the blood that stained her arms to the elbows. She smiled at him, while biting her bottom lip. To Gerard, she was beauty incarnate. Her eyes became pinpoints of seduction, and even had he wanted to, there was no way he could've resisted her at that moment.

"Come," she softly commanded. "We don't have much time."

She led him to the water, a place far enough away from the camp that the firelight didn't quite reach them. The Moon was dim, but Gerard had no trouble seeing her milky white skin as she unlatched her leather armor vest and shrugged it away. She rinsed her arms in the water, then unlaced her leather britches. Her breasts were apple sized with puffy, pink areolae the size of a coin. Gerard felt the hardness of her nipples through his shirt when she pressed herself against him. Her arms went behind him and pulled his shirt up. She giggled when it caught there. He fumbled with the lacings to get it clear of his head. When he finally got it off and could see again, she was moving away from him back toward the water. She had taken off her pants. Her perfectly formed buttocks jiggled lightly as she went. The sight of it made him so hard he could barely unlace his britches.

He joined her in the river. She was at a place that was neck deep. It was cold, and he would've grown soft if she didn't take his manhood in her hand and begin to squeeze and pull at it under the water. She kissed him, and with her free hand, she moved one of his hands to her breast. Her nipples were like tiny pebbles. He moved his other hand between her legs and felt her heat, even in the chilly water. He wanted more than anything to be inside her then. He was completely under her spell.

She found that she wanted him there, too. So much so, that she forced herself to distance the moment in her mind. He had a purpose to serve, she reminded herself. He was a toy. No, he was a tool. She would be done with him before long, and continuing this would only serve to make it harder to lose him later. He was different, though. There was something about him. He wasn't a boring noble-born prude or an ignorant farmer. Nor was he a gruff and hardened fighter, or an oily thief. She had never known this type of man. He, as boyish as he seemed at times, was a grown man. The proof was right there in her hand.

Gripping him, the ache to have him inside her filled her mind again. The way his fingers moved deftly inside her was driving her mad with desire. His kisses were hot, and his tongue insistent. She felt a wave of relief, mixed with regret, when he shuddered against her. He wrapped his arms around her, and clinched her buttocks tightly as he came. His intensity caused the tremors in her belly to quake through her as well. When she finally found herself again, she had to force the anger out of her expression. What was she doing? She didn't have time to feel for this man. She didn't have time to feel at all.

"We must go now," she said, rather flatly, into Gerard's dreamy daze.

He didn't want to let go of her. He felt he would've drowned himself in the lake then and there if she only asked him to. Confused by her blank expression, he reluctantly released her and followed her out of the water.

They rode through the night again and all of the next day. Dennly and the other Valleyan hadn't returned the previous night, so it was only the six of them heading south down the river road. The swell of the river was so wide, Gerard lost sight of the opposite shore the first night. He had a hard time thinking of that body of water as a river. The shoreline forced them on a southeasterly course for some time. The Belly was a massive swell, but eventually its width narrowed again and the road resumed its place at the flowing river's side. It was nearly full dark at that point, so Shaella stopped them for the night.

Throughout the day, Shaella hadn't said a word to Gerard. He watched her though. She had a firm command of the group. Cole and Flick sometimes bickered with her, but would obviously follow her to the ends of the world. Ultimately, they were all so obedient, it seemed to Gerard she had some sort of spell cast over them. None of them seemed weak, though.

Cole and Flick were both imposing and strange. The robes they wore were split up the front and fastened together with little bone buttons painted black to match the material. Under the robes, they wore loose-fitting pants and vests, made of the skin of some scaled creature Gerard had never seen before. The scales looked small, but they were bright and glittery. The two magi wore boots decorated with more pieces of bone; they seemed too large for their feet.

Greyber kept to himself. It was clear that he would have no problem wielding the huge, two-handed sword slung over his back.

Apparently, Seawardsmen didn't wear clothing above the waist. At least Gerard could never remember seeing one do so. The tattoo-covered warrior wore ordinary deerskin britches and good Valleyan horse-hide boots, just like the ones Hyden purchased for Gerard. Steel-plated gauntlets covered the big man's arms, from wrist to elbow, but otherwise, he wore no armor.

Trent looked deathly pale throughout the morning. His chainmail shirt was laid across his horse's back, behind the saddle. Through the tear in his shirt, Gerard could tell his wound was no longer bleeding. By evening, the man regained some of his color. Now that the camp was set, he seemed even better, as if the light of the cook fire finished the healing Shaella's magic started. He made a jest over Greyber's so-called road stew that caused the big man to smile through his gloom.

Gerard was so tired from the long ride that he didn't have time to wonder if Shaella would come to him in the night. He thought about going to her briefly after he'd eaten a share of

Greyber's concoction, but exhaustion and the warmth of the food in his belly consumed the thought. Only moments after he ate, he fell into a deep, heavy sleep.

The next morning Shaella woke him with a kiss, but its sweetness was lost in the commotion of the breaking camp.

He was starting to feel as if she were ignoring him. The feeling grew stronger as the day wore on. He caught her eyeing him once, but her strange expression only caused him to worry more.

Finally, late in the day he used the power of his ring to get her attention. He silently told her that she should come and kiss him. The wonderful feel of the ring's magic in his veins was nearly eclipsed by her sudden appearance at his side. She guided her horse alongside of his, then leaned over and kissed his cheek.

"You're wicked," she whispered to him. "You need not use your great magic to get a kiss from me, my young warlock. Just ask."

He wanted to feel her against him, to smell her hair while he held her in his arms, to feel the warmth of her breath on his skin. "When are we making camp?"

She blushed despite herself at the obvious undertone of the question. She thought she had distanced herself beyond such foolish feelings, but apparently not.

"We're not stopping," she decided as she said it. "We'll ride at least until we cross the Everflow River into Wildermont."

His expression showed his disappointment. His look touched her deep inside, and that scared her. She was supposed to be a sorceress of the dark. She was supposed to be cold and ruthless like her marsh-witch mother had been; like her father was. But hadn't her mother loved once? A wicked enough thought crossed her mind. Didn't a cat love to taunt and tease the mouse, before devouring it? Gerard could be her mouse. She leaned in close to him then, and spoke in a conspiratorial whisper.

"We will be able to lodge at an inn when we reach Castlemont. We can have a private room all to ourselves."

He smiled at the prospect of having her alone like that. He could only imagine the possibilities. It didn't matter, though. He could wait forever, as long as he knew she would be there when the wait was over.

"What's it like?" he asked.

At first, she thought he was still being lascivious. Then she recalled he was from the mountain clans and had never even seen a real town, much less the grandest city in the entire realm. He was asking about Castlemont, the capital city of the Kingdom of Wildermont. She smiled at him as she answered.

"We will be at the town known as High Crossing soon. That is where we will cross a river called the Everflow. The river separates the Leif Greyn Valley from Wildermont. High Crossing is more of a village than a town. As we pass through, imagine a place more than a thousand times as big, with buildings built on top of other buildings, and towers that reach all the way up into the sky, like the Spire."

He asked about the people and their ways, and she answered him as best as she could. Money, it seemed, was what made one strong in the kingdom cities. He understood. It was just a larger, more permanent version of the Summer's Day Festival. He couldn't wait to get there and see it all for himself.

Night settled on them quickly. The sky was gray and cloudy, the early summer air thick and warm. The bridge Shaella spoke of seemed to come up out of nowhere. It was wide enough for two wagons to cross at the same time.

The roar of the dark river that churned swiftly under the span filled Gerard's ears. The bridge was a lot longer than it had looked at first. It took a few minutes for the horses to trot all the way across it. The bridge didn't cross the Leif Greyn. It spanned a smaller river that met the bigger flow there. Gerard could only imagine the skill and the time it had taken to build such a thing. It amazed him. Even in the dim light of the few lanterns that wavered at intervals along the span, he could see the stonework was carefully crafted. The flowers and leaves carved into the retaining wall lining each side of the bridge looked almost real, and the gargoyles that held the lantern poles seemed to snarl and growl as he passed them.

"Why are there none of these buildings on the other side of the river?" he asked as they entered the village of High Crossing.

"We just left the sacred valley," she answered. "It's still considered sacrilege to build or claim land there, but this side of the river belongs to King Jarrek. Welcome to Wildermont."

Just then, a dozen or so armored horsemen emerged from the shadows. Gerard didn't even hear the jingle of their tack as they moved to block their passage.

Light could be seen coming from a few of the windowed buildings that lined the road, but most of the structures were only hulking shapes in the darkness. A nervous-looking man brandishing a torch strode out of the building nearest the end of the bridge and motioned for them to halt. Cole, who had been leading the group while Shaella rode with Gerard, turned and looked back at her sharply as he reined his horse in.

"A copper a man, or a silver for the lot of ye to pass," the old toll man called out. The presence of the soldiers on the road lent confidence to his voice.

Shaella spurred her horse up to the old man.

"Here!" she snapped, as she flipped him a silver coin. "If King Jarrek is too poor to make change, then I'm the Queen of Westland," she added with a chuckle.

Cole and Flick both gave her a warning look.

"We would have you come with us!" a commanding voice boomed at them. It was the Captain of the Redwolf Guard troop, who was now completely blocking their way.

From his place at the rear of their group, Gerard saw Greyber's hand reach up over his shoulder to his sword's hilt. He looked again at the men blocking the road. Bright, polished, plate armor and shiny chain mail reflected back at him in the torchlight. Above the soldiers, a stalking wolf's silhouette danced crazily in the wind on a fluttering crimson banner. Even the horses they rode were strapped with leather and steel. The idea that Greyber would even think of drawing his blade against men such as these made Gerard's stomach clench. What was about to happen here?

As beautiful as Shaella was, as much as Gerard wanted her, and as much as he wanted to be on this grand adventure, he suddenly found the only place he really wanted to be was home.

Chapter Nineteen

Lord Gregory spent the whole of the day learning why the plant Vaegon prepared for him was called Squat Weed. He had to make for the bushes so many times throughout the day, he was walking bow legged and crying openly from the soreness. Worse than that, up in the northern reaches of the Leif Greyn Valley, there weren't very many bushes. Modesty wasn't an option when the only features of the landscape were rock-strewn hills and shin-high grass.

The people of the Skyler Clan pitied the Lion Lord. The Westlander thrilled them with not one, but two great Brawls in the last few years. To see him in such a state was heart wrenching. They, without a doubt, respected him, and if Hyden thought to help the man, they wouldn't intervene. But for reasons other than the fact his frequent stops were slowing their progress, they decided to leave Hyden, Lord Lion and the elf to travel at their own pace.

"That guard captain paid far too much attention to our friend," Vaegon said. He and Hyden were walking side by side, leading Lord Gregory, who was slumped in his saddle.

"Why do you insist on talking about me as if I'm not even here?" Lord Gregory shot weakly. "It's maddening."

"The men of the kingdoms think in different ways than I do," Hyden replied to Vaegon absently.

His attention was focused on Talon. The bird was trying to chase an insect that was darting through the air in short, zagging spurts. It seemed the bug was mocking Talon. Talon couldn't change direction as quickly as the insect could, nor could he stop and hover. He could barely fly, and the poor bird was growing frustrated. Finally, Talon gave up and flew off in a different direction, leaving the irritating bug seemingly forgotten.

"He will tell his superior officers I'm alive and where we're going," Lord Gregory spoke again. "It isn't wise to...wise to... Oh blast that fargin stuff you gave me, elf! Help me down again! Hurry now!"

Vaegon did so. He turned his back to the Lion Lord and watched Hyden watching Talon as Lord Gregory noisily handled his business.

Talon hadn't lost interest in the bug, after all. It had been a trick. Hyden was absorbed in the ordeal now. He could feel what Talon was feeling, but only in the back of his mind. Still, it was exciting to feel the bird's eagerness to get his taunting prey.

Talon was higher up now, circling, watching and calculating. Suddenly, he dove, wings back, neck outstretched, eyes focused sharply. He was coming down fast and at a sharp angle. The insect buzzed along from place to place lazily now since it no longer felt the presence of the pesky and clumsy young bird. It had no idea its doom was swiftly swooping in from above. Talon adjusted his little wings a bit, then thrust out his claws. In one fleeting movement, he came out of the sky and snatched the insect. It didn't have a chance. The bug was crushed in the bird's grip instantly. A few moments later after munching his prize and swallowing it down, Talon reared back his head and let out what was intended to be a proud, fierce shriek. It sounded more like a long, thin squawk to Hyden, but he didn't dare laugh.

"Is there no mercy left for me?" Lord Gregory wailed miserably from where he was squatting down in the grass.

"He needs a lot of water now," Vaegon said. "Much more than we can carry."

"One of the streams that flow into the main river isn't too far," Hyden told him. "My people will cross a lot farther upstream. When they do, they will leave the Redwolf soldiers they hired behind. If we go across now, we will be able to avoid crossing paths with that greedy captain you spoke of." The last was directed at Lord Gregory.

Vaegon nodded his agreement.

"In the lore of my people, there are stories of men like you, Hyden Hawk, men who bond with the creatures of the world. Those types of men grow to be very powerful and their actions tend to have a great impact upon all of the lands." The elf paused searching for the words he wanted. "Are you—no—do you feel such a power brewing inside you?"

The question caught Hyden off guard. He thought briefly of the old fortuneteller's words and the words of his grandfather back at the harvest lodge.

"I feel Talon's instincts in my mind sometimes, but nothing more."

"I would rather you left me for dead," Lord Gregory interrupted.

He was back on his feet, walking with his legs stiff and making an obvious effort to keep them from rubbing too close together. His buttocks were raw and chafed, and one of his shoulders was swollen to twice the size of the other. He was so pale that if he stood still long enough, he could pass for a stone statue. All in all, he looked to be on the verge of death, which truthfully he was.

"Lead us to the river," Vaegon said softly, then went to help the Lion Lord back into his saddle.

Hyden sensed the urgency in the elf's voice. Talon must have felt or heard something too, for he fluttered down and landed on Hyden's shoulder.

The foothill river was icy cold, fairly narrow, and flowing rapidly where they decided to cross. If it weren't for the numerous rocks that pocked the deeper main channel like a dam that had broken away, they never would've gotten Lord Gregory's horse across. Vaegon's soothing words and sharp commands in the strange, elven tongue sent the beast leaping from boulder to boulder, like some huge, malformed rabbit. They floated Lord Gregory across. The man was glad to get into the water. He savored it, as he let its bitter chill soothe and cleanse his tender backside.

They filled their skins after the Westland Lord drained them, then they filled them again. There was still enough daylight to travel, so they tried to take full advantage of it. They didn't make it very far before the squat weed forced the Lord to make for the bushes again. The river formed a shallow pool nearby that had a small copse of trees growing at its side. They decided to camp there, since there was plenty of dead fall. Hyden made a rather large fire so they could dry their clothes.

Lord Gregory sprawled out near the blaze and began moaning softly, while Hyden laid all but their small clothes out to dry. Talon sat perched on a nearby tree limb, watching Vaegon curiously. The bird's attention to what the elf was doing was so intense that Hyden was forced to watch as well.

He was standing shin deep in the middle of the pool. His leather pants legs were pulled up and bunched at the knees. The elf's head was down and his arms were spread out wide, with his fingers hooked into claws. Hyden almost laughed at him. He was mimicking a bird of prey, but he looked more like one of the scarecrows the Westland farmers sold at the festival, the ones with glittery yarn for hair, and bodies made from straw, sticks and old clothes.

There was a flash of movement then, so fast it startled both Talon and Hyden, forcing them to blink several times in wonder. Vaegon snatched a fat, silver-bellied whisker trout right out of the water. It was wriggling crazily in his grasp as he charged through the pool toward them. He kicked up huge splashes as he raced for the shore. The fish squirmed and curled its long, thick body trying to twist and slip itself free. For a moment, it looked like it might succeed, but the elf was smart. Just before the struggling fish got loose, he tossed it toward the shore. The trout literally swam through the air, its tail searching for a purchase that wouldn't come. Even before it smacked into the rocky bank, Talon was after it. As soon as the fish landed, the bird was on it, pecking at its eyes and doing his best to hold it in place with his little claws.

They ate well that night. Even Lord Gregory managed to hold a stomach full of the tender white meat down.

After the sunset, Vaegon worked his elven magic on the sick Westlander again. He healed the damage the poison had done throughout the day, but the poison was still in the man's system. The squat weed went far to thin the toxic stuff flowing through the Lion Lord's veins, but only time would tell if it had done enough. When Vaegon was finished, he covered the Westlander's body and washed the man's clothes again in the river. As he was laying them back out to dry, he spoke. "Do you know the story of the wizard, Dahg Mahn, and how he and King Horst helped save the elves, the giants, and even the dwarves?"

The word dwarves was said with an expression that showed his distaste for the vanished race of little men. "Have you heard how he brought them all together to rid the world of the soulless Abbadon?"

"Aye," Hyden answered. It was Gerard's favorite story. When they were boys, Gerard often pretended to be the legendary wizard Dahg Mahn when they played. Berda told them that tale far more times than she ever wanted to, Hyden was sure of it. "I've heard the story many times."

"Have you been told the tale of how Dahg Mahn became the king's wizard? Of how he became Dahg Mahn?"

Vaegon had Hyden's attention then. There was nothing Hyden loved more than a story, especially one he had never heard.

"No, but I'd love to hear it now."

Vaegon finished laying out Lord Gregory's clothes, then took a seat across the fire from Hyden. After he was comfortable, he took a long pull from a water skin, glanced at Lord Gregory's soundly sleeping body, and began the story.

"Pratchert was a hunter, and the son of a woodsman. He grew up in a village whose name has long been forgotten, but which stood very near where the town called Tip sits now."

"Where is that?" Hyden asked, trying not to sound too ignorant.

"The Southron River forms the natural border between Seaward and Valleya, but in Pratchert's time, it was all one kingdom. The Evermore Forest trails southward along the river's banks into the plains. Where this extension of forest ends, sits the town called Tip. King Horst was young then and ruled over all of those lands, along with what is now the Kingdom of Highwander, too. The world was relatively peaceful in those days. The Abbadon wasn't yet strong enough to threaten the lands, but it soon would be.

"Pratchert's father was commissioned by King Horst to travel to the frozen sea. A quest it was called, a quest to kill a great white bear, the fur of which the king wanted, for some reason or another. Pratchert, along with a large group of men led by his father, set out on this long and dangerous journey.

"They traveled across the continent and made it to the frozen sea in the west. They killed the mighty white bear, but the bear managed to kill more than half of the group in the battle. The survivors were strung out across the icy lands, along the bloody trail the dying bear made them follow. The great beast was hearty, and it led them for dozens and dozens of miles before it finally died.

"Young Pratchert was one of those who got lost along the way. A pair of men who were too lazy to make a proper search, led his father to believe his son had fallen into a chasm and frozen to death. Pratchert was left to survive on his own in the vast, frozen wilderness.

"Having been raised by a hunter and woodsman, Pratchert learned many things about survival. He was both smart and resourceful. He used the sun to determine his direction and began traveling south, away from the colder climate. As he went, he came along an injured wolf, which was in the process of giving birth. Only four pups came into the world, and two of them died the first night.

"Pratchert hunted for the injured mother wolf with a bow and arrow he made out of a fallen limb and some sun-dried rabbit gut. He managed to keep her and himself fed long enough for the two pups to wean themselves from the teat, but she died soon after when a harsh, late winter storm hung over them for a few long days.

"When the weather finally relented, Pratchert found one of the pups had disappeared. Knowing he did all he could for the wolves, he started south again with the last of the pups right on his heels."

Vaegon shifted on his rocky seat, leaned forward, and prodded the dying fire back to life with a stick.

"Somehow, he and the wolf ended up cutting east through the forest your people call the Reyhall."

"Not my people," Hyden corrected. He couldn't help but stare at Vaegon's wild yellow eyes. They were like cat's eyes, or an owl's. "My people aren't kingdom folk."

"Yes, yes," the elf nodded. "I forget all of you humans are not sworn to a king. Anyway, Pratchert took his time. He and the wolf wandered the forest for a few years. No one really knows why."

Hyden almost stopped Vaegon to tell him that though he wasn't sworn to a human king, his people did reside in the Giant Mountains, and were more or less sworn to obey the laws of King Aldar. He let it go though, because he had never actually seen the giant king, or the fabled city of Afdeon, from where he ruled, much less had he ever sworn any sort of oath of fealty.

"...finally crossed the Leif Greyn River and made it to the Spire." Vaegon was saying. "There, our lore says Pratchert was visited by a great, blue dragon. The two of them supposedly spoke for many days.

"After the dragon flew away, Pratchert and his wolf came through the Evermore Forest. He was traveling toward his childhood home, but before they could get that far south, they encountered a problem. His wolf's familiar thick, white fur was making the animal sick in the warmer climate. Even after it shed its winter coat, the wolf was suffering in the warm, southern air. After much deliberation, Pratchert and his wolf decided to stay together. He used his dagger to trim the fur from the wolf's hide so that it could stand the heat. It was for the best, they both learned. When they came into Pratchert's village, the people were afraid of the wolf, even though he looked more like a mangy dog than the ferocious creature he could be. If he hadn't been half-shaved, he would've terrified the simple folk to drastic measures.

"Pratchert learned his father died of a lung sickness the year after he returned with the king's prize bear skin. His mother died the year after. Naturally, he was saddened by the news, and he returned with his wolf and grief to the Evermore Forest. He planned on going north so he and the wolf could range and explore in comfort, but before they could get away, they were stopped by a pair of frightened squirrels.

"The squirrels communicated with him through the link he had formed with his wolf. They told him men were destroying the forest in the east, and they practically begged him to help them make it stop.

"He took them seriously. It was no small matter that would cause a pair of squirrels to grow brave enough to approach a wolf and a man. Other animals heard the squirrels' pleadings, and since the wolf hadn't tried to eat them, they cautiously approached as well. Soon, a crowd of birds, deer, a fox, a rabbit, even a bright green tree snake and a wild hog gathered around them. They convinced Pratchert to at least go and see what might be done about the matter."

Vaegon sipped from the water skin and then continued.

"Pratchert and the wolf were sickened by what they found there. An entire valley had been cleared of foliage. It looked as if an angry god hacked away the trees with a giant scythe, like they were so much wheat.

"Pratchert rounded up all of the strongest forest creatures, the ones with teeth and claws, and the ones with venom and size. One day while the men were starting to chop and saw at the trees, Pratchert led his army of animals out of the forest. They took a position and held firm, directly in the men's way. The terrified men sent for their foreman, who in turn, sent for the Captain of the King's Guard. Days passed, and eventually King Horst came to see the spectacle for himself.

"For days, hissed and growled insults, and the foul-worded threats of men were hurled back and forth. Luckily, King Horst saw they were getting nowhere. His need of these timbers was as great as that of the animals, so he agreed to talk to Pratchert.

"The king explained an army of demons and devils led by the Abbadon himself, was marching toward them as they spoke. They were coming for the Wardstone. He told him of the need for catapults, spears, ships and all the other devices the men of the world might need to fight such an enemy. He spoke of how this foe burned everything in its path: homes, crops, and even the forest. King Horst ended his speech by suggesting it would be better to take a few of the trees than to let all of the forest be burned to ash by this evil foe.

"Pratchert went back to the animals and explained the situation. They agreed losing some of the forest was better than losing all of it. Reluctantly, the animal army disbanded, and the creatures began to migrate from that part of the Evermore so the men could continue.

"King Horst was so astonished and impressed with the man who could speak to animals that he asked him to come and be his wizard. Pratchert felt bound to help fight the Abbadon and the terrible legions it commanded. When he found out King Horst's castle was located in the city of Xwarda, up in the Wander Mountains where the weather was cool and crisp, he accepted the offer. You know the rest, I think," Vaegon finished.

"Aye," Hyden nodded. "When the soulless one came, Dahg Mahn called forth the animals from the forest. The animals brought the giants, elves, and dwarves with them. In Berda's tale—she's a giant, a goat herder's wife who comes to my clan's village and tells us stories every so often. In her tales of Dahg Mahn, the animals turn the tide of the battle and save the races of men from the Abbadon."

Hyden yawned and scratched his head curiously.

"If his name is really Pratchert, why is he always remembered as Dahg Mahn?"

Vaegon laughed deeply.

"I should make you wait and ask your giant friend Berda, but I'm starting to like you, so I'll tell you, Hyden Hawk. It's really simple, and I'm surprised you haven't figured it out yet. The wolf looked like a mangy dog," Vaegon said, as he moved to lie down by the fire. "And Dahg Mahn means dog man in the old tongue."

"Ah," Hyden nodded, as he, too, found a place to lie down for the night.

Chapter Twenty

The coronation of young King Glendar went smoothly enough. The sadness of the past week was replaced by the hope for a greater future. The good people of Westland, for a few days at least, were led to believe the days to come still held promise. The ladies and wives of the noble born and common folk alike were busy with their gossip. It appeared Lady Zasha caught the young king's eye, and they all had a comment to make about the development.

"She's such a beautiful girl."

"What a wonderful queen she will make."

"With fat Lord Ellrich as her father, what will the heir look like?"

"The daughter of the Marsh Lord has done well to draw his eye."

Then there was Glendar himself. The whole of the nobility watched him as he grimaced and clutched at his face, and then finally broke into tears when his father's crown was placed upon his head. The outcome pleased Pael immensely. The stupid boy had grinned as the crown was presented. Pael had to act quickly. He sent an invisible, but sizzling hot, particle of dust into Glendar's eye, which wiped the smile from his face, and caused all the flinching, grimacing, and tears. Yes, Pael mused, it had all gone extremely well. So well, in fact, no one noticed Ironspike was missing.

Even better was the news Pael received from Shaella. Summer's Day had turned into a battlefield. The sacred Leif Greyn Valley was thoroughly bloodied. He intended to put the kingdoms against each other with his covert and indirect aggression, but a full scale battle was even better. In fact, it was perfect. And who would've thought Lord Gregory would've been so inadvertently helpful, before he crawled off and died from Inkling's poison dart.

Pael's plans went so well that King Glendar's present foolishness didn't bother him at all. It didn't matter how many heads the boy piked in the court yard, or whose heads they were. As a matter of fact, Pael welcomed any distraction that kept the new king's mind off of his father's sword.

Now that the news of the massacre at Summer's Day was finally getting back to the Westland people, Lord Brach's forceful recruitment of young, able bodied men didn't seem so alarming to the common folk. The whole of Westland would soon be chomping at the bit to avenge the death of the well-loved Lion Lord.

The latest rumors pinned the blame on Seaward and the Valleyans. The noble trading houses and major landholders were already sending their extra men to join in the upcoming campaign. It wouldn't be long before Pael could send the whole of the Westlander army, King Glendar included, off to war with the east.

The only piece he needed to complete his puzzle was Ironspike. He didn't want the blade for Glendar to wield on his fool's quest to conquer the eastern kingdoms, though. Pael needed the sword for other reasons. One of which, was that its presence would solidify the claim of the one who would soon replace Glendar as the ruler of the west. Another reason was Ironspike's great power was the only possible thing that could stop his plans from playing out.

Upon hearing the news of Lord Gregory's death, Lady Zasha pleaded with King Glendar to let her and her father, Lord Ellrich, be dismissed from court so they might escort the Lady Trella back to her home at Lake Bottom Stronghold. Zasha wanted to help her through her troubled time of grief.

Lady Trella came to Lakeside Castle for the king's coronation, and to help Zasha woo the new king. The excitement of the times flared like a bonfire inside of her. Little Zasha's mother died while birthing her, and Trella always acted as a matronly figure for the girl. The fact Trella had no children of her own only made the bond stronger.

Lake Bottom Stronghold was only a few days' carriage ride from Settsted Stronghold, where Lord Ellrich and Lady Zasha resided. Being that the two families were the most powerful in all of Southern Westland, they visited each other often. That Zasha would ask for Trella's advice and confide in her so much was heartening. Lake Bottom Stronghold was the most boring of places when Lord Gregory and his men were away. It wasn't much better when they were there. Lady Trella reveled in the giddy excitement that women share when love is blossoming, and she was proud when Zasha asked her to act as her matron during the courtship. Trella's blaze had been extinguished rather abruptly, though. Like an entire keg full of water being dumped over a single candle flame, the news of her husband's death snuffed all of her cheer instantly and sent her tumbling into darkness.

Lady Zasha could not, and would not, let the closest thing to a mother she had ever known go home feeling so miserable and alone. The Stronghold at Lakebottom was a great and mighty place, but it was a lonely place. For each of its breathtaking balcony views and high-arched windows, there was an empty, unused room, full of dust and gloom. It was not a place for grieving, Zasha knew. She had to do something that would help Trella cope with her loss. What that something was, she had no idea, but leaving the woman to mourn alone was out of the question.

King Glendar, in a show of kindness and understanding, very publicly granted part of her request. Zasha was allowed to return to Lake Bottom with Lady Trella, but with all the trouble brewing in the east, her father could not be spared. War was most certainly on the horizon, and the commander of the Marsh Border Garrison would be needed.

Lord Ellrich sent a small attachment of his most trusted men to accompany the two ladies on the journey around Lion's Lake. He did his best to hide it, but he felt fairly certain it would be the last time he saw his daughter. He secreted a letter to her through one of his men for her to read when she was finally out from under Glendar's wickedly deceitful thumb. The letter pleaded with her to find a way to dissuade King Glendar from making her his queen, and if she couldn't manage it, he wanted her to kill him in his sleep, for the good of the people of Westland.

"Send Lord Able all the supplies he has requested," Pael told the men seated at his end of the long, glossed oak table in the council hall. "As a matter of fact, double the quantity of the supplies he wants. After all, more men are gathering at Eastwatch as we speak. This request is a week old. The four thousand men it speaks of will be doubled by the time the wagons get there."

For the moment, Pael was leaving the actual planning of the battle to King Glendar and Lord Brach. The two of them were at the other end of the table, hovering over a sprawl of maps and charts, conferring to themselves and oblivious to Pael and the others. A thin-haired, old scribe wrote Pael's order up quickly and passed it to him. He blobbed it with wax, then put the King's Seal on it without even batting an eye at Glendar. Pael was in sole charge of the preparations, a duty he chose to perform himself, so he wouldn't come across any surprises when he took over the rest of the campaign.

"Lord Ellrich, it says here you're only able to supply your new king with two thousand men. Is that correct?" Pael asked rather loudly.

"High Wizard Pael," Lord Ellrich started diplomatically, as he leaned back and rested his meaty arms across his huge belly. His bulk caused the chair to groan in protest. "As you know, the garrison at Settsted is our great kingdom's only protection in the south. If men are not left there to guard the border, then the creatures of the marshes will slither right into Westland."

Pael harrumphed loudly and stood, making sure that the scraping of his chair legs and the swiftness of his movement caught the attention of everyone in the room. He waited until he was sure King Glendar was listening and he spoke harshly, while throwing up his arms in exasperation.

"Marsh creatures, m'lord, are you serious?"

The men sitting at Pael's end of the table blanched, as if some wild magic was going to come flashing forth from the wizard's hands. Lord Ellrich, though, didn't even bat an eye. He held Pael's gaze steadily.

"We are about to wage war on the east!" Pael ranted. "They have butchered our people—innocent people—and in cold blood. One of our peers, Lord Gregory, lies dead at their hands. How many men does it take to fend off snakes and lizards?" Pael turned toward the king. "Can't the farmers fend for themselves for a while?"

"May I?" Lord Brach asked the king respectfully.

Glendar nodded. He was interested and amused by the argument.

"How many men are left at Settsted?" Lord Brach asked.

He had been to the marshes and understood that Lord Ellrich had a valid concern here. Some of the creatures of that area were far more formidable than just snakes and lizards.

"Some two thousand men would remain," the big lord answered.

He had never liked Lord Brach, but he could tell that the boot-licker was going to back him. The man understood the dangers hidden within the swampy lands along Westland's southern border.

"They are spread along the river, in the outposts from Depin all the way up to Locar. The rest are manning the garrison at Settsted that supplies the outposts."

"We need those men, Lord Ellrich," Brach said flatly. "Half of them, anyway." He turned to King Glendar, and spoke with just a hint of sarcasm in his voice. "A thousand soldiers should be able to keep the denizens of the swamp from taking over Westland while we are at war."

Pael snorted contemptuously at Brach. The Lord of the North had over-stepped his bounds.

"Two hundred men should be able to manage that task, Your Highness," Pael snapped. "Not in a hundred years has a viable threat come out of those marshes."

The room was silent. All eyes fell on King Glendar. He seemed to be relishing the moment. It was one of the few times Pael left an important decision open for him to make. The intensity of the wizard's glare wasn't lost on him as he pondered his response. Pael was right, he decided. A few hundred men should be able to fend the snakes away. He didn't want to offend his friend Lord Brach, though. He thought it might be wise not to offend Lord Ellrich either, at least not until after he and Zasha were wed. If it weren't for her, Ellrich's fat jelly head would already be decorating one of the pikes by the gate. Ellrich was a greedy, sneaky man. Pael was probably just mad at being argued with.

"Five hundred should do on the marsh border," Glendar said. "Leave two hundred more men at Settsted to supply the outposts."

He glanced at Pael who looked no less angry at the decision than he had before. The wizard finally nodded to the scribe to make the order and sat back down.

The king went back to his maps, mildly gloating over his own diplomacy. The fact the scribe waited for Pael's nod went over his head, but it wasn't lost to Lord Ellrich, or Lord Brach.

Pael was furious, not at the king's decision, but at himself, for letting the issue slip out of his control. To quell his rage, he shot a verbal blow at Ellrich.

"You'll want to resume command at Settsted when we march, I presume?"

Pael paused to enjoy the look of relief that played across the big Lord's face, before continuing.

"We have no horse strong enough to carry you into battle, nor any armor that will fit you. And obviously, you'll be of no use here at the castle."

Ellrich wasn't shocked by the jibe. The comments about his weight didn't rankle him in the least. He was too busy reveling in the hope he might actually get to keep his head on his shoulders for a little while longer. He truly never expected to make it back to Settsted in one piece.

"If it pleases the king, I'll leave immediately so the troops needed can be given their new orders and set to march for Eastwatch as quickly as possible." He gained his feet quickly for a man of his size, and rested a hand on the scribe's shoulder, hoping to have his own orders in writing before anyone could change their mind.

Pael looked over at Glendar. The boy was oblivious. He was back to his planning with Lord Brach. As if he were the king himself, Pael looked first to the scribe, then to Lord Ellrich.

"It pleases the king." His smile was wickedly powerful. "Make it so."

As soon as the order was written, Pael pressed the King's Seal into the soft wax and excused himself. Inkling, the imp, was scratching at the inside of his skull from up in the tower. A message bird had arrived, or something else was happening. Whatever it was, it was likely far more important than the farce happening here.

Pael made his way through the castle as quickly as he could without drawing attention to his haste. He could've flown to the tower like a bird, or teleported himself there had he not been so spell weary.

In the past few days, he used his magic and a chest full of kingdom gold to influence hundreds of decisions, both here in the castle and afar. His time was coming, he knew, and he was preparing for it well. The bloody events at Summer's Day not only served his ultimate purpose, but also set the eastern kingdoms on each other like a pack of dogs fighting over a scrap of meat.

Already King Broderick, the ruler of Valleya, was treating with his cousin, Queen Rachel of Seaward. Broderick wanted her to grant his army safe passage through her lands so his attack upon Highwander could be carried out that much more swiftly. He wanted to punish Willa the Witch Queen for letting her Blackswords fall on the innocent people at Summer's Day. Queen Rachel was not only willing to grant his men passage, she was contemplating joining him with troops of her own.

Her people wanted Westland blood, though. The tale of the death of Bludgeon, the Seaward Monster, had been embellished and blown out of proportion. It was now a story of intentional murder and riotous bloodshed, all brought upon by crazed Westlanders. According to Pael's spies, Queen Rachel was going to decide where to send her army soon. The fact she was going to send it somewhere seemed inevitable.

The Dakaneese nobles and merchants who had somehow managed to avoid getting involved in the blood-letting at the Festival, were now demanding that their leader, King Ra'Gren, do something about the massive amount of wager winnings that weren't being paid to them. The Wildermont gambling houses who were supposed to back the wagers wouldn't even give people back their initial bets. King Jarrek, the old Redwolf himself, was trying to investigate the whole mess, but he couldn't imagine that gold would be such an issue after so many innocent lives had been lost under the Spire.

All those people leaving the festival, the survivors, had to cross the Everflow River at High Crossing. A troop of King Jarrek's men was there, interrogating everyone crossing the river. Only those foolish, or brave enough to cut through the Evermore Forest could avoid it.

A soothsayer from Kandor Keep, who had no love for anything but coins, had sent word to Pael that several battles had erupted right there on the bridge into Wildermont. The whole of the realm was in chaos, and Pael couldn't be more pleased with himself for orchestrating it all.

As he stepped into his lift, Pael was thinking that it was probably only a bird returning with news from the sorceress Shaella that had Inkling so excited. He wondered if all he had done for her would go unnoticed. So much of what was happening was for her, and she had delivered much more than he had hoped possible. He found he was proud of her, and all that she had accomplished. He hoped she didn't get greedy. It pained him to think it, but he told himself that if she got out of hand, he could eliminate her without pause. He could do that, and would, but only if she forced his hand.

As the lift rose up into the room full of squawking, little caged hawkling chicks, Pael saw that Inkling wasn't there. He closed his eyes and warily probed for the imp.

Inkling was up on the floor above, in the room that held the Spectral Orb. Immediately, the wizard grew excited when he realized it wasn't Inkling who had been trying to get his attention: it was the demon Shokin.

When Pael stepped off the lift this time, all of his exhaustion had been forgotten.

"Take down the lift," he ordered Inkling, who was wiggling excitedly in his natural red devil form.

"Yesss," the imp hissed as he scampered to the lift.

Before the platform even cleared the floor, Pael began cranking down the orb. Before it was in place, a small square of floor off to the side lifted on creaking hinges. Inkling crawled up through the trapdoor, shivering with glee, and let it slam closed behind him.

Pael wasted no time getting his ritual chanting started. If it cost him all the energy he had left in him, he would hear what Shokin had to say. Never in all of the eighty-seven years that he had possessed the Spectral Orb, had it beckoned to him as it did now. The message to come must be one of great importance.

The huge crystal swirled and churned in its depths as Pael's voice grew from a singular intonation into a ghastly chorus. The gathering misty cloud filled the orb, and pulsed a deep crimson.

"THE PACT HAS BEEN BROKEN!" Shokin's voice ground through the air, like a slab of stone being dragged across gravel.

Pael noted the excited tone in the spectral demon's voice. The sound of it sent Inkling skittering under a small wooden table.

"I had hoped as much," Pael said calmly.

It was taxing his essence greatly to hold the powerful spell he used to communicate with the demon, but he didn't show it.

"Already, you're able to reach out of the blackness and summon me."

"When will you open the seal?" Shokin asked harshly. "I have felt the power of the sword, wizard. You need me more than you know."

Inkling rocked to and fro under the table. He was terrified. The air in the room was full of static energy and becoming hot. It was making him frantic.

It took a moment for the implication of what the demon had just said to register in Pael's tired mind.

"How can that be? King Balton's only son is here and the sword is not."

"There is another with Pavreal's blood flowing through his veins," the specter growled. "He has used the sword, and it has honored his lineage."

"Where?" was all Pael could think to ask.

"Where the land of the giants begins, in the forest that feeds off the Life Giver. That is where the sword was used. The seal, wizard! WHEN?"

"There is still the matter of the dragon to contend with," Pael explained weakly.

He didn't like the commanding and demanding tone of the mighty creature before him.

"Soon," he went on. "Are you not strong enough to lend me aid?"

He asked the question to subtly remind Shokin of his helpless state, and of his need of help, if he ever wished to escape the Nethers.

For a few heartbeats the room was deathly silent. Pael could feel the weight of the magic pushing in on him, as if he were at the bottom of the sea.

Suddenly, a jagged bolt of searing, yellow lightning shot forth from the crystal. It hit Inkling and the imp was engulfed by it. It held the trembling imp in its glowing grasp. The table he had been under was now nothing more than so much ash and smoke. The humming bolt slowly undulated through the air, like some wild electric snake.

The imp's black eyes opened wide and filled with terror. His scaly skin bubbled, hissed, and swelled, as his shape shifted this way and that. The fist of magical energy that gripped him slung him against the wall of the tower, smashing a hole the size of a large wagon cart that revealed the dim evening. From below, shouts of alarm and pain rang out as blocks of bricks and broken stone rained down on the people.

Pael shuddered and collapsed. It was no longer his power holding the spell, it was the demon's power. It was all the wizard could do to keep his eyes open to see what was happening to his familiar.

It was no quick process. The imp stretched, swelled, and screamed horribly into the night as the demon reshaped him. His body grew long and feline, like a giant warhorse-sized panther whose tail was barbed and as long as a whip. The imp's wings elongated and spread wide, like those of a wyvern, or a great dactyl. His claws grew long and razor sharp, and every inch of his body became as dark as the deepest night. Teeth, eyes, claws, fur, and scales were all nearly indistinguishable for the quality of their blackness.

The brilliant kinetic display ended abruptly, leaving the menacing-looking result flapping its huge wings in a hover, just outside the gaping hole in Pael's tower.

"Use this gift wisely, Pael, for this is your familiar now," the fading, yet still powerful voice of the spectral demon commanded. "Open the seal for me, and do it soon!"

With that the voice, and the ozonic power that it radiated, disappeared with a sharp pop.

Pael felt, as much as heard, the sound of the demon's departure, and he was more than relieved by it.

Apparently, he had underestimated the spectral demon's power. This alarmed him. The demon did need him though, that was obvious. He would just have to make sure that when he opened the doorway to the Nethers, he had a way to bind Shokin to his service. That was a dilemma for another day though. He needed rest.

Almost as an afterthought, he turned toward the hellcat waiting outside his tower. He could still feel the familial bond with the creature, but he knew that it was no longer Inkling.

"Kill the one that wields Pavreal's blade, and bring the sword to me!" Pael rasped the order, then closed his eyes and crumpled to the floor.

Chapter Twenty-One

As they traveled deeper into the foothills of the Giant Mountains, Hyden found himself thinking about the tale the elf Vaegon had told him, or more precisely, of the things that he hadn't been told in the story.

He wondered what had happened to the other wolf pup, the one that disappeared into the blizzard. Had it starved? Maybe it grew up to be strong and fierce, like the wolf that attached itself to Pratchert.

He glanced up into the clear blue sky and saw Talon circling protectively above them, and then he went back to his thoughts. Dog Man! What a nickname: the Great Wizard, Dog Man? What a title. He laughed at the thought of some colorfully dressed herald calling that out at some royal ceremony. That provoked another series of thoughts and ideas, which only served to create more questions in his curious mind.

"Lord Gregory, who announces people at a kingdom...uh?" he stammered, and stuttered, searching for the word he was after. "A...uh...Council meeting?"

"We call it the Royal Court," Lord Gregory answered.

The Western Lion had been feeling better with each passing day. He had even climbed off his horse and walked for half of a day, to help work the poison that remained in him, out of his muscles and joints.

They had been going downhill that morning. He tried walking uphill in the afternoon, but he wasn't quite ready for that yet. The exertion had him back in the saddle, feeling weak and exhausted.

"The Court Announcer at my stronghold in Lake Bottom is also the local Sail Master," Lord Gregory told him. Thoughts of his home put a smile on his face. "He's a tiny little man with a big, deep voice. The king's Royal Court Announcer at Lakeside Castle is as big as a whale and he stays in his cups. No one in the whole Kingdom of Westland can figure out how he gets all the names and titles right, even the strange foreign ones, especially while he is so stupendously drunk."

"What's a whale?" Hyden asked.

"It's a giant sea fish, as big as that hill over there, and it breathes air through a hole in the top of its head," the nobleman answered.

"Just because I'm not a kingdom born man," Hyden said with a hint of anger in his voice, "don't think you could have me believe just anything."

Vaegon was at the top of the steep hill they were climbing, curiously scanning the evening horizon behind them. His glittery hair sparkled, as it blew about his shoulders in the cold mountain breeze. Hyden thought that even from where they were, far below the elf, he could see Vaegon's strange, yellow eyes. It made him shiver, and he wondered if such fantastical things as whales really existed.

He liked Vaegon well enough, but no matter how many times he looked at him, he would never become comfortable with the fact that he wasn't human.

"It's no jest, Hyden Hawk. There are also smaller fish that are still five times bigger than a man, that have rows of teeth the size of dagger blades. They call them sharks, and believe it or not, they sometimes eat the whales one big bite at a time."

"If that is true, then the sea is a place I'd like to see someday." Hyden's attention trailed away.

He noticed that Vaegon had been staring at the same place for quite some time now. He sensed that something alarmed the elf. He quickened his pace, forcing Lord Gregory to spur his horse to keep up with him.

Vaegon could see the question form on Hyden's lips as he gained the top of the rise.

"Someone, or something, is behind us," he said.

"Where?" Lord Gregory asked sharply, as he turned his horse.

"There," Vaegon pointed to an area a few hilltops back. "It's in the valley now, out of view. I just caught a glimpse of movement before it went down out of sight. A dark horse maybe, or some other large creature."

Hyden was peering from beneath his hand trying to see what they were talking about.

"About a day back you think?" he asked, when he saw what set of hills were in question.

"No more than that, if it's men with horses," Vaegon said, with growing concern in his voice. "Far less though if it's a predator."

"We'll have to wait for it in the next valley then," Hyden said with some disappointment and a sigh. "My village is close. I dare not lead anything or anyone else into it. Already, I am going to feel the full wrath of the Elders for bringing you two there."

"What if it is a predatory beast, as the elf suggested?" asked Lord Gregory.

Before Hyden could answer, Talon came out of the sky and fluttered down to his shoulder gracelessly.

Though he wasn't very big yet, Talon's body had taken the true hawkling form. He was still too small to lift a field mouse into the air, but not too small to swoop down and kill one, a feat which he had proven the day before. When he was fully grown, he would be able to snatch a fat rabbit off the ground and fly away with it in his claws. His wings would be as wide as a man's outstretched arms. At the moment though, he wasn't much bigger than a crow. For all his smallness, the bird still found a way to posture itself proudly on Hyden's shoulder.

"Go see what it is that's following us, and then come back and tell me," Hyden said jokingly to the bird.

To everyone's surprise, save for Vaegon's, Talon leapt back into flight, and started toward the valley where the elf had spotted the pursuit.

Hyden was confounded tenfold, when a weird, yet familiar, sensation came over him. It was just like the dreams he had been having as of late, yet he was awake. The sensation of seeing Lord Gregory and Vaegon in front of him, while seeing through Talon's eyes, was overwhelming. It was too much for his mind to handle, and he was forced to close his eyes. When he did, it was as if he were in Talon's body, flying over the foothills, with the cold mountain air streaming through his feathers.

Only the tops of the western facing hills were in the sunlight. The rest of the world was drowned in shadow, and the valley bottoms were even darker than the rest. He found them though: two men with four horses, two of which looked to be carrying a log. The group was moving slowly through the shadows, snaking their way down through a scatter of pine and scrub brush. They didn't appear to be in a hurry. They were obviously not hunting Lord Gregory, but their direction of travel would lead them dangerously close to Hyden's village.

Talon swooped in closer, and landed on the gnarled branch of an ancient oak. It was tall, and it towered over the whole of the valley bottom. Near its base, a stream trickled and gurgled through the rocky area, where spring's thaw had washed away the plants, and most of the soil. Even though there was very little light, the hawkling's sharp eyes could pick out the details.

"What are you seeing?" Vaegon asked excitedly. The idea that the human boy was really seeing through the eyes of the hawkling was thrilling, yet it made the elf feel more than a little jealous of Hyden.

Vaegon's question seemed to shake Hyden's concentration free of the vision, but only for an instant. With closed eyes, and from miles away, Hyden refocused on the approaching horses, and spoke softly.

"Two men, four horses— Hold on."

He squatted down, and put his elbows on his knees, as if perched. He heard Lord Gregory whispering softly to Vaegon. The western lord seemed as astonished by this as he was. The elf seemed to have expected it.

The tale of Pratchert came to Hyden's mind then. Was he destined to be like Dahg Mahn? It was an incredible thought, one that would seem absurd, were he not watching these travelers come toward him through the eyes of a bird. It was as if he himself were sitting in the tree that Talon was now perched in. "Hawk Man." He tried it on the tip of his tongue, and then dismissed it. He would have to try to remember to ask Vaegon what the word for hawkling was in the old tongue. He would also have to... Wait, what was that? Voices? He gasped loudly. Not only could he see these unsuspecting travelers, he could hear them as well. They were talking.

"What is it?" Lord Gregory asked.

"Shhh!" Hyden hissed.

Being a high Lord of the most powerful kingdom in the realm, Lord Gregory wasn't used to being hushed. It offended him momentarily, but the idea that he was feeling well enough to get offended was enough to keep him from reacting rashly. Most likely, he would've died had it not been for Hyden and the elf. He owed them all the respect he could give. If he had to take being shushed by the village boy, then he would take it like a man.

Hyden was amazed, thrilled beyond words. He could hear the crickets in the distance; the scuttle of a varmint; the song of the jay bird telling its mate about the berry bush by the stream. He even registered the disgusted huff of a fox coming from the ridge behind him, after it had missed a meal that it had been hunting. The steady crunch and shuffle of the approaching horses, and the jingle of tack, then a voice, came to his ears from closer by. He almost shushed again, but he realized that it was one of the travelers speaking, not the Lion Lord.

"—you're not lost?"

"Nay, Mik," a deeper voice responded. "The village is not far now, I think. I traded there with an old man named Hardin, or Halden, maybe. I never forget a place where I made a profit."

"You're lost," the first voice said flatly.

Hyden could see them clearly now that they were out of the trees and the gloom. The younger one, the one that was following the big tattoo-covered Seawardsman, was the one speaking now.

"You keep telling me you're not lost, but you're just trying to convince yourself of it."

"Aye, Mik!" the Seawardsman laughed. "Maybe so, maybe so. Either way, I know we're getting close."

Hyden realized he recognized the bigger man. He had once wandered into the Skyler Clan's village accidentally. Hyden had only been a boy then, but he would never forget the big, tattooed trapper. He hadn't traveled out of his village at that point in his life, and the sight of those tattoos, the slick bald head, and the bulging muscles, was etched into his mind forever. Hyden remembered that the man had saved himself by naming several of the giant folk that he had bartered with. Had he not done so, the Elders would have killed him. It had been one of the most exciting things that had happened in Hyden's youth. He remembered the man telling several stories about the land of Seaward, where ships lined the shores, and a queen ruled, instead of a king. He tried, but couldn't seem to remember the man's name.

Talon leapt into the darkening sky then, and Hyden's vision went abruptly black. When he opened his eyes, he was glad he was squatted down. The world at hand hit him like a forge hammer. He rolled onto his back and covered his face with a loud grunt. The wealth of emotion that churned through him was unbelievable. He had heard the animals, what they were doing, what they were calling out, and what they were feeling. He wasn't sure what you would call it. He wasn't sure there were words to describe the sensation. He had been right there among them, seeing, hearing, and even smelling, what was around Talon. He had watched them like a hawk! He burst into a joyous peal of laughter at the insanity of it all.

"Well it doesn't look like trouble is coming," Lord Gregory observed.

Seeing Hyden's manic joy caused him to smile, despite himself. He looked at Vaegon, searching for some sort of explanation.

The elf was scowling at first, but his expression soon softened, and then broke. Hyden's joy was contagious, and Vaegon eventually smiled down at him. His jealousy faded into the hills with the setting sun. Who was he to feel wronged by the decision of the gods to gift Hyden so wonderfully?

When Hyden finally regained his composure, he told them all of what he saw and heard. They decided to make camp right there, on the lee side of the hill, and wait for the travelers to catch up with them.

Lord Gregory thanked the heavens that Mikahl was alive and well. When Hyden had told him that the Seawardsman had called the other man "Mik" the Lion Lord had cried.

Hyden shared in detail, particularly with Vaegon, the wonders of the experience. The amount of innocent fervor that Hyden displayed, while expressing himself, made the elf feel more than a little ashamed for having let his selfish emotions get hold of him. Hyden, Vaegon found, was as good and pure-hearted as any man could be, which was most likely exactly why the gods had chosen to bless him so. With this realization, nearly all of Vaegon's hidden contempt evaporated like water on a hot stone. He had to admit that he was still a bit jealous, but it wasn't the dark sort of envy that brings about hatred. It was more of a healthy, competitive sort of feeling. He grinned ear to ear, and slapped Hyden on the back.

"Well, at least we now know how a mere human archer could come so close to beating an elf," Vaegon jested. "With the eyes of a hawkling to aim with, how could you miss?"

Hyden couldn't seem to find a response to that.

Loudin decided that he and Mik would camp in the valley by the tiny stream that trickled through it. They built a fire across the flow from an old oak tree and ate the last of Mikahl's cheese. Loudin warmed a bit of the small, feral pig he had killed the day before on a stone by the blaze, and then split the meat with his companion. The meal and the cold stream water filled their stomachs to bursting. Only moments after they stretched themselves out by the fire, they were asleep.

Mikahl's sleep was so thick and heavy for the few days that followed his killing of Duke Fairchild that Loudin had to boot him awake in the mornings. That all changed the previous night. Mikahl's sleep had been fitful, fevered, and full of dark dreams of even darker creatures.

This night, the dreams were even worse, because the creatures seemed to recognize him. One of them in particular was after him, a black hulk of muscle and claw, driven by nothing less than pure hatred and evil intent. In his dream, it was searching for him so that it could destroy him. It wanted something from him, but Mikahl had no idea what it could be. He was only a squire, he tried to tell the dream creatures as they chased him through his dark, empty dreamscape. The highest ranked squire in the realm, but a squire nonetheless.

"You're a squire no more! The king is dead," they cackled and howled at him. "Everyone you know and love is out to get you now!"

Occasionally, the dream creatures would retreat, as something monstrous came near: something so much darker and more sinister than the rest of them, something that seemed to leech the life force from everything around it. This hulking, evil monstrosity radiated hatred and foulness, like a desert radiates heat. Evil shimmered from it in wavy sheets of blackness. When it would move off, the others came right back at him, snapping, growling, and cackling with their lustful desire to tear his flesh from his bones. There was always the one beast though, the one that had singled him out to hunt in the darkened dreamscape. That one had form and substance to it now, unrecognizable still, save for the glossy reflection of menace in its black eyes. It stood before him snarling and ready to pounce. Then it did.

Mikahl woke with a start. Thunder boomed, and then grumbled from not so far away. A peal of lightning streaked across the sky, silhouetting the jagged peaks of the mountains that loomed over them to the north. The air was frigid, and steam billowed from Mikahl's lungs, as he fought to get his breath. The waning moon was still in the sky, its pale blue glow highlighting the tops of the clouds that were rolling over the mountaintops toward them. He shivered. The clouds were thick, black, and churning violently. It took only moments before they completely blotted out the moonlight. Suddenly, the whole world was engulfed in blackness, just as in his dream.

Mikahl's hair suddenly stood on end. A massive crackle of thunder exploded, and a jagged streak of white lightning filled his world.

It struck no more than a dozen paces away from the camp. The concussion from the blast was so great that it literally took away Mikahl's breath. Loudin came up with a raspy yelp. One of the horses screamed in fright. The others pulled at their tethers, trying to get away. Across the little stream, the old gnarled oak tree showered the night with orange sparks, as it slowly split in two. Already, its lesser limbs and branches were consumed in dancing flames.

Mikahl wasn't sure why he did it, but the urge to do so was irresistible. He got up, hurried over to Windfoot's saddle, and untied the straps that held Ironspike to it.

Duke Fairchild's blade lay alongside his bedroll, but it was completely forgotten. He sat back down with the king's blade in his lap, ready to draw it from its scabbard at a moment's notice.

While he and Loudin huddled silently, waiting for the storm to subside, Mikahl watched the slow, flaming death of the once mighty oak tree, and found that he was thankful beyond words for its dying light.

Chapter Twenty-Two

When dawn broke, Lord Gregory mounted his horse and started back toward Mikahl. He was feeling as well as he had since before the Brawl, despite the wet and gloomy weather.

If Loudin, or Mikahl, had seen him coming, then most likely they would have set a trap or an ambush for him, but they didn't catch sight of him until he topped the ridge opposite the one they were on. They spotted the lone rider and knew without a doubt they had been seen. There was no need for trickery after that, only caution.

It was nearly midday then, and the rain that had been drizzling for hours was starting to subside. Out over the Leif Greyn Valley to the south, the clouds were letting go of their burden fully. A steel gray wall of natural fury could be seen inching its way over the sacred grounds. The lightning storm had been a brilliant display, and the continuous thunder made sleep all but impossible. The day was cold, damp, and somewhat depressing. It was as if the storm left a dismal stain, both in the sky, and in the tired minds of those who had witnessed its power.

"Should we keep going?" Mikahl asked from Windfoot's saddle.

Loudin was sitting on his mount beside him. Both watched as the lone rider approached, with seemingly excited haste. Loudin was annoyed at being so exposed. What if it had been a dozen armed kingdom men across the way instead of only one? What if it was an angry band of rock trolls? What if? What if? What if? Be happy, he finally told himself. It's just a single man. At least it's not worse.

"He's about to fall out of his saddle, for all that waving and hollering," Loudin observed. "Could be a trap. There could be a handful of men waiting on the other side of that rise." He didn't sound convincing, not even to himself. Still the possibility was there.

Since Mikahl had killed the Westland nobleman, since that eerie magical blue glow had filled the forest around them, Loudin let Mikahl have a say in things. He would put the facts and possibilities out there, and Mikahl would ask questions, and give his opinion on the situation. Loudin knew that there was something special about the boy. He also knew that the boy had no idea that he was special. Loudin was trying to help the lad see the complexity of the situation. Mikahl, most of the time, seemed oblivious.

"Nah, nah," Mikahl finally said, more to himself than to his companion. He turned to Loudin. "Let's go on down and see what he's about. Maybe he isn't lost."

"Bah!" Loudin cursed through his tired grin. "I'm not lost, blast you!"

Lord Gregory, after seeing they were going to continue coming his way, sat back into his saddle, and hurried his horse down the slope. He wasn't satisfied to wait for them at the bottom of the valley. Their pace, hindered by the big, long object that their pack horses were carrying, was so slow that he couldn't stand the wait. He met them a quarter of the way up the slope they were descending, in a semi open area, which was spattered with young pine trees, old oaks, elms and sycamores.

"Mikahl!" The Lion Lord shouted, in a voice that was thick with emotion. "Oh, Mikahl!"

The sound of Lord Gregory's voice was startling. He was the last person Mikahl would've expected to come across out here. He shook his head, and rubbed at his eyes, wondering if he was hearing and seeing things.

Loudin recognized the embroidered patch on the king's-man's saddle and drew his dagger with a muffled curse. Loudin's bladed pike, his favorite weapon, had been shoved through the center of the lizard-skin roll to keep it from sagging in the middle.

Mikahl's hand went to the hilt of Duke Fairchild's sword at his hip, while his other hand felt behind him to make sure that Ironspike was still secure in its place on Windfoot's saddle. Only when he was sure that it was safe, did he let his full attention fall on the familiar man reining up his horse before them.

It took half a minute for Mikahl to register that the pale, sickly man really was Lord Gregory, but when he did, the dam of emotion he was holding back burst forth in a teary flood.

Both Westlanders dismounted and embraced each other fiercely. They held on for a good long moment, before Lord Gregory moved Mikahl back to arm's length. The Lion Lord of Lake Bottom eyed him proudly.

A small hawkling alighted on a tree limb nearby, drawing Loudin's attention away from the reunion. The young bird seemed unafraid of them, and that was a curious thing to the seasoned hunter.

"Are you well?" Gregory asked.

"I should ask you the same question, m'lord," Mikahl returned.

The man before him was but a shadow of the mighty warrior he remembered. It seemed strange to Mikahl that the Lord of Lake Bottom would treat him so cordially. It seemed like a lifetime ago, but it had only been a few weeks since they had crossed paths outside King Balton's chamber.

"No more m'lords from you, Mikahl," Lord Gregory said firmly. "Never again. This isn't the place to explain, but I promise I will." As if he had just remembered something hugely important, Lord Gregory looked at Mikahl's hip. Alarmed, he asked, "Where is it?"

"It's safe," Mikahl answered, taking a step reflexively.

There was no doubt what the it was he was referring to. King Balton hadn't said anything about giving Ironspike to Lord Gregory, and as much as Mikahl loved and respected the man before him, he wouldn't let him have the sword.

"I don't want it," Lord Gregory nodded his understanding. "The sword is your charge. Now that we're both free of Glendar and his dark hearted wizard, it's you that I must keep safe. King Balton spoke to me just before he spoke to you. Do you remember?"

Mikahl relaxed a bit. He remembered.

"Aye, m'lord," he acknowledged.

"I should be saying that to you," the Lion Lord ruffled Mikahl's hair like he had, after sword drills and grappling practice, a thousand times before.

A memory from one of the summers when Mikahl squired for the Lion Lord at Lake Bottom caused him to smile. Looking back, Mikahl realized that Lord Gregory personally groomed him to be the King's Squire.

"Who is your companion?" Lord Gregory asked.

"I am Loudin Drake," Loudin said. "And I know who you are, Lord Lion. I saw you take down the Valleyan Stallion a few years back. I never forget someone who makes me a profit."

"If I'd only done as well this year…" Lord Gregory let his voice trail off.

He turned his horse tactfully, avoiding further explanation. It was obvious that these two men hadn't attended, nor heard about, the massacre at Summer's Day. If they had, he didn't think a Seawardsman would be interacting so peacefully with a Westlander.

"I have some interesting friends waiting up ahead; warm food and a hot fire as well." Lord Gregory let out a strange uneasy laugh. "One of them is among us now. Would you like to meet him?"

Mikahl and Loudin both looked around the area curiously. There was not even the hint of another person about.

"Yes, we would," Loudin answered for the both of them.

Lord Gregory pointed toward the young hawkling that was perched in the nearby tree.

"That's Talon. A sort of friend of a friend, I should say."

In response to his introduction Talon tried to shriek out a fierce cry. It came out sounding more like an angry caw. He leapt from the tree, and fluttered gracelessly down onto Lord Gregory's head.

Mikahl burst out laughing at this. Loudin joined in the mirth, but his mind was wondering about the nature of the Lion Lord's friends. In his experience, the type of men, if you could call them men, who kept the close company of animals, were the sort of men one should avoid. Friends aside, it was quite funny seeing the mighty Western Lord with a bird perched on his head.

"I have much to tell you both," Lord Gregory said, after brushing Talon back into flight. "Grave news from the Festival, but I would rather you heard the tale from my companions, for they can tell it firsthand. I would like to hear the story, though, of how you came to be wearing the Coldfrost Butcher's sword, Mikahl."

He patted the boy on his back and climbed back into his saddle with a groan.

"The telling of it will kill the time between here and there, I hope."

Mikahl told Lord Gregory the whole story while they rode. From his meeting with King Balton at his deathbed, all the way up until the present. He told of the two bandits he had been forced to kill after fleeing the castle, the terrifying ordeal with the barkskin lizard, and the grisly battle with Duke Fairchild and his henchmen. The only part left out was how Ironspike lit up with its wild magical glow when he used it. He glared at Loudin when he was done to let the hunter know that part of the tale was to be kept between the two of them.

They were well met just after dark, when they rode into the camp. The smell of rabbit stew cooking was pleasant, and the fire was blazing bright and warm. They made introductions and small talk while they ate.

Mikahl was clearly awed, and mildly disturbed by Vaegon's feral yellow eyes. Hyden's strange friendship with Talon didn't seem to sit too well with him either.

In turn, Hyden was shocked by the enormity of the bark lizard skin. He had seen plenty of bark lizards in the Evermore Forest on his clan's journeys to and from the Harvest Lodge, but nothing remotely close to the size of the one Loudin and Mikahl had killed. He readily agreed that Borg, or any other of the mountain giants who roamed the range, would pay handsomely for such a prize.

During all of this, Loudin sensed their unease at his presence, and after the meal was done, he asked about it. It was then that Vaegon calmly, and with the political neutrality that only a non-human could muster, started the tale of the massacre at Summer's Day.

Both Hyden and Lord Gregory added bits and pieces as it was told. They also watched Loudin closely, gauging his reaction to it all. The hunter seemed saddened, yet impartial about the events, and when Vaegon had finished, Loudin told them of his long ago departure from the ways of the kingdoms of man in general. He was a hunter and trader now, a free man who had paid his dues, both on land, and at sea. He held no ill will toward Lord Gregory for killing the Seaward Monster during the Brawl. Nor did he seem to harbor any opinion about Willa the Witch Queen using her arrows to turn the volatile situation into an outright battle. It wasn't his business. He wasn't too keen on the idea of war, though. War wasn't good for the hunting trade, save for the selling of meat to the troops.

Mikahl, having never been out of Westland until now, seemed oblivious to the politics and the ramifications of what he was hearing. He was more interested in the hawkling and the elf.

Lord Gregory seemed irritated by this, and several times throughout, had over-expressed his opinion to him. Mikahl wanted only to find the giant named Borg, and deliver King Balton's messages and the sword, as he had been instructed to do. He was wanted in the west now, most likely dead or alive, and for a healthy reward. He didn't feel that he could afford to concern himself with wars and such. He would be a hunter, like Loudin, or maybe he could move to Valleya and raise horses, or maybe sign on to a ship and sail to the distant land of Harthgar. The possibilities were endless. He decided that he would worry about all of that when he was finished with his duty to King Balton. It was getting late and, at the moment, all he wanted to do was get a good night's sleep.

He didn't get his wish. The strange, dark beast haunted his dreams again. It was hunting him, and he could feel it drawing near. He could feel its hot, fetid breath on his skin, and its slimy drool as it salivated for a taste of his flesh. He woke in the night and took Ironspike from Windfoot's saddle, and then lay back down with the sword in his arms. Only then did the monsters leave his mind so that sleep, deep and dreamless, could take him.

The next evening, Hyden Hawk called the group to a halt. They were dangerously close to his clan's village, and he didn't want to bring them all into it with him. He and Loudin would go and ask the Elders' permission to bring the kingdom folk and the elf.

Vaegon agreed to stay and make sure that the two Westlanders didn't try to follow. Hyden only took Loudin because the old hunter had been there before. The Elders would probably be angry with the big tattoo-covered man for attempting to lead Mikahl to the village, but not so angry as to not let him purchase the mountain gear and hides he was seeking. After the way the festival had ended, Hyden was sure that his people hadn't rounded up all of the seed, tools and supplies that they wanted to. Loudin's coin would be needed later when Uncle Condlin and Hyden's father, Harrap, made their annual end of summer journey down into Wildermont to stock up on things for the long mountain winter. Once upon a time, getting to make that journey with his father and uncle was all Hyden could think about. Now, the idea of it seemed insignificant.

Loudin forced himself to leave the lizard skin behind, and go with Hyden. It was hard, but after Mikahl assured him that he would protect it with his life, the hunter relented.

In the darkness, the Skyler Clan village was nearly invisible to the naked eye, and had Loudin not been there before, he would've missed it entirely. He found he was glad that they happened upon Hyden and his group. Without them, he might never have found the place, and would've had to listen to Mikahl's chastising forever.

Though the clansfolk were all inside their dwellings, enjoying the warmth of their hearth fires, not a speck of light could be seen from outside. Their homes and common areas had been carved into the sides of the valley ages ago by the giants. Huge scallops of earth were scooped deeply out of the rock, and then squared rooms were constructed out of stone slabs. The rubble and scree was piled back over, covering them completely. The same had been done with the long, winding entry tunnels that led from the outside world into the rooms. The natural shape of the valley was restored over the halls and dwellings, and after a few seasons of growth, it appeared, to the unknowing eye, as plain and empty as any other valley in the area. Well placed wooden doors, which the clansmen hung to keep out the weather, sat a dozen or more feet inside the entry shafts. The only way anyone unaware of their location would ever see one of them, was to wander into one of the dark, overgrown cave-like holes that pocked the sides of the valley. Some of the underground rooms were so vast, the clansfolk housed herds of rams and goats in them during the harsh winter months. At night, only the smell of cooking, and the occasional noise that escaped up through the many hidden ventilation shafts, would give them away. It was different during the day. In the light of the sun, the valley crawled with life. A life kept joyous and peaceful by keeping the kingdom folk and the elves out of it.

Hyden knew someone would be watching them approach from one of the many hidden nooks and precipices along the ridges. They would signal his location with tiny mirror flashes that seemed to be no more than flighty fire bugs in night. It came as no surprise to Hyden when a sudden light pierced the darkness ahead of them. It was Harrap, Hyden's father, and he was standing in the entry tunnel that led to the Elders' council chamber. By the way the shadows moved about in the swath of steady blue light that spilled across the valley floor, he could tell that his father wasn't alone. The Elders were waiting for him.

Harrap made a piercing whistle as they came upon him. His look was quizzical, as he recognized Loudin. He looked at his son, and a dozen questions swam across his eyes. Talon came flapping down out of the sky and landed on Hyden's shoulder. That alone seemed to answer many of them, but it was obvious that his father wanted to know what had happened to the elf and the Westland kingsman.

"Take our guest," the word guest was stressed, "to the gathering room, and feed him," Harrap commanded to the darkness.

Out of the gloom, Hyden's slightly older cousins, Tylen and Sharoo, stepped to each side of Loudin.

"Make a comfortable place for him to sleep."

Harrap turned and faced the hunter then.

"Well met, Loudin Drake. The business that we have with my son will take some time to finish. I apologize for the rudeness."

Before Loudin could reply, Harrap gestured for Hyden to enter the tunnel he'd been blocking, and a moment later, closed the door behind them.

The medium-sized room seemed overcrowded to Hyden. In its center, the huge skull of a dragon sat. The top of its brain cavity had been long removed, and inside the brain pan, a torrent of magical blue flame raged wildly.

All of the Elders were there, sitting anxiously around the frightening-looking horned skull. Hyden could tell that something was amiss. Their faces all looked grim as they reflected the eerie blue light.

Talon shivered on Hyden's shoulder. Hyden could sense the bird's fear, or maybe he could sense the bird sensing his own fear. He wasn't sure. The one thing that was certain, was that he and Talon both were afraid.

As Mikahl slept, less than a mile beyond the rim of the valley of the Skyler Clan, the creature from the blackness stopped hunting his dreams. The evil things still imprisoned in the Nethers howled their jealousy as the beast left them behind. It was coming now, and getting closer. It had broken free of the horrific nothingness that had held it before. The hulking evil that had let it loose laughed at his accomplishment. Something was coming for Mikahl in this world now, not in the dream world. It knew where he was, and it was coming quickly.

When Mikahl woke, he seemed to know these things. When he took Ironspike from Windfoot's saddle this night, he found that it was of little comfort. He knew that his nightmare had somehow come to life, and that one of the creatures from his dreams would be coming for him soon. He had to let the others know. It was only right to let them know the risks they faced by helping him go deeper into the Giant Mountains. He would understand if they chose not to accompany him. It was their right. He wasn't really sure why any of them seemed to want to help in the first place. Alone or together, either way, he would have to stand and face the beast that was coming for him. What other choice did he have? For a long time, he watched the dying flames of the campfire, and pondered that very question, but no answer came to him.

Chapter Twenty-Three

In the days that passed since they crossed the Everflow River into Wildermont, Gerard Skyler had seen a hundred wonders, each more amazing to him than the last. As he lazed in the morning sun, on the foredeck of the riverboat Shaella had chartered, he thought about the past few days and the sights he had seen.

They had been lucky at High Crossing. The Redwolf soldiers only wanted to talk with them, to question them about the Summer's Day Festival. A lone rider had come across the bridge before them and told the soldiers that some sort of bloody skirmish had broken out under the Spire. Shaella's party had apparently left before it had started, so they had nothing to offer the bridge guard. What Gerard couldn't figure out was how the rider had passed them on their way south. Shaella reminded him that they followed the river, not the wagon road, and that he'd slept all of a day recuperating from the saddle soreness of that first night's ride. After being reminded of that deep, dreamless sleep that Shaella's potion brought on, he had to concede that a dozen riders could have passed them without his knowledge.

As Shaella promised, that first night in the northern outskirts of Castlemont City, they took a room at an inn. She had made love to him there, and it was breathtaking.

The following day they rode toward Castlemont proper. It was an entire day of traveling, down a crowded, building-lined road, just to get to the heart of the city that had been built in the shadow of King Jarrek's palace. The buildings near the inn they stayed in, had been single- and double-story affairs of wood and crude stonework. They were widely spaced, with large, fenced pens full of goats, chickens, and sometimes squealing children. Most had wooden slat roofs and dingy exteriors. Some were decorated with signs advertising their particular type of business: taverns, leather works, bakeries, and so on.

As the day's journey wore on, the size of the buildings grew, while the spaces between them shrunk away to little more than alleyways. The crude construction gave way to more solid and symmetrical brick and mortar block work. The roofs were steeper, and some were shingled with colorful baked tiles. A picket fence surrounded a home here or there. The air was full of the smell of hot steel, and the sound of smiths' hammers clanging away could be heard from behind many a door.

The road wound its way through the foothills of the Wilder Mountains. The small mountain range rose up out of the earth on the eastern bank of the Leif Greyn River. While the roadside along the riverbank was packed with building after building, the lush, green hillsides were dotted with larger stone structures. Long dry-stone walls snaked over the dips and rises of the rolling landscape, penning large herds of cattle or sheep. Some of the larger buildings were crenellated, and had squat, round towers built up alongside of them. "Strongholds," Shaella called them.

Gerard was amazed by all of this. Berda's stories told of cities and towns, but Gerard had only been able to imagine a larger version of his village, with huts and shacks, instead of underground burrows. The idea of three- and four-level structures, built of carefully fitted together pieces of rock, was astounding.

About midday, when they came upon the first real towered stronghold, Gerard thought he was seeing a castle. He hadn't seen the formidable stronghold at High Crossing because they crossed the bridge at night. If he had, then the one they looked at that afternoon might not have seemed so massive.

From there, the streets grew more crowded, with both people and structures. It became hard to see the surrounding lay of the land. The smell of refuse, and the press of the populace, was overwhelming. That evening, when they came to the center of Castlemont and stood in the city's wide open square, Shaella pointed up and to the east, and showed Gerard what a real castle looked like.

Wildermont was easily the richest kingdom in the east. The small mountain range was full of iron and copper deposits. Nearly all raw iron ore, and the majority of worked metal products in the entire realm, came from here. Brackets, axles, fittings for wagon building; banded hinges, frames and latches for construction; swords, steel spear and arrow tips, and armor all came from Wildermont. It was no wonder the ancient kings had built into the side of the mountains a monstrous palace-like structure that dwarfed any other kingdom seat in the realm.

Half the mountain was bricked, blocked, tiled, and arched, all in the same pale gray stone. Half a hundred towers reached into the heavens, while in their shadows, twice as many more tried to do the same. A dozen wide crenellated walls, with wagons, and groups of people scurrying along the tops of them, snaked across the mountainside. Here and there, huge wooden gates were set in the sides of them. The tiny colorful specks of a thousand different banners flickered in the breeze. All of this seemed to glow dully in the evening as the sun slowly set.

As darkness slipped over the world, Gerard's amazement grew a hundredfold. Thousands of window-arches and doorways began to glow golden, as torches and lamps were lit all over the palace. Large barrel fires blazed forth from along the tops of the walls and bridges, making them all look like elevated roads that floated in the air. It was a sight to behold.

They had taken an inn again that night, but Shaella hadn't come to him. She told him she had other business. He didn't complain. He drank a mug of dark ale, in the common room with Greyber while a bard sang a ballad about a pirate who had his entire ship snatched from the sea by an angry blue dragon. The pirate's lover was so stricken by the loss that she rowed a skiff out to sea and was never seen again.

Later, Gerard went back to his room and fell fast asleep. His dreams were full of the wonders that the rest of the world might hold for him to see. Only a small portion of his dreams concentrated on the fact that, soon, he was going to be very close to a dragon himself.

The next morning, they rode further south. The familiar Leif Greyn River found the road again and flowed along beside it. Here, the river was so wide that he could barely make out the opposite shore line. Westland was over there. The roadway was wider here, too. Carts and horse-drawn wagons came and went, three abreast. They passed, but didn't cross, the incredibly huge bridge that led over into the Westland City of Locar.

"Locar Crossing," Shaella called it. She paused and studied the impossible span for quite some time.

The bridge was colossal: four wagon lanes and a pedestrian lane. Gerard watched as a barge slipped under one of the seven arches that the viaduct made on its way across the river. The center arch was bigger than the others. At its top, the bridge seemed to be impossibly thin, yet it held fast as three fully loaded wagons, five horses, and a large huddle of squealing pigs went across it at the same time.

While Shaella studied something farther across the bridge, Gerard studied the diverse types of fashion he saw people wearing. Here was a pair of men in red robes, and over there, was a peasant in rags. A lady, in a fine yellow dress on horseback, being led by a fully armored knight, had the crowds parting before them, as if they had the plague. A man in baggy silk pants the color of emeralds hurried past, a long, shining cape wavering after him. The variances were endless. But almost everywhere he looked, there was at least one uniformed man sporting a red wolf's-head patch.

After finally leaving the crowds of Castlemont behind them, they came to yet another river bridge. This one was called Low Crossing. It spanned a small river that came out of the Wilder Mountains, just before it joined the main flow of the Leif Greyn. The town there, also called Low Crossing, was full of warehouses, and seedy-looking men who wore the garb of river men.

They didn't cross this bridge. While Shaella secured them a room for the night, Cole and Flick spoke with some workmen near a dock, where several barges full of wooden crates were moored. Gerard saw Cole pass a pouch to one of them, but didn't concern himself with the matter. Shaella was returning, and he could tell by the look on her face that she was going to spend this night with him. They didn't make love, but instead, stayed up late kissing, laughing, and talking of the sights and wonders that had amazed Gerard. Eventually, they fell asleep in each other's arms.

When they left there this morning, they did so by boat. The horses had been left behind. This fact concerned Gerard as much as getting onto the boat did. He had never been on a boat before. Shaella explained that their destination was deep in the southern marshes, and horses couldn't travel there without sinking.

"We're leaving the world of men behind," she said, leaving him to wonder what other sort of worlds there might be.

It didn't occur to him that there would be terrible dangers on this portion of the journey, at least not until he was brought out of his pleasant recollection by the sound of steel being drawn directly behind him on the river boat deck.

The huge Seawardsman, Greyber, swung his big sword in a wide sweeping arc slicing the abdomen of one of the deckhands open, and gashing into the thigh of another. Terror jolted through Gerard's blood like ice. What was happening? Why? His eyes searched for Shaella, but he couldn't see her anywhere. Not on the fore deck. Not down either side of the railed walkway that ran past the sides of the box-like pilothouse, sitting in the middle of the boat's flat-topped deck. He didn't see her inside the pilothouse either. He did see the boat captain's head suddenly twist to an impossible angle, before he slumped out of view. Where was she? What was happening?

There! He saw her! A brief glimpse when the pilothouse door had swung open as Cole left it. She was on the rear deck. He started to go there, with this heart hammering in his chest, but his way was suddenly blocked.

From around the walkway, to the right, men were approaching. Greyber stepped in front of Gerard protectively, and took up a readied stance. Gerard was forced back into the triangular area formed by the side rails coming together in a point, and Greyber's rippling tattoo-covered back. From where he was, he could see Flick standing on top of the pilothouse. The black-robed mage was chanting and pointing a finger down at something on the rear deck. Gerard thought he saw tiny streaks of crimson light shooting forth from Flick's fingers, but he wasn't sure. The man's back was to him, and the sun was bright. It could have been glinting reflections, but he was fairly certain that it had been some sort of magic.

One of the men in front of Greyber lashed out with a long dagger, forcing the big man to jump back. Gerard was pinned into the bow rails, and had to lean out over the water to see around his protector. Another man had appeared, making it three. This one held a crossbow, trained in their direction, but he was behind the others, so he couldn't fire it yet. He was jostling to get past his mate at the corner of the pilothouse so that he might get a clear shot at Greyber.

What happened next was more instinct than decision. Had he thought about it, he might've curled up into a fetal ball. Instead, Gerard dropped down to his hands and knees, and crawled forward between Greyber's legs. He felt them tense as the big man swung his sword. Gerard didn't rise up immediately, for fear of the blade. When he was sure he was clear, he rolled to the right, and screamed into his mind for the crossbowman to fire into his fellow's back.

Instantly, the rush of the ring's magic filled his body. His senses grew sharper, and the fear was forced completely out of him. He rolled to his feet in front of the two men, just as the crossbow bolt flew. The face before him contorted in shock and pain, as the steel-tipped bolt tore into him from behind. He started to fall to the ground, and Gerard wasted no time making his move. He reared back, and swung his fist as hard as he could into the face of the bewildered man, who had just shot his friend. The man stumbled down the walkway, and fell in a tangle of limbs. Before he could recover, Gerard began to savagely kick him. Within moments, the man was a bloody, unconscious heap.

Leaping over the man's limp body, Gerard charged to the rear of the boat. Shaella's sword was glowing pale yellow, where it wasn't streaked with blood. At her feet, Trent and three of the deckhands lay dead or dying, and before her, a huge, burly man seethed with anger, while clutching a severe gash in his side. A few hundred yards behind them, shouts erupted from the deck of a flat barge that was heavily loaded with crates.

"Go!" Shaella commanded.

Gerard looked up at where Flick was standing over them on the top of the pilothouse. The bald man's image shimmered and sizzled into a misty, blue color. Then, to Gerard's open-mouthed amazement, Flick disappeared altogether. Cole stepped out of the pilothouse then. He glanced approvingly at Gerard, and then strode toward the back of the boat, fading into nothingness as he went.

"Look!" Shaella ordered the man before her. She pointed her blade tip toward the barge behind them. She looked fierce and beautiful. Her face was mottled red with rage and exertion, causing the tear-like scar on her cheek to stand out in its paleness. She's a force to be reckoned with, Gerard thought proudly. She's a natural born leader, with a wicked magical blade glowing in her hand, and I'm her lover. It was all he could do to pull his eyes away from her, to look at what she was pointing out to her wounded captive.

On the barge, Flick and Cole were stalking across the tops of the crates, blasting anything that moved with hot, crimson bolts of magical energy.

"Do as I say or you'll die," Shaella told the terrified man.

With a grim nod, he conceded defeat.

"As you wish," he said, as he limped into the pilothouse.

Shaella flashed Gerard a triumphant grin as she followed the man. She was enjoying herself, he saw, and he found that he was, too.

Of the men that were on the boat with them, only her prisoner was moving about. He began doing something in the pilothouse that caused the boat to slow in the river's current, so that the barge was suddenly coming upon them most swiftly. Beyond the barge, Gerard saw a huge, billowing plume of black smoke rising up into the air. He started to ask what it was, but the barge was coming at them so fast now that his train of thought was forced into preparing himself for the coming impact.

Just before the collision would've taken place, a handful of frightened men, under Flick's watchful eye, came down off the crates, and bodily guided the river boat around the barge. Once they were beside the barge, Gerard saw the source of the dark smoke. A push-boat, or the flaming hulk of one, was drifting behind them in the current. A few men, and a lot of debris, were in the water around it. Some of them were cursing and splashing. Another was screaming horribly, and a few others were floating lifelessly in the flow. A rather large splash sounded, and the man who had been screaming disappeared under the water. A large, rippling wake could be seen trailing toward the marshy side of the river channel. The others in the water suddenly grew very still.

It became obvious to Gerard what they were doing. They had pirated the barge. They were going to push it with the boat they were in. Gerard learned that the man Shaella had spared was a Water-Mage. Berda had told of them in one of her tales.

Water-Magi came from Highwander, and used some sort of magic, Gerard remembered. They could make a boat move up or down a river, or in the case of Berda's tale, across a stormy sea. Shaella confirmed this when Gerard asked her about it. She explained that the magi could only work their power on ships and boats fitted with transoms lined with Wardstone. It was the stone that held the power, she explained. The ability to command the stuff was a specialized skill though. One could only legitimately learn the art at the Port of Weir, in the Kingdom of Highwander. Willa the Witch Queen's Castle, Shaella told him, was built on the only place where the magical rock could be found.

"It's what gives her so much power," Shaella said, with a teasing look in her eyes. "That, and the fact that she eats her soldiers after they die."

"Don't fill his head with old wives' tales," Cole said, with a grin. "He did too well today to get less than the truth out of us from here on out."

Gerard felt a bit of pride after hearing this, but no one told him anything more. As the day wore on, things settled. The four men, who were taken forcibly from the barge, were told that they would eventually be paid and released if they served and obeyed. Mutiny, of course, meant death, so they really had no choice. The Water-Mage, however, knew better than to believe the lie. He knew he was as good as dead. He cooperated more for the sake of the four bargemen's lives than for his own. He thanked Shaella sincerely after she healed his gashed side, but she was no fool either. She caught him eyeing his possibilities, and placed Greyber in the pilothouse to watch over him, just in case he got any ideas.

Later in the afternoon things got tense. Ahead of them, the river split into a Y, and down either branch there were people and buildings. To the right was the Westland flow, and to the left, the channel that eased along the Kingdom of Dakahn. Several docks reached out into the river from each side and hundreds of people could see them pass. Cole and Flick both pulled up their hoods and stayed where the barge men could see them. Shaella joined Greyber and the Water-Mage in the pilothouse. If any of them were going to attempt something foolish, this would be the best opportunity for it.

No one did.

They took the Westland branch of the river. Gerard saw that what spread out between the two channels wasn't really land. It was shallow, marshy muck. Grass grew up out of it, thick, lush, and as tall as a man, giving the terrain the illusion of being solid underneath. The illusion was shattered though, when the rolling wake of the boat made the grass dance and waver with the flow. The expanse of grassy marsh seemed to spread out endlessly to the south and east. The solid shoreline to the right of the boat though, was Westland.

Bright, green, rolling hills, dotted here and there with rocky formations and small clusters of hardwood trees, filled the spaces between crop fields and grazing pastures. A hard-packed road ran alongside the river, boasting what might be considered a small town every now and then. Wooden docks stretched out to the edge of the main river channel's flow. Some were empty.

Others had small fishing craft tied to them. A few fishing boats could be seen working out in the swamp grass. They looked out of place, like they had been washed up in a field.

Soon, they passed a stone building with armed soldiers standing on its crenellated parapet.

"An outpost of the Westland Marsh Patrol," Shaella told him as she studied the place intently.

Less than a mile later, they passed what could've been called a city. There, the docks and piers were large and sturdy enough to load and unload barges. To the left of them, the marsh was only growing thicker and deeper as it filled the space between the boat and the horizon. Gerard could see places where the ground humped up out of the muck, and large droopy trees had taken root. Around each of these swamp islands, a plethora of birds swooped and swirled about like a cloud. Some of the birds were as big as men, with wingspans easily twenty feet across. Flick called them dactyls.

At dusk, after a long stretch where nothing but farmland could be seen along the Westland bank, Shaella ordered them to turn directly into the marsh. Gerard could hear and feel the abundance of life out and around them as the boat was swallowed up. Like a horse-drawn wagon charging through a cornfield, they moved through the tall swamp grass. Several times, he saw patches of the grass shake as the surface of the water was churned by some huge thing underneath that was darting away from their passage. Chirps, humming buzzes, and distant splashes, along with bellowing croaks and the occasional groan, filled the night. Eventually, they lit torches, which only served to make the swampy marsh seem that much vaster. A cloud of biting gnats formed around Gerard's head, and a not so distant splash, which was so big its ripples made the whole boat rock back and forth, caused a tremor of unease to run through him.

He decided to sit down and close his eyes for a while. He fell asleep against the pilothouse.

He woke once, when it felt like the boat had stopped moving. He heard foreign voices that had an almost animalistic hissing quality to them, but he was too tired to pull himself out of his slumber to investigate. After a while, Shaella joined him. She was silent, as she took his side and let her head rest on his shoulder. His sleep was deep and sound.

The sudden lurching of the boat woke him again. Shaella was gone, and the sun was coming up off to the far left. He could tell they were heading south. The barge that they had been pushing was no longer anywhere in sight, and the riverboat was moving swiftly.

The surrounding terrain was as much above the water level as below it now. It looked like they were in a scattered forest that had suddenly been flooded with grassy water. The places that were above the water level were dense and thick, with tall, yet drooping, trees, and even thicker, leafy undergrowth. The sounds of grunting land animals could be heard, and once, Gerard saw a dark shape swinging from a shaking tree. None of it seemed to take his attention fully away from the dominant feature of the deep marshes though. Far ahead of them, rising up like a mammoth fang to tower hundreds of feet above the swamp trees, was a sharp and slightly curved formation.

"That's our destination," Shaella said excitedly.

Actually seeing Dragon's Tooth Spire, and knowing that Shaella expected him to climb to the top of it to steal the egg of a real dragon, made Gerard's stomach roil. It was all he could do to keep from vomiting over the rail.

Chapter Twenty-Four

"Once upon a time, it was a fire mountain," Shaella said, as she slipped her arm around Gerard's waist.

They were still on the riverboat, leaning against the bow rail. She felt she had gone crazy, allowing herself to feel for Gerard. It was stupid and unwise, she told herself over and over, but knowing it didn't make the feelings go away. "What is youth for, but to make mistakes?" A quote from some obscure text she once read came to mind. The words somehow made her foolishness seem all right, like the words of a priest cleansing away a sin. Gerard pulled her closer to him, bringing her wandering mind back to the moment.

The afternoon sun made the air thick with humidity. The chattering, chirping hum of the insects around them filled the air. Occasionally, they found themselves in a cloud of pesky gnats or tiny biting flies. A larger, scarier looking thing, half-dragonfly, half-scorpion, hovered and buzzed about them menacingly until Cole came out and zapped it with one of his sizzling, crimson bolts.

"I can climb it," Gerard's voice held only the slightest trace of bravado when he spoke.

To Shaella, he seemed to be speaking more to himself than to her. She only nodded and smiled sweetly at him.

"Once, it was wider than it is tall. You can see what I mean if you look at it from the sides." Shaella indicated the Dragon's Tooth Spire looming ahead of them in the distance. "The entire river used to flow down the channel we're in now. It was far deeper then. Somehow, it split around the fire mountain. Over the centuries, it wore at the sides and deposited all of this." Her arm swept around broadly, indicating the whole of the marshes around them. "The marsh is bigger than Westland." She turned to face him, and her look grew serious as if what she were about to say was of great importance. "Right now we are in the biggest, most powerful land in the entire realm. What's more, is not a single one of those self-righteous and mighty kings even knows it."

"But it's empty," said Gerard. "There's no one out here."

"Oh, but there is." She kissed him on the lips quickly. "You just don't see them, but you will."

"When?"

"Tomorrow night, if the Water-Mage's strength holds out," she answered.

He pulled back from her quickly, swatted at a buzzing sound near his ear, and then ducked reflexively. Whatever it was, it had already absconded. Grinning at the silliness of how he must look, he recovered.

"So, do you have a plan yet? Have you decided what I'm to do once I climb to the top of that thing?"

"Yes, there is a plan," she answered coolly.

She didn't want to think about it. She didn't want to consider what she might have to do while he was up there inside the dragon's lair. She wasn't so sure now that she could do it.

"We'll talk about it later." She kissed him again, deeply this time, trying to drive the worry from her mind and the subject from his.

That night, they made love in the moonlight on top of the pilothouse. They tried to be quiet, but it was impossible. The act ended up being humorous and awkward. They spent most of the night giggling like children.

When Gerard woke, he was alone. He sat up and looked around. The sun was only slightly above the horizon, and only one or two white fluffy clouds were in this part of the sky. Far behind them, the entire northern horizon was a dark gray line.

The loud CHOOK! CHOOK! CHOOK! of some creature grabbed Gerard's attention. A large, hairy, mannish thing sat in a tree, voicing its disapproval of their presence in its domain. Somewhere not far beyond the beast, a whole tree shook violently, sending a squawking flock of angry birds up into the air.

For the most part, the marsh had risen up out of the water around them. Very few open spaces could be seen now. The jungle that surrounded them was dense and steamy. The trees along the edges of the waterway leaned out over it. Their limbs hung down, the sagging branches heavy with beards of blue-colored moss and long, stringy leaves.

As he climbed down from the pilothouse and its higher vantage point, Gerard began to feel enclosed. It was like moving down a roofless corridor or a narrow, forested wagon trail.

The site of something so personally familiar to him that it was startling caught his eye. A large, full grown hawkling was perched solemnly on the back rail of the boat. It was as out of place as anything he could imagine. It cocked its head toward him and blinked. It was big and healthy, but to Gerard, it seemed that something, some glint of existence, was missing. It didn't seem to be proud or even aware. A flash of sunlight reflected off something at the bird's neck and Gerard moved closer. It was a jeweled leather band, a collar. He went toward the hawkling, half-expecting it to launch away, but it didn't. It sat there passively as he fumbled at the band around its neck. He tried to unclasp it, but found it was held in place by a solid silver ring. Perplexed, he started to look for a dagger to cut the thing off.

"Don't release it," Shaella barked angrily from the pilothouse. "How can I reply if you cut it loose?"

"How can someone keep such a creature bound like that?" He wasn't sure how he knew that the collar was like a shackle around the bird's spirit. Maybe it was the ring's magic telling him, maybe he just felt it. Either way, he knew.

"How could you, of all people, ask such a stupid question?" she snapped.

"What do you mean?"

"You and your people are the very ones who plucked this creature from its nest before it was even hatched!"

She made a sharp clucking sound. The hawkling flew over to her and perched on the edge of the pilothouse roof. She tied a finger-sized scroll case to another band that was clasped around the bird's ankle. When she was done, she stood on tiptoe and fiddled with the collar while murmuring a few words that Gerard couldn't quite make out. As soon as she dropped back to her heels, the hawkling leapt into flight and headed off on a swift, northwesterly course.

"What did you think happened to the eggs your people stole from the nest and sold?" she asked. Her eyes trailed after the bird.

Gerard winced. He knew and never ever really thought about it much. Were his people no better than that? Were they just villainous egg thieves who stole something more precious than gold? The idea was unsettling. How could his people respect and revere a creature so much, yet make a profit by selling its young into slavery? Maybe it was true. Maybe the Skyler Clan was nothing more than a band of bird-soul stealers.

The slight bit of guilt and unease he'd been feeling about leaving his people the way he had suddenly evaporated. Who were they to judge him for leaving? What reason could they possibly have to disapprove of what he was going to do for Shaella? His people wouldn't shun him for stealing a dragon's egg for her. They would be proud of him. What greater harvest could he make? The Elders even used a dragon's skull for their fire pit. The memory of the size of that skull sent a chill through him. A hint of the dangerous nature of what he was going to do became real to him, and his mind went off on another track.

It was one thing to wave off an angry hawkling mother while you plucked one of her eggs away. Shooing off a dragon probably wasn't an option. He wasn't sure if dragons really breathed fire like they did in Berda's tales, but he didn't think it would matter. The jaws on the skull in the Elders' council chamber back home were large enough to pluck him from the fang-spire and swallow him whole. There were claws and blasts of turbulent air from the powerful wings to think of as well. If the dragon really did breathe fire, and it caught him, he was done for anyway. He could almost imagine being roasted like a stag's loin while he clung helplessly to a sheer face of rock.

"Where did you go?" Shaella asked him. He was staring after Pael's hawkling with a look of deep concern on his face, but the bird had long since disappeared from sight.

"Your plan better be a good one," he said a little more sharply than he intended to. He meant for his voice to convey his concern without showing his fear. The result simply sounded angry.

Her brows narrowed and she stepped away from him while holding his gaze. She searched his eyes deeply. The quality of his manner that caused her to fall so hard wasn't there to be seen at the moment. She hoped it hadn't flown away with the hawkling. Maybe it would make it easier if she… NO! She stopped herself from thinking that way. She wouldn't. She couldn't. She huffed out her frustration. She had fallen in love with him, and already she was fighting with the possible regret. The task he was here for was dangerous, and she couldn't let it affect her judgment.

The worry he was feeling was showing plainly on his face. She felt it, too.

"Tonight, we feast with the marsh men," she said, with a forced smile. "After the formalities, Cole and I will share our ideas with you. Our plan, if you will. If we have to make a few changes, if you can add anything, or if some part of the plan needs to be adjusted to help you succeed, we will work it out then."

His eyes softened while she was speaking. That glint of whatever it was she adored returned to them. She found herself relieved it was still there. She was irritated though, that the presence of some silly twinkle meant so much to her. Before she could think, he stole a quick kiss. The smile that resulted came across her face of its own accord.

The boat came aground just as the sun was starting down below the horizon. Before Gerard hopped down off the pilothouse, he took a long, last look at the distant fang-shaped spire. He was sure he wouldn't be able to see it once he was under the jungle's thick canopy. As he hurried into the gloomy swelter to catch up with Shaella, he found he was right.

It had been uncomfortably humid out in the open, but once he was in the jungle, he found the heat stifling. The air was so thick with moisture, he felt like he was swimming through it. The trail led away from the boat. Gerard thanked the goddess for it. The journey through the tangle of greenery would've been impossibly slow without the path.

Cole led them. He was followed by Greyber. The Water-Mage came next, and Shaella was behind him, prodding him along with her sword. The soft, yellow glow of its blade helped with the dimness created by the density of the vegetation.

Even if the sun had been directly overhead, Gerard thought it would've been dark in this claustrophobic place.

Flick stayed with the boat. The two deck hands that hadn't gone with the cargo barge were with him. The further Gerard moved away from the boat, the more he found himself looking back over his shoulder into the dark nothingness.

Some sort of thorny vine spiked into his arm sharply. He tried to pull away, but it was embedded in his flesh. He pulled again with gritted teeth and finally broke free of it, but not before dragging several feet of the ropey plant down the trail behind him. The rustling of bushes and the sound of heavy footfalls as some large, grunting thing bolted away from them, hurried his pace. When he caught up to Shaella and the comforting glow of her sword, he decided this wasn't the sort of place where one should lag behind.

The clamor of a hammering bird's beak and the chirping sizzle of a million different insects wafted up through the thick air to his ears. To his right, for a fleeting instant, he thought he saw two tiny specks of yellow light, spaced a hand's breadth apart, bobbing slowly along beside them at head height. By the time his mind registered that what he was seeing was two eyes reflecting the light from Shaella's sword back at him, they were gone.

Off in the distance, the ear-piercing shriek of something huge caused a moment of total silence. The whole jungle, even the insects, stopped to listen. Then slowly, hesitantly, the cacophony of noise resumed, as if the creatures hadn't been disturbed at all.

The ground seemed to grow less spongy as they continued, but it never stopped being slimy. The ever-present moisture dripping from the leaves and vines above wouldn't allow it. Gerard figured they were slowly moving up onto higher ground. His new boots were probably a ruin. He wondered absently what Hyden would think of all the places he had seen so far on this journey.

He glanced at his arm to find it was swollen and bleeding. So much moisture was clinging to his skin that he hadn't noticed it. The wound began to pulse with pain, and he wondered if he would be feeling the growing throb if he hadn't looked at it. For a moment, he panicked. He had to climb soon. He couldn't afford to have a swollen arm and be in this kind of pain. Go away! he screamed inside his head. Before the thought had completed itself, he felt the ring on his finger heating. The usual rush he felt in his blood was dampened by the pain in his arm, but only for a moment. The magic quickly scoured away all traces of the injury, and he soon felt its luscious tingle coursing through him. A thought came to him as he rode on the rush of unnatural power. Light! He commanded in his mind. To his great surprise, an apple sized ball of bright white light appeared in his palm.

He heard Shaella gasp as she turned to see what had happened. It was a gasp of surprise, and maybe wonder. The sound of the Water-Mage's gasp, though, was clearly one of shock and terror. Gerard reluctantly peeled his eyes away from the glowing light in his hand, and saw what frightened the man. In the trees all around the group, were glittering pairs of reflection. Hundreds of black orbs set in slithery, slick reptilian faces, were staring at the light. The lizard-like creatures were standing upright and armed to the teeth with human weapons. A bright, pink tongue flickered from a split in a snouted turtle-shaped head, then another. The parts of the creatures' bodies not covered with ringed leather armor or scraps of chain mail were scaled and as green as the jungle around them. Skeeks, Gerard decided correctly, right out of one of Berda's stories.

Everyone seemed to be captivated as well as irritated by the light. More than one of the lizard men moved to shield its eyes from the brightness. More flickering forked tongues appeared, accompanied by a severe hissing sound, as their heads began to dart around nervously.

Gerard was sure they were about to be attacked, but then one of them spoke to Cole in a strange, clicking, sibilant language. Gerard recognized it as the language the two bald-headed wizards used when they spoke to Shaella and each other. Gerard noticed something else. It was the blackness of the eyes, maybe, or the elongated torso and head of the lizard men—he wasn't sure. He tried to pinpoint the similarities, but couldn't. They were subtle and many. He was sure beyond a shadow of a doubt, that both Cole and Flick were related to these unsettling creatures somehow. As if to confirm this thought, Cole responded to the beast in a casual, yet commanding tone.

Gerard waited for the lizard man's response, but the next words were spoken to him.

"Extinguish the light!" Cole commanded harshly in the common tongue.

"Do it, Gerard," Shaella added softly. "The light will draw things to us we don't want to run into out here."

Gerard tried several silent commands to make the light go away, but none of them seemed to work. Off, Dim, Dark, Darkness. It grew very quiet. The air was crackling with tension, as everything alive inside the reach of the magical glow held its breath. The silence became deafening. No matter what command Gerard gave, the light would not extinguish. Finally, under the intense gaze of all those strange pairs of eyes, he did the only other thing he could think to do. Reluctantly, he pulled the ring off his finger. A dozen hisses and sighs of relief emitted from the suddenly darkened jungle around them. Gerard made a short prayer to the goddess that the light would stay gone when he slipped the ring back on. He let out his own sigh of relief when it did.

What seemed like days, but was really only a few hours later, they came to a clearing in the trees. Gerard gasped in shock when he saw a bowl-shaped depression, lit like a field full of burning stars by hundreds upon hundreds of campfires. Illuminated in the wavering orange glow around them were thousands of Skeeks and other strange swamp creatures. A few big four-legged lizards could be seen carrying small groups of their two-legged kin around a perimeter of bigger bonfires. A dactyl bird, like they had seen soaring out over the marshes, was sharpening its long beak on a chunk of the black porous rock scattered about in the clearing. It looked to Gerard as if all of the creatures there were, in one way or another, preparing for battle.

"An army of Skeeks?" he asked Shaella quietly.

One of the lizard men escorting them hissed out sharply.

"This is only one of several armies. And don't call them Skeeks."

She sheathed her sword and took his hand. "They prefer to be called Zardmen or the Zard. Come now, let's feast, and then we can work out a plan to steal the dragon's egg that pleases all of us."

Gerard couldn't help but wonder what they would be eating, and just who all of us really was.

Chapter Twenty-Five

After being out in the cool, crisp mountain air for the past few days, the Elders' council chambers seemed stiflingly hot. Every single pore on Hyden's body was running freely with perspiration. His condition wasn't caused solely by the temperature, though. He was nervous, and more than a little bit afraid. He wanted to leave, but that wasn't a possibility. The Elders would deny his exit and probably lock him in a goat burrow if he so much as complained.

Talon was miserable, too. He fluttered over to the tip of one of the dragon skull horns that curved up out of the dancing blue flames and perched there, but only for a heartbeat or two. Apparently it was just as hot up there. The hawkling finally flapped his way down to the floor and found a place between Hyden's boots.

The stool Hyden was sitting on was directly in front of the dragon skull. The wicked blaze burning in the skull's brain cavity made the dragon's eye sockets seem alive, and made the semicircle of Elders gathered around it look like a bunch of hungry ghouls.

Halden, the Eldest, sat directly across the sapphire blaze opposite Hyden. The dragon skull's curved horns framed a disturbing picture, with Hyden's grandfather at its center. The old man was now chanting and raising his arms in a series of lunatic gestures. At precise intervals in the Eldest's manic song, the rest of the Elders spoke the powerful words of invocation in unison. They shouted, in short bursts, phrases that seemed to make the walls of the cavernous burrow they were in hum with reverberation. Slowly it became repetitive and hypnotic, and Hyden found himself slightly swaying to the flowing rhythm they created. How long this went on, he couldn't say. He became lost in the moment.

Eventually, the walls of the chamber faded. All around and above them was nothing but a deep, empty blackness. Hyden looked up into it. A pinpoint of light appeared, then another, and then several more.

Suddenly, Hyden was looking at the open night sky. It looked exactly the same as it would have if they were outside around a campfire in the very same place. Or did it? Hyden questioned. Hadn't the real sky been gray and cloudy?

Hyden became aware of the stark silence around him. Between the dragon's horns, a thin wisp of smoke began to swirl up from the blue flames. The tendrils thickened and twisted like a miniature funnel, then spun crazily until a small, featureless, humanoid form appeared. It was about as tall as a man's forearm was long. A pair of arms rose away from its sides. Hyden could see the back and buttocks of a shapely woman slowly define itself. Long flowing hair, curvaceous hips, and smooth tapering legs formed in perfect miniature out of the swirling smoke. It was the White Goddess, but she was facing away from Hyden. He wanted badly to move to the other side of the dragon skull so he could look upon her face, but he dared not do anything that might startle her away.

Halden spoke a greeting in a strange language and bowed his upper torso to the misty woman before him. The rest of the Elders remained silent, but all of them bowed their heads to her in a show of respect. Hyden bowed his head, too, even though he didn't think she could see him. Looking down, he noticed Talon was standing alert like a statue, with his raptor eyes glued to the apparition floating in the shimmering air over the fire.

The goddess spoke. Hyden couldn't understand the words, but he knew he was the subject of the conversation. He could feel it. Halden responded to her, and then their words switched to the common language.

"The Pact has been broken," she said gravely. "The guardian of the seal is no longer bound to protect it."

There was a long silence. After the pause, the voice of the goddess grew angry and harsh.

"This is what happens when old men grow jealous and covet another's abilities. You changed tradition. It is shameful that a foolish squabble with the elves would cause grown men to act like children." Before Halden could respond, her smoky form turned to face Hyden.

His breath left him and his heartbeat quickened. His eyelids felt like they might peel back over his skull. She was beautiful, perfectly formed, and naked. He was glad to see her expression soften before she addressed him.

"For now, you must follow your heart, Hyden Hawk. When you're lost or confused, Talon will help you find the right path to follow. Eventually, you must get back the ring your brother wears. It was not meant for him. It was meant for you to find."

She glanced back over her shoulder at Harrap and the other Elders, with distaste showing clearly on her tiny, smoky face.

"The balance of things is out of kilter. The entire nature of prophecy has been fractured. Not even I can know what to expect until the balance has been restored. You must follow your heart, Hyden. Your heart and your familiar will guide you until the time comes when you can get the ring back from Gerard."

She turned back toward the Eldest then, leaving Hyden staring after her.

"The power of prophecy is useless now," she said, with a quick, nervous glance up into the false sky around them. "Fractured and uncertain is the only future I can see—"

She paused again, and for a moment seemed confused. Her suddenly fearful expression, along with her words, created a wave of panic among the Elders. More than one pair of shame-filled eyes fell on Hyden. Even the Eldest glanced at his grandson with an expression full of dire concern.

"There is no sure path for him to follow," she continued. "Any deed of honor might prove to be horribly destructive. A cold betrayal might prove to be the most righteous act ever committed. No one can say with any certainty."

She spun and half-ducked reflexively, then looked up into her starry sky with an arm held out protectively over her face. High over her head something as dark as the night glided by. Had it not been eclipsing the stars it was passing under, it would have been invisible to them.

"Evil approaches as we speak! It is upon them. You mus—"

Her voice ended abruptly, and her image turned into a shapeless swirl as Talon shot through her, toward the dark thing that was gliding overhead.

"NOOO!" Hyden screamed at the bird, but it was too late. The spell had been broken. The night sky had been replaced by the stone ceiling of the chamber and Talon struck it with a sickening thump. The Elders gasped as the brave hawkling tumbled to the floor like a feather-covered stone.

The door to the chamber burst open then, and young Derry Skyler came in huffing and covered with sweat, with eyes as big as saucers.

"Something has attacked them!" he said between breaths.

Being a seasoned climber, the boy was in spectacular shape. Hyden knew he would've had to run a long way to be so out of breath. Hyden's stomach clenched as he realized Derry had been watching over Vaegon and the kingdom men.

"It was coming down out of the sky on them when I left to warn you. They…they were asleep. Oh, Hyden," he sobbed. "I should have warned them awake instead of…of…"

He fell apart then. He was crying and very confused.

"I pa...panicked. I thought...thought there...thought there might be more of them...come...come...coming here."

Mikahl's eyes popped open. His hand went to Ironspike's hilt and he took in a long deep breath to clear his mind. The beast from his dreams was there! As he exhaled, he tried to force out all of the fear and anxiety the nightmares had left inside him.

The sudden screeching roar of some creature, followed by the wet ripping sound of one of the horses being brutalized, saved him from having to wake the others. Mikahl spun to his feet and drew the king's blade in one fluid motion. Its soft, bluish glow filled the night around them. He didn't advance toward the beast. Instead, he stood over Lord Gregory and Vaegon protectively until they were both on their feet and armed.

Lord Gregory stared open-mouthed at Ironspike, then at Mikahl.

"So it's true," he muttered in astonishment. It was all he could do to keep from falling to a knee on the spot.

At the edge of the blade's light, the horses brayed and nickered in terror. Beyond that was total darkness.

"Should we cut them loose?" Mikahl asked, indicating the frightened animals. One of them was already a bloody mess, and the scent of its death was traumatizing the others.

"Aye, Your Highness," Lord Gregory said, then went to release them. Mikahl had heard the Lion Lord's words, but was too intent on the matter at hand to make sense of them.

Vaegon turned in a whirl and fired an arrow up into the air above and behind Mikahl. Mikahl felt the presence of evil there. He also felt and heard a distant, musical vibration. He wasn't sure, but he thought it might be coming from the sword in his hands. He didn't have time to contemplate the sensations though; he had to duck. He turned and came back up quickly with a sharp thrust, but missed the dark thing. Luckily, its big, swiping claw missed him, too. He saw the elf's arrow. It was stuck into the creature's shoulder, and there was a black wetness where it penetrated.

"It bleeds!" he yelled more to himself than to the others.

It was an odd relief to know the creature from his dreams was made of flesh and blood, that it had form and substance, and it could most likely die.

As fast as the hellcat had come, it disappeared back into the darkness. Above, the sky appeared empty, but the thick grayish clouds were backlit by the moon.

"Look for the shape," Vaegon called out, "the shadow in the sky."

A sudden sound swept by in the darkness. A horse? Mikahl hoped so. It was probably trying to get as far away from the light of his blade as possible. He also hoped it wasn't Windfoot that was slaughtered, but he didn't dare take the time to go and check.

Lord Gregory came hurrying back into Ironspike's radiance. Mikahl saw it then, a speeding shadow coming at them from the side. He cringed and felt his heart drop to the dirt. Not even a warning shout could save the man he respected and loved so much.

Vaegon loosed another arrow and it struck true, but it didn't help the Lion Lord. The hellcat's claws dug deep into Lord Gregory's back and shoulder, and yanked him screaming up into the darkened night. Vaegon started to launch another arrow, but thought better of it. As good as his aim was, under these conditions, he could easily hit the Westland Lord by mistake. He wondered for a fleeting moment if that might not be the merciful thing to do, but then the chance had passed.

"I think it's afraid of the sword," said Vaegon. "Or maybe, it's just the light it's weary of. Otherwise, I think it would land and fight us tooth and claw."

"Aye," Mikahl agreed absently. He was in a state of shock now. His confidence had been snatched away into the night with the Lord of Lake Bottom.

From behind them came the hellcat's shrieking growl. Mikahl nearly dropped Ironspike and ran. They turned and Vaegon made to loose the arrow he had nocked, but the spiked tip of the hellcat's tail caught him square in the face. He went down hard on his back, his bow tumbling uselessly to the ground as his hands shot up to protect what was left of his ruined eye.

Mikahl swallowed his fear and swung at the beast with all he had. A glancing slice was all he could manage, but the contact of the blade on the beast's skin caused it to howl out in rage and pain. It gnashed its teeth together and snapped its catlike head out, as if it were a striking viper. The sharp, blackened maw smashed closed just inches from Mikahl's nose. The beast's hot breath stank of burnt steel, rotten flesh, and hatred. It reminded Mikahl of how the body-strewn field at Coldfrost had smelled a month after the snows had melted. He had to choke back the urge to vomit.

Mikahl used his backswing to hack at the thing's extended neck, but it withdrew its head even faster than it had lunged. The miss would've carried him off balance had he been a fraction less agile. Instead of stumbling away as he came around, he pulled his arms in close to his body like he once saw a dancer do in a mummers' play. It made him spin faster. He did a full revolution and as he came around the second time, he extended the blade out as far as he could and caught the surprised beast.

From shoulder to shoulder, the hellcat's narrow chest opened up like a bright red maw. Mikahl noticed two things before his momentum twisted his legs and sent him tumbling to the ground. The first was Ironspike's glow briefly changed from blue to red before turning to the bright white radiance that it was emitting now. The second was he missed the vital tendons and veins in the hellcat's neck by only inches. He had sliced too low and only caused a flesh wound.

The feline monster snapped out its wings for balance and reared up on its hind legs like some nightmarish horse. The roar it let out was bone-chilling. It seemed angrier than hurt by the wound Mikahl inflicted.

To Mikahl's side, he saw Vaegon fumbling with his bow. The elf's face was a bloody mess. There was so much blood that it was a wonder he could even see. By the way he was handling his weapon, Mikahl thought maybe he couldn't.

Mikahl started to rise, but before he could sit up or even bring Ironspike up to protect himself, the hellcat pounced. Its savagely graceful leap landed its bulk right on top of him. Its fore claws found his chest and shoulders and pinned him in place. The beast's great weight forced the breath from him, causing him to gasp a lungful of the hellcat's fetid breath. Warm saliva dripped from a blackened tongue, some of it found its way into Mikahl's mouth, causing him to retch and gasp for more rotten air. Black, empty eyes he recognized from his nightmares raged down at him with nothing less than death reflecting from their glossy depths. He felt as if he were about to choke on his own vomit. Mikahl tried desperately to raise Ironspike, but the beast's paws were huge and covered his upper arms, chest, and shoulders. He could barely turn his head.

Vaegon's bow thrummed as he loosed an arrow into the creature's rear flank. The hellcat tensed and roared out its anger at the assault, but didn't move to get off of Mikahl. Instead, it reared back its head and opened its foul, toothy maw.

This is it, Mikahl thought, remembering the way the monster lunged out its head before. It's going to tear my face off with those teeth. I've failed King Balton and I'm about to die. I've come all this way and I've failed.

The beast's head darted down. Mikahl could see that his own head would easily fit into the hellcat's mouth. He hoped the thing would rip it away quick. He didn't want to die slowly, half maimed out in these foothills. At the last moment, he squeezed his eyes shut, turned away, and waited for the pain.

It never came.

The hellcat suddenly stiffened and froze in place. Its head slowly drew back far enough for Mikahl to see that those hungry, evil eyes had grown wide with shock, or maybe confusion. The beast's brow furrowed. Mikahl heard a solid thump, then another. The monstrous winged feline jerked with each of the sounds. Suddenly, it leapt to the side, writhing and shrieking in frustration.

Mikahl couldn't possibly imagine what was happening to the thing, and he didn't wait around to try to figure it out. He sucked in a deep, well needed breath of fresh air, drew his knees up to his chest, and then kicked out while arching his back. The move brought him acrobatically to his feet and he was in a defensive stance, facing the hellcat less than a heartbeat later. The beast had at least half a dozen arrows sticking out of its back now. Another arrow came streaking down out of the sky and stuck into the ground between Mikahl and the monster. Not daring to take his eyes off of the raging and confused creature before him, it took Mikahl a moment to figure out what was happening.

The hellcat started toward Mikahl again. As he steadied himself to make a swing with Ironspike, another of the arrows slammed into the creature's back, but it didn't stop the animal. It took one long, lunging leap, then another, and then launched itself into a crushing pounce. Mikahl stumbled over the ring of rocks they placed around their campfire as he instinctually backed away. He brought his sword up and managed to hold the blade out steady, even though he fell and landed hard. The hellcat's great weight would impale it on the sword when it came down on him this time.

Mikahl waited with his eyes clenched shut to feel the beast come crashing down, but it didn't happen. The heavy THUMP! of leathery wings catching air came instead. The nightmare come to life flew over Mikahl's head and disappeared back into the darkness.

He passed a few anxious moments waiting to see if the hellcat would return, but it didn't. As soon as he was sure the beast had fled, Mikahl went to Vaegon's side.

"Go! Find your Lion Lord," the elf said waving him away. "I'll be all right."

"What if that thing returns?" Mikahl asked.

"Then we will deal with it," a breathless voice spoke from the darkness beyond them.

It was Loudin, Mikahl realized in a flood of relief. He was coming out of the darkness with a handful of the hawkman's people.

"Is it hot?"

One of them kicked a booted foot at the barely visible fire ring where Mikahl was just sprawled. The tiny swirl of sparking embers was stirred up by the kick. He poured liquid from a flask into it and flames leapt up. Wood that had been set aside for the morning's cook fire was thrown into the blaze by another man.

"We have light here now," Harrap said sternly. "And we have torches on the way. Use the sword's light to search for the other man."

He turned to a pair of young men who were not much older than Mikahl. "Tylen, Derry, go and help him."

Even though each and every one of the hawkman's people had deeply tanned skin and sported the same long, slick, black length of hair, Mikahl could tell the man giving the orders was Hyden Hawk's father. It was clear he was an authority figure here, and the resemblance was unmistakable.

It was dawn before they found Lord Gregory. He was just over the next ridge, half in, half out of a huddle of pine shrub. He was still alive, but barely. He had been dropped from a great height, and it appeared nearly every bone in his body was broken. He also had several puncture wounds in his back and a wide, open tear from his chest to his chin. When they got him back to the camp, Vaegon tried to heal him, but it didn't work. He wasn't strong enough. One of the elf's eyes was swollen shut and the other was blood red. A deep, jagged tear ran from his slightly pointed ear to the closed eye.

The men from the Skyler Clan ended up making a travois for Lord Gregory, then toted him back to the village, where a burrow had been cleared out just for the outsiders.

Hyden helped only slightly in the search for the Westland Lord. He hadn't raced down into the camp, either. Instead, he stood on the ridge and used his bow and his hawk-like vision to put those arrows into the hellcat's back. As soon as he was sure the creature had fled, he went to tend to Talon. Only after the hawkling had come out of the half-stunned state his collision with the ceiling of the council chamber had caused, did Hyden leave the village to help the others in the search.

The women cooked a stew chocked full of healing herbs and goat meat. Poultices and liniments were administered. Mikahl took several stitches in a wound on his chest he didn't remember getting. All that could be done for the outsiders was done.

Vaegon would survive. One eye was probably ruined, but it was too soon to say for certain. Lord Gregory, though, was nearly torn in two. Vaegon did what he could do, but even with the elf's magical healing abilities, the Lord of Lake Bottom would most likely die. If the gods decided to let him live, he would never walk again, the elf told them.

With all of the swelling from his broken limbs and the ghastly purple color of his pulverized flesh, Lord Gregory was not a pretty sight to look upon. He looked worse than dead. Late the second night when he suddenly opened his eyes and croaked out a request to see Mikahl, it came as a shock to everyone.

Mikahl had to be rousted from sleep, but once he knew why he was awakened, he hurried to Lord Gregory's side. The dying man's voice was weak. The gleam of life had left his eyes completely.

"Is that you, Mik?" The words came out in a scratchy hiss. "Are you there?"

"I'm here, m'lord," Mikahl told him. He wanted to take the man's hand as a show of support, but it was so swollen, it looked like the skin might split.

To Mikahl, his onetime teacher and mentor looked more like a tangle of gnarled tree roots than a man.

With appalling effort, Lord Gregory swallowed.

"He was your father, you know," he croaked. "He made sure, in the best way he knew how, that you were prepared for your birthright."

"What are you talking about?" Mikahl asked, with a panicked look at the woman who had been watching over the Lion Lord. "You're fevered and confused."

"Maybe so, Your Highness, but you're still the intended heir to your father's throne." He blinked and lulled his head to the side so he could look into Mikahl's eyes. "Ironspike's magic only ignites to those of Pavreal's blood line, Mik," he coughed.

His body wracked with terrible pain, but he fought it back. Mikahl felt hot tears streaming down his cheeks. He realized he loved this man just as much as he had loved King Balton.

"Glendar is a greedy fool; Pael's puppet, you'll see. King Balton saw it a long time ago. There's a third, but—"

It looked as if the Lion Lord passed on then, but his chest still rose, fell and wheezed as his body struggled on.

Mikahl stayed there the rest of the night, lost in teary-eyed sorrow, hoping the mighty Lion of the West would speak to him again, but he didn't. Mikahl couldn't help but wonder what the third was Gregory began to talk about, nor could he keep from being swallowed up by the confusion of the things the man told him. Had Lord Gregory not turned and looked into his eyes, he might've dismissed the words as rambling, but now he couldn't because he knew it was the truth.

Chapter Twenty-Six

"We've taken the bridge!" someone yelled from outside King Glendar's command pavilion.

An excited cheer came from the sea of Westland soldiers gathered and waiting in formation around it.

"Don't crowd the bridge!" a stern voice commanded over the ruckus. "Third, Fourth, and Fifth Cavalry, you'll cross next! Stay in order! Your captains will lead you! Once you've cleared some room on the other side, the rest of us will follow. Now go! Take the city! Go take Castlemont!"

More cheers erupted as the orders began to be carried out.

Inside the hastily erected command tent, King Glendar stood with his arms across his chest, tapping a foot impatiently. He was waiting for his two new pageboys to get the carpets unrolled, so his desk could be situated in the center of the pavilion the way he pictured it in his head. The pages were testing his patience to the limits.

Lord Brach led the First and Second Cavalry personally and took control of the massive bridge leading from Westland into Wildermont. He had done well. The taking of the bridge was paramount to this initial operation. Without it, there could be no mass troop crossing. No mass troop crossing meant there would be no element of surprise.

It was just after dawn, and King Glendar was tired and cranky. It was one thing to plan a secret early morning attack, but it was another thing entirely to have to get out of bed to carry it out. He would've much rather been back at Lakeside Castle, sleeping until midmorning, only to be awakened by the hot mouth of one of his many servant girls. But no, Pael insisted Glendar lead the army of the west on this attack. It seemed to Glendar that Pael insisted on a lot of things lately; far too many things. There was no doubt he owed Pael a boon or two for all the help he had given him over the years, but he was king now.

King! It seemed at times that Pael ordered him around as if he were still a child. He'd heard the sniggers in the castle halls, whispering things like, "Wizard's puppet," or "Puppet king." They called him worse when he was growing up. Not anymore, though. Nearly a hundred disloyal sniggering heads decorated the castle yards back at Lakeside. No one dared to say an ill word about him now. He gave one of the pages a glare that promised severe punishment if he didn't hurry up.

"The rest of you go now! Steady, keep it ordered!" the voice outside the tent sounded loudly. "Infantry, you go next! You already know what to do after we cross! Ready to march now! On my command! And march!"

The carpets King Glendar insisted on using each weighed as much as a full grown man and were nearly impossible for the two adolescent boys to manage. On top of that, the youngsters were scared to death of the ill-tempered new king. The younger of the two boys stumbled over the corner of a carpet that was already unrolled and went down in a face-first sprawl. The other page went to help him.

Glendar yelled. "I should mount one of your heads on my desk, to remind your replacements of your clumsiness!"

Neither of the boys considered the threat an idle one. Tears welled in the eyes of the fallen boy. The other wet his pants while trying to help his companion to his feet. At that point, all the work stopped completely. Glendar had scared them stiff.

"What?" Glendar screamed. "What is wrong with you two? It's not complicated! You unroll the blasted rug and move the desk! How hard can it be?" Spittle flew from his clenched teeth. "I guess I'll have to mount both of your heads!" He drew a sword that looked quite similar to Ironspike, but had no magical properties whatsoever. He would've used it to cut off their heads, had Pael not entered the pavilion just then.

"Put the blade away," the wizard commanded sharply.

Glendar spun and looked at Pael as if he had just told him the sky was yellow instead of blue.

"Not now, Pael," he shot back dismissively, then turned his attention back to the trembling boys.

Pael mumbled some unintelligible phrase and made a grasping gesture with his hand, like he was choking the air. The look on King Glendar's face went from anger, to shock, to fear. An invisible hand gripped his throat and was threatening to crush it. It was all he could do to draw in a breath.

"Leave us!" Pael ordered the two pages. They wasted no time starting toward the tent flap.

When they were about halfway to it, Pael stopped them.

"Report to Lady Trella at Lake Bottom Stronghold."

Pael looked each of them in the eyes in turn.

"I may call upon you someday for repayment of this favor. When I do, don't forget that I just stayed your execution."

Seeing that they understood, he dismissed them and turned back to Glendar's purple, gasping face.

Pael didn't loosen his grip on Glendar's neck.

"Are you daft?" he asked the new King of Westland. "Look outside!"

As if dragged by the hand that held his throat, Glendar stumbled forward and peered out of the tent flaps. Of the more than twenty thousand men and horses that had been gathered there in the pre-dawn darkness, only the tail end of the last infantry division and the supply wagons could be seen. King Glendar had been left behind. Only the riff-raff, the whores, the blade sharpeners, and the civilian scavengers hadn't crossed out of Westland yet. King Glendar's personal guard attachment was milling around outside the Command Pavilion, trying desperately to not look embarrassed when the stragglers jeered and pointed at them.

"I told you to lead this army," Pael said, shaking Glendar in his magical grip forcefully. "Those boys you would have killed are on your side, you buffoon! Your blade should be out there in that city, raised against the Redwolf soldiers, not against Westland children!"

As if discarding trash, Pael threw his hand off to the side. Glendar's body followed the motion perfectly, and he ended up sprawled on the trampled grass floor.

"You are nothing, KING Glendar!" Pael ranted as he turned his back to the armed man he had just humiliated. "You're spoiled, stupid, and have no respect for those who placed you where you are. Even your lowliest infantrymen will question your fortitude now."

Glendar wanted so badly to charge across the pavilion and bury his sword in the wizard's back. He wanted it more than he wanted his father to hurry and die after Pael poisoned him. He couldn't bring himself to do it, though. Partly because he needed the wizard: Pael had guided him from childhood, like his father should have. Pael helped him take the throne, and Pael could crush him like a fly if he chose to. And partly because Glendar was afraid, afraid his blade would find nothing but thin air when he struck, or if it did sink into flesh, Pael would only laugh at him and pull it free. He was also afraid he might actually kill the only person in the kingdom he could depend on, or the wizard might go away and never return.

"I thought you—" Glendar started, but was abruptly cut off.

"You THOUGHT Glendar, that is your problem!" Pael turned to face him, his voice brimming with anger. "Someday, boy, you will be in control, and when that time comes, you will make the rules. For now, I am making them. Do not think or wonder why I tell you to do something. JUST DO IT!"

From his knees, Glendar flinched, as if a bolt of lightning might fly from the wizard's hand. Pael sighed, then strode over and extended his hand to help Glendar to his feet. Reluctantly, Glendar took the hand and allowed Pael to pull him up.

"Have I ever lied to you, son?" Pael asked, in a softer voice. "Didn't I hand you the Westland throne on a silver platter? The whole of the eastern kingdoms will be yours as well, if you'll just do as I say."

Glendar still raged defiantly in the back of his mind, but he lowered his head like a scolded schoolboy.

"I will try to listen better, Pael," he said with a heavy exhale of breath.

"Good!" Pael clapped his hands together, then began pacing back and forth across the tent. "The rest of Lord Ellrich's Marsh Guards, from Settsted Stronghold, should be here within the hour. Have a handful of them move this pavilion into Castlemont City and erect it directly in front of King Jarrek's palace."

Pael looked at Glendar for a moment, then added, "Be sure it is out of the wall-top archers' range."

Pael turned and came gliding back across the half-rolled carpet toward the king. His finger went to his smooth chin and his other hand found his elbow. Glendar could see a greenish-blue vein pulsing under the taut skin of Pael's chalky white forehead.

"As soon as this turns into a siege, which it surely will, I want you to send Lord Brach and all the men that can be spared, up into the Wilder Mountains."

King Glendar started to protest, but Pael raised a hand to stop him.

"Trust me, Glendar. Lord Brach is to find, and secure, a route through the mountains that will allow us to gain a favorable position on the Valleyan city of Dreen."

"Our plan was to march south and take as much of Dakahn as we can before winter sets in!" Glendar blurted out.

He and Lord Brach had spent weeks planning. Now Pael was throwing those plans to the dogs and he couldn't hold his tongue.

"King Broderick and Queen Rachel have joined forces," Pael explained. "They are gathering up to march east against Highwander. King Broderick has taken it upon himself to punish Queen Willa the Witch for starting that mess at Summer's Day. They will be beaten back badly by Willa's treacherous Blacksword Warriors.

"If we can get the bulk of our troops through the mountains before winter sets in, then we can take the kingdom seat of Valleya, while King Broderick and his army are still battling in Highwander. By then, Queen Rachel's forces and possibly even the Blacksword Warriors of Highwander will be weakened enough for us to overrun them all."

Pael moved closer to Glendar, stopped his pacing, and looked the young king directly in the eyes.

"I assure you that King Jarrek, the old Redwolf himself, will either bow to you, or he will die when I bring his mighty fortress to the ground. Either way, you will soon assume command of what's left of the Redwolf army, thus doubling the size of our force."

"How will you bring down Castlemont?" Glendar asked doubtfully. "It's as big as the mountain it's built into."

"I will make that palace crumble!"

The force of Pael's words left no doubt in Glendar's mind that he could and would do it.

No army Glendar knew of had ever taken the mountain castle, and he'd recently studied its history fairly well. It was built to survive a dozen years of siege. The original structure, the heart of Castlemont, was connected to massive mine chambers cut into the mountainside. Those chambers were filled with stores upon stores, and a surplus of defensive weapons built for just such an event.

It was rumored that before the dwarves disappeared into the earth, they made several secret ways in and out of the castle. Even if the massive amount of reserves were depleted, they could be restocked through the hidden passages.

Glendar knew Pael would not be the first wizard to try and break Castlemont. Pael was a determined and a powerful Master Mage, but there were other wizards in the realm just as capable, and some of them served King Jarrek and Wildermont. After all, it was the richest kingdom in the realm. Still, it was impossible for Glendar to doubt Pael. The egg-headed wizard, as cocky and controlling as he was, had always kept his word. Always.

"As soon as I tell you to," Pael continued, resuming his back and forth pace across the pavilion, "you will personally travel south to Dakahn and give King Ra'Gren a wagon train full of the Wildermont Wolf's gold in exchange for as many ships as we can fill with our reserve men. While Lord Brach and his group are occupying the capital city of Valleya, you and the others will sail to Seaward City and surprise Queen Rachel while her troops are still aiding King Broderick. No one would expect you to sail out of Dakahn, so you'll take her off guard. After that, it's just a matter of bringing yours and Lord Brach's forces back together again in Highwander to take Xwarda from the Witch Queen."

Then I will assume complete control of the fantastical power contained in all of that Wardstone she guards so dearly, Pael continued in his mind. With that much power and you, KING Glendar, dancing at my fingertips, I'll be able to conquer the giant lands, the elven forests, then the rest of the world as well!

Pael's plan was so perfect it left Glendar speechless. With Dakahn as their allies, they wouldn't have to expend men to commandeer ships or to sail them. Nor would they have to wait for Westland's own ships to make the long journey, from Portsmouth and Southport, down around the islands and the marshes. Even if Queen Rachel managed to aid her cousin by sending troops to help defend the Valleyan Capital from Lord Brach's army, she would only be depleting her own forces in Seaward City. When Glendar and his troops landed at her doorstep, she would have no choice but to bow down to him. The bulk of her army would be scattered about Highwander and Valleya. Pael's plan made the fall of the eastern kingdoms seem inevitable. It would be nothing less than a rout.

Glendar's silence snapped Pael out of his glorious reverie. He wasn't one to get caught up in daydreams. What was it King Balton used to say so often? Oh yes, "Think, then act." They were wise words from a goodhearted king; a king Pael despised and disposed of.

He looked at Glendar, and the boy's stupid expression put him back on track.

"Of course, my King, this glorious battle plan was your own idea. You will be remembered as one of the greatest strategists and commanders of all time."

Pael bowed mockingly, then snapped back up screaming his next words. "NOW DO AS I SAY!"

The wizard's breath shot forth like a blast of wind, hitting Glendar full in the face. It felt like an arctic gale, icy and cold. Glendar had to lean forward to keep from being bowled over by the force of it. His hand instinctually went to shield his face, but by the time it was in place, the demonstration was over and he was stumbling forward to catch his balance.

"The men from Settsted are arriving," Pael continued as if nothing out of the ordinary had just happened. He acted as though he were on the outside of the pavilion and could see the men with his own two eyes, as if King Glendar wasn't wiping ice crystals from his eyelashes.

"I suggest you claim a few of them to attend to your command pavilion. The rest of the Southern Muster should arrive on the morrow. Have them round up every single Wildermont man, woman, and child who can't wield a weapon or pull a cart. When the siege begins, have a detachment of soldiers march them down through Low Crossing and on to O'Dakahn. Send a scroll presenting them to King Ra'Gren as a gift. He and his slavers will like that. It will help his Overlords to see things our way when we need their ships later."

Pael stopped pacing again and searched Glendar for some sign that he had been paying attention. When he was satisfied with what he saw, he made for the tent flap. He had more pressing matters to attend to this day.

"Pael," Glendar called as the wizard was about to leave.

"What is it, boy? I have business elsewhere."

King Glendar's eyes found the ground somewhere between the two of them. "Thank you," he mumbled.

"You're welcome, son," Pael replied almost warmly. Then he disappeared out the tent flap.

Pael spent half of the day flying back to his tower in the form of a crow. He could have transformed himself into a larger bird, an eagle or a condor, and made the trip in half the time, but he didn't want to attract attention to himself. He wasn't so much worried about the old and infirm, mothers, and small children who were all that was left inhabiting the Kingdom of Westland. It was more of a precaution, born of careful habits, and distrust of those who might try to detect his movements. He was certain there were still plenty of enemies about. They would expect him to fly as something powerful and proud. None of them, he hoped, would question the flight of a common carrion bird, such as a lowly crow.

While he was flying, Pael thought about King Glendar. He wondered how the boy could've turned out so completely ignorant and pig-headed. He could just picture the fool stepping out of his Command Pavilion into a flurry of Wildermont long arrows because he set the tent too close to the wall. He had to bite back the chirping cackle that passed for a crow's laugh. As he neared his destination, his thoughts drifted toward Shaella's last message. He hoped he had enough time to properly prepare for what was to come. There was much to do.

Once he was in sight of Lion's Lake and Lakeside Castle, he made for the gaping hole the demon Shokin had left in his tower wall. Inside, he returned to his human form and took his lift down to the darkened library, where a dozen ancient texts were spread out across an old reading table. With a point of his finger, the lamp hanging from a brass wall hook flared to life, and the dimness of the musty room abated. Grotesque forms of melted dripping wax spread away from tiny used-up candle nubs at the table's corners.

Most of the last few days, Pael had been there gathering in every bit of knowledge he could find on the subject of binding a spectral demon. He had learned much, but not enough.

He made a note to himself to send for more candles and not for the first time, found that he missed Inkling. Having to seek out a lamp after the candles guttered out while in the middle of reading an account of the Priests of Kraw was a great reminder of how the minute details of a thing can suddenly become paramount. He could've just cast a light spell, but then the forty-odd pages of the priests' tediously scribbled writing he had been committing to memory would have to be reread. It was easier to snatch a lantern from the laboratory below. Now he smiled at the wisdom of that decision. It had been far easier than traipsing through the castle in search of candles.

The Priests of Kraw were necromancers and seemed to know all sorts of useful things about dealing with demons, devils, and the undead. Why they so carelessly let the journals and manuscripts detailing some of their greater achievements get out of their hands, Pael didn't know. Once he had control of the Wardstone and all the power that came with it, he would go to the Isle of Borinia and ask them himself.

In the years that passed since Pavreal created the Demon Seal, the Priests of Kraw had become nothing more than second-rate cultists, but Pael wasn't about to set foot on their island without enough power at his command to defend himself. As pitiful as they appeared to be now, he was far too wise to underestimate them. That was for another day, though. What he needed from the priests was right before him.

Pael's library shelves were many; all of them were crowded with books, both new and old. The texts were from everywhere one could imagine, and from some places that defied what the untrained mind could fathom. Ancient volumes from the Dwarven Eminence, the journals of a dozen elven druids, and an entire shelf of manuscripts that Pael couldn't yet translate supposedly from the lands beyond the Giant Mountains, took up only a corner of the room.

Pael had even collected, in his vast travels, a dedicated set of drawings that detailed Afdeon, the Giant King's massive stronghold. The shelves along the library's walls were crammed to the point of bowing. There was a set of calfskin volumes so old that to open them without the aid of powerful, protective spells would destroy the pages. There were also Pael's spell books, immaculately bound and neatly scribed. His three compendia of arcane knowledge sat on a crate on the floor, looking like the other crudely stacked piles of forgotten texts. To touch them without speaking the proper phrases was to invite a most horrible death. Pael didn't want those who tried to violate his precious secrets to die quickly. He wanted to be able to interrogate them while they withered.

The books he had out on the table all referenced the Dragon Pact, Pavreal's Seal, or the binding of spectral demons. Pael was searching for a way to keep Shokin's dark and mighty power under his control after he opened the Seal and released him. He needed a way to bind the demon to his will, to enslave its vast power, and control it for as long as he needed to. He would need the power to manipulate the Wardstone to its full potential, and the added might wouldn't hurt when he returned to Castlemont to fulfill his promise to King Glendar.

He read on through the night and through the next day as well until finally, he found what he had been looking for. A sorcerer from the wild and distant land of Harthgar had kept a diary. The Priests of Kraw made a copy of it. Pael obtained it years ago and now after scouring it, he knew what he needed to know. With the Harthgarian sorcerer's spell and a human sacrifice to bind the deed, he could open the Seal, release Shokin, and make the demon's will and power his own. He didn't need to find a sacrifice, though. One would be waiting for him when he got there. Shaella was going to send an excellent offering up into the dragon's nest to do her bidding. Pael laughed merrily, because he couldn't have planned it more perfectly.

Without regard for his need of sleep and sustenance, he excitedly began gathering the things he would need to perform the ceremony. He had no time to rest. His timing must be just right. Too early and Shaella would fail; too late and the sacrifice would've come and gone.

He wasn't feeling spell-weary, even though he had flown half of the day while holding a transformation spell on himself, so he took what he needed and made to position himself.

Exactly as Pael predicted, the battle at Castlemont City slowly turned into a siege. Westland's armored cavalry swept through the streets swiftly and easily. Resistance was met in many places, and hundreds of Glendar's men died.

The Redwolf soldiers lived up to their reputation and fought hard for every inch of ground, but it wasn't enough. In the end, Westland's overwhelming numbers, coupled with the suddenness of the attack, allowed young King Glendar's army to gain control of everything outside of the castle's massive outer walls. Siege engines were in place now, and once unleashed, the mighty Wolf King would have to retreat behind the castle's formidable secondary wall. The lay of the mountain would be in King Jarrek's favor after that. New siege engines would have to be built, because there was no way to get anything larger than a wagon through the steep, crowded lanes between the two walls. Glendar didn't care though. He was confident his wizard would come soon.

There was plenty to do to keep his men busy until Pael came to crumble the castle for him. After ordering Lord Brach to take his troops and carve a path to Dreen through the Wilder Mountains, he ordered another group of his soldiers to begin gathering and herding the innocent folk of Wildermont into pens. Later, he would have them escorted south to O'Dakahn and give them to King Ra'Gren, but for now he would go pick out a few of the prettier women and make them service him while he waited on Pael. After all, the King of Westland, if anyone, was due his share of the spoils of war.

Chapter Twenty-Seven

Gerard Skyler was scared, but not of the climb he was about to make. He was comfortable with that. He was also comfortable with the plan they had come up with—at least he was comfortable with it after he removed all of the Geka lizards, rope ladders, and pulley wheels from the proposal, then simplified it.

Gerard decided the Zard weren't the smartest of creatures after hearing what they had originally been planning to do. And as reptiles, they were instinctually afraid of the dragon's lair. At the moment, though, all Gerard could do was tremble and pray to the goddess that Flick was capable of keeping the huge creatures swimming in the water around their canoe from eating them.

He felt like he was sitting right in the water with the huge, toothy snappers that looked to be all around them. Most of the long, thick, gator-like beasts were as big, if not bigger, than the canoe. It would take only one swift chop to splinter the craft to pieces, and it was all Gerard could do to keep from covering his eyes and whimpering.

He didn't want to know what made that powerful thumping splash behind them. The waves caused by the ruckus threatened to come up over the sides of the little boat. He would have to stand up in the canoe soon, and he was trying not to think about it. He had no idea how he was going to keep his balance while he stood. The only thing he was sure of was he didn't want any part of his body in that murky, tooth-filled water. Not even a boot tip.

He did his best to focus his attention on the towering formation he was about to climb. He decided it was correctly named for it rose up out of the marsh and tapered to a sharp point, while curving slightly to the east, exactly like a fang. It was completely black, formed out of a rough and porous type of stone. The way it rose up out of the swamp and loomed over the tiny canoe did little to ease his discomfort.

Gerard motioned for Flick to take them to the western side of the Dragon's Tooth. The way the east side of it curved slowly outward, it would be impossible to climb. If he tried that side, he would be dangling from his handholds after the midway point.

To the common eye, the western side looked no easier. It was dauntingly steep, but to Gerard it appeared to be a simple climb. To him, it was like a ladder leading up to where the curve started laying over toward the east. After that, it was more like a steep stairway. It would be one of the easiest climbs he had ever made.

His destination was a cavern that went all the way through the formation, up near the sharp tip of the fang. It was like a giant worm had bored a hole from east to west, all the way through the black rock, a thousand feet above the surface of the swamp. The dragon lived in that hole, but Shaella had a plan to keep it occupied, while Gerard snatched away one of its eggs.

He looked at the surface of the stone as they drew closer, then craned his head back and looked up toward the dragon's lair. There were plenty of hand and toeholds, no slick hawkling dung to contend with, no angry mother birds pecking and clawing at him, no sheer freefall down to the Lip, or to the rocky canyon floor below it. If Shaella could keep the dragon away, this would be easy. If Shaella couldn't keep the dragon away—Gerard didn't want to think about that.

Shaella and half a hundred of the creepy Zardmen were to handle her part of the plan. She swore to Gerard over and over since the night of the feast that she would keep the dragon from its lair until he was down and safely back in the canoe with Flick. Last night, as they lay in each other's arms, she had sworn it again.

"You'll never even see the dragon after it comes out to feed," she said, and he believed her.

Even though she wanted him, he hadn't made love to her last night, or the night before. This confused her. He explained having sex before a rigorous climb weakened a man's legs and softened his heart. He told her that was the reason the Skyler women weren't allowed near the harvest lodge when he and his clansmen took the hawkling eggs each year. They laughed together when he told her that his grandfather called the complication love legs and that his older brother, Hyden, had to explain to him what it meant, because his mother was too embarrassed to broach the subject with him. Gerard told Shaella only a fool would climb after a night in bed with her. She took that as a compliment and spent the night nestled against him with her head on his shoulder.

From the western side, the Dragon's Tooth Spire looked more like a fish fin than a fang. It made sense to Gerard, when he remembered Shaella's explanation of how the water had been flowing past the formation from north to south, eroding it for ages upon ages. He looked up and could see rays of the morning sun shining through the Dragon's Wormhole. He studied the spot, letting the location firmly imprint in his mind.

The idea of standing up and maneuvering from the canoe to the rock face sent a ripple of nerves through him. He found himself scanning the water along the base of the spire for any sign of the ferocious-looking snappers that might be lurking there. He didn't see any but felt little relief for it.

"Get us directly under the dragon's hole," he said quietly to Flick.

He went about checking the backpack sitting in the floor of the canoe between his feet. It was fairly heavy, and going through it again helped him forget about the water and the things swimming in it.

The pack contained over a thousand feet of thin but strong cord, a makeshift sling cradle to put the dragon's egg in, a few pieces of dried and salted snake-meat, and two skins of water.

The plan was simple enough: get up there, locate the eggs, and lower one down. Cole would be waiting for it on the eastern side of the spire, where the curve of the formation caused the Wormhole to open up over nothing but air and water. It was simple. The climb down would be easy, because the pack would be empty, and he would be using the western face again. It seemed the whole thing was going to be too easy. Something Berda had once said, a saying, was floating at the back of Gerard's mind, but he couldn't quite grasp it.

"We're below the lair now," said Flick.

From the moment Gerard had fought alongside the group on the riverboat, they began to treat him as one of their own. They respected him and seemed to trust his abilities. The look on Flick's face was a mixture of reverence and worry as he eased the little boat up close to the base of the formation.

"Are you sure you can do this?" he asked Gerard. "It's a long way up to the lair." His voice was hushed, as if speaking too loudly might bring the dragon's wrath down upon them.

"Just make sure Cole is there to take the egg, and that you're here to get me when I come back down," Gerard chuckled nervously. "I can make this climb in my sleep, but I don't know how to swim."

"I swear I'll be here," Flick said, with an honest grin on his face. "You're a brave young man. Shaella chose well."

Gerard wasn't sure what Flick meant, so he didn't reply to the man's words. Instead, he stated the obvious, in a hesitant tone that betrayed just how tense and high-strung he was feeling at the moment.

"I guess…w…we just wait for th…the dragon to leave now."

Shaella and her troop of lizard men used two of the big four-legged gekas to drag their bait into the dragon's feeding ground. The gekas' riders were having a hard time keeping the big creatures calm. The harsh smell of rot coming from the uncooked remains of the dragon's previous meals was thick in the air, and the fresh meat they were dragging was far too close to them. Every creature in the deep marsh understood who the highest predator of the area was, and the dragon almost always carried its kills to this clearing to roast and consume them. Had the gekas not been as afraid of the Zards' whips as they were of the dragon, they would have been nowhere near the area.

Greyber and his detachment of Zard stood alertly by, ready and waiting to do their part of the plan. Once Shaella's troop had the giant snapper they were dragging in place, he and his Zardmen would be responsible for skinning the carcass. Shaella had been adamant: blood, plenty of blood, and exposed meat. The Zardmen all knew the drill. They had been feeding the dragon here for months in preparation for this very day.

Shaella had been on edge all morning. Those around her assumed it was because of the danger in which her lover was putting himself. That or the pressure she would be under to keep the dragon distracted long enough for him to do his deed. It was more than that, though. She tried to get Gerard to let Greyber climb with him, but he refused her, saying he could manage far better on his own.

"The man might be strong and handy in a sword fight," Gerard said, "but on the side of a rock face, he would be nothing more than dead weight."

Shaella stormed away after that, with what might have been tears in her eyes. She couldn't change his mind. Gerard was climbing alone or he wasn't climbing at all.

She was worried for Gerard, but for a different reason than anyone suspected. Another hawkling had arrived bearing a message from Pael. It was Pael she feared. He wanted her to make sure that her climber stayed in the dragon's lair until he arrived. She tried and tried to send Greyber, or one of the Zard, up into the cavern with him, but Gerard was as hardheaded and proud as any man she had ever known. She just wanted someone up there to watch his back. She knew she should've explained the situation to him, but she hadn't been able to. Tears began to flow when she tried, and she would have rather died than to have her Zard army see her as a worried, lovesick girl. Her mission, and Pael's, had to come first. No matter how much heartache it caused her, she had to keep everything in perspective.

Maybe Pael wasn't going to do anything drastic to Gerard when he came. If Gerard didn't dally after he did what he was supposed to do, then he would be down before Pael arrived anyway. If that happened, she knew she would have to deal with Pael's wrath, but she could handle it. She held out hope she could get Gerard out of there safely, even if Pael did catch him unawares. It was a slim hope that would require a great deal of good fortune and more than a little bit of skill on her part, but none of it would matter at all if they couldn't get the dragon to come out of the lair to feed.

Once the snapper was in place, the gekas were ridden away. The stubborn hesitance they had shown only moments before evaporated when they realized they were being directed to move out of the feeding grounds.

Now it was Greyber's turn. He and his group charged out and began hacking through the thick-plated skin of the creature. When they were through it, they peeled back the hide to expose the fresh pink meat. Blood flowed freely. There was no shortage of fresh gore-scent to draw the dragon.

Just to be sure, Cole cast a spell that carried the aroma wafting right up into the dragon's lair. It wouldn't take long to arouse the great red wyrm. The Zard had been placing snapper here regularly for half a year, and those meals had been left plain and unskinned. This offering was being prepared specifically to entice the dragon, and at an interval at least a week longer than usual. All that was left to do now was take cover and wait.

As if tempting fate, Shaella boldly walked out to the would-be feast and began slinging some specially prepared liquid contents from a fat wineskin, over the most readily available meat. Only after the bladder was completely empty did she join the others in the cover that surrounded the wretched-smelling bone-strewn clearing.

Gerard and Flick didn't have to wait very long. A deep, rumbling roar sounded from above. It was so loud that it could have come from an arm's reach away. Gerard thought he saw tiny ripples radiating away from the rocky formations he was about to climb.

When the dragon finally leapt from its lair, there was a moment of pause as its wings unfurled, then a heavy whooshing THUMP! as they caught air. It was huge. Far larger than Gerard imagined it could be. It was easily a hundred feet long, maybe more. Gerard found himself trembling in place and otherwise unable to move.

"I hope she can keep that away from here," Gerard whispered in a quavering voice.

His mind raced for an excuse to back out of this madness, but his thoughts kept going back to all the macho bravado he spouted during the planning of it. He decided he would rather die than to face Shaella and the others as a coward.

The whole canoe was trembling now, and he was certain it wasn't just him. Only a fool wouldn't be afraid of the sight of such a perfect predator, and Flick was far from a fool. Gerard found some relief in knowing the mage was scared, too. He took a few deep breaths and decided he was as ready as he ever would be. He shouldered the backpack into place and, ever so gently, stood up in the canoe. For a heart stopping moment, the craft jerked and wobbled under his feet. Only after his hands found the rock face and he gripped it tightly, could he still himself and let the flock of birds flying around in his rib cage settle down.

The hardest part was getting that first foot to leave the floor of the canoe. Once he managed that, it was all instinct. He was so intent on getting this over with, he didn't hear what Flick was saying. Apparently, it wasn't that important.

Flick's voice died away as he watched Gerard racing like a madman up and away from him. He shook his head in amazement. He'd seen lizards that couldn't climb as swiftly. He decided Shaella couldn't have chosen a better person for this task. The young man was amazing.

As Gerard expected, the climb was easy. The weight of all that coiled line in his pack was the only inconvenience. He could bear the burden though, and the knowledge he wouldn't have to carry it all back down gave him comfort.

Each time he gained a new foothold, he found himself thanking his brother Hyden. The new horse-hide boots were gripping the strange black rock extremely well. The stuff was crumbly, though. More than once, he had to resituate before pushing or pulling his body upward.

Thoughts of being roasted to the wall by spewing gouts of dragon fire came and went, as did thoughts of how pleased Shaella would be when this was all done. The physical and emotional rewards she had already given him outweighed any amount of gold she could offer. He could only imagine how she would reward him later this night, when his body was too tired to move, and the dragon's egg was safe in her custody.

He smiled as he climbed on. He'd learned long ago from his Elders and cousins that the only thing you couldn't think about while climbing, was falling. He wasn't afraid of falling. Falling didn't hurt a bit. It was the sudden stop at the end that got you.

There was too much going on in his head for those sorts of thoughts to linger. He began to contemplate Shaella's army of skeeks. What was she planning to do? It was obvious she was their leader. They were definitely planning something more than just stealing this dragon's egg. The idea Shaella might really be a lizard woman in disguise came to him. After he shivered the revulsion away, he stopped climbing, and laughed at himself.

When he started up again, he wondered what Hyden was doing these days. He was probably lolling around the clan village or out roaming the hills with his bow. He definitely wasn't doing anything this exciting. Maybe he was chasing the little hawkling around. It was probably big enough to fly now.

He wondered if Hyden won the archery competition at Summer's Day. If there was one thing Gerard regretted about leaving the way he did, it was that he didn't get to see the competition. He would've loved to stay and watch Hyden beat those snotty elves.

It was at that moment in his thoughts, that he remembered the stupid, old fortune teller he and his brother had seen. He was just over halfway up to the dragon's lair. The climbing was so easy now that he barely needed his hands for more than balance.

What had that old crone said? His blood grew cold. Shaella was supposed to betray him up here. The old hag had almost choked on her own words and died, but he had seen the vision play out in his mind's eye as the old woman was speaking to him. He had been watching Shaella, and some older, stronger-looking version of Cole argue vehemently in a cavern. The dragon was there, too. What else had she shown him? He searched his memory. He couldn't give the crone credit for her prophecies. It was absurd. All those people couldn't possibly be about to converge on the dragon's lair. How would they get there? Suddenly, it came to him. He remembered the rest of the old hag's words. He would find the power he sought in the depths of the dragon's cave. Depths? He laughed. There were no depths at this height. The rest was just as silly. What was it? He would die, live again, then die and live again. Why had she said it twice, he wondered?

The question was still fresh in his mind when he pulled himself up into the mouth of the bone-strewn dragon's lair.

Shaella's plan wasn't going as well as expected. The dragon had already killed, scorched, or eaten half of the Zardmen in the troop. The beast was a thousand times fiercer and agile than any of the dragons written about in the accounts and stories she studied. A beast such as this could destroy an army of men at its leisure. How the Giants of Afdeon had once killed such a creature without the aid of magic was beyond her.

Red-scaled fury filled the clearing. Huge, yellowed teeth and bright, backlit amber eyes glared and scowled as the dragon spewed forth gouts of flame. Crushing claws and a whipping tail came out of nowhere to dispatch any who were within reach; such was the wrath of the dragon.

Greyber was writhing on the ground, his screams slowly fading away with his life. He lost his sword arm and most of his shoulder to a snap of angry jaws. As if to silence a pesky insect, the dragon stomped on the Seawardsman's body with her huge hind claw, and ground him into the bloody mud.

The dragon seemed content to stand and battle with them. It wasn't the least bit injured, and was in complete control of the situation. In fact, like a cat toying with a mouse, the great wyrm seemed to be enjoying the sport.

That was the problem. The sleeping potion Shaella doused the meat with should have been enough to at least tire the ferocious beast, but it wasn't so. The dragon was quite a bit larger than she expected it to be, and it charred the snapper meat to a sizzling crisp before tearing into it. The heat of the flames must've evaporated most of her concoction. It was a costly mistake, one she was doing her best to compensate for.

"Run and get a hundred more Zard here as swiftly as possible," she ordered a bug-eyed, green-scaled archer. "Have some others bring a geka, two, if they can manage to get them here."

"Yes, Masteress," the lizard man responded before scampering away gratefully on his long, webbed feet.

She hated to sacrifice so many here, but the egg and the bargain with Pael was paramount to the larger scheme of things. He had the Staff of Malice, and she needed it to free the Breed beasts that King Balton imprisoned at Coldfrost. She needed those huge savages to help her hold what she was about to take. Pael needed the dragon out of its lair, so he could access the ancient Seal the beast had been guarding. Now that the pact that bound the dragon to guard the Seal was broken, she could trick it into service by threatening one of the eggs. It was a complex plan, and she was dancing on a delicate, razor-sharp edge here. She might have scrapped the plan because the loss of Zards was going to be so great, but now Gerard's safety factored itself into the equation. She had no choice but to feed the great wyrm bits of her army a few at a time until Gerard got an egg down to Cole. Only then would she attempt to get the situation back under her control.

Thinking about the greater plan and all that went into preparing for what was to come, she conceded she might have to give Gerard to Pael, but only if it became necessary. The cold and relentless fury of the dragon was rubbing off on her. She loved Gerard, but she was a sorceress of the dark arts, and she knew if she wanted to have all that she desired, she had better start acting like one.

A roaring blast of heat sent her scrambling to the side. Luckily, it was aimed at the dragon's main course and not at her. The Zard weren't faring too well. Their swords were useless, as were mere arrows. There was only one way to end the dragon's tirade, and the only way she could get it done was to keep it here, distracted from its lair. The icy resolve she found gave her strength. A human man's fleeting life could never really come between her and all she had worked so hard for. At least, she hoped it couldn't.

After tearing another huge slab of scorched meat from the snapper carcass, the dragon raised her head and wolfed the morsel down. As Shaella gained her feet again, Cole scrambled across part of the clearing toward her. All the while, the great wyrm swiped and lashed its treacherous tail at the Zard, as if they were only flies disturbing its meal.

"Flick says that he's in the cavern," Cole said, in a way that showed his surprise and respect of the speed of Gerard's climb.

"You should go then! He could already be lowering the egg!"

She had to yell over the dragon's rumbling growl. Her voice was full of equal parts of apprehension, worry, and excitement. Cole pretended not to notice.

"What a waste it would be if a snapper were to snatch the egg up as soon as it was floating in the swamp," she added, in an attempt to hurry him.

"I'm off then," Cole responded and began casting the spell that would take him where he needed to go. Just before he began to shimmer away, she stopped him.

"Return just as soon as you have it!"

Her voice had become hard and commanding. "No matter the cost!" she added.

Cole's response was a slight smile and a knowing nod, as his form wavered and faded from the clearing.

The dragon roared again and reared up as if it were about to leap into flight. A cold chill of horror ripped through Shaella. She couldn't let it leave yet. Not now, not when they were so close. She spun around, searching for the replacements she had requested. They were nowhere to be seen. Only a handful of the lizard men that started this with her were left, and they were hiding at the edges of the clearing. Unable to think of another option, she drew her sword and charged out into the feeding ground, waving her pale yellow, magical blade around crazily. She screamed out challenges and curses in an old tongue, a language the great wyrms were supposed to understand.

It was a gamble born of desperation. She hoped she could draw the beast's attention and keep it there. When the dragon cocked its head and eyed her with curious fury, she felt her knees turn to water. Suddenly, she found she wished it had flown away, that it would fly away now. As it pulled its wings back and lowered its head toward her, the great beast drew in a long, slow breath.

Shaella couldn't help but ask herself the obvious question, "What was I thinking?"

Chapter Twenty-Eight

The dragon's lair was a deep, bubble-like pocket which swelled off to one side of the huge wormhole. It was lit by the sun shining into the eastern mouth of the tunnel. The bright rays illuminated over half of the rocky passage's floor. From the opening in the western face where Gerard was standing, it was less than two hundred paces across to the gaping sunlit maw on the other side. Piles of bones, from creatures both large and small, were scattered among the rubble. The horrid smell of decaying flesh would have been unbearable had there not been the natural breezeway caused by the wormhole, continually drawing in fresh air while venting the foul.

Gerard started into the dragon's lair. The only thoughts in his mind were to get in, lower the egg out the other side, then climb back down, and do it all quickly. To keep his fear or any other distracting emotion from creeping in and getting hold of him, he repeated those thoughts over and over again. Get in, lower the egg, climb down, and hurry.

He made his way to where the cavern opened up into the actual dragon's lair. It wasn't easy. He had to climb over several odd-shaped pieces of broken stone, and had to wiggle his way between others. He had to hold down his bile while climbing over a wet, matted tangle of hair, bone, and gore.

Some of the skeletons he saw were alarmingly large. Others were undoubtedly human. One was still covered in rusted and crushed armor. A series of fist-sized holes ran in a line across the breastplate. Teeth marks, Gerard thought, and then he shivered.

He spotted the eggs easily enough: three of them. They were in a shadowy nook at the back of the lair, nestled in a pile of animal hides that had been crudely thrown over a bowl-shaped pile of bones.

"I guess dragons don't like to sit on their nests like hawklings do," he said the thought out loud.

The sound of his voice was comforting. In the back of his mind, he repeated his mantra again. Get in, lower the egg, climb down, and hurry.

On his way across the rank, musty lair to retrieve one of the eggs, he noticed something peculiar. The cavern bottom here wasn't rough and rocky: it was level like a floor. After further examination, he found that it actually was a floor. It had to be. It was perfectly smooth. It even had a design carved into it. Most of the circular inscription was buried under bones and scree, but he could see its center. The dust-filled grooves were a finger's breadth wide, and easily as deep. A circle, twice as big as a wagon wheel, framed a strange symbol. Around it there were other, smaller symbols, like ancient writing. These went all the way around the inner ring. There was another ring outside that. It reminded him of an archery target, only with a strange symbol for its Wizard's Eye. Sure enough, a few feet farther across the floor, he saw yet another ring that shared the same center as the others. He found himself staring at the markings, as if he were momentarily hypnotized.

Get in, lower the egg, climb down, and hurry, his mind screamed, snapping him out of his daze.

"Get the egg, lower it down, then get out," he said the words aloud and kept repeating them as he moved to the nest.

The eggs were the size of summer melons, and when he hefted one into his arms, he realized lowering this thing wasn't going to be quick and easy. It weighed about as much as a full sack of grain.

"This is going to take some doing," he mumbled under his breath.

He had to keep his mind on track. He kept feeling the urge to go back and stare at the strange markings carved into the floor but his fear of the dragon and of failing Shaella kept him from it.

He carefully carried the egg out of the lair. It was no easy task, getting over and around the rough bottom of the wormhole, without the use of his hands and arms to steady himself. More than once, he stumbled and nearly let go of the egg. Absently, he wondered why a dragon would need a floor like that, and if it did, why hadn't the floor of the whole place been leveled out? It sure would have made getting the egg over to the eastern cavern mouth a lot easier. He was nervous. He had assumed it was going to be an in and out sort of thing. Now he wasn't sure at all. He knew he had to hurry; he knew Shaella couldn't keep the dragon occupied all day.

Gerard cradled the egg among the rocks near the opening and yanked off his pack. He hurriedly started pulling out the coils of rope.

Suddenly, he stopped himself. He couldn't afford to get it tangled, so he took a deep breath and went about laying the coils out, so that they would hopefully unroll without snagging on anything. Once he began lowering the egg, he didn't want to have to stop for any reason whatsoever. The sling for the egg was nothing more than a net sack, and once he had it slipped over the prize, he tied the rope to it securely. After that, he took one of the water flasks and drank.

He studied the opening. When he had come up with this part of the plan, he had figured that the egg would be a lot lighter. He had imagined himself lying on his belly with his head, arms, and shoulders hanging out of the opening. He planned to play out the rope while watching the egg go down. This egg was far too heavy for that. If he so much as jerked it while it was going down, it would probably yank him out of the cavern mouth. He found he wouldn't have been able to get his body into that position, anyway. Two big formations like jagged bottom teeth jutted up from the opening. He decided that he could use them to brace his feet on, and lower the egg from a sitting position. The only problem was the place between the two rock teeth was rough, and might wear the rope apart as it slid over.

He drained the last of the water from the skin and tossed it to the side. Whatever he was going to do, he had to hurry. He stepped to the edge and looked down. He saw nothing but an endless expanse of green, spreading away from the black, murky water below him. The thought that if just this tiny bit of rock beneath his feet crumbled he would be falling made him pull back into the cavern. Never, in all his life, not once in all the hundreds of times he had looked down from the heights, had he felt such a dizzying and disorienting feeling. He knew why he had felt it, too. It was because there was nothing there: nothing to cling to, no cliff, or rock face. It was just open air all the way down. No sooner had he mastered that fear, than the sunken feeling that he had already taken too much time started to creep into his mind. He had to move. After a few deep breaths, he came up with an idea.

He darted back through the wormhole, covering the rocky, uneven floor with ease now that his hands and arms were free to help him stay balanced, and went to the nearest of the larger skeletons. It had been some monstrous winged thing. Probably a smaller dragon, which had come into this one's territory, or some other kind of beast he had never heard of. There was no skull, so it was impossible to guess. After a few moments of grunted effort, he had what he wanted: a bone. It was roughly as big around as his forearm, and about as long as his whole leg. It was perfect for what he intended, and he thought for the first time he just might get this thing done and get out of there before the dragon came home.

He got back into position, laid the bone across the base of the two teeth-like rocks, and then situated himself on his butt, with his feet against the teeth. With a grunt of effort, he lifted the egg up and over the gap between them, and let the rope slip a few feet down. The friction heated his hands quickly, but he didn't let loose his grip. He had to be careful. He needed his hands to make the climb back down, and he couldn't allow them to get rope-burned. He chided himself for not thinking to bring gloves with him. Greyber suggested it, but since Gerard didn't climb with gloves, he'd dismissed the idea. He hadn't figured the egg would weigh so much. It was a mistake that he wasn't about to let himself forget.

The rope ran through Gerard's hands, out over the rounded middle of the bone he had placed across the teeth, and then it disappeared down toward the marsh below. Where the rope would've been dragged over coarse and abrasive stone, it now slid smoothly over the hard, yellowed bone. Only the slightest edge of the rope even touched the rocky cavern's mouth.

As if trying to pull a spear out of his sternum, Gerard played out the rope hand over hand. He was tempted to use his boot to clamp the rope against the bone, and let the egg fall at a controlled speed, but he thought better of it. If he failed to stop it, or slow it down, it might splatter into the water below. If that happened he would have to pull the seemingly endless rope back up, and start again with another egg.

Already his body was screaming at him, sending hot wires of tight, burning heat from his fingertips, up his arms, and over his shoulders into his back. A glance at the coil of rope that remained told him the egg was barely halfway to the bottom. The idea his arms might get too sore for him to make the climb back down crossed his mind and added to the panic swirling in the back of his head. His shoulders and back were throbbing. His grip was getting looser and looser; his palms were starting to feel raw and slick with blood. He had to stop and rest, but how?

Cole shimmered into being on a tiny island, which was only large enough to hold the roots of a single drooping tree. A huge snapper had crept up alongside the canoe he left there. It probably thought it was another of its kind, lazing in the sun. It was as startled by Cole's sudden appearance as Cole was by its unexpected presence. Cole stood stock still and let the bird flying loose in his chest settle, while the big beast slithered casually away into the water.

Once he calmed himself enough to move again, Cole glanced up at the opening in the eastern side of the Dragon Spire. Nothing was there yet. He was glad he didn't have to hurry. He found he was greatly troubled by appearing so close to a deadly predator. One could make plan after plan and be as cautious as possible, Cole thought grimly, and still end up the victim of pure chance and circumstance. The concept was eye-opening to him. Until that moment, he firmly believed in Pael's theory that careful planning and well-timed execution could overcome anything. It was the first time he ever came close to thinking against what his mentor had taught him.

Pael was wrong about this, he understood now. There was always the random chance that something out of your control would force you to improvise. Of course, that's why Pael so adamantly studied the situations in which he might find himself. Cole chose to re-evaluate his ideas just a little bit. Unlike Pael, he didn't have an endless supply of research material, and the quantified power of a master wizard. Had he only appeared a few feet closer to the snapper's maw, the creature could have gotten hold of him before he even knew what was happening. He decided later he would think about ways to avoid such a predicament. That's what Pael would tell him to do, but right now he had other things to attend to.

He stepped into the canoe and shoved off in one fluid motion. He didn't have far to go to get into position. He had chosen the tiny island because it was impossible for him to appear in a drifting canoe. Unlike a larger craft, the canoe would spin and twist with the currents and the wind, even if it was anchored. As with the snapper, being just a few feet off could mean appearing over open water.

Once he had the egg, he would have to row back to the island before he could transport himself back to Shaella. It wouldn't do to shimmer into existence in the middle of the body-strewn clearing while in a sitting position, with an egg in his lap. He would have to be ready for anything, and on his feet in case he had to duck and run, or otherwise flee the dragon when he appeared.

He looked up again, and was relieved to see the egg coming down. He had his doubts about the mountain-clan boy's plan, but hadn't been able to doubt his confidence. The boy had been certain his plan would work, and since Gerard had proven his loyalty back on the riverboat, Cole gave him the respect he deserved. He didn't want to doubt him openly, or do anything that might take away from the boy's confidence. And besides, the plan was a fairly good one.

In a small way, he was jealous. He was supposed to have been the one to get the egg for Shaella, but every time he attempted to teleport himself up to the dragon's cavern, he failed. Whether the place had wards against such comings and goings, or it was just too high from the surface of the earth for his magic to take him, he couldn't say. Maybe it was because it was surrounded by water. He was sure that if he could shape-change, he could fly up into the cavern, but that level of spell casting was beyond his ability as of yet. He once thought Shaella was powerful enough to change forms, but now he wasn't so sure. If she could've gotten the egg without risking Gerard, she would have.

Cole saw how much she had come to care about the young man, how protective of him she was. He knew it would soon be a problem. He only hoped that she would make the proper decisions when the time came. If she chose well, Cole was certain she could have everything she was after, including Gerard, but too much was at stake to let love blind her. Far too much was at stake.

When Cole looked up again, he saw the egg had been lowered a considerable distance. He stared up at it from the drifting canoe for a long time, before he realized it had stopped coming down. It was just hanging there a few hundred feet above him, swinging slightly with the breeze.

Suddenly, Cole was alarmed. His mind raced through the myriad possibilities that could have forced Gerard to stop lowering it: injury, not enough rope, a tangle, or another creature might have been lurking up there. He was just about to panic, when the egg lurched down a few feet, causing his heart to jump up into his throat. As he tripped through possible spells that might help the situation, the egg started gliding down slowly and smoothly, as if it had never stopped.

Cole cursed his stupidity, not only for letting his brain run rampant with foolish fears, but for not telling Gerard he could have dropped the egg once it was this far down. Cole had a number of spells that would slow its fall. He could even make it drop right into his boat, or slowly levitate it down to the water so he could scoop it up on his way back to the island. He shook his bald head while he waited for the lowering egg. So much for perfect planning.

Gerard had never in all of his life felt as relieved as he did the moment the rope in his hands went slack. The brief reprieve he gained by looping the rope around one wrist for a short while, and then the other to rest his arms, had been probably the smartest thing he could have done. As it was, he would have to rest his upper body and let the circulation begin flowing again in his legs before he could start his climb back down. Even though there was a voice in the back of his head screaming he was out of time, there was no choice in the matter. He wanted to start his descent, but he knew his body wasn't ready yet.

He ate the dried snake-meat he packed and sipped from the remaining water skin, all the while listening to his panicky subconscious warnings. The dragon is coming back to roast you for your thievery! If you don't leave now, the beast will catch you on the rock face and char you to a crisp!

After he finished the meat, he shouldered the pack and headed back across the cavern. The food seemed to have energized him, and he stopped at the lair to consider an idea. As he stood there, looking at the rune-marked floor and the unnatural smoothness of it, the words of the old crone came to him in his mind.

"You will find the power you seek in the depths of the dragon spire," she said, or something to that effect. He found himself looking around for a tunnel, or hidden stairway that let down into the formation, but there was nothing to see. He laughed at his foolishness and stretched his back and arms. He squatted and pushed himself back up with his legs a few times, while holding his arms straight out before him as he did so.

He was feeling much better now. He was glad the first half of his descent was so easy to make. He really wouldn't need his arms until the lower part of the rock face, where it became almost a sheer drop. He was confident again that he could make the journey down without faltering now that his body had recuperated. He was feeling so confident, in fact, he decided to act on the idea he just had.

He would bring down another egg in his pack. The eggs were heavy, but not any more so than the coils of rope he carried up with him. He became excited. Oh, how Shaella would be pleased with him when he gave her the second egg. He could only imagine how this night would be spent. She would be doubly happy, and he would get doubly rewarded.

He wasted no time getting the pack open as he gained the nest. It took some effort to squeeze the egg into the pack because its girth was as wide as the pack's opening. The egg was so big that part of it stuck up out of the pack, but that was all right.

HURRY! the voice in his head screamed at him. The dragon's coming back any moment now! That was all right, too, Gerard told the voice. I've got it, I'm done, I am out of here! With a triumphant smile on his face, he shouldered the pack and turned to go.

He was thinking how easy this had been and how light the pack felt on his shoulders, when a figure shimmered into being directly in front of him. For a fleeting moment, he thought it was Cole, but the evil grin on the pale, bald-headed man's face told him he was mistaken. It was the ghastly, white-skinned older man from the vision he had seen back in the old fortune teller's tent.

In the wizard left hand was a gnarled, old wooden staff with a head-sized crystal mounted at its crown. On his face was the most confident of snarls, and in his eyes there was something far more certain than death.

Gerard was so utterly stunned by Pael's appearance, he didn't even feel the dagger the creepy wizard had thrust into his chest until Pael twisted it and laughed at him with manic glee.

Chapter Twenty-Nine

The dragon was fierce and quick, but it seemed to enjoy playing the cat to Shaella's mouse. It gleefully toyed with the brave little girl, who wielded the insignificantly magical sword, and more than a few times intentionally kept from killing her out of sheer curiosity.

Shaella spun, twirled, dived, and twisted out of the way of the dragon's razor-sharp claws, its whip-like tail, and its fiery maw so many times now that she exhausted herself. She was certain the beast could have destroyed her at any time. She was glad it let her survive long enough for her reinforcements to arrive. It was their turn to occupy the beast now. She had to catch her breath.

Some of the new Zardmen were already running into the clearing. When she saw them, she wasted no time getting herself into the cover of a clump of trees, so she could rest. She stumbled more than ran as she went. With new mice to play with now, the dragon would hopefully stay around a little while longer. Cole would have the egg soon, she hoped. Then the tables would turn, and she would get to be the cat. For the moment though, she was content to just sit against a tree trunk, and breathe.

She felt a sharp pain across her scalp above her right ear. She went to investigate the sensation with her fingers and found a big, watery blister where her hair should have been. After a moment of vain panic where her hands frantically touched every inch of her skull, she cursed the dragon's very existence. Her once beautiful raven black heir was a ruin.

From her right temple, straight back over her ear, and down to her neck, her hair was gone. Her scalp was a hot, puffy blister; her ear was raw, scorched around its edges, and the shoulder of her custom armored leather vest was ruined beyond repair. The sleeve on that side of her shirt was nearly burned away. All that remained was the cuff and some tatters. The rest of her head seemed to be all right, though. She didn't care about the wounds, or the terrible pain they caused. Her only concern was how she would look to her Zard soldiers and her lover. She could deal with it, she decided. She had lived with a tear drop scar running down her cheek for years now.

The screeching, skittering sound of a big geka lizard rose over the general clamor of the tussle briefly. Shaella turned to see it fighting the Zard, who were trying to lead it into the clearing for the dragon. The dragon heard it and flung out its massive wings, sending a blast of concussive wind blowing through the area.

Shaella felt it in her chest. Without standing, she peeked around the side of the tree trunk to see what was happening. Panic swept over her as the dragon jumped into flight. "NOOO!" she screamed. Not now! Not when we're so close.

She had to twist her head and roll away from the tree to see where it went. She forced herself to her feet. She had to go back out into the clearing to get a better view because the gargantuan, red-scaled beast had disappeared from her sight completely. Once in the clearing, she half-stumbled, half-fell back to the ground. One of the studs on her armored vest gouged the blister on the side of her head when she landed. She felt warm liquid running down her neck and back, but she ignored it. The relief of seeing the wyrm again overcame all other sensations.

Apparently, the potion she splashed on the snapper meat was starting to take effect, after all. The dragon, half-flying, half-skipping like a drunken sailor, was stumbling and crashing through the trees, trying to get to the terrified geka. It growled, hissed, and sent jets of flame out of its cavernous nostrils at random. Trees snapped and fell, some of them roots and all, under the beast's massive hind claws. Had the jungle been any less wet, it would have been consumed in flames by now. As it was, the foliage on and around several trees was smoldering, sending up dark, roiling plumes of smoke into the sky.

The geka had gotten its lead ropes tangled during its thrashing panic and was pulling frantically, trying to get itself free. The Zards that had been leading it abandoned it to its fate.

The dragon was now slithering through the forest like a fat snake in the grass, inching ever closer to its prey. It was almost comical how the huge predator was still attempting to be stealthy in its approach. Every creature within a hundred miles surely knew exactly where it was at the moment. Yet, it crashed through the trees ever so slowly, as if it were stalking something, and the trees were merely blades of grass. The geka was lurching and twisting, threatening to yank the tree in which its lines were tangled up out of the soft earth. The dozen or so Zardmen that had left it there were now hiding in the shrubs a good distance away.

The geka's writhing and jerking seemed to be about to pay off, as the tree it was tethered to pulled up and fell over. The escape wasn't meant to be, though. Just as it started dragging the tree away, the dragon belched forth a long river of fire that cooked the moisture out of everything, living or dead, in its path. While flames took hold of that particular strip of jungle, the dragon wallowed forward and took a huge piece of the still twitching and sizzling geka into its mouth and chomped away. After watching the dragon's drunken craziness and the sheer magnitude of power it displayed in the destructive attack, Shaella was suddenly very happy all she had lost was a patch of hair and an armored vest.

While Gerard lay gasping and dying on his side, Pael, with only a dismissive wave of his hand, summoned a gale-force blast of wind. The air shot through the wormhole with a fury, and swept around the dragon's lair like a tornado. Every bone, animal skin, and piece of debris that wasn't embedded in the rock or piled in a corner, was caught up in it. Even the dragon's nest rattled and fell apart into the twister. The remaining egg fell to the smooth floor with a thumping crack. The whirlwind of bones and skins rode the thrust of Pael's magical force around the lair a few more moments, then shot down the wormhole, and out into the sky. All at once, the cavern was silent, save for Gerard's ragged breathing.

Pael sat the gnarled, old staff down among the larger pieces of stone at the edge of the lair's opening. He knew it was a slight risk to open the Seal before Shaella had collared the dragon, but it was too late to wait now. He had already mortally wounded the boy. It was only a matter of time before he bled out.

Without further hesitation, he strode over to where Gerard lay and dragged him by the feet into the center of the rune circle that was etched into the floor. A wide swath of glossy crimson marked the path. Gerard's blood was flowing freely from around Pael's blade, but it wasn't pooling on the floor. Instead, it found its way into the grooves of the carvings, and began to chase the path they created. It took only moments for the center rune and the circle around it to be clearly lined in glistening red.

Pael concentrated on his task. He took a tapered vial out of his black robe and poured its bright green contents into the outermost ring of the symbol, and a little more into the next ring. When the vial was empty, he tossed it away, letting it crash and shatter on the back wall of the lair.

The green liquid took on a luminous quality as it oozed through the grooves and filled the runes between the two outer rings, just as Gerard's lifeblood filled the inner ones. Then, like a blaze catching on oil spilled over water, the green stuff ignited. A shin-high emerald blaze worked its way around the runes until both outer rings, and the symbols marked between them, were alive and dancing with green fire.

"Yes," Pael hissed wickedly under his breath.

He stepped over the magical emerald fire into the area it surrounded. He had to hurry now. He had to have the Seal open while the last of the sacrifice's blood was leaving his body. It was the only way the mighty spectral demon would come out of the Nethers bound to Pael's will. With only the slightest of missteps, Shokin could come out free to do his own bidding. As glorious as the destruction would be in that case, Pael wouldn't have any control over the demon. He had to have control of that great power. It was what he came for, what he had been planning and scheming to attain because, with the demon's might at his beckoning, taking the even greater power of the Wardstone away from Willa the Witch Queen would be easy.

Pael raised his arms up high and started his low, mumbling chant. It was a summoning spell, similar to the one he used to activate the Spectral Orb up in his tower. The only difference was this chant contained subtle binding phrases. As in the tower, he began pacing slowly around the center of the symbol. Gerard's dying body lay there, the slight rise and fall of his chest as his body continued to pull and push air from his lungs while his blood pumped slowly away, showed he wasn't quite dead yet.

With each pass around the body, Pael's chants grew stronger and clearer until they became rhythmic and musical. He was almost there. It was perfect.

Gerard felt his life pulsing slowly out of him. With each heartbeat, another jet of hot, liquid life leaked down his chest. He could see the evil wizard and the green flames dancing around him, and he could hear the dark song being sung. He even felt the world around him, alive as it was with crackling static, but no matter how hard he tried, he couldn't seem to move. The dragon's egg in his pack kept him from rolling onto his back, and the dagger sticking out of his chest kept him from rolling forward. His arms felt like they were made of jelly. A powerful thump from underneath him sent his feeble heart sputtering.

Gouts of blood flowed now. It seemed as if something deep within the spire had hammered the rock a few feet under his body. Again, it struck, and the shockwave of the concussion nearly lifted him off of the floor. He tried to swallow. The world around him was starting to fade.

The jolting blow came again, but this time, the sound abruptly stopped mid-bang. He blinked his eyes, not sure he was seeing correctly, but when he looked down again, he found that his eyes were not deceiving him. The floor had vanished and he was suspended in midair over a large, circular pit. Dark things, both small and large, were rushing up at him as if they were chasing their last meal. Around the walls of the pit, a staircase spiraled down into the seemingly endless blackness. A few of the dark things, a winged panther as black as night, and a pair of dark, scaly beasts swept past him. As life began to fade from him completely, his mind caught on a scratchy old female's voice speaking to him from far away.

"You'll find the power to control legions in its depths," said the old crone.

Maybe she hadn't been a crackpot after all, Gerard thought hopelessly. So close to that destiny, yet so far away. Nothing could save him; he was beyond help now. He was about to close his eyes and die, when he remembered the ring on his finger.

Pael hadn't expected the lesser devils and demons to come flying up out of the darkness, but they had. The ones that cleared the mouth of the pit had actually been fleeing Shokin's approach. The freedom they gained from their hellish prison was a thing of sheer luck. Shokin was at the opening now, and none of the dark things, not even the other demons, dared to get close to him. Had the Abbadon, the King of the Nethers himself, bothered to come up out of the depths of the lower planes, even he might've shied away from Shokin's determined rage.

The evil that Shokin was radiating at the moment was so focused and raw, it made the blackness around him seem like daylight. He was about to come back out into the world from which Pavreal had banished him, and he wanted nothing less than vengeance. Nothing from the Nether World seemed brave enough to test his wrath, but in the world above, there was Pael. With lustful excitement, and nothing less than violent intention, more shadowy shape than physical form, the ancient spectral demon began climbing up out of his blackened prison into the world of men.

Shaella was about to pull what hairs she had left out of her head by the fistful. All of the conceding and self-convincing she had done, all the grim realizations that she would sacrifice Gerard for the sake of her own plans, had been premature. The moment she achieved her goal with the dragon, she was going to try to save Gerard from Pael. She hoped she could get to him quickly enough.

Thankfully, Pael said he wouldn't even approach the Seal until she had the dragon collared. Without the egg, she couldn't collar the dragon, so it wasn't a race yet. She wanted so badly to save Gerard, complete her objectives, and satisfy Pael. She wanted it all.

She screamed out in frustration and hacked at the corpse of one of her Zardmen with her sword. No sooner had the scream died out, then she turned to see Cole hurrying toward her with the precious dragon's egg cradled in his arms. She didn't even allow herself to feel the wave of relief that washed over her. Instead, she recklessly started off toward the dragon.

"Follow me!" she commanded over her shoulder.

After all the time he wasted trying to find a dry place to stand and transport himself back to her, Cole didn't dare argue. It turned out he hadn't planned all that carefully, after all. He hadn't considered the ocean's tides. While he had been busy getting the egg, the tide had risen and submerged his island. He had to row himself nearly a mile before he found a suitable place to teleport himself back to Shaella.

As they passed one of the Zard captains, a Sarzard as they were called, Shaella barked an order so harshly that Cole nearly fumbled the egg.

"Bring the collar! NOW!" she yelled.

Wisely, the Sarzard didn't waste time with any sort of formalities. His only response was a quick, "Yes, Mastress," as he darted off to do as she had bidden him.

Without any fear or hesitation, she stalked purposefully to a place between the dragon and its newest meal. The dragon's head was raised, and it was chugging a chunk of geka meat the size of both she and Cole put together, down its gullet. That didn't seem to faze Shaella. Cole, on the other hand, was terrified. He wasn't sure who he feared more. Shaella, at the moment, seemed far more fierce and determined than the dragon.

"Set the egg down before me," she commanded.

When Cole had done so, she finished giving him his order.

"Go! Help get the collar ready."

Then up to the dragon, she screamed with all the urgent fury she could muster. It was no small amount.

"You have a choice! Hey you, dragon bitch!" She waved her sword in the air, until the dragon stopped chewing, and eyed her. "Look! Look at what I've got!" She reached down and touched the dragon's egg with the tip of her glowing blade.

Hissing sharply, the dragon brought her head down with a quickness that was unnerving. The potion-wrought haze in her huge, amber eyes seemed to fade as her sense of alarm grew.

Shaella had to master herself. She wanted to do nothing other than turn and run as the great beast's red-plated head loomed in close to her. The black slits in the dragon's eyes were as long as Shaella was tall. Its bloody teeth were just as big, and as sharp, as swords. A piece of geka meat that weighed easily as much as Shaella did, hung loosely from between two of those teeth. Heat coming from cavernous nostrils, big enough to walk into, blew her hair back like a strong wind might. The smell of its breath was sulfurous and rotten, like burnt steel and spoiled meat. Had it not been for the hope that she could still save Gerard, she thought she might crumble in her tracks.

"I have no time to waste with you, dragon," she forced herself to say. "Either you will put on a collar, or all of your hatchlings will be born into one."

The dragon's plated brows narrowed between the trunks of her curving, yellowed horns. Angrily, she reared back and began sucking in a vast lungful of air. Her intention was obvious. Shaella had to hold the hair back from the left side of her face, as it was being sucked back toward those massive nostrils. The dragon's flames wouldn't harm the egg, Shaella knew. Dragons used flame to incubate and hatch them. She had to speak quickly and loudly, and make sure the dragon understood.

"You might burn me to ashes, bitch! You'll save this egg, but what about the others?" She paused, letting her bluff sink in. Pael told her that there were three eggs. She hoped that he had been correct. "If you even try to burn me, they will be smashed to bits!"

The dragon paused, flames swirling in her big eyes, her expression overflowing with hatred and anger.

"If you refuse, then I'll ruin this egg while you roast me!" Shaella threatened. The point of her sword rested on the egg at her feet. All it would take was a firm push to render the egg unable to hatch.

"Then the Pact hasss been broken?" the dragon asked.

The thunderous hissing voice was more in Shaella's head than anywhere else, and the sound of it was full of confused malice. When Shaella nodded that the Pact was indeed broken, the dragon raised her head and roared out to the heavens. The earth shook as a tower of flame shot up into the clouds. As angry as the dragon was, it knew it was beaten. Shaella knew it, too. The curse of all maternal creatures had trapped the mighty beast. Her natural born instinct to protect her young allowed her only one choice in the matter.

"Bring the collar!" Shaella called out urgently.

Chapter Thirty

Shokin was halfway out of the Seal, held there by the binding words in the wizard's wicked song. Pael shivered with glee. The spectral demon hadn't expected to be bound.

With a deep, growling rumble of respect it accepted this condition of its release into the world. It knew that it could find a way to unbind itself later. The wizard Pael wasn't as powerful as he liked to think he was. Eventually, Shokin could get rid of him. For now, the important thing was to escape the Nethers, even if it meant pledging his service to Pael.

Shokin had been trapped in the black nothingness for far too long to quibble over technicalities, not when he was this close to freedom. He wanted vengeance on he who banished him. He had sworn it, and if he wanted to vent his wrath on Pavreal's ancestors, for now, he had to grant the wizard Pael his boon. He would lower himself to serve Pael for a time. After all, it was only temporary, and the wizard worked very hard to get the Seal open for him. Yes, he would accept Pael's binding. For now, he would obey without hesitation.

Pael's voice was like a distant macabre chorus howling in Gerard's ears. He had a thought, a hope, for a fleeting moment, but it slid from his mind when the icy cold, ghost-like form of the demon rose up through him.

Its evil filled him for a moment, and was filling him again. With each pulse of his dying heart, a little more of himself was forced away. It wouldn't be long now. His lifeblood was nearly gone. He wondered absently about what had changed the future that the old fortune-teller had seen. Shaella was too close to him to have betrayed him, and Gerard didn't think she had. He was supposed to be brokenhearted, and climbing down the steps underneath him to seek out some great power. The seer had almost seen the right future, but not completely. He had to admit he was glad Shaella hadn't betrayed him. In a strange way, that would have been worse than this. He could face death. He would rather die than feel his heart crushed by the woman he loved. The old crone got part of it right. He had known and felt true love. What else had the woman said? He had been thinking of it only moments ago when he was climbing up the Dragon Spire, but now the train of thought eluded him. He forced open his eyes, hoping he might be able to see the thought lurking in the dragon's lair somewhere, as if it were some tangible thing.

It took some time for his eyes to work. The world was a collage of blurring splotches, but it all slowly came back into focus: green flames dancing crazily, spittle flying from the black-robed, egg-headed sorcerer's mouth as he chanted and circled. Then the light of the cavern suddenly blacked out, eclipsed by some huge, glittering scarlet thing. Then, then he saw Shaella.

"NOOO!" she screamed, as she slid down the side of the newly collared dragon's neck. Her heart hammered at the sight before her.

"HELP ME!" a terrified voice called out.

One of the deckhands, from the barge they had pirated, was clutched gingerly in the dragon's jaws.

"OH! PLEA—" His voice stopped abruptly as the dragon gave him a warning squeeze with her teeth.

"Stop it!" screamed Shaella. "I have your sacrifice right here!"

She stormed over toward the ring of flames, pulling her sword from its sheath as she came. Around her neck was a collar similar to the one she had put on the dragon. It linked her to the beast, and her anger caused the dragon to let out a low, rumbling growl, which made the cavern tremble.

When she was close enough to see Gerard, she froze. There was so much blood. She couldn't believe what she was seeing. She had just left a feeding ground full of gore that was strewn with dozens of dragon-torn bodies, but she was still shocked. How could Pael have done this? He was supposed to have waited until the dragon was collared. She promised him a sacrifice, but she hadn't wanted it to be Gerard. It felt like her heart was being squeezed by some giant icy cold fist. Why hadn't Pael waited? She had his offering clutched there in the dragon's jaws. Oh, Gerard!

Her rage at the wizard melted away as she met Gerard's eyes. His eyelids were fluttering closed. He was so gaunt and sickly looking, so close to death. She looked back at the wizard and was about to make a plea for the life of the man she loved, but Pael's expression sent a tidal wave of fear and anger washing over her.

The dragon dropped the trembling deckhand to the cavern floor and loomed in close behind Shaella, ready to attack at her command.

As Pael came around the circle, he was pacing, still singing his binding chant and entranced in his ritual. Shaella charged him with her sword held high. The outer ring of flames leapt up like a shimmering emerald wall before her. The power radiating from them gave a clear warning. Unlike regular fire, demon fire would burn her flesh for ages. As angry and scared for Gerard as she was, she dared not pass through those flames.

"I hate you!" she screamed at the wizard. Then she broke down, and fell to her knees, letting her sword clatter to the floor beside her. She put her face in her hands and cried for Gerard. It was all she could do.

Gerard heard her sobbing voice through the exotic symphony that Pael's spell created around him. She truly loved him, she was truly sorry, and she hadn't meant for any of this to happen. Had she somehow betrayed him? He wondered. It seemed more as though the wizard betrayed her. Gerard wanted nothing more than to run to her and comfort her in his arms. He wanted to tell her that everything was going to be all right, even though he knew that it wasn't. He didn't even have the strength left to open his eyelids. The coldness of the black thing was moving through him again.

"Oh, Shaella, I loved you," he rasped, as the last drop of his life blood ran down his chest. I don't want to die. Please don't let me die! were the only thoughts he could manage to think, as death's maw finally closed over him.

Pael almost lost his grip on the complex strands of magic he was weaving when Shaella arrived. The dragon startled him, too. In the back of his mind, he remembered that he started this even before the dragon had been collared. If Shaella somehow failed him, the dragon could've returned and ruined everything. He had placed total faith in Shaella's abilities, and she had come through.

Listening to her howl, cry, and carry on over something as trivial as love made him wonder if he were a fool for having faith in her. He was giving her what every father alive wanted to give his little girl, what every little girl wanted from her father: a kingdom of her own to rule. Power, and the means to hold it all, was hers. Didn't every little girl dream of being a princess or a queen? Now here she was, on her hands and knees, cursing his name, threatening him, and babbling on and on right in the middle of the most important moment of his life. She was so much like her mother, he swore. So impossibly hard to please, so ungrateful for the sacrifices he made. Years of manipulating and planning; schemes upon schemes he hatched and played out for her. He misdirected the eyes of kings and queens, and tricked the nobility of entire nations, to get Shaella into this position. Here he was, on the cusp of dark glory, as much for her as for himself, and she was crying over a dead boy. Pael cursed himself a fool for even trying to please a woman. He-he—

He suddenly felt that something was very wrong. The binding was holding perfectly, but Shokin was slipping away from him. How could this be? The demon wasn't trying to break free, either. It couldn't. It was being drawn back into the Seal. Something had gone terribly wrong, but what? Pael searched the depths of his knowledge frantically for a solution.

For the briefest instant, there was nothing but Gerard. No sight, no sound, no emotion. Just death. But the surge of magic from Gerard's ring as it made to carry out his last command, caught hold of him just in time.

Like a mother's fingers squeezing her child's skin between her thumbs to force out a splinter or thorn, his pectoral muscles clenched against the dagger blade. It didn't leave his body, but its tip slipped out of his heart. The powerful magic of the ring couldn't fill his empty body back up with blood, but it could heal the mortal wound, and it did.

The ring's power held him there, on the brink of death, long enough for his heart to start beating again. Gerard's soul was clinging to his body with all the strength of his love for Shaella. The surge of magical energy gave him the strength to hook his thumb in the dagger's hilt, and pull it out of his body. The momentum of his falling arm caused him to roll onto his stomach. He couldn't think. Every move he made was on instinct, or guided by some other force. The magic couldn't hold him in life much longer, and his body needed liquid to make more blood. These realities came to him as afterthoughts, fragmented truths, telling him how dire his situation was.

Riding the tiny bit of strength the ring's magical rush afforded him, he pulled himself across the empty space he was suspended over to the landing of the stairway that spiraled down into the depths. He found that his hands slipped down through the invisible plain that supported him.

The first step felt real enough when he touched it. The cold, dark thing that he felt earlier was pulling at his will again. It wanted desperately to keep him from going down. Gerard's will wasn't his own though, it was a thing of instinct, so the demon's desperation was wasted. The magic of the ring was guiding Gerard. First one step, then another; he used his hands to pull himself down. Then his upper body went over, and he went sliding. His blood-soaked front acted like a lubricant, and it was several steps later before he came to a rough, jumbled halt against the curving wall of the pit.

The sound of the wizard's musical chanting disappeared, and the cold, black thing seemed to have found a way to crawl completely inside of him. It was screaming horribly in protest, and the sound echoed through Gerard's head. With the last bit of magical strength left in him, he managed to pull one arm out of the shoulder strap of his pack. He wiggled himself a step or two down from it, so that it was at the level of his head. He then jabbed a finger-size hole in the top of the dragon's egg, and put his mouth to it as if it were his mother's breast.

He looked upward as he greedily drank in the dragon's yolk. His bloodless body was craving the nutrients, and he didn't deny it.

Above him, the world was a black smear, backlit by bright, wavering green light. It was as if he was seeing the world from underneath a frozen lake. He could make out the shape of someone as they stalked around, throwing out erratic gestures, but everything else was a blur. Somehow, he knew that it would be a very long time before he could get himself back into the world above him. As the screams of the icy, dark thing in his head clashed with the fiery heat of the dragon's yoke settling in his guts like lava, he began to wonder if he might be better off dead.

Shokin felt the revival of the sacrifice and began to panic. Pael's binding held the demon to both the wizard and the dying boy, and now it was being pulled apart. Pael felt it, too, but the persistent wizard wouldn't let the spell break. Shokin screamed out in horror. He was bound to each of these men. He reached into the boy's mind, found the place that controlled human thought, and told him to stop; ordered him to stop, but it was no use. Pael wouldn't let the spell break. Then the boy tumbled through the Seal and down the stairs, and Shokin, the mighty spectral demon, was torn in two.

The demon's horrified yell blasted through Pael's concentration, thus breaking the wizard's spell, but it was too late. The demon's essence was contained in two separate pieces of dark shadow, each with no form of its own. The part of Shokin that was free of the Seal was bound to Pael, and the quick-witted wizard was gathering it all in.

Shokin wasn't just a place in Pael's mind now, nor was he another spirit in the wizard's body. He was Pael now, and Pael was him. The demon's power was Pael's power, and the binding was holding true.

Shokin was a prisoner in two separate places, bound to Gerard in the world of darkness, and to Pael, in the world of men. The demon raged and screamed, his anguish slowly turning to a desperate kind of madness. How had the sacrifice regained its life? Why hadn't it gone into the Nethers? The answer was irrelevant; all that really mattered was the fact that he was Shokin no more.

Pael felt the spectral demon being torn apart and concentrated all his will and power into his binding. He didn't let himself panic; he had worked far too hard to make this moment possible. He would do his best to salvage as much control over the demon as possible.

When the spell was finally broken, he was rewarded for his diligence. As the emerald fire faded away around him, the surge of spectral power filled him like a lightning bolt. It was awesome and breathtakingly electric, glorious, and enlightening. It was like a whole new world—no—a whole new universe of possibilities had suddenly come into being. It couldn't have happened more perfectly. Now, instead of having a demon to do his bidding for him, he had the demon's power for himself. He wasn't exactly sure how it happened, how the boy kept himself from dying, but Shokin's blood tingled with vast demonic power and he found he didn't really care.

So long and so badly had Shokin longed for revenge, that Pael felt the demon's desires coursing through him now. All of that rage and determination would serve Pael's purpose well. He found he was laughing maniacally, and it felt so good that he didn't try to stop when he saw his daughter, Shaella, crying hopelessly on the floor. He didn't even stop laughing when the huge red dragon behind her reared back its head and sucked in a great breath of air.

Claret wasn't really the dragon's name, but it was the name she had given Shaella to command her by. Her true name was unspeakable in any of the languages of men, elves, or dwarves. It pained her deeply to be collared as she was, but she had to protect her eggs. Nature dictated it. It was instinctual. Now, she found she was glad to be where she was. As the green demon flames around Pael died away, Claret saw the egg the wizard's tornado blast had left broken on the floor. In her growing rage, the dragon sent out magical feelers for her other eggs.

Shaella had tricked her, she learned, but in doing so, saved one of her eggs from being destroyed. Through the magical link of the collars she and Shaella wore, the dragon could read the girl's heart plainly. Shaella had not wanted to hurt the eggs, nor did she have any personal reason for trapping and collaring the dragon. All that Shaella did was to please her father or protect her lover.

Claret could tell the only egg left unharmed was the one Shaella captured. She also knew when the girl was done with her, that she would return the egg to her. Therefore, protecting the girl's interests became important to her. The hysterical wizard, rubbing salt into the girl's wounds by laughing at her sorrow, was the one responsible for destroying two of her unhatched babies. Thus, when Shaella looked up at her father and wished him dead, Claret gladly warned Shaella out of the way, and prepared to roast him in his tracks.

Shaella wiped the snot from her nose and looked at the vile old man she had been trying so hard to impress all her life; her so-called father. The man spent his entire life raising a kingdom prince instead of raising her, his own flesh and blood. She had asked him why he was always away when she was a little girl. "It is all for you," he would tell her, and she would believe him.

She desperately wanted her father to love her. He promised her a kingdom, but that's not what she really wanted. She wanted him to teach her as he had Cole and Flick, and spend time with her, but it never happened. Her mother, who had been a Dakaneese Marsh Witch, had cursed him with every breath she ever took, even her last one. Now Shaella understood why. He was so heartless that she doubted him even human anymore.

She bent down, picked up the gnarled old staff he left lying there, and then spat at his raving laughter. Then she wasted no time getting clear so Claret could avenge her unhatched babies.

The blast of fire that spewed forth from the dragon's maw was long and white-hot at its core. Pael was completely consumed in its path, but even through the ear-splitting roar that accompanied the huge gout of flame, his laughter never ceased.

The rock at his feet began to glow red, like coals in a fire pit, yet the laughter carried on. When the blast finally subsided, Pael was still there, unharmed. He glanced at his daughter's giant eyes then, and the mirth and joy he was feeling evaporated like a single raindrop in a hot skillet. His brows narrowed, and his lips pulled back in an angry snarl.

What Shaella saw before her wasn't her father anymore, but something else altogether, something terrifyingly powerful, and out of control.

Pael raised his right arm and choked the air exactly like he had done in King Glendar's pavilion tent, but this time, when he thrust his grasp back, it was Claret's huge, horned head that felt his grip. The great plated head slammed into the back of the cavern, causing huge pieces of stone to come crashing down on the floor.

Smoke curled up from behind Pael, where all of Gerard's blood was sizzling like grease on the surface of the red-hot Seal. Claret started to scrabble for purchase with her sharp foreclaws, but a squeezing shake of Pael's grip made her think better of it. It was all she could do to get air back into her emptied lungs.

Somewhere close to the dragon, the deckhand made a sound that was a miserable, pleading howl. Pael flicked at the air with his free hand, and a huge chunk of the cavern ceiling broke free and fell. The sailor's whine ended in a sickening crunch.

Shaella swallowed hard. Through the link of her collar, she could feel the dragon's growing fear. After seeing Claret so easily destroy a hundred or more of her Zard soldiers, she could only imagine the power this thing in her father's body now commanded. She hated him. He could have waited until the dragon was collared, like he said he would. He could have used the deckhand for a sacrifice. His greedy lack of patience caused Gerard's death, nothing more, nothing less. None of this had been for her. She saw it plainly now. It had all been for him; for him to gain more power.

"Let her go!" Shaella yelled at him.

She wanted to draw her sword and charge, but she knew it would be useless. He would easily find a way to stop her. Besides, she had left her blade lying on the cavern floor where she collapsed earlier. It didn't matter to her now. The sword had been a gift from Pael, and she found that she no longer wanted it.

As if he could read her mind, Pael spoke.

"Ungrateful bitch!"

His voice was as hard and cold as his expression. "I would crush your life away if you weren't my daughter! Love is a fleeting thing, little girl. You're too good for a mere egg thief. I saved you from being a slave to your own emotions. You have Valldian blood in your veins, the blood of the ancients, and you'd do well to never forget it. I spared you a lifetime of heartache!"

Spittle flew from his lips and his veins bulged, like blue and green earthworms under the slick, white skin of his forehead and neck.

"I've left a kingdom virtually unguarded for your taking, and I showed you how to take and hold it. I gave you the dragon collar and the means to trap the feeble beast, and all you can manage is to try to use it to burn me to ashes!"

A long, ropey strand of saliva dangled from his chin, but he was oblivious to it. "How dare you scoff at all I have done for you!"

Claret writhed bodily in his grasp, her huge body knocking loose pieces of the walls and shaking the whole cavern as she did so.

Pael knew she was about to choke to death. He gave her a rough final squeeze, and with eyes that glared deadly lightning into her, he let her go. Wisely, she recoiled into a cowering position and gulped precious air back into her lungs.

Shaella found she felt more than a little ashamed. Pael was right, and she knew it. Still, she hated him no less. She glared back at him coldly as she strode over and took up her sword. As she stood there fuming with the staff of malice in one hand, and softly glowing blade in the other, she thought she saw in his eyes the thing she had sought for her entire life. For the first time she could remember, she saw his respect there.

"Use your rage and hatred, for what I have done is to help you take Westland for your own."

The look in his eyes faded into something colder than ice and darker than pitch, and his voice grew distant. She wasn't sure then if it was still her father who was speaking to her.

"I have my own agenda to tend to. You owe me. Do not forget it again!"

What Pael had become she couldn't say, but whatever he was now, he vanished from before her with a static pop of emerald sparks.

Looking beyond where he had stood, she saw the dark stain of Gerard's blood smoldering on the floor. It was all she could do to bite back her grief and keep from breaking into tears again. The knife scar that ran down her cheek tricked her into thinking a tear had escaped her newfound force of will. As she went to brush it away, she couldn't help but think she lost far more than just a lover this day. She lost her father as well.

Chapter Thirty-One

Mikahl shivered inside the thick Shagmar fur coat he was wearing. It was still early summer, but in the Giant Mountains, it was snowing. Not actually new snowfall, Hyden had explained to the castle-born Westlander, but windblown snow, left over from the previous winter. Mikahl didn't care how it got there; to him it was snowing. The stuff was swirling about them, getting down his collar and whipping into every little tiny opening of his warm wear.

And the blasted wind! The wind was driving him crazy. Even up in Coldfrost, where the sea freezes solid for most of the year, it wasn't this cold. The numerous valleys they had already traversed hadn't been so bad; they were almost spring-like. The ridge they were passing over at the moment, however, was caked in ice, and so bitter and frigid, so slick and narrow, that Mikahl thought he might lose his digits to the bite if he didn't tumble off the side of the mountain first.

He had been forced to lead his horse, Windfoot, the last few days. How the others walked up and down the treacherous slopes was beyond him. His legs were sore, he was tired and confused, but as he shivered again, he decided the worst thing about all of it was that he was so blasted cold.

Loudin had been leading the two horses that carried his precious bark lizard skin. In the valleys, he rode the lead horse awkward style, just like they had back in the Reyhall Forest, but it was far too treacherous on this narrow pass for either of them to ride. More than once, the lizard skin almost caused disaster. They had to untie the roll so the horses could make a few tight turns; once around a washout, and again where the pass turned, hugging the mountain. The skin grew stiff in the cold and wouldn't give at all. It was just like hauling a log.

Once the front horse was startled by a chunk of falling ice. It tried to bolt forward, nearly yanking the rear horse off its hooves. This in turn yanked the front horse. Both horses and the bark lizard skin, along with Loudin as he grabbed after his prize, almost went over the edge.

After that, the bulky skin came off the horses at even the slightest sign of trouble. Mikahl was certain that Loudin expected a small fortune for the skin. Only great wealth, or the prospect of it, would give a man like Loudin cause to make such a miserable and treacherous journey as this one was turning out to be.

Mikahl found the other two often left him shaking his head in wonder. They had been on foot the entire way, and had jogged for days alongside the horses in the lower passes and valleys. Not once had they slowed the group. Not once had they complained or asked for rest. Even though the elf's wounded eye was obviously troubling him, he never voiced his discomfort to his companions. And Hyden Hawk, to Mikahl's great surprise and respect, hadn't even been winded after jogging uphill most of a day. Neither of them seemed affected by the sharp bite of the wind, or the slick, icy terrain.

Hyden and Vaegon took turns leading the group. The elf led more often than not. When the wild-looking, bone-thin creature wasn't out front, he seemed troubled. It was more than just the loss of the eye or getting used to the leather patch he now wore over the ugly hole. The elf seemed to be hurting on a deeper level.

Mikahl wasn't exactly sure what Vaegon's problem was, until one night when the golden-haired elf ceremoniously gave Hyden his longbow at the campfire. He saw the problem a little more clearly then. Vaegon had lost his aiming eye, probably the worst injury an archer could sustain.

"Hyden Hawk," Vaegon always called Hyden 'Hyden Hawk,' whether he was speaking to him or about him.

Hyden took the bow with a silent nod of understanding, and had since treated it with nothing less than reverence. This obviously pleased the elf, but not enough to shatter his bouts of depression.

Hyden Hawk, it seemed to Mikahl, was part animal, part wizard. He could see through the eyes of his hawkling friend, Talon, and he could hunt up a meal in the middle of an icy rain storm, as if it were a clear spring day. He spoke with his bird as if it were just another traveler among them. He obviously had a lot on his mind, but he made for excellent company at the fire. He loved to laugh, and he loved to hear a tale almost as much as Loudin loved to tell them.

Loudin, Mikahl learned, was more than just a trapper and hunter. He had once been a mariner of sorts, and he often spent the evening stretching a story about the strange and distant lands he visited in his adventures. He had been to all of the seven kingdoms, including the Isle of Salazar. He had even been across the Great Western Sea to the land of Harthgar. He told them of the strange customs of the people of the outer islands and of the great shipbuilding yards on the big island of Salazar. He told them of the slave-fighting pits in Dakahn, of the exotic women one could purchase there. He even told them all about the Seaward custom of skin marking. He hinted at the vast and powerful magic that the Witch Queen of Highwander had at her disposal, and the strange little men called dwarves that were rumored to stay in the city of Xwarda at her magnificent palace.

Hyden asked many questions, and was disappointed to learn that these later tales were more from secondhand sources. Loudin had never been to Xwarda himself, but he had been to Highwander's port cities of Weir, Old Port, and New Port. Loudin had seen enough magic on those docks to know a lot of what he heard about Xwarda wasn't exaggerated.

Mikahl listened intently and wondered at it all. He heard a lot of things while serving as King Balton's Squire, but he chose to keep his knowledge and speculation to himself. He let Hyden do all the questioning, and gained even more respect for the mountain clansman. Not only was he in supreme physical condition, his mind was sharp and his queries were well chosen.

Thinking about chumming around a campfire reminded Mikahl of just how cold he was at the moment. He was miserable, and felt that if he ever stopped shivering, he would freeze into a solid statue of ice. He hated the cold and was glad this was the last high altitude pass they would have to traverse for a while.

According to Hyden and the elf, a rich, warm valley lay on the other side of this ridge. They would hopefully be able to lay up there and wait for the giants to come to them. Both Loudin and Hyden Hawk agreed it was a strange thing that Borg had not already found and questioned them. They said no group of men ever made it this far into the Giant Mountains without the Southern Guardian greeting them.

It came as a welcome relief to all of them that they would be making camp soon. Hyden explained over the icy wind that Talon had spied a cave that looked big enough to hold all four of them, and the three horses as well. It was ideal, because from there, they could reach the protection of the valley early the next day. A good, warm fire and a long needed rest would benefit them all. Six days of rough up and down mountain traveling had taken its toll on even the hardiest of them.

They reached the cavern with plenty of light left in the sky, so while Loudin tended to the horses and Vaegon helped Mikahl scrounge up enough wood to start a fire, Hyden and Talon went off to hunt up some fresh meat. Mikahl ended up chattering, pacing, and rubbing his hands together, trying to thaw out enough to be of assistance, but by the time he quit shivering, a fire was burning and the horses were unsaddled, eating oats from muzzle bags.

The cavern was featureless: rocky walls, a rocky ceiling, and an uneven, rocky floor. Remnants of past travelers littered the place: most of a torn jerkin, a good length of poorly made braided rope, a single well-worn boot, among other things. Luckily, there were a few sticks of firewood. Someone had once used soot to draw a scene of stick men and horned creatures on one wall, but it was faded. There were also a few strange symbols daubed in something more permanent, possibly blood, by the entryway. To Mikahl, it was just a cave; a cave that was getting warmer and more comfortable by the moment.

"You'd think you were the one from way down south," Loudin joked at Mikahl. "I know it snows and freezes around that castle you were raised in. I've been there. You act like you've never been cold before."

"You've said the exact same thing three nights in a row now." Mikahl shook his head. "Are you getting forgetful in your old age?"

Loudin laughed at this and sat down by the blaze Vaegon had created.

"What about you, elf? Does it get this cold in the Evermore Forest?"

Vaegon put down the small leather-bound journal, which he sometimes wrote in while the others carried on around the fire. He tilted his head thoughtfully, as if he were remembering something fond.

"Not so cold in the Evermore, no," he answered. "But there are places my people travel, places we visit, that have a climate very similar to this one."

He pointed at the old cavern's roof. Hundreds upon hundreds of campfires had blackened it.

"Places far less hospitable than this cozy cavern." The last was said with a slight grin at Loudin.

"Bah!" Mikahl blurted. He finally felt warm enough to open up the front of his fur coat. He eventually stood and removed it. "I can't imagine any place less hospitable than these mountains." He plopped down on a rock near Loudin with a long, loud groan.

"You dare call me old, boy?" Loudin laughed. "You'll never make half my age if you're in such bad shape now. That sounded awful."

Mikahl gave him a severe stare, but couldn't keep his mouth from curving upward at its corners.

"Bah!" he said again, with a roll of his eyes.

"These are but foothills, compared to the heart of this mountain range," Vaegon told Mikahl. "There are places so high above the sea that even the valleys stay frozen year round, places none of us could survive an hour in, much less a whole day."

"Well, the giants can keep those places for themselves. I've already gotten my fill of the Highlands. If I didn't have to be here, I would've left long ago."

"Aye, we shouldn't have to be up here this far anyway," said Loudin. "Old Borg is either caught up in something nasty, or he's grown lax and forgetful of his duties. I'm fairly certain his old mind hasn't begun to slip just yet. I imagine somewhere along the border, something has attracted him and is keeping him occupied for the moment."

Loudin shrugged off his fur coat and piled it into a cushion, then leaned back into it.

"The two other times I came up here, he met us after the first big pass. No one travels long in these mountains without his knowledge, I assure you."

"You said that the last four nights as well. How can one giant guard the whole of the giant kingdom?" Mikahl was skeptical. He asked Hyden the same question one day, but all he got for an answer was a shrug and, "I wish I knew."

"He doesn't," Loudin answered, with a sly glance at the elf. "He just guards the southern border." They chuckled at the frustrated expression that came across Mikahl's face.

"Bah!" Mikahl growled. "You know what I meant, old man." Then to Vaegon, who was struggling to bite back his laugh. "You too, Cyclops. I want to know. How does one giant guard thousands of miles of foothills all by himself?"

Whether stunned by the well-placed, but good-natured insult to his one-eyed condition, or maybe just pondering his response, Vaegon paused with raised brows for a moment before responding. The elf looked angry and possibly a bit wounded by the jab. Seconds turned into hours as the tense moment passed. Finally, as he started to reply, a grin crept across the elf's face.

"Well, Mikahl, he's only guarding his kingdom from mere humans. How many more giants do you think he would really need?"

Mikahl didn't realize at first that the elf had mocked his humanity. His mind had gone back to a memory of the bloody ordeal at Coldfrost.

He, King Balton, and Westland's Northern Muster battled the giants there for most of a winter a few years back. Mikahl had been told those weren't full-blooded giants. They were a wild and primitive cross-Breed, driven by an animalistic instinct. They had been eight and nine feet tall, overly hairy, with slightly snouted faces and mouths full of sharp, carnivorous teeth. They fought like they were demon-possessed.

He had just been promoted to King's Squire then, and hadn't earned King Balton's full trust yet, so he hadn't been privy to why the battle was being waged. He hadn't been allowed to fight, even though he was one of the better swordsmen on the field, but he saw the carnage firsthand. He also witnessed the power of Ironspike. King Balton took quite a few giants down with it before using it to create the magical boundary that still imprisons those Breed Giants to this day. Mikahl couldn't realistically imagine a single giant being able to stand against Ironspike's might, so it took some time for the joke to register in his mind. When it finally did, he didn't think it was all that funny, but since he liked the one-eyed elf so much, he faked a laugh.

It became clear to Mikahl that neither of these two would-be jesters knew exactly how the giant named Borg did his duty.

In the silence that followed, Mikahl let his mind wander further. Of course, his thoughts went to the sword and Lord Gregory's unfathomable proclamation. Mikahl spent a lot of time dwelling on the possibility that he was actually King Balton's bastard. He had come to the conclusion that it was the truth. The king went to great lengths to train and educate him in everything, from table manners and mathematics, to military tactics and weapons play. He was taught the qualifications and proper duties of all of Westland's lords and nobles. He knew, from page to prince, what every titled person in Balton's kingdom was supposed to be doing for the throne.

The only exception was Pael. He had never been told what the Royal Wizard's true duties were and when he asked, his instructors always avoided the subject. King Balton made sure he understood his numbers and the history of the land, and that he read and understood certain books out of the castle's library. King Balton often inquired about the contents of a book while they rode out to a stronghold or went on a hunt.

Mikahl remembered fondly the trips to various lords' and nobles' holds for weddings, funerals, and other functions. King Balton never rode in the Royal Carriage. That was where Prince Glendar and the wizard always traveled. King Balton rode his horse, Firewind, Windfoot's sire, and everywhere he went, he kept Mikahl close at hand.

There were days he and King Balton rode surrounded by guardsmen who kept their distance, so he and the king could speak quietly. There were nights where the titles of king, captain, duke, and squire somehow got lost in the flames, as flasks of brandy-wine were passed around the campfire.

Looking back, Mikahl could see that he was being trained and tested all along, a lot of the time by King Balton himself. He had been raised by a father who didn't dare claim him as his son. The idea of that stung, but not so bad that it tainted the memory. Mikahl had faith that King Balton had good reason for the subterfuge. It was the idea he was supposed to someday rule Westland that seemed so preposterous to him. Prince Glendar was the king now, and he surely wanted his father's sword back. He probably ordered that creepy wizard, Pael, to send that beast after them. Thankfully, the thing fled. Hopefully it would stay gone.

Mikahl had to admit to himself that he liked the feel of Ironspike in his hands. Its magical symphony was glorious and thrilling to experience, but he wasn't sure if he really wanted to be a king. The elf, who had been in the sick bed next to Lord Gregory when the old lion told Mikahl who his father was, later said, "Your lack of want is most likely why you were the one King Balton wanted to be his heir."

When Mikahl asked Vaegon what he meant, the elf said, "One who wants to be a king, obviously wants the title for all the wrong reasons. No good, reasonable, or honorable man would want to have the responsibility of ruling over others. He might accept that responsibility as his duty, but he would be wary of it, not crave it."

Mikahl thought long and hard about that, and it made sense. Prince Glendar always wanted to succeed his father, and Mikahl couldn't imagine that spoiled brat being either fair or honorable. He hated to think what sort of shape Westland was in at the moment. Mikahl figured chaos reigned between the landholders, the nobility, and the new king.

He was torn from his thoughts by the sudden appearance of Talon fluttering into the cavern. The hawkling landed near the fire and began chirping, then pacing back and forth excitedly. Mikahl and Loudin both looked at Vaegon with alarm on their faces. The elf had been traveling with Hyden when they met them, so it was up to him to interpret what the bird was trying to convey.

The possibilities of mishap were endless in this sort of terrain; falling rock, falling ice, collapsing footholds, not to mention the vast array of predators that called these inhospitable mountains home. Everyone's mind raced through the myriad possibilities of harm that might have befallen Hyden. Loudin went so far as to throw on his coat and start digging through the packs for rope.

"Is Hyden all right?" Vaegon asked Talon.

He wasn't as worried as the other two. He was sure if Hyden were in a dire situation, Talon would be pecking on one of their heads with his sharp beak or trying to pull one of them up to his feet with a claw full of hair. Neither Hyden, nor his hawkling familiar, were capable of much subtlety.

The bird squawked in response to the question. Vaegon took that as a negative.

"What then?" he asked.

Loudin paused his rummaging.

"Has he found Borg?" he asked hopefully.

Talon cawed out and leapt into the air. After circling the cavern once, he landed on Loudin's head and cooed. An almost visible blanket of relief lifted from them all.

"I think we should make up some sort of code to talk with Hyden through Talon," Mikahl said, while giving the hawkling a peculiar look. "Hyden, have Talon peck Loudin's head twice, if you agree."

Talon cocked his head to the side for a moment, then leaned over and sharply pecked the old hunter's forehead twice. Before Loudin could react, Talon flew to the other side of the fire, landed near Mikahl, and bobbed his head up and down with glee. Mikahl and Vaegon burst into a fit of hysterical laughter. Loudin scowled at them and rubbed the red spot on his forehead briskly. Hyden, like Mikahl, had a great sense of humor.

The giant, Borg, stood just over fourteen feet tall. He wasn't even close to being the tallest of his race. The club he carried—he called it a staff—was made out of the trunk of an old pine tree, whose resin-like sap was hardened in the Cauldron at Afdeon. The base of it was as big around as Hyden's waist, and so were the giant's upper arms. Borg's hair was long, dark, and streaked with silvery gray, as was the thick beard that trailed down his chest. His pants and knee-length vest coat were a patchwork of thick furred animal skins. The long-sleeved shirt he wore underneath was made from a dark and well-tanned elk's hide. His boots looked to be made of a thicker sort of pelt. The fur was as white as the snow he was standing in. Mounted on the bridge of each foot was a toothy skull that matched the one mounted on his belt buckle. What the giant's hair, mustache, and beard didn't cover of his face, the long, bushy eyebrows did. Even though his eyes were the size of plums, they seemed hidden underneath the hair. The huge slab of Borg's forehead was the most prominent and most exposed of his features.

Hyden saw a glint of curiosity sparkle from the depths of Borg's sockets, as the approaching giant mused over his sudden burst of laughter. Hyden didn't think he could explain the long distance jest that had just played out on Loudin's skull, so he did his best to suppress his mirth.

Borg was more than a little intimidating, even to one who had met him before. Hyden wanted to be taken seriously by the Southern Guardian, because he was sure Mikahl's business with King Aldar was important, as well as urgent. He put on a face, similar to the ones he'd seen his father and grandfather use when dealing with the giants: stern and serious. He then searched his memory of Berda's tales for a hint of the proper etiquette and greeting to use in the situation.

Confident now he wouldn't make a fool of himself, Hyden started through the ice and snow to greet Borg. He caught himself fighting back a grin as he went. He hadn't been able to see Loudin's expression when he told Talon to peck his head, but he imagined it was a sight to see. His grin faded, when the deep creases of concern splitting Borg's huge forehead became clear through the swirling snow. It was an intense look, a look that cut far deeper into Hyden than the icy blast of wind that preceded the giant.

"What business would cause you to guide two kingdom men and an elf into these lands, son of Harrap?" Borg asked harshly.

Hyden couldn't believe the giant recognized him as his father's son, but he had.

Obviously the giant wouldn't know which son he was, so he clarified the matter.

"I am Hyden, eldest son of Harrap," Hyden said. "One of the kingdom men, a tattooed hunter called Loudin, says he knows you. He has brought something of value he thinks you will want to barter for."

Hyden paused to gauge Borg's reaction. He hoped the giant actually knew Loudin and remembered him. The giant's nod assured him this was so.

"The other kingdom man has urgent messages for King Aldar. He carries those and a sword that—" He let his voice trail off there. He wasn't sure how much information he should divulge. He didn't want to mislead Borg, nor did he want to betray Mikahl's trust. He found he suddenly wished he hadn't mentioned the sword at all.

Borg was silent for a long moment. He looked haggard and worried over serious matters beyond the issue before him. Hyden noticed there were dark stains all around the base of the giant's big staff. Some were old and a brownish black in color, but some were slick and glossy red. A patch of yellow could be seen where a piece of the wood had been chipped or torn away recently.

"What about the elf?" Borg finally asked.

"The elf," Hyden searched for an explanation that made sense, but couldn't come up with one. He ended up saying the first thing that came to his mind, which was also the least believable of any answer he could have given. "Vaegon is my friend."

With a doubtful scowl, Borg seemed to accept this. He let out a deep sigh and nodded for Hyden to lead him. As Hyden complied, Borg spoke from behind him.

"It is a sign of strange times when any member of the Skyler Clan chooses to befriend an elf, but a bridge between the two races has long been needed."

Hyden had to hurry and scramble to stay ahead of Borg's huge strides. He wanted to ask about Berda, but couldn't find the words or the moment to speak them. He cared deeply for the giantess who educated him through the telling of her tales, while her husband grazed his big horned goats in the valleys around the Skyler Clan village. He had a feeling that if he didn't see her while he was here in the mountains, it would be a long while before he had the chance again. He wanted to ask her about the man named Pratchert, who eventually became the wizard, Dahg Mahn. He wanted her to see Talon and to ask her what she knew about such a bonding. All of that aside, he just plain wanted to see her and hear her soft voice, as she carried him away to some grand and far off place for an adventure. It came as a shock when Borg, seeming to have read part of his thoughts, asked him a question.

"So Hyden Hawk, where is your familiar?"

Hyden took two more steps, then stopped abruptly and turned.

"How do you know about Talon?" His tone was as curious as it was fearful.

"I talk with the animals as you do, Hyden Hawk." Borg made sure his tone wasn't severe. He hadn't meant to alarm the boy in any way. "They help me with my duty. Sooner or later, I hear of everything that happens in these mountains. How else do you think I could guard such a vast border by myself? For the moment, you and Talon are the envy of the skies. All the birds are chirping about it."

"I can only communicate with Talon," Hyden said, as he turned and started walking again.

"You will grow into your power far sooner than you'd like," Borg told him. "It's something that takes time to develop. Usually, necessity brings out the abilities you have happened upon. And I am afraid that using your gift will become a necessity before too long."

The giant sighed again, as they continued stalking through the snow.

"Bad things have been loosed upon the world recently. I think maybe you and your group may have met one of them already."

The idea that there were more things out there like the hellcat that killed Lord Gregory and half-blinded Vaegon made Hyden shudder. He wondered what sort of things they could be and what they were after. The hellcat had seemed concerned only with Mikahl, or maybe it was that magical sword he wielded. Either way, Hyden was sure he would find out more about the kingdom men than he really wanted to.

He was relieved when they finally reached the cavern, and at least for a while, his mind wouldn't be idle to dwell on such dire possibilities.

Borg had to duck into the cavern, and ended up sitting cross-legged by the fire with his head brushing the soot-blackened ceiling. Hyden introduced him to everyone and them to him.

When Mikahl rose and bowed formally, as Westland custom dictated, he got a good look at the massive Southern Guardian. He was shocked and relieved at what he saw. The things his countrymen had fought at Coldfrost hadn't been giants at all. He couldn't picture them as even being half-Breeds.

Borg was just a great big human, where those things had been semi-intelligent beasts. The contrast between what Mikahl had expected and what was before him confounded him so much that he forgot to ask Borg the questions that had been eating away at him for the last few days. He was so relieved that he forgot about everything for a while, at least until he caught the giant eyeing King Balton's sword.

Chapter Thirty-Two

After everyone was introduced and all the formalities had been taken care of, Loudin attracted Borg's attention by carefully unrolling a few feet of the bark lizard skin. The size of the cavern wouldn't allow him to show any more of it, but he didn't need the extra room. Like some monstrous baby, Borg crawled on hands and knees over to the roll to examine it more closely.

The horses whinnied as Mikahl, Vaegon, and Hyden were forced to cram against them in the now overcrowded space. For a moment, Vaegon thought the giant's fur-covered boots were going to end up in the fire, and Hyden had a flashback of watching Gerard riding his father's back around the fire when he was a boy. If any of the group dared to climb on the giant's back, it would have looked about the same.

Mikahl, with his hands protectively on Ironspike's hilt, was still trying to get his breath. The giant was huge, and Mikahl kept comparing him to what he expected him to be like. The Breed giants at Coldfrost had been eight to nine feet tall at best. Their faces were crude with wet, slightly upturned noses, jutting jaws, and a single thick brow that ran unbroken over both eyes and across the bridge of the nose. They were wild and primal, half-man, half-beast. Borg, even on all fours cooing like a farm wife at a cloth merchant's lace display, was nothing like them at all. He was more like an excited child, an excited human child. Since the giant's attention shifted from Ironspike, Mikahl let himself relax, but only a little bit. He absently patted Windfoot's flanks and watched as Loudin and Borg hogged most of the space the cavern offered and argued about a price for the skin.

Borg wanted the thing; that was obvious. He said he would have to take a short journey to fetch the amount of gold and other items Loudin wanted in exchange for the roll. He explained to Mikahl he would take the scrolls to King Aldar and bring back the king's responses. It might take him three days to return, but they could wait for him in the relative warmth of the valley beyond this ridge.

"What of the sword?" Mikahl asked dutifully, if a little reluctantly.

King Balton told him to present it to the giant king, but in truth, Mikahl didn't want to part with it now. He had grown attached to the strength and confidence it gave him. He wasn't about to let Borg take it. If he had to hand it over, he would only hand it over to King Aldar himself.

"If my king requires it, he or I will return for it," Borg said, with his eyes glued to the jeweled hilt. "It is far easier for my people to travel in these lands than it is for you."

"Aye," Mikahl agreed with a grateful bow. "I agree with you completely."

He could spend the rest of his days happy if he never saw another snow-capped mountain peak in his life.

"If King Aldar does have to have the sword, I would only give it to him personally. I hope you understand."

"So be it," Borg replied flatly.

Hyden interrupted the exchange and asked Borg if he knew the whereabouts of Berda, and a short private conversation between the two of them ensued. Eventually, Talon introduced himself by fluttering down and landing on Borg's shoulder. The giant smiled broadly and commented on the healthy condition of the hawkling. Soon after, the giant bade them farewell.

Outside the cavern, a bitter wind howled through the darkness, but inside, it was warm and cozy. Hyden wished he had the chance to make a kill. Fresh meat would have been a blessing, but dried meat and herbs would have to do this night. While Hyden helped Vaegon prepare the evening meal, Loudin joked with Mikahl.

"I would only give it to his grace!" the old Seawardsman said, in a mocking aristocratic tone, accompanied by a fancy bow.

"It's formal courtesy," Mikahl defended. "Manners and etiquette, things you'll never understand."

"It's highfalutin nonsense." The hunter laughed. "You should've just licked his boot."

"Bah!" Mikahl waved him off. Then to the others at the fire, he said, "Did you see those skulls on his boots and belt? I wonder what sort of beast those are from."

"Dread Wolves," Hyden and Loudin answered in unison.

"When I was younger, they used to be as thick as the plague in these parts," said Hyden. "They moved on, or died out after the bulk of them were killed off by the giant herdsmen."

Mikahl suddenly remembered that some of the Breed giants at Coldfrost had big, savage wolves for pets. One of them tore Duke Silion and two of his men to shreds. Mikahl hadn't seen it happen, but he saw the aftermath. The bodies had still been warm and steaming in the crimson snow. A trail of silvery blue innards twisted away from the body of one man, who looked utterly shocked to be dead.

Mikahl had seen the wolf, too. It had looked more like a huge porcupine, with all the arrows and crossbow bolts sticking up out of it. When the king's guardsmen rolled it over, he saw the thing's huge head and teeth. A man's forearm was clamped in those jaws, the hand still gripping a nasty-looking dagger hilt.

"I don't think they died out," he mumbled more to himself than to the others.

"You don't think that Pratchert's wolf was a Dread Wolf, do you?" Hyden asked the elf.

Mikahl looked at them as if their heads had just shrunken to the size of peaches.

"Not likely," Vaegon answered. "Thanks to the giants, there are plenty of Dread Wolves roaming the Evermore Forest now. None of them seem to need to be shaved to survive the summer heat as Dahg Mahn's wolf did. Pratchert's wolf was most likely an Arctic Great Wolf, or one of its high range kindred."

"Who in the Seven Kingdoms is Pratchert?" asked Mikahl.

Excitedly, Hyden goosed the elf.

"Go on, tell him the tale," he urged. "I'd love to hear it again myself."

"Yes, Vaegon, tell us," Loudin encouraged. "I'd be happy to get to listen for a change."

"All right," Vaegon conceded, "but after we've eaten."

As Vaegon was telling the story, Mikahl often glanced at Hyden. He caught Hyden sneaking glances his way as well. Both of them were feeling a strange connection. Could Hyden be like the great wizard Dahg Mahn? Could Mikahl be the king who would someday need his aid to fight off the dark ones and unite the human kingdoms? On the surface, the idea of it was silly. There was no great evil loose upon the land for them to battle. King Glendar might be a horrible person, but Mikahl did not think he was a servant of evil. Likewise, Hyden couldn't see himself leading an army of wild animals from the forest to save Mikahl and his kingdom men. Still, there was a bond forming that couldn't be denied.

Earlier, when they pranked Loudin through Talon, it had been like they were reading each other's minds. Everything Mikahl intended, but didn't say aloud, Hyden understood clearly. Mikahl had known that Hyden would get the hint. It was strange, and even now as their eyes met, each of them felt the odd connection gaining strength, though they chose to say nothing about it.

By the time Vaegon finished the story of Pratchert, Loudin was snoring softly by the fire. Not long after, the others were asleep as well.

Sometime in the early morning, the fire died out. The cavern was freezing when Loudin stirred awake. After he sat up and bundled himself in his fur coat, he noticed Hyden wasn't in his bedroll. The hawkling and the man's cold weather gear were gone as well, so he didn't think much of it. He grunted his stiff, sore body into a standing position, and gave Mikahl's sleeping form an angry scowl.

It was as if the boy's constant joking about his age and condition was the reason he felt the pain and ache of every inch of his body. He liked the boy though, and was glad he hadn't abandoned him back in the Reyhall Forest. Loudin found that he saw himself in the younger man. He wished he were still as young as these lads. He could tell their future held many great adventures, but he didn't know how much longer he would be traveling with them.

Once Borg paid him for the skin and he gave Mikahl his share, he had a mind to build himself a little cabin and retire. He would clear a spot in the Reyhall; maybe just use that clearing by the pond where they killed the big lizard. He would grow a garden and make a trip into Locar a few times a year to buy supplies. He could hunt for his meat. Maybe he would get lucky and find himself a woman that hadn't had the dowry to get herself married off in her younger years. With his half of what Borg was bringing back, he would want for nothing. He might even get a place in one of the smaller towns and open a trading post or something. He wouldn't need to turn a profit; it would just be something for him to do with his time. The possibilities were endless.

The only thing he knew for certain was that Mikahl was right. He was getting too old to traipse around the woods all the time, and he was forgetting little things here and there. How long would it be before he forgot something important, something that put him in harm's way?

Something Loudin heard while playing a high stakes game of Rune Discs on the Isle of Salazar kept coming back to him. A Harthgarian Sail Master had just won half the markers at the table, and was counting it up to cash out. One of his mates asked him why he didn't stay and try to win more. The man chuckled and shook his head. "If you don't leave the table while you're winning, then you don't win."

Loudin was winning now and he knew it. He would follow those words of wisdom, and with his prize, he would be able to live to a ripe old age in relative comfort.

"If I don't freeze my fargin arse off first," he grumbled under his breath.

He had to laugh then. He knew he would've never said those words aloud had Mikahl been awake to hear them. He would never hear the end of it. He leaned against the cavern wall for support as he pulled on his boots, then went to see if he could find some wood for the fire pit. He didn't want to hear the spoiled castle-born lump whining about the cold, he told himself, but deep down he knew the truth was that he really wanted the boy to wake up warm.

Hyden always loved the hunt, so much more so now with an elven crafted longbow to loose with, and Talon's sharp vision to see by.

Hyden understood Vaegon had lost his depth sight. The elf had to be deeply pained by the loss. Hyden understood. At least, he thought he did. He couldn't imagine how it would affect his mind if he lost his ability to aim properly. When Vaegon offered him the bow, he almost refused it. Something, some odd intuitive feeling, made him think better of denying it though, and graciously he accepted the gift.

The elf's smug and superior attitude had all but disappeared, but that change started before Vaegon had lost his eye. Vaegon wasn't himself anymore. His wound wasn't just of the flesh, and

Hyden had spent a lot of time on the trail and by the fire thinking of ways to cheer his elven friend. It was the least he could do to repay Vaegon for the wonderful gift he had given him.

Vaegon was spending more and more time scribbling in his little journal, and it worried Hyden. He wished he could think of something suitable to do for his friend, something that would fill at least part of the void the loss of his eye had created. So far, nothing he thought of seemed even close in comparison to his gratitude toward Vaegon and his sorrow over his friend's loss.

"Life is not kind, nor is it fair." Hyden repeated the words he recently heard his uncle Condlin grumble under his breath. "Sort of like now."

A few hundred yards away, a ram was leading two of his females up the mountainside, completely unaware of Hyden and Talon's presence. Through the hawkling, Hyden watched the animals come up out of the distant valley and slowly make their way toward him. He could've killed one of them long ago, but decided to wait. As long as they were moving toward him, he would let them come. If they started changing course, he would try to herd them his way with Talon. The swooping hawkling might be able to frighten them right up into the cavern entrance. It would take a while, but it would be faster and far easier than having to drag one of the carcasses all the way back. If Talon couldn't keep them on track and they started moving away, then he would just have to kill one and move it the old-fashioned way.

While he watched and waited, he found himself thinking about Pratchert again. The story was fresh in his mind, and the strange question kept forming in his head.

In the story, the wizard and his wolf stopped at the Summer's Day Spire, and a dragon had come. They had a conversation that supposedly lasted several days. What kept nagging Hyden's mind was the subject of that conversation. What would Pratchert have to say to a dragon, or a dragon to him, and for days, no less? Hyden couldn't imagine what he would want to say to or ask a dragon if he were given the chance. Knowing himself as well as he did, he figured he would ask the dragon to tell him a story.

What sort of story would a dragon tell? Maybe that's what dog man had done. It would had to have been an awful long story to last for several days, but then again—

"Still too long of a shot, eh?" Loudin asked softly, but with an intentional sharpness in his voice.

Hyden almost jumped out of his skin at the sound. He hadn't heard the old hunter approaching at all. He took a moment to let his thundering heart settle before he replied.

"You startled me," he whispered.

"Nearly scared a turd right out your arse is what I did," Loudin chuckled. "It would've been far worse for you if you didn't have my breakfast in your sights."

He hunkered down beside Hyden and patted him on the shoulder. Fog swirled from his mouth with his breath.

"Consider it payback for the knot you had your blasted bird put on my head yesterday."

Hyden felt his face flush with embarrassment, but couldn't help but smile at the memory. For a long while neither of them spoke, they just watched the ram lead his females ever closer.

"They've been in my range for a very long while now, Loudin," Hyden bragged the answer to the Seawardsman's original question. "I'm just saving myself the work of having to carry one of them up that hill and back to the cavern."

Loudin squinted at the three specks moving in the distance, then turned to look at Hyden.

"It's those hawk eyes that allow you to shoot so accurately," Loudin guessed correctly.

Loudin raised himself back up to his feet and managed to do it without an audible groan this time.

"I'll have a fire waiting," he said, then made his way back toward the cavern.

Hyden chided himself for letting the hunter sneak up on him like that. That kind of carelessness would not do. He hadn't told the others yet what Borg said about there being more of those dark creatures about.

It wasn't until he heard the story of Dahg Mahn again that he began to truly believe that the power of Mikahl's sword had something to do with the attack. If the sword truly made Mikahl the King of Westland, then more of them would surely come for it. Hyden wasn't learned in the way of kings and kingdoms, and he knew even less about magical swords, but it was obvious that whoever was running Westland at the moment wouldn't want Mikahl showing up and ruining his plans.

A warning shriek from Talon brought Hyden's attention back to the ram. It was getting closer to him laterally, but working its way higher up the mountain. He sent Talon to swoop down the slope at it. He was as anxious to see if the bird could harry the ram where he wanted it to go, as he was about preparing to kill one of its mates.

Vaegon woke to the first crackling sounds of Loudin's fire. The pain in his empty socket had lessened considerably, but not the pain in his heart. The empty space there was like a raw, open sore. He felt like part of him, the part that made him elven, had been ripped away from him by that beast.

None of his companions could know the true extent of his loss. Only an elf would understand. The night vision, the ability to see the life force of living things, and the currents of magic flowing around and through the rest of the world was so distorted now that it was useless. For him, seeing was now like a human trying to hear with his nose, or smell with his tongue; like trying to wield a sword with a booted foot, or trying to run with only one leg. He felt empty and useless.

As much as he had been missing the Evermore Forest, he no longer found the idea of going back very comforting. His people would be accepting and loving, of course, but the whispers as he walked past the flower gardens, without being able to tell the shapes the scents made as the sunlight reflected through them, would be unbearable. They would laugh as he missed the signs of the trail that the forest showed him to follow. They would be consoling, polite, and their good intentions would be a constant reminder of the myriad things he could no longer sense with his elven vision. It was sickening to think about. Even now, the flames that danced to life before his eyes were like a single cricket call where before, they would've blazed forth in his vision, like the entire nocturnal symphony of the forest.

It had pained him dearly to give his longbow to Hyden Hawk, but he could have found no better owner for it. Not in all of the races, including his own, would a person respect the gift more than Hyden Hawk did. The young human was special, as was Mikahl. In all of Vaegon's seventy-three years of life, he had not met anyone, be they elf, giant, fairling, or dwarf, that had the power of life radiating from them like those two did. He couldn't see it anymore, but he saw it before losing the gift of his elven sight.

A gift was all his wonderful vision had been, he realized now. He shook his head, thinking how his kind took such things for granted. That thought humbled him even more than the actual loss did. In truth, his race was not much different than the humans, just a few more gods-granted gifts. Take them away, and they were the same. He couldn't believe he used to think he was better.

Vaegon knew Hyden Hawk needed someone to help him come into his power. Mikahl's power came from the sword. That was something Vaegon wouldn't even try to understand. The Westland boy had a great deal of potential coursing around his aura when they met outside of Hyden's village. The sword had no part in that, he remembered. It was strapped to the horse that day. Still, the Westland boy needed some guidance, too. They both did.

Vaegon sighed. If it had not been for Hyden Hawk's brilliant shot that destroyed the arrow the Witch Queen's archer aimed at him, he wouldn't be here at all. He still owed his life to Hyden. That simple fact gave him purpose, which in turn gave him a little hope. He needed that.

Not just as a life debt anymore, but as a friend and mentor, Vaegon silently and willingly pledged his existence to Hyden Hawk. He wasn't sure what sort of help a Cyclops elf could offer, but he would give it nonetheless. He smiled brightly and seemed to forget about his troubles when Hyden Hawk appeared at the cavern entrance, slightly winded and blowing clouds of steam from the burden of hauling his kill.

Mikahl woke to the rich smell of cooking meat. The cavern was warm and toasty. As he blinked and rubbed the sleep from his eyes, Loudin handed him a flask of cold water. A moment later, Vaegon placed a piece of bread in his lap with a flourishing bow, then Hyden gave him a dagger that had a hot, sizzling chunk of fresh roasted meat stabbed on its point.

As Mikahl started to take a bite, he looked around at the faces that were staring at him. All three of his companions were about to burst into laughter. With mock severity they all bowed deeply. When they rose back up, they spoke in perfect unison, and the sarcasm dripped like honey from their words.

"Mighty King Mikahl, your most gracious Highness, we are at your service." Before they even finished, their laughter exploded through the cavern.

Mikahl smiled broadly, gave a regal nod, then broke his fast.

Chapter Thirty-Three

Lord Ellrich was happy to be back at Settsted Stronghold. The familiar stone walls around the keep with its little bailey yard, single tower, and its bird's eye view of the seemingly endless and empty green swamp marsh that began on the other side of the river channel, made him feel comfortable and safe.

The smell of Rosila's cooking wafted up from the kitchen, and the reassuring sound of the men—the few of them King Glendar and his wizard left him—drilling in the practice yard, were sensations he had never thought to enjoy again. How he managed to keep his head from being piked at Lakeside Castle was a mystery. He was sure it was more to do with King Glendar's interest in his daughter than anything else.

Thank the heavens Zasha was safe at Lake Bottom with Lady Trella. His only hope was she still might be able to turn Glendar's eyes away from her. Maybe Trella could get him interested in another maiden. He would send her a message as soon as he was settled and invite them to visit. Lake Bottom was probably a sad sort of place without Lord Gregory around to lend it his cheer.

The week had been extremely busy. Riding out daily to cull men from the garrisons had been no easy task. His huge, old horse could only go so far, so fast with his great bulk riding on its back, so the work took some time.

The soldiers were mostly river folk, his folk. No matter who Lord Ellrich sent off to Wildermont to fight, he found protesting mothers, fathers, and wives. Some he managed to appease, others were still cursed his decisions. They were his people, and he was their liege. It pained him to do his duty, but the new King of Westland was waging war against the east, and Ellrich would sooner anger a few families than donate his head to the cause.

The river folk were only a portion of Lord Ellrich's responsibilities. Besides guarding the stretch of Westland shore that contained the Leif Greyn River's western channel, he held sway over a huge section of the kingdom's southern lands. Farmers, herders, and craftsmen alike all lived and worked under his banner. Lord Brach's recruiters had come through and hauled every able-bodied man and boy away from their homes to fight. Very few people were happy in this part of the kingdom. Ellrich couldn't imagine it being much better anywhere else. His people might not be happy with him, but at least it was his people that were around him now. He was home.

On the desk before him was the remainder of the petitions and grievances that had piled up during his absence. Dealing with King Balton's funeral, Glendar's coronation, and the matter of sending the king most of his men had taken well over a month. What matters his captains weren't able to resolve were left here for him to review. It seemed they hadn't resolved much. He had thinned the stack down a bit over the past few days, but since the news of his return had spread, it was growing again.

Several people sighted flocks of the big swamp dactyls flying into the farmlands. Dozens of goats, a few sheep, and even a milk cow had been reported missing. The next report said a handful of barges had sunk or been pirated before reaching their destinations. This was a fresh copy of an old report and he quickly tossed it away. A young girl had been raped by men in uniform, probably Lord Brach's recruiters. Ellrich's men knew better. She had just come forward with the claim. Her family most likely bade her to wait for Lord Ellrich's return before she made the accusation. It was probably too late to find the men responsible, now that the invasion of Wildermont had begun. Lord Ellrich sighed and rubbed at the folds of his chin with his sausage-like fingers. What a shame.

Another report said a rash of burglaries along the riverfront had occurred in more than one town. "Highly organized," Captain Long had written in the margin of the report. Ellrich tried to remember if Long had been sent to the Wildermont front or not. If he had investigated the thefts enough to learn how organized the perpetrators were but still hadn't managed to find them, then maybe the battlefront was the place for him. Or maybe Captain Long would like to lead an excursion out into the marshes to wipe out some of the pesky dactyls. Ellrich liked that idea better. A few of the big, leathery birds hanging from the trees in the towns along the coast would make the people feel a little bit better. He started to read the next page, but sighed again and tossed the stack of papers onto his desk.

Since being home, he had been forced to deal with these sorts of matters personally. He used to assign a man to each and see what came about, but he didn't have the resources of his garrison anymore. A few thousand men suddenly turned into a few hundred. He would deal with it on the morrow. The scent of Rosila's meal had him salivating. Not even the upsetting matter of the molested girl, whose father he knew personally, was going to disturb his dinner this night.

The table was loaded with his favorites. Rosila cooked and cared for him since he was knee-high to a swamp bug, and knew just what would satisfy his vast hunger. Since he had been home, he had been too busy culling the outposts and making the rounds to sit down at his own table and enjoy one of her feasts, but she insisted he stay put this night. She also invited his advisers and warned them what would happen if they didn't leave the Lord to get a good night's rest after supper was finished. They knew better than to argue with her, as did Lord Ellrich. She was as old as Settsted itself, and as stubborn as the stone from which it was built.

Captain Layson, a tall, thick man in his graying years with a clean military demeanor and a balding head, had been invited. He was Lord Ellrich's second in command here at the stronghold.

Captain Munst, a slightly younger and bulkier version of Captain Layson, was there as well. He was over all the men who manned the string of outposts that Lord Ellrich had just gutted.

Sir William, the wily old Weapons Master who had trained nearly every man that served under Lord Ellrich, was there as well. He was getting on in years, but his wild explosion of snow-white hair and his hardened physique were still imposing, especially on the training yard, where he often proved why he was still the Weapons Master.

The rock-walled dining hall wasn't very large. It held only one long table and was lit by torches spaced evenly along the long walls. The big fireplace at the foot of the table was blocked off with a wooden folding partition, and was painted the same dark, dreary shades of green and brown as the two swamp scene tapestries hanging on the walls that ran alongside of the dining board. Even this early in the summer, a fire would have made the heat in the windowless room unbearable.

The occasion was informal; old friends who trusted and respected one another, just socializing and enjoying the return of their Liege Lord. These were the three men who had shaped Lord Ellrich's ideals and raised him after his father passed away many years ago. His title meant little in their company; they were like family, and none of them would hesitate to speak his mind. All three of them were pleased to get to enjoy Rosila's feast. It was rare that she let them share the Lord's table.

Not much was said while they ate. Roasted game hens and sliced pork drenched in gravy seemed to keep their fingers and mouths busy enough. Fresh-baked and heavily buttered loaves of bread, sweet jellies and a mix of green vegetables weren't ignored, either. The best cask of red in the cellar had been brought up, and Rosila and her daughter kept the goblets full. Dessert was sugared moss cakes with candied gar root, a swamp land delicacy that was as rare as snowfall to the men. They ate their fill of all of it.

The conversation stayed light until Lord Ellrich, who was sweating profusely and bloated like a boar hog, had a pair of candelabras brought out so the torches could be extinguished. After wiping the grease and sweet jam from his hands, he belched loudly, then touched on the subject of King Glendar's campaign against the east. He was buzzed from the wine and had a green smear of icing from the moss cake on his cheek. His manner and tone were almost comical.

"You think this war is a winnable thing?" he asked the table.

"Why that Highwander Witch would set such a thing off at Summer's Day, I cannot imagine," Captain Layson offered.

"I heard it was a Seaward bastard who started the blood flowing, after Lord Gregory killed their fighter," Sir William said.

The mention of the Lion Lord caused a long moment of head-shaking reverie as they all thought about the much loved and greatly missed Lord of Lake Bottom.

"He was a fine man," Lord Ellrich slurred. He raised his flagon up in toast. "To a fair and noble warrior, who will be sorely missed."

"Aye, he was that," Sir William added.

"Here, here," the others agreed.

"They say ol' King Jarrek is already holed up in that castle fortress of his like a scared rabbit." Sir William changed the subject before the loss of Lord Gregory ruined the mood of the evening completely.

"Those Redwolves like to snarl and bark a lot, but when it comes time to really fight, what do they do but run like curs."

This came from Captain Munst, who was obviously the least intoxicated of them. He had only been sipping at his goblet while the other men had been drinking deeply. He had three daughters and an anxious wife at home. With the loss of manpower along the riverfront, he was sure he wouldn't get another chance like this for a good long while. Always traveling from outpost to outpost limited his time here. He had the chance this night to go and see them, and he wasn't about to come home in a drunken stupor.

"If they had policed the festival like they were supposed to," Munst continued, "then none of this would've happened. They brought it upon themselves."

"THAT FOOL'S PUPPET, GLENDAR!" Lord Ellrich roared out quite loudly.

Only here in his home, with these men whom he trusted completely, would he speak what was truly on his mind.

"He and Lord Brach would've found a reason to go after Wildermont sooner or later. They've been scheming on it since long before King Balton died."

"Another great man who will be sorely missed," said Captain Munst, hoping to detour his Liege Lord's treasonous line of thought before it went too far. "To good King Balton," he toasted. "May he lie with the gods for all eternity."

"Agreed," the others chimed in, getting the drift of Captain Munst's intention.

None of them wanted to find out what their fate would be if Lord Ellrich got his head spiked for being treasonous against the new king. They had all heard the rumors about how the bailey yards and the garden gates of Lakeside Castle were sporting the heads of those who so much as irritated young Glendar. It was also said Lord Brach had spies everywhere. Between the resourceful Northern Lord and the king's strange wizard, Captain Munst feared that Glendar's ears might be privy to the words Lord Ellrich spoke, even here in his own stronghold.

Sir William started to speak, but the wooden fireplace cover fell flat onto the stone floor with a sudden and resounding, WHACK!

Lord Ellrich didn't seem to notice, but Captain Layson and Sir William both snapped their heads around, instinctually alarmed by the sound.

Captain Munst, who was at the foot of the table and had his back to the hearth, chose to gauge the reaction of the others, instead of twisting in his chair. Only when Captain Layson's brows narrowed over squinting, quizzical eyes, and when he stood and strode toward the sound, did Captain Munst's curiosity get the better of him.

"What caused that?" he asked as he made to join Captain Layson's investigation.

Lord Ellrich noticed them and became only mildly concerned.

"Probably the wind," he said with a dismissive wave. "Leave it be."

"What in the name of—?" Captain Layson's voice was cut short, as he leapt back from a cloud of soot that erupted suddenly from the back of the stone recess.

"It's a fargin Widow Worm!" Captain Munst yelled when he saw the venomous marsh lizard.

It was as long as his leg, covered in grey ash, and it was already streaking across the floor. It leapt sideways into Captain Munst's empty chair, paused for half a heartbeat, then jumped onto the foot of the table, and shot full speed across it toward Lord Ellrich's wide-eyed jiggling head.

As if he were the only man in the room, the determined thing came at the oversized Lord of Settsted. Its claws and teeth were about to find flesh, but Sir William brought his dagger down, and pinned the Widow Worm through its back to the wooden table. Its vicious, toothy maw snapped shut only a hair's breadth from Lord Ellrich's face. It lurched and scrabbled in place, its claws seeking purchase on the well used, but polished surface of the table board. It snapped, writhed, and twisted, still trying to get at the huge man as if it had no other purpose than to sink its teeth into him. Its tail whipped around, sent the remainder of a serving platter clattering to the floor, and managed to knock over the candelabra, but its thrashing was in vain. The old Weapon Master's dagger held it fast.

Thump! Thump! Thump!

The sound of someone beating heavily on the wooden door startled them all.

Sir William doused the overturned candles with what was left of his drink. Rosila came barging into the hall from the kitchen to see what the racket was about, saw the lizard flopping on the table, and screamed loudly. Her daughter, who had come in on her heels, fainted at the sight of the bloody thing.

Thump! Thump! Thump! at the door again.

This time Captain Layson went to answer it. On his way, he attempted to bat the ash from his shirt, but only managed to smear it across the front.

"Kill it!" Lord Ellrich commanded as he raised his bulk from his seat.

The Widow Worm was still straining and snapping at him. He stumbled drunkenly and nearly fell over his chair. He wasn't sure which was worse, the insistent swamp creature, or Rosila's ear-piercing shriek.

Sir William was still coherent enough to keep from pulling his dagger out of the writhing thing to stab it again. It wanted to get at his Lord too badly. Instead, he grabbed his empty goblet, and began pounding the creature's head. Blood and pieces of wet, goo-covered scales flew everywhere.

Rosila backed away and fell over her daughter. Captain Munst made an alert move and managed to catch her before she went all the way down, but her screaming continued in loud, hysterical bursts. Sir William hammered away at the creature as Captain Layson opened the door and let in a terrified-looking, sweat-covered young soldier.

"Enough!" yelled Lord Ellrich.

Captain Munst recognized the boy and immediately began trying to ease Rosila's ample body into his empty chair. This couldn't be good news.

Sir William hadn't heard his lord, and was still pounding the lizard into the table. Its body was twitching now, and its hiss had become a gurgling, spewing sound.

"Enough!" Lord Ellrich roared it this time.

Everyone in the room froze in place. Sir William was a sight, with his bloody cup raised for another blow, his expression a mixture of childish glee and utter befuddlement. The newly arrived young soldier's heavy panting, Rosila's whimpering sobs, and the slow scratching of the dying lizard's claws as they raked across the table, filled the sudden and relative silence.

The young soldier looked desperate to speak, but afraid to make a sound. One could only imagine how he was interpreting the scene before him. Captain Munst unceremoniously dropped Rosila into his chair and stepped around.

"What is it?" he asked, with a tinge of fear in his voice. He knew the boy had come a very long way to bring whatever message he was carrying. "Tell us now!"

"They've come out of the marsh, Captain!" The words came like water bursting through a breaking dam. "I've run all the way from the Mids. It was happening at Half Point when I passed, and now here. Dane, a rider from Last Post, has just come into the yard bearing the same news from the other end." The young man gasped for another breath, before continuing. "They're armed to the gills and coming in swarms. We haven't the men left to stop them."

"What in all the bloody hells are you saying boy?" Lord Ellrich asked.

Neither of his two captains waited for the answer. They were bolting out of the hall to assess the situation for themselves. Sir William understood that something was very wrong and waited, still frozen in place, with his cup held high over his head, for the young soldier to answer his Liege Lord.

"We're under attack, m'lord," the boy said, with tears pooling in his eyes. They were obviously tears of terror. "We're being overrun by the Skeeks!"

"The Zard?" Lord Ellrich looked to Sir William stupidly.

The Weapon Master's arm finally fell to his side, and his mouth formed a perfect O.

The Zardmen were hunted to extinction in the days of Lord Ellrich's grandfather, or so they had thought. Sightings had been reported from time to time over the years, but they were dismissed as hoaxes or mistakes. In all his life, in all of the treks into the marshes to hunt snapper, dactyl, and geka, during all the deeper excursions to hunt wibbin and skirlsnake, not one of his men, nor any of his father's men had ever produced a shred of evidence that the Zard still lived. Ellrich couldn't believe what he was hearing, and neither could Sir William.

"Master William," the boy went on, after wiping away his tears. "They number in the thousands. We should see to our lord's safety."

Shaella looked down from the dragon's back at the squat, blocky shape of Settsted Stronghold with an expression of deep concentration and purpose on her wind-raw face. Her satiny black cloak fluttered at the collar, and anywhere it wasn't pinned between her shapely bottom and the dragon's scaly hide. Her mind was clear and focused on her purpose. All thoughts of Gerard and Pael were pushed aside for the moment. She was invading Westland. She couldn't afford to think about trivial matters. She was the Dragon Queen now, come to conquer Westland and make it her empire.

All along the river border, Shaella's Zard army was attacking. The whole stretch of Westland was being overrun. The military outposts, cities, and towns that sprouted up around them were getting the worst of it. She concentrated her forces in those heavily populated areas. They were the only places where enough people remained to put up any sort of organized resistance. Smaller groups of Zard were attacking the fishing villages, and it was her soldiers, riding on the backs of the big geka lizards, who were now patrolling the river roads. The metropolis of Southport would have to wait. She would use terror tactics to take hold of its people's fears. That would have to work in Portsmouth to the north and Castleview at Lakeside as well.

"Nothing like a great big fire-breathing dragon to get the city folk in line," she mused.

Between Claret and the savage Breed giants she was about to let loose on the northern parts of Westland, she was sure there would be very little resistance. Who could stop her? All the able-bodied men in the land were off with King Glendar. Westland would fall like wheat before a scythe.

When she was finished with Settsted, she had to fly to Locar, then to Coldfrost. She couldn't allow word of Westland's demise to reach King Glendar with enough time for him to pull out of Wildermont and come home. She would use the half-Breed giants to cut him and his army off soon, but she had to get Settsted out of the way first. It was the only place in Westland, save for Lakeside Castle, where a sizable group of trained soldiers remained.

The destruction of Settsted would be an example to the rest of the land. The fall of the much loved and overfed southern marsh lord would be a blunt statement to those he had been sworn to protect. The message would be clear. Westland has fallen. You were never safe. Bow to your new queen or be roasted in a blast of dragon fire. Pledge your allegiance, or face slavery and torture or a fate worse than death. The geka, after all, had to be fed.

The thrill and glory Shaella thought would accompany this moment was absent. So was the anger and passion she felt in the dragon's lair with her father. That night was intense, yes, but her mood and demeanor were cold and deliberate. Her actions and decisions seemed almost mechanical. Her emotion had been left up in Claret's lair with the blackened stain that was once Gerard.

Mindlessly, and without feeling, she would take this kingdom and squeeze the life out of it. She was too drained by the loss of her lover to even savor the revenge she was taking out on King Glendar for stealing her father's attention her entire life. She just didn't care anymore.

The gluttonous lord hadn't shown himself on the walls yet, but his two old captains had. Time was running short. She had to make a calculated concession. Lord Ellrich was probably somewhere in the stronghold, shoveling food into his face. Shaella thought he might be too fat to get himself up onto the wall, anyway. What she had to do in Coldfrost couldn't wait much longer.

Through the magical link of the collar, she commanded the dragon to destroy the stronghold. With barely a tweak of her huge wings, Claret started her dive toward the dark stone structure, drawing in a deep, billowing breath as she went.

Captain Layson sent half the men of the stronghold garrison, about a hundred of them, out to meet the attackers. The rest were scrambling up onto the walls with long bows and pikes.

Captain Munst ordered the fire pits to be fueled and lit, and the tar pots to be brought out. The mile or so of town between the stronghold wall and the riverfront was already half in flame. The men outside the walls were holding back the armed lizardmen, but barely.

"There are hundreds of them," Captain Munst observed aloud. "And there are more of them riding on the backs of those geka. Why don't they just rush the walls?"

"Probably too stupid," Captain Layson spat. "They're just Skeeks! They might…"

He was about to say more, but Captain Munst's pointing finger and sudden wide-eyed gasp of breath stopped him.

"No, they're staying out of the way of that!" Munst's tone was deflated. He knew then and there, beyond all doubt, that he would never see his wife and daughters again. All he could do was close his eyes and say a prayer for them.

"Gods," was all Captain Layson could manage, before Claret's flaming breath charred them and the men around them to smoldering husks.

Lord Ellrich bodily pulled Sir William toward his office. The young soldier followed nervously. He was too afraid to put his hands on his lord to help the Weapon Master stop him even though his superior, Sir William, was ordering him to do so.

Sir William wanted Ellrich to go with him to the stables. There, they could gather enough men to escort Ellrich away from the fighting, but the Lord of Settsted wouldn't hear of it. After glimpsing the burning town from one of the arrow slits in the long hall, he had only one thing on his mind. He remembered as clearly as if it had been an hour ago, Pael and King Glendar arguing for the soldiers of his border guard to be taken away. The wizard had a hand in this, Ellrich was sure of it. And if it was so, then all of Westland was in trouble.

He ordered both Sir William and the boy to get out, then changed his mind, and ordered the young soldier to follow him to his study. The Weapons Master was doing everything short of physically assaulting his lord, to try to get him to see reason, but it was no use. Ellrich just dragged him along as if he were a child.

Once in the study, Lord Ellrich sent Sir William stumbling across the room with a heavy shove. Sir William slammed into the wall and decided he had tried as hard as he could. His lord was determined to do whatever it was that he was about to do.

Lord Ellrich took a parchment and quill, and after clumsily spilling ink all over the stacks of unanswered petitions and reports on his desk, he began writing with furious intensity. He sanded the paper, and burned his hand lighting a wax candle in the torch flaming on the wall sconce. He showed no regard, not even a wince, as the flames licked and blistered his knuckles. The room filled with the acrid smell of burnt hair. Lord Ellrich didn't care. He blew the sand from the note, rolled it quickly into a scroll, and then blotted a globule of wax on it to seal it. After pressing his ring into the cooling stuff, he handed the scroll to the boy.

"You are to ride!"

He said it quickly, placing a hand on each of the young man's shoulders for emphasis. They were eye to eye then, and the lord's order took on a deadly weight.

"Ride like the wind to Lakebottom, and give that to either Lady Trella, or my daughter, Lady Zasha. Do you understand? Lady Trella or Lady Zasha only!"

"Yes, m'lord," the soldier answered dutifully. The idea he was being ordered away from the slaughter taking place around him, the hope that he might not die this night, filled him with confidence.

"Stop for no man. Not even for the king himself!" Ellrich said sharply. "And take as many horses as you need to make it through without stopping. Now go!"

The boy didn't hesitate. He was off in a flash of boot heels and elbows, leaving Lord Ellrich and Sir William alone in the room. A bright, orange blast of light suddenly shone through the shuttered window that overlooked the training yard. It was accompanied by an earth-shaking roar, which chilled both men to their core. There was no time to even think after that. The building shook, and pieces of the ceiling beams splintered downward. A huge piece of stone flooring came down on them from above, crushing both of them to death in an instant. The last sound either of them heard was Claret's battle roar as she tore Settsted Stronghold to the ground.

Lord Ellrich would never know it, but the young soldier managed to get clear of the stronghold and the Zard army closing in around it. The horses he chose were fast, strong, and more importantly, they were rested. There was a good chance that he would manage to escape the two geka that were chasing him.

Chapter Thirty-Four

The siege of the Redwolf's mountain castle had lasted a week so far. According to the lists before him, King Jarrek knew they could go another half a year or more. Considering they had over three thousand soldiers behind the secondary wall, and nearly eight thousand other people that were waiting, they had plenty of stores hidden away in the caverns.

Women, children, nobles, and dignitaries, as well as the castle staff and personal servants, were all inside the castle. It seemed amazing to him. What amazed King Jarrek even more was that the castle folk spoke of the siege as if it were an event: a ball, a concert, or a mummers' show. Even the lords and merchants whose homes were being torched and looted just outside the secondary wall seemed oblivious to the reality of the situation. They just didn't understand. They were all certain they were safe because the castle itself, in all of history, had never been taken. The first, second, and third baileys had fallen a few times during the bloody dark wars of Jarrek's great, great-grandfather, but the castle's innermost wall, known as the Gate, had never been breached. The fortress was designed to wait out a siege.

The castle was a city in itself, built into the side of the Wilder Mountains, thus the name Castlemont. Many of the people who lived there had never gone outside the outer walls in all of their lives. Day to day life inside the huge palace seemed almost normal to most of them, as if war wasn't waiting just beyond the secondary wall, as if an enemy army wasn't waiting to storm in, ravage them, and march them into slavery.

King Jarrek shook his head in wonder at the ignorance of his people. He had no doubt the siege would be broken soon, but someday an enemy might really threaten to take the whole place. He could only imagine how the castle folk would act if a time like that really came.

He and his advisers were in his conference room, planning. The table at which they were seated was forty feet long. Its eight legs were carved into perfect wolf's paws, and its oak surface was varnished and polished so perfectly that it looked wet. The chairs were just as impressive. The crown of each sported a growling wolf's head above a back thick with padding and covered in red velvet. The armrests were wolves' forelegs, and the chairs' feet matched the table legs in miniature.

All along the walls on both sides of the table, realistic paintings of heroic battle scenes and other historical events were separated by fancy, brass oil lanterns hung on ornate sconces on the gray-and-white-swirled marble walls. Like the tabletop, the black marble floor resembled a body of water. The room's two huge carved oak doors were shut and barred, giving the dozen men inside the room total privacy. They were planning to break the siege.

One of the two wizards in attendance was from Highwander. His name was Targon. He stood a head taller than any other man there. His height and plain white robes made him stand out quite dramatically in the rich, colorful council chamber. His long, silver-streaked black hair, his dark eyes, and well-trimmed goat's beard gave him an almost sinister look.

Willa the Witch Queen sent him to Wildermont as soon as she heard the reports of Blacksword impostors flying her banners and firing arrows into crowds. She claimed that though some of the merchants and traders of her land had surely attended the festival, no one that represented Highwander or her Blacksword army in any formal capacity had been there. She and her kingdom held no ill will toward any other in the realm at the moment and Targon assured King Jarrek if she did, she would handle the dispute swiftly and in the open.

Targon had come there to assist in the investigation and to find out who it was that impersonated the Blacksword. He got caught up in the Westland surprise attack. Now, acting on his newest orders from Queen Willa, his full services as a War Wizard had been offered to King Jarrek and Wildermont in this time of need.

The other wizard, Keedle, had been born right there in the castle eighty years earlier. The riverside villa he had been raised in was now being used as a Westland Command post, and he was none too pleased about it. His bitter anger at King Glendar was the only thing keeping him from being jealous of Targon's presence in his kingdom.

With his long, white hair and beard flowing over his red-and-gold-trimmed black robe, Keedle stood looking out the glassed-in window wall at his city. The audacity of Westland's new king showed. Placing his pavilion tent right there in front of the main gates, as if inviting them to charge out and take him, was maddening. The fact that, for days now, he had paraded the women of Wildermont in and out of his tent as if they were his was infuriating. Keedle decided that he would show no mercy if he had a choice in the matter. Glendar wasn't just a bad neighbor or a land-greedy tyrant. He was a menace to humanity.

Others in attendance were General Coron and two of his captains, all three representing the army of the Redwolf; Lord Marshal Culvert of the Castlemont City guard; one of his deputies; and the King's Investigator, Lord Greenwich and his page. A few nervous but busy scribes sat to the side, scribbling away as the orders and suggestions were thrown out on the table for discussion.

"Why would he leave so few men to hold us?" Lord Marshal Culvert asked the room. The he he was speaking of, was of course King Glendar of Westland.

"He's keeping us pinned up while he gets the bulk of his army through the mountains," General Coron explained. "Is it possible that once they're through, he will pack up and follow them?"

"That's a very optimistic question, General," King Jarrek commented politely. "If that were his plan, though, I doubt he would've looted the outer city and marched all of our women and children south toward Dakahn."

For a moment, no one spoke. Courtly manner dictated that the king be allowed several moments to add to his own statements before anyone might interrupt his Highness's thoughts.

"I agree," Lord Greenwich, the King's Investigator finally said. "Why give us a hundred reasons for vengeance and retaliation, then just up and march away?"

"Not to mention the fact that Westland has got to be nearly defenseless," said General Coron. "Twenty thousand men have marched across that bridge, maybe more. Who's guarding the henhouse while the young rooster is out strutting?"

The General spoke in a way that made it clear that he didn't really believe what he suggested a moment ago. "They have to hold that bridge no matter what happens here. If we break the siege, we'll be able to march right into Westland."

"Oh, we'll break the siege, General," King Jarrek said with confidence. He turned to Lord Greenwich. "How many men did you estimate Glendar had left in our city?"

"At best, twenty-four hundred, a few hundred more on or around the bridge, maybe."

"We have as many, if not more, men inside the walls with us!" Marshall Culvert blurted out, his overly optimistic enthusiasm showing again.

His city guard had been routed in the streets. He was as bitter as he was embarrassed by the fact. Those men had not been trained to handle a full scale attack on the city. They were there to protect the people from each other, not from an invading army. That was the job of General Coron's men, most of whom had been too busy dealing with the myriad problems associated with

Summer's Day to muster a defense. Marshall Culvert didn't blame the General. His men put up so little resistance, they may as well have not been there. They mostly died in vain. He manfully accepted his share of the blame. He took no comfort in the truth, and he lustfully wanted to break the siege. He wanted to take back some of the pride that had been stripped from him.

"I've got three hundred men up at High Crossing, maybe a few more," General Coron offered. "They retreated into the lower Evermore on the Leif Greyn side when the Westlanders turned north. If we can get word to them, they should be able to at least break through the encampment where the fargin Lion's men went into the mountains."

"I can help you there, Your Majesty."

Targon, who had been listening intently, finally spoke. His voice was deep and radiated a sort of confidence that was greatly needed among them.

"Not only with getting orders to those men." Smoothing his robes, he stood and faced the window, where the other wizard was brooding. "I can help protect them when they sack the encampment, and with the help of my colleague, Keedle, we can communicate and make sure the arrival of those men here is timely to your cause."

"Yes," the general nodded, and mumbled under his breath as the plan formed in his head. The idea that it was put there by the Witch Queen's Wizard was lost on him.

The king was about to ask the General to share his thoughts, when Keedle spun and strode toward the table. The look on his face demanded that he be heard next. King Jarrek gave him a nod and steepled his fingers, intent to listen to his trusted old wizard's words.

"When you send your men storming out the gates, General, I'll make them appear to be twice as many as they really are." Keedle's anger made his words sharp and cold. "If King Jarrek will allow it, I'll take the outer wall so I can be over them and wreak as much havoc as I can manage. I'll draw the attention to me. With Targon coming with those other men to catch them from behind, and my surprises, we should be able to break the siege and take our city back with minimal losses. At worst, we could run the cavalry right over that pavilion tent, and crush the young Westland dog in his sleep."

"Now you're the one being optimistic," said General Coron.

Though he would love nothing more than to flatten the cocky young bastard just as Keedle suggested, the fact remained they didn't hold the outer wall anymore. A charge out of the secondary gates would allow the Westland King enough warning to be long gone by the time they got there. He shook his head side to side.

"I have no doubt you'll be able to do as you say, but we can't run all of our men out of the secondary gates, Master Keedle. It will take at least half of them to hold the castle, if something should go wrong. Even fifteen hundred wolves would have a hard time taking on all those fargin Westlanders. It's almost two to one."

Keedle's brows narrowed as he realized the truth of the general's words. Even with two wizards working together, two to one odds would be hard to overcome in open battle.

"We mustn't forget about Pael," Targon said in his deep voice. "The Westland wizard is no mere conjurer."

"I pray I get the chance to face Pael!" Keedle said hotly. "This whole attack stinks of his rotten influence."

"General," King Jarrek spoke, then placed his steepled fingers to his chin and pursed his lips for a moment before continuing, "if it were an even battle, man for man, so to speak, do you think this plan would work?"

The General's nostrils flared and his chest swelled proudly.

"Man for man, your Redwolf Army can beat anyone."

"So, if I allowed you to march out of here into the city with two thousand men, with Keedle's and Targon's help, along with the men from High Crossing to surprise the Westlanders, you think you can come out victorious?"

"I'm sure of it," the General said flatly.

"Of the thousand men who stay behind, I think four hundred should be left inside the gates," said King Jarrek. "The rest should be our best archers, and they should take to the secondary wall when you go out, to keep your men from getting trapped between the secondary gate and the outer walls. Once your men are clear and into the city, they will be shut out, General Coron. As I'm sure you're aware, this is an all or nothing sort of gambit."

The General had to fight to suppress the smile. He could never remember loving his king's boldness more than he did at that moment. Jarrek, he decided, was a warrior through and through.

"I will proudly lead them myself, Your Highness." He stood, and bowed his head in respect. "I understand the risks fully, and relish the chance to overcome them."

"I want all of you to think on this plan while we break our fast," King Jarrek told them. "Keep in mind that we don't have to do this. We can just sit and wait for a better opportunity to present itself. If we have to, we can wait out the whole of fall and winter." He rose from his seat and ran a hand through his dark hair. "But don't forget those of our people whom Glendar marched south. They might not have the luxuries we have. We have to get them home."

After they ate and had time alone to think, the king took a consensus of the men's thoughts on the matter. All of them agreed. The plan was sound, the situation would probably never be more opportune, and they had to do something about the women and children King Glendar had sent south before they were sold into the Dakaneese slave market, or worse. They were all fairly certain that Westland would soon send in reinforcements. Right now, the odds were surmountable. They might soon become impossible.

King Jarrek privately decided that he would ride out with his personal guard attachment through a secret exit way. The expert swords would be needed, and he wanted to get his own steel into the enemy as badly as anybody. He ordered the plan to be executed, and the wheels of the Kingdom of Wildermont's fate clicked into motion.

Young King Glendar was enjoying the company of the wife and daughter of one Wildermont's most prestigious merchants. Outside his tent, six of the bloodiest, most ruthless men Glendar could find in his troops after the battle for Castlemont City stood guard. They weren't bloody now. Glendar had given them the pick of the armaments and weapons that had been collected from the many smithies and armories around the city. They were now his personal guards. They stood brilliantly in the hot summer sun, in gleaming chain and plate mail, under a pair of Westland's biggest banners. The weapons were newly forged and razor sharp. A few were works of art, with extreme value. They were the envy of the Westland troops that remained in Wildermont. Their only duty was to protect their king, with their very lives if necessary. They pledged to do so with their own blood.

Inside the tent, Glendar was just finishing up his present business. The shade that the canvas provided did little to cool his sweating body, and the aroma of many couplings hung heavy in the thick air. He had taken, or been offered in some cases, the virtue of many a Wildermont woman while he waited for Pael to return.

He had done exactly as Pael ordered and sent the bulk of the women and children south to O'Dakahn. Of course, he handpicked the ones that he fancied, and imprisoned them at a wealthy nobleman's mansion near the city's edge. The duke, or lord, or regent, or whatever title the man held, didn't mind. His head was drawing crows on a pike in the house's yard. Tonight, very soon in fact, out of sheer boredom, King Glendar was going to start terrorizing King Jarrek and his men from afar. It could be weeks before Pael came back to help him take the castle and King Glendar figured to weaken their spirit while he waited.

The idea of his tent sitting just outside of the fortress's outer walls gave him a sort of smug satisfaction. It showed a cocky lack of fear or respect for his enemies. Besides that, it made him feel superior. At first it unnerved him. The idea that a horde of Redwolf soldiers could, at any moment, come storming out of those open gates had been overwhelming. Only after he toured the area beyond the gates, with the smoldering buildings, body-strewn streets, and the clouds of carrion that attended them, did he realize he had nothing to fear. He would have moved his pavilion in front of the secondary wall's main gate, if doing so wouldn't make it too hard for all those eyes way up in the castle to look down upon it. Where it was now, any who looked out toward the west were forced to see it. Glendar was about to decorate the area around his tent properly, so that all those peering eyes had something substantial to see when they gazed out.

"Out now!" he ordered the two women who were trembling and naked in his bed.

They rose quickly, and began searching for their clothes on the floor. "I said now!" he screamed, and shoved the mother out the tent flaps into the dirt, sniveling and bare-skinned. He gave the daughter a swift boot in the rear as she stopped to grab her mother's dress. She went sprawling out behind her mother, her arms so full of bundled clothes, that she couldn't stop herself from smacking into the ground. The mother, shamed and terrified, helped her daughter up. They huddled together right in the middle of the street, until a soldier from a group of Glendar's attendants came hopping over to lead them back to their prison.

"Roark!" Glendar yelled through the closed flap of the tent.

The biggest and meanest of the guardsmen turned and stepped into the tent. He quickly averted his eyes, while Glendar pulled his leggings up over his spindly white legs.

"Yes, Your Majesty?"

The big man had to stoop awkwardly, because the pavilion's roof pressed down on the sharp horns of the helmet he sported. Glendar found it comical and chuckled.

"From now on Roark, remove your helmet before entering the tent."

Glendar laughed again as the man fumbled the helm off like a scolded child.

"It's a rule now. Tell the others." Glendar's voice turned serious, almost sharp. "I don't want the canvas ripped by those fargin helmets."

He looked around the room for something, then sighed heavily and continued.

"Send a handful of men over to where Lord Abel is holding the rest of the Wildermont City Guardsmen and help escort them all here."

He gestured through the tent wall toward the open gates outside.

"As you command." Roark nodded. He bowed in his gold chased plate armor as if the heavy steel weighed nothing on his frame, then spun and exited the tent.

He froze three paces later, with this helmet held nearly in place over his head. King Glendar was calling out his name. He turned to go back inside, but Glendar stuck his sweaty grinning head out saving him the trouble.

"Have Captain Stimps bring some torches and the chopping block. Oh yeah, pikes, Roark. We're going to need plenty of pikes."

Chapter Thirty-Five

King Glendar expected a reaction over his gruesome display, but not so soon. The sun had long illuminated the sky, but hadn't risen over the mountains that cradled Castlemont quite yet. Glendar's pavilion was deep in the morning shadow.

Glendar's evening had been spent laboring. Now he was being ripped from a deep, well earned sleep. The kind of sleep a lumberjack might find after a day of felling trees, or a blacksmith after swinging his hammer all day; or maybe like a young tyrant might earn after a night of piking men's heads.

"Your Majesty!" Roark yelled for the third time. This time, he pulled the silken sheets off of his king and added a threat. "I'm going to yank you out of bed and carry you out of here! Get up and dress!"

"What is it, man?" Glendar growled. "Didn't last night's display teach you better manners?"

Glendar held his hand up in front of his eyes to shield them from the brightness of Roark's lantern. He was naked, save for his small clothes. To Roark, he looked like a bleached wood scarecrow with a dark mess of a wig on his head.

"They're riding out to break us!" the big guard said excitedly. "Captain Hinkle's man said there are at least four thousand of them between horse and footmen. Maybe more!"

Suddenly, King Glendar was fully awake.

"What? Four thousand men?" King Jarrek couldn't be foolish enough to send out the whole of his forces. Blast!

That's more men than Glendar had left himself in the city. Panic tore through the young king. He had no idea what to do. He sent the bulk of his forces through the mountains, just as Pael had instructed him to do. Pael! Where was Pael anyway?

"Get dressed, uh, um, if you please," Roark stammered, holding out the king's leggings and an undershirt.

"Bring my chain mail," Glendar barked, as he took the offered clothes. His stiff attitude did little to hide his confusion, though it did mask his growing fear fairly well.

He could hear the distant sound of battle now, the chink and clang of steel on steel, the clattering of horses, and the occasional death cry. The sound was coming from somewhere beyond the open gates. He could tell by the sounds of his own men riding in from the encampments around the city and the hustling of his troops outside his tent that there was not much time to waste.

Suddenly, an explosion shook the earth. A brilliant flash of light lit the morning shade so brightly, its glow could be seen plainly through the thick canvas walls of the pavilion tent. The sheer volume of the noise was deafening.

In the long, relative silence that followed the blast, the shriek of a man died away slowly. The terrified "oohs" and "aahs" of the men outside of his tent, made Glendar tremble.

What could've made that explosion? He had no idea what was happening. He heard the words, wizard and magic shouted in fear outside. He vaguely remembered Lord Brach once warning him about King Jarrek's old sorcerer, Keedle. He had scoffed at the warning, saying Pael was far more capable. Where is Pael, anyway? Glendar needed him right now, and badly.

A few moments later, King Glendar emerged from the command pavilion into a world of utter chaos. This was no dominating rout like the taking of the city had been. Already, some of the Redwolf Cavalry were getting through. The men holding the inside of the outer wall, Glendar's men, or what was left of them, were falling back. Most of them were covered in something black, soot or oil maybe, Glendar couldn't tell exactly what it was.

Roark yanked him out of the way of a volley of arrows that came thumping down in a tight grouping where he had just been standing. The other men of the king's personal guard swarmed around them. They forced King Glendar to fall back away from the battle that was taking form right there in the gateway of the outer wall. Glendar looked around frantically for some indication, some sign of what he should do.

More Westlanders were charging in from the north and south to clog the way, some in organized groups and some in stumbling tangles. From the road that led out to the Locar Crossing Bridge, a huge band of Lord Abel's Cavalry came charging past with weapons drawn and faces set for grim and bloody work.

Seeing them, Glendar sighed with relief. Up until that moment, he'd thought King Jarrek's soldiers held the advantage. He had thought it was all but over. Now, with so many of his men in sight, ready to drive the Wildermont soldiers back behind the walls, he began to feel that smug confidence returning to him.

Suddenly, from the top of the wall, a sizzling streak of yellow blazed down into the crowd of Westlanders at the mouth of the gate. Where it impacted, a man-sized divot of dirt and debris exploded up from the earth, causing the horses and men around it to go flailing blindly into the heated battle. A figure robed in black with his hands raised up high sent another blast, then another, into the fray below him. At first, Glendar thought it was Pael, but through the smoke and distance, he saw a long, white beard trailing from the sorcerer's chin. It was Keedle.

As if he had sensed Glendar's eyes on him, the old wizard stopped his attack, and met Glendar's wide-eyed gaze. Across the great distance, Glendar could see the rage and hatred burning on Keedle's face.

Then the moment was gone. The wizard's next crackling blast was larger than the others had been. It shot like a bolt of lightning from his fingers across the open air and over the battling men below him, toward the piked heads in front of Glendar's pavilion. They, and the pavilion tent, exploded in a roiling ball of flame. In the sudden light from the blaze, Glendar could see Redwolf soldiers were pressing out of the gateway now. More of them spilled out into the bloody mix, and his Westlanders were beginning to fall.

From the north, more of his men were charging through the city to join the battle, a few hundred it appeared. He wasn't sure if that made him feel more confident or not. As he gained the saddle of an offered horse, he stood in the stirrups and looked southward. There, a small group of soldiers, maybe three dozen Wildermont cavalrymen, were casually riding up toward the gates. A few of them ranged ahead and dispatched any Westlander who dared to get in their path. At the front of the main group, a rider carried King Jarrek's personal banner. Glendar's strained eyes could tell by the brilliant red enameled armor that those men wore, and by the glinting ruby-eyed wolf skull mounted on their leader's helmet, that it was the Wolf King himself and his infamous Blood Pack.

The realization sent a chill of terror and confusion racing through him. Why would King Jarrek risk himself when Wildermont was losing the battle so badly? It didn't make sense. Again Glendar wished Pael was there. The wizard had promised to take Castlemont down for him. It seemed Pael had forgotten him.

Roark's gasp brought Glendar's attention back to the men riding in from the north. Glendar cursed at what he saw. Then he cursed Pael for not being there.

"I think we should get you to the bridge," the big guardsman suggested.

Glendar didn't have the heart to argue with him. What he had thought were a few hundred Westland soldiers coming in from the north to tilt the battle in his favor, were really only a few dozen Westlanders fleeing from several hundred Wildermont soldiers.

To make things worse, another wizard, this one with dark hair and white robes, was sending bright blue bolts of energy into the group of fleeing Westlanders by the dozens. Like glowing sapphire arrows, the magical blasts shot forth from the wizard's finger, one after another, as fast as he could point out a new target. Each magical pulse struck true and the victims fell, only to be trampled flat as the Redwolf Cavalry rode them over.

Glendar didn't want to watch, but he couldn't seem to tear his eyes away. He wasn't in immediate danger. At least he didn't think so. He still had six guardsmen now mounted and surrounding him, each of them looking more eager than the next to be allowed to go join the battle. Only a short gallop away was the bridge. He knew for certain that enough soldiers remained there to discourage any pursuit back into Westland if he was forced to cross back in retreat.

A knot of Westlanders who had been too crowded into the mass at the gateway to be effective, peeled off at the order of a screaming captain. Fifty men or more turned their horses and rode out to meet King Jarrek's fearsome-looking Blood Pack. One, two, then a third Westlander fell to the huge swords of the crimson-clad wolf's men. The Westlanders appeared to be outmatched until a pike found a painted breast plate, and one of the Redwolf's men flipped off of his horse and crashed to the ground.

Encouraged, the Westlanders roared out and went forward. The battle graduated into a gleaming, bloody frenzy. Swords rose, fell, and swept through the air in blood-slinging arcs. Men screamed in agony, horses reared, and came twisting down on their sides as pikes were rammed through their chests and flanks. A helmet flew spinning through the air, smashed from a man's head by the blow of a huge war hammer. King Jarrek, in his crimson armor, cut through Westlanders like an explorer hacking his way through jungle vegetation, with big heavy slashes that cleaved everything in their path.

Most of the Westlanders that faced the King's Guard were down now, but more were quickly coming. Half of King Jarrek's red armored honor guard was dead as well. A pair of them had been unhorsed and were now fighting viciously back to back on their feet. The half dozen Westlanders surrounding them looked weary.

Along the top of the wall, a troop of archers, followed by the black-robed wizard, ran southward, trying to get into a range that might help their struggling king.

To the north, the white-robed wizard had reined his horse to a halt, letting the Wildermont soldiers he had been leading ride past him. They broke off into groups of four and five and met, with a sickening crash, the Westland archers who had been firing up at the men on the outer walls. The rest of them charged headlong into the knot of men still battling outside the gates and began hacking, stabbing, and slashing their way through.

Glendar's breath caught in his chest, and a powerful wave of sadness and shame came over him. It was a hopeless situation. The siege was broken. The battle was lost. He had failed.

Targon, Willa the Witch Queen's man, sensed something in the air. It alarmed him so much that he steered his horse out of the road and away from the many skirmishes that were taking place there.

The complexity of the spell he needed to cast required his full concentration. He had to find out what it was he was feeling, because it seemed horribly wrong to him. The spell he wanted to cast would identify the source of the strangeness, but already the sensation had gotten so much stronger that it might be too late.

Off the horse he stepped and strode quickly to the semiprotective shelter of a nearby building's awning. It wouldn't do to take a stray arrow while he was distracted. He backed himself up against the rock and mortar and began his casting.

Some of the soldiers were feeling it, too. Some of them so much so, that they stopped in their tracks trying to identify the odd sensation.

The air was becoming static and electric, like it would right before a lightning storm. Hairs rose on the backs of necks and cold shivers ran down spines. A low, vibrant humming sound began to fill the air. For the briefest of moments, it seemed that save for the humming vibration, the whole world stood still. Even the fighting stopped. Then the hum became a droning buzz, and the sound of battle slowly resumed as if it had never ceased.

On the far side of the gates, Keedle was raging from atop the wall. He was so lost in his anger, he didn't even notice the strange sensation, or the way it was affecting the soldiers below him.

From either side of him, Wildermont archers rained deadly steel-tipped arrows down into the crowd as quickly and as accurately as they could. From the smoldering remains of Glendar's pavilion, a few Westland archers loosed back up at them, but not many. One of them struck their mark. The man next to Keedle fell into him, with a Westland arrow sprouting out of his chest. Keedle, seeing how close he had come to being hit, stopped his assault on the Westlanders for a moment. He cast a spell that would shield him from the arrows flying up at him. The spell would protect him as long as he didn't leave that particular section of the wall. As soon as the magical barrier was in place, he was back at it, sending hot sizzling bolts down at any man or horse that ventured too close to King Jarrek and his crimson armored guards.

The bone-tingling buzz had turned into a deep vibration, a tangible feeling in the guts of all of the men. It frightened a lot of them. Wildermont soldiers and Westlanders alike were staring at each other wide-eyed, making ward signs with their hands, and mumbling prayers. Roark, who looked like the Dark One's own champion in his gleaming plate armor and devil helm, was terrified.

But not Glendar, who thought the sensation had a familiar quality to it, a quality he recognized all too well. He wasn't about to leave just yet. King Glendar shrugged Roark's heavy arm from his shoulder.

"Just a few minutes more," he growled at his big horn-helmed guardsman.

Targon came out of his visional trance with a start. What he had just learned defied almost every law of magic and demon lore he knew, and he knew almost all of it.

He had to think. Soon, every ounce of available magical energy would be gone from the area, sucked out of this little part of the world into a thing that was part man and part demon. Pael, Shokin, whatever it was, was right here. It was about to unleash all that power it was drawing in, and Targon wanted no part of that horror.

His mind raced through his cataloged memory of spells and protocol. He couldn't just flee. Queen Willa despised cowardly actions. Targon was no coward, but he was wise enough to know when to retreat. Every base instinct he had was screaming for him to flee. In his mind, he repeated the orders she had given him when she sent him here. A plan formed, and an appropriate spell revealed itself. Without concern for stray arrows, crossbow bolts, or even the straggling Westland soldiers, he hurried out into the middle of the lane. He faced toward the cluster of still battling men by the gates and began his casting.

It wasn't an easy choice for him to make. The very act of getting into position went against everything he had ever learned about self-preservation – a subject of great importance to a wizard of his abilities and skill. He couldn't fail to warn Queen Willa of the thing Pael had somehow become, for whoever or whatever it was now, it would sooner or later set its sights on the Wardstone foundation of Xwarda.

He couldn't abandon King Jarrek, either. He had no choice but to leave his body open and vulnerable to the physical. As risky as it was, it was his only choice. He was in a race to harness enough of the depleting magical force to cast a spell before the demon-wizard took it all. Just like the attempt to break the siege, from here it was all or nothing.

The explosive blast of energy that accompanied Pael's sudden appearance amidst the smoldering remains of Glendar's pavilion shook the very earth like a quake. The world fell into a deeper sort of chaos as terrified horses bolted this way and that, and men fell to their knees, grabbing at the sides of their heads. Blood pulsed from the ear holes of any man or beast that had been close to Pael when he arrived. Equilibriums were thrown off kilter, and a few men simply died from the concussion. One of the northernmost towers up on the mountainside tilted slowly, starting its slow, arcing fall down into the clustered buildings below. The battle had all but stopped. All eyes were drawn to Pael.

King Glendar and his men were behind Pael, and far enough back, that it only took a moment to get them and their horses back under control. The earth-shaking boom scared them all senseless, save for Glendar. He sensed Pael's signature on the grand entrance, like a child senses his mother's mood. The young King of Westland raised his fist and let out a primal yell that trumpeted out what little bits of fear and doubt remained inside him. He had nothing to fear now. Pael was here!

The sight of the wizard standing there, his arms stretched wide in his flowing black robes, the golden embroidered patterns on the belled sleeves and collar sparkling in the new sunlight that just peaked over the mountaintops, was awe inspiring.

Pael's right hand shot out toward Keedle up on the wall, and a huge swathe of blazing white light flashed forth toward the stunned old wizard. The power of the blast shot straight through its target, taking a huge bite-shaped chunk out of the wall as it went. The blast exploded into the southern part of the castle, in a brilliant shower of rock and flaming debris. It cleaved two of the castle's massive towers in the middle. One of them fell straight down on top of the stub that had just been its base. The other canted slowly over until its upper half failed, and the whole thing went tumbling into the castle proper.

King Glendar, emboldened by the blatant display of power, spurred his horse into a trot toward the gates.

"To me!" he cried out, raising his sword up high. "To me!"

It was all Roark and the other guardsmen could do to pull themselves out of the stunned trance that Pael's blast had put them in so that they could follow their king.

"Westlanders to me!" Glendar kept screaming at the top of his lungs. He stopped his horse while still out away from the gates. He wanted to draw his men away from the Redwolf soldiers. He knew Pael wouldn't hesitate to level them if they were in his way. It was a brilliant move, and it probably saved the lives of half of his remaining men, for Pael's wrath knew no colors.

The Wildermont soldiers were stunned, as much by the fact that the Westlanders were pulling back, as by the wild magic the white-skinned, egg-headed wizard was hurling about.

Pael's second massive charge of white-hot magic went arcing across the sky like a monstrous flaming arrow. It was brighter than the sunlight, which it eclipsed at the apex of its flight. When it came down toward the castle, into what remained of the mountain's shadow, it blazed like a falling star. When it impacted, the explosion and the amount of devastation that resulted were heart-rending.

The whole front of the castle proper fell into a crumbling heap, leaving partial rooms and hallways exposed in the swirling dust. Distant colorful specks that were people tumbled out and fell to their deaths as floors collapsed and the smaller towers came crashing down into the main structure. A large piece of the castle, as big as a merchant's mansion, came free from the southern corner. It rolled once on its way down the mountain like it was a boulder, then slammed into a landslide of rock and timbers as it rolled over dozens of lesser buildings and homes.

Pael glanced back over his shoulder at where all the Westland soldiers were gravitating. King Glendar was there. A few hundred men were struggling to form up into some sort of order behind him. A huge plate-armored warrior with a wicked looking horned helmet caught Pael's eye as he barked out orders and threatened the soldiers into their ranks. Pael sensed a dark and brutal quality about the man and marked it in his mind for later recollection. Satisfied with what he had seen behind him, he turned back to the matter at hand.

With only the slightest flicker of motion from his hand, he sent a crackling yellow streak of jagged lightning into the chest of a nearby Wildermont soldier. It held the man in place for a heartbeat, shaking him and smoldering his flesh. From his back, two more bolts shot forth and found other bodies to decimate. One was a limping Westlander, who was trying to reach his king; the other, a Wildermont soldier who was on his knees and still holding his ears from the concussion of Pael's initial coming. From each of them, the lightning branched again, and soon more than twenty men were curled on the ground, writhing and smoldering, or dead.

Pael laughed hysterically. His expression was that of a gleeful child. Oh, how he loved the power he had gained. The gods had been kind. Shaella's lover somehow ruined his intended binding spell and the result left Pael in full control of the demon essence that was trapped inside him. The demon's power was at his fingertips. It didn't matter to Pael that he could still hear Shokin's protests echoing in his mind. He walled the lunatic ravings out. The threats were empty. Pael was in complete control. Shokin was part of him now.

He laughed again and sent the lightning streaking into another soldier near the gates, starting another deadly chain reaction. Then he focused his energy into creating another concussive blast. He almost quit the spell when the sudden presence of another magic tainted the air. He quickly detected that the other wizard was no threat to him, dismissed it, and continued building the huge, magical sphere of destruction he had started. After he hurled it at the castle and enjoyed watching it destroy hundreds, if not thousands of lives, he would deal with the remaining wizard.

Targon was in a daze from his spell. The massive booms and crumbling explosions around him seemed like a distant disturbance in some faraway place. Before him, a swirling tunnel formed itself into being. Outside its roughly ten foot diameter, the battle raged on. Inside, it was like looking down a huge empty pipe that lead straight through the battling soldiers, right past the demon-wizard, over the litter of dead and dying men around him, and ended directly in front of King Jarrek and his men.

"Come! Now! Before it's too late!" Targon screamed out to the King of Wildermont. He repeated the words as loud as he could manage.

This time, King Jarrek heard him, but barely. The concussion of Pael's arrival had left him and his men nearly deaf.

King Jarrek looked down the strange telescopic tube at the Highwander wizard. He mouthed a question. Targon nodded in understanding. After calling out an order, King Jarrek spurred his horse down the shaft toward the Witch Queen's Mage. Three, then another of the red-armored honor guard followed.

A bright, eye-searing flash from somewhere beyond the king and his men nearly caused Targon to falter and lose the spell, but he managed to hang onto it. Then a fifth soldier came galloping down the magical tube. He was wearing the red enameled armor of Jarrek's honor guard as well.

Trembling with the effort, Targon held the spell as long as he could. It was already failing when Jarrek and the first four men shot out of the magical portal past him. Though it pained Targon greatly to do so, he had no choice but to let go of the spell, or get lost in its collapse. The fifth guard's scream filled his head as the magical tube came crashing in on him. The sound of the man and his horse yelling in terror as they were crushed into oblivion echoed for long hours in Targon's head as he, King Jarrek, and the four red-armored guardsmen fled northward as swiftly as their tired mounts could carry them.

No one would ever know it, but the man who lost his life in Targon's magical throughway didn't die in vain. His sudden screaming appearance a few dozen yards directly in front of Pael saved the group from being marked for pursuit. Pael was so surprised by the man that he instantly blasted him and the horse into a cloud of bloody mist. The realization of what had actually happened there came to Pael later after the entire city of Castlemont and its castle were nothing but a dusty ruin and a litter of mangled, bloody flesh.

Later, while the carrion feasted, Pael used Shokin's power to summon some of the dark things that had escaped from the Seal before Shokin had been torn in two. A pair of nether-born wyverns, all acid-mouthed and angry, answered the call. He ordered one of them to track down and kill the wizard who had defied him. The other he commanded to find and aid the hellcat that had once been his familiar, Inkling.

The search for Pavreal's sword took on a new sense of priority in Pael's mind. The part of him that was Shokin feared it, and for good reason. Though Pael thought it very unlikely that a mere squire might find a way to thwart his plans, the boy was apparently King Balton's son and therefore he was a threat. Actually he was the only threat. Ironspike's magic was the only thing in the realm that could possibly stop him now. Once he had it and the power of the Wardstone in Xwarda, the whole world would be forced to kneel before him.

Pael couldn't help but laugh out maniacally at the thought. Things had changed. He was in a far better position at this point than he ever expected to be. New plans would have to be made. Pael couldn't see any reason to wait until spring to attack Xwarda. With his newfound power, he could conquer what was left of the mainland kingdoms before the weather set in and spend the winter months learning how to manipulate the Wardstone. When spring arrived, he would tear through the elven forests on his way to take Afdeon from the giants.

Of all the men who could hear the demon-wizard's hysterical giggling glee, King Glendar was the only one who wasn't unnerved by it. To him, the psychotic sound was akin to the cooing love words a young mother might speak as she kissed her child on the brow at bedtime.

Chapter Thirty-Six

In the Giant Mountains, they found it hard to leave the sheltered cavern. Especially Mikahl. Even after the daylong descent into the warmer, almost spring-like forested valley below, he found he missed the place.

He decided later while they set up camp in a densely canopied area of the valley floor, that it was the moments of camaraderie and brotherly affection, more than the cavern itself that had marked it in his mind. If the death of his king and Lord Gregory's dismal fate hadn't been lingering in the back of his mind, he would've considered the last few days good times.

After the fire was blazing and a haunch of the meat Hyden had hunted was roasted, they all bundled down and listened as Vaegon told them the tale of King Speran.

King Speran was the first of the great Kings of Men. Until he came along, many lesser kings ruled the divided lands, but Speran marched an army of magi across the lands south of the Giant Mountains and united all the humans under his banner. In his honor, they called the great, unified kingdom Speraland, but that was long ago.

The elves, until then, had kept themselves hidden in the Evermore Forest.

"Our magical cities were impossible for you humans to find," Vaegon chuckled kindly, and added, "They still are."

Illvan, an influential elf in those days, feared the might of all of the humans put together could prove to be a threat to his people. He decided to send forth emissaries, bearing gifts in hope that the two races might coexist in harmony. A magical bow was one of those gifts.

King Speran treated with the elves willingly, and a relationship began to form. Through the elves, the humans learned about the giants, fair folk, and many other things as well. For an age, all was well. In that time, the human king slew a giant serpent, sailed the seas, discovered the island that is now called Salazar, and the other smaller islands around it. The humans fought, but couldn't kill a mighty dragon, and later with the help of the dwarves, found the Wardstone.

As Vaegon told of these deeds, Hyden found himself thinking of the betrayal King Speran's great grandson made against the world.

Berda had told of the sacrifice of the firstborn, the Awakening of the dark ones, and all of the horrible times that had followed.

For the first time in his life, Hyden began to understand why the elves loathed the humans so much. There was a reason why all of the other races kept a wary eye on human happenings. The merry race of dwarves had been all but killed off in the many wars that followed the Awakening. The fair folk, who once sang and danced around the Monolith without a care in the world, had supposedly hidden themselves away from the rest of the world. It made Hyden feel a little ashamed of his race, especially those kingdom-born men whose lives seemed to only revolve around status, wealth, and power.

Hyden was glad Mikahl wasn't like that. If what Lord Gregory had said was true, someday Mikahl might be the king of all those men. Hyden decided it would be a grand thing if Mikahl could reunite the kingdoms and bring about an age where even the fair folk would feel safe enough to come out and dance again. What a time that would be.

Hyden drifted off to sleep on those thoughts. He dreamt of a time, a distant world, where all was truly well. Then he soared over a future just as wondrous on the wings of his hawkling familiar.

Mikahl woke early. He was determined not to be the butt of another jest.

As frigid and chilly as the valley was this morning, he found he wasn't freezing. His companions—his friends—he corrected himself, had meant well enough. They just didn't understand the way a royal court worked. The idea he might someday have to try to fill King Balton's boots was daunting. The fact he might have to face down King Glendar and the creepy wizard, Pael, to earn that position was unfathomable. He had no direction, no idea what to do, or where he should go to find allies. He was as lost as he could imagine a man could be. So what if the sword glowed when he used it. How did that make him a king? How was the strange symphony that filled his mind when he held Ironspike supposed to help them?

He was hoping beyond hope that King Aldar, the Giant King, might lend him aid. With an army of giants behind him, removing Glendar from the throne wouldn't be so hard. He didn't really think that would happen, though. He had no idea what to expect from the giants. Out of respect and his sense of duty, he hadn't broken the seal on King Balton's letters, but he held hope that they might explain some of this madness.

He decided that some hard labor might clear his head, or at least warm his blood. The sky was rosy, lit by the rising sun. No direct sunlight had found the deep valley shadow depths yet, but there was enough light to work by. He took the ax that Hyden's uncle had given them and made his way out into the woods.

He found an open clearing with a still standing, yet dead pine tree, at its edge. He decided he was far enough away from the camp that the noise shouldn't bother the others. After unbuckling Ironspike and laying it out of the way, he started to chop down the old tree.

Mikahl's steady and repetitive chopping brought Vaegon awake after a while. His elven vision might be ruined, but his other senses were the keener for it. The idea of having to actually chop a tree went against all his elven beliefs. He could tell by the sound the steel ax head made as it thumped into the wood, that the tree had died a few winters ago. The horror the sound might have caused him was thankfully avoided.

Curious as to why a castle-born man might be chopping wood, especially when they had all agreed the night before to find a more suitable campsite in which to spend the next few nights, Vaegon bundled in his fur cloak and trekked out after the sound.

Just as he stepped into the clearing, the long, straight shaft of the dead pine started its slow, creaking arc down toward the open ground. The thick trunk slapped the ground hard, breaking off several of the branches that radiated out from it. It rolled slightly and finally settled.

Vaegon saw Mikahl wince at the loud crash and the crunching noise of the breaking wood. Did the boy actually think he could quietly fell a tree?

Mikahl greeted him with a smile. Vaegon's face must have shown his curiosity because Mikahl answered his unasked question between chops as he took the ax to the lower limbs that still remained.

"Hard work is a sure cure for a troubled mind," Mikahl repeated the mantra that the old Weapons Master of Lakeside Castle had drilled into his head after his mother had died.

The ax fell again and a piece of bark flew off to the side.

"I apologize if I woke you, Sir Vaegon." Another chop, and this time a thick, white triangular piece of wood went spinning away. "Did I wake the others?" Another chop, then Mikahl put the ax head in the dirt, leaned on the shaft, and looked at the elf through troubled eyes.

"I don't think so," Vaegon replied with a dry smile. "It's time to greet the day anyway."

He held up a hand to stall the next swing of the ax. He had been tempted to add Your Majesty to the end of his comment, but thought better of it. Instead, he clarified his feelings on the matter of titles right then and there.

"If you don't want me to address you as Your Highness, Your Majesty, or King Mikahl, then please quit calling me Sir Vaegon." He chuckled, because he couldn't help but end his little gripe with a bow and the sarcastic words, "If it pleases."

Mikahl shook his head slowly, and a wry grin started to curl the edges of his mouth, but the effect of his next swing of the ax wiped the mirth away. The blow was hard enough that it cleaved through the remaining half of the branch he had been working on.

"Point taken," Mikahl huffed, and then let the ax fall to the ground.

He was about to take a seat on the trunk of the fallen tree when the sharp crack of a small stick being stepped on came from the forest at the clearing's edge.

Instinctually, his hand went for Ironspike's hilt. Panic raced through his body when he didn't find it there. The sense of relief that came over him when Talon fluttered out of the woods where the sound originated was overwhelming, because at the same moment he saw it was the hawkling, he remembered where he had laid his father's blade, and saw it was still there.

Hyden stepped out of the woods and yawned. He looked at Mikahl curiously, letting his eyes take in the felled tree from top to bottom. Then he turned his gaze on Vaegon and shrugged.

"Kingdom folk," he said, as if that explained everything.

Vaegon bit back a laugh. He couldn't figure out how he could've ever hated the sometimes clever and witty humans. The elves were always so stern and serious, save for when they were celebrating. In contrast, these humans were determined to laugh and make light of the problems that weighed them down. Vaegon could never remember laughing and smiling so much as he had the last few days. Even with pain, sorrow, and uncertainty threatening to swallow them whole, they found a way to make each other smile. Vaegon wasn't sure, but he was almost certain, that all humans weren't this much fun to be around. He decided he would catalog some of his curiosities today when he took time to write in his journal.

Hyden sat on the tree trunk. Talon swooped in, and landed on a branch beside him. Mikahl sat as well and wiped the sweat from his brow. A light mist of steam radiated out from his skin up into the cool morning air.

"Did I wake the old man, too?" Mikahl asked.

"He was sound asleep, and making more noise than you when I left him," Hyden answered.

Loudin's snoring was a well-known subject among them.

"I'm going to miss him when he leaves us," Hyden confided. "Without the terrible sound of his sleeping to scare away the creatures of the night, we'll have to start posting watches."

"Aye," Mikahl chuckled, but found no mirth in it. He had been wondering what Loudin would do after he collected the money for the bark lizard skin. "You think he'll go, then?" he asked the others.

"I think he is still trying to decide," said Vaegon.

"I see him spending his gold in his mind when he talks of it," Hyden said. "But I see his concern for you as well, Mik."

A sound came to Vaegon's ears then, a high-pitched wail. Talon heard it, too, and with a glance of his raptor head toward Hyden, he leapt into flight.

Hyden looked at Mikahl and shrugged. Neither of them had heard the noise. The next time it came though, Hyden sensed it through his link with Talon. He could tell by Talon's instinctual recognition that it was a wounded animal, something in great pain, and full of fearful sorrow.

Without another thought, he jumped up and started after the hawkling. Vaegon made a frustrated grunt and followed them, leaving Mikahl standing there full of curiosity and more than a little excited. All the traveling he had done over the last few weeks had been monotonous for the most part. Whatever these two were chasing after, it had to be more interesting and distracting than chopping wood. It was no wonder he forgot all about Ironspike lying there in the dewy grass when he raced off after them to see what all the fuss was about.

The sounds led them beyond the clearing, through a dense section of the forest. It was no easy chore picking the way through the tangle of branches and undergrowth, but they managed it. Up a rough hillside, and down again, and across a tiny stream in a wide, rocky bed, they went. Hyden paused there. He clenched his eyes shut and sought out Talon's vision.

Using the hawkling's ultrakeen senses and using the bird's-eye view, he followed the sound to its source. At the bottom of a ravine, a dusty, gray-colored ridge wolf lay wounded and dying. At her belly, a couple of good-sized pups suckled for milk, with desperately futile effort.

Hyden could tell they had been weaned for a while, but hadn't learned to hunt yet. The mother had probably stopped producing milk a few days ago, and had been trying to teach them. If she wasn't helped, all three of them would starve or be killed by scavengers.

From the ravine, he guided Talon back to the streambed and marked the way in his mind. It wasn't far, just downstream a bit, then around a forested hillock. It took only a few minutes for him to get there.

Hyden went over the edge of the ravine with urgent quickness. His climbing skills had been honed to near perfection over his lifetime, and he was at the bottom in seconds. He spoke softly to the wolf as he approached, but she growled at him anyway. Her instinct to protect her pups was strong. Only after Talon came swooping in and landed on Hyden's shoulder, did the wolf relax its toothy snarl and let him get close.

Had she fallen? No, Hyden decided, she would have been battered and broken, and her pups wouldn't be at her side if she had taken a tumble into the ravine. After carefully and cautiously inspecting her fur while sending calming reassurances to her through his link with Talon, he found two rows of deep puncture wounds down her side. Bite marks. It was as if a huge predator had clamped its teeth down over her back. An icy chill ran down his spine. What could have done this?

"Vaegon!" Hyden called out to the elf. "I need you to come down and heal her. She's not in very good shape."

Vaegon looked cautiously over the edge. With only one eye, he couldn't tell whether the bottom was forty feet down, or a hundred. What's worse is that what he did see spun dizzily in his head, and he nearly stumbled over the edge. Had Mikahl not caught up and grabbed him from behind, he would have gone over the edge. It shamed him to say it, but he did so anyway.

"There's no way I can make it down Hyden Hawk. No way."

Hyden noticed the drastic changes in Vaegon's demeanor since he had been wounded. He didn't doubt what the elf was saying, but he was determined to help the beautiful wolf live long enough to raise its pups. He sent Talon soaring along the ravine searching for another way down. There was one, but the journey required to get to it would take longer than the wolf had left to live.

"What do I do?" Hyden called out desperately.

"I could fetch a rope and we could haul her up to him," Mikahl yelled down. He wasn't really sure he could find his way back to the camp on his own, but he was willing to try.

The idea of pulling her up with a rope had crossed Hyden's mind too, but the wolf's injuries were too severe to allow it.

"Thanks, Mik, but she wouldn't make it."

Hyden started to panic in fear for the animal's life. One of the pups yapped and growled at him. Its stance was awkward: half-afraid and half-protective. Its neck fur stood on end, but it was ready to dart away if it had to.

"You'll have to heal her yourself!" Vaegon called down matter-of-factly. "You have the ability. I know you do!"

The idea seemed ridiculous. "What? How?"

"You'll have to calm yourself down, Hyden Hawk. You have to relax and clear your mind."

Vaegon sat at the edge of the ravine, not too close to the drop, but close enough that he could communicate with Hyden without having to yell.

"Once you do that, I'll talk you through it. If you really want to help the wolf, then we'll get it done."

Mikahl watched in wonder as Vaegon talked Hyden into a relaxed state. In the back of his mind, something was nagging at him, but the revelation of what it was never came. The elf was speaking of envisionment, perceptual clarity, and intangible likenesses. Mikahl had no idea what any of it meant, but he was listening raptly whilst watching his friend below.

If by force of will alone, if he could've made Hyden understand the confusing things Vaegon was describing, the wolf would've already been rambling away with her pups. As it was, he heard the expressions, and the careful instructions that followed them, but couldn't even begin to grasp what they meant. Still, the intensity of the situation, and his deep-felt hope for Hyden to succeed, held him glued to the scene unfolding below.

Hyden Hawk felt tingling, felt the magic start to work his will in the wolf, but the amazement of the feeling caused him to lose concentration. Now, he was frustratingly trying to calm himself down again so that he might find that level of mental clarity once more. Deep breaths, envisioning a completely empty space, a void, as Vaegon's smooth-flowing words had suggested. Hyden Hawk formed the scene that was actually before him in the void of his mind's eye. He was overcome by an electrical feeling as the magic found him once again. He kept from losing its flow this time, and into the wolf's flesh he delved.

He wished he understood the creature's anatomy better, and resolved to ask Vaegon how he might learn of such things. He had heard Mikahl speak of the great library at Lakeside Castle. In all his life, he had never held a book, much less tried to read one. He had seen books at Summer's Day on peddlers' tables and in some of the finer merchants' tents, but not even once had he picked one of them up. He could do numbers till the sun went down, but he could neither read nor write a single letter. A book was as foreign a thing to him as a castle or a ship, or the inside of a wounded ridge wolf. He vowed to learn all he could, and he knew that the first step was to learn his letters.

Some of the wolf's wounds were obvious to his untrained eyes. The dark clots of pooled blood he removed, and the holes in the wolf's thick, furred skin he laced together with glowing yellow strands of magic, using the same type of stitches he had seen his mother use to patch the holes in his and Gerard's britches when they were boys.

The slight crack in the big bone, which connected the wolf's spine to its hind legs and tail he would have overlooked had Vaegon not told him what to search for. He filled the tiny fracture with the strange, yellow magical glow in the same manner he once mortared a loose stone back together on his grandfather's fire-chute. The work was intense and taxing and, when he finally finished, he collapsed in a physically drained, yet pride-filled heap of sweaty exhaustion.

"It worked!" Mikahl exclaimed excitedly. "The wolf is getting to her feet. You did it!"

Vaegon dared a look over the edge and sure enough, the mother wolf was on her feet nuzzling and licking Hyden Hawk's face. This delighted Vaegon. He had actually only suspected that Hyden could perform the deed.

"Amazing," he muttered and, for the first time, he held absolutely no doubt that Hyden Hawk was destined to be as powerful a wizard as the great Dahg Mahn had been.

Hyden scratched behind the appreciative wolf's ears absently. He could barely move. The pups nipped playfully at his other hand while he lay there lost in the moment.

He had done it! He actually healed the injured wolf with magic. What would Gerard think about such a thing? It was ironic, Hyden thought, because it was Gerard who had always wanted to be a great wizard. Now, here he was, healing wolves and flying with hawklings.

An odd thought occurred to him then. Gerard might actually find all that power he longed for in the depths of the Dragon Spire, like the old soothsayer crone said he would. The thought had come from out of nowhere and was lost again as Talon sent a shrill warning through him from the sky above.

Hyden looked up, searching for the bird, but the large, dark shape of the beast that had killed Lord Gregory swept past overhead. Suddenly, true panic set in.

Mikahl's first thought when he saw the beast gliding by overhead was of Loudin, but when he reached for Ironspike, his heart sank. It was lying in the grass back in the clearing, like so much dead wood. The guttural urge to get to King Balton's blade and protect it was almost washed over by the shame of his carelessness.

Vaegon saw the look of despair come over Mikahl and, after only the briefest of glances at the boy's hip, did he understand what had happened.

"Go!" Hyden screamed from below, saving Vaegon the trouble of thinking of what to say.

Hyden's concern was for Loudin. He had no idea that Mikahl had left the sword out in the open.

"Talon will show you the quickest way! Follow Talon!"

The Sword and the Dragon

When Vaegon set out, he was three steps behind Mikahl. Mikahl had spotted Talon and was already headlong in his charge to get to the sword. It was all the fleet and nimble elf could do to keep up with him.

Chapter Thirty-Seven

In the pit of his stomach, Mikahl felt a certain icy dread as he ran toward the clearing where Ironspike lay. Talon's direct path spared him the short jaunt through the overly thick forest. Using the semi-dry stream bed, they went around it. The way was faster, but rockier. Even through the sparsely treed area in which Mikahl was charging, the footing was loose and gravelly. At one point, a hook-thorn vine ripped at his face, and now his cheek was bleeding freely from the wide-open gash the vine caused, but he paid it no mind.

The last stretch of the way was uphill and through trees dense with undergrowth, which threatened to trip him up with his every stride. He'd left Vaegon far behind, but he didn't dare wait for the elf to catch up with him.

Ahead, he could hear Loudin's voice cursing defiantly over a deep, snarling growl and the heavy thumping of wings. He had to hurry. He had to secure King Balton's sword.

By the time he came stumbling into the clearing, he was out of breath, but that didn't matter to him. He was forced to reorient himself because he entered the clearing from an entirely different point than he had left it. The tree he had felled was aiming in the direction they had gone to find the wolf. It lay across his path now, pointing off to his left.

To his right, by the trunk, was the hellcat that had killed Lord Gregory. It was hovering on slow, flapping wings, while clawing down at Loudin. The tattoo-covered hunter was shirtless and bleeding, but doing a fair job of keeping the creature at bay with the ax Mikahl had left behind. Somewhere under Loudin's bare feet was the sword. Mikahl wasted no time charging across the clearing after it.

As he approached, he saw that Loudin's injury wasn't mortal. It was only a gash across his tiger-striped back that was bright and glistening with blood, even in the valley's morning shadow.

The Seawardsman yelled and swung the ax up wildly at the huge, menacing beast. It appeared to Mikahl that the creature wasn't trying very hard to attack Loudin. Surely, it could maul the hunter to pieces if it really wanted to. It became clear that it was after the sword. The hellcat was too big and too bulky to go crashing into the forest. Ironspike was at the clearing's edge, and Loudin was right there with it.

Roaring with frustrated determination, the hellcat put its hind legs on the ground and while folding in its wings, lashed out savagely with its fore claws. Mikahl was only ten paces away and closing fast. He didn't even see the other dark shape swooping through the shadowed clearing at him. He heard Vaegon cry out a warning from somewhere behind him, but by the time the elf's words registered in his brain, he was off his feet and flailing through the air sideways.

As the world cartwheeled before his eyes, pain tore through his shoulder. He caught a glimpse of a sleek, shiny, black-scaled thing just before the grassy earth came up and slammed the air from his lungs.

Hyden, still lying exhausted in the ravine, cringed at Mikahl's rough impact. He saw it all through Talon's eyes. He wanted nothing more than to raise himself up and go running to help his friends, but his body wouldn't cooperate with his will. The wyvern had been a surprise. At first, he thought it was a small dragon, with its sinuous body and great wingspan, but the memory of seeing a half-rotted thing in the snow as a young boy came to him.

The village men of the Tuska Clan are very much like the men of the Skyler Clan, but they live in the easternmost reaches of the Giant Mountains, where the range borders the desert. They had wing-wounded a wyvern and followed its blood trail all the way into the lands hunted by the Skyler Clan.

Being distantly related to each other and aware of each other's existence primarily due to Berda and other nomadic giants, the Tuska Clan eventually sought out the Skyler Clan, seeking shelter and supplies for the long trip home. Stories were shared over a celebratory feast and Harrap brought out a skin of fire brandy he had purchased at that year's Summer's Day Festival.

The next day, Uncle Condlin took a handful of the curious young boys out to see the mysterious beast, whose diluted blood could supposedly be used to shape stone. Hyden remembered it now as clear as if it had been only yesterday. That wyvern hadn't been black, though, it had been a grayish brown, the color of the rocky caves in the east. Hyden remembered that its dark blood had eaten away the shafts of the spears that finally killed it.

As he watched Vaegon try to get around the clearing to where Loudin was by skirting the tree line, Hyden racked his brain, searching his memories of what the Tuska Clansmen said about the wyvern. He hoped to remember anything that he, or Talon, might be able to use to help them.

Vaegon darted around the edge of the forest like a startled deer, ducking this branch, leaping that root, and twisting around every clump of dead fall and undergrowth that presented itself to him. He closed the distance between him and Loudin in only a handful of hear beats. He wasn't fast enough, though.

The hellcat's front claw caught Loudin in the chest, and ripped a trio of gouges down his body. As the hunter fell to his knees, a glistening bulge of intestine and gore bubbled out of the center furrow. The hellcat's other foreclaw clenched around Ironspike's scabbard beside him. Awkwardly, it began backing away from the tree line with the sword in its grasp and Mikahl's belt dragging behind. Its wings unfurled, with a heavy snap and lifted it a hand's breadth into the air.

Vaegon snatched the ax from the ground, and ran out after the beast. He raised the heavy-headed tool over his head with both hands and hurled it at the fleeing creature as hard as he could. The hellcat rose a few more inches off the ground as the ax flew through the air, head over handle, and struck blade first into its neck just behind the ear. It stuck there a moment then fell away. The wound was deep and probably painful, but it was far from lethal. The beast roared its displeasure at Vaegon but still made to get away.

Loudin, still on his knees, fell forward, reaching his arms out as far as he could. His hands clasped around Mikahl's belt and as the horse-sized creature lifted away, he used the strength of his arms to yank at the sword. Deftly, the hellcat latched its other foreclaw onto the sheath and held it tightly.

Loudin grimaced and pulled with all he had left in him. He came up to his knees as the furious beast started to lift up again. He felt his guts bursting out of him, fought the pain, and the knowledge that he was as good as dead. With a mighty heave, he pulled himself to his feet, and managed to hook his arm between the hellcat's claws, over the sheathed sword. He felt the surge of power from the hellcat's next wing-beat lift his feet off the ground. The pain in his guts was incredible, but he held on. He swore to himself the beast wouldn't have Mikahl's sword as long as he could draw breath. The beast then lifted him higher.

Vaegon felt helpless. He started to grab onto Loudin's legs, but after seeing the two-clawed grasp the creature had on the sword, he was sure he would have only pulled Loudin free of it. The hunter's guts were spilling now. The lining that had bulged out of his abdomen was tearing, and a coiled loop of slick, silvery intestine, dangled down by his knees.

Vaegon was certain that at any moment, the pain of the injury would cause Loudin to let go and fall back to the earth. He grabbed up the ax, intending to take a swipe at the beast, but by then, the only things low enough for him to possibly hit were Loudin's dangling feet. A wing beat later, even they were up and out of the elf's range.

A different type of roar, higher in pitch and more avian, came from where the wyvern was swooping back down at Mikahl's prone body.

Talon was fluttering about it, slashing and clawing at the beast's horny, black-scaled head, trying to take it off its intended course. Vaegon charged across the clearing toward them, raising the ax over his head as he went. Apparently, Talon got a claw into the wyvern's eye, because it forgot Mikahl for a moment and thrashed its head about in agony while hovering a few feet off the ground. Through some warning from Talon, Mikahl managed to roll his half-dazed self out from under the angry beast. Vaegon saw the opportunity and heaved the ax at the creature, just like he had at the hellcat. Talon barely managed to flap clear of the heavy wooden handle, as it came whooshing by. Vaegon had thrown it so hard, that Mikahl heard the powerful WHOOMP! WHOOMP! WHOOMP! of it spinning through the air.

The blade hit the wyvern in its face with a sickening crunch, sending it flailing into the ground, where it landed hard on its side. The splatters of blood that sprayed both Talon and Mikahl began to sizzle and burn through feather and flesh. Instinctually, the hawkling made for water. The stream was close for the bird whose tiny, hollow bones and body would be devastated if the hot, acidy stuff got through its layers of feathers.

On the ground, the wyvern wheezed, sputtered, and managed to slink a few feet away, before finally falling still. All around it everything, even the grass, was being eaten away by its corrosive blood.

Loudin's horrifying scream filled the air, and echoed off the hard surfaces around the valley's rim. Mikahl rolled to his feet and followed Vaegon's gaze with a knot of dread growing inside him. It was an awful sight to look upon, and seeing it broke something inside Mikahl.

Loudin's intestines had gotten hung in the branches of a tree. A few yards of guts had been pulled out of him, yet he still hung onto the sword with both arms, as the powerful wings of the hellcat pulled, and the beast twisted and yanked, trying to get free of him and the tangle. Another cry of anguish and pain erupted from the Seawardsman that chilled Mikahl to the bone.

"Let it go, old man," Mikahl whispered under his breath, but he knew in his heart Loudin wouldn't do it. He felt the sizzling pain of the wyvern's blood burning his face and arms, but he ignored it. At the moment, there was no room in him to feel such trivial discomfort. He would rather lose the sword and live his whole life in the shame of doing so, than to see his friend die this way. His very soul cried out for Loudin to let go. Tears welled in his eyes and he started to look away.

Loudin screamed again. This time, it was cut off, as another few feet of his intestines were yanked out of him. Like some macabre kite, he hung there, suspended in midair. One arm came loose from over the sheathed blade and it looked as if the hunter was about to fall, but his other arm was crooked over the sword, and he refused to let it go.

Loudin was beyond pain now. He felt the pull against his insides, and he felt the raw, cold mountain air touching places inside him that were never meant to be exposed. He felt the tearing when the hellcat lurched and tore more of his guts loose. Something ruptured that time, and the world was growing fuzzy and gray, yet he still refused to let go. He tried to scream again, but only a hot whoosh of air came bubbling out of him from somewhere besides his throat. This was it then, he conceded. It was over.

Better to die for a friend than to rot away in some woodsy cabin all alone anyway. He was done for, but as futile as all his effort seemed to be at the moment, Loudin still thought he could beat the beast.

You fargin, flying, panther-horse hell-born bitch, he tried to yell, but no audible sound came. "You'll not have Mik's sword!" he finished anyway. With the last bit of his strength, he reached out with his free hand, grabbed Ironspike's leather-wrapped hilt, and started sliding it out of its scabbard.

Mikahl hadn't been able to watch. His carelessness had not only cost him King Balton's sword, but had cost his friend his life. He failed his father and king. He let Lord Gregory's death be in vain. He wasted the Giant King's time and on top of it all, he killed Loudin.

What a fool he had been to have even entertained the notion he might be a king of some sort. A king's bastard-born fool is all he was, a squire who had grown too big for his britches, and had carelessly thrown away his honor and a dear friend's life on a whim. He had failed. He wasn't worthy to be called king. He was just a fool.

Vaegon's sudden gasp carried a tinge of hope in it. Just enough to bring Mikahl out of his shame, to look up and see what it could possibly be that mocked him so. What he saw made his own breath catch and drew him stumbling forward. First one step, then another, and then he was running. Ironspike was flying through the air. Its mirror-smooth blade reflected the pastel colors of the morning in sparkling turns as it came spinning toward the ground. It landed blade down, sinking two thirds of its length into the earth from the momentum. Mikahl stopped and stared at it. It wavered there a moment, then stilled. It looked more like a glimmering, jeweled cross than a sword. He turned away from it just in time to see Loudin's body fall crashing into the trees.

The old hunter didn't even grunt as his body slammed and broke over the heavy limbs. Mikahl prayed his friend died with an inner peace. Loudin's valiant death saved Mikahl a lifetime of shame. The man could have easily let go long ago and died somewhat intact without so much excruciating pain. Mikahl swore then and there he would never give up. Neither Loudin's, nor Lord Gregory's, sacrifice would be in vain.

The angry roar of the hellcat as it circled around and dove back toward him made Mikahl's blood boil with rage and vengeful anger. As he pulled the sword free of the earth, he welcomed the beast's approach. Loudin's death couldn't be avenged this day, Mikahl told himself. This beast was just a weapon or a tool sent by another, but he could send a message to whomever it was that wanted Ironspike so badly, a message that was plain and clear.

Ironspike's blade lit the clearing like a star, and a symphony of magic filled Mikahl's ears. The hellcat lowered its hind claws, and at a blinding speed came swooping down on Mikahl. The surge of static heat that filled Mikahl was tremendous. A dozen different voices sang into his brain, each one a separate melody that added to the angelic chorus in his mind. Each voice represented a different means of magical attack and all of this, somehow, became crystal clear to him in that moment. He knew he could access them with a thought, but he knew he didn't need them for this. He felt the time around him slow, as if the whole world, save for him, was moving through molasses. That effect and the heat of his rage was more than enough to mark this dark thing.

The hellcat was on him now, and even though the world had slowed, the beast was coming in hard and fast. As Mikahl leapt and spun in the air, the blue glow of his blade went through all the shades of lavender and purple, until its glow was a deep, bloody red. His head came up under the creature and he twisted in his spin, so that its dagger-like foreclaws missed his shoulders and its hind legs swept past him. Only then did he complete the now white-hot blade's blinding arc.

Vaegon watched in fearful awe as Mikahl pulled the sword free of the ground and strode forward to meet the streaking approach of the beast. The sword was bright, radiant, and quickly became the cherry color of forge-heated steal. Mikahl leapt into the air, his acrobatic movement so swift that all Vaegon could make out was a furious blur. It was all happening so quickly that it made the elf's head spin.

One second, it looked as if the hellcat would grab onto the boy and carry him off like it had Lord Gregory. A fraction of a heartbeat later, Mikahl was behind the beast, his sword sweeping like a white-hot sheer through the creature's rear thighs as if they were nothing more than butter. As the beast's hind legs tumbled to the ground free of its body, the would-be bloody stumps sizzled and smoked. The intense heat of the white-hot blade cauterized them cleanly. A third piece of the hellcat spun smoking through the air like a half-embered piece of firewood. Later, Vaegon would find out that it was the spiked tip of the beast's tail, the very thing that gouged his eye out of his face and ruined his elven sight.

The creature was ten feet past Mikahl, raising its bulk up on its wings so that it might clear the trees and come around again, when it realized what happened to its hind-legs and tail. The primal shriek of terror and pain that it let out was earsplitting. It was all the legless hellcat could do to stay aloft as it fled howling over the trees and out of the valley.

Mikahl felt no pride or joy in the rush of emotion that came to him after the beast had gone. Instead, he fell into a crumbling heap of sorrow, and cried out for the loss of his friend.

The tattoo-covered Seawardsman, who would be forever immortalized in the histories of both elves and men as "Loudin of the Reyhall," was dead.

Chapter Thirty-Eight

Vaegon watched over Mikahl until Hyden finally returned from the ravine. Both the humans were exhausted so the elf took on the task of cutting Loudin's body down out of the trees.

It took most of the day, and as horrible as the work was, he knew he was the best one for it. Not only did he know the trees and have a way with them, as all elves did, but the fact that he wasn't human made the death of the hunter a thing he could accept more peaceably than his two companions might.

Once the body was on the ground and intact, Vaegon rolled it up in a woolen blanket and set an old elven warding around it that would protect it for the night. Mikahl would need to take part in the burial, but only after he rested. Where elves might let their dead decompose back into the ecosystem, Vaegon understood the nature of the short-lived humans and their delicate mentality made the funerary process a necessity. Not so much for the deceased, but for the friends and relatives that survived him.

While he was working, Vaegon heard the trees whisper of the great evil they were feeling among their roots. The wyvern's blood was in the soil now, and they feared what it would do to them. They could sense that the unnatural beast's presence in the world was just the beginning of something far worse.

Vaegon listened, and a tiny speck of fear took root in his heart as well. It was no mountain-born wyvern that he had killed this day. That thing was evil and born in a place unnatural; a place from which things shouldn't be allowed to escape. He understood then that some great, dark force had let it and the hellcat loose, and just as the trees feared, far worse was more than likely on its way.

The next day, when the three companions came to the clearing to bury Loudin, they found the strangest of things. In the middle of the clearing, a perfect circle of fragrant blue flowers had grown overnight. The center of the circle was exactly where Ironspike had pierced the earth after Loudin had thrown it, and the whole thing was easily twenty paces across. Mikahl chose that spot to bury his friend. The sign of the good cross that the sword had made as it wavered there was fresh in his mind. He felt it would be an ill omen to bury the hunter anywhere else.

The coincidence that he met Loudin in a clearing not unlike this one wasn't lost on Mikahl, either. Where that glade had a pond full of sparkling water, this one had an island of magical flowers. It was thoughts like this that kept Mikahl from breaking down as they piled up a great mound of stones over the grave.

The chore was done slowly and carefully so as to avoid damaging the flowers around the burial mound. When it was done, even the trees blessed the old hunter's passing. The magic from the sword that had leeched into the soil and caused the sapphire blooms to suddenly erupt, had also spread through the earth and eaten away the corrosive power of the wyvern's black blood. Vaegon heard the trees whisper a promise to watch over the sacred place, and told his companions as much as they returned to the camp just after dark.

That night, they started using a watch system. Vaegon would be first, then Hyden, then Mikahl. Mikahl insisted on being last. He didn't explain why and no one asked.

The next morning, as dawn lit the valley shadows, they learned the reason. The young Westlander was going through a furious series of workouts with his softly glowing blade. Hyden and Vaegon both woke, and watched with respectful awe as Mikahl went through grueling combinations of slashes, thrusts, and turns, each more strenuous and graceful than the last. When he was done, he bowed deeply to the four corners of the compass and even managed a thin smile at the others, as he toweled himself off with one of Loudin's old shirts.

Through the darkened part of his watch, Mikahl tried to adapt the sheath from Duke Fairchild's sword to fit Ironspike's blade. He managed to work its narrower width so that he could slide his blade down to the bottom, but it was still a hand's width too short. When the belt was around his waist, a small part of Ironspike's blade rose glowing up out of it, and the pommel rubbed at his ribs uncomfortably, but it would have to do for now. Ironspike's scabbard was gone.

After breaking their fast on some dried meat and stream water, Vaegon grew tired of watching Mikahl fiddle with the ill-fitting scabbard and excused himself from the camp. With a troubled look on his face, he trekked out into the forest and disappeared.

Hyden was lying down. He appeared to be asleep, but he wasn't. Talon was out exploring the valley, and through the hawkling's senses, Hyden was soaring with him.

The old wolf mother had made it out of the ravine with her two pups in tow. She managed to kill a slow hopper for them to eat. Hyden observed them from the branches of a nearby tree as they picked the bones clean, then crunched them between the teeth.

Satisfied that they would be all right, he and Talon circled high and soared over the whole valley. Movement not too far from the camp caught the bird's keen eyes, and sent mild alarms jangling up Hyden's spine. He was glad he didn't react rashly and get Mikahl all excited, because it was only the elf. Vaegon was walking around, mumbling to the trees in a sort of half-dazed state. Not wanting to intrude on his friend's privacy, Hyden and Talon flew on.

He saw the wyvern's carcass in the clearing. It looked like a scab on an otherwise healthy patch of forest. Not even the carrion would touch it. The perfect circle of blue flowers made the place seem unnatural, though. Talon alighted briefly on top of the stone mound that was Loudin's grave. Hyden wondered what sort of place the hunter's spirit was in now. He didn't dwell on the question because it saddened him, and the curious thought was soon forgotten as Talon shot back into the sky.

The hawkling found a column of warm air rising up from where the sun was heating a patch of dark stone, and rode the currents into the heavenly heights. From there, Hyden could see several hundred valleys in every direction he looked. The only real visible change in the terrain was to the far north: the white-capped mountains were taller and seemed far less hospitable, while to the south, the sharp peaks and jagged precipices gradually rounded and smoothed, giving way to warmer, greener foothills.

Talon soared around into a dive, and with his wings tucked back, came streaking down toward the valley where they were camped. It was exhilarating. Even lying on his blanket at the camp with his eyes clenched shut, Hyden felt the rush of it.

The joy was suddenly eclipsed by another warning sensation rippling up his back. More movement—the flashes of something white and fleeting—darting through the trees at the northernmost ridge above their valley had caught Talon's eye. He aimed his diving descent in that direction to investigate. There was another, then there was a third snow-white creature, scrambling through the woods.

They were four-legged creatures, running friskily about the trees without a concern in the world. At the ridge, the density of the canopy thinned, and three of the beasts came leaping out into the open. They were wolves—big wolves—and white as snow. Two more darted out, and the pack pranced in the clearing anxiously before scattering off in the same general direction on five different trails. One would chase another for a bit, then break off and playfully take up pursuit of another of its pack mates. They were coming down into the valley toward the camp, and Hyden counted nine of them in all.

These weren't the gray dusky wolves that lived in the valleys and foothills of the lower mountains, like the one he had healed in the ravine. These were the Great Wolves from the high peaks around the giants' hidden city of Afdeon. These were the wolves that Berda told him about on more than one occasion, and recalling that, he knew suddenly why they were here.

Hyden grew excited and sent Talon up over the ridge from where the wolves had come. Sure enough, he found them there, three giants striding purposefully up the valley toward the ridge.

Borg and a young giantess walked side by side, and behind them came another huge male, whose bearing and stride were so regal that Hyden could only assume it was King Aldar himself.

Hyden jumped to his feet, grinning with anticipation. The sorrow of Loudin's death was lost for the moment in his excitement. In all his days, he never thought he would ever get to meet the Giant King that Berda had spoken of so often. She had held such obvious regard for this being that Hyden had always envisioned him as some sort of god on earth. And now, he was going to meet him.

At once, he sent Talon to go land on Borg's shoulder so he would know they had been seen and were expected. Then he turned to Mikahl's worried expression and explained why he had suddenly grown so excited.

"We'll have to meet them somewhere more open," Hyden said, as he started to gather up things around the camp. "This is too low. There's a place by the stream pools where the branches are higher, and the stream bed is open to the sky. I think that will be best."

"What are you so nervous about?" Mikahl asked. "It's my future and my destiny that King Aldar is about to unveil, not yours."

"Aye," Hyden laughed lightly. "It's true, but I've heard about this king all of my days. He crossed the desert and treated with the Krags that live on the other side. He's killed vipers that Berda said were at least a hundred paces long, and his grandfather and a few other giants once killed a dragon. Its skull sits in the council chamber of my Elders. To the kingdom folk, we Clansman seem to live as free men, and we are, but we live in the Giant Mountains, under the protection of King Aldar."

He paused to take a reverent breath. The importance of this meeting to him radiated from his expression like the rays of the sun.

"It is no small honor for any Clansman to meet the King of the Giants."

"Aye," Mikahl nodded his understanding. "It's no small honor to meet any king." He was thinking of King Balton when he said the words, but he found they awakened something inside of him.

According to Lord Gregory, he was a king, and he decided he would try to act like one when he met King Aldar. He began double-timing his work then. He hoped to be able to wash himself, and he wasn't sure, but he thought there might be a fairly decent set of clothes stashed in the bottom of Windfoot's saddle.

The wolves came to the pool in the early evening. The sun had sunk below the mountain tops, leaving the valley bottom in a dusky light, but with a bright blue sky overhead.

The creatures were mildly hesitant as they inched to the water's edge and lapped from it. After a few moments of pacing back and forth, one of them came splashing across the narrow end of the pool. Once on the companions' side of it, the animal fiercely shook itself dry. His pack mates quickly followed. They didn't seem to fear Vaegon's fire, and it took only a few minutes for the bravest one to inch up to Hyden and sit down.

Hyden, trembling with a mixture of more excitement than fear, let the wolf sniff at him. The wolf's head was twice as wide as a man's, and its fangs were the size of a child's fingers. He was sitting on a big knee-high rock, and still the wolf's head was higher than his own. When he tentatively reached up to scratch the pack leader behind its ears, he found it was like putting his arm around an old friend's shoulders. The huge wolf leaned in, nuzzled him, and gave his cheek a lick with its damp, sandy tongue. Its fur was thick enough to lose a hand in.

After a few minutes of ear scratching, the wolf eased away, then stretched out its fore paws and lay on its belly. The others of the pack weren't as ready to make friends yet. They paced anxiously about, or laid down a safe distance from the campfire.

All of the wolves, save for the pack-leader, jumped to their feet when a not-so-distant whistle erupted from the woods. The pack-leader only raised his huge head and tilted it curiously. About half of the pack re-crossed the stream and darted into the forest after the sound. The others grew excited; their pacing became restless in anticipation of their chosen master's coming.

Borg was the first out of the trees. Mikahl found he had to look up from where his eyes had expected a head to appear. The Southern Guardian was more than twice the size of a man, and the sight of him standing erect instead of hunched down in a cavern was startling.

He wore the same dark elk-hide shirt and patch-worked britches as he had before. His similarly patch-worked vest coat was open, displaying the big Dread Wolf skull belt buckle he wore like a trophy. His long, silver-black hair and beard wavered in the breeze. He leaned his weight on his tree trunk staff and stepped across the stream in a single stride to join them. As he approached, his dark eyes moved under a heavy brow, from face to face, nodding respectfully to each of them. He could tell instantly that something was amiss.

"Where's Loudin?" he asked.

"He's dead," Mikahl answered, sadly. "I apologize, but I'd rather only tell the tale once, so I'll wait to tell it. The bark lizard skin is yours, my friend. I'm sure Loudin would've wanted you to have it."

Borg's head lowered, and he mumbled something that might have been a prayer, but sounded suspiciously like, "Not for free he wouldn't have."

He threw a fat leather bag to the ground at Mikahl's feet. It was loosely tied, and the mouth of it fell open. Inside was a chunk of raw gold, as big as Mikahl's fist, and there were a few smaller pieces as well.

"I'm sure he would've wanted you to have that," Borg said, in a way that left no room for argument.

Just then, the other male giant stepped from the trees, and the group all stood to greet him.

With a rap of his staff and a sweep of his arm, Borg spoke in a deep, resounding voice.

"May I present King Colossi Aldar, Master of Peaks and Valleys, Lord of Afdeon, ruler of these mountains and all who call them home. The pillar of our—"

"Enough, Borg," King Aldar interrupted, with a shake of his head. "I get enough of that bunkum at home."

He absently patted at the two wolves that were prancing at his feet. Another joined them, wagging not just its tail, but its whole body as it vied for the Giant King's attention.

King Aldar was a full head taller than Borg, but looked much the same. His long hair and beard held quite a bit more silver and gray than the Southern Guardian's, but his sapphire eyes were not as deeply set. His clothes, while being skins and made of a similar cut to Borg's, were far better tailored, and all made from the same animal, so that they didn't appear to be patched together.

His staff was made of bone or ivory. Unlike Borg's, it was no weapon. Its base was shod in silver. Its shaft was carved into a flow of leafy vines, and its head was shaped into a great white wolf. Amber jewels glittered in the eyes of the carved beast, and lent it the unsettling quality of appearing to watch everyone around the King of Giants.

Where Borg's face was dominated by a huge forehead, King Aldar's wide, but sharp nose drew the eye. He was wrinkled and old, ancient most likely, but still fit. Wisdom oozed from him like fragrances in a flower garden.

He studied them all for a moment, then stepped across the stream. He looked down at Hyden and smiled kindly.

"My daughter has befriended your hawkling it seems. I hope it is no inconvenience. She only came because she's never seen a human before, and now she's grown too bashful to present herself."

He motioned to Borg, then pointed at a boulder a short way downstream with his staff. Wordlessly, Borg went to the massive rock to roll it to where the king indicated. When it was in place at the edge of the firelight, King Aldar sat down with a sigh and motioned for the others to do the same.

"Princess Greta is shy," he continued speaking about his daughter. "She's not yet a woman, but trying desperately to keep from being considered a child. She's curious, which is good, I suppose."

He looked around toward the forest from where they had come and looked like he was about to call her, but must have decided against it. Instead, he touched one of the wolves at his feet. Its ears perked up, and with a, "Yip!" it and another wolf scampered back across a stream and disappeared into the woods. With his long staff, the Giant King reached over to the wolf by Hyden's feet and touched it softly.

"Hunt," he whispered.

The wolf rose up, stretched, and after a long tongue-curling yawn, it growled at the rest of the pack and strode off up the creek bed. All but two of the other wolves followed excitedly.

Turning to meet Mikahl's eyes, Borg spoke.

"Before the princess shows herself, I would like to hear about what befell Loudin of the Reyhall. He was a man I held much regard for."

Mikahl started to speak, but thankfully, Vaegon cut him off. The elf told the tale concisely and completely, leaving no important detail unspoken. From the physical descriptions of the two dark beasts, to the radiant magic of Ironspike's blade as Mikahl wielded it against them, the elf painted the gruesome scene.

Mikahl was thankful. He could barely hold back his tears while listening. If he had to tell the story himself, he would have broken down, and he didn't want that to happen, not in front of King Aldar.

As the elf told of the burial of Loudin and the strange circle of blue flowers, Mikahl saw that Princess Greta had come, and in an attempt to not be rude and interruptive, she wandered about on the other side of the pool. At the moment, she was chasing Talon here and there, like a young human girl might chase a butterfly. The two wolves King Aldar had dispatched after her were lolling nearby, watching her and the area around her. It became clear they weren't just lazing. They were intently guarding her.

Hyden noticed the princess as well, and studied her as Vaegon spoke. She was his size, but by her girlish manner, it was clear she was only around ten or eleven years old. Her dark hair fell in ringlets around a wide, but pretty face. Even from across the stream, he could make out the spattering of freckles that ran across the bridge of her nose from cheek to cheek. She wore a long, doeskin shirt that hung to her knees and loose-fitting britches underneath. A bright, rose-red pair of furred boots matched a coat or cloak that lay in a bunch near the stream.

Hyden couldn't tell if the boots and cloak were dyed that color or if it was natural. He couldn't think of a creature whose fur was that bright a shade of red, but there was no telling what sort of animals lived way up in the heights that the giants called home. It was another question he would have to ask Berda when he saw her again. If he saw her again, he corrected the thought. The feeling he wouldn't seemed to grow stronger every day.

By the time Vaegon had finished the telling, the sky was starting to darken and the faces of the two giants looked grave. There was a long, reverent silence, then King Aldar called over his daughter and introduced her.

Princess Greta blushed and hid behind him while he spoke. She curtsied at the appropriate time and managed to keep from giggling. When the introduction was finished, she made off with Talon as quickly as she could. Her two great wolf guardians followed her dutifully as she went back across the stream to explore. More than once, Borg's cautious eyes glanced protectively toward the area where she was playing.

The King of the Giants was silent for a very long time after she left. His eyes kept finding Mikahl, then lingering on the few inches of Ironspike that were exposed and softly glowing at his hip. He pondered the news of more dark creatures attacking people in his kingdom. Before running into this group, Borg killed a red-eyed Hell Boar as it came up out of Westland's Reyhall Forest into the mountains. The thing had run rampant through a herd and almost killed a herdsman.

The leader of the wolf pack returned just after dark. His muzzle showed pink and bloody in the firelight. Borg went off after the beast and returned with a freshly killed doe. It was obvious the wolf pack killed more than one deer because they all had bloody snouts and paws, and the doe Borg carried was intact, save for a small chunk that had been torn from its neck.

While Borg and Vaegon dressed the meat, King Aldar politely told Mikahl that he would speak to him later after they had eaten, and in private, if Mikahl wished it so. Mikahl declined the need for privacy. As far as he was concerned, his friends could hear anything King Aldar had to say to him about the scrolls, the sword, and King Balton's wishes. They were wrapped up in all this now as much as he was. At least it seemed so.

The savory smell of the doe's haunches roasting over the open flames should have given Mikahl an appetite, but the fear and uncertainty of what was written in King Balton's scrolls, and what the Giant King might tell him, turned his stomach into an icy knot.

Sensing his discomfort, the leader of the wolf pack nuzzled his side and sniffed at Ironspike's exposed blade until Mikahl started scratching him behind the ears. Again, the big wolf leaned into him.

Oddly, Mikahl found a deep and calming comfort in the weight of the powerful creature. He was thankful for it.

Chapter Thirty-Nine

"I don't know how much you know about what's going on," King Aldar said after they had all eaten. "I think it would be best if I just tell you everything I can remember."

The sun had long since left the sky. From behind a small bank of clouds, a half moon shone brightly, lining its edges in silver. Around that, hundreds upon hundreds of twinkling stars spread out as far as the eye could see. The air was chilly, but the fire was warm and blazing brightly.

Hyden used his bedroll to make a palette for Princess Greta, who insisted on sleeping near the horses. The horses didn't mind the oversized girl so much as they minded the wolves, who were constantly watching over her. Mikahl and Hyden had done their best to soothe the animals, and for the moment, they seemed to be at relative ease.

"The blood recently shed on the sacred ground of the Leif Greyn Valley around the Monolith violated a pact that was made a very long time ago."

The Giant King produced a pipe from a pocket inside his fur. He looked into its chamber, seemed satisfied with what he saw, and lit it with a flaming twig from the fire. The chamber glowed as he puffed, and a billowy cloud escaped his mouth as he continued.

"Four or maybe five centuries ago, I forget exactly, but it's not important. Way back then, a foolishly curious human wizard called forth a demon. This demon came to the earth unbound, and it quickly consumed that wizard's soul. I forget the wizard's name, but what's important is that he was the High King's Wizard.

"After tapping all of the wizard's knowledge, the demon consumed the High King. His name I remember. King Steven he was called. He started war upon war, and by the blood of the dead, called forth more of his demon kind until he had an entire army of dark beings to command.

"It is also said that those human warriors, whose hearts and battlefield deeds were cruel enough, were sometimes granted a dark gift as well. When they were mortally wounded, they didn't die. As undead they fought on, and the Demon King's army grew stronger and stronger, attacking us, the elves, and even the dwarves when they could root them out of their holes.

"The Demon King was an abomination to all that is natural, and eventually even the dragons, who rarely meddled in human affairs, took offense at the dark power he had amassed. The elves lent their unique might, as did the dwarves, and of course the humans. Together, they battled the dark hordes for what seemed like an age. Back and forth the battles turned, back and forth, until it seemed like a hopeless fight.

"The demons were winning, even when they were being beaten on the fields. The very act of fighting them, of defending oneself, gave those dark things a feast of hatred and fear to feed upon."

Hyden, excited and into the story, almost blurted out, "What happened then?" but he caught himself, remembering who it was that was speaking.

"Then one day," the Giant King continued, "a human man came forth, a brave swordsman who was willing to give his life to right the wrong the human wizard committed. He really just wanted vengeance for the death of his lover, but the bards, I think, like to leave that part out of it. He wasn't afraid to die trying to exact his revenge, though, so that gave him a sort of power over the demons."

"Pavreal," Hyden said aloud. He flushed darkly at the stern glances King Aldar, Mikahl, and Borg gave him for his interruption.

"Yes, Hyden Hawk, Pavreal," King Aldar finally nodded.

Hyden blushed even harder hearing the King of Giants use his nickname. He glared daggers at Vaegon, who had a slight grin on his feral-looking face.

"He was also known as a Marked One. The Marked One really. As a child, he'd been a pit slave in one of the Demon King's forge furnaces and the soot and ash that settled in the whiplashes that crossed his back healed, leaving him marked with stripes like some wild beast."

Mikahl thought of Loudin and his tattoo-striped body. He didn't think the Seawardsman had ever been a slave. Maybe it was a religious thing, or a rite of passage. He remembered something from his lessons about why those southern men marked themselves, though he couldn't recall what it was at the moment; something to do with the sea, maybe? He chided himself for not paying better attention to his lesson master. Then he chided himself for not paying better attention to King Aldar. He didn't want to miss any of what the king was saying, so he shoved the abstract thoughts out of his mind for now and listened.

"...such was Pavreal's hatred of the Demon King."

King Aldar paused, and puffed deeply on his pipe. He exhaled a fat, swirling ring of smoke, watched it waver and rise for a moment, then blew it into a misshapen cloud. His eyes fell to rest on Ironspike.

The small section of exposed blade glowed softly, bathing Mikahl's side and upper thigh in pale, blue light. King Aldar's brows narrowed, then he brought his gaze up and gave Mikahl a look that conveyed the importance of what he was about to say.

"A great gathering of the leaders of all the races was held, and a decision was made. A plan was formed. We giants supplied the purest of ores that these mountains hold: iron, titanium, and silver, among others. The dwarves forged the metal under dragon's fire, and the elves weaved spell after spell into the weapons that were made that day. Then once the items had been dipped in the magical waters of Whitten Loch, the great human wizard, Killton Alx, put enchantments on them as well.

"They were still far too hot for a man to handle, though. They were placed on a block of Wardstone, in a secret cavern in the eastern range of mountains beyond Xwarda. After almost a year, they finally cooled, and then the War Hammer of Doon, the Arrows of Tayllah, and the Sword Errion Spightre were ready. The name Ironspike grew out of the old language's strange pronunciation of 'Errion Spightre,' which means Demon Fighter, in the old tongue of lore."

Hyden wanted badly to ask where the Hammer of Doon and the arrows were now, but was afraid to draw the wrath of the Giant King.

Mikahl looked down at the blade glowing at his hip, trying to imagine dragon's fire bathing it while dwarves hammered it into shape. He couldn't quite fathom such a thing.

"To get to the point of the matter," King Aldar continued through another cloud of pipe smoke. "Pavreal somehow used the sword to draw the demon's essence out of King Steven. Then he and the wizard, Killton Alx, went to the place in the southern marshes we giants call the Black Tooth, and made a passageway back into the world of darkness. They put a lock on this passage that they called the Seal. The demon was banished from the blade through this Seal, back into the hellish Nethers where it came from.

"Pavreal hunted demons with the sword his whole life. Each time he took one, he brought it to the Seal and banished it back to the darkness. Pavreal had become the unquestioned leader of the campaign against the demon hordes, and soon all the humans called him king. For an age, hope prevailed while things were rebuilt and restored. Slowly, the dark things that lingered were hunted down and sent back into the hell from which they had come.

"Generations passed, and it was learned that the demon, while in King Steven's body, had spawned several children. They had children, and the demon seed was passed on. Most of those demon-kin were only mildly evil in nature. They lived as slavers, tyrant lords, or dabblers in the dark arts. Nothing seriously dangerous to the world, but then came Shokin. Birthed from a half-penny whore and more demon than man, Shokin was obsessed with reopening the seal. Eventually, he found a way to do it. That was just two and a half centuries ago.

"Shokin was no fool. He bound the power of the greater demons to himself as he released them, and used their power as his own. Once he had gathered enough power, he stole their essences and killed them. The things he did, the horrors he committed, the evils, the torments, and all the sinister connivery he brought to the world, earned the respect of the Abbadon. The Hell-god himself granted Shokin eternal life by making him a fully fledged demon.

"He was eventually pulled onto Ironspike's magical blade by your ancestor King William, but not before he destroyed much of the land and divided the kingdom into all its warring factions.

"For years to come, the seeds of his subtle lies and deceit would keep sprouting. This time, when the demon essence was banished into the seal, a wizard summoned a dragon, and with King William, they made a blood pact. The dragon, not wanting to be trapped by the pact forever, made stipulations. For some reason that only dragons know, dragons have a deep regard for the Monolith in the Leif Greyn Valley, and since that dragon knew the humans gathered there every year, and sooner or later there would be a bloody battle, it chose that as the focal point of its conditional binding to guard the seal.

"As long as the humans continued to meet every year in peace and shed no innocent blood in the earth of the Sacred Valley, the dragon would guard the Seal so no other could come along and open it as Shokin had. Recently, the pact was broken."

King Aldar nodded questioningly at Borg. The Southern Guardian gave a short grim nod of agreement in return.

"The dragon no longer guards the Seal," the Giant King continued. "I fear it has been opened. I fear Shokin may be loose again. We all know firsthand some of the lesser devils and dark creatures are about.

"These things, these hellcats, wyverns, and hell boars, are only minions. They're being sent and commanded by some far greater evil."

The Giant King shifted positions and gazed at Mikahl square in the face.

"What your father intended for me to tell you is meaningless now. He wanted me to help you take Glendar and Pael out of power, to help seat you on the throne of Westland, but the kingdom cannot be your concern anymore. The fate of all the kingdoms has been placed upon your shoulders."

After another long pull on the pipe, followed by a heavy sigh, King Aldar finished what he was telling.

"In the place called Coldfrost, a few years back, your father used Ironspike's power to create a boundary. This was done for the sake of my kingdom as well as Westland, so I am indebted.

In the letter you carried to me, King Balton wrote that the act of creating the boundary drained the sword's power almost completely. One of the things he wanted you to do, something you still must do now more than ever, is rejuvenate the blade.

"You must take Ironspike to the secret chamber where its Wardstone cradle is hidden and let it replenish its strength there. It will draw power from the cooling stone until it is saturated again. Only then will you be able to use it to banish Shokin back into the Nethers."

King Aldar turned to face Hyden. His expression was stern and grave. Hyden's eyes were open wide and his jaw was slack. King Aldar had his full attention.

"As with any resident in my kingdom, Hyden Hawk of the Skyler Clan, you were born free, so I will not command you to do anything. But I will ask that you accompany King Mikahl on his journey, and that you protect and aide him as best as you can in my stead."

"Yes, Your Majesty," Hyden said.

He found he regretted ever teasing Mikahl about having courtly manners. He was glad at the moment that he had learned from Mikahl the simple response he had just given.

"How will I find the secret cavern?" asked Mikahl. "How will I fight a demon? Will you not help us?"

"I'm helping you now!" King Aldar snapped, a little more harshly than he intended.

He liked humans well enough, especially King Balton, Lord Gregory, and the great, fat lord of the marshlands in the south, but for the most part, humans irritated him, badly.

Mikahl was special, though, and for some reason, that irritated him even more. He softened his voice, and a smile that was only half-forced, came to his lips.

"If the time comes when Errion Spightre cannot cleanse the land, then yes, we giants will go to war against demon kind. Until that time comes, I am bound by the ancient traditions of my people to stay out of human affairs. We gave the precious metals used to make the blade. That is all we could or can do until we as a race are actually threatened by this dark force. I will repay our debt to your father, though, for his aid in imprisoning the foul Wedjakin Breed at Coldfrost.

"The cooling cavern is in the eastern range of mountains, in the Kingdom of Highwander. Its precise location is a secret, but the sword itself should lead you to the exact location. To even our debt with King Balton, I can help you get there in a handful of days, where it would take you more than a full cycle of the moon, or more, to get there on your own."

"But what of Shokin?" Mikahl asked, with uncertainty and confusion showing plainly on his face. "How do we kill it or trap it, or whatever?" He looked to Vaegon for help, but the elf only shrugged and nodded for Mikahl to pay attention.

"In the ancient city of Xwarda, the capital of Highwander, there's a place called Whitten Loch," said King Aldar. "It's just a lake, but there's a little known temple there as well. You might seek the wisdom of the White Goddess there. She will be able to tell you more. It is said that there is a prophecy pertaining to the breaking of the Dragon's Pact. If there really is a prophecy, then she would know it."

King Aldar's expression showed he wished he could help Mikahl further, but could not.

"I would advise you to seek her out," he finally said, knowing it was the best advice he could give.

"She said the whole of prophecy has been fractured!" Hyden interrupted, with a voice full of concern. "The White Goddess said I was supposed to have the ring that my brother ran off with and—"

His voice trailed off as Gerard's destination came to his recollection. The place King Aldar called the Black Tooth had to be Dragon Tooth Spire. Hyden was suddenly overcome by dread.

"My brother went with a Dakaneese woman to the Dragon Spire to try and steal a dragon's egg. She had to know the pact you spoke of would soon be broken, because they left the day before the Highwander Blacksword soldiers started the blood flowing at the Monolith."

Borg, who had been sitting in the near darkness at the edge of the firelight, spoke for the first time since they had eaten.

"My spies tell me a woman invaded Westland immediately after King Glendar rode his whole army across the Locar Bridge to attack Wildermont. They call her the Dragon Queen, because she rides on the back of a great, red fire wyrm. Could this be the Dakaneese woman?"

Hyden tried to answer Borg at the same time that Mikahl tried to ask a question, but the Giant King's deep voice cut over both of them.

"It's clear then, that the White Goddess knows far more of this than I," King Aldar huffed.

He tapped the dying embers out of his pipe on the rock at his feet and put it back into his pocket, then looked at Hyden.

"If your brother had any part in opening that Seal, then you will bring him before me for judgment when this is all done. Is that clear?"

Hyden felt like he was about to vomit, and the harsh look on King Aldar's face filled him with fear for his brother.

"I understand," he said with a gulp, then quickly added "Your Majesty."

"I am honor bound to accompany Hyden Hawk," Vaegon said respectfully. "Since we must travel east anyway, would it be possible for us to stop in the Evermore? I would like to share with my people this dire news and ask for their advice on these matters. It would only take a day at the most, and I think what the slight delay will cost us in time, will be made up tenfold in the end of things."

"It can be so," the Giant King said as he rose to his feet. "You must decide now, Mikahl."

Looking down, he gave both Hyden and Mikahl stern and imposing looks.

"Each moment it is loose, the demon grows stronger, and every time you're forced to use that sword, the blade grows weaker. By my dragon-bone staff, you'll leave with the speed of wolves on the morrow, if that is the path you choose. If you choose another way, then on the morrow we will bid you farewell."

With that said, he found a relatively smooth stretch of earth under the trees and lay down, leaving the companions alone in the fire's light.

In the shadows, Borg rose and took his leave as well. It was a long while before any of them dared to speak.

Hyden couldn't stop worrying about Gerard. What had his little brother gotten himself into? The old soothsayer said that he would find the power to lead legions in the depths of the Dragon Spire, but those depths were where all the demons and devils had been banished. And the ring! How would he ever get it back from Gerard? The White Goddess said that it must be done. What if Gerard wouldn't willingly give it to him?

It was too much to think about all at once. He knew he would do what must be done, but he chose not to think about how terrifying it might be, or how hard it would be to actually do it.

Oh, Gerard, what have you done, little brother? He asked the question in his head over and over. He wondered if Shaella, the beautiful Dakaneese fighter who recruited Gerard, was the dragon rider Borg had spoken of. He wondered if Gerard was alive and at her side, or if he chased his foolish dreams into the darkness of the Nethers.

He glanced at Mikahl across the fire. Had his own brother helped take Mikahl's kingdom? He shook his head, hoping to clear some of the questions away. He knew what he had to do for now. The White Goddess told him to follow his heart, so that's what he was going to do. The choice was Mikahl's to make.

"I'll see it through with you, Mik," he said softly. "To whatever end we come."

"And I as well," Vaegon added.

"Then it's decided." Mikahl's voice was firm. He had already sworn to avenge Loudin's and Lord Gregory's deaths, as well as King Balton's. He figured King Balton's death was on Glendar's hands, but the others had been killed by demon kind. Still, he was certain all three deaths were rooted in the same sort of evil. He hoped the White Goddess would help them. He also hoped the people of Westland were all right. It troubled him deeply to think that King Balton's good and loyal subjects were under the command of some dragon-riding wench.

They didn't post a watch that night because they knew the Great Wolves were guarding them, but long after everyone was asleep, Vaegon was still awake and busy. First with writing the day's passage into his journal, then later, mending and remaking what he had retrieved for Mikahl earlier that day in the forest.

The next morning, Mikahl was up before dawn, going through his rigorous array of exercises with Ironspike. The pack of wolves found this curious, and formed a ring around him. They watched the display of will and dexterity from their haunches intently. King Aldar sat up and watched as well. When Mikahl was finished, the king approached him and spoke quietly.

"You're going to replenish the sword, then?" he asked the question, even though Mikahl had made the answer plainly clear with the intensity of his workout.

"Aye, King Aldar," Mikahl said as if speaking to an equal. "Is it not the only choice to make? Ironspike will do me little good without its power. What's a plain old sword against a demon or a dragon? I'll need all the help I can get."

"That you will." The Giant King gave Mikahl a fatherly pat on the back, his huge hand touching both shoulder blades at the same time.

"I have something for you. It was going to be a gift for your father, a token of gratitude for walling back those half-Breeds at Coldfrost."

He produced a thick gold chain. On it hung a medallion made of the same yellowed bone as his wolf's-head staff.

"This is dragon bone. It has some power of protection to it, a charm, so to speak," he said as he leaned down and placed it over Mikahl's head.

Mikahl took the piece of dragon bone in his hand and examined it more closely. It was the size of his palm, and carved in the shape of a lion's head. Its mane was worked with golden inlays and the eyes were two sparkling emeralds. It was beautiful. Mikahl tucked it away into his shirt and bowed in thanks to the towering giant. Already, he was trying to think of a way to protect the piece from the chain mail shirt he favored. It wouldn't do to scratch and scar such a wonderful gift while in battle.

When Vaegon woke, Mikahl received another gift. The elf had gone out into the forest and found where the hellcat dropped Ironspike's original sheath. The belt was ruined and the scabbard itself damaged, but Vaegon had taken part of Duke Fairchild's sword belt and sheath, and made a shoulder rig for Mikahl to use. It fit awkwardly, placing Ironspike's blade across his back diagonally, so that its hilt jutted up just over his right shoulder, but it worked. The whole of the blade fit perfectly into the familiar, hardened leather scabbard, and what's more, the sword's magic went dormant when it was seated, as it was supposed to do. Thus, the sword wasn't slowly losing what little power it had left when it wasn't being used.

Mikahl drew the blade several times, and figured he would grow to like the accessibility that the shoulder rig gave him. With deep gratitude, he thanked Vaegon for the kind gesture.

They learned that they would be riding on the wolves' backs across the thousand miles that separated them from the eastern mountain range. It excited but pained Mikahl, because he would have to say goodbye to Windfoot.

Borg promised to take the horses back to the Skyler Clan village, where he would personally enlarge the entry of one of the herd caverns, so the horses could survive the bitter winter if they needed to. Still, it was a long and slightly tearful goodbye for Mikahl, one that brought tears to Princess Greta's eyes and Hyden's as well. It was as if Mikahl was saying goodbye to everything he had ever known.

Neither Hyden nor Vaegon had ever ridden a horse, much less a Great Wolf. Straddling one of the huge, husky creatures on their bare backs was strange to Mikahl as well. A fourth wolf was rigged up to carry the saddle bags and blankets. They ate what remained of the doe the wolves killed the evening before. Then King Aldar introduced each of the animals to the companions by name. After a brief exchange of goodbyes, including a girlish kiss on Talon's beak from the princess, they were off.

They covered over a hundred miles that first day. It was amazing how swift and sure the Great Wolves ran, even with the weight of grown men on their backs. By the end of the third day, they came out of the foothills of the Giant Mountains, right into the legendary and mystical Evermore Forest. The thick, lush canopy came as a welcome relief, for it had started to rain that last day in the mountains. By the looks of the dark, cloudy sky, it wouldn't stop for some time.

Even with the sad state of affairs and the dreary weather, Vaegon found he was excited. He was on familiar ground now. Even the myriad dangers the Evermore Forest harbored seemed to welcome him. Home, the elf decided, was like that.

Chapter Forty

Pael felt the sudden and terrible agony that the hellcat felt when Mikahl crippled it. If it had not been for the great power of Shokin flowing inside him, the debilitating surge might have done him permanent harm. That particular hellcat was still bound deeply to the wizard. It had been formed from Inkling's substance, and the imp's familiar link to Pael was apparently still potent.

Pael had never been one for trivial affections, but the imp had been his familiar since he was a young man. Long before Shaella had been born, before his toy prince had come along, and long before he had stolen the Spectral Orb from the Palladian wizard Ah-Rhal, Inkling had been there. The imp helped Pael kill his mentor, Allagar, after the old Master Mage tried to punish him for stealing the Staff of Malice from the not-so-distant continent of Murga. Pael couldn't fathom missing a lover or a friend, but he missed his devilish little companion greatly.

It was old Allagar who inspired the imp's name, Pael remembered, with a sinister chuckle. When Allagar would catch Pael dabbling in the darker things, he would snatch away the books or devices, and say: "You haven't got an inkling, boy! Do you know what damage you might cause with that?" or something like: "You haven't an inkling of what the effects of that spell might be!" Pael hadn't liked that. So what did he do? He went and summoned for himself an Inkling. He and the imp ended up sacrificing old Allagar to the Abbadon in exchange for the location of the Spectral Orb. It was one of the fondest memories and greatest triumphs of Pael's younger life.

Pael wasn't sentimental, but Inkling deserved better than to spend his life trapped in the form of the horribly crippled hellcat. After he recovered from the brunt of the sensation that Mikahl had caused him, he reached deeply into Shokin's knowledge and found a way to spare the imp that fate. Like all powerful spells of transforming, this one required a sacrifice. In this case, a living body to house Inkling's soul and essence after it was removed from the hellcat. Inkling would lose most of his powers in the process, but Pael figured it was a small price to pay to keep his life. After all, Inkling had failed to bring Ironspike back to him.

It took Pael a while to decide in whose body Inkling could best serve him. When he finally made his choice, it came as a revelation of pure, ironic joy. Pael would make Inkling a king, King Glendar to be precise. Glendar had served his purpose by leading Westland's army out of Westland. He was nothing but a figurehead now, an obnoxious, spoiled-rotten figurehead. Pael had Shokin's power now. He didn't have to hide behind a king. With much excitement and manic glee, the wizard went about making his preparations to return to Wildermont. He would enjoy very much putting King Balton's horrible, sniveling son in his proper place.

On Claret's broad back, between two large triangular spinal-plates, Shaella rode comfortably through the cool, thin air of the higher altitudes. Far below her, King Glendar and his wagon trains were just leaving Wildermont's southernmost city and were heading steadily toward the Dakaneese border. She had waited patiently for this moment, and would now fly directly to Coldfrost to hear the answer the Breed giants would give to her proposal. Of course they would agree. She had no doubt. They had no other option.

The days that passed since she made the offer would have stirred their spirits. They would be greedy for freedom by now, she figured. Their mouths would be salivating for the feasts of vengeance she would allow them to reap across the northern half of her kingdom.

After years of imprisonment on that river-formed island, bound behind the invisible magical walls King Balton erected around them, they could not possibly refuse to take the deal. After all, to be allowed to ravage the lands and the families of the very men who had hunted them, the men who drove them onto the miserable island and trapped them there, was just about the sweetest gift they could be given. To be considered free folk and to be able to claim that same land for their own was simply icing on the cake.

Shaella was glad to have loosed them. A few bloodthirsty bands of giant half-Breeds terrorizing the streets of Crossington and Portsmouth would go far in bringing the rebels and resisters under control, but that wasn't her priority. Having the Breed destroy the great bridge over to Wildermont so she could seriously begin to fortify her holdings was.

There were more personal reasons for her wanting the final part of her Westland takeover to be finished. She found her father's tower at Lakeside Castle. She hadn't managed to figure out the lift yet, but she had accessed his vast library by going through the gaping hole in the upper chamber from Claret's neck. From there, she climbed down through the trapdoor to the library.

She had already been there several times. She studied some of the writings on the power and qualities of the Seal that Pael left out on the table there. It was the books that spoke about the Spectral Orb and her father's own notes on that subject that were driving her savage curiosity, though. Something Claret shared with her about the fate of Gerard back in the dragon's lair had sparked a fire in her. Once the final phases of the Westland conquest were complete, she would have the time to focus on what she now truly hoped she could achieve. It was that furious drive that motivated her actions even now, as Claret carried her down in a slow, descending circle toward the river-formed island called Coldfrost.

It was too cold this far north for her Zardmen or any other of the marsh creatures to survive. She leveled Northwatch, Westland's northernmost stronghold, with Claret's might. It was an example for the people who lived up here. From a wealthy fur merchant's keep nearby, Flick held reign for the time being. Lord Brach had left behind only women, children, and just enough able men to hunt and care for them. All were terrified of what the dragon had done, but a few of the men who had been left at Northwatch escaped the destruction and had managed to get into the Reyhall Forest. A veteran Captain named Bittercosp was leading them, and had futile hopes of starting a rebellion. She already knew about them, and if Flick hadn't tortured the location of their hiding place out of the common folk yet, then the feral Breed giants would soon root them out.

Those simple folk who dared to come out of their homes into the whitewashed, snowy world on this beautiful day, soon scattered like cockroaches from a lantern's light. Claret announced Shaella's arrival with a blood-curdling roar that left no room to question what creature it had come from. A few low passes over the nearby villages helped the stragglers find their way home. Soon, only the heavily bundled figure of Flick was braving the outdoors to witness the huge dragon's landing.

As brutal as any winter blizzard, Claret's great wings started up an icy, blasting gust as she swooped down out of the sky into a scampering run. The run died into a lunging sinuous walk as she folded her wings back to her sides. She finally stopped and lowered her head. Shaella slid deftly off of her back, down to the snow before Flick.

"Mastress," Flick said with an intentional Zardish hiss and a flourishing bow.

"Oh please, Flick, where's the fire?" she asked, with a half angry shiver. "Or should I have Claret torch this little keep to keep me warm?"

He laughed cautiously and led her into the place.

Inside, a central stone and mortar walled room was built around a large pit that was raging with flame. Shaella laid the Staff of Malice to the side and went straight to the blaze. She was glad for its heat. The spell she had been using to keep herself warm while on Claret's back was a simple one, but maintaining it hour after hour while riding was taxing, to say the least. Claret was warm, but Coldfrost was bitter. She decided she would eat and recuperate in the glow of the fire. Later, after she was rested and the moon was high in the sky, she would turn loose the Breed giants on the sleeping, unsuspecting people of Northern Westland.

Flick watched her from afar. He liked and respected Gerard, but he found that Gerard made him jealous. What Flick felt for Shaella, he wasn't sure. Something between awed respect and total adoration, but not quite romantic love. Or was it? If it was, it was foolish.

She still felt so deeply for Gerard that it showed plainly in her every move and expression. He was sure she thought nothing of the sort toward him. Maybe in time he could win her. No! It was improper. She was his queen and he was her sworn servant, but that didn't mean he couldn't hope and dream of a day when he might feel her desire.

It was with those thoughts swirling through his mind that he covered her sleeping body with a thick blanket and went about making a meal that would fortify her for what she had come here to do.

"How many men did you leave guarding the bridge?" Pael asked Glendar in a sharp hiss, as he suddenly appeared beside him.

Watching the shock and fear of his unexpected appearance explode across everyone's face thrilled Pael to the bone.

His suddenness startled them all, especially Roark, who spun quickly while drawing his sword, only to find himself held solid by some magical force halfway through the motion. The weight of his armor and his off kilter balance in his now paralyzed state left him about to fall from his horse. Mercifully, Pael released him so he wouldn't tumble like a statue into the road and be trampled.

Surrounded by his personal guards, King Glendar was leading some four hundred of his men southward into Dakahn. Four horse-drawn wagons full of gold, jewels, and other valuables rolled amongst them. A few other wagons full of kegs, crates, and stacks of weapons, armor, and other various looted items straggled not far behind the procession. A dozen more wagons full of jewels and gold bars, along with the finest of the forged things, had been sent across the bridge into the Westland City of Locar. Eventually Glendar wanted them hauled to Lakeside Castle and added to the kingdom vaults. King Glendar, it seemed, still had no idea Westland wasn't his kingdom anymore. Shaella's Zardmen had apparently done a thorough job of intercepting and forging responses to the communications he had sent since he had marched out of Castlemont.

"A hundred men to guard the bridge in rotation," Glendar answered Pael proudly. "There are fifty each in Locar and Castlemont, and a handful more to guard Westland's piece of the pie."

Pael chuckled at the young king's total lack of awareness and gave the boy a nod of respect as he silently complimented Shaella on the patience and diligent care she used to keep her conquest from being discovered by the fool. She didn't know it yet, but King Glendar just made her kingdom that much richer by delivering all those wagon loads of loot to Locar. Pael wondered when she would loose the Wedjakin Breed beasts from Coldfrost. It never ceased to amaze him how his past failures sometimes could be used to his advantage later on.

"It's late in the afternoon, my King," Pael said. "Why not let these men rest? Open a few kegs; have the cooks make a rich stew. These men fought hard and deserve a victory celebration. And I would like to speak with you in a more comfortable and private, environment."

"Master Wizard Pael," Glendar leaned down from his saddle so that no one but Pael might hear him. "I believe that is the wisest idea I've heard in days."

Pael didn't doubt it.

Rising up in his saddle, Glendar projected his next words to make sure many heard them. He also made it sound like the whole thing was his idea.

"Roark, break the men. Tonight we feast and toast our victory over those Redwolf curs."

A small cheer rose up from the ranks nearby and spread, as the order was repeated shoulder over shoulder to those in the rear. By the time Roark rode down the line to make the command official, the troops were already breaking formation.

Pael instructed Glendar to have his new, far larger pavilion erected away from the bulk of the soldiers. He then pulled Roark to the side and told him that he would be on full duty this night, guarding the king's tent soberly and diligently.

The rest of Glendar's personal guards were dismissed to celebrate with the others. Once he began his work, Pael wanted no interruptions, and when he was finished with the king, he had something he wanted to try on the big horn-helmeted soldier.

The celebration was taking place in a field just off the open road south of Low Crossing, but still shy of the Dakaneese border. The feast went as well as any roadside celebration might be expected to. Every man was allowed double rations, and the cook added far more meat than usual to the pots. Enough of the kegs were opened so each man would be able to get good and inebriated.

King Glendar made a victory speech from atop a pyramid of barrels. When it was done, toast after toast was offered between congratulatory cheers and prideful boasts. Not long after, the mild sleeping spell Pael placed on the food began to work. Glendar passed into such a comatose state, that Pael had to enlist Roark's help getting him into the tent. Once that was accomplished, Pael casually stopped Roark's heart with a hot, sizzling lightning bolt from his finger. The huge warrior crumpled into a smoldering heap.

Pael cast the spell that would summon the wounded hellcat that was once his familiar, Inkling, directly to the pavilion tent.

It took more than half the night to complete the process, but when it was done, Glendar Collum was no longer the one in charge of his body. He was still there and had somewhat of a voice in the thought process, but for the most part, Inkling had taken over and was wickedly grateful to Pael for freeing him from the crippled and pain-wracked body of the hellcat.

Pael then turned his attention to Roark. In his search through the depths of Shokin's knowledge, he stumbled upon a necromantic spell the Priests of Kraw had supposedly used to bring the dead into service. As he finished casting it on Roark, the crumpled soldier stirred and slowly rose before him. The big warrior made a daunting sight, with his huge horned helm and eyes that glowed red, like the embers of a campfire when a breeze strikes them. The once brilliant shine of his armor had been dulled to a flat gray by the electrical power of the bolt that stopped his heart. Pael wasted no time before casting a binding spell to make its will his own.

Pael was so pleased with himself, he decided to experiment more with the necromancy spell he had cast on Roark. He cast the same spell on the soulless hellcat, but only after he had Roark and Inkling-Glendar hack it into pieces.

Disappointed that the bloody parts didn't squirm or twitch with attempts to reform a unified body, Pael had the haunches, and other meaty parts of the beast, skinned down, and placed by the cook's pots. The rest, he had Glendar—Inkling, he supposed now—bury.

After that, he summoned the mightiest of the dark things that escaped the Seal before Shokin.

A Choska was no lowly minion, like a wyvern or a hellcat. It was an intelligent lesser demon that could command such things on its own. Somewhat bat-like in build, it was large enough to carry a man as big as Roark on its stout, leathery wings with ease. It had a wide, mastiff-like head, with tiny eyes that glowed deep and cherry. Its mouth was full of sharp, dagger-length teeth, and its clawed feet could snatch a man or even a horse off the ground, or just as easily mangle them to bloody ribbons.

When the Choska demon came gliding down into the grassy plain in the pre-dawn light and landed among the sleeping soldiers without a sound, Pael was delighted. He was further pleased when the thing moved before him and bowed its dog-like head in supplication.

"Shoo-Keen," it hissed. "How might I repay the one who released me?"

"The sword that might return either of us to that dark, empty place is in the hands of a boy," Pael said. "Errion Spightre has recognized him as Pavreal's heir. I tell you that in warning, but the boy has no idea of the true power and purpose of what he carries. He is the last of his line, and if he dies, so does the power of the Banishing Blade. Accept my gift: this undead human warrior is yours to command. Use him as you will to eliminate our shared threat, and your debt to me will be paid. Either kill the boy or relieve him of Errion Spightre."

"Yesss, Shoo-keen," the Choska demon hissed and gave a bob of satisfaction toward Roark.

Silently, the demon ordered the undead warrior to mount his shoulders, and was pleased that Roark did so obediently. After the big steel-clad man was situated, the Choska asked Pael, "Where might I find this boy?"

"You'll find his trail in the lower region of the Giant Mountains. I trust you'll be able to track him from there. Use all you must to aid you. Failure is unacceptable."

"I will not fail you, Shoo-keen," the Choska demon hissed. "When I bring you the blade and the boy's head, my debt will be paid in full, for all eternity."

"Bring me either, and I will grant you whatever you desire: an entire kingdom to feed upon perhaps? Or a place of power beside me as I send the world into chaos? Do not fail me, and whatever you desire is yours."

"Yesss, Shoo-keen. Yesss!" the Choska replied greedily.

It didn't linger further. It turned and leapt once on its big hind legs. After a second hopping leap, it snapped out its wide leathery wings and took to the air. Roark rode solemnly on its shoulders, looking like some ancient battle lord on his way to face something far worse than death.

Pael shivered at their departure. He could only imagine the terror that the sight of the dark armored warrior riding atop the Choska demon would instill in those who saw it coming. He was almost certain that the sight of his daughter, Shaella, on the back of her massive red dragon didn't exude as much pure, evil-born fear as the two red-eyed, dark things that just left.

The memory of Shaella's wrathful eyes on him the last time he had seen her caused him to re-evaluate his estimation. Nothing, Pael decided, was more terrifying than an angry bitch on a dragon's back.

Save, of course, for the wrath of Pael.

Morning came, and the hungover soldiers unknowingly stood in line for their rations of hellcat stew. The meaty slop helped take the edge off the residual ale-induced grogginess. The hellcat's haunch-meat had a succulent sausage flavor. That pleasant taste masked the evil taint that Pael's experimental spell casting had left upon the meat.

Pael was gone. King Inkling, in Glendar's body, explained Roark's absence to his other bodyguards, with the suggestion of a secret mission involving Pael. They wanted as little to do with the wizard as possible. They accepted the information, and as good soldiers do, asked no questions and showed no further concern.

Inkling spent the day's march getting used to riding a horse and feeling out the confining body of King Glendar. The imp was pleased that Glendar's mind was cruel and weak. At least the mental aspect of his new home was comfortable. A few nights later, a bit of Glendar's consciousness fought to the forefront long enough to get Inkling to experience a woman at a roadside inn in the Dakaneese Town of Pearsh. After that night, Inkling gave his host enough headway to allow himself to tap Glendar's knowledge of human ways. It wasn't long before Inkling was enjoying the flesh of women as much as, if not more so, than Glendar ever had.

The towns of Owask and Osvoin were ripe with Wildermont slave women. Inkling didn't know it, but his obsession with human sexuality kept him in perfect character. Not even the Duke of Portsmouth, one of Glendar's captains and a man who had spent much time around Glendar over the years, suspected the king was not in control of his own faculties.

For Inkling, the farther south the march took them, the more he grew to like his new place in the world. He figured he would be disappointed when they finally reached O'Dakahn and they had to start looking for ships to carry them on to Seaward. He was wrong, however.

O'Dakahn was a cesspool of lust and greed, full of whores and gambling halls. Anything you could imagine could be had for a price. It was all free to Glendar, of course. The new King of Westland had brought with him gifts, which caused King Ra'Gren to cater to his every whim. As King Inkling and Glendar's four hundred soldiers boarded the three ships King Ra'Gren provided for them, he found he was more than content. As they say, "It's good to be the king."

It was only later that Inkling began to have regrets about his situation. A human body can sometimes get very uncomfortable. He and most of the men aboard his particular ship began to fall ill, and when the men began to vomit blood and die horribly, the other two ships started to keep a distance. As it turned out, being a king held little weight with superstitious sailors and ships' captains at sea, especially when everyone on your ship had the plague.

Chapter Forty-One

At the moment, King Jarrek was a bitter man. Not only had he been forced to flee his own lands, but he watched as some of his closest companions died trying to defend his exit. He'd seen the wizard Keedle, his longtime adviser and confidant, blown from the wall like so much fodder. Men, nobles, friends, and family alike died around him in their hard-earned, red King's Guard armor.

He had watched on helplessly as the Westland wizard toppled the Ladies' Twin Towers. Inside them, his own mother and his betrothed, along with most every notable mother, daughter, and sister in all of Castlemont, had been killed in the devastating crumble.

He had seen soldier after soldier sizzled in their tracks, then was held in shocked horror as the pride of this kingdom, the millennia old mountain fortress Castlemont, was leveled by the magic of a single man.

Targon, the Highwander wizard, said it was done by demon's might, but King Jarrek had seen with his own eyes that it was Pael. When he attended Glendar's Coming of Age celebration a few years ago, the spindly, old egg-headed wizard had given him the shivers. And Glendar, oh what a disappointment to old King Balton that boy must've been. The only thing keeping Jarrek from crumbling himself was the hope that he might someday get the chance to face Glendar and Pael; that, and the fact that somebody had to go to Dakahn and free his people from the slavers.

King Jarrek suddenly thought about the warning message he had sent to King Broderick. The rider was Marshal Culvert's son, Brady. The Marshall had died in the battle. Jarrek hoped Brady would make it to Dreen, the capital city of Valleya, to warn them of what was marching their way. Brady would be safe there. The young man had trained hard with both bow and blade to earn his Redwolf armor, and was a capable woodsman, too. With two of the four cavalry men they had picked up in High Crossing riding with him, Jarrek figured that Brady had a better chance of getting through than most would. Old Marshal Culvert would've been proud of his son. Jarrek hoped he had remembered to tell Brady as much before he sent him off.

As his mind drifted from horror to horror, Jarrek stared absently at the dark clouds rolling down from the Giant Mountains to the north of them. A light drizzle fell now, but the downpour was coming. He could feel it in his weary bones. The storm mimicked his mood all too well, and the precipitation hid the occasional tear that trailed down his cheek. They would be in the thick of the lower Evermore soon. The forest would offer at least some protection from the coming weather.

King Jarrek, his three remaining red-armored guardsmen, the Highwander wizard Targon, and two cavalrymen made up the party. The cavalrymen were nothing more than glorified bridge guards who had probably fled at the first sign of attack. Jarrek couldn't be angry with them for it, though. After all, what was he doing?

The group had crossed out of Wildermont and somehow managed to escape the Westlanders' pursuit. They made it into the fringes of the Evermore Forest, where it touched the northern tip of the Wilder Mountains and borders the Leif Greyn Valley.

For days, they had ridden up and over rocky ridges, then down through thickly forested valleys. Up and down, over and over again, until finally they were about to put the hills behind them. They now descended the last unforested hillock and were about to enter the thick of the Evermore Forest.

Targon had tried desperately to get word to his queen of what had transpired, but it wasn't yet to be. He had drained himself so completely when he'd made the tunnel-like tube through the fabric of the world to save the King of Wildermont that he was only now, days later, beginning to look alive again. Jarrek had thought that the man would die. At first, Targon had looked like a corpse. If he hadn't insisted on coming with them, Jarrek might have left him in one of the mountain villages they had passed recently. The wizard's intense desire to share his ramblings of demon might and broken bindings with his queen, and the simple fact that Jarrek wouldn't deny a man who saved his life anything, kept him from it.

King Jarrek wasn't sure he wanted to meet with the Witch Queen. She was rumored to be a strange and powerful woman, who had lived for hundreds of years. Just thinking about the unnatural mess of it made Jarrek shiver.

He doubted most of the tales were true. Targon had told him they weren't; that she wasn't really an old witch, and she would most likely help them in any way she could. But who could trust the ramblings of a half dead wizard. The remoteness of her kingdom and the strange ways of the people who ventured out of it, lent to the spooky image of Highwander like butter lends flavor to bread.

King Jarrek's practical side knew that the place, however magical and mystical in nature, was once the seat of all the human lands. The palace in the city of Xwarda was ancient and had once been the home of many of the realm's heroes and legends.

Targon didn't have to defend his queen or the kingdom she ruled over. King Jarrek most likely wouldn't be alive if it weren't for him. As a man of honor, Jarrek would dutifully repay his debt by escorting the man anywhere he wished ago. What could a Witch Queen do to him compared to what King Glendar and Pael had already done? She couldn't be as bad as rumors would have one believe. Maybe she would lend him enough men that he could ride to Dakahn and try to free some of the people Glendar sent into slavery there. It was a big hope, but enough to keep him from sinking into the gloom and sorrow that threatened to consume him.

The rain was coming down hard now, but the end of the storm was in sight. To the north, along the tailing edge of the black swirling clouds, was a golden line of sunshine. A few days of clear, blue sky seemed to be pushing the storm southward. Another dark line was on the horizon beyond the expanse of blue. It was no surprise. In the heat of summer, storm after raging storm came rolling down out of the Giant Mountains. His only realistic hope was that the sun would still be in the sky when the rain finally passed over them, so they might dry out before nightfall. A glance ahead of them reminded Jarrek they would be entering the forest soon. The sun wouldn't be able to penetrate that canopy, he knew. The sun would heat the soggy woods like a steam bath. He decided he wouldn't even begin to look forward to dry clothes until they had a fire raging.

The wyvern's first swooping attack was so smoothly carried out, no one in the procession even noticed the cavalryman in the rear being clawed out of his saddle and hurled to his death. The rumble of distant thunder, and the chink and jangle of the horses plodding along on the heavy earth masked what sound the steady thrum of the rain on their steel plated armor didn't drown out. The wyvern's second attack wasn't so successful, though it might have been, had its first victim's horse not whinnied out in fright and confusion.

The noise brought Jarrek's head around. A dark flash of movement caught his eye just as the wyvern's claw clamped down on his shoulder plate. He couldn't do more than avoid the beast's other claw, but the fact he was looking in the right place at that moment saved him from having his face ripped off. Such was the force of the wyvern's momentum, that Jarrek was unhorsed. He fell from the creature's grasp and landed heavily in the sloppy mud. Captain Proct of the King's Honor Guard snatched up the reins of Jarrek's horse and called out orders.

"Hargh and you!" he pointed at the remaining cavalrymen. "Get the wizard into the forest! Now!" He paused, seeing his king struggling to get to his feet in the slippery mud. "Markeen, help me cover the king!"

The edge of the tree line was just a good, hard gallop away. The red-armored King's Guard, Hargh, had already snatched the reins out of Targon's hands while the terrified bridge guard spurred his horse ahead of them toward the trees. The fact that he separated himself from the others so quickly cost him.

The wyvern came thumping down on heavy wings directly in front of the man's horse. The horse rose up and lashed out with its hooves, but the toothy maw of the black-scaled terror shot past them like a striking viper. The horse and rider fell, the animal thrashing in its death throes as it did so. Half of its neck and throat was already being chugged down the wyvern's long snaky gullet. The man screamed again as the horse's body crushed his leg, but the sound was drowned out by the thundering storm.

Hargh led the wizard swiftly toward the forest in a route that arced around the feeding creature. Captain Proct took a chance and deftly strung up the bow he'd taken from an abandoned shop at High Crossing. He knew the gut string wouldn't hold its tension long in the rain, but he hoped to get at least two or three arrows loosed before it stretched and was wasted.

In a move that surprised everyone, the wyvern left the screaming bridge guard pinned under his horse and darted across the muddy ground toward Hargh and Targon. Its hind claws sent up great splashes of dirty water as it threw back its wings and dove in for a headlong attack.

Hargh slapped Targon's horse in the rump with the flat of his blade, then came around with his sword held high. The wizard was carried out of harm's way. Hargh's steel met black scales, while razor sharp claws came ripping upward. The man's sword bit deeply, nearly severing one of the wyvern's foreclaws, but its other claw caught Hargh under the chin. Hargh's jaw was nearly torn from his face and his helmet went spinning through the air, slinging strands of water at odd angles through the downpour.

Black acid-blood spurted from the wyvern's wound across red armor and horseflesh. The wyvern took two steps back, shrunk in on itself like a compressed coil, and leapt into flight directly at Hargh. As it passed over him, it used its hind claws to rake him out of his saddle. A corrosive hiss and a small trail of smoke trailed up through the rain from his writhing body as it crashed back into the earth.

Captain Proct loosed an arrow at the beast. Then, as quickly as a man in full armor could manage, he sent another. The second struck the wyvern near where one of its wings joined its body. The creature roared out in pain, and the long, snaky thing veered clearly to one side in its flight. The wyvern roared again as it tried to alter its new course with its injured wing. It did no good. The creature came crashing into the wet earth in a tumbling, flailing splash.

Hargh's wild-eyed horse went screaming and bucking toward the trees. The cool rain was no comfort to its burning, dissolving hide. Already, a large swathe of its flesh was corroding away where the wyvern's blood had splashed it. It didn't look like the animal would suffer much longer.

King Jarrek and the other red-armored guardsman, Markeen, went charging toward the struggling wyvern with their swords held high, hoping to kill it before it regained its senses.

Captain Proct checked the tension on the bowstring. He almost regretted that it was still holding true. He put an arrow to his string and rode swiftly over to the writhing, growling body of his longtime friend. Hargh's face was a misshapen, acid-eaten ruin, and Proct mercifully put an arrow through the man's breastplate into his heart.

Just as King Jarrek and Markeen gained the wyvern, it rose up onto its hind legs. One of its wings was folded in naturally, but the other was half open and twisted skyward. It scrambled forward at the approaching men, snapping its teeth and hissing. The wyvern's one good foreclaw was raised to defend itself. The other dangled uselessly from a small thickness of bloody sinew.

"I thought I'd never wish to see a pike again!" King Jarrek yelled, letting his memory of King Glendar's beheadings fuel his courage and anger.

Wishing he had one of Glendar's pikes now, he broke away from Markeen and started around the creature's right side.

"Go around it, Markeen, so it can't see us both at the same time!"

Markeen did as he was ordered, and was rewarded for it by a jarring crack across the side of his helmet by the wyvern's thick tail. The force of the blow nearly knocked him from his horse. For a long moment all he could see was blackness, filled with tiny exploding stars. In a berserk rage, he shook it off and went charging in at the creature.

His sword made hard, slashing arcs. His horse stopped and started as Markeen's knees commanded, but it balked and hopped when the wyvern's tail came sweeping back across the ground. Markeen landed a solid blow, slicing a deep gash in the beast. The blade would have done massive amounts of damage had the stumbling motion of his horse not carried them both away from it. It was a stroke of luck that the destrier had faltered, because the wyvern's jaws came `round and snapped shut with an audible crack exactly where Markeen's head had just been.

King Jarrek, not one to go into a reckless battle rage, spurred his mount in close enough so that he might thrust into the wyvern's body deeply. The thing was focused on Markeen and paying little mind to where he was, so Jarrek took advantage. His attack was thwarted by the beast's broken wing as it came around and nearly clipped him from his horse. It was then that Jarrek heard the Highwander wizard's voice screaming out hoarsely.

"Away! Get away from it!"

Targon, on foot with a growing sphere of magical blue force in his hands, was half-stumbling, half-charging from the tree line. No sooner had Jarrek reined his horse away and got clear of the thing than a bright, sizzling sapphire crackle came streaking from the wizard's hands like a shooting star. The blast went right into the wyvern's side and exploded. A head-sized chunk of its meat and bone was blown into an acid mist. By then, both King Jarrek and Markeen were spurring themselves toward Targon at a full gallop.

Seeing that his companions were finally out of his way, Captain Proct let another arrow fly, but his effort seemed pointless when Targon sent two more of his wicked, blue blasts at the thing. The last magical blow hit the wyvern in the side of its viper-like head. Upon impact, skull, scale, and a grayish black mass of bloody muck splattered to the ground with a sizzling hiss. A moment later, the long, sinuous neck and body fell sputtering and twitching into the mud.

Exhausted and half dazed, Targon crumpled to the grass where he stood. Captain Proct raced over to see to him. King Jarrek dismounted and ordered Markeen to follow suit. They took a long time inspecting each other's armor for damage.

The king's breastplate had been splattered, and when Markeen tried to wipe it clean with a piece of blanket, the red enamel and a thin layer of gritty steel smeared across it.

Jarrek's plate mail had been crafted generations ago and was far lighter than it appeared to be. Apparently, it was still semi-resistant to the wyvern's acid blood, because Hargh's armor was eaten completely through. The smear left on Jarrek's breastplate resembled a streaking fireball, but the integrity of the armor seemed intact.

Luckily for Markeen, whose armor was of the same make and material as Hargh's, his was free of the corrosive stuff altogether.

Once Jarrek saw the tip of Markeen's blade, he was glad he hadn't stabbed the wyvern with his. Like his armor, the sword called Wolf's Fang, had been passed down from king to prince for generations. It wouldn't do to have an arm's length of its tip eaten away like Markeen's sword.

"Was it a dragon, Highness?" Markeen asked his king.

Jarrek told him no, but further explanation was cut off by the wizard's weak voice calling for him. The captain had run down Targon's horse and gotten the spell-weary man back in the saddle. He was leading the slumped-over wizard toward the others.

"Hellborn Wyvern," Targon rasped to them. He wiped some rain from his face and looked at King Jarrek sternly. "It is a creature of brimstone, which until recently was banished behind Pavreal's Seal." He looked like he wanted to say more but didn't have the strength.

"Say a prayer for our countrymen," Jarrek ordered. "There's no time to bury them. We have to get into the forest. We'll be safer there. We're about ten days out of Highwander, and I, for one, don't want to wait around and see what else is lingering about out here."

Maybe it was guilt, or maybe Jarrek just had to say it, but when he was back on his horse, he spoke clearly.

"They would understand and forgive us."

After a few moments of silent reverence, Captain Proct barked out an order.

"Salvage what supplies you can from the Bridge Guards, Markeen." He pointed at both the fallen cavalrymen. "I'll go see where Hargh's horse fell and get what's worth saving from it."

The rain seemed to be falling harder now, and the line of golden sunshine Jarrek spotted earlier was nowhere to be found. He and Targon waited at the tree line for the other two to finish pilfering the dead. In any other situation, Jarrek wouldn't have allowed such sacrilege, but the food, wine skins, and other necessities that might be stashed away in those packs couldn't be left behind. They had a long ride ahead of them, through one of the most formidable forests the gods had ever created. Anything that might help them get through was welcome at this point, no matter how it had to be acquired.

The soldier who was unhorsed and killed before the wyvern announced itself properly, had a sword that Markeen gladly took up. The same man's horse was found by Captain Proct and used as a pack animal to carry the blankets and other gear they gathered from their fallen comrades. They had enough rations now to go a few days without being forced to hunt. This was a small comfort, after all the death and destruction they had seen and survived over the last few days, but a comfort, nonetheless. It meant they could make haste and put some distance between themselves and all the horror. The farther into the forest they went, the better. Or so they hoped.

Strangely enough, the rain slacked off, then stopped right after they entered the Evermore. It was late in the day and they were spared, for that evening at least, the miserable humidity the sun would eventually draw out of the soaked woods. They traveled long into the night before sadness and exhaustion forced them to make camp. When they finally did, King Jarrek looked long and hard at the weak and sickly form of the Witch Queen's wizard. He couldn't help but feel squeamish about going to Xwarda, but there was no way he could doubt Targon anymore. Twice now the Highwander wizard had saved his skin in the heat of battle. If that didn't warrant his complete trust, he didn't know what did.

As King Jarrek drifted off into a wary sleep, his mind and heart went out to the thousands and thousands of his people that King Glendar had sent to Dakahn to be used as slaves. Just the chance that Queen Willa might aid him in rescuing them was enough for him to feel a spark of hope. He was glad for it, because that tiny spark was all he had.

Chapter Forty-Two

Grrr, the biggest of the four Great Wolves, the stern and serious pack-leader, carried Hyden Hawk. Oof, the fearless, carried Mikahl. Huffa, the fastest of the four and only female in the bunch, carried Vaegon, and Urp, with only his lighter burden of packs to carry, ran circles around them all.

Through the mountains and the foothills, the wolves had been able to keep a strong and steady pace, but as they went deeper into the Evermore Forest and further out of the cooler, higher altitudes, the heat began to take its toll on them.

The companions wisely made camp in the later part of the morning and sleeping away the heat of the day. This schedule went far toward helping the wolves cope with the climate, and they appreciated the men for their consideration. The wolves showed their thanks by sharing the meat they hunted with them, and by keeping their keen eyes and ears open for possible dangers along the way. It had been a long time since any of the companions had eaten so well, and so often.

The wolves worked up a ferocious appetite carrying them and they made off to hunt at every break, save for their regular midnight water stop. Now it was late afternoon, and all of the wolves except for Grrr, who attentively stood guard over the camp, were off to find a meal.

They had been camped in the same place for two days now, patiently waiting for the elf. The spot wasn't quite a clearing, it was more of an opening in the dense forest, an area with just enough room between the tree trunks for them to stretch out and build a fire. Even during the heat of the day, they were shaded by the emerald canopy of oak, elm and poplar. Only a few rays of sunshine dared to penetrate through the leaves, and those were long gone now, as the unseen sun was getting lower in the sky.

Vaegon was growing increasingly irritable. It had become obvious to Hyden and Mikahl that the elf's missing eye was causing him a sort of pain that wasn't physical. It was keeping Vaegon from seeing the subtle auras he needed to see to find his people, and in turn was causing some deeper agony inside the elf. Vaegon's temper grew short, and he was sharp with his responses and comments.

Hyden tactfully broached the subject, and pointed out they had no more time to waste. Vaegon finally admitted defeat. Two full days of travel, it turned out, was more than even he thought they could spare. He tried to explain to them about the powerful concealing magics, and the mobile nature of his people's secret home.

"Our city, if you could call it that, doesn't actually exist at the location where you might find and enter it," Vaegon said, with sadness and longing in his tired voice. "It moves as our people move. The Queen Mother is connected to the forest through the Heart Tree. If we were so inclined, we could be found in the Reyhall Forest in the west, or in the Gnarish Tree Wards, beyond the Giant Mountains. We have forests that we favor. The Evermore is one of these. We were visiting it when I was born nearly a century ago, so to me, this is home. To get back to my people, to find my home though, has become impossible. To find the entry points in the powerful wards that conceal it, one must have a certain, and uniquely elven vision, and I have lost that."

His hand fiddled with the patch over his empty socket as he spoke. The sorrow and agony he was feeling was plain in his voice. It was as if he had been utterly defeated.

It wasn't easy for the haughty and superior elven archer to admit his newfound weakness, or to accept the fact that he was blind to his homeland, but he swallowed his pride and let reality set in. After he finished his explanation, he started off into the woods again. They agreed that he would look the rest of this day, and then they would move on. He would look again when they stopped, for the entrances were many and could be found throughout the great forest. He knew he had kept them there too long, but it was only because he hoped the elves would have noticed him blundering about and would send a party out to investigate. If any of the elves noticed him, they would surely tell his father or brother, if not the Queen Mother herself. After all, he was well known amongst his people for a skill he no longer had.

Neither Hyden nor Mikahl had realized how old Vaegon actually was. In terms of appearance and in relation to the human aging process, he wasn't much older than they were, but in actual years, Vaegon was old enough to be one of their grandparents.

Mikahl couldn't conceive of the idea of Vaegon's age very well, but he understood the elf's inability to get home. He was haunted by the same feeling. Sure, he could find his way back to Westland, but according to Borg, it wouldn't be his home that he found when he got there. His mind carried him back to a memory of youth then. A time long before duty and responsibility had swallowed up the promise of the future.

Once, as a boy of seven or eight, when his most important duty in life was the nightly candle snuffing in all the great halls of Lakeside Castle, he and some of the other castle brats had pulled a prank. Had big old Lord Ellrich's daughter, Zasha, not been involved, he and his conspirators might not have survived King Balton's wrath.

A feast was being held for some local event, a name day, a wedding, or such. Lord Ellrich from the south and a few of the northern dukes were the only attendees of note other than the king.

The main course was to be a huge glazed pig, complete with an apple in its mouth, and served on a bed of green lettuce on a silver tray.

For hours it had sat there in the kitchen, sprawled on the rolling cart it on which it would be presented. Mikahl remembered its pinkish-brown skin, all slick and shiny with honey glaze, as clearly as if he were looking at it now. The troop of castle brats and the visiting Lady Zasha, who at that time was a long way yet from being a real lady, had hidden with their surprise behind the heavy curtains of the bard's alcove in the dining hall. They fought the giggles, grunts, and the wiggles that always seem to plague children when mischief is about, while desperately trying to remain undiscovered. They peeked through the curtains at the unsuspecting feasters, and waited patiently while the servers brought out the courses one at a time. Keeping their surprise quiet and still was a chore, which caused many a snort and a few squeals of worry and mirth.

First came the cold greens, and after those dishes were taken away, soup and loaves of aromatic, freshly baked bread arrived. After that, a dish of sea crawlers was presented, and all the while, big Lord Ellrich listened intently as King Balton spoke enticingly of the great glazed ham that was yet to come. The king described the main course in such a way that all of the attendees were salivating for it. He was just jesting with Lord Ellrich's great hunger of course, but he made it sound as if it was the last pig left in the realm that they were about to eat. The whole room full of merchants, lesser nobles, and all of their wives went excitedly still in anticipation when the head cook rang the bell.

Proudly, with his chest puffed out, the man said, "The main course, Your Majesty, sweet pork on the bone."

A half second before the cart came rolling in, the castle brats let go of their surprise. The big sow that they had been struggling so hard to contain was let loose through the curtains, into the dining hall. It charged out of the bard's alcove, propelled into a fleeing squeal, as one of the children slapped it sharply on the rump.

The stage they were hiding on was elevated, and the terrified pig soon found itself running through midair, as it raced off the end of the platform. It was only a two-foot drop to the dining hall floor, but the fall frightened the sow so much that her fearful shriek was nearly deafening.

The ladies at the table squealed, and cried out as well. Chairs shot back and swords were drawn. As soon as the men realized they weren't under attack, a few of them tried to chase the pig around the room. The event quickly turned into a study of chaotic disaster. Mikahl remembered it had been riotously funny to the small group of perpetrators, until old Master Hinten cornered them and called for the king.

Mikahl pictured clearly the smile King Balton had been fighting back as he paced back and forth in front of them, deliberating whether the dungeons or the chopping block would be their fate. In the end, the head cook got to handle most of them, a fate far worse than the dungeons might have been.

Mikahl, until this very moment, had never understood why he had been spared the cook's wrath. Zasha, of course, was to be punished by her father, because she was a noble-born lady. To punish her openly wasn't proper, but Mikahl was told that he was going to be sent away. He had cried his eyes out to his mother, thinking he would never see her again, but King Balton had only wanted Lord Gregory to evaluate Mikahl over the summer.

He spent his time at Lake Bottom Stronghold in Lord Gregory's stable, learning the proper care of horses and how to ride. Looking back, Mikahl realized that King Balton used the incident as a reason to get him out of the castle. Working for the Lord of Lake Bottom that summer was just another of the many subtle steps King Balton took to educate him over the years. He returned to his mother and Lakeside Castle in the fall, with a new job as the Royal Stable Master's Assistant. No one thought twice about it when Lord Gregory took him on as a page a year later.

Mikahl wondered what had become of the castle brats. Only one had become a soldier. Flint was his name. Had the Dragon Queen killed them? Peter was a scribe now, and Dotty went on to work in the kitchen with her mother after her father died one winter. Maybe they were alive and well, maybe not. Mikahl hoped that they were just doing the same jobs they had done before, only for a different ruler.

But what of Zasha? She was most certainly Lady Zasha now. The last time he had seen her, she looked as beautiful as anything he could imagine. He hoped she was all right. The idea of soldiers having their way with her sickened him. Any joy that remained from his memory faded on that thought.

He asked himself where this so-called Dragon Queen had gotten the men to take and hold Westland. Surely, the Dakaneese weren't in this with her. A hope formed in his heart. Westland was huge. She would have to have spread thin a fairly large force to hold a kingdom that size.

He put the thoughts of retaking his father's kingdom aside a moment later, when he realized that no matter who occupied the place, to him, it would never be the same again. His mother, King Balton, and now Lord Gregory were dead. Glendar had most likely branded him a thief and a traitor. It all suddenly seemed so impossible to overcome, that even an attempt to do so would be nothing more than a fool's quest. His tone was far angrier and far sharper than he intended it to be when he spoke.

"I'm fargin tired of this!"

Mikahl hadn't specifically meant that he was tired of the waiting in the forest, but that's how Hyden seemed to take it. Vaegon's sharp ears picked up the comment as well, but the possibility that the words were spoken about something other than his situation never crossed his mind. The elf started angrily back to the camp to respond, to defend his unexpected lack of ability, but Mikahl's next words stopped him.

As Mikahl stood and began pacing, Grrr eased up to Hyden's side and lay down close to him. Hyden sensed the big wolf was as worried for his friends as he was. Feeling his concern and despair as well, Talon came fluttering down out of the trees and perched on his shoulder.

"I don't even know who I am!" ranted Mikahl. His voice was tired and desperate. "I was raised and trained as a commoner, by a king who always spoke to me and treated me as a father might, but I was never his son. I never had a father. The kingdom I grew up in has now been taken over by some dragon-riding wench. Everyone close to me seems to die because of this sword, and now I'm supposed to save the world from a fargin demon! This is insanity!"

Mikahl was about to pull his own hair out of his head in an act of sheer exasperation, when Vaegon strode back into the camp.

"WAAAAAHHH!" the elf made the sound of a baby crying and threw a wadded piece of cloth at Mikahl, as if it were a heavy stone. The mocking tone and rude sarcasm in the gesture caused Mikahl to look at the elf as if he had just burst into a shower of golden coins. Vaegon fought back a laugh.

"Quit your crying, Mik! Dry your tears! I've already cried enough of them for the both of us."

The last few words were spoken through a sincere grin. Mikahl's tirade reminded Vaegon of just how much he hadn't lost. It forced him to see that he wasn't the only one suffering.

Mikahl's angry expression softened when he realized that the elf was trying to cheer him up. Seeing his yellow-eyed friend come out from under the dark cloud that had been smothering him for the past few days went far toward lightening his own gloomy load.

"I suppose you cried your eye out." Mikahl tried valiantly, but couldn't bite back his laughter.

Hyden burst out as well, causing Grrr to sit up suddenly.

Vaegon's face went blank as his mind registered exactly what Mikahl had just said, then he too joined in the chuckling. For the first time in days, they were all smiling at the same time.

Urp, Huffa, and Oof returned in the midst of the newfound mirth. Huffa had a limp creature clutched in her jaws. She dropped it at Vaegon's feet, and the elf wasted no time preparing it for the spit.

"What is that?" Mikahl asked.

"I have no idea," Hyden responded, with a curiously crinkled nose. "I've never seen anything like it before."

The animal was the size of a spring fawn, but looked nothing like any deer or antelope the boys had ever seen. Its head was small and similar to that of a badger or an opossum, and sported two small, forked antlers. Its fur was the same muted shade of green as most of the forest's undergrowth and its long, bushy tail had darker rings around it, like a raccoon's.

"It's a ring-tailed buck squirrel," Vaegon told them with a satisfied smile on his face. "This is what we elves like to call one fine supper."

And it was. The meat was succulent, buttery, and seemed to melt in the mouth. The wolves liked it, too. When he had finished with his portion, Vaegon gathered up the small bones and skin, and started off into the woods.

"One last look around," he said, meaning that he would be gone for a little while.

Oof and Urp began to snarl and growl over the last piece of the meat. Heads lowered, hackles bristled, and it seemed for a long moment that they might actually fight over the scrap. When they began to circle each other, Grrr gave Huffa some silent command. The she-wolf strode calmly over between the two would-be combatants and snatched the morsel for herself. With a challenging posture, she strutted back to her place near Mikahl and munched it down. Both of the younger males stood there and watched her stupidly. A short while later, while Talon picked the big bone clean of the meat the wolves had missed, Oof and Urp were nuzzling and yapping at each other as if nothing had happened.

Hyden watched all of this transpire with an attentive eye. He could tell the wolves' moods clearly by the way they moved and the positions of their tails and ears. The message Grrr sent Huffa had been simple: "Your kill, your claim."

Oof and Urp's lack of response when she took the meat had been more than just a look of shock and longing. There'd been embarrassment and regret in their postures as well. Not regret for taking the last scrap of meat or fighting over it, mind you, but regret for not making the kill themselves in the first place.

It amazed Hyden, looking at the wolves through Talon's eyes, when they were traveling. They radiated a soft, glowing aura, which Hyden had come to think of as their life force. All creatures had it to some degree, but the higher predators were bathed in it. Other birds of prey, the tree cats, and sly foxes that they had seen, even the few long, slithery snakes hiding in the trees, all glowed with it. In the rabbits, squirrels, and the flirty songbirds that called the forest home, the radiance was more of a timid and fleeting glimmer. Hyden longed to study the sensation and the creatures he could define by it, as well.

He asked Vaegon and Mikahl both about books that held such information. Mikahl told him they could be purchased in the more sizable kingdom cities. Vaegon said he had some books at his home. They weren't about animals or magic, but he could use them to help teach Hyden to read. That excited Hyden to no end, but now it looked like Vaegon wasn't going to be able to find his way home. Hyden would have to wait to get himself a book.

Hyden didn't dare voice his disappointment. His problems were insignificant compared to Vaegon's and Mikahl's. He could wait until they reached Highwander. A temple of his goddess, Whitten Loch, was in the city called Xwarda, and he had enough coin to purchase plenty of books when they got there. He wished he had the foresight to buy a book or two while at Summer's Day. He had seen them there, but never once thought about them, or the wealth of knowledge they might contain.

Thinking about the festival made him think of his brother. He hoped Gerard was all right. He was glad it was nearing time to get back under way. Riding on Grrr's back, with Talon winging through the trees beside them, was as exhilarating as it was exciting. He could free his mind, and like an animal, live only in the moment, forgetting all other concerns. It was the greatest feeling he had ever felt, save for soaring through the heavens with Talon. The joys of both were amazing.

Grrr's ears pricked up suddenly. Hyden sensed the alarm in him immediately. Oof and Huffa rose quickly, while Urp sniffed at the air. Without warning, Urp let out a low growl and darted off into the forest.

Hyden nudged Mikahl awake.

"What is it?" Mikahl asked. He had fallen asleep leaning against the tree.

"SHHHH!"

The urgency and warning in Hyden's tone brought Mikahl fully awake. Silently, he took Ironspike's sheath rig from his lap and looped it over his shoulder. When he had it buckled in place, he looked over and saw his chain mail shirt lying on his blanket. Too late now, he decided regretfully, as Urp's distant bark caused Grrr and the other two wolves to charge off toward the sound.

"At first, I thought it might be Vaegon returning," Hyden whispered. "It's not. The wolves feel threatened. There's something out there."

Mikahl looked up through a small break in the forest canopy. The sky was a deep, dusky blue. Not much daylight left above, even less down there under the trees.

One of the wolves suddenly let out a long, angry series of snarling barks. Another wolf, Urp, thought Hyden, echoed the sentiment. The first had been Grrr. Something unknown was upon them. Something that the wolf wasn't sure he should attack or not. Grrr's uncertainty was a good sign. If it had been some dark, evil thing, Hyden figured they would already be attacking it. Talon was gliding into the trees above the wolf pack now, and Hyden closed his eyes so that he could see.

Mikahl saw Hyden close his eyes and huffed out a frustrated breath. He didn't wait for his friend's explanation. Vaegon might need them. He charged off in the direction the wolves had gone. He drew Ironspike as he ran and noticed that its magical glow was noticeably dimmer than it had been when he used it to kill Duke Fairchild. The sound of its magical symphony was still in his head, though, only it was as if it was coming from a great distance. Through his grip on the leather-wrapped hilt, he could feel the power of the blade slowly fading away.

"It's all right!" Mikahl heard Hyden call out to him from back at the camp.

He hoped that it was all right, because all he saw as he came crashing into the clearing were snarling great wolves, dozens of angry yellow eyes, and a whole bunch of razor-sharp arrow tips trained on him and his four four-legged friends. It wasn't until after he had blinked his eyes several times that he realized that all of those yellow eyes staring back at him belonged to elves.

Chapter Forty-Three

It took Shaella most of the night and cost the Staff of Malice all of its power to undo the magical barrier King Balton created around the island of Coldfrost, but the deed was done. Once the boundary's soft, static hum finally ceased, the Breed giants came stampeding off the island like the half-intelligent, half-feral beasts they were.

Straight across the deep and sluggishly powerful river channel they came, with little to no regard for the freezing temperatures and the deadly current. More than a dozen of the hairy man-beasts ended up floating stiffly out to sea, trampled, drowned, or frozen solid by the icy cold water. The smartest of them, the older males and the naturally protective mothers, waited on the other side with their children. They came across in the sunlight at a safe, shallow ford. There was a narrow place a few miles upstream from where Shaella vanquished the barrier. There, one of the younger, brighter males boasted he could make a bridge. It turned out that one wasn't needed. The water there never reached more than knee deep.

The wildest of them, the toothy, crazed males driven by rage and testosterone, were already ravaging the nearby villages and towns, and were slowly working their way south in small packs. The biggest and meanest of them, though—the smarter, more terrifying self-proclaimed leader of all of the Breed giants—was leading a band of his kind to Locar to complete the bargain they had made with the Dragon Queen.

Bzorch was nearly ten feet tall, and like all of his kin, his body was covered with a thin yet coarse fur everywhere, save for his face and palms. Bzorch's fur was light brown in color, and still thick enough for him to be considered young, but the grayish-white patches along his spine and chest showed his maturity.

A lot of the Breed giants were born with white or silver fur. It was much harder to tell the ages of those beasts. All of them were large, had wide wet snouts, and jutting lower jaws. Their mouths were full of ferocious-looking teeth that tore into raw flesh easily, sometimes the flesh of their own kind.

Bzorch had fought ruthlessly with dozens of contenders to become the alpha male. Lately though, the challenges had ceased. His hard and violent victory displays, where the loser was dismembered and consumed before those who chose to watch such combats, had gone far to dissuade further attempts to take over his role.

The Breed giants hadn't been cannibals until King Balton imprisoned them on the island. Up until then, they had hunted the northwestern arctic for bear, wolf, and lazy tusked seal. They eventually ranged far enough inland from the icy coast to stumble upon some of the true giants' herds, and some of Westland's northernmost villages. Herds were devoured, women were raped, and men and giants were slain. Eventually, the Breed started eating the flesh of the two-legged creatures they killed. This wasn't cannibalism yet, for they were neither men nor giants, and the taste of man flesh was succulent. It drove them mad for more.

Lord Brach and his hearty northern troops hunted, tortured, and did everything they could to dissuade the beasts, but the Breed eventually lost all fear of humans. They were the hunters, and the men were their prey. That's when King Balton stepped in.

The kingdom folk thought the Breed were half-bears, or the fabled Yetin. The fact that they were obviously two-legged, mannish creatures capable of semi-intelligent thought was the only reason King Balton and King Aldar agreed to spare them from complete annihilation.

The Giant King claimed they were a mutated form of a race called the Wedjakin, which hailed from beyond the other side of the Giant Mountains. What caused them to turn so violently feral was unknown to the Giant King, though. There was a hope that the wildness would eventually be bred out of them.

Bound to the island of Coldfrost, the beasts couldn't kill, rape, and savage the good folk of Westland, or plunder the giant herders' flocks any longer, and that was all that really mattered to the two kings. On the island there was little to hunt, and the bitter climate made growing anything impossible. Soon, the Breed beasts were forced to resort to eating each other to survive. The transition from human and giant flesh to the flesh of their own kind was easy to make, but the fact they had been forced to that extreme wasn't easy for any of the sentient ones to forget. Especially Bzorch.

The Breed had been hunted, killed, captured, and tortured by Westland's king and his northern lords. Like animals, they had been herded out onto the island of Coldfrost and imprisoned there. Until then, the Breed hadn't understood the idea of borders and property lines. The beast in them, the instinct that drove them, was to feed, to claim territory by way of scent marking, and to mate. There had been no evil intent to their raiding and marauding. There were no greed-driven designs of conquest involved. They were just creatures migrating and feeding.

Now all that had changed. Now they were driven by hatred and vengeance. Now they knew what it was like to be caged and forced to eat each other to keep from starving. The imprisonment had only lasted a few years, but what, to a half wild animal, is time? Especially in a place that is bitter cold and icy white year round, a place where the changing of seasons is a barely conceivable notion.

The Breed giants were loose now and they were having their way. To the people of Northern Westland, this was a most terrible thing. There was no one left to protect them. Almost all of their capable men had gone to war. The rampaging groups of huge wild creatures left a trail of blood and death in their wake. As for the more intelligent group, led by Bzorch, who had a specific mission to accomplish, the savaging was no less horrible. In fact, it was worse.

After gathering his chosen and leaving the Isle of Coldfrost, Bzorch led his band eastward through the town of Riverbend. They stopped only to feed on a few of the townsfolk there. No women were raped, no children pulled apart piece by piece, but only because Bzorch had more meaningful victims in mind.

The group consisted of thirteen of the most brutal of their kind. Bzorch had chosen them not only because they were strong and vicious, but because they weren't bright enough to plan and think on their own. They were the most primal of the Breed beasts, and the most obedient to his role as alpha male.

Bzorch himself was fairly intelligent. He had negotiated himself something more valuable than land or gold from the Dragon Queen. He had gained two of the most important things one could have among the humans. He had gained a position of authority, and he had garnered respect. Once he completed his end of the bargain, the city of Locar would be his to rule. Lord Bzorch, the Lord of Locar. He relished the sound of it on his thick, wide tongue as he led his chosen on a southeasterly course for the town of Greenside.

Bzorch had some unfinished personal business there, and his pack needed rest and food. Three days of nonstop travel had taken its toll on them. A night of pillaging and feasting, followed by a day of rest, would do them all some good. Greenside was the perfect place for it. The man who had earned the nickname "The Coldfrost Butcher" resided in that town. It was the home of the heartless torturer, Duke Fairchild.

Queen Shaella explained to Bzorch that the duke was most likely off on the new Westland king's fool's quest, but Bzorch didn't care. His father and two siblings had been captured, and taken to North Watch back before the imprisonment. They had been tortured and then displayed, like some macabre artwork, to serve as a sort of warning to the Breed. They had been laid out in the bloody snow, in so many pieces, among giant loops of their own entrails.

Bzorch remembered looking on that scene all too clearly, for all of the winter months. He had an inclination to display the Coldfrost Butcher's many women in a similar fashion. The warmer climate this much further south wouldn't preserve his exhibition like the frigid north had preserved his family's remains. Not being able to see such a sight for weeks and weeks on end wouldn't have the same effect on the humans, as seeing his family had had on him. He couldn't waste that much time, anyway. He had a city to take, a bridge to destroy, and a title to claim.

A night and a day of rape and torture would have to quench his thirst for vengeance. Maybe Duke Fairchild's wife would bear him a child. He would try his best to plant his seed inside her, and maybe eat one of the many sisters she was rumored to have, right there in front of her. He could make her eat some of the meat, too. The idea caused him to let out a low, guttural growl as he loped along.

The stronghold at Greenside wasn't hard to find. The half dozen armored men guarding the place fell like frightened penguins before the Breed assault. While most of them tore through the village, Bzorch and two others brought the wrath of the Breed into the duke's stone-walled home.

The duke's wife and her gaggle of sisters screamed, pleaded, and begged for mercy, but none was given. The plumpest of the women had her face bitten off by one of Bzorch's companions, who then raped her body, while her feet sputtered and thumped on the floor.

One of his other raiders sunk his teeth into an ample bosom, and didn't stop until the floors were soaked in blood and gore. Women fainted, whimpered, and huddled in the corners. A few made it out of the stronghold, only to find as much savage chaos outside.

Bzorch singled out the lady of the house, who had collapsed into a heap on the bloody floor. Her jeweled necklace, and the many rings on her fingers, gave her away. He carried her to the dining hall, and none too gently laid her out on the heavy walnut table. With a single rake of his hand, he tore way the front of her dress, revealing pale goose-pimpled skin and heavy breasts. He didn't rape her then. First, he went back into the sitting room, and grabbed a whimpering girl up by the hair. Before the terrified girl knew what was happening, her neck was twisted to the point of tearing free of her body. Bzorch was hungry, and he tore into her, as if he were a starving dog. He drenched the half conscious Coldfrost Butcher's wife with blood as he feasted on her niece's raw flesh, then savagely penetrated her again and again.

When he was done with her, he swept her body from the table, into a pile of cool, sticky human remains as if she were so much trash. A good while later, he ordered his chosen to get some rest. It was a long way to Locar, and only the small trading town of Halter lay in between. Once he had made sure that the chosen would comply, he lay down upon the Coldfrost Butcher's table board and slept.

At Lake Bottom Stronghold, where Lord Gregory had once taught Mikahl how to ride and fight, the Dragon Queen's Zardmen had rooted themselves in thickly. The watery lowland terrain was comparable to the swampy marshlands, and the warm water of Lion's Lake agreed with their slithery, scaly skin.

The Breed would not come this far south. Not only had Queen Shaella forbidden it, but the Breed preferred the cooler climates of the north, just like the Zard wouldn't, and couldn't for any extended period of time, suffer the colder northern portions of the Dragon Queen's kingdom. She had allowed some groups of the primitive man-beasts to terrorize the cities of Portsmouth and Castleview.

The city of Castleview was built around Lakeside Castle. By road, it was a few days' journey on geka back, from Lake Bottom to Lakeside, but to the Zard, it was only a short swim across the lake. Having the Breed so close kept the Zardmen at the stronghold constantly on edge.

Shaella had made it clear that she wouldn't tolerate fighting amongst the Zard and the Breed, but that didn't stop the Zard from feeling the internal instincts of hatred and fear that the Breed instilled in them, nor did it stop the Breed from wanting to kill and eat them.

The Zard soldiers and their Sarzard captains loathed the idea of Shaella loosing the Breed giants, but they understood the need to protect the north and had faith in her judgment, if not faith in her ability to use her dragon to keep the primal savages in line. Still, the idea of chancing upon one of the wild packs of tree-tall monsters ranging this far south was driving the Zard mad. The not-so-exaggerated rumors they were hearing about the Breed giants' rampage through the north distracted them enough for Lord Gregory's messenger, Wyndall, and a few others, to escape from the cellar where they had been held prisoner for some time now.

After receiving Lord Ellrich's disturbing message, Lady Trella and Lady Zasha had begun preparing to flee the kingdom by ship. Being well-bred ladies, they went about it all wrong and spent far too much time worrying about all the wrong things. They wondered what plates to save, which paintings and dresses to stow in their trunks, and then ran out of time. Now, they were slaving away in Lake Bottom Stronghold's kitchen, scrubbing pots and cooking slugs, turtles, and other strange bug-like things for the Zard who had taken command there.

Wyndall had grown up around Lion's Lake, and knew every step of ground around its shores. He had hunted every stretch of the thinly wooded hills around the area, too. His father, he had learned, had died fighting futilely to save the family's farm during the initial Zard attack. His mother had been sold to a Dakaneese slave merchant a few weeks later. These things he learned from other captives at Lake Bottom, and from those who were forced to serve the Zard there.

He had delivered Lord Gregory's message to Lady Trella, but it hadn't been a timely delivery. He had run into the musters of soldiers gathering in the villages around Eastwatch. Mistaken for the page of one of the attending lords, he was forced to carry out a few miscellaneous orders, but quickly got himself away from there.

After that, he traveled on foot and off the roads. Groups of Lord Brach's men were on keen alert for those who tried to sneak past their call to arms. It was no easy task to avoid them, but somehow, he had managed.

He had gotten to Lake Bottom only a week before the Zard attacked Settsted. He fought them when they came, but there'd been swarms of the slithery Skeeks, far too many to hope to overcome. Along with several others, his life was spared, and he was locked in the cellars. The rumor was that another Dakaneese slave ship was coming, and they, and several of the women including Lady Zasha and Lady Trella, were to be put on it in exchange for supplies that the Zard needed.

Wyndall enlisted the help of the young rider from Settsted, and a few of the locals, who were loyal to Lord Gregory. Together, they were about to risk their lives, as much for the two ladies, as for their own sake. The only thing that might hinder the scheme, the only thing that worried young Wyndall, were the ladies themselves. Already, their foolish desire to hold onto things from the past had cost them their freedom. He hoped they had learned their lesson, because what they could carry in a pillow sack was about all they could bring with them this time, and only if it was ready when he came for them.

That night was rainy and dim, which was all the better for their cause. Wyndall and Bryant, the Settsted rider, huddled in the drizzle, the precipitation doing little to ease their nerves. The summer nights weren't much cooler than the sweltering days around the lake. The rain did keep the insects away, and that alone was enough to be thankful for. Not to mention the fact that it made the two young men nearly impossible to see.

"There it is," Bryant whispered harshly. A lantern was shuttered twice in a row in the stronghold's kitchen window.

"I see it," Wyndall confirmed. He took a deep breath, and checked to see that the rusty sword he had found hanging in old man Gander's barn was still at his hip. "Set them off then."

"I'll see you at the boat, Wyn," said Bryant. His eyes held Wyndall's, searching for something. "You'll wait for me, won't you?"

Wyndall smiled reassuringly. He understood Bryant's concern.

"On my word, I'll wait until we can wait no longer. That's all I can swear to."

"Aye," was all Bryant could reply to that.

Wyndall waited until Bryant was gone, then said a prayer. When he finished, he made the sign for luck, and moved toward a little supply gate at the rear of the stronghold. He counted thirty paces from it along the wall to the right, and after a panicky moment of searching, found the tiny wooden door hidden there. A few moments later, he had the old rusty sword slid through the jamb, and was jimmying the bar loose.

Just as the Lion Lord's ancient priest who died in the cellar cell next to him had told him, he found himself in the back of the stronghold's chapel.

Outside the main gate, four men draped in cloaks made of burlap and goat hide approached on jury-rigged stilts, howling, snuffling, and demanding entry. They growled, yelled, and pounded wooden clubs together insistently, trying to make as much racket as possible.

The Sarzard on command stood atop the wall and hissed at them.

"Comesss closersss."

He was terrified of these Breed giants that defied the Dragon Queen's orders, but he wanted to see how many of them there were. He wanted to see if the rumors were true about them being twice the size of men. The Zardmen that recently returned from Lakeside Castle had been saying all sorts of things about the ferocious creatures they had seen there. The whole stronghold was astir. Already, a group of Zard was gathering in the yard below the Sarzard captain, making a clamor. Some of them had been ordered there. Others came out of curiosity and concern.

"Wilds savages at the gates," a Zardman hissed.

"The ones from Portsmouths, that ates all those humans," added another.

"Breeeds giants from Lakesides!"

The whole ordeal lasted only a few minutes. The savage Breed giants cursed about the drenching rain and finally gave up when it was clear that the gate wasn't going to be opened for them. They stalked away into the rainy darkness, leaving the Zards inside the walls hissing a breath of relief.

"Where's Lady Trella?" Wyndall asked Lady Zasha in an exasperated whisper. He had only found one of the women he was trying to rescue waiting for him in the chapel, and was furious about it.

"She had to get something while the lizards were distracted," Zasha responded fretfully.

At the moment, Wyndall's expression was easily as terrifying as the prospect of getting caught by the Zardmen.

"It's important," she added in a mousy whisper.

As terrified as she was, she couldn't help thinking how handsome this brave boy was that Lord Gregory had entrusted with his dying words. Without realizing it, Zasha inched closer to him. He made her feel safe, a feeling she hadn't felt in quite some time.

Fargin women, Wyndall thought.

One had boiled his blood already without even being in his presence, and the other melted his heart with her timid voice and liquid eyes. He was pleased that he didn't have to wait long. Lady Trella soon eased through the double doors that lead to the corridor beyond the chapel. She was struggling with a pillow sack, which appeared to be far too empty to warrant such effort. As she drew closer, the dull clank of precious metal explained why the sack was such a burden to the gaunt woman. Wyndall took it from her, and noticed her hesitation before she finally released it.

"Come, milady," he said, forgetting his anger.

He knew that the value of the jewels and gold in the little sack he now held might make the difference in the success of the escape in the grander sense of things. There would be more to surviving than just getting away from the Zard.

"Follow me, and hurry. It is slick, and we've not much time."

His voice was soft and reassuring now, and the strength and surety of it went far in easing the angst the two women were feeling.

Through the dark drizzle, they made their way down to the river to a place just a few hundred yards from where the headwater came spilling over the natural dam that formed Lion's Lake. The roar of the powerful waterfall filled the night, but the darkness hid its beauty from the eyes.

Clayton Widden, a local farmer's son, was waiting with the little boat. It looked to be a struggle for him to hold it there in the roiling current.

Wyndall helped the ladies into the craft, then handed Lady Trella her bag. She nodded her thanks to him, but wasn't sure if he saw. A moment later, he handed each of them a makeshift shield. They were old wagon wheels with fence pickets nailed to them.

"If we are fired upon as we drift out, these will help protect you," he said over the sound of the waterfall.

Worriedly, he glanced back up the hill they had just descended.

"Lady Zasha, could you please hand up that bow?"

His tone had become suddenly urgent. He took it from her, strung it, and threw the quiver of arrows over his shoulder.

"Clayton, be ready to shove off at my command," he ordered, then moved off the dock back toward the hill.

"It's past time to go," Clayton was saying, but Wyndall didn't hear him. Bryant had topped the hill.

There were two dark shapes, and only the slight glimmering reflection off their rain-soaked clothes as they ran made them noticeable. One was Bryant. The other was a young stable boy of about ten years of age, named Dort. Three, maybe four, Zard were not too far behind them. As soon as Wyndall had a good aim, he loosed an arrow. One of the Zard tripped forward, and went into a tumble of scaly limbs and tail.

"Don't wait! Go!" Bryant yelled.

"We'll swim for it!" added Dort.

Wyndall loosed another arrow, but missed his mark. He was drawing back a third when he felt the gut bow string stretch to uselessness. The rain had gotten to it.

Clayton urged him back to the boat, and as soon as he got in, they were off, swept downstream by the raging current. Already, Bryant and Dort were being forced to angle their mad dash down the hill toward them.

"Hold up the shields!" Wyndall commanded, as he drew his sword and moved to the boat's prow, which was momentarily facing the unfolding scene of the chase.

Dort leapt out over the water, his small legs churning, as if he were running through the air. Arrows rained down from above, some thumping into the wood of the boat and the shields, others plunking into the river's dark water. Bryant barely escaped the claws of a Zardman and dove headlong into the river. That Zardman, and a few others, came in after him.

From beneath the surface, a slithering, snakelike wake formed just behind Dort, who was swimming toward the boat with all the effort he could muster. It was all Wyndall could do to plunge his rusty blade blindly into the river behind the boy as he reached the boat. The sword felt like its tip grated across the river bottom, until it violently shook itself free from his hand and sank away.

Bryant surfaced just behind the boat, but a leaping lizardman came splashing down into the river right on top of him. The huge sheet of water thrown up by the splash, and the swell of the impact, rocked the boat violently. Wyndall fell awkwardly onto the floorboards, but Dort used the motion of the wave to pull himself up. The two women did the rest, and hauled him over the side like he was an oversized fish. The last thing Wyndall remembered before slipping into unconsciousness, was the gasps of horror from the two women, and Bryant's blood-chilling scream as the swift-swimming Zard tore him apart in the water.

Bzorch's thirteen chosen tore through the trading town of Halter with a sickening fury. After feeding on the slower of the townsfolk, they spent two nights raping and recuperating from their long trek through the fields and forests of central Westland. Then they were off again, loping away toward Locar. What they found when they got there was more daunting than anything their simple minds had ever conceived.

The size of the bridge city was overwhelming. It was bigger than ten of the other towns they had seen put together. Why anyone would dwell in a place so crowded and noisy, none of them, save for Bzorch, could fathom.

As they had been ordered to do by the Dragon Queen, they waited on the outskirts of the city for nightfall, killing anyone who ranged too close to their hiding place. That night, just as planned, the dragon came.

As Claret set upon Locar with Queen Shaella riding proudly on her back, the Breed giants tore into the city with a vengeance. While most of the chosen wreaked havoc in the city, Bzorch, with Claret's help, went about doing the important work. Together they demolished the crossing bridge. Claret, with her massive claws, crumbled and crushed huge sections of the stone worked archways, and burned anything flammable to ash, while Bzorch bashed away the smaller parts of the structure. It wasn't long before the deed was done. The only bridge over the wide and mighty Leif Greyn River, which crossed from Westland into the eastern kingdoms, was uncrossable. Westland was isolated now, and Shaella's conquest was complete. No army could march into the west without first going through the Giant Mountains, swimming the Leif Greyn River, or sailing around the great expanse of the Marshlands, and those three occurrences would be easy to defend against.

Just as Bzorch became the undisputed Lord of Locar, Shaella, Dragon Queen and Master Sorceress, leader of the half-beast Breed giants and the Mastress of the Zardmen of the marsh, became the sole ruler of Westland. And her Westland, unlike Glendar's, was a kingdom that no one could take from her.

Chapter Forty-Four

Hyden had to explain to Mikahl how the elves felt about the humans. How human folly, over and over throughout time, had brought trouble to the lands, and how the elves had come to the rescue, again and again. He also tried to explain that unsheathed, Ironspike's presence might bring more dark creatures down upon them at any moment.

Mikahl put the sword away, but he still fumed at the idea that they weren't welcome in the elven forest city, or whatever it was. The fact that they were being detained out in the regular forest while Vaegon gathered his things appalled him.

"Here we are, going off to try and save the world from the likes of demons, and these fargin yellow-eyed bastards won't even let us stop in for a visit!"

"Sounds like something my father would say," Hyden said, more to himself than to Mikahl.

The wolves didn't hunt that night, nor did Talon fly through the forest. They, and the companions, just waited there in the camp for Vaegon to return.

Hyden laid down and stretched out to rest. The wolves, save for Grrr, did the same. Grrr sat close to Mikahl, who was sitting against his tree with Ironspike lying sheathed across his lap. All around them, seen and yet unseen, elves guarded their position. They didn't do it in an obvious manner—they weren't ringed around the group with drawn weapons—but they were there, and not trying to hide the fact completely. That glint of yellow eyes over there, a rustle of undergrowth, and a muffled whisper over here. They could have been utterly silent, Mikahl knew; he had observed the way they eased through the forest while they were leading him back to the camp earlier. He guessed that they had relaxed and let their guard down but didn't understand why.

Hyden had caught up to Mikahl when he had come upon the distressed wolves and the armed elves just in the nick of time. Mikahl had been certain he was about to become an elven porcupine, and still his instinct had been to attack in order to defend the wolves. Hyden's shout had been the only thing that stopped him from it.

The elf called Deiter, who Mikahl later learned was Vaegon's younger brother, explained the situation to Hyden after they each placed an open palm on the other's chest, over the heart. After the gesture, bows lowered, and stances relaxed. Hyden spoke soothingly to the Great Wolves and calmed them enough for them to stay quiet. Reluctantly, Mikahl slid Ironspike back into its sheath, but unlike the elves, he didn't relax his guard. Neither did Grrr.

There was no doubt that the elves didn't want them there. It was plain in their expressions and the way they narrowed those wild, yellow eyes. It was a look one might give after taking a big bite of a piece of rotten meat. Distaste.

Why was Vaegon so different? Mikahl asked himself. Maybe he's not so different, maybe he just hides his feelings better. A glance down at the shoulder rig in his lap made him regret ever having that thought. Vaegon was different. The elf had been kind, thoughtful, and most helpful to him. Mikahl decided not to judge any of them yet. He didn't have to like the way he was being treated, but he also didn't have to blame the whole race of elves for this lack of hospitality.

He closed his eyes and used his breathing to clear the anger from his mind. He hadn't gotten the chance that morning to go through his routine of exercises, something he had done relentlessly every day since Loudin was killed. He needed that release of sweat and stress to balance his anger and fear. He knew that if there was even a remote chance of beating the odds that were piling up against them, he would need total clarity to see it through.

How long he slept, he wasn't sure, but he was startled awake by a nudge from Grrr's cold wet nose and the sound of Vaegon returning.

He must have slept for some time, because it was full night now. Vaegon brought two other elves into the camp with him. One had silvery blue hair, which reflected in the campfire's light like icicles. The other's hair was another shade of blue entirely. It was the color of a cloudless summer sky. This elf was ancient. He moved with a slight tremble, his eyes were more amber than yellow, and had a depth to them that one might get lost in. He nodded at Hyden respectfully, then looked directly at Mikahl. He spoke in the elven tongue, and Vaegon translated for him.

"It would be a great honor, friend, if you would allow me to look upon Pavreal's sword with my own eyes."

Mikahl looked at Hyden askance. Hyden nodded that it was all right.

Mikahl drew the sword. The soft, bluish glow was barely enough to light the radius of the camp, but it still caused a look of awe to form on the faces of the two older elves.

"Tell them it's no longer Pavreal's sword," Mikahl said sharply. "Ask him if it were Pavreal standing here, instead of me, if this would have been a more courteous meeting. We've been traveling for weeks, and haven't even been offered water."

Mikahl's words put a mortified look on Vaegon's face, but a gentle urging from the older elf caused him to repeat them, word for word.

The old elf's response was quick and hard.

"He said his grandfather helped to forge that blade, and that there is a cool, crisp stream only a stone's throw from here."

"Pavreal was my ancestor," said Mikahl, who was still riled. "You all should be ashamed to be afraid to bring your grandfather's work among your people, no matter what sort of trouble it might bring with it."

The old elf listened to Vaegon's translation, then smiled sadly. After a moment, he spoke in a far softer tone. Again, Vaegon translated.

"He apologizes for the lack of hospitality and courtesy shown to you, to our group, to us. It was not his doing. He says that his wisdom is sometimes relied upon to make decisions, but he is not a true decider. The Queen Mother, after seeking the guidance of the forest through the Heart Tree, made the decisions that offend you so much. He only wishes to lay his eyes upon the fruit of his grandfather's labors. If it were up to him, the sword would be displayed at every gathering with pride and honor for its intent."

Vaegon added his own words now.

"He is a respected man among my people, Mik, and one of the oldest of my kind. Please don't be rude to Em Davow."

Vaegon gestured at the forest full of glittering yellow eyes that surrounded them. "This is not his doing."

"Then I apologize for my rudeness," Mikahl said, with a nod of his head. He took Ironspike by its glowing blade, and offered the hilt to Em Davow.

The instant he let go of the blade, the bluish glow vanished, leaving the insufficient dancing orange flames of the campfire to illuminate their faces.

The aged elf took the hilt, moved closer to the fire's light, and studied the sword reverently. The fact that its magical inner radiance didn't acknowledge him was a statement unto itself, and more than once Em Davow glanced up at Mikahl curiously.

The other elf and Hyden were having a quiet conversation. Mikahl saw the resemblances to Vaegon in Deiter and the older elf, and knew that he was their father. He took another long gaze at Em Davow. If the ancient elf was related to Vaegon, it didn't show.

Mikahl hoped he hadn't offended or embarrassed Vaegon's family. His intention had been to make the old elf aware that he disliked being guarded in the forest, when they might be bathing, eating a warm meal, or resting somewhere more comfortable. He also didn't like the fact that the whole realm was currently threatened by some dark and evil power, and the elves didn't even seem to care.

Vaegon started translating Em Davow's words again. "He says he hopes that the evil we must face is swiftly defeated, and that after it is done, you might return. He hopes then that his tree can be open to you as it should be now."

"Tell him..." Mikahl paused. He wasn't sure what he wanted to say.

Em Davow was probably full of ancient wisdom. It showed in his deep, amber eyes. Now that Mikahl's anger wasn't clouding his mind, he wished the meeting had started differently. He could have gleaned a thing or two from the ancient elf if he had been a bit more diplomatic. Now, he felt too awkward to ask anything of him.

"Tell him, thank you," was all he could think to say as he took Ironspike back and quickly inserted it into its sheath before its glow became pronounced.

He felt more than a little ashamed at his inability to keep his anger from controlling his mouth. In a feeble attempt to reconcile his rudeness, he put his right hand out, stepped up to Em Davow, and placed his palm over the old elf's heart. Em Davow returned the gesture, and then made a deep, respectful head bow, which surprised Vaegon. The fact that Mikahl was Pavreal's sole heir, the rightful king of not only Westland, but of the entire Seven Kingdoms, didn't slip past the old elf.

"I think it's time for us to be on our way," said Hyden.

"Yes," Vaegon agreed, he was relieved, and as pleased as he was surprised, at the way Mikahl and Em Davow's exchange ended. He took a moment to introduce his father to Mikahl while the camp was being broken. It was a short affair, with only names and the human gesture of clasping hands taking place, which was fine with Vaegon.

Hyden paused his rigging of Urp's pack harness only long enough to make the palm to heart gesture with Deiter, who had come out of the woods to escort his father and Em Davow back to the Elven Heart.

Before they left, Drent gave Vaegon a palm-sized leather pouch and hugged his son fiercely. A few more goodbyes were spoken, and the companions climbed onto the backs of the restless wolves and disappeared into the forest night.

Mikahl couldn't help but reflect on the way Vaegon and his father said farewell. It seemed as if they both knew that they would never see each other again, or something equally as drastic. The idea of it left a hollow feeling in Mikahl's gut that didn't go away until long after the sun had filled the sky again.

They rode swiftly around the massive tree trunks of the deeper forest, over shrubs, and through silvery moonlit glades. Dawn broke quickly, but the wolves paid it no heed. They ran until well after midday, when the stored energy of the last few idle days started to wear off, and the heat started to get to them.

A mossy, pebble-strewn creek ran through the forest where they stopped, and while the wolves lapped up bellies full of its cool water, Vaegon began making a ring of stones for a cook fire. He wasted no time gathering up some dead fall and setting it to blazing. Then he curiously took out a small tin pot from a pack he had taken from home and began boiling water.

Huffa and Urp went off to hunt, and Hyden followed them for a while from above, through Talon's vision. Feeling the hawklings hunger, Hyden had the bird inspect the area around the camp. Once he was satisfied that there were no immediate dangers about, he let Talon go hunt for his own meal.

The hawkling had grown quite a bit, and was nearing full size. His appetite was amazing. Talon could eat most of a rabbit now in a single sitting, and be hungry again only a few hours later. It made sense, though, Hyden thought. Talon's outstretched wings were almost as wide as Hyden's open arms, and if the hawkling were to stand on the ground beside him, its head would be just above his knees. The incredible amount of energy it took to sustain flight through the dense Evermore required a good bit of sustenance. There were no warm thermals to glide upon when racing through the trees with the Great Wolves.

"Here," Vaegon offered Hyden a small tin cup of aromatic tea.

Mikahl was already sipping from his. The little leather pouch Drent had given his son was lying open on a flat stone, and a smattering of dark leaves could be seen inside. The ingredients of this drink, Hyden could only guess. It was tart, but refreshing. It seemed to reach down into the nooks and crannies of Hyden's body and cleanse away the grit that had collected there over the years. After only a few sips, he found he was relaxed in a way he had never been before: not tired, yet soothed and content.

"I apologize to you all," Vaegon said to them.

He was including the wolves in his apology, even though he wasn't sure if they understood him, or cared to hear his words.

"You have to understand that my people are afraid. Their fierce pride causes them to recognize the emotion as anything but fear. The sword seems to draw the dark creatures to it, and if one of them were to find you in the Elven Heart, then this evil might learn where the Elven Heart truly exists. To allow the dark creatures to know that place is to doom my people. The Heart Tree is rooted there, and without the heart tree, we cannot survive. Its location must forever remain secret to all but us. I hope you understand."

Mikahl didn't, but he held his tongue. Hyden, however, lived in a village that was built to remain hidden from the kingdom men and other dangerous things. He sort of understood and nodded his understanding to his elven friend. Grrr yawned with a curling tongue, as if Vaegon's words meant absolutely nothing to him.

Vaegon was about to continue, but was saved from the embarrassing subject by a nod and a tiny, little screaming sound.

"That's an odd-sounding bird," Mikahl said, with his ear cocked curiously to the sky.

"Was that cursing?" asked Hyden.

"Might have been," Mikahl replied.

The little screaming voice was moving rapidly toward them and coming from the level of the treetops. The sound was now obviously angry words, not some animal call, but the voice was little and childlike. The curses, however, could have been coming from a drunken seaman. The source of the voice suddenly became clear, and it was as astonishing as the sound itself.

Talon came swooping out of the trees from downstream, and was quickly approaching them. Clutched in his claws was the little creature that was causing the racket. It was a little man! A tiny little man!

Talon landed as softly as he could manage, then held the little guy pinned, shoulders under one claw, legs under the other. The bewildered companions stared as the man grunted and huffed under Talon's weight. The bird was forced to keep flapping his wings sporadically, as the little man squirmed, wiggled, grunted, and cursed.

Grrr rose quickly, and with a curious way about him, stuck his muzzle in close and sniffed at Talon's victim. His hackles rose, and he stepped back, snarling. The companions all had the same wide-eyed, open mouthed expression, but Hyden broke free of it and spoke to calm Grrr. He had to say a word or two of restraint to Oof, who was coming in close to investigate as well. Hyden could sense the wolves' reaction was not from anger or a feeling of danger, but from a sense of uncertainty.

"Oh, mighty mushrooms!" the little man chirped. "Let me be, let me be! I done naught to deserve to be a white-furred monster's turd!"

Mikahl looked at Hyden and Vaegon in turn. Hyden was busy soothing the wolves, but Vaegon looked just as shocked as he felt. This only served to further Mikahl's sense of disbelief at what he was seeing and hearing. This was the forest that Vaegon called home. Nothing in it should surprise him. But this did.

"Let him go!" Hyden ordered Talon aloud.

The hawkling obeyed, but only stepped back off the little man. Talon kept behind him, ready to snatch him back up should he try to make a run for it.

The little guy stood up and dusted his britches off indignantly. They were a faded green color, as was his vest. The garments looked to be made from frog skin, or maybe leaf lizard hide. On his tiny feet were leather sandals, and his hair and beard were gray and neatly trimmed.

"Who? What are you?" asked Hyden.

"I'm minding my own business, is who I am!" he chirped back angrily. "What's a sorry lot like you bothering with peaceful folk out here, anyway?"

"Sorry lot!" Mikahl shot as he sat up and loomed in on the little man.

The little man pointed at Vaegon first.

"An elf who can't see straight and a wizard who can't read."

His finger had moved to Hyden. Then he pointed at Mikahl.

"And what's this? A king with no kingdom!" The little man clutched at his belly and laughed with mock hysteria.

"Callin ya a sorry lot is being far too kind!"

"I ought to let the wolves eat—" Mikahl started, but cut himself off abruptly when the little man's eyes widened and pointed up over Mikahl's head. The tiny man's mirth had vanished, and his jaw hung slack in a gasp of terror.

"A dragon!" he squeaked. "Mighty mushrooms, no!"

They all turned and looked right into the sun. Even the wolves had followed the little man's finger. The brightness of it put colorful, blooming patches in their eyes. By the time any of them had blinked the searing splotches away, the little man was darting into the leafy underbrush at the tree line with Talon hot on his heels.

Mikahl had to laugh at the clever trick the rude little guy had played on them. Vaegon, however, didn't seem to think it was funny. Hyden was too busy seeking out Talon's vision to react, but he was smiling like a boy with a piece of cake.

Hyden and Talon followed for a bit, but finally lost the little man in the underbrush. Grrr offered to follow the scent trail, but Hyden told the leader of the wolf pack to let the little man be.

They spent the evening talking about the event, as if it had been a hallucination brought about by Vaegon's tart tea. The elf assured them that it wasn't the drink.

"One of the fairy folk," was his explanation.

He said that several races of the fabled little people lived in the Evermore Forest. Fairies, sprites, gnomes, and pixies had once lived all over these lands. But he had to admit this was the first time he had ever seen one of them firsthand.

They rode again after sunset, and did the same the following few days as well. The wolves took turns hunting, and Vaegon assumed the role of camp cook.

Hyden spent the down time trying to make sense of the letters Vaegon was teaching him. Mikahl, as was his daily ritual, woke and went through the grueling series of exercises each evening before they started off.

At the end of the fourth day's run, around midmorning, they came upon what they thought was only a large clearing, or a break in the forest. To their great surprise, the Evermore Forest had come to an end. Beyond the tree line, the landscape rolled away gently. A mild, emerald sea of low, rounded, grassy hills dotted here and there with small copses of poplars and oaks, spread out before them. A herd of some sort of brown and white domesticated beasts grazed on a fenced hillside to the south and the west, and even farther away, a cloud of gray smoke rose up from what looked to be a small city, or at least a large grouping of buildings. It was too far away to say for certain.

To their left, or eastward, the hills grew sharper, and upthrusts of grayish-white stone could be seen among the larger clutches of trees. Farther away to the east, the Evermore wrapped its dense vitality around the base of a small range of mountains, the tops of which showed only the slightest bit of snow capping.

Being that the night's traveling was already near to an end, they eased back into the forest a safe distance and made camp.

Hyden watched through Talon's eyes as the hawkling rose up into the heights over the edge of the forest. The prospect of seeing an actual city excited Hyden no end, and it was to the southwest where they had seen the rising cloud of smoke that he urged the hawkling to explore first.

As Talon gained altitude, Hyden saw that not too far to the south of their camp was what he decided was a road. It ran east to west, curving as it followed the valleys and skirted the larger of the hills. It was wide and looked well traveled. On the road a good ways east, the dust cloud from a train of wagons moved away, but to Hyden, they looked to be the size of beetles crawling across a mossy creek bed.

As Talon neared the city, Hyden saw another group of wagons. These had riders on horseback darting around them, and they were coming out of a crude picket wall that was built around the heart of the place. Outside of the wall, a few dwellings could be seen, some with fields of crops around them in rows, others with large fenced-in animal pens. Inside the wall there was a huddle of roofs and smaller yards, some larger than others, but far more crowded together than Hyden had expected.

The road cut through the town and out the western side of the wall. It ran due east into a finger of the Evermore Forest, which clung to the banks of a southward flowing river. The road split at the river, one path going across a small wooden wagon bridge that spanned the modest flow, the other going south following the river's course. Both of those roads were empty of travelers as far as the hawkling's eyes could see.

Talon swooped lower and circled over the town. It was nearly deserted, and several of the buildings within the walls were burning. A few were already charred and blackened husks. As Talon turned back toward the east, Hyden saw that the wagon train going out of the gates was surrounded by armed and armored soldiers. The banners they displayed were white with Highwander's Blacksword emblem emblazoned on them. Hyden shuddered. These were Willa the Witch Queen's men. Hyden noticed that the women and children, some riding in the wagons, some on horses of their own, didn't appear to be afraid of the Blacksword Warriors, though. It became clear that the soldiers were protecting these people's passage. Protecting them from what? Hyden wondered. Talon circled up high again, riding the waves of heat from the buildings burning in the town. In moments, he was up in the clouds, soaring back toward camp, just a tiny speck in the sky above the road.

Hyden was disappointed. He had been looking forward to seeing how so many people, cramped inside the walls of a city, interacted with each other. All he had seen in the city was a few dozen men loading up a few wagons, and a few ducks and chickens running loose in the empty streets. He decided not to give up, but to follow the road eastward for a while, instead of going back to camp just yet. He was glad he did, because what he found was a sight that amazed him even more than the little fairy man had.

Nestled in a green valley at the base of the eastern mountains was a massive hub of buildings and life. From Hyden's great vantage point, the city looked almost like an archery target. The center was a mass of white stone buildings and towers with shiny, sparkling rooftops. In front of the main structure sat a deep sapphire-blue lake, with a fountain spraying up out of its middle. Several walls ringed that center jewel. The innermost was wide enough to drive a wagon along the top of, and the taller, outer wall was as wide, if not wider, than several of the roads that led up to the various gates. Between the walls were squares and rectangles of brown, red and gray split by narrow roads that were speckled with busy people. To Hyden, they looked like ants scurrying around a mound.

From the south, three other roads led into the ringed walls like the spokes of a wagon wheel. Hyden urged Talon to dive down into the city for a closer look, but something large and dark passed beneath them. It was big and bat-like, easily twice the size of the hellcat they had faced in the mountains. Luckily, neither the dark beast, nor its horn-helmed rider, seemed to notice the tiny hawkling gliding above it.

The thing's aura was hot and repulsive. It exuded malice freely. What was worse was that it was heading on a northwesterly course directly toward the camp. From above, Hyden followed it for a while just to be certain. When he was sure, he pulled himself out of the hawkling, and as a thick feeling of dread threatened to overwhelm him, he warned the others. It was coming for Mikahl's sword.

"Make ready to fight!" he said sharply, as he made his way to the pile of packs that Urp had been carrying. "Something huge and evil is winging its way toward us."

He described the creature and its rider as he strung the elven longbow Vaegon had given him.

Grrr rose to his feet and started pacing anxiously. The other wolves watched him, awaiting his command with alert eyes, high pricked ears, and ready stances.

Vaegon took out a long, skinny pouch, and made to dump the contents onto the ground in front of him. Three arm-length shafts of intricately carved wood, and a wicked-looking curved and serrated blade fell out of it. In a matter of moments, he had threaded them together into a pike-like bladed staff, which was a head taller than he was. He made a few thrusts with it to check its balance. "I'm ready!" he said when he was satisfied.

Mikahl reached over his shoulder and grasped Ironspike's hilt. He didn't want to draw it and have its magic give away their position. Feeling that it was there was enough for now.

"Let it begin, then," he said harshly, remembering the brutal message he sent when he crippled the hellcat, instead of killing it.

He pictured King Balton, all sweaty and breathless, dying on his bed. Then he pictured Lord Gregory, sprawled out on the ground, his bloody body so swollen and broken that it was almost unrecognizable as human. Then the scalding image of Loudin of the Reyhall forced its way through. His friend's guts hung in the trees as he clung onto the sword, with the last tendrils of his life spilling away from him.

Mikahl seethed with rage and anticipation. He felt nothing resembling fear at the moment. He was eager to face whatever was coming. Through teeth clenched as tightly as a closed vice, he repeated the words again.

"Let it begin!"

Chapter Forty-Five

Dreen, the kingdom seat of Valleya, sometimes called the Red City due to the color of the sun-baked bricks that make up its notably long wall. Its modest castle and most of the other dwellings are made from the readily available resource as well. It sits in an arid but grassy plain, just below the foothills on the eastern side of the Wilder Mountains.

King Broderick, the current ruler of Valleya, had received warning of Westland's army's march through the mountains toward his capital, but only a few days before the force's expected arrival. He had taken those days to set up the defenses of the city and to call the wealth of Valleya inside the walls for protection. The horse herds were the pride and primary commodity of the kingdom. They had to be protected at any cost.

The wall that encircled the city was taller than any building inside it, save for the twin towers of the modest Royal Castle. The wall stood thirty feet high, and the city was so widely spread that it took a perimeter patrol a full shift to march all the way around on the top of it.

There was a lot to defend. Unlike most cities, the spaces inside the wall were open and uncrowded. Nearly every building, be it tavern, mercantile establishment, warehouse, or home, sported a fenced-in stockyard, complete with stables and troughs. Some even had lush, magically fortified grazing pens, which were larger than an average family's farm plot, which stayed green year-round.

Even with all of the people and animals filtering into the city, Dreen didn't have the feel of a place that was about to be attacked or besieged. The atmosphere and the attitude of the people were more like that of an open market day, or a minor festival. None of them had any idea of what was headed their way.

The Royal Castle itself was only a three-story rectangle, with a pair of crenellated towers rising up above it. The castle's defensive wall was more like a tall fence, made to keep the Royal Herd in, more than to keep others out. The Valleyan way had always been the same. Save the horses, let the enemy tear the city down. There was enough of the easily worked red clay in the foothills to rebuild the city a hundred times over. It was in this spirit that King Broderick, who had only a month ago sent the better half of his men to march against Highwander, went about gathering up the best of his personal herd, with the full intention of fleeing with them to the south.

If the Westlanders took the city, then so be it. He would never take the knee to young King Glendar, thus Valleya would never really fall to the west. Already, he had riders speeding with orders to recall those troops he had sent to Highwander. He also had riders on their way to Seaward City to beg his cousin, Queen Rachel, to send those men of hers that were about to march on Highwander, back to help save Dreen. She would not refuse him. After all, they were blood relatives. Since King Broderick's wife died childless, and he was without an heir, Princess Rosa, Queen Rachel's daughter, stood to claim his throne, as well as her mother's. As long as he didn't take another wife, Queen Rachel would do anything he asked. Keeping the Red City out of Westland's hands was in Queen Rachel's best interest, anyway.

King Broderick was confident that King Glendar wouldn't expect a force of nearly ten thousand Valleyans and Seawardsmen to come bearing down on him so quickly. Glendar's army would be driven right back into the mountains and chased all the way back to Westland.

The Westland army was too small to occupy much more than the Red City, King Broderick told himself. Valleya was far too vast. From Dreen, it was nearly three hundred miles south to the sea coast, and just over a hundred miles east to the Seaward border. If by chance Glendar did get rooted into Dreen, it would only be a matter of days before King Broderick's southern forces arrived and besieged the invaders. If the rumors out of Dakahn and Ultura were true, if a million lizards and a dragon-riding sorceress had risen out of the swamp and invaded Westland, then the foolish young king of the west couldn't afford to meddle with Valleya very long.

All things considered, King Broderick decided he could better manage the defense of Dreen from afar. In truth, he was as cowardly as a man could be. He was afraid for his life. Along with the rumors of Westland's new Dragon Queen, he was beginning to hear tales of the wizard Pael's display of destructive power on Wildermont. He had no intention whatsoever of getting caught up in something like that here. Thus, as dawn rose on the day his scouts expected the lion hordes to come calling, he and a dozen guards, along with two dozen handpicked horses from the Royal Herd, started south toward Stroud.

Pael stood alone, on a ridge looking down over the city of Dreen from a distance. The wind ruffled his silky, black robes, and threatened to blow the hood back from his chalk-skinned head. The gold worked embroidery on the belled sleeves and collar of his garb glittered in the morning sun like star-fire. Far below and to his left, Lord Brach led a long, winding snake of some eight thousand men out of the mountains, toward the irrelevant red wall. Inside the walls, Pael could see the Valleyan soldiers swarming like maggots on old meat. The fact that Lord Brach's snake wasn't spreading out or marching toward one of the gates was confounding them. Pael wished that it was Xwarda below him now instead of Dreen, so much so that his actions were mechanical and his mood dismissive. The manic joy he had found while destroying Castlemont was absent, the exhilaration of the raw demonic power he possessed seemingly forgotten.

In a moment, he would breach the wall for Lord Brach's men, so that the hungry snake might feed on the maggots, but now Shokin was forming an idea in his head. The idea made him regret sending Inkling and those poisoned men to sea so far to the south, but only for a moment. When the idea fully bloomed in his mind, he laughed aloud, because neither the three ships full of men, nor the Imp King leading them, mattered anymore.

There might be joy in this day yet, Pael told himself.

He had just come up with a new plan of action, one that wouldn't force him to have to wait out the winter here in Dreen. If it worked, he could take Xwarda and gain the power of the Wardstone long before the snow started to fall. He would be able to launch his assault on Xwarda in days, not months.

As he transported himself down to appear before the big, red wall of clay, he couldn't help but laugh again. This time, the manic glee was abundant in his countenance.

The idea was wondrous. It would take a bit of quick work to pull it off, but he could manage it. Knowing this created a sense of urgency about him. This day would be a grand one, after all. Riding his high spirits and the possibilities of the days to come, Pael unleashed a blast of searing energy into the wall before him.

The hole it created was enormous, easily wide enough for a half dozen wagons to ride through abreast of each other. The force of the blast and the debris that it sent flying into the city left a swath of chaos and death deep into the refugee-crowded streets. Lord Brach and his winding snake of men came charging in to fill the void, and the battle was underway.

Pael could've started blasting away groups of Valleyan soldiers and large portions of the overcrowded city itself, but he chose not to. Instead, he cast another sort of spell, and he cast it not only on the Valleyans, but on the Westlanders as well. The second spell, an old favorite of the necromancer Priests of Kraw, was the same spell he recently used in its singular form to resurrect

Roark. Pael wanted this battle to play out. The more casualties there were here, the better. Spell weary after casting the long and powerful incantation of reanimation, Pael used the last bit of his energy to transport himself back to his elevated perch. From there, he watched the battle unfold, while he worked out the details of his new idea.

As soon as Lord Brach got the first few hundred of his men into the breach, the Valleyans threw open a nearby gate and charged forth. It made sense. With a massive hole leading into the city not far away, keeping the gates barred was pointless.

Cavalry met cavalry in a shining clash of armor and steel. The red-and-yellow-checked Valleyan banner whipped proudly in the wind. The dark shield upon it was an ancient and constant reminder to defend the horse herds. The golden lion on its field of green roared and reared back at them as the Westlanders pressed forth intensely.

A troop of cavalry broke free from the middle section of Westland's procession, thus ruining the snakelike appearance of the army. The group raced away to meet a knot of Valleyans that had come out of some unseen gate around the wall. The Valleyans were charging to attack the Westland flank. The collision of men, animals, and sharpened steel happened at a full gallop, and the sound of it was sickening. Men and horses screamed in protest as they were slashed, pummeled, and crushed in the violent explosion of natural force.

Arrows filled the sky like streaks of windblown rain. The Valleyan archers up on the walls made full use of the advantage they had over those below them. Lord Brach ordered his archers to shoot at them, to make cover for the men trying to get into the city. He sent other troops of archers to fill the open gateways with flying death. The ranks of pikemen and the untrained slashers were ordered to crowd the breaches and get through any way they could manage. Before long, the battle was raging on both sides of the wall.

Inside the wall, the Westlanders pushed into the Valleyan crowd, inch by bloody inch. Then a man went berserk, wildly hacking into the knots of people, felling bodies like wheat before a scythe. From the rooftop of a structure near the breach, a brown-robed mage rained streaks of fire down upon the invaders. The men writhed and burned as they fell. They were replaced immediately by others pressing into the space.

Outside, the sheer number of Valleyans that came from the other open gates broke what remained of Westland's serpent formation into knots and clumps of frenzied battle. A large skirmish was forming about a thousand yards out from the wall. Valleyan riders, carrying long jousting lances, were charging into the mix of foot soldiers. They were skewering Westlanders and then withdrawing at will. The length of their weapons allowed them to stay out of range of their victims' blades, and their superior warhorses were quick, well trained, and knew their duty well. Most of Westland's archers had been ordered to the front, to cover the penetration into the city, but a few squadrons remained, and they were doing their best to slow the assault of the fearless and greedy Valleyan spearmen.

The gateway nearest the breach had become choked with fallen bodies. The Westland archers had done extremely well there. Already, it was next to impossible to get a horse out of the opening, and the clog of Valleyan riders trapped there were falling in droves to the Westland foot soldiers who had stormed the breach.

The brown-robed Valleyan mage had been joined by another, and together they created several bonfire-like piles of smoldering Westland flesh. They had become so effective at charring away the bodies of Lord Brach's men that Pael decided to intervene. He didn't want the bodies of the dead all burnt and ruined. He needed them.

Pael appeared with a crackling pop, right amongst the Valleyan archers along the top of the wall. A cheer erupted from the Westlanders who saw him. Rumors of Pael's might followed Lord Brach's army as it marched through the mountains. Those who had seen and survived the leveling of Castlemont had made Pael the hero of that particular battle.

With no regard for the archers firing arrow after arrow at his person, Pael gazed out across the two hundred or so yards of clanging bloody steel and death that separated him from the two brown-robed magi. Arrows exploded into splinters as they hit the invisible field of energy that surrounded the demon-wizard. Some of the arrows glanced off and continued into the knot of men on the opposite side of him. Some of the arrows just passed right through. Either way, they were of no concern to Pael, for they could not find his flesh.

With a wave of his hands and a muttered word, he pointed at each of the magi in turn. Seconds later, green flames erupted at their feet and licked slowly upward, until each man was consumed in a white-hot inferno. A few heartbeats later when the fire died away, only a whirl of ash and dissipating smoke remained.

As quickly as Pael had come, he was gone again. Without the magi to thwart them, the Westland surge broke loose into the city. A stream of almost two thousand bloodthirsty men came riding or charging into the general populace, unhindered. More were on their heels.

After Pael reappeared on the ridge, he studied the battle below. Not the logistics of the formations and the chaos that threatened them, nor the way the soldiers fought. Pael watched the way they died. The idea he had earlier had just refined itself in a pleasing way.

He cast a ward of protection over himself, sat down, leaned back against a boulder, and dozed as the battle raged into the afternoon.

The spell of mass resurrection he cast earlier cost him more than he had expected it to. He was drained and needed the rest. As he slept, the demon dreams of Shokin shed even more light on the evolving plan he had conceived. When he woke feeling sharp and refreshed near sunset, the continuing battle below was of little concern to him. What he needed was a book that was back in his tower library. Before he could go there though, he had to make sure that Lord Brach was fully aware of what he was to do when this battle was finished.

The sudden shock and fear in the faces of the men Lord Brach was giving orders to, and the smell of hot ozone that reached his nose, told Lord Brach that Pael had just appeared behind him. Without batting an eyelid or showing the fear and unease that the wizard instilled in him, he dismissed the men and turned to face his kingdom's greatest weapon.

Brach was no fool. He knew Pael was the true force behind King Glendar and the conquest over the eastern kingdoms. He didn't like it, and he was far too intelligent to oppose it, but it didn't matter anyway. The teeth-jarring jolt of Pael's touch on his shoulder killed him instantly.

The wizard caught him as he slumped down, and though there was no need to do so, he spoke the words of a spell into the corpse's ear.

Pael didn't have the patience to wait until dawn when the mass resurrection spell he had cast would take effect. Sluggishly at first, then slowly growing into his full strength, Lord Brach regained himself. Where the tiny, white glimmer of life had just been in his eyes, there was now an ember, a little red sparkle of evil instead.

As soon as Pael flashed away, Brach ordered his men, all of them, to storm the breach. It was an alarming order for the captains to swallow, but none questioned their commander. As they formed, and pressed their way in, those waiting to squeeze through were left exposed. The Valleyan spearmen outside the wall were left to pike them apart at will.

Long after sunset, when the last Westlander had gained entry into the city, the Valleyans found that there was nothing else to do but follow them in. It was a strange scene they found inside. As battle upon battle played out in the city streets, handfuls of Westlanders, at the command of their leader, were dragging the corpses from both sides back into the buildings and alleyways, as if trying to protect them.

The Valleyan fighters didn't stop to question this occurrence, as they were still outnumbered considerably. It was all they could do to stay alive and find a way to keep the Westlanders from getting deeper into the city, where most of the innocents and the horse herds were.

Eventually, the Westlanders found some of the fenced pens where the precious animals were being guarded. Lord Brach ordered that all the horses be killed, and several more groups of his men broke loose from the main body and began running them through with brutal efficiency.

The surge of anger this action sent through the ranks of the Valleyans caused a resurgent rally of their defense just before dawn. But when the sun finally did break the horizon, the sounds of battle died away and were replaced by shouts and screams of utter terror. The battle resumed, but it wasn't Westlander against Valleyan anymore. It was the dead against the living. The corpses were rising and engaging those still alive with a jealous fervor.

Dead horses stampeded through the streets, and broken-bodied soldiers limped or crawled with determined expressions on their faces, each trying to kill or maim the living men that mocked them. Before long, only the dead and the undead could be found in the red city of Dreen and they were all forming up, following the orders of Lord Brach, to begin the long march directly to Xwarda.

A few men made it out of Dreen alive. One of them was King Jarrek's elite Redwolf guardsman, Brady Culvert. Wearing his red plate armor like a shroud, the son of Marshal Culvert had warned King Broderick of the coming of Westland's forces, then dutifully stayed on to lend his sword.

He fought beside the Valleyan soldiers all night long, but when dawn broke and the dead started rising, it was every man for himself. He battled like a cornered animal and eventually won free of the encroaching death and wild necromancy taking place inside the walls of Dreen. He witnessed firsthand the awakening of the dead, and now found himself terrified and fleeing eastward ahead of them, as fast as his still-living horse could carry him.

The idea that the evil force that destroyed his homeland could have grown stronger was beyond the grasp of his reason, but it had. These soldiers couldn't be killed, because they were already dead. They probably wouldn't need rest or food, and they would fight on mindlessly, while arrows and steel tore apart their lifeless flesh. What was worse was that they were going to Xwarda next.

Knowing that was where King Jarrek had gone to seek aid gave Brady reason enough to get there and warn them. He would warn those along the way as well. As much as he wanted to put his steel to use against them, he understood that it would be a waste of effort. He had to get to Xwarda and give testimony to the insane magnitude of the evil that followed him. He only hoped he could stay ahead of the undead army, and if he could get to Xwarda in time, they wouldn't think him a lunatic for his tale.

Chapter Forty-Six

"How far away is it, Hyden Hawk?" asked Vaegon.

"Not very far," Hyden answered grimly.

Grrr's hackles rose and he darted into the thicket, beneath the forest canopy at the northern edge of their camp. He growled, then pealed into a series of savage barks. The other wolves wasted no time going to him.

"Someone—no—a group of people approaches," Hyden spoke the feelings Grrr's warning conveyed to him and the wolf pack.

No sooner were the words out of his mouth then the sound of jangling tack and the nervous whinny of a horse came to his ears. Oddly, Hyden heard Grrr's growling tail off into a whimper of confusion before it ceased altogether.

A pair of riders moved confidently out of the trees. Another was behind them, and two more followed. The camp was so crowded by then that the last two men had to stop more in the trees than in the clearing.

The person in the middle of the other four was a woman. She was draped in glittering chain mail, which was belted at the waist with a large, steel-plated girdle. She wore no helmet. It was dangling from her saddle horn. Her hair was in a long, fat yellow braid that trailed over her shoulder and ended somewhere near her bosom. She wasn't young, but was far from being considered old. It was hard to say, but she was probably quite shapely under all that armor, at least Hyden thought so. Her fair-skinned face was probably beautiful as well, but her narrow-browed scowl was hiding its potential. She looked to be the one in command, sitting atop her gray horse with its fancy cropped mane and even fancier saddlery.

The four men with her were rugged-looking. The two in front were cloaked and dressed in uniform leather woodsman's attire, all shades of gray, brown, and green. Their bows were drawn. One had an arrow trained on Vaegon. The other had his pointing at Hyden's heart.

The two men behind the woman were armored as well as she was, though theirs was in far worse condition, as if it had been put to its proper use on more than one occasion. They wore their helmets with the visors up, and though they were crowded and still mostly in the forest, neither seemed to be worried about it affecting the swing of their drawn blades.

Besides feeling the full anticipation of the coming dark-winged creature he had just seen through Talon's vision, Hyden was aware that the wolves were completely silent and nowhere to be seen.

"Where are my white furred friends?" he asked sharply. His bow was drawn and held as steady as the other men's, but his arrow was aimed at the woman's heart.

She spoke a strange word and snapped her fingers. Instantly, Grrr's whine of confusion seemed to start from halfway through. Then the wolves were leaping back into the camp, taking on aggressive stances and growling savagely at the intruders. By the amount of distance Grrr kept from them, it was obvious he was wary. His feelings were conveyed to the other wolves by his posture. More than once, he glanced at Hyden for some indication of what he should do.

"You picked a bad time to come upon us, lady," Mikahl said, with polite urgency. His face was a study in raw emotion. "Some dark and deadly beast approaches our camp as we speak."

"A trick!" One of the leather clad men up front barked.

"Just like them little buggers," agreed the other.

"Silence, rangers!" the lady commanded. Then to Mikahl, in the same demanding tone, "Why are you here? It isn't wise to sneak into a kingdom that is under attack. Willa the Witch won't be pleased by your trespass. You don't look like Valleyans, or Seawardsmen, for that matter, and you travel with wolves and an elf. Who do you align with?"

Turning to face Vaegon, she asked, "What do these human's affairs concern you?"

"M'lady, on my word of honor, we can parley later," Mikahl said quickly.

His grasp on Ironspike's hilt had tightened, but he didn't draw the blade for fear of the rangers' arrows that were aimed at his friends. Through his grip, he could feel the magic warning him of thc fast approaching danger.

"This is no place for you or your men. There is—"

The shadow of the Choska demon passed over them then, three full heartbeats of shadowed eclipse. The woman started to give a command, but her horse tramped sideways nervously, and the air filled with a high-pitched wailing shriek.

Vaegon fell to his knees and clasped his hands over his ultra sensitive ears. Mikahl pushed Hyden to the side and drew Ironspike. The ranger in front of Vaegon almost loosed his arrow, but showed great restraint by thinking better of it. Ironspike's glow wasn't bright or radiant, but it was visible. A sword with only blue light where its steel blade should be apparently warranted his discretion.

"Get the lady clear of here, man!" Mikahl yelled over the horrible shrieking sound. "It is no ordinary beast that comes for me."

Hyden closed his eyes and found Talon's vision. The hawkling was still circling high overhead, and it was clear that the winged monster had come around to dive in for its attack. Hyden whirled and loosed an arrow at the open sky above the trees at the edge of the clearing, earning a snort of disgust from one of the rangers. The snort turned into a gasp of terror, when the Choska demon came streaking over the treetops and met the missile. The steel point stuck deeply into the dark-furred flesh of the Choska demon, but it showed no concern. Hair flew about wildly, and swirls of leaves and debris leapt from the ground as the beast slammed into a hover on powerful, thumping wing beats.

The huge, horn-helmed rider on the Choska's back leaned over and slashed with his long, two-handed blade. He held it in only one hand, as if it weighed nothing. One of the rangers cursed, loosed his arrow, and tried to duck away from the slicing steel. He wasn't fast enough. His body, cleaved from collarbone to abdomen, twisted sickeningly out of the saddle. The woman did well to spur herself clear of the Choska's dangling claws while Hyden and the remaining ranger loosed arrow after arrow at the beast, to no real effect.

The Choska didn't even flinch when the arrows struck it. With a hiss of effort, it flapped back up out of the camp and made to get a better position. As it went, a cracking jag of yellow streaked upward from the woman's hand into the creature's underbelly. The Choska didn't ignore that. It bucked wildly in the air, nearly tossing the horn-helmed rider from its back, while shrieking in anguish and fury. A heartbeat later, it was beyond their line of sight. Without thinking, Hyden sought Talon's vision, and saw it was already turning to attack again. He called out exactly what he saw.

The fallen ranger moaned horribly. Vaegon raced to his side with every intention of saving the man, but there was so much blood on the ground that he slid in it, and nearly fell on him. Vaegon found the man's side, but the expression on his wild, yellow-eyed face when he rose back to his feet said it all.

Mikahl made his way to the center of the camp's open space, shooed back the others, and assumed an aggressive stance, as if he was going to fight the beast by himself. Oddly, the wolves ringed around him at a distance, like they did every time he put himself through his grueling exercise routine. Grrr raised his head and let out an angry growl of savage intent at the empty sky. First Huffa, then Urp and Oof, joined in the din.

He's gone mad, Hyden thought.

"That's no hellcat, Mik!" Vaegon yelled, as he dashed to Mikahl's side with his pike-like bladed weapon held high.

"Just stay clear of my sword, elf!" Mikahl snarled.

Vaegon saw the look in Mikahl's eyes, and took a healthy step back. The memory of the Westlander's dexterous and acrobatic skill with the blade caused him to take a few more.

This time, the Choska came down and landed hard. Its heavy body forced Mikahl to roll away or be crushed. Vaegon managed to thrust up into the thing's chest, and black blood spilled over him from the wound. It seemed no more than a thorn prick to the angry demon. The elf stabbed up again, but was knocked away this time by a defending claw.

From beside Hyden, the woman raised her hands from her reins and sent another streaking yellow blast of lightning at the Choska. The demon took the assault with a breathy grunt, then sent out its own magical blast in response. Its cinder-red eyes flared brightly, and a crimson fist of energy shot forth from them, sending the woman head over heels, clear out of her saddle. She landed hard in the dense thicket at the tree line, and instantly, the two armored riders charged their mounts in, to form a protective barrier between her and the creature.

The remaining ranger was in the trees now, still loosing his arrows futilely at the demon. Hyden was firing with his bow, too, but his arrows were now aimed at the horn helmed warrior instead of the beast. One of his arrows struck Roark in the heart, and he expected the big warrior to fall, but he didn't. Instead, the dark knight leapt from the Choska's back and landed a few feet in front of Mikahl. The Choska moved between the archers and its rider, thus cutting off Hyden's view of them. He knew Vaegon was over there somewhere too, but didn't have any more time to think about it as the Choska turned its attention on him.

The sound of one of the wolves attacking erupted viciously from behind the Choska. Another flash of white fur, streaked heavily with crimson, darted through the trees nearby.

As Mikahl rolled to his feet, Roark attacked him with all his might and skill. The undead warrior was bigger, stronger, and fueled by hellish intent, but Mikahl was quicker, and smarter. They were evenly matched, and the battle that ensued wasn't over quickly.

Grrr started to leap on the horned man attacking his two-legged friend, but Mikahl's savage and unpredictable quickness kept him from it. Seeing Oof and Huffa bound toward the Choska demon's unprotected flank and tear into it, Grrr decided to join them instead.

White fangs tore into dark, foul tasting meat, while heavy steel crashed against Mikahl's magical blade in a shower of sparks and humming power. Each of the swordsmen pressed, but was met with a cunning misdirecting defense or bone-jarring solidity. Blow after blow was thrown, sweeping arcs of radiant sapphire and glimmering steel. Lunge, parry, and thrust, as sparks and spittle flew through the air.

In Mikahl's head, Ironspike's symphony was there, but it was barely audible. Even if it had been stronger, Mikahl wasn't sure how to use the sword's power. He didn't have time to ponder the matter, either. It was all he could do to use his natural skill to avoid Roark's heavy-handed blade.

He feigned a turn one way, then spun the other. The shining silver of Roark's blade followed the misdirection, but the undead man's strength was enough to recover and block Mikahl's thrust. Twist and duck, Mikahl's mind screamed as Roark brought his steel back around. Mikahl came up behind the stroke and swung his sword wildly into the bigger man's blade, adding to its momentum as it carried on around. It was then that Mikahl finally saw an opening and went for it.

As Roark went spinning around off balance, Mikahl jabbed Ironspike into the unprotected area behind the bigger man's knee. Mikahl was stunned when it didn't drop the man. He had barely pulled the blade free of Roark's rotting flesh, when the undead warrior's sword finished its revolution, and came slashing across his rib cage. It sliced with ferocious force, splitting the little rings of Mikahl's chain mail and biting hotly into his flesh.

Not knowing what else to do, Mikahl reached up, and yanked at the stub of the arrow protruding from Roark's chest. The lack of reaction from the assault sent waves of panic through him. He noticed that Ironspike's symphony of power had faded completely from his ears. He brought his sword up just in time to deflect an overhead blow, which would have split him in two. As it was, the blow forced Ironspike down so hard that its failing blue blade bit into his own forearm deeply enough to hit bone. He tried to spin free of the horn-helmed warrior, but Roark was too strong for him. Mikahl's side burned, and he could feel the warm liquid life running down over his thigh, under his leather britches. For the first time since he had drawn Ironspike against Duke Fairchild back in the Reyhall Forest, Mikahl's confidence began to falter.

On the other side of the camp, Urp had managed to sink his teeth into the demon-beast's foreleg and was holding on for all he was worth. Like a terrier shaking a rat, the Choska kicked and whipped its clawed limb around, trying to sling the wolf free.

Hyden loosed at the demon's head, hoping to get an arrow into one of those fist-sized, ember-colored eyes. He missed, but his shaft shot into the beast's nostril, causing it to rear up and scream out that terrible shriek again. A deep, red pulse flared from the Choska's eyes, and Hyden was hammered by a powerful concussive blast that sent him cartwheeling into the trees. He came to an abrupt halt against the trunk of an unyielding oak. In the darkening haze that followed, Hyden's only thought was that he no longer held the elven longbow Vaegon had gifted him. After that, there was only blackness.

Vaegon rolled to his feet and saw the horn-helmed warrior bearing down on Mikahl. Like a fleeing deer, he darted through the forest and circled around them until he gained Roark's undefended rear. Mikahl, bloody and grimacing, looked to be about to crumble under the pressing onslaught of the warrior. Mikahl was on his knees, using his forearm to block the press of his own sword, and his whole right side was wet and slick with blood.

Vaegon let his outrage strengthen him and charged forth. He thrust the serrated blade of his pike into Roark's back with all the strength he could muster. Mikahl felt the surge of Vaegon's attack jar his raw, exposed arm bone. The front of Roark's breastplate dented outward from the savage force of the elf's pike tip. Mikahl instantly felt the huge warrior's strength ebb, but when he looked up, the red-eyed, undead face showed not the slightest bit of fear or pain. Roark didn't as much as wince when Vaegon violently jerked the pike blade out of him. When the serrated teeth of Vaegon's weapon caught on flesh and steel, he did stagger back a step. In that instant, and in a state of utter panic, Mikahl spun out from under Roark and attacked. He brought Ironspike around in a sweeping arc, aiming at the neck. Roark saw the stroke coming, and brought up a steal-clad arm to deflect the blow. Had he been a fraction quicker, or had luck been on his side, he might have fully thwarted the pale blue blade. He managed to knock the swing off course, but not far enough. Ironspike hit Roark's head just under the ear, at the jaw. The horned helmet did little to stop the sword. The warrior's head would have been severed completely, had his armor not tipped the blade up. It didn't matter, though. Roark's head, though still attached to his body, fell over at a crazy angle and hung there. The lower jaw was still attached to his neck, but the rest of the mass hung grotesquely canted. A hard boot from Vaegon sent the huge warrior tumbling over, and one of the wolves peeled away from the Choska demon's flank to worry the head the rest of the way off the still-twitching body.

Mikahl turned toward the Choska. It was reared up and screeching loudly, but facing the others, not him. He surged to his feet, and took two running strides, but it sent icy shocks of pain tearing through his side. He ignored the pain and drove Ironspike into the demon's flank, up to its jeweled hilt. For the briefest of moments, he felt his sword's magic trying to draw out the demon's life force, but it just wasn't strong enough. Had it been, the fight would have been over. The demon's essence would have been trapped in the blade, like so many others before it.

It wasn't to be, though. Ironspike had exhausted all of its magical power, and Mikahl found that he was in serious trouble. He yanked the sword free, but not before the raging Choska spun and slung him. Mikahl didn't let go of his sword. He couldn't let go, no matter what happened next. Loudin had held on, and so would he. He didn't even let go to use his hands to cushion his tumbling fall.

Urp's toothy grip broke free of the Choska's foreleg, and the wolf went slinging away, just as Mikahl had, only Urp didn't land before crashing into the forest.

Mikahl came down hard on his injured side, but managed to roll with the impact. He ended up on his back, with no air in his lungs whatsoever. He saw the Choska demon's slavering, yellowed teeth coming down at him and tried to scoot away. Hot pain shot through him from the bottom of his feet up to the base of his skull, as if his nerves and tendons were white hot wires. He was barely able to keep his grip on Ironspike's hilt. His back was broken, he was sure of it. Even with all of the pain, his legs should have moved, but they didn't. Terror chilled his blood. All he could do was look on helplessly as those dagger-sharp teeth came gnashing down for him.

Vaegon charged, seeing the terrible fate that was about to befall his young kingdom-born friend. Even as he did so, he knew he wouldn't be fast enough to get between the demon and Mikahl. Stopping in mid-stride, he launched his weapon at the Choska demon's head as if it were a javelin. At the same moment, a flash of white fur leapt onto Mikahl and Grrr's growl erupted into a peal of savage barking. It all ended with a wet, sickening crunch. From beyond the demon's bulk, a skittering, crackling boom concussed through the whole forest like a thunderclap.

The trees, the ground, and even the air, shimmered for a moment, like an expanding ring of desert heat exploding outward.

Vaegon fell to his knees, and in the mind-numbing silence that followed the blast, he saw the Choska demon's body twist crazily up and over his head. Its great bulk had been blown like a leaf off the forest floor by the force of whatever had made that sound. The beast didn't crash into the forest, though. It threw out its leathery wings crazily as it whirled over the treetops and caught the air. With long, ropey strands of thick, black blood slinging away from its body, it righted itself and winged away westward.

Vaegon ran to Mikahl's side. He was lying twisted at a sickening angle, his thigh bone jutting up out of torn and punctured flesh. Mikahl rolled his head to one side and made a deep growling sound. He focused on something. Tears then welled and spilled out of his eyes, just before they rolled up into his head. Vaegon couldn't help but turn to see what Mikahl had been looking at.

There on the ground lay Grrr, the pack leader of King Aldar's great wolves. He was a bloody heap of mangled fur, still and lifeless, eyes open and empty. Huffa whined sadly, and sniffed at her mate's unresponsive body. Oof whimpered as well, then suddenly looked up, and started searching for Urp. Urp was limping slowly over toward them, his fur a tangle of leaves and debris, his maw bright with crimson gore.

Vaegon glanced around frantically, looking for Hyden Hawk. He spotted him, half in, half out of the forest, looking with wide-eyed bewilderment at where the Choska had just been. He was down on one knee. His right arm was outstretched, and his hand was open, as if he had just thrown something at the beast.

The well-armored lady wasn't far away. She was staring up at Hyden with a look of shock on her dusty face. She was ruffled and had twigs and leaves in her hair, but otherwise seemed fine. She shrugged off the help of her plate-armored soldiers, and with a look of disgust at them, strode over toward Vaegon.

Seeing that Hyden Hawk was alive, the elf forced everything else out of his mind, and began using his magic to tend to Mikahl's wounds. A moment later, he raised his head back and let out a horrible, keening wail.

Mikahl had serious internal damage, more than even he could begin to heal. All he could do was what he had done. He stopped the bleeding and put Pavreal's last heir into a form of stasis that might or might not keep him alive a little while longer.

"Will he live?" The woman asked, with sincere concern showing plainly on her face. "There are extraordinary healers in Xwarda, if we can get him there."

"How far?" Vaegon asked, with a glint of hope forcing its way through his anguish. His head felt like there was a hive of bees swarming in it, and his ears most likely had permanent damage from the Choska's horrible scream. He ignored his pain and looked at the woman, waiting intensely for her answer.

"If he can ride, we can make it by dawn, I think."

Vaegon closed his yellow eye a moment, and fingered the patch over the empty socket of the other. He doubted the stasis spell he had cast to keep Mikahl alive would last that long. After a few deep breaths, he looked around and stopped his gaze on Huffa. She was licking at Grrr's unresponsive muzzle lovingly. It was obvious that she knew he was dead, it showed in her posture. It only made the sight that much harder to look upon. Her eyes met Vaegon's gaze, and the elf could feel her sorrow. He could also sense the pride she felt in knowing that her mate had died trying to save another. An idea struck him then, and he looked back up at the lady.

"If you can ride a wolf, then you can have him there by nightfall!" His inner ears hurt horribly and his sudden excitement was intensifying the sensation. "I assume you can get him to these healers quickly once you get there?"

She nodded and glanced at Oof for a moment, then nodded again, though with a lot less confidence about her.

Vaegon looked toward Hyden, who was struggling to get to his feet.

"Will you help my friend?" he asked her. "I need him over here."

Without another word, she went to help Hyden.

As soon as she moved away, Vaegon gingerly straightened out Mikahl's broken leg, and did his best to magically knit the bone back together. It was all he had the strength left to do, and he couldn't even do a good job of it. The flesh wound there was deep and uneven. He reverted to a more primitive form of healing; he tore strips of cloth from his sleeves and bound them around Mikahl's thigh. There was nothing he could do for the internal injuries. After trying to help the fallen ranger earlier and what he had just done for Mikahl, he was drained completely. He hoped beyond hope that he had done enough to keep Mikahl alive until he could get better care.

Talon and Hyden fell to the ground at Grrr's side at the same moment.

"Oh, by the Goddess, no!" Hyden cried out, as he clutched his arms around the great wolf he had come to love.

Talon let out a mewling coo of sorrow. Through the dead wolf's fur and his own unashamed sobs, Hyden asked Vaegon about Mikahl.

Vaegon explained to him that if Mikahl didn't get to the healers in Xwarda quickly, he was as good as dead. He explained his idea, and Hyden listened intently. When Vaegon was finished, Hyden grabbed Huffa around her neck and hugged her close, while whispering desperately into her ear. She let out a rolling yelp of concern when he was done.

"Yes, we'll look after him," Hyden replied, speaking of the injured wolf, Urp.

Vaegon began re-rigging the pack harness that had been used to strap their supplies to Urp's back during their long journey. Huffa yipped, nuzzled, and waggled at Oof's side, then pranced over to Vaegon and stood proud and still for the elf.

While Vaegon rigged Mikahl's body to Huffa's back, the lady ordered her men to gather the horses. The two armored soldiers who had stood guard over her instead of helping to fight the Choska and its rider, threw the fallen ranger's body over the lady's horse as if it were a sack of grain. They were none too pleased to learn that as punishment for their inaction, they would be walking back to Xwarda. It was clear the woman held rank over these men. They turned over their horses without a word of complaint, so Hyden and Vaegon could ride them. The other Ranger, whose name was Drick, was to lead them to Xwarda.

Hyden wondered who this brave woman was as she mounted Oof's back with only a minimal pause. It was just moments after she and Mikahl's limp body were racing away on the wolf's back, that he realized she might be after Mikahl's sword, too. A flash of panic swept over him, and he looked to Vaegon. The elf was sheathing Ironspike, and securing it to his saddle. This came as a comfort, albeit a slight one. If Mikahl lived, Hyden wouldn't have wanted to be the one to tell him they had lost the sword.

Hyden wished he wasn't so slow and dazed at the moment. He felt as if he hadn't slept in weeks, and his head felt as if it were full of mud. He had done something out of sheer desperation, and repeated the word he heard the lady say as she released one of her lightning blasts. The explosion of power that resulted from the word he used had been the concussion that sent the Choska twisting up and away from them. He had used magic, and now he was paying the price for it. His mind was a jumble of sorrow and confusion, and he couldn't hold a thought. He was sure that a moment ago, he had been alarmed or excited by something, but now he had no idea of what it might have been.

Drick urged them to get onto the horses. After riding on a wolf's back for days and days, the saddles looked relatively comfortable.

As he swung a leg over the horse's rump and settled into his seat, Vaegon asked the ranger a question, reminding Hyden of what it was that had alarmed him.

"Who is that woman?"

The ranger looked at the elf, and unease spread across his face as he took in Vaegon's wildness.

"I'm not sure you really want to know," said the man.

There was no hint of jest in his voice, and the look Hyden shot Vaegon sent chills of alarm up his weary spine.

Chapter Forty-Seven

With the invasion of Westland complete and the border now secure, Shaella found she didn't have much use for Claret. Through spells she found in her father's library, she learned to transport herself directly from her royal bedchamber to the tower library, so the dragon was no longer needed to fly her up to the gaping hole in the wall.

The Breed giants that sacked Portsmouth and Castleview had been rounded up and herded back northward, away from the Zard and human population centers. A big show was made about getting this done. Shaella came out looking like a savior and her dragon a fully trained pet.

If the city folk ever questioned her power or her ability to keep the massive red dragon restrained, then the ease with which she used it to get the marauding Breed out of the cities and towns removed all of their doubt. Though she had no immediate purpose for the dragon to serve, she kept the collars in place. She wanted to be able to call Claret to her at a moment's notice, but she released the dragon from duty until that time arrived. She also returned Claret's remaining egg. The dragon had taken it and flown back to her nest in the fang spire.

Claret lay on the smooth surface of the Seal. She was curled protectively around the last of her eggs, deeply brooding. She could incubate the egg by bathing it in her fiery breath at any given time. She had refrained from doing so for centuries, because she didn't want to have hatchlings to worry about while she was bound to guard the Seal.

Now she felt guilty. Had she incubated the eggs sooner, they might have had a chance to survive. Now she was bound to the collar. She couldn't hatch this one, because Shaella could call her away at any time. She was used to these helpless and trapped feelings. She had been bound by the Pact for as long as she could remember. If it hadn't been for that, she would have left this land full of pesky humans behind long ago.

It took her a few days to make her lair feel homey again. She flew down and picked choice bones from her feeding grounds. She put her remaining egg on a pile of Zard skulls. Then she scattered geka bones and freshly killed snapper carcasses around the smooth floor, until it once again began to look and smell like what it was.

At idle times, she tried to stretch and rip the collar from her neck, but it wasn't to be removed. Its ancient and powerful magical properties dictated that it could only be removed by the person wearing the collar's mate. Claret knew that long ago. On another land mass, a place far away from this one, the collars were regularly used. When possible, dragons were taken when they were young and raised with the collars on. Those dragons grew up used to the idea of being servants. They never got the chance to know what it meant to be the highest predator alive, to be the ruler of the roost, to be the true master of all that inhabited its territory.

Claret had known those things once. Long before she was bound by that tricky human wizard to guard this place, she was once the queen of a land not so much different to this one. She had watched those silly humans fight over this and that, each faction trying to prove dominance over the other. Every so often, she would swoop down among them, remind them of their folly, and give them a common enemy. She would burn down a few buildings, ravage a few herds, and maybe even snatch up a stray human or two. Then she would sit back and watch as they forgot their personal quests for dominance and banded together to rebuild. A few years later they would forget, and the whole process would start anew.

She didn't long for that sort of freedom anymore, at least not for herself. She would die content, and destroy half the world before she went, if she could guarantee that her last unhatched egg would hatch and live its full life free and unbound.

She pondered these things while munching the meat from a snapper she had just roasted. For now, pondering was all she could do, but she knew that sooner or later the situation would change. With humans, it always did.

Shaella tried for the hundredth time to ignite the power of her father's Spectral Orb. Claret told her that she had seen Gerard crawl down into the Seal while her father had it open. Shaella had no choice but to believe the dragon. With the collars on, there was no way that Claret could lie to her.

Dead or alive, Gerard's soul was beyond the Seal now, and according to her father's books, the orb would allow her to communicate with him. First, she had to figure out the minute inflections of the chant that was supposed to activate the orb's power. She wasn't sure if it was her rhythm or the pronunciation of the words that she was getting wrong. The only thing she was sure of was that she was getting it wrong.

She glanced out of the crumbling hole in the tower wall at the darkness. It was late. The moon was already sinking down into the black expanse of the Western Sea. With a heavy sigh of frustration, she went back down the trapdoor ladder, through the nest, and down into the library. With a flick of her wrists, she set flame to the dozen candles that she spread around the room. She went to a book that lay open among many on the desk. She read and reread the passages about calling out the orb's power. Another passage pertaining to the orb followed the inadequate instructions that were trying her patience. The crystal sphere didn't have to remain so large and bulky, it stated. She could shrink it so that it might be moved.

She had hoped to get it to work at least once before she attempted to move it, but she hadn't been able to as of yet.

The gaping hole in the side of the upper chamber was letting the weather in. Several times, it had rained hard enough for water to pool on the upper floor. The floorboards were going to rot, and already water had seeped through and dripped into the nest and the library below it. If she knew the commands to use Pael's lift, she could bring up some masons and have the damage repaired, but she didn't.

She needed to rearrange some of the ancient volumes so the weather wouldn't damage them. She had a mind to move the orb and the contents of the library out of Pael's tower to somewhere more convenient. If Pael had anything to say about it, she would tell the truth, at least about the books. She was fairly certain that a little rain or even a long fall through the rotted floor would do little to no damage to the powerful Spectral Orb.

She sighed again. Moving the texts and the crystal could wait till morning. She transported herself back to her bedchamber, wondering if the staff she had commissioned to be made was finished yet. If it was, she would shrink the orb and place it as the staff's headpiece so she would be able to carry it around with her.

Cole was overseeing the staff's creation. He was laying spells of protection and binding into the materials as well. She was confident he wouldn't fail her. He never had before. He had known Gerard, and how she felt about him. He knew how important trying to contact him was to her.

As she strolled through the castle in her blood red silken robes, she wondered at how smoothly things were going. The people of Westland seemed to be carrying on as if nothing had changed. Sure, they mourned their losses, but those losses were mostly due to Glendar, not her.

They had all seen the amount of power she wielded, both as a sorceress and a dragon rider. It seemed to her that as long as she didn't start blatantly abusing her power, she would go on unchallenged as the new ruler of Westland. Crops were still being tended and herds were still being sheared or brought to market. Trade and commerce continued as it always had, save for the addition of Dakaneese slave ships in the Westland ports.

The Zard weren't accepted in the cities very well, but they found their places to work and dwell, and they stayed to themselves as much as possible. There was a lot of animosity between the three races, but Shaella made it clear that open violence against each other wouldn't be tolerated. The Breed giants were having a hard time trying to settle into the northern reaches of Westland. Farming and raising animals had never been a part of their heritage. They would eventually figure it out if they wanted to survive. There would be no more raiding and pillaging. Shaella, with Claret's effectively persuasive abilities, had driven that message home. The message was clear: learn to associate and work with each other, or die.

Bzorch, her Lord of Locar, was the exception to her rule. He was given some leeway in his dealings with the humans in his little part of her kingdom. Shaella was pleased with the effort he was taking to strengthen the defenses along the riverfront. His idea to build towers along the banks not only had created work, but would go far in keeping barge thieves and smugglers from sneaking in and out of her territory. Already, men were harvesting the lumber for the construction from the Reyhall Forest, and barges were being readied to float the wood into place.

She refrained from telling Bzorch that the idea was far from original. The Westlanders had done the very same thing along the marshland border a few hundred years earlier. Settsted Stronghold and all of its outposts were farther apart than Bzorch's towers would be, and they were made of stone; but Shaella saw no point in bruising the Lord of Locar's feral ego by telling him this.

She wandered into her empty, torch-lit throne room, and touched the burn scar on the side of her head absently. The wound Claret had inflicted there was now healed over, but her hair still hadn't grown back. From a line that ran across her left temple, up and over her ruined, but still functioning ear, then down to the middle of her neck, there was nothing but scar tissue. At times, she felt like a monster. Only those quick and fleeting glimpses in the reflecting glass, where she saw only her right profile, reminded her that she was still quite beautiful.

The low feelings she was having as of late had more to do with losing Gerard than with her personal appearance. She was the woman who let her father send her dying lover into the blackness of the Nethers, and the guilt of not protecting him better was where her saddened state was rooted. Other than that, she just plain missed Gerard.

She tried not to care what people thought about her, but it was hard. She was the Dragon Queen after all, the Conqueror of Westland. She couldn't let her emotions show. She had to appear confident and in control. As much as she hated the idea, appearances did seem to matter. So, she spent a lot of her time in public trying to mask the turmoil that roiled inside her.

She was startled by the sudden, sizzling pop of someone snapping magically into the room. She was even more startled to see that it was Pael. He looked angry, anxious, and spectacular in his glittering black robes. His pupils were dilated, his eyes open wide, and the deep purple bags of exhaustion under them gave his head a skullish look. He moved skittishly, as if he were wound up as tight as a drum. Shaella realized she was more than a little bit frightened of him.

"Where are my texts?" he asked sharply.

The question threw her because she hadn't yet moved any books out of the tower. After a moment's thought though, she realized that he was most likely referring to the volumes she had moved to protect them from the rain.

"The hole you left in the wall up there was letting in the weather."

She spoke the words slowly and then paused, letting the idea that they might have been ruined have a chance to sink into his slick, white head. The way his angry eyes flared and his hands wrung nervously together caused her to cut her pause short.

"I moved them so they might not take damage."

Pael slowly stopped his fidgeting, and let out a long sigh of relief.

"Show me!" he ordered.

"Come," she snapped back as she turned and strode away.

She wondered if this was the way other fathers and daughters got along. She would have been surprised to learn that her relationship with her father wasn't that much different than many others. Most young women were traded like chattel to other men, not for money, but for position and favor.

"If you will show me how to use your lift, I will have repairs properly made to the tower walls, so we don't have this problem again."

She spoke over her shoulder as she led him through the castle. The people and Zard that they passed parted for them, as if they were contagious, but every last one of them gave a bow or curtsy of fealty.

"You'll have to kill the masons when they're done," Pael said conversationally.

He suddenly stepped around Shaella and led them from the semicrowded corridor down a narrow servant way. She followed him through a maze of stairways, corridors, and even through a hidden passage, which was cleverly disguised as a stray run of wall. It was all she could do to take in the route as they went.

When they finally arrived at what looked like a storage pantry set into the wall not too far from the entrance to the upper dungeons, Pael spoke a word that released his wizard lock and the false door vanished. He spoke the word to make the door reappear and raised a querying eyebrow at Shaella. She repeated the release word for the magical door, and it went away again.

Pael smiled at her approvingly, giving her a good look at his crooked, almond colored teeth. Then he called down the lift.

As they rode it up, he went through a series of command words, and showed her what they all did. After she repeated them all correctly, he had her take them the rest of the way up. She only cared about the commands for up, down, and stop. Since she had no need to sneak around the castle because a king's wandering eye was on her or nosy servants might report her movements, she didn't think the lock or several of the other commands would be necessary for her. She learned and repeated them anyway. When the lift was moving upward by the command of her voice alone, Pael gave her another nod. A look of fatherly satisfaction was in his eyes. Seeing this gave her the courage to ask him about the Spectral Orb. Pael didn't hesitate to tell her a lot more about it than she really wanted to know.

"This human you're so concerned with, this Gerard, has absorbed part of what is empowering me," he told her. "Through some ethereal bond, I can feel him in my mind sometimes, like a pesky mosquito. He buzzes around in a daze of confusion and occasionally stops to suck off bits of information from Shokin's—no—from my mind, as if it were a drop of blood."

He met Shaella's gaze then, his expression as dire as ever.

"You must never even so much as attempt to release what he has become from the Seal. He is no longer human. He consumed the yolk of the dragon's egg. At the moment, his power is infinitesimal. It's doubtful he will be able to survive amongst the evil he's bound with, but if he does find a way to survive the Nethers, he has the potential to become a power beyond imagining."

"I just want to communicate with him," she lied.

"If you'll make a Binding of Blood with me that you'll not attempt to set him free as long as I live, then I'll show you how to use the orb, but I want a future favor in return."

A Binding of Blood is a magical binding, which forfeits the life of one who breaks the oath the instant the oath is broken. The ancient spell was specifically created to keep powerful wizards from cheating each other. Still, Shaella thought, Pael should know better than to try to make an oath that a woman couldn't find a way around. Even the least clever woman could work her way around such a promise, be it binding or not, and Shaella was as clever and deceitful as they came. Without hesitation, she agreed to Pael's terms.

She wanted desperately to reach out to Gerard. She was confident that eventually she would find a way to set Gerard free from the Nethers, especially since Pael seemed so worried that it might happen. If it wasn't a possibility, then the mighty Pael wouldn't be concerned about it.

She couldn't conceive of Gerard being some ultra powerful force, though. He wasn't a greedy or lustful person. Even if he did have power, he would be content with it, and not yearn for more. Pael's concern seemed rooted in fear for himself. If what Pael said was true, that the same power that had manifested in him also manifested in Gerard, then it made sense that Pael would fear Gerard if he were released. After all, it had been Pael who shoved the dagger into Gerard's heart. He of all people would expect Gerard to come seeking vengeance.

Shaella had to force the excitement from tingling through her body. She had to be clearheaded when Pael had her speak the blood oath. She couldn't be filled with daydreams and delusions of Gerard. The exact words of a given oath were sometimes the undoing of it. It wouldn't do to have her head in the clouds when she spoke hers.

Once they reached the floor below the library, Shaella halted the lift. She showed Pael where the books were stacked up off of the floor on a plank of wood that she had sat on a couple of stone blocks. The room stank sharply with a mixture of scents that were foreign to the common nose. A cask of bear urine and an open jar of pickled griffin livers were the main contributors, but a crate full of dried bat wings and many different bags of the herbs and powders used in spell crafting added to the fierce aroma.

Pael ignored the stench as he hurried to kneel on the dust-caked floor before the stack of books. He ran his finger down the spines, searching the titles. More than once he growled in frustration. Before long, he had the once neat piles scattered across the floor, and had created a new stack. Flipping through the pages of these with a feverish intensity, he ended up discarding all but two of them into the disarray.

The two that he kept, he sat on a shelf next to a jar full of grayish, yellow liquid, labeled Plague Pus. In the jar next to it, a fat, black spider with a bright yellow star-like design on its back, floated in clear liquid. Shaella studied it all as she waited on him. The shape of the spider's mark was like three double jagged lightning bolts, all crossing in the middle. Shaella and Cole had been trying to decide what symbol she would use on her banner, and now the choice had been made. Cole's dragon design was fierce and impressive, but this was not the dragon's kingdom, nor was it Cole's. Shaella would have the lightning star.

"What kind of spider is this?" she asked her father.

Pael was making a halfhearted effort to restack the texts he'd strewn about, but he stopped long enough to look and see what she was referring to.

"One you don't ever want to get bitten by," he said, as he went back to what he was doing. "It's called Arachnid Voltonimous, common name, the Luminous Weaver, or just the plain ol' Shock Spider. Its web glows a soft, yellowish color at night, and with a single bite, it can kill an animal as big as an opossum or lemur with a shock of lightning-like intensity. The shock is not quite powerful enough to kill an average human, but its venom is acidic and painfully lethal. The venom is excellent for etching and enchanting steel with a rune or a symbol."

Her eyes drifted to the cover of the book Pael had left exposed. It had the letter P scribed ornately upon its leather-bound face four times. She had to peer in closer, to see the smaller script between the letters. Plants and Potions for Poison and Preservation, the book was titled.

A brief tremor of paranoia passed through her, only subsiding after she convinced herself that her father had no reason to kill her and if he did, he didn't need poison to get it done. Neither Cole nor Flick, who would each die for her in any other situation, would do anything to thwart Pael. They both emulated him in every way they could. If Pael wanted to kill her, all he had to do was kill her, or possibly order one of them to do it for him. She shook her head and cursed herself a fool for being so stupidly suspicious.

Pael stood and was making a feeble attempt to get the dust off of the hem of his fancy wizard's robe. The sight made Shaella smile in spite of herself.

Seeing her mirth, Pael snarled. He passed his hand over his face, down his body, and with the gesture, his robe was instantly pristine again.

Shaella wasn't impressed.

"The Spectral Orb?" she prompted, seeing that he had already forgotten their agreement. She hoped he had forgotten the oath that he wanted her to swear as well.

"Very well," he said, grabbing up the two books he had chosen. "Take us up out of this foul place. I have a dagger up in the nest."

Disappointed that he hadn't forgotten the Binding of Blood, but excited beyond reason about finally getting to learn the trick to using the artifact, she spoke the command that took the lift up into the library.

Pael snarled with disgust at having to crawl up through the trapdoor to get to the nest, and then the floor above it, but he went.

The first thing he showed her was how to raise the orb out of the floor by the chain crank on the wall, so it didn't block the lift from coming all the way up. He didn't raise it far, just enough to show her how the mechanics of the crank worked. He then took a dagger from a table, and before she had a chance to think, he slashed her palm open.

"By your own life's blood, do you swear to never attempt to release the one you seek, the human boy named Gerard, who went to the Seal? Do you swear to never try to release him from the dark place where he is bound?"

Shaella wasn't very pleased with the broad range of possibilities that Pael's words had encompassed, but already a loophole had presented itself to her.

"As long as you live and breathe father, my blood is my oath. I swear that I will never attempt to release the human boy named Gerard from the Nethers."

Pael spoke a chant of binding, and then closed Shaella's bleeding hand in on itself. He went on chanting in the ancient tongue of the magi to finish the spell.

She understood most of what he said. If she broke her oath, her own mind would stop her heart from beating, freeze her blood, or something to that effect. Basically, if she ever tried to break the oath she had just given, she would die. This was acceptable to her. The oath she had given wouldn't stop her from having someone else help Gerard get free of the Seal. And besides that, her father had already told her that he had changed. Drinking the dragon's yolk had turned him into something other than a human boy named Gerard. Whatever he had become, she hadn't sworn not to help it escape the Seal. If Gerard's mind hadn't survived, then it didn't really matter anyway. She hoped she would know one way or the other, soon.

She paid close and careful attention as Pael instructed her on the ways of the orb. The session reminded her of so many others they shared in the past. Him, speaking with precise expert knowledge of the subject at hand and almost forcing the information into her mind with his intensity. The only thing missing was the scratching of Cole's quill as he feverishly tried to keep up his notes, and Flick's odd, yet relevant questions.

Shaella realized that, even though she didn't like her father very much, he was no fool. In fact, he was as knowledgeable as all the men she had met in her entire life put together. He was half-mad, power hungry, and rotten to the core, but ignorant, he was not. His dark mind was meticulous and thorough, and with his newfound power, Shaella figured that there was nothing he couldn't do.

Pael set the orb off with his circling chanting song, as if it were no harder then plucking an apple from a tree. She hadn't been using the right inflections of voice at all. The syllables of the ancient words she had read were formed all wrong in her mouth, and she hadn't even known about the three black candles that needed to be lit and spaced around the orb.

Pael explained that the candles weren't actually necessary to open the connection, but they helped focus his mind on the task. He also explained that the gaping hole in the wall was letting in minute distractions, such as the whispering of the late summer breeze or a distant bird's call. This hadn't been helping her concentration at all, and if she acknowledged those distractions and singled them out of her mind, it might help.

Once Pael had the orb alight and swirling with purple smoky power, he took his books and disappeared back from where he had come.

Shaella trailed her fingers around the huge crystal as she circled it. She spoke Gerard's name softly at first, then more aggressively, if not a bit desperately. For what could have been a few heartbeats, or half of the night, she poured her heart and soul into the effort. After a time, her legs grew watery, and she fell to the floor at the base of the humming lavender sphere. When she opened her eyes, the light of dawn was just starting to lighten the sky outside the gaping hole in the tower wall. She wiped a tear from her face, and seeing that the Spectral Orb was still radiant, made one last attempt to call out to Gerard.

"Gerard, hear me my love. Can you hear me? Gerard?" The static caused by the sphere's power pulled her hair to its surface as she leaned in, hugging the huge orb, and yearned to touch her lover's soul.

Her heart nearly stopped cold when a faint and distant voice rasped out her name in a bewildered response.

Chapter Forty-Eight

When Hyden Hawk tried to mount the horse he had been provided, he fumbled and fell into a collapsed heap. Vaegon waved off Drick's attempt to help, and simply said, "He needs rest."

The ranger nodded his understanding, ordered the two chagrined soldiers to stand guard, then took the reins of everyone's mounts and picketed them. When he was done, he sat back against a tree. He didn't like the idea of his fallen companion just lying there, dead over a horse's back, but what could he do? The elf and his exhausted friend had seemed about to fall over when they were burying the big wolf. Now they could barely move, much less ride.

Drick could go ahead and dig the hole for his fellow forester, but poor, dead Arnell had a wife and a father who might not want him buried out here in the forest, even though it would be any ranger's obvious choice of places to be laid to rest. He didn't like the idea of burying his friend so close to that foul, half-rotted, headless corpse they had dragged into the woods. If he could talk to Arnell's father, maybe they could find a nice, peaceful glade somewhere. Absently pondering the matter further, he noticed that one of the armored soldiers was staring at the elf and wondered what he was thinking.

Drick had seen an elf before, but it had been from a great distance. The wild yellow of Vaegon's good eye kept stealing the soldier's attention from the big, white wolf that crawled up beside Hyden.

It's like one of those fargin old tales, he thought. Demon beasts, wolf-riding elves, and a Westlander with a magic sword. And right in the middle of a war no less. Ah, the war!

No one in all of Highwander, least of all Drick, could understand why Valleya and Seaward were attacking them. Queen Willa probably knew the reasons, but not he.

A hawkling came swooping down through an opening in the trees and landed beside the young mountain boy. It had been among them during the battle with the Choska demon, and had even managed to get a raking claw across one of the demon's cherry eyes. Its presence only added to the strange, surreal mood that Drick was feeling. At this point, it wouldn't have surprised him if a herd of tiny finger-tall deer came swarming out of the forest and started talking to the mushrooms.

These folk will fit right into Queen Willa's strange court, mused Drick. What with her dwarven castellan, her bearded dwarfess confidant, and her little blue fairy counselor, a one-eyed elf and a man who looked to be now having an intelligent conversation with a Great Wolf and a bird, would complete the mummers troop with which Queen Willa surrounded herself. Drick decided he would be glad to deliver these folks to the castle so that he could be off. He would go back to his mundane forest patrol and never complain of boredom again.

Of his own accord, Talon followed Mikahl, the woman, and the wolves. He tried to force his hawkling vision into Hyden's head, but Hyden was too dazed to make sense of it. The impact with the oak tree and what had happened after took its toll on him. Talon watched the woman and Mikahl's limp body as they raced away, and followed them until he was confident the lady intended no trickery, and that Mikahl's body wouldn't fall off of Huffa's back. These visions helped Hyden get through the burial of Grrr without breaking down.

Vaegon lay down alongside Hyden, and placed Ironspike between them. As if the wolf understood the elf's concern, Urp curled up into a furry ball at their feet. Talon alighted on the sword's hilt and began preening himself.

Vaegon wasn't feeling very safe around the Highwander soldiers, so he wasn't taking any chances. It was men, just like these armored soldiers, that Hyden Hawk had seen loosing the arrow at him back at the Summer's Day Festival. Vaegon wasn't ready to trust them just yet.

As he drifted off to sleep, his thoughts and worries weren't for himself, though. It was Mikahl he was concerned about. Hopefully the Xwardian healers were as good as the woman had said. They would have to be to save him.

When Hyden woke, it was nearly dark. It took him several long moments to figure out where he was and what had happened to him. He had been dreaming, and the visions of his slumber clung to his waking mind like a bad smell.

He had dreamt of the dragon skull that lay in his village's council chamber. In his vision, the White Goddess was calling out to him frantically from the dancing blue flames that filled the open brain cavity. Her voice had been thin but insistent, and he was having a hard time shaking the image from his head. What was worse was that he couldn't remember the span of time from when he was knocked into the oak tree, until they sent Mikahl off to Xwarda with that strange woman.

He sat up, and his movement caused Urp to do the same. The wolf's white fur caught the moonlight that filtered through the trees, and was glowing the same magical blue that the flames from the dragon skull in his dreams had. Again, he heard the voice of his clan's goddess calling out to him. This time, it sent chills up his spine. Absently, he rubbed Urp's head, and decided that he needed to answer her call. King Aldar had spoken of the temple in Xwarda, called Whitten Loch. As soon as he saw to Mikahl's condition, he would seek it out and pray to her for guidance.

It was late the following evening when they arrived at the massive gates of Xwarda's huge, white rock outer wall. All of them, even Drick, had been dazzled for the last hour or so by the way the setting sun reflected off of the western face of the mountains and the Witch Queen's sparkling castle city. Hyden couldn't imagine anything looking more glorious. He'd seen the city from above, but that sight hadn't prepared him for this.

He counted seven great round towers rising up from the castle's main structure. Several smaller towers rose up around the city as well. All of them were topped with shiny metal sheets, which made them look like they had been dipped in molten gold as they caught the rays of the sinking sun.

The wall itself was easily fifty feet tall, and half as thick. Drick told them that there was normally a great congregation of tent dwellers and hawkers who lived just outside of the wall, but Queen Willa had ordered them inside the gates so the military might prepare the terrain for the Valleyan/Seaward attack. Only the trampled debris they left behind remained, and most of that had been saturated with flammable oil.

Hyden and Vaegon marveled at the tunnel-like passage they went through to get into the city. Hyden asked about the slits and holes in the walls and ceiling of the entry tunnel, and Drick explained the horrific nature of them. Hot oil and burning pitch could be poured on trespassers, while archers loosed through the slits. It made Hyden shudder just thinking about it. When they finally emerged from the entry tunnel, both Hyden and Vaegon gasped at what they saw.

A great colored mosaic of leaded stained glass spread high across the castle's main building. It was still a good distance away, but the paneled depictions rose up over the city like a painting hung for the gods. The backlit scene was indecipherable from their current distance, but the ruby reds, sapphire blues, and emerald greens shone like a dragon's hoard of jewels in a band across the castle's front. The breathtaking majesty of it all managed to overshadow the feelings of unease that the hundreds of Blacksword banners flitting in the breeze instilled in Hyden and Vaegon. The uncertainty and fear was still there under the surface. Neither of them could forget the amount of bloodshed that the Blacksword soldiers had started at Summer's Day.

Inside the walls, a stench of refuse and foul body odors assaulted them, and the streets were packed with people, wagons, various farm animals and all their filth. It was crowded beyond imagining. Everywhere one looked, there were wagons piled with the belongings of the people who were huddled around them.

"People coming in from the western towns and farmsteads," Drick explained. "They come for the protection of yon walls."

He pointed back at them, and Hyden noticed for the first time that the top was crenellated. He also saw that the slots he had assumed were windows or vents before Drick explained them as arrow slits, were nowhere to be found on this side of the wall. The ranger's distaste for the crowded city showed plainly on his face as he nervously urged them on into the throng of chaos.

"It will be less cramped once we get past the next set of gates."

They had no problem getting through the crowd. The people parted like a cornfield might if a bear went wandering through it. Many of them pointed and gasped at the sight of Vaegon's elven features, but Urp's raised hackles and steady, menacing growl were enough to cause the hungry and disheveled folk to give the group a wide berth.

A few groups of people cheered their passage, as if they were some great heroes coming to save them from the approaching Valleyan and Seaward hordes. More than once, Vaegon, Hyden, or both of them had to talk Urp down from his fearful and excited state.

Hyden felt sorry for the brave wolf. Urp had limped the entire way from the camp to the city without slowing them, or making a sound of pain or protest. Sore and tired, there was no doubt he was intimidated by the masses and all their strange scents. Vaegon had commented that the wolf watched over them intently the whole time they rested and hadn't slept much. Hyden reminded himself to make sure that ample food was provided for Urp, and that there was a quiet place for the animal to rest.

Drick had been correct. When they passed under a slightly smaller, older, yet no less formidable looking wall a short while later, the space beyond it was far less crowded than the outer city. There were plenty of people and wagons spread around the cobbled streets, but it was obvious by the quality of the clothes people wore, and the possessions piled into the carts, that these were a different class of refugees.

The sun was gone now, but its rays still touched the tips of the mountains, leaving them looking like some golden bronze crown over Queen Willa's palace.

Hyden struggled to read aloud a street sign advertising fresh baked goods and the best cheese in the world. Vaegon prodded, and helped him through the words. Over the last few weeks, he had been learning, but hadn't gotten far. Writing was even harder for him. He could spell out his elven friend's name, Talon's, and Mikahl's in the dirt, but he had come to the conclusion that without parchment, ink, and quills, he would get nowhere fast. He would surely be able to find those items, and a few books here. The idea of looking for a place to purchase them in this mass of people and buildings so crowded in together was daunting. He was discouraged and overwhelmed by it all, but he was still determined to learn as much as he could about everything he could. Learning to read and write was the obvious first step.

The color of the sky reminded him of his dream from the night before. A glance at Urp's soft white coat brought forth the image of the White Goddess, pleading for him to respond to her call.

"Do you know of a temple called Whitten Loch?" Hyden asked Drick, as they closed in on yet another gated wall.

"I know of Whitten Loch, yes," Drick answered. "But to call it a temple, is to call a single dying tree a forest. It's a swan shelter, and a small filthy one at that. It sits along the elevated rim of the lake's retaining wall, at its westernmost end."

"Whitten Loch means White Lake," Vaegon said matter-of-factly.

"I wouldn't know what it means," shrugged Drick, "but you're about to see it for yourself."

Unlike the other gates they had come to, the one before them was closed. The wall, some twenty feet tall, was covered in vines and moldy growth and had a single row of arrow slits up high, with a wicked-looking, spiked iron overhang running along its top.

Before Hyden could study it further, a gruff voice spoke out to them.

"You're expected," the gatekeeper said while eyeing Urp cautiously.

He let out a loud whistle, aiming his head up toward someone unseen on the wall. From deep within the stonework came the sound of rattling chains. Slowly, the ironbound gates began to creep open, and beyond them, Hyden saw all the splendor of the world revealed before him.

In the foreground was a fountain lake. Around it, stretching a way to either side into the dusky night was a well tended, forested park. It was illuminated by lanterns, hanging from evenly spaced poles, along white marble tiled pathways that wound through the trees, around manicured gardens, and perfectly trimmed shrubberies. Beds of multicolored flowers were scattered here and there among private benches and open plots of lush, trimmed grass.

Beyond the lake and reflecting dizzily on the surface of the rippling water, was the palace of Xwarda: a castle of white marble blocks that thrust up out of the earth and looked like a growth of crystal shards. The glittering stained glass panels were brilliantly backlit. The scenes that each of them depicted were clear, vivid, and at least forty feet tall. Hyden recognized a few of them from stories he had heard Berda, and more recently, Vaegon and King Aldar, tell.

There was the wizard, Dahg Mahn, surrounded by all of his animals on a battlefield, across from a horde of monsters. Another panel showed the forging of the Hammer of Doon and Mikahl's sword. Two dwarves, with faces aglow with dragon's fire, were hammering away at the creations. A wizard and a group of elves hovered around behind them, while a long-haired giant watched over them all with his huge, muscled arms folded across his chest.

Another depiction showed a trio of dragons. One was a bluish-green color, another white as snow, and the third was a dark, ruby red. They were circling in flight around what Hyden thought was the Summer's Day Spire. The center depiction was of a golden armored warrior fighting a horde of dark and familiar-looking creatures. A hellcat, and what might have been one of the bat-like creatures that killed Grrr, and a dozen other crimson-eyed things with fangs and claws faced down the hero.

"Pavreal," Hyden mouthed in awe.

Another depiction showed a mountain split in two, with legions of ax and hammer-wielding dwarves racing out to meet a mass of greenish-skinned trolls.

The rest of the scenes, thirteen in all, were no less spectacular. Hyden figured that if one of the panels was laid on the ground, it would be twenty paces wide and just as tall. He figured that only the greatest magic could have created such a wonder.

Below the row of monumental masterpieces were several underlit peaked archways, which were divided by great spiraling columns. Under each archway was a set of curtained window walls, save for the center arch. Under it was a widening, ornate marble stairway, and the castle's grand entry doors.

Above the row of glittering stained glass portrayals were half a hundred relatively normal-sized windows, reaching up the smooth marble walls in symmetrical rows. Each window was shaped as a perfect miniature of the grand arches below.

Vaegon was speechless. Even with magic, it must have taken a thousand years to build this place. He was certain that only the long-lived elves could have accomplished such a feat. The way the lake reflected the stained glass like a shimmering sheet of jewels; the way the towers rose up out of the reflected light into the darkness, only to be haloed by their liquid bronze rooftops; the way the white marble absorbed, reflected the kaleidoscope of color, and glazed it across its own surface like a sheen of oil polish – those were details he would have thought to be beyond the creative ability of humans. Yet, here it was before him.

Urp had taken off at a dead run toward the lake, and was now lapping at the water greedily. The swans Drick had spoken of took to flight in a noisy, honking procession, and the emotional depth of their protest at the wolf brought Hyden out of his daze of awe. Then the sound of the gates booming closed behind him drowned it all out.

He searched the shoreline and saw the modest square building Drick had called a swan shelter. The ranger was absolutely right with his assessment. It looked nothing like a temple. It looked more like a solid block of marble that had been left over from the construction of the palace. If there were any doors, windows, or features whatsoever, they had to be on the side of it that faced the lake and the palace entryway because all Hyden could see was smooth, weathered stone.

Two of the swans Urp unsettled glided out of the gloom and back into the torch light. They landed in the lake with a graceful splash, then swam toward the structure. They came to a ramp-like rise and waggled out of the water, seemingly up into the far side of the place. Hyden was just about to spur his mount over to investigate further, when the swiftly growing sound of hoofbeats approaching on one of the tiled stone paths filled the night.

An ornately garbed troop of suspicious-looking soldiers, all sporting the Witch Queen's Blacksword emblem, came riding up out of the darkness and met them. A nod of understanding passed between Drick and the commander of the twelve-man detachment that set off alarms in the minds of both Hyden and Vaegon. The men behind the commander were darting their eyes this way and that nervously, which only served to raise the two companions' level of suspicion. Hyden instinctually called out to Talon to help keep an eye on them.

"These men will escort you two the rest of the way," Drick said, with a halfhearted smile. "Luck and leisure to you. I have to go tend to my fallen comrade now."

Hyden looked at Vaegon. The elf's sad expression showed no less concern than Hyden felt, but he indicated with a nod of his head that they should follow the soldiers anyway.

Hyden sought out Talon's vision as they made their way through the maze of cobbled paths that led to the palace. He half expected to see groups of Blacksword soldiers waiting in ambush behind shrubs and in the trees, but there were none. That in itself was alarming.

It was a mild, late summer night. The sky was clear, and the stars were starting to shine overhead. Hyden couldn't see the moon yet, but the point of his observation was that there should be people out in this clean and beautiful expanse of greenery. As a matter of fact, the whole place should be filled with the refugees, who were crowded in their own filth on the outskirts of the city.

Suddenly, Talon's sharp eyes saw something flashing through the trees at great speed toward them. Hyden left his thoughts and focused in on the sight, and then it all made perfect sense to him.

Huffa and Oof were tearing through the forest toward the lake at breakneck speed. By the way their tails danced about in the air, Hyden could tell there was no alarm; they were just excited to see Urp. No one was out in the park, because the wolves were loose in it. Hyden figured the wolves had caused the nervous looks and uptight demeanor of the soldiers that were escorting them as well.

"Have they been fed?" Hyden asked one of the men, as Huffa came streaking by. A few of the horses balked at the sight, but the men riding them did a good job of keeping them under control.

"A leg of lamb for the two this morning," the commander answered. "She ordered a hunt be made this afternoon, so there should be a doe or two about, any time now."

"Could you put out another leg while they wait?" Hyden asked. "Urp, the wolf that came in with us, is injured and exhausted. He needs rest and food badly. His master, King Aldar, of the realm of giants, would appreciate the kindness, I'm certain."

The last bit he said with an air of authority, doing his best to imitate Mikahl's stately tone. The way the blood drained from the man's face at the mention of the Giant King told Hyden the matter would be promptly handled. He would have asked about Mikahl then, but they had come up under the long entry that sheltered the grand stairway leading up into the intricately carved entrance to the Palace of Xwarda.

Men were waiting to take the horses. When they dismounted, both Vaegon and Hyden nearly fell to the ground in agony. The ache in their inner thighs and lower backs assaulted them as soon as they were on their feet. Neither had ridden a horse before the long ride from the camp. The saddles had looked more comfortable than a wolf's back, but now, it was all the two of them could do to stand upright without moaning or stumbling over.

Hyden's will to make a good impression and not show weakness to these people, who may or may not be an enemy, helped him master his pain. Vaegon cheated and spelled his pain away. Under another circumstance, Hyden might've made a jest about the discomfort, but Mikahl's dire situation hung heavily in the air and smothered away any mirth that tried to manifest itself.

They were greeted at the top of the stairs by a dwarf. Neither of them had ever seen a dwarf before, and it was shocking. The man was apparently used to the reaction, and didn't take offense to the slack-jawed expressions he received. Hyden wasn't sure, but he thought the dwarf might have never seen an elf before either. Either that, or the patch over Vaegon's ruined eye socket held a particular interest to him. A silence hung over them all as they took each other in.

To Hyden, the dwarf looked as if a normal-sized man had been smashed down to just over waist tall. His shoulders and waist were as wide and thick as any man's, only compressed down, as if a Mammoth Shagmar had stepped on him. The dwarf's hair was a nested mop-like explosion of graying tangles that seemed to erupt up out of his uniform, and spilled down over his shoulders. A huge, bulbous nose parted a set of heavy, white eyebrows, under which the sparkle of dark, yet merry eyes could be seen. His beard flowed down over his ample belly, the tip of it nearly touching the floor, and only a trace of bottom lip could be seen under his mustache.

"Dugak's the name," he said in a deep, grumbling voice.

He bowed, and might have been smiling, but it was hard to tell through all that hair.

"She has been waiting for you in the dining hall. There are refreshments to be had there as well."

He indicated for them to enter through the open doors. Hyden went first. Vaegon followed, and was glad that no one tried to take Ironspike from him, because he wouldn't have let it go.

Hyden wondered who she was. At first, he assumed it was going to be the woman they met in the forest, but now as they walked, with loud, echoing steps through the beautifully decorated corridors of the palace, he began to think it might be Willa the Witch Queen herself who was waiting for them.

The palace didn't seem like the sort of place a witch would live in, mused Hyden. It was definitely fit for a queen, though. Tapestries depicting sceneries of all sorts lined the walls of the wide passage they were in. Every so often, a small but bright lantern was ensconced on the wall. They passed a few open doorways, which gave the impression that the darkened rooms beyond them were cavernous and as majestic as the rest of the place.

At a crossing of hallways, four suits of armor stood at the corners. Hyden couldn't tell if there were men standing perfectly still in the suits, or if they were just for decoration. He tried to peer into a face plate of one helmet, but couldn't get a good enough look to tell. He found himself peeking back over his shoulders to try and catch one of them moving.

*

Vaegon was contemplating the lighting in the corridor. It didn't correlate with the widely spaced lanterns, or the limited amount of illumination they were providing. He noticed that the high ceiling wasn't marble, like the walls and floor were. It was bright to look at, and probably made of Wardstone, spelled to a soft and steady glow.

They eventually ended up entering a dim, formal-looking dining area. The room was multi-leveled, and on the lower floor, three long identical tables sat empty. At the far end, on an elevated stage-like rise, was another table. This area was lit up with flickering torches on ornate stands, and the table was laden with platters of food and drink.

The woman who had brought Mikahl back from the forest rose to greet them as they came in. She wasn't wearing her armored girdle or her riding boots any longer, and her hair was no longer in its single braid. Her golden locks flowed like a waterfall over her shoulders. The pale, blue formal gown she wore fit her shapely body well.

Another dwarf, a servant or attendant, rose beside the lady. This dwarf might have been a female; it was hard to say. It had well-groomed hair, long lashes, feminine brows, and even the pronounced bulge of breasts under its garments, but the beard that flowed down to its waste was thick, full, and disorienting. Neither of the companions pondered the dwarf's gender very long because the look on the human woman's face was so sad and grim that their concern was only for Mikahl.

Hyden was so suddenly consumed with grief that he didn't even hear Dugak introduce the woman.

"Welcome to the Wardstone Witch's hall. Willa Undite, the Queen of Highwander, has been expecting you."

Chapter Forty-Nine

"Shoookin," the wounded Choska demon called out an ethereal feeling for Pael.

It sensed the demon wizard at the edge of the Evermore Forest, north of the ruined city of Castlemont. Pael was not far from where King Jarrek and the Highwander wizard, Targon, had killed the wyvern that attacked them. The Choska found Pael there on his hands and knees.

The wizard was searching the ground for a certain type of mushroom, one that only grew in the shadow of the Evermore's gray oak, because the spore fell to the ground in the droppings of the scarlet sparrows that nested there. He had already collected several dozen of the purple-and-yellow-spotted mushroom caps, but figured he needed twice as many more to get the yield that he required. He was growing frustrated over the amount of labor involved in his search, and he missed Inkling, who excelled at tasks such as these. As the morning wore into the afternoon, the sun's rays began dissolving the poison out of the mushrooms, leaving them white, chalky, and useless. In the shadows of the gray oaks, he was still finding the potent ones.

Pael, so used to getting his way now, was discovering that even great magical power had its limits. As much as he wanted to, he couldn't stop the sun from ruining the mushrooms, and he couldn't just make the mushrooms appear in his basket, either. Therefore, the most powerful wizard in the realm was reduced to crawling around in bird droppings to find what he needed to execute his master plan.

The Choska demon's sudden appearance hadn't startled him, but it had effectively stopped his search for the day. He huffed out a sigh. There was no way around it. He would have to hunt Blood Caps again in the morning to meet his need. He checked the wicker basket he carried to make sure the ones he already harvested were covered with cloth and protected from the sun's rays. It wouldn't do to have them turn to chalk while he conversed with the Choska demon.

Rising to his feet and brushing the muck off of his robes, he noticed for the first time that Roark wasn't on the Choska's back, and that it was bleeding thick, black blood from several wounds.

"Did you get the sword?" Pael asked with growing excitement.

"Nooo," the Choska hissed. "But the boy has been mortally wounded."

"Wounds can be healed!" Pael snapped. "Why didn't you stay and finish the deed?"

"There were others helping the boy, Great Wolves from the northern mountains, and the Witch Queen and her archers. There was a young Beastling as well, but it matters not." The demon paused, and breathed in deeply.

One of the wounds in its side made a slow, wet, sucking sound.

"Look at the wound, Pael. The blade was alight with its power when it sank into me! I thought I was doomed, but it was too weak to draw in my essence. Errion Spightre's power is no more!"

Pael looked. The blade had entered just in front of the Choska's hind leg. The wound was deep, wide, and near the skin, but more of a stab, than a slash. Black blood had clotted around the opening, but hadn't been able to seal it in scab. The Choska's flight had opened the gash again and again with its wing beats.

With a resigned sigh, and without bothering to wash the poisonous residue of the mushrooms he had been picking from his hands, Pael probed the wound. He spoke a word under his breath, and his right hand began to glow a dull, yellow color that was barely discernible in the bright daylight. Without prompting the Choska, he pushed his arm deep into the wound and went to work.

The Choska let out a gasping roar, but managed to hold itself still. The pain was tremendous and probably not necessary. The demon-beast knew Pael was punishing it for not keeping the promise to bring back the boy's head or sword. It had no choice but to take the pain Pael was inflicting. Its wound was as mortal as the boy's was, and only Pael would bother to heal it. No one else had that kind of power, or would dare to get close enough to do such a deed. The Choska had no choice other than to suffer the excruciating torment until Pael was done.

When the sword wound was repaired, Pael went around the creature, pulling arrows out of its hide and healing the minor wounds. There were far more arrows than Pael first thought. The one in the demon beast's nostril was the one Pael saved for last, and he was far from gentle when he yanked it free. All of the Choska's agony was quickly flooded over by relief then. Of all the wounds, that one was the most irritatingly painful.

"I'll need you soon demon," said Pael.

"Shoookin, you owe me my freedom," the Choska hissed with as much respect in its voice as it could muster. "You said that—"

"NO!" Pael cut the demon off with a fierce shout. "You were to bring me the boy's head or the sword! You brought me neither! And now, you not only owe me your service, you owe me your life!"

Pael seethed and veins bulged out on his rage-mottled, egg-shaped head. A drop of saliva trailed down his trembling chin, and his eyes flared with promises of violence.

The Choska cowered in fear, for Shokin spoke the truth. Pael had saved his life, and it hadn't completed the bargain they had struck. The Choska demon could not yet claim its freedom from the demon-wizard's service.

"I will come when you summon me," the Choska conceded before it leapt into the air and winged away in search of a place to rest.

Pael let the heat in his blood cool a little bit, then transported himself back to his temporary laboratory. He had taken over the modest twin-towered castle that sat in the center of the Red City, Dreen. When he got there, he carefully put the Blood Caps in a stone box, covered it securely, and lay down to rest. The healing of the Choska had taken its toll on his strength. The plain fact that it took far more energy to heal than it did to destroy wasn't lost on him. As he drifted off to sleep, he wondered if someone would expend that much power to heal the boy, and if Ironspike had really exhausted itself of its power.

He found that the low, wailing cries of frustration and anger coming from the crippled undead that were scattered about the city helped him sleep. Nearly a hundred burned, broken, or semi-dismembered men and women who couldn't die had been left behind in the city. Pael contemplated sending someone around to behead them, to send them to true death and put them out of their misery. Eventually he would, but not yet. For now, he let the sounds of their restless agony and their horrid cries of frustration, carry him into that deep place of sleep were Shokin's powerful dreams came to him.

"I'm sorry General Chatta, those are my king's orders," General Vogle, the commander of the Valleyan forces King Broderick had sent to invade Highwander, said dejectedly.

"But why?" General Chatta asked.

His queen, Queen Rachel, after much deliberation and as much, if not more reserve, had agreed to aid King Broderick in this attack on Highwander. Now after they had taken two

Highwander cities, made the plans, and gained the position to attack the city of Xwarda itself, King Broderick was ordering the Valleyans to pull out. It made no sense.

"Westland's new king has attacked Dreen," General Vogel said, shaking his head with disbelief. "Apparently, he already sacked Castlemont, and carved a passage through the Wilder Mountains. I just don't see how."

"That's preposterous!" exclaimed Chatta.

The two generals were in an abandoned city house, getting ready to take supper. Vogel had gotten the message from King Broderick the night before but had only gotten enough liquor into himself to find the courage to tell General Chatta this afternoon. The two had planned and worked so hard preparing to take Xwarda. The new orders were a grave disappointment. It shamed Vogel to have to pull out now, but if his kingdom's capital city was under attack, as the messenger said, there wasn't much choice in the matter. He had already delayed leaving an extra day, and that was far too long.

The combined Valleyan and Seaward armies had already taken the Highwander border city of Tarn, and here they sat, about to dine in the newly taken trading town known as Plat. They were barely a day's ride from Xwarda, and the siege engines and towers were nearly completed. The new developments back in Dreen made everything they had accomplished and all the blood they had shed seem like a waste.

Plat hadn't been hard to take. Most of its people had already retreated to the protection of the great wall of Xwarda. There had been some resistance, and a score of men had died, but eventually the Highwander troops who had been waiting for them there retreated into the hills between Plat and Xwarda. Both generals agreed they were waiting there to ambush the advance, an advance that wasn't going to come, now that half of the army was pulling out to ride home.

The skin around the black tattoo on General Chatta's bald head was bright and splotchy, with flustered redness. The tattoo ran from the tip of his nose, where it made a fine point, up and over his head, widening gradually until it disappeared, neck wide, into the collar of his ringed leather armor. Sometimes, especially when Chatta was angry, General Vogle thought it looked like Chatta's head had been split with an ax. Such was the case now, because underneath his civil demeanor, Chatta was fuming with rage.

A sharp rap at the door saved Vogel from Chatta's hot, disgusted glare. Outside the door, a muffled argument was cut short, and the door flew open. An armored soldier strode in. He looked haggard and road weary, like he had been riding for days. His normally bright red armor looked brown, due to the grime and dirt caked on it. The man showed no respect for the two generals' rank, and it was obvious he was at a point that was beyond that sort of triviality. Chatta stood quickly, and with the rage over Broderick's decision in his bearing, started to voice his protest of the rude interruption, but the sound of the man's raspy voice stopped him in his tracks.

"They're coming," Brady Culvert croaked. "The dead are coming!"

"What?" Chatta asked incredulously. Then to the soldier who had supposedly been guarding the door. "Is this man mad? Get him out of here before I have you flogged!"

"WAIT!" General Vogle shouted over the room. "He's one of the Redwolf's personal guards. Look at his armor!"

Vogel strode over to Brady and wiped two fingers across his breastplate. Twin streaks of bright crimson shone through the dust and filth where General Vogel's fingers had been.

"My king and a few others escaped the wrath of the Westland sorcerer." Brady swallowed hard and pointed at the table.

Vogel understood. He handed Brady the pewter goblet that he held in his hand. Brady downed it in one long swig.

"Fetch water, man! And bring the food," Vogel ordered the nervous guard in the doorway. When he hesitated and looked at General Chatta, Vogel added a sharp, "Now!" to the command. The soldier disappeared to comply, and Brady continued.

"King Jarrek ordered me to ride and warn Dreen of Westland's plan to march through the Wilder Mountains. Your king got out just in time. He went south to Stroud, I think. The Westland wizard blasted the red wall away and in the morning, he raised the dead."

Brady looked at the two generals in turn, trying to make them believe with his eyes.

"They all march for the Westland wizard now. Westlanders and Valleyans alike. They've been a day behind me, maybe I gained a day, so it could be two now, but it matters not. They're coming this way. I saw them cross the Southron River at the village called Tip, so I'm sure Kasta Keep fell as well. I–they are dead–walking, fighting, dead men. I gave them warning, but they wouldn't listen."

He fell to his knees, with the clank of his heavy plate armor. He was emotionally overwrought and exhausted. Tears streamed down his dirty face, and he sobbed.

"I…I…I…did what I could…all I could do… What else…against the dead?"

"Well, General Vogel," General Chatta started in a somewhat satisfied tone. "So much for pulling out to go save Dreen!"

The next morning, the two Generals pondered what course to take. Over the night, Brady Culvert had escaped, stolen a fresh horse, and rode out toward Xwarda, leaving them to wonder about his tale. General Chatta suggested that it was a ruse to stall their advance on Queen Willa's palace city. Vogel sent out riders to see if an army was really coming from the west. In the meantime, he prepared his troops to make the long march back to Dreen.

Brady had to knock out a Seaward watchman as he snuck out of town. He hadn't relished the idea of assaulting an unsuspecting common soldier, so he rationalized his actions any way he could. If the man had been doing his duty, Brady figured, he wouldn't have been able to sneak up on him in the first place. The knot on his head would remind him to be more vigilant when he was on guard.

Brady figured that when the sun came up and his absence was discovered, he would have an insurmountable lead on any pursuers who might try to follow. The ride to Xwarda would be a short one for a single mounted man. With his midnight start, he could be there before anybody even knew to look for him.

He had eaten and rested, but not well on either count. He wouldn't succumb to his exhaustion—couldn't succumb to it—until Queen Willa had been warned of the coming force. His hope was that King Jarrek would already be there. King Jarrek wouldn't question his seemingly insane claim of an army of walking dead. They had to know it wasn't just Pael and Westland's army coming. It was something far worse.

Xwarda was the undead army's destination, Brady was certain. Xwarda was the oldest city in all of the known kingdoms. It had been the kingdom seat back when all the kingdoms had been one. He remembered from his lessons something about a great magical force that embraced the place, but couldn't remember the details. All he knew for certain was that if the Westland wizard took control of that ancient power, then the kingdoms were all probably doomed.

Brady was so consumed with these dire thoughts he didn't see the rope leap taught across his path. It caught him across the breast plate and stopped his momentum cold, as his horse ran right out from under him. All he saw before blackness consumed him were the faces of other soldiers looking curiously down on him. He couldn't tell where they were from. It was still too dark, and his head was swimming. He tried to raise his body up, but couldn't. It didn't matter who they were. Now no one would be able to warn Xwarda. He fought to pull air into his emptied lungs, but before he found out if he succeeded in drawing breath, he slipped into unconsciousness.

The next morning, Pael collected his Blood Caps alone with haste. As soon as he was satisfied with the weight of his basket, he went back to his little red castle with a crackling flourish and began preparing his concoction. He took special care to ward himself from the effects of the potent poisons he was combining with a deadly virus he cultivated a few days earlier. Not only would his potion be lethal to all who ingested it, but its deadly effect would spread like wildfire among the rest of them. After a few hours, the virus would die out, but it would be too late by then: everyone in the Valleyan/Seaward encampment would already be dead.

He methodically boiled, mixed, strained, and stirred, stopping every now and again to read and reread the pages of the open book lying on the table. When he finished his concoction, he stoppered the vial of murky black liquid, shed his goat hide gloves, and shimmered away.

It was dark in the city of Plat when Pael appeared behind a row of empty buildings, out of sight. Hundreds of campfires burned along the western portion of the city and beyond its limits. Both armies were still here, and he was pleased. The more the merrier, he told himself, as he ran his hand down his front, turning his fancy black robes into coarse, homespun rags.

He pulled the hood up over his gleaming blue-and-green-veined head. The top of his scalp had blistered when he'd taken the time to heal the Choska demon. The healing had lasted well into the afternoon, and Pael hadn't thought to protect his head from the sun. Now the rough material irritated the sunburn, and Pael growled at the pain. He had to force himself to tolerate the sensation so that he might savor the moment at hand.

He took his time strolling around the occupied city, and the many encampments at its fringes. He studied the siege engines, the catapults, and the boarding towers the Seawardsmen had pieced together and mounted to the tops of big horse-drawn carts. He estimated the numbers of horses and men as best as he could in the insufficient light of a hundred small fires.

As he walked around and gathered in all that would soon be under his control, he began to formulate his plans to the next level.

He found the command post in a deserted building and studied the displayed maps of Xwarda there. The city hadn't changed in years, and Pael had to smile at the fact that a few of the little known ways into the walls were on his own maps, but not on these.

He then found the building that was being used to heat the huge cauldrons of gruel that would be bucketed out to the different divisions of soldiers at sunrise. A handful of men, full of yawns and curses, went about stirring meal mix into the boiling water, cutting fruit, and readying eggs to be fried for the officers. The smell of baking bread filled the place and oddly reminded Pael of a time when Shaella was but a baby. The memory was fleeting.

The men didn't seem to notice him standing there watching them. He was far from invisible; he had only wanted himself to be unobtrusive to the eye of those who might pay attention to him. He trembled with glee as he dripped a few drops of his brew into each of the cauldrons. He had a strange moment of déjà vu, remembering how he poisoned Glendar's father's goblet, but it was overridden by his deviant mirth.

When the vial was empty, he tossed it aside and began casting the spell that would reanimate those who died from his poison or the plague it hosted. These undead soldiers would rise from the earth, whole and unwounded. No gaping gashes or broken armor for these undead troops, and what was more, they were already in position to take Xwarda for him.

He sank into his work with fervor, and soon the casting was under way. He had already given Lord Brach his new orders. Brach would arrive and assume command of this new set of battalions very soon. Pael planned it so that he could concentrate his full focus, and sink all his power into the casting of the powerful, dark spell that would raise these men after they died. He held back only enough power to transport himself to his warded bedchamber in the castle at Dreen.

As he finished his casting, he shook his head in disbelief. The power of the demon Shokin that had come into him by luck, or maybe fate, gave him the tools to achieve his goals far sooner than he ever expected to. He had grossly underestimated the number of troops he would find here in Plat. It was all he could do to fight away the giddy, manic shivers that tried to course through him as he thought about the Wardstone. Soon he would be able to wield endless amounts of raw, natural power. With a mountain of Wardstone to fuel his desires, the giants, dragons, and even the rest of demon kind, would be forced to kneel before him. It was with much pleasure that he finished his spell and transported himself wearily back to Dreen to recuperate from his exertion. By the time he woke from his slumber, his undead armies would be enjoined, and he would use them to take Xwarda for his own.

The next day, the three undead commanders, Lord Brach, General Vogel, and General Chatta all prepared their undead troops to march on Xwarda.

They split into three groups, each over ten thousand undead men strong. Each group was to make for one of the four main gates that opened into Xwarda's massive outer wall. The last gate, the one with the road that led eastward through the foothills of the Wander Mountains to the city called Jenkanta, was to be left unguarded. Pael wanted the Witch Queen and her refugees to have a way to flee the city when they saw the army of undead coming. Even a heartless being like Pael had some reservations about destroying the wonder of Xwarda's palace. He could hunt down those who ran later, at his leisure. If he could avoid destroying the city and the palace within it, Pael wanted to do so. Besides, the idea of watching the pitiful folk flee in terror entertained his ego to no end.

Sooner or later, Queen Willa would see the futility of fighting his army. His was no ordinary siege force. They had no need to worry about raining arrows, or pots of boiling pitch pouring down upon them. They didn't need food, nor did the weather concern them. They couldn't be deterred by fear or pain, and none of them were afraid to die because they were all already dead.

Chapter Fifty

Save for the raspy and laborious rise and fall of his chest, Mikahl lay perfectly still. The healers had done everything they could. It may or may not have been enough. His chain mail shirt and his ruined travel clothes had been stripped away. In their place, plain white robes covered his body. His skin had been cleaned, and his long, blondish brown hair brushed to shining.

He lay atop a raw block of Wardstone in a plain room at the back of the castle, in a wing designated to the healing arts and the recovery of those who might need them. The room was formed of the same white marble blocks as the rest of the structure and was illuminated by a soft, magical glow that seemed to radiate equally from every direction so no shadows were cast whatsoever. Darkness had little chance of taking hold in this room. There were no chairs, no windows, no tables, just the featureless room, and Mikahl lying up on the Wardstone block, like a forgotten altar sacrifice.

To Hyden Hawk, Mikahl looked like some saint of old out of Berda's stories, lying there after a battle. To Vaegon, he looked as good as dead. To most any other, it looked like the room held a sarcophagus, with the likeness of the occupant carved and painted on its top for visitors and mourners to see.

"We know what he was about. Shall we continue it?" Vaegon asked Hyden.

He raised Mikahl's sheathed sword in his hand to indicate what it was. He had been tempted to lay it on Mikahl's chest and clasp his hands to the hilt, but that seemed like such a final gesture, he couldn't bring himself to do it just yet.

"Aye," Hyden answered, his voice thick with emotion. "I think I'll go to the temple of the White Goddess and seek counsel. I'll ask her the location of the cooling stone King Aldar spoke of. Hopefully she'll tell me what needs to be done now."

"After seeing that grand depiction of Ironspike's forging, I think Queen Willa or one of her people might know of the cooling stone's location. I'll ask Dugak, the dwarf, while you visit Whitten Loch. Maybe he will know something about it, or who to ask."

"Aye," Hyden wiped away a stray tear. "I'll send the wolves home first. King Aldar will—"

He didn't finish. Looking at Mikahl and thinking of Grrr's brave sacrifice overtook him. He turned and strode out of the room, nearly bowling over a pair of serious-looking, robed and bearded men in the hallway. Seeing which room he had come from, they kindly waved his apology off and made way for him. The pair of uniformed Blacksword soldiers posted at the end of the hallway did the same.

It took Hyden a while to find his way out of the castle. He felt claustrophobic, and more than once had to wipe away the salty tears that clouded his vision and added to his growing sense of panic. Once outside, the clean air and openness of the park around the lake was so refreshing that each breath he took forced out some of his grief and replaced it with crisp lungfuls of not quite hope, but relief at least.

He sought out Talon, and through his hawkling familiar's keen vision, located the wolves. He made his way along a stone path that led to them and found them with the ease of one who was watching his way from above. When he came upon them, all three crept close and greeted him with much licking and tail wagging. They picked up his mood easily, and as he settled amongst them in the grass, they spoke of Grrr, Mikahl, and the Lady Queen. They conveyed their need to return to King Aldar, so that he might know his proud and ferocious pack-leader gave his life trying to save Mikahl.

As he, Talon, and six soldiers from the inner gates escorted the great wolves through the city, Hyden noticed how much more crowded it had become. He and Vaegon passed through only a day and a half ago and, already, the number of refugees packed into the streets had doubled. He remembered the other roads leading into Xwarda, the spokes of the wheel he had seen from above. He wondered how many more might be wedged in before the Valleyan and Seaward armies attacked.

Last night at dinner, Queen Willa's denial of having any knowledge of her men starting the bloodletting at Summer's Day had been believable enough. With demons loose upon the land, and a Dragon Queen in control of Westland, the idea that servants of some dark force started this mess while posing as Highwander soldiers made more sense, especially now that Highwander was under attack.

The soldiers escorting Hyden Hawk and the wolves motioned for them to squeeze to the side of the lane. Another procession of soldiers passed on its way toward the castle. Among them, Hyden saw two men wearing red armor, one with a ruby-eyed wolf skull mounted upon his helmet. Hyden had heard tales of the red armored guardsmen of Wildermont at Summer's Day. It was Wildermont soldiers who policed the Festival every year, and every one of them revered the Redwolf Guard. These men looked haggard and road weary. Another of the group, a dark-haired man with a beard and robes that had once been crisp and white but were now filthy with forest grime, looked at Hyden curiously as they passed. The Great Wolves had drawn his attention, Hyden hoped, but the man's eyes stayed glued to Hyden and the hawkling that was riding tall on his shoulder.

Once the two processions passed each other, the way to the outer gate became easier to manage. The other group had caused all the debris and belongings to be cleared out of the roadway. When they passed through the tunnel-like gateway of the outer wall, Hyden imagined that it was full of soldiers, all ready to pour out and defend the city when the time came.

Once outside the gates, they found a semiprivate niche, and Hyden and the Great Wolves crowded together. He tried not to cry, but it was hopeless. He'd grown to love them. Urp's frisky and never-ending playfulness, Oof's cocky and proud attitude, and Huffa's motherly authority had found a place deep in his heart of hearts. They were as much his friends now as Vaegon and Mikahl were.

He spoke with them, and they reminded him they would meet again. It was far too warm for them here, and they were needed at home, to run the borders with Borg and the other Guardians.

Hyden understood. He hugged each of them in turn, and used their fur to dry his tears. Huffa gave his face a thorough licking, and then he stood and watched as the wolves raced away to the northwest toward the Evermore Forest and beyond. Talon winged after them for a while. Hyden watched through the hawkling's eyes. It was good to see his friends running free and without burden, as they were meant to do.

One of the soldiers finally mastered his awe and fear of Hyden, and told him that the gates needed to be closed. Hyden didn't respond with words; he just turned, and quietly followed the men back through.

Vaegon, with the help of some tired and worrisome servants, found Dugak. It amused the elf to think that he was the strange one here, in a place as strange as any he could have imagined. To Vaegon, Dugak was the oddity among all these humans. Vaegon's good eye might be yellow and wild-looking, and his ears a bit sharp at the tips, but at least he wasn't built like a tree trunk with so much facial hair that only his nose poked through. How the squat, thick-bodied little people once ruled the realm, Vaegon couldn't fathom.

He found the dwarf in the queen's council chamber, where he was as shocked as he was welcome.

If Dugak and his bearded wife, Andra, seemed strange to him, then the little blue-skinned, winged fairy man who hovered a few feet in front of Queen Willa left Vaegon bewildered. The tiny man was no taller than a handspan, and hovering there in the air on glassine wings that were but a blur to the eye. The sight of one of the flying fair folk left the elf utterly speechless.

"Starkle," Queen Willa introduced the tiny man as Vaegon approached with a wide eye and an open mouth. "This is the elf, Vaegon. Vaegon, this is Starkle. As you can see, he's a pixie. He's one of my most trusted advisers."

"How do you do?" Starkle said, in a voice that was entirely too big for such a small creature.

Vaegon was awestruck. Here was this man, the size of a sparrow, wearing a white robe tied at the waist with a golden thread. The robe's back was split to accommodate the wings, and on his tiny feet were laced sandals. He was half the size of the little man Talon had caught in the Evermore Forest, but his neatly cropped hair and beard were the same exact shade of dull gray.

It was all Vaegon could do to muster a response to the friendly greeting.

"I'm better than my companion seems to be," he finally said, trying to suppress his awe with the gravity of his reasons for being there.

"Sir Vaegon is seeking the cooling stone," Dugak announced, saving Vaegon the trouble of explaining.

"Why do you seek the cooling stone?" Queen Willa asked pointedly.

Vaegon noticed that her eyes went from his, to the sword he was carrying, and back to meet his gaze without a hint of emotion showing on her face.

Vaegon glanced around the room. It was empty, save for the four of them. He wasn't sure what he should say so he said as little as possible.

"I do not seek it for myself, but for my companion. The reasons are his to say."

"So, that is the mate to the Hammer of Doon, then?" She didn't wait for an answer to her question. "Ironspike, the westerners foolishly call it. We have waited a long time for it to find its way home." She paused as if remembering something. "Why didn't it extract the demon's essence when King Mikahl drove it into the Choska? The boy is of Pavreal's bloodline, no?"

"Its power was drained by Mikahl's father, in a deed performed for the benefit of the giants and the people of Westland."

Vaegon chose his words carefully. He didn't want to betray Mikahl while trying to help him. He wasn't sure what Queen Willa was inferring by calling this Ironspike's home, either, and he was beginning to feel uneasy. He decided to lend a little weight to what he was saying.

"King Aldar, the ruler of the giant realm, told Mik, uh, King Mikahl, that the sword had to be placed in the cradle it had formed in the cooling stone in order to replenish its power."

"Dugak?" Queen Willa looked at the dwarf expectantly.

Starkle buzzed around behind Queen Willa's head and perched on the crown of her chair's back. Dugak scratched at the side of his head. His whole hand disappeared into the tangle of his hair.

"It can be done as he said, Your Highness." Dugak looked a little uncertainly at Vaegon. "The people of the deep might not like the trespass, but the sword has every right to lie in its cradle."

"The people of the deep!" Starkle blurted out in his big, little voice. "Your people, Dugak, should have no concern over a trespass into a shallow place that they left behind and forgot." The pixie shoved off from his seat and took back to the air. "If the people of the deep had concerns over the cooling stone, then they should have taken it with them!"

"It's underground," Dugak replied in a yielding tone, as if any argument would be futile. "Is it wrong to respect the domain of my kin? They could surface just as quickly as they went underground."

"They've been to ground for centuries—"

Queen Willa waved the pixie quiet with an attempted swat.

"If your people return to blame anybody for the offense, Master Dugak, then the blame shall be mine." She spoke diplomatically to the dwarf. "Just so there is no question, I will command you to lead Sir Vaegon to the chamber. That way you bear no responsibility, for you will be following my orders."

The queen's voice and expression changed to show her distaste as she turned to scold the little blue pixie man.

"There are not one, but two kingdom's armies at our doorstep, Starkle. You have messages to deliver, and duties that do not include worrying about the dwarves and their domain."

The pixie bowed in the air.

"Yes, Your Majesty. Please forgive me."

Before she could respond, he was off on a zigzagging streak toward the open door.

Dugak's expression appeared as if it wanted to be smug, but he couldn't quite complete the look.

The dwarves of Doon hadn't been seen in ages, save for the small group that wandered to the surface by accident a little over a hundred years ago. Those dwarves were Dugak and Andra's ancestors. Those short-lived dwarves who had shown up in Xwarda by mistake, had all but died out. Half a dozen families still lived in the mountains near Jenkanta, and a handful served the kingdom here in Xwarda. The rest of the race was hopefully still living in the depths of the earth, where they had retreated after war and the quickly growing human population drove them away.

Dugak seemed content with his orders. Vaegon couldn't tell whether it was the act of trespass into the earth, or the idea that he might be punished for it that bothered the stumpy man so much. He was glad the dwarf was taking the order seriously. Dugak wasted no time ordering preparations to be made, and supplies gathered, for their short journey out of the city.

Dugak explained that the way would only take a few hours on foot. For obvious reasons, the dwarf didn't want to make the trek on horseback. Vaegon wasn't disappointed with this decision. He too would rather walk. His main concern was he had no idea how long they would have to remain with the sword at the cooling stone. He wanted it to fully reenergize, but had no way to know if and when that state had been achieved. One thing he was certain of was that he wouldn't leave the sword there. He told Dugak to make sure they had enough supplies for a week or more. He figured the dwarf would balk at this news, but he didn't. Instead, Dugak was completely excited by the prospect of getting to spend a few days underground.

Vaegon started to leave Hyden a note, but remembered his friend probably wouldn't be able to read it. In an effort to spare Hyden Hawk the shame of having to ask someone to read it for him, he left the message verbally with Dugak's wife. The dwarfess was more than happy to deliver the simple explanation of where Vaegon was going and why.

As Dugak led Vaegon down through the castle to the hidden exit, a commotion began somewhere outside the place. The dwarf did his best to dutifully ignore the hubbub, but the news that the wizard, Targon, had arrived at the gates with the Redwolf King still found its way to his and Vaegon's ears. Neither of them bothered to comment on the happening, because it didn't affect their present mission one way or the other. They were about to leave the safety of Xwarda, and make a short hike east into the hills to visit a catacomb.

Hyden stood before the boxy structure King Aldar referred to as a temple. He was certain the ranger had told him wrong. This place couldn't be the temple of Whitten Loch. It was only three slab walls with a slab roof, and a stone bench inside. The bench was placed so that one might sit on it and watch the fountain play upon the lake's surface. The floor and the bench were covered completely with greenish, gray splatters of swan dung. In one corner was an empty nest, save for a few feathers and some broken egg shells.

As he stood there debating whether to enter the place or not, Talon came swooping down out of the sky and flew into it. The hawkling landed on the bench and bobbed up and down in a strange little dance, beckoning Hyden to come in. Hyden understood that Talon wanted him to sit there, so reluctantly, and with a grimace at the slime that covered the bench, he did so. The castle staff had already cleaned his leather breaches once. He hoped they would do so again. When he sat down, he was discouraged, but then he looked out across the water and knew immediately he was in the right place.

The angle of his position reflected the pure white marble of the palace across the lake's surface, making it look like a great pool of rippling milk. The sparkles and spray from the fountain caught the green of the forest park and the blue of the sky, making it look as if emeralds and sapphires were spewing up out of the lake and falling back in. Hyden figured after sunset it would be an even more spectacular sight, because the yellows and reds of the stained glass panels would lend their colors to the mix as well.

The droplets and rolling ripples danced a colorful and mesmerizing dance that soon pulled Hyden into a hypnotic state of tranquility. His mind began to empty of all but the dazzle before him. His worry for Mikahl, and the situation they were in, slipped away, and a hazy voluptuous shape began to form in the mist of the fountain's spray. She turned slowly toward him, opening her arms as she did so, and a sad smile crept across her beautiful, mist-formed face.

"You've found the right place at the right time, I think," she said to him in a soft, musical voice. "Your heart has led you well."

"My friend...he...oh, milady, I don't..." Hyden had no idea what to say or how to say it, so he blurted out what was in his heart. "Can you help him? Can you help me help him? He is so close to death, and I don't know what to do. My heart tells me to stand and fight against this great evil that hunts the sword, but...but..." He wiped a stray tear from his cheek. "Without Mikahl to wield the sword, I don't think we stand a chance."

"Where there is hope, there's always a chance," she told him. "As for Mikahl, he is locked in a battle within himself, as well as without. The Dragon's Prophecy says that an unknown son of the blood of kings will take up Errion Spightre and replace the true heir to his father's throne. This contradicts the situation, and since the core of prophecy has been fractured, I cannot decide what is best for Mikahl."

"Mikahl is the true heir!" Hyden said defensively.

"Isn't he also the unknown son? Or did King Balton have another?" the Goddess asked. "Mikahl's fate will be decided by the victor of the battle going on inside him. The elf has set out to find the sword's cradle and replenish its power, but you, Hyden Hawk of the Skyler Clan, friend of the feathered and the fanged as well, must prepare yourself for your own battles. Your heart has told you that you must fight that which has been hunting you and your companions. This dark force grows stronger each day and it will not relent in its quest to destroy love and hope. With or without Mikahl and his sword, the demon must be sent back into that black place from which it came."

"But how?" Hyden asked. His head was swimming with confusion. He had no idea what to do.

"There is a crystal shard in Dahg Mahn's tower that can force the evil that has broken free to go back and rejoin its other half in the Nethers. The crystal must be dissolved into the grooves of the Seal that Pavreal carved up in the Dragon's Tooth Spire. Doing this will make the demon whole again, but it will also close the Seal forever, with the demon trapped behind it."

The White Goddess reached out toward Hyden and trailed a misty finger down his cheek. "This is no easy task, Hyden Hawk Skyler. Just getting into Pratchert's tower will be a trial. How to get the shard to the Dragon Spire before the demon destroys Xwarda and makes use of the Wardstone is what you must figure." Her tone became motherly and full of love. "Use your wits, your cunning, and have faith that the kind deeds and hard work you have done will be rewarded."

Hyden tried to absorb the information, but something was nagging at him. He had no proof of it, but he felt it inside his heart.

"What about Gerard and the ring? My brother went to the Dragon Spire. A soothsayer told him that he would find the power to lead legions down inside it. I know my brother. Gerard couldn't, wouldn't, resist such a temptation."

"He has taken the ring, which belongs on your finger, into the Nethers?" the Goddess asked with sudden alarm in her voice.

"I cannot swear it, Lady, but my heart tells me it's true," Hyden answered solemnly. "Either he went into the depths of the Dragon Spire, or he tried to and died."

"Then victory now might mean disaster later," she whispered, more to herself than to Hyden. Then directly to him, she said. "The core of prophecy is truly broken, for there is no clear path I can see for you to follow. I know not how to direct you other than what I've already told you. You must follow your heart and your hawkling familiar. There is no certain way for you to go."

"What of Pratchert's…I mean Dahg Mahn's tower, then?" Hyden asked, trying desperately to find a morsel of hope in what she was telling him.

"To gain entry, you must only be who, and what, you are." Her tone softened, and she took on a curious look as she continued. "Remember this: you are as much your familiar as your familiar is you. Becoming one together will help you see what's truly ahead of you."

He felt her misty hand caress his cheek again.

"I do not envy you, Hyden Hawk Skyler. You may very well have to seal your own brother into the dark of the Nethers to stop the demon. Yet some day, you will have to take the ring back from him, so that the nature of prophecy can be restored. Doing both seems impossible. Your heart is the only true guide you have now. Follow it, and you cannot fail."

With those words, she began to shimmer away.

Hyden wanted to call out to her, to stall her departure, but he couldn't form a question or find a real reason for doing so. He knew what he had to do first. Pratchert's tower was looming over him even now. He hoped beyond hope that his instincts about his brother were wrong, but no matter how much he wished it to be different, his heart told him the truth of the matter.

Chapter Fifty-One

Not long after he returned to the castle, Hyden was summoned to Queen Willa's council hall. With Talon riding tall on his shoulder and occasionally flapping to keep his balance, he made his way through slanting bars of sunlight that shone like mote-filled splashes of gold, across the softly lit corridor. Andra, the dwarfess, greeted him at the heavy double door and quickly told him what Vaegon was out doing with Dugak and Ironspike. There wasn't time to question her before the door came creaking open, and he was approached. A tired-looking man with long, straight dark hair, a well-trimmed beard, and wearing a white bell-sleeved wizard's robe stepped in front of him and bowed deeply. Talon cawed at the action, and Hyden realized that this was one of the men he had seen riding into the city earlier. Not sure how to respond to the deep bow, Hyden nodded slowly and slightly dipped his knees.

"Lord Hyden Hawk," the man said, rising back up to his full height. "It is an honor. Queen Willa has spoken highly of you and your companions. My name is Targon. I'm the High Wizard of Xwarda, and I am at your service."

Hyden wished that Mikahl were there to coach him about what was proper to do and say around all these fancy people. He also wished he hadn't just come from sitting on a bench covered in swan dung. He felt like a fish that had chased some bait up the bank, out of the water, clear into the tall grass. What could he say to that introduction? What should he say? He was at a total loss for words until he heard the White Goddess's soft, whispering voice in his ear. "Follow your heart," it said.

"When this is done, Master Targon," Hyden indicated the table, and gathering that was about to commence inside the chamber. "Could you please show me Pratchert's...I mean, Dahg Mahn's Tower?"

The master wizard's head cocked slightly to the side and his eyes squinted, as if he were trying to see through to the inside of Hyden's skull. A wry smile soon crossed his face, and he nodded in the affirmative.

"There are things you might want to be aware of before you open that door, Lord Hyden Hawk. I will explain, as you said, when this is done." He put a hand on Hyden's back, turned him toward the door, and gently ushered him into the council hall. "I saved you a seat near mine." Targon indicated the chair he had reserved for Hyden. "I hope you don't mind."

Hyden let himself be seated. There were a half dozen people in the room that he had not yet been introduced to and none of them, at the moment, seemed to even notice his existence. A couple of the men looked to be high-ranking soldiers or guardsmen. The others looked to be lesser royalty or wealthy merchant types. All of them looked important. He was glad none of them could see the swan refuse caked to the back of his britches. Nonchalantly, he sniffed at the air around himself, and was happy to find that he didn't smell of the stuff.

He was just beginning to relax in the strange environment when everyone who wasn't standing jumped to their feet. Not sure what else to do but stand with them, he did so, but he was careful to keep his behind against his chair's back.

"King Jarrek the Redwolf of Wildermont!" an announcer called out in a booming voice, while a staff thumped heavily on the floor.

From behind a row of heavy curtains, a tall, worn-looking man limped into the room. As he gained his chair near the head of the table, the announcer called out again. "General Spyra, Commander of the Blacksword, and her Majesty, Queen Willa."

"Enough! Sit please. Please, sit!" The queen's voice was adamant. "This is a war council not a Summer's Eve dance."

She looked the part of a warrior queen, thought Hyden: fierce, commanding, and seemingly ready for battle. She was in the same plated, leather girdle over glittering chain mail that she had worn when they met in the forest.

Earlier in the day, Hyden learned from Andra that Queen Willa had dreamt of his, Mikahl's, and Vaegon's coming. Obviously, the Queen of Highwander didn't ride out to meet with everyone who rode into her lands. He hadn't had a chance to talk with her about any of that yet, but he wanted to. He was curious to learn if her dream also included the attack of the Choska, or if the prophetic nature of her dream had revealed some other happening that never had a chance to take place.

The nature of prophecy is fractured, he reminded himself, but still, he was curious. After some prodding, Andra revealed that in the queen's dream, Mikahl had flown on a horse of fire and light, and had somehow saved Xwarda from coming under siege. Hyden didn't think Mikahl would survive, much less be able to do anything on any sort of horse, anytime soon.

General Spyra was a big, round-faced man, with the build of a barrel keg. He wasn't fat or even plump; he was just round and big. His head was balding, and the little hair that remained was grayish white and ran in a strip around the back of his head, from temple to temple. He wore old ringed leather armor that looked to have been put to proper use over the years, and he carried a dull gray helmet under his arm. At his hip was a sheathed blade, which was probably as wide as Hyden's thigh, and at least four feet long. The look on his face showed that he was anything but pleased about the situation at hand.

From behind the heavy curtains, Hyden saw a huge moth come fluttering toward the queen. Only after Willa put her hand out and the thing landed on it, did Hyden see that it wasn't a moth. It was a little blue fairy man, right out of one of Berda's tales. He tried not to stare, and it was all he could do to keep Talon from instinctively going after the little guy.

A servant brought around goblets full of a light, fruity wine. When he was gone, the announcer banged his staff on the floor again in three sharp raps. Crack! Crack! Crack! and the council of war began.

"King Jarrek, you've already heard the tale of the demon that escaped us in the forest just north of here," Queen Willa started. "Please tell us all of the battle at Castlemont so that we might better understand what sort of enemy we are up against."

"Forgive me, Your Majesty," General Spyra cut in, before Jarrek could start his tale. "We have an army, no, two armies, marching freely through the kingdom with the intent of taking this very city. What happened in Wildermont between them and the Westlanders has no real bearing on our current situation."

"I understand your concerns for the well-being of Highwander and Xwarda, General, but I believe that the same dark force that was behind the attack on Wildermont is behind all of this madness."

Queen Willa reached over to the general, who was sitting immediately to her right, and gave his hand a pat of reassurance. "We will get to the defense of Xwarda, I assure you." Then to King Jarrek, who was waiting patiently for his chance to speak: "Please, go ahead."

Jarrek stood and spoke with heavy emotion of the fall of his castle city, the herding and selling of his people to the Dakaneese slavers, even of the way that young King Glendar had so casually beheaded several of his kingdom's notables, and displayed their heads like trophies. But mostly, he spoke of the Westland wizard's incredibly destructive power. When he was done, he slipped down into his chair, as if utterly defeated and yielded the floor to Targon, who had witnessed the happenings as well.

"The power Pael wielded was beyond mere human capability. Not even the great wizards of old could have wrought so much destruction with so little effort. I sensed the taint of brimstone in the air as well."

Targon spoke as if he were lecturing a classroom full of students.

"It was as if one of the greater demons had lent Pael his power. He even—"

"The demon was torn in two!" Hyden burst out over the Master Wizard.

He had jumped to his feet so quickly that Talon had to flutter his wings over Hyden's head, to keep from tumbling to the floor.

"The White Lady, the Goddess of my people, told me only part of the demon has escaped the Seal. The other half of it is still trapped in the...the...the..."

Hyden couldn't remember the word she had used. In his awkward pause, Talon flapped down onto the table before him.

"Nedders," he finally said, knowing he hadn't gotten it quite right.

He looked around the table at all the strange faces staring back at him, and with a face hot with embarrassment, quickly sat back down. Talon's fierce gaze met those faces, though, and many of those eyes were abruptly averted. Hyden was never more thankful for his feathered companion. The hawkling's pose was unyielding, and full of swell-chested pride.

General Spyra used the moment of silence to stand and face down Targon.

"That army, and that demon power is not what we're facing, sir. There is a pair of battalions marching up from Plat as we speak. The mages among them are arrow diverters and fire starters, at best! I don't see how a single sorcerer could—"

An icy breeze fluttered through the room, and a deep, sizzling hum suddenly popped like a miniature crackle of thunder over the table.

Everyone was startled. Talon cawed out a warning cry, and General Spyra drew his sword with uncanny speed. A figure had appeared, hovering a few feet over the table. Talon leapt into flight at it, and passed right through the man-sized form. Queen Willa stopped General Spyra from attacking the apparition, and held the room still, as the vision slowly gained definition and detail.

The figure was robed and booted in shiny black. At the sleeves, collar, and hem of the robe, glittered rows of crimson shapes that strongly resembled droplets of blood that sparkled and dazzled the eye. Inside the upraised hood of the robe, Hyden could see a menacing smile on a pale, grayish face.

The little blue pixie man took up a hovering position behind the queen, and Andra made the hand sign to ward away evil from her cowering place half under the table.

"A sending only," Targon said quickly, in a voice full of forced reassurance.

To demonstrate, he reached out, and passed his hand through the apparition.

"See, it's just a vision sending, it has no substance."

"Sort of like your feigned confidence," Pael chuckled softly.

"Who are you? What do you want?" Queen Willa snapped.

Her voice was harsh and commanding, but her eyes plainly betrayed her fear.

"Hmmm," Pael's voice, shimmering with magical energy, tinkled coldly into the room from seemingly everywhere, yet from nowhere at all.

He reached up and slipped the hood back from his head. The color of his skin so perfectly matched the white marble walls of the room, that for a moment, the shape of his skull was hard to define. His gleefully evil expression and cold, dark eyes were perfectly clear though.

"I want you out of my castle. All of you," Pael said menacingly. "You have until the end of tomorrow to vacate the city. My army will leave the Jenkanta Passage unmolested for those who are wise enough to flee me."

He indicated King Jarrek with a flourishing, outstretched hand.

"As the former ruler of Wildermont can tell you, I can and will tear this ancient place to the ground. If you swear fealty to me though, Willa the Witch, I might let your citizens repopulate Wildermont. The place is completely empty at the moment."

Pael chuckled coldly and turned away from Jarrek's outraged, crimson expression.

"If you do not, then my Dakaneese friends will be pleased to sell your people afar."

It wouldn't have surprised Hyden if smoke began rolling out of King Jarrek's ears. The man was fuming with anger, but somehow managed to keep his tongue in check.

Seeing his effect on Jarrek's demeanor, Pael laughed more deeply, then strode through the air and across the table, toward Queen Willa.

"I would rather not destroy this place, but have no doubt that I will if you resist me, witch."

"We will not run from you!" Willa said fiercely.

From somewhere high in the room, Talon cried out a proud shriek of support. The hawkling's call reverberated around the stonewalled room harshly, causing Pael to flinch and glance about. Once the wizard determined there was no threat to him, his temper flared.

"You fools will think differently when you gaze upon my army."

Pael turned, and strode back over the table toward where Targon, Hyden, and Andra were. Clasping his hands behind his back, he continued his tirade.

"My daughter, who incidentally is now known as the Dragon Queen of Westland, was only supposed to cause blood to be shed on the sacred soil of the Leif Greyn Valley so that the Dragon's Pact might be broken. With the dragon unbound to the Seal, I had my way. The fact that her little band, dressed as your Blacksword soldiers, caused King Broderick and Queen Rachel to attack you was a boon I couldn't have conceived and better planned myself."

He stopped and turned back toward General Spyra. From across the length of the table the General met his eyes.

"By the way, General, you needn't worry about the Valleyans and Seawardsmen now. I've killed the lot of them. You'll find out when the dawn breaks that they march for me now!"

Pael strode quickly back toward that end of the table, where he stopped and bent forward to meet Queen Willa's eyes. She was standing rigid, clenching her fists over and again. The set of her jaw looked painfully tight, and her eyes were alight with fear and fury.

"They are already dead, witch!" Pael yelled at her. "Take the morning to gaze upon them. Loose a few arrows into the ranks and see for yourself. They will not fall. And when the morrow ends, they will set upon Xwarda. You'd be wise to flee before I arrive to oversee the occupation!"

"We have the sword, and we will stop you!" Hyden stood and yelled at Pael's back.

Targon put a restraining hand on his shoulder, but Hyden shrugged it off, as Pael turned and almost ran back down the table at him.

Pael recognized the boy, and it startled him. It wasn't the specific face he remembered, though. It was the brother's face, and he remembered it well enough to immediately recognize the relation.

"It was your brother's life blood that opened the Seal and bound the demon for me, boy!" Pael was trembling with fury, and spittle flew from his mouth as he spoke. "My daughter used him to collar the dragon and left him for me to sacrifice!"

Talon swooped down from somewhere above and landed on Hyden's shoulder. Hyden was terrified by the white-skinned abomination. He didn't know what to do or say, or why he had said what he did. It was all he could do to hold the defiant look on his face as Pael took a knee, and leaned down to look him in the eyes. For a long moment, the demon-wizard just stared at him. Then, in a half pouty, childish voice Pael spoke.

"Little Fawlkra Mahn, you should've taken the ring from your fool brother when you had the chance. It was meant for you, and without it, you are nothing to me." Pael's voice grew hard and menacing. "And tell that idiot squire, if he survived the Choska, that I will chew him up and spit out his pieces all across MY FARGIN KINGDOMS!"

The last few words were screamed in a demonic voice so deep that it rattled the cups on the table.

Pael jerked upright and whirled toward Queen Willa. His voice grated like a massive stone slab being dragged across a gravel road.

"On the dusk of morrow, if you are still here, you will all be slaughtered!"

Then, with a flourish of his robes and a hissing pop, his apparition was gone.

Later, as the sun set, Targon showed Hyden the door to Pratchert's Tower and gave him a dire warning.

"You either pass Dahg Mahn's trials or you never return from beyond that door."

"How many have passed?" Hyden asked, hoping to be able to speak to one who had done so.

"None," Targon replied simply.

Hyden nodded his understanding. He wasn't ready to enter yet, and he knew it. Ready or not, he would have to enter soon though. The demon-wizard wasn't about to wait for him to prepare.

His problem wasn't fear of the trial. He had faith that the White Goddess wouldn't send him off to die in some ancient wizard's trap. What troubled him was what he would do with the crystal if, and when, he recovered it from the tower. It could take weeks to get it across the land to the marshes where the Dragon Spire was located. By then, it would be too late. If it was small enough, then maybe Talon could carry it there. But even if it was small enough, how would Talon dissolve it into the carving of the Seal's symbol?

He sighed and tried to sort out all the questions forming in his mind. Then he changed his train of thought altogether.

"Is there anything you can do for Mikahl?" Hyden asked, as he followed Targon away from Pratchert's door.

Somehow, knowing Gerard's fate caused him to see that this was as much his war as it was Mikahl's. His personal responsibility for his brother's actions, and the burning feeling, a longing for vengeance that was growing inside him, seemed to give him strength and resolve. With or without Mikahl and Ironspike, he would face the darkness ahead, but he would much rather face it with his friend by his side.

"There are possibilities, but none that would prepare him for the upcoming battle," Targon answered honestly. "Queen Willa said he was, is, a brave soul."

"Aye," Hyden agreed. "And he is vicious with a blade. Not just Ironspike, but any length of steel."

After a moment, Hyden asked, "What was it that Pael called me? Fawlkra Mahn?"

"It means hawk man, like Dahg Mahn means dog man."

Hyden thought of Vaegon then. If he were to be remembered, which he doubted he would be, he would rather be remembered as Hyden Hawk. Fawlkra Mahn sounded more like a food dish, or maybe a wagon part. Thinking of the elf and the fact that Vaegon was out doing something instead of wandering around, blowing hot air, caused him to strengthen his resolve even further. He forced himself to focus his attention.

"Do you know of a magical crystal that Dahg Mahn possessed?" Hyden asked hopefully.

"I assume you mean the Night Shard."

Targon stopped their procession through the bustling corridor they had entered.

"There's a text that mentions it in the Royal Library. It came from deep within the earth, and was given to Pratchert by the dwarves for some great act of wizardry he supposedly performed for them."

He paused and put his finger to his chin.

"There is a tapestry depicting the ceremony in which it was presented. The Shard was one of his most prized possessions, they say."

"Can you show me this tapestry?"

Hope was beginning to rise in Hyden's heart. Once he knew how big the crystal was, he could start forming an actual plan. Surely the depiction showed the artifact's size in relation to a man.

As they traversed the mile or so of stairways and passages that led to the hall where the old tapestries were stored, Hyden explained what his goddess had told him to do with the crystal. At one point, Hyden looked around and realized that they were outside under the stars, crossing an open-air courtyard that was big enough to contain his whole village.

Targon's pace had quickened as they spoke of the crystal's size and weight. If it was too large for Talon to carry, there were other ways that it might be transported to where it needed to be. If Talon could carry a small marker to the exact location, then Targon would easily be able to send the crystal there. Dissolving it, Targon said, was another matter altogether.

He lectured Hyden on crystalline structure, which Hyden barely grasped. Learning that salt was a crystal that dissolved in water and that ice was actually crystallized water that thawed with heat, only served to confuse Hyden. Some crystals dissolve with corrosives, some just took time. There was no way to know what would dissolve the Night Shard without testing samples of it. To sample it, Hyden would have to beat the tests set by Pratchert hundreds of years ago, tests that had caused every one of the hundreds of aspiring mages and fools who had entered the tower, never to be seen again.

With a flick of his wrist, Targon lit the torches that were ensconced along the walls of the old musty room they were entering. The big, open storage chamber was full of statues, armaments, paintings, and other relics from the history of Xwarda. There was so much stuff, they had to squeeze between dusty piles and teetering stacks to get through the room.

"One of my students is supposed to have inventoried all of this recently, but by the dust and clutter, I think I might have been shammed."

Targon eased away from Hyden and cast a spell, while calling out the name of the student. A moment later, a sheepish-looking boy caught in the awkward stage in between youth and manhood, appeared in a blurry apparition before the master wizard.

"But I did!" Hyden heard the youth blurt out defensively.

"How did you inventory all of this, without so much as stirring up the dust in here, Phenilous?" Targon asked the boy, dubiously.

"Your instructions were for me to catalog the contents of the room without disturbing anything…Sir." The last was added as an afterthought.

"But how, Phen? How did you—? No, never mind how, it's not important. Do you remember a tapestry showing the presentation of the Night Shard to Dahg Mahn?"

The boy thought for a moment, and then a smile crept across his face.

"Who's going into Pratchert's Tower?" His eyes found Hyden and flared hopefully.

"Phen, tell me where the tapestry is or you'll be scrubbing pots in the kitchen for a month," Targon ordered.

The boy's smile vanished.

"It's in the third rack, along the display wall, but won't you at least tell me—"

Targon, with a dismissive wave of his hand, made the apparition of the boy vanish.

While Targon went over to the rack that was holding the tapestries, Hyden studied the one nearest the door. There were dwarves and elves fighting desperately against a cloud of dragons, ridden by what Hyden could only assume were humans. Hyden noticed that the dragons, as well as the riders, all wore collars.

"My daughter used him to collar the dragon and then left him for me to sacrifice!" Pael's cold words echoed in Hyden's brain.

The vile demon-wizard had said it proudly, like a taunt or a brazen boast. Hyden, once more angry and disgusted, walked away from the scene, trying to calm himself and keep his mind focused.

"Here," Targon exclaimed after a few moments.

As Hyden approached, he saw that Targon's expression had grown doubtful, but when Hyden reached his side, the wizard's lips curled into a grin. He crossed his arms across his chest, and gave Hyden a smug look, that showed he had confidence in whatever scheme he had come up with in his head.

When Hyden looked at the tapestry, he gasped in a breath so quickly he nearly swallowed his tongue. It showed a man who looked remarkably like himself holding a glittering, smoke-colored crystal, which was roughly the size of a newborn child. Before him, the Dwarven King, or at least a dwarf of high nobility, bowed before the legendary wizard. Beyond them, a horde of dwarven soldiers bowed as well.

"This can be accomplished," said Targon. "Now all you have to do is pass the trials of Dahg Mahn so that I can dissolve a sample of the Night Shard."

Still feeling the rage of Pael's insulting words echoing in his head, Hyden said flatly, "Then it's as good as done!"

Chapter Fifty-Two

"How many, and how long will it take?" Queen Willa asked General Spyra and his two advisers.

They were back in the council chamber. They had taken a break after Pael's interruption, but had now resumed the war council in earnest.

A pair of Targon's High Magi, one that specialized in defense and fortification, and the other, whose area of expertise was magic as a weapon, had come and taken the Master Wizard's place. The queen excused Targon and Hyden Hawk to, "Pursue other avenues," as she had put it. The pixie, Starkle, and Andra, the dwarfess, had been excused as well, but King Jarrek was still present, as were Parooka, the Mayor of Xwarda City, and his man, Commander Strate, head of the City Guard.

"Maybe three thousand men between High Port, Old Port, and Jenkanta," one of General Spyra's subordinates answered timidly. "They are gathering in Jenkanta as we speak. There, they will await new orders. It will take two days at the most, if we send a bird." He paused and glanced awkwardly at the High Magi. He knew a messenger bird wasn't necessary, but didn't even try to understand how else a message could be delivered. "...immediately," He finished.

"What of the people, Highness?" Mayor Parooka asked quickly, before anyone else might get the floor. "If we use the tunnel to bring in more troops from Jenkanta, then how will we evacuate the city?"

"And who will protect the citizens once they are in the hills?" Commander Strate added.

"Who said we would evacuate? I need those men!" General Spyra's voice was sharp. His narrowed eyes darted from the queen, to the mayor, and back. He had risen from his seat as he spoke, and was now leaning down with both fists on the tabletop. He was an intimidating sight, just as he intended to be.

"Sit," Queen Willa commanded softly, but firmly, to the general.

Grudgingly, he complied.

"If what Pael says is true, that these soldiers of his won't fall from normal battle wounds, then I don't see how the extra men will help you, General."

Willa took a long, sorrowful breath before continuing.

"I have a duty to the people. I have to protect them no matter what the cost. But I have a duty to stay and guard the Wardstone as well."

She paused long enough that the general felt he could speak. He ran his hand back over his sweat-slicked head as if there were still hair there. His hand ended up squeezing at his fleshy chin.

"How do we fight such an enemy?" He looked at the two magi as if they were his corporals. "Tell me!" he ordered.

Master Amill, the mage who studied defenses, looked at the queen askance. He was showing the proper respect for his not-so-elevated station. She smiled at his manners and nodded for him to respond. The look she gave the mayor and the general showed that they might try to remember their etiquette as the mage had.

"General Spyra," Amill stood. "Can a man with one leg walk? Even a dead man would have a time of it. Can a man wield a weapon when his muscles and sinews are burnt and stiff? If his arm is no longer attached, can he strike at you? There's only one way to completely incapacitate the necromatized, besides burning them to ash. That is to separate the head from its body. However, there are many ways to defend against them, or render them ineffective. The most obvious way is to burn them, but that is an offensive stratagem. I'll let my colleague tell you more."

Master Amill indicated with his hand the other mage. Master Sholt seemed surprised to be called upon so soon, but he stood and cleared his voice. He took a sip of wine from the goblet on the table before him, and took a few seconds to gather his wits.

"Fire is the most potent form of attack that comes to mind."

His confidence grew as he spoke to the most powerful people in his bookish little world.

"But the fire must be sustained long enough for the heat to deteriorate or cook, if you will, the meat of the corpses. The eyes of the undead are not how it sees, so blinding or burning the face is pointless. Also, there is a theory about…"

And so it went well into the night. Ultimately, Queen Willa ordered that the people would be evacuated into a tunnel, which led from a mock cathedral behind the palace, out under all of the city walls and into the foothills near Jenkanta. The tunnel was nearly two miles long, and wide enough for two wagons to pass each other. The dwarves had dug the passage ages ago. No one was certain why, but it was there, and they were going to use it.

The Blacksword soldiers from Jenkanta and the port cities were massing at the far end, to guard it from Pael's soldiers. There were several collapsible sections, so if Pael's undead came after them from the palace end, the way could be blocked off. Willa's intent, though, was to pack the people into the passage and use it as a shelter. Only in the event that Xwarda was about to fall, would she give the order for the Jenkanta guards to open the other end of the gate and let the people chance a run through the hills to Jenkanta. If it came to that, Willa knew that her people would be alone in their struggle to survive. The best she could do if Xwarda fell was guarantee that they weren't being pursued when they started out of the passage.

While General Spyra and the magi made their defensive and offensive battle plans, the mayor, the queen, and the commander of the City Guard made the plans to evacuate the city.

Queen Willa insisted that the poor folk, the ones packed into the space between the outer wall and the secondary wall, would go into the tunnel first. Mayor Parooka argued that the merchants and the nobles of the city should go first, but Willa would not budge. Even as they worked out the details of food and water distribution, and relief stations for the evacuees, she had Commander Strate start the common folk in from the outer bailey.

Her reasoning was sound. She was sure that Pael's undead army would be visible at dawn, exactly as he had promised. It would be better for the simple-minded people to be long into the tunnel before the rumors of undying men and dark-hearted wizards started coming down from the walls. The terror and chaos that would ensue might turn riotous, and ruin any chance of moving troops through the city.

She told Mayor Parooka that it was the duty of the noble-born and the wealthy to take care of those who give them station and coin, not the other way around. The mayor could only nod in agreement and hope to find a way to sneak to the front of the procession the families of the men who had already paid him bribes for protection.

Confident that her orders would be carried out, Queen Willa took her leave of the council and made her way through the castle, down into its bowels, to the ancient temple of Doon.

It was only a small room in the depths of the palace's main structure; hard to find if you didn't know what you were looking for. The god of the underground was only worshiped these days by the few dwarves that lived on the surface, and a handful of others. Queen Willa wasn't one of them, but she hoped to find Andra there, and she did.

The dwarfess was in the almost completely darkened chamber, sobbing and huddled on one of the stone-worked pews. She was up near the altar, which was made entirely of carved jade, chased in gold and silver, and studded, here and there, with precious stones. It sparkled wildly under the scant flickering light of a three-pronged candelabra that rested atop it. It was the only illumination in the high-ceilinged room, and its light faded before reaching any of the walls, save for the one directly behind the altar. Andra's sniffles and snorts reverberated up into the darkened heights, but stopped when the sound of Queen Willa's footfalls came upon her.

"It'll be all right, dear Andra," Queen Willa said, stepping over Andra's stumpy legs, so that she could sit beside her friend.

"Oh Willa, he's out there! He's outside the walls, with that elf, and all those dead men!"

She turned to the queen and clung to her, burying her bearded face in the queen's bosom. Then she let out a sobbing wail of despair.

Queen Willa lovingly patted the dwarfess and hugged her tightly.

"Come now. Dugak knows the tunnels as well as any alive. He will come back soon."

Willa's eyes were looking over Andra, and settled on the shadowy shape of the horn that rested on top of the altar.

"But he doesn't know to use the tunnels." Andra looked up miserably at the queen. "He and Vaegon don't know about that horrible wizard yet."

She sniffed, and with a child-like swipe of her forearm, wiped the mucus from her mouth and mustache, and tried to gather herself.

"If I blew the horn, would they come?" Willa asked absently.

Her eyes looked forward, but they were focused on another time and place, somewhere far beyond the walls of the darkened temple.

Andra followed the queen's eyes to the glittering altar.

"That is the promise that King Malachite made." Her tone was hopeful, but her eyes betrayed her doubt.

"Would you really summon my people back to the light of day?"

"I may have no choice, but King Malachite is long dead by now."

Queen Willa pulled herself back into the moment, and looked at Andra seriously.

"Would they keep a promise made a thousand or more years ago?"

"A promise made by a king should be kept by his successors. A dwarf's word is his bond. A king's promise, I think, should hold even more weight."

"And the Hammer of Doon is as mighty a weapon as King Mikahl's sword!" Willa added, with growing confidence.

She stood, eased back past Andra, and approached the altar.

The horn was lighter than she expected it be. It was a plain curl of ram's horn, save for the mouthpiece, which was crafted of silver. All around the curling body, there were runes etched into the rough surface. There was a leather thong fastened to it so that it might be carried in the field. Willa pulled that over her head, letting the horn hang just below her breasts.

"If the need be great and the times be dark, then sound the horn, and the might of Doon will come forth from the depths of the earth to lend its strength to protect the Wardstone."

Willa muttered the words of the promise spoken over a thousand years ago, just before the dwarves had gone to ground. At the moment, the need wasn't so great, she decided. Pael could be bluffing or exaggerating his strengths. Just wearing the thing around her neck seemed to give her some strength. The confidence that Pael's display had shaken from her earlier seemed to be returning. Nevertheless, when she and Andra left the temple of Doon to try and get some rest, the horn remained looped around her neck.

Shaella was sitting on her throne, in the empty Grand Petition Hall in Lakeside Castle. Hours had passed since the courtiers and petitioners of the day had been dismissed. Cole, her right hand, and the functional ruler of the castle and the city outside its walls, had reluctantly left her there at sunset.

He was worried for her. He knew she was strong and far from a foolish girl anymore, so he left her to her statuesque silence, and retreated.

Shaella simply didn't want to move. She was recuperating still from her most recent use of the Spectral Orb. For two consecutive days and nights, she had been with Gerard in spirit and mind. She was exhausted.

Through the orb she could feel him, but he was weak, and had been transformed somehow. He was alone and seemingly lost in the darkness he was bound to. She spoke, and he seemed to hear her. Sometimes he even mumbled a coherent response, but mostly he rambled off strange phrases, or cried out in confused terror.

He was alive though, and that's what mattered most to Shaella. She would not, could not, give up hope for him now. As soon as she rested and regained enough strength to open the orb-way again, she would do so. At the moment though, her mind was numb. She didn't even start when Pael appeared, suddenly and crisply, before her. In fact, she didn't even seem to notice him there.

Pael looked at her with a father's eye of concern for a moment, but his attention shifted when he saw the object sitting across her lap. His Spectral Orb had been shrunk to the size of a cantaloupe and mounted on an intricately carved wooden staff. He eased up to her curiously and reached out to take it, but when his hand came close, the shaft flared a bright crimson arc and bit into him sharply. Shaella jumped from her daze, and raised the staff to strike Pael.

Pael yelped in surprise and pain from the staff's magical defense, and his head grew pink with his growing rage.

When Shaella realized who it was before her, she relaxed the staff and made a quick apology before her father could unleash something horrible at her. As a sorceress, she was fairly powerful. She had memorized a wealth of spells, and was learning more each day. She could cast them effortlessly and with supreme confidence, but compared to her father, she was a kitten to his saber cat. She dared not cross him. She knew that the bond they shared as father and daughter was, at best, as thin as a strand of spider's web. His anger alone would burn it through before it could be checked, especially if she provoked him.

"Father," she said meekly as he tried to calm himself.

"I see you have warded MY orb well." The stress on the word my wasn't lost on Shaella, but Pael's voice betrayed little animosity, and most of his anger had dissipated by then.

He stared at her, but the look softened. He had no further use for the orb, he decided. Xwarda's vaults held much more powerful things, if one knew how to use them. Luckily for Pael, Shokin had that knowledge right there for him to take.

"Why are you here?" Shaella asked kindly, and then stood. "Can I have something brought for you? Food? Wine? Anything?"

He took her hand, and helped her down the three steps that formed the dais for the Lion's throne. Her mind raced through the possibilities. His strange, suddenly fatherly manner suggested he wanted something. But what could Pael want that he couldn't just take?

"No, my dear, I need no refreshment." He put a hand on each of her shoulders and looked her in the eyes. "You have made me proud, Shaella." He seemed as earnest as one could be, but Shaella wasn't fooled by the act; at least not completely. "I wish to have you by my side when I take Xwarda on the morrow. I wish to share the victory with you, and I hope to make you as proud of me as I am of you."

She would have thought that he just wanted her along to gain the advantage of intimidation and might that her dragon would bring, but she didn't even have the collar on at the moment. It interfered with her use of the orb, allowing the dragon's thoughts into hers and Gerard's moments, so she had stopped wearing it. As it was, Pael could have just summoned the collar to himself, put it on, and taken control of the dragon. There was no question in her mind that Pael knew exactly where the collar was, but he hadn't tried to take it.

She dared not believe in this sudden burst of fatherly tenderness. Her mother's voice rang through her head, spewing myriad curses at his lack of such an emotion, warning her not to be taken in by his act.

Shaella returned the loving gaze into Pael's cold, dark eyes and searched them. Try as she might, she didn't see or sense any sign of deception or mockery. He seemed as sincere as one could be. She found that this moved her, and without a moment's more thought on the matter, she agreed to join him in his conquest of Xwarda.

Starkle woke Queen Willa just after the sun broke the horizon. In a hurried zigzagging flutter, flown at a respectable distance from the waking queen's bed, he spoke to her in his deep, excited voice.

"It is as he said, Highness; the necromancer didn't lie. You have to see it for yourself. Hurry now."

He had to zip out of the way of a thrown pillow.

"I am only the messenger!" he said indignantly after he had recovered. "General Spyra and the High Wizard, Targon, sent me. They await you at the Coast Road Gate. Hurry now, Majesty."

"Would you excuse yourself so that I may dress, sir?" Queen Willa snapped sharply. A little tiny pixie man was still a man, and she was still a lady, no matter how serious the emergency.

"Of, of course Highness, forgive me." Starkle bowed in midair, then erratically zipped across the room and out the slightly cracked door.

"Milly!" Willa yelled coolly. "I know your ear is glued to the door! Someone had to open it for that little blue gnat!"

A middle-aged woman, blushing furiously, eased into the room. Willa was hurriedly swapping her nightclothes for a heavy pullover gown.

"Why wasn't it you who awakened me?" the queen asked. "Find my hooded cloak while you answer. No, the darker one."

Milly hid her face in one of Willa's large closets.

"Who can say the ways of the fairy folk, Highness. Surely not I," she called from inside.

Willa found a black leather belt and buckled it around the velvety lavender gown she had chosen, and then took the cloak Milly offered.

"It's not the ways of pixies that concern me, Milly," Willa said, while bunching her hair into a ponytail. "Pixies can't turn door knobs by themselves."

Willa's grin showed that she was just teasing her maidservant. Suddenly, her face turned serious, and she looked sternly into Milly's eyes.

"I want you to gather a pillow sack full of your dearest things, then report to Lady Andra. Do it just as soon as I leave, and tell her I said to take you to the tunnel herself."

A half hour later, Queen Willa came up from the endless switchbacks of stairs, up to the wide roadway-like top of the outer wall. It took a few moments for her to catch her breath and gather her bearings, long enough for her to locate the general and Master Targon.

In her cloak, with the hood up, no one bothered to acknowledge her, much less direct her. This was fine with her. She didn't want to distract the men. Looking around at them, she decided that she could have come up to the top completely naked, and not a one of them would have been able to peal their eyes away from what was holding their attention.

When she gained the side of her advisers, she was finally close enough to see for herself. Out and down from her vantage, standing boldly within bow range, row upon row of soldiers stood in perfect formations. Thousands of men, among them huge ladder towers and great battering rams, stood at the ready. Catapults and wagonloads of head-size boulders for ammunition were spread evenly just out of bow shot, in a row parallel to the wall.

"Look," General Spyra pointed down and helped the queen lean out past the arrow crenellations, to see what it was he was trying to show her.

Below them and a bit to the right, directly in front of that particular set of gates, stood half a dozen soldiers at attention. They had so many arrows sticking out of them that they resembled porcupines, yet none of them had fallen. In front of them was a pyramid stack of three-barrel kegs.

"What of the other gates?" Willa asked.

She felt as if she were sinking in sand and had the weight of the world pressing down on her shoulders.

"The same," Spyra answered, with little or no emotion in his voice. "Around ten thousand men who are unhindered by our arrows, and ready to set all of the outer gates on fire with those casks of oil."

"Curse the gods of the heavens and earth," Willa said to herself, fingering the horn she had snatched from her bedside table as she left her room.

Just then, a small mule-drawn wagon, pulling a load of supplies up one of the long, slow sloping ramps that ran on the inside of the wall, broke free from its tethers. Men shouted and screamed to make way as the cart wobbled and scraped against the wall on its unhindered way down the ramp. Men dove and leapt out of its way as it gained careening speed, then smashed into the next mule cart, which was halfway up the slope. A man and a mule were crushed to death, and a few men were injured from the tumbles they took while trying to avoid a direct hit.

Queen Willa decided not to mock the gods anymore, and also decided that never in all of her life had she felt more helpless than she did just then.

"What is it that you and Hyden Hawk have come up with?" she asked Targon, with her last bit of hope hanging in the balance.

"There is a plan," Targon answered with a doubtful look on his face, "but it cannot even be started until he returns."

"Returns?" She didn't understand.

With an expectant wince at what her reaction would be, Targon explained.

"He has gone into the Tower."

"Wha–what Tower?" Willa asked.

The sand she felt like she was sinking in was about to suck her under because she knew the answer to her question before he spoke it.

At least ten would-be heroes had gone into Pratchert's Tower in her lifetime. Not a single one of them had ever been heard from again. According to the records, over a hundred wizards, sorcerers, mages, and fools had tried to beat Dahg Mahn's trials over the ages. None of them had succeeded.

She didn't even think before she took the Horn of Doon from inside her robe and put it to her mouth. The loud, blasting sound it made startled General Spyra, who almost tumbled over the edge of the wall. It was all Targon could do to wrestle him back to safety. The scene before her only served to confirm that, without a doubt, it was indeed a time of great need.

Chapter Fifty-Three

Vaegon sat patiently beside the big, bland block of Wardstone, waiting for something to happen. On top of the stone, Ironspike lay in the exact place where it had melted itself a snug cradle into the semi-smooth surface a few thousand years ago. A depression shaped roughly like a war hammer, and a few smaller ones shaped like large arrowheads, were empty alongside the sword.

Nothing had happened when Vaegon placed it there, nothing at all. He had half-expected a flare of light, or a telling glow, or maybe even a hum, but there was nothing to indicate that the great sword was replenishing its power. He had slept for awhile and was now growing restless. Dugak's long, powerful snores filled the cavern. The sound reverberated off the stone walls, and came closing in on the elf.

If there was one thing that Vaegon, or any other elf, for that matter, didn't like, it was being enclosed underground. The smoky torch flame that wavered in its crude sconce by the entryway was the only movement, save for the grotesque shadows it threw across the roughly hewn walls.

"There's no breeze to sway the grass and the trees, even if there were grass and trees to be swayed..." Vaegon sarcastically butchered the words, while singing a verse of an old elven tune in a soft, musical voice. "There are no songs, for the birds and the bees are all gone, and all they left here is the decay..."

Worse than the dead air and the suffocating feeling was the fact that this wasn't just a cavern: it was also a catacomb. There were no corpses in this particular room, but just outside, there was a tunnel lined with rooms just like this one, and they weren't so empty.

Vaegon shivered at the thought and forced it away. He didn't want to think about it. He didn't want to know. All he wanted was to get back into the open, to see the sun, the moon, or the stars overhead, and to breathe in the fresh air. He had been sitting there so long, he wasn't sure if it was night or day anymore.

He decided that when Dugak woke, they would go. There was no way he or the dwarf could tell if the sword had been replenished. The important thing was that he now knew where the cooling stone was hidden. He could bring Mikahl here if... No, he corrected his thought. Not if, but when, Mikahl recovered from his injuries.

Vaegon stood, looked at the sword, and seeing that it appeared no different than it had the last time he had looked, let out a frustrated sigh. He began to pace the dusty gravel floor of the chamber, trying to fight off his claustrophobic feelings and his unease in general. The crunch of his footfalls gave him a strange comfort in the otherwise silent catacombs. He was sure he would have felt much better if he still had his elven vision. Seeing in the darkness is one of the things he had taken for granted all of his life. He could still make his way in the dark without the torch, but with his vision he could have... Could have what?

"No use in might've been, foolish elf!" he said to himself out loud. "It's the lot I've been left with so I must accept it and move on."

"Who are you talking to?" a wavy, liquid voice said from the doorway.

The sound of it and its suddenness startled Vaegon so badly he almost fell to his knees. He looked for the source of it and found a ghostly form standing there; a man in a long, flowing robe, sporting a crown upon his head. The figure had no substance and very little color, but was still defined in smoky white, and vivid detail. The ghostly thing had been human once with a sharp nose, high cheekbones, deeply set eyes, and long, straight hair.

"What? Who are you?" Vaegon asked, as he eased his way back toward the cooling stone.

"I was once a king," the ghost said sadly. "But now, I'm just a harmless ghost."

There was a hint of sarcasm in the tone of his voice.

"There are so many undead up and about that I decided to go look for a conversation. It's lonely down here, you know. I felt the sword there, and heard you singing." The apparition pointed a bony finger at Ironspike on the cooling stone. "It's not every day a power such as that comes around. It's driving them away, as I suppose it should do. No undead soul wants to feel its edge biting into them. It's such a final thought, don't you think?"

"What?" was all Vaegon could manage to get out of his mouth. The dwarf's powerful snore filled the silence that followed.

The ghost looked at Dugak curiously, and then back to Vaegon.

"Well, sir, there are no ghosts or undead in here, and I doubt you can relate to my situation well enough to sustain a decent parley, so I'll be on my way."

The ghost bowed regally.

"Good day," it said, just before it disappeared entirely.

Instantly, Vaegon felt the air begin to warm around him. He had been too frightened to notice how cold the chamber had gotten. He spent long moments blinking his good eye, trying to figure out whether he'd really seen the thing, or if he'd gone crazy down here in the underground. It didn't matter, he decided. Crazy or not, the thing had felt Ironspike's power, so it was time for them to go.

He put the sword back in its sheath and, as politely as he could manage, he woke Dugak.

They started back the way they had come. Vaegon had never been happier to see the light of day than he was when they came out of the mouth of the necropolis, into the afternoon sun. The moment they were drenched in the bright, welcoming warmth of it though, he knew something was wrong. He turned, and saw the source of the rancid stench that had assailed his nostrils. A troop of soldiers was there, looking just as surprised as he and Dugak were. Every one of them was dead and rotting on the bone, but coming at them with murderous intent, nonetheless.

Mikahl was back in his childhood bed, in his mother's tiny apartment, in the servants' wing of Lakeside Castle. His mother was in the old, creaky rocking chair in the corner, needling something or other out of a peach-colored yarn. The fall of her golden hair shone with angelic radiance, and he was bathed in her feelings of love for him.

Creeek…Krooth…Creeek…Krooth…Creeek…Krooth… the chair sounded, as she slowly rocked it to and fro. In a nearly inaudible voice, she hummed an old lullaby in time with the rocking of the chair.

Quietly, so as not to disturb the tranquility of the scene that he found himself in, Mikahl crept out of bed and tiptoed to the window.

Outside, he saw the ocean rolling and swelling in the distance. A deep, dark sea wasn't supposed to be outside that window, but he accepted it as if it was. He felt a comforting presence ease up beside him and peek its furry head out, to see at what he was looking. It was Grrr, and sensing him there caused a coldness to churn inside Mikahl's belly. As he scratched the wolf behind the ears, he realized he was no longer a boy, and that the sound he was hearing wasn't his mother's rocking chair, but was the creaking and groaning of a ship. He looked from the wolf, back out the window, and it was there, passing very close to them.

Creeek…Krooth…Creeek…Krooth…Creeek…Krooth… the timbers slowly groaned and the taut ropes protested.

The ship's deck was littered with bodies. A small group of tired and haggard-looking men worked to throw them overboard one at a time by the limbs, like sacks of grain. Each of their faces was full of fear and defeat. At the front of the ship, leaning out like some half-dead bowsprit, was King Glendar.

Glendar turned and looked at Mikahl with eyes as cold and black as jet, and smiled a grin of needle sharp teeth. It wasn't a smile of victory or menace. It was a smile full of contempt; contempt for the living, for the ship was floundering aimlessly at sea now. There was no crew in sight, only King Glendar and a few Westland soldiers, tossing corpses out into the vast, cobalt expanse, while drifting to their own certain deaths.

Mikahl turned from the window and hurried to the door of the little room, but it wouldn't open for him. He tried and tried to turn the knob, but it wouldn't budge. Terror shot through him like wildfire.

"There has to be a way!" Loudin's voice spoke from the chair where his mother had been sitting.

Mikahl's fear ebbed away, and he smiled at his big, tattoo-covered friend.

"Aye Loudin, but what is it?"

"There is only one way!" King Balton's hoarse voice croaked from the bed.

He was buried under a pile of blankets. The skin of his face was greenish pale, and slick with sweat. The poison was still eating his life away, and he was gasping for breath.

"Think...Then act...Think...Then act...Think...Then act..." the raspy mantra echoed on and on.

Suddenly, Grrr rose with his hackles standing on end and a deep rumbling growl in his throat. Mikahl turned to the window. Peeking in, with a gleeful smile on his sickly, white face, was Pael. His cackling laugh echoed through the room, and it all collapsed into a sudden blackness that overtook Mikahl.

Alone again, back in his coma, the only sound Mikahl could hear in that dark, empty place was the sound of his own broken body trying desperately to draw breath.

Creeek...Krooth...Creeek...Krooth... Creeek... Krooth...

After he stepped inside, Hyden Hawk closed the door to Pratchert's Tower behind him. Talon flapped up from his shoulder with a start, and he jumped a little himself.

There was no room or hallway there. He found himself in a forest. Sort of a forest, anyway. Leading out ahead of him was a tunnel-like corridor formed of greenery. What little space overhead that wasn't closed in by branches and leaves, was filled with tangles of colorful, flowering vines and clumps of hanging moss. The moss seemed to glow a radiant yellowish color, which lit the underside of the canopy like a lantern might. Thick trunks of the trees lined the archway in nearly perfect rows, wrapped in spirals of ivy and creepers. Between and behind the trunks, an unforgiving wall of thorn-bearing shrubs filled every conceivable space. Beyond that, there appeared to be nothing but blackness.

Talon flew up to the peak of the arch and tried and tried to get through where there should have been sky, but the effort was futile. There would be no bird's eye view of the layout of this place, Hyden decided.

After further investigation, Hyden found that the walls of this passage were just as impenetrable as the roof was. Seeing there was nothing else to do but find where the forest tunnel led, Hyden set off down the leaf-strewn, grass-covered floor with Talon winging along beside him.

Clumps of wildflowers sprouted up here and there, some with tiny white petals, some with big, drooping orange and red blooms. Around the base of a rather large tree, a cluster of purple and gray mushrooms sprouted up, like a little city of toadstool buildings. A bright yellow butterfly fluttered by on its way to an even brighter, cerulean-colored flower, which bloomed from the thorny shrub beyond the trees. Hyden half expected a group of fairy folk to troop out and dance a jig for him.

Before long, he came to a junction. The tunnel ended, and he could either go left or right. A few dozen yards down the righthand tunnel, a man sat. He was huddled with his head between his knees, and his back against the trunk of one of the trees that lined the way.

Cautiously, Hyden walked toward the man, while Talon flew further down the right-hand passage to explore it. Hyden called out, but there was no response. When he moved closer, Hyden got a strange feeling in his gut. He nudged the man's shoulder with his boot, and wasn't too surprised when the skeleton fell over, with a rattling thump of dusty bones.

Through Talon's eyes, he saw that the right and lefthand tunnels were identical mirror images of each other. Each went on straight for a ways, than ended in a T-junction, just like the first tunnel had. He decided that he would turn right at each intersection he came to, that way he could find his way back to the skeleton by making left hand turns on his way back. To his great surprise, when he turned his second right, the skeleton was there ahead of him, laid over exactly as his boot had left it.

Hyden pondered this for a while, then sent Talon back to the first junction. When the bird flew left at the corner, there he was, coming right back at Hyden, again from the righthand corner of the other end of the passage. This was unexpected, and confusing. Hyden decided to go left then. There was no surprise when he made his second left hand turn, and saw the toppled skeleton laying there ahead of him. Talon came flapping down and landed on his shoulder. The bird let out a frustrated squawk and started preening himself while Hyden pondered their dilemma further.

While he was standing there with his chin in his hand, he heard a chirping giggle from the trees nearby. Again, he heard the sound. He looked around and spotted a couple of tree squirrels peeking over a root at the edge of the thorny wall. A few other squirrels scampered along the limbs as they went about their business, but they didn't seem to notice him. The two squirrels by the tree trunk, though, were watching him intently, and giggling.

"You think it's funny, then?" Hyden asked lightheartedly. He didn't expect a response, and was shocked when he heard the squirrels plainly speaking to each other. Sure, he had communicated with animals, but it wasn't a very verbal sort of communication. This was something altogether different. The squirrels were articulate.

"Can he hear us?" one squirrel asked the other.

"He can, I think!" the other replied.

"That's far better than most that come here."

"Is there a way beyond this, this…" Hyden indicated the tree-formed passage, but didn't know what to call it, "…beyond this, this loop?"

"My, my, my, this one might just do," a squirrel passing by on a limb overhead said to the others.

"He didn't ask for a way out!" one of the squirrels by the root nodded reverently. "He asked for a way forward. That's a start."

"He asked for a way beyond, is what he did," the squirrel beside him corrected. "A wise word beyond. A wise question to ask, not a foolish one."

"I'm here!" Hyden snapped. "You talk about me as if I'm not, or as if I couldn't hear you. You're awfully rude squirrels. You should know that I have friends who love to eat squirrels." The last was said lightly, but the possible threat caught the little creatures' full attention.

"Your friends may eat careless squirrels," one of them replied, indignantly. "But we're not careless."

"Not careless at all," the other added.

"Careless or not, it's rude to talk about someone as if they weren't there," Hyden scolded. "Now that you're talking to me, instead of about me, would you please answer my question?"

"No," one of the squirrels answered simply. "You already know the answer to the question that you asked."

"Use your head and ask the proper question," the other one told him. "We will only answer one."

Hyden made a face at the squirrels because he knew they were correct. Of course, there was a way out of the loop. The right question became obvious then, but Hyden thought it through before asking it.

"What is the way to get beyond this place?"

"Follow your heart!" a squirrel giggled from the trees.

"Follow your familiar!" another added.

The two squirrels by the root started bounding away, into the thorny wall. Just before they were out of earshot, one of them turned, and said, "Try going both ways, at the same time, and looking through all of your eyes at once."

It took several attempts and as much concentration as it did for him to climb the nesting cliff of the hawklings, for him to be able to see through Talon's eyes with his own eyes open, but he finally managed it. It was even harder to keep Talon moving through the lefthand tunnel in a restrained hover that matched the speed of his jog through the righthand side. When it finally happened, when four eyes looked together down both corridors at once, it all became clearer. When he turned left, just as Talon turned right at the T-junction, they met in the middle, and the forested passages shimmered away. The trees were replaced by a long torch-lit hallway. At the end of the featureless passage was a single door.

Beyond the door, there was an empty room. As before, when Hyden closed the door behind him, the room shifted. The door vanished, and he found himself somewhere that was as beautiful as it was terrifying. Talon was holding a steady hover, over and just behind his head, and cooed out a sigh of relief at seeing the open sky overhead.

They were standing on a slow, rolling plain of fertile green, an emerald sea of turf, which stretched as far as the eye—or eyes, in this case—could see. Right behind where he stood was a single, monstrous old oak. Ten men might not have been able to put their outstretched arms together to form a ring around it. Littered among the leaves and deadfall at its base were the bones of a score or more men. Some were scattered about, some were in neat little piles. Others were still connected at the joints, and sitting there in half-rotted clothes, with packs and pouches strapped to their bodies. A few empty water skins, a handful of books, and even a sword or two lay among them in various degrees of weathered decay.

Suddenly, movement caught his eye. A huge, dark knothole in the tree trunk had shifted, he was sure of it. Cautiously, he took a few steps back. Talon landed on a shoulder and sunk his claws firmly, and reassuringly, into Hyden's muscle. A breeze cooled his skin, and the leaves rustled about him.

It was warm, probably hot, beyond the shade the tree provided. He was about to send Talon off to explore the lay of the land, when the knothole moved again. There was no mistaking it this time. The knot closed and puckered, like a mouth, and then in a voice as deep as the ancient tree's roots, it spoke. The rhyming riddle came out slowly and rhythmically.

"A guide will come, if your heart's been true, and lead you to a door of mine.
Ponder this, while you wait, if you want to go inside;
A pyramid, a patterned knock, made up of only ten.
You must start from the bottom; if you do, I'll let you in."

After the voice stopped, Hyden spoke the words to himself, over and over again. It was hard to do, considering the shock and bewilderment he was feeling after being spoken to by a tree. He didn't dare forget the words, though. They made little sense to him now, but he would think about the meaning later. At the moment, all he wanted to do was commit the riddle to memory. By the look of the others waiting, he figured he might have plenty of time to sort it out.

He grimaced at his morbid sense of humor. His faith that the White Goddess of his clan would send him a guide hadn't wavered, at least not yet. He was certain she wouldn't let him whither and rot like these others had.

Only after he was sure he had the rhyme memorized, did he try to communicate with the tree. It didn't respond to anything he asked, or commanded. Nor did the tree do more than rustle its leaves at him, when he pleaded. After a while, he gave up, and sat back against the tree trunk among the remains of the others, and began going over the riddle in his mind.

"A pyramid, a patterned knock, made up of only ten.
You must start from the bottom; if you do, I'll let you in."

He had no idea what the answer was, and after saying the thing a few times out loud, he found he had grown sleepy. It was only a matter of moments before slumber took him to a deep, dark place, where not even dreams dared to go.

Vaegon, having no other weapon at hand, and cursing his lack of foresight for not bringing one, drew Ironspike from its sheath. Dugak raised his walking stick as if it were a club. For a moment, the undead soldiers hesitated. The sword had scared them. Vaegon knew this only because of what the ghost had told him earlier. He also knew they were slowly starting to realize that he wasn't Mikahl, and that Ironspike's power wasn't unleashed.

"Run for it, Dugak," Vaegon yelled.

He shook the sword at the undead nearest him, and spoke some strange words in the elven tongue. The dwarf started away on his short, stumpy legs. The rotting soldiers cringed back, as if the sword might suddenly flare to life and waste them where they stood. The ruse didn't last long, and soon, Vaegon was turning to run after Dugak. The undead were swiftly in pursuit.

On his own, Vaegon could have easily outpaced the soldiers. They ran on atrophied muscle, moved by decayed tendons that were covered with putrid skin. The armor they had worn proudly as a second skin in life, now encumbered their failing bodies, making them slow and clumsy. Dugak, however, was churning his little legs madly, and was still falling behind. Finally, after gaining the top of a small hill, the dwarf stopped.

"You know the way! Go on!" Dugak said between huffing breaths. "I'll lead them astray. I'm only slowing you down."

"I won't leave you, dwarf," Vaegon said sternly. "So save your breath."

With that, he turned, ran out into the path of the leading soldier, and swung Ironspike with all he had in him. The silvery steel blade bit into the mushy flesh and bone at the shoulder and the undead soldier's arm fell away. The thing toppled forward, and Vaegon had to kick it away from him with a booted foot. The stench was so strong that the elf's keen senses revolted. He could almost taste the rot on his tongue, and he doubled over to vomit.

A rock twice the size of Vaegon's skull went sailing over him, at the approaching knot of undead soldiers. Dugak's strong arms had thrown it as if it were a child's toy. It impacted with a thumping smack, which sounded both wet and bone-crunching. Two of the attackers fell from the blow. The others hesitated. The next rock caved in the side of one of their heads and splattered the others with grayish, yellow goo.

Vaegon stood, raised the sword, and charged toward them a few steps. There were four of them left. Two of those turned and loped away, as if the encounter had never happened. One of the others moved forward to meet the elf's charge. The last one just stood there, as if it had been suddenly frozen in place.

Vaegon cut down the soldier before him with one vicious swing of Mikahl's blade. The remaining undead stayed stock-still. It just stood there as motionless as a statue. Not so far away though, mumbles and grunts could be heard. There were more of them out there in the hills.

Neither Vaegon nor Dugak cared to know why the thing had just stopped. They were too busy running toward the little passage that was hidden in the rocky foothills almost a mile away. If they could get to it, it would lead them back into the relative safety of Xwarda's walls.

Chapter Fifty-Four

Mikahl's dream about his half brother, Glendar, wasn't far off the mark.

The ship carrying the young King of Westland's undead body was drifting aimlessly at sea. The bodies that were being thrown overboard, however, were not willing to stay dead. Nor were the ones doing the throwing. The other two ships had abandoned the king's plague-stricken vessel. They had gone so far as to pull down most of its rigging with a half dozen well placed harpoon shots, and even made an attempt to set the craft on fire by hurling clay pots full of flammable oil at it. No one wanted to chance the king surviving his ordeal, making shore, and then calling them out as mutineers or deserters.

Just as Mikahl had seen him standing at the prow of the doomed ship, Glendar, or Inkling, or some measure of them both, stood in the wind at the front of the craft. He was calling out desperately to Pael.

Pael was a thousand miles away, and too busy to notice the pleas. Even if he could have heard them, he was too preoccupied to care any more about the fool, Glendar, and his bond with Inkling had fizzled to insignificance.

Glendar had gained a bit of control over the undead men by sheer force of will, but that meant he could only keep them from attacking him. He couldn't stop them from attacking each other. The tainted hellcat meat that Pael had let them eat left its bit of evil inside them, and chaos prevailed onboard the ship. Soon, it was all-out battle for everybody just to stay out of the sea.

When the first of them went into the water, the sharks came. After the first man was hit and shredded into a rotted, brown cloud of gore, the sharks fled in search of a more wholesome meal. The scavengers came though. A whole flotilla of crabs and sucker fish arrived, and most of the undead men were skeletons before their still-animated bodies had hit the sandy ocean floor. Now, only a few of King Glendar's men remained on the ship. None were really alive.

The sun overhead was fleecing them of their flesh almost as fast as the denizens of the sea were consuming the fetid meat of their sinking comrades. For a half mile behind the drifting craft, a wake full of tattered clothes, and churning waters alive with fat, dinner-plate sized pink crabs followed them. Further down in the depths, a small group of bewildered skeletal soldiers roamed the seabed, searching for a place where they might climb back into the light of day. They were caught in a state of perpetual animation, doomed to wander the depths.

They won't go wandering aimlessly for long, Glendar or Inkling thought, with a smile full of contempt. He would be forced to join them soon and, maybe someday, he could lead them up out of the sea and exact his revenge on Pael. Maybe someday.

"Dragon guns?" King Jarrek asked, with equal shares of amazement and doubt in his voice.

He was looking at one of the huge crossbow-like mechanisms mounted along the top of Xwarda's outer wall. Men were greasing its spindle with lard and working over its other moving parts with intense scrutiny. The sun was about to set, and there was a great sense of urgency about. The morrow Pael had given them was almost over, and time for preparation was running out as swiftly as the daylight.

"They're rigged to shoot flaming spears from up here," General Spyra said with confidence. "And they're rigged in pairs to loose simultaneously from thirty feet apart, down in the avenues. They launch with a taut wire strung between them."

"A taut wire?" Jarrek asked.

This time there was nothing but doubt in his tone. Who do these people think they are up against? Hadn't he made it perfectly clear what Pael alone was capable of? Had they even been listening?

"Look, sir," the general stopped their casual tour of the defenses, with an irritated scowl. "It comes off like a thirty-foot-wide razor blade, flying at waist height. If those things get through the outer walls, they," he indicated a group of his Blacksword soldiers, "need time to work their way back behind the secondary wall. There are whole sections of the city set to go up in flames, and most of the major avenues are rigged to cut the enemy, literally in two. We've got three Master Wizards, five magi, and three times as many apprentices running around setting pitfalls and fire bombardments all over the place. Those things will wish they never came here if they win their way past this wall!"

To emphasize which wall he spoke of, General Spyra stomped his boot down heavily, and crossed his arms across his wide barrel-keg chest.

King Jarrek nodded away his doubt of General Spyra's preparations. He hadn't meant to rile the man. He still couldn't help but feel that it was all for naught. Pael would level this wall, then the next all by himself, just like he had leveled Castlemont. Xwarda's palace might be spared that fate, but only if Pael chose to spare it. If it were only these undead soldiers they were facing, Jarrek told himself, then no doubt they could find a way to prevail. There was no accounting for Pael though; at least no way that Jarrek knew.

They resumed their stroll along the top of the wall. Jarrek scrutinized a catapult, rigged to sling barrels of oil and pitch into the formations outside the wall. Then he watched as a procession of chanting apprentices, led by one of Targon's underlings, went by. They were sifting chalky, white substances through their fingers, and sprinkling what might have been goose feathers, as they went. The pungent smell of the powder wasn't much better than the reek of the undead wafting up from below.

The long day of sunshine had ripened the air with the smell of them, to the point where a brigade of bucketeers had been put into service, so that the men on the wall might have a place to vomit. Now the evening breeze was helping to dissipate the smell, but earlier in the afternoon, the air had been thick with it.

"General," King Jarrek called out to the busy man, who was now lecturing an archer on the placement of his loose quivers of arrows.

"I would like to prepare, if you'll excuse me. My armor is back at the castle, and I would prefer to be here on the wall when it begins."

"I'll have a man show you the quick way back," Spyra said, with a polite bow.

He pushed his hand back over his balding pate, as if there were still hair there, and let out a sigh of frustration. He then turned to a man who was stacking javelins near one of the dragon guns.

"Gratton, finish this later. For now, King Jarrek has need of a swift return back to the castle."

Turning back to King Jarrek, he added, "I'm amazed that we got the outer portion of the city cleared at all. Gratton here will get you past the choked-up secondary gates by way of an underground passage."

Grattan led him down one of the long ramps that lined the inside face of the outer wall. Jarrek noticed a large wooden section of it that was rigged to collapse, if certain pins were knocked out. A few well-placed hammer blows would leave any attackers who had gained the top of the wall with no way to use the inclines. There were switchback stairways and narrow passages going all over the place inside the wall, though. They led to several levels of arrow slits and murder holes that opened up on the outside.

Bratton led them to a stairway, which went down several flights before it opened onto a wide and busy tunnel. Crates of spears and arrows, along with barrels and boxes, lined the walls, and there were rooms full of other stored wartime goods, opening up off the main artery.

Inside one room, Jarrek saw men suiting up in their armor, like he was about to do. The long, slow process of strapping plate and chained steel to one's body was ritualistic by nature, and none of the men in the rooms were trying to hurry. Further along, a knot of already armored Blacksword soldiers joked over a cup of ale by a keg. One of them recognized King Jarrek and elbowed his fellows into a slight bow of respect.

Xwarda is ready for war, thought Jarrek, but are they ready for Pael?

All in all, the city would be well defended if they were facing any normal foe. Come to think of it, no normal foe really stood a chance of getting past the outer wall, and with all of the city's tunnels and secret passages, a siege would be pointless.

The enemy who was outside the gates was anything but normal, though. The demon-wizard was worse than all those undead men put together. Jarrek hoped they would find a way to best Pael and his death brigade, but honestly, he reserved little hope of any of them making it through this night alive.

It was well past sunset when Vaegon and Dugak came up through a trapdoor in the floor of a wine cellar, which was located in the lower part of the palace. The dwarf quickly emptied the water from the skin he had carried and refilled it from a tapped keg of stout. He offered Vaegon a sip, but the elf declined with a grin. He waited patiently while Dugak gathered his wind and recovered himself, then asked him to lead the way to where Mikahl was housed.

Vaegon had a general idea of where the healers' wing was located, but the castle was huge, and crowded with soldiers and refugees alike. He didn't want to chance getting lost. Dugak drained off his skin in three big gulps, filled it again, and then started off into the castle.

The rooms and corridors were as crowded as the streets were the first day when Vaegon and Hyden came through with the ranger, Drick. These people weren't filthy and poor, though. These were the families wealthy enough to buy their way into the castle, the dukes and lords, the landowners, and the mayor's other favorites, Dugak told Vaegon.

The rumor that the enemy was going to attack at midnight was being passed amongst them all. Both Dugak and Vaegon could tell that it was no mere gossip, so the dwarf quickened his pace.

The wing where Mikahl lay was far less crowded than the rest of the palace, but it was busier than it had been the last time Vaegon looked in on his friend.

Mikahl lay just as he had before, seemingly peaceful and still, save for his labored breathing. Only the rise and fall of his chest, and the slight rasping of his breath, indicated he was still alive at all.

Fighting back a tear, a rare thing for an elf to be doing, Vaegon placed Ironspike atop Mikahl, just like it would be placed if he truly were dead.

The sheathed tip of the blade rested between Mikahl's shins, and the cross-guard sat on his chest, near his heart. Vaegon gently took his friend's hands and grasped them to the leather wrapped hilt. They closed around it reflexively, and a moment of hope flared in the elf, but it was only a fleeting feeling. There was no strength in the grip; it was more like a baby's hand grasping an offered finger.

Mikahl made no further movement. Vaegon stayed for a good while to make sure. He wasn't sure why he did it, but the urge to slide the sheath off of Mikahl's sword was overwhelming. He was blinded with relief when the revealed section of the blade bloomed with brilliant blue light. It shone so brightly that it threw deep shadows across the magically lit room.

He studied his friend for a few more moments, hoping to see some sort of reaction to the reenergized blade's magic, but none came. Feeling disappointed, but not completely so, because the sword had regained some, if not all of its power, the elf let out a long, frustrated sigh.

"I've got to find Hyden Hawk," he said to Dugak.

The dwarf was slouched against the wall, finishing the last of his second bladder of liquor. When he was done, he tossed the skin aside and belched deeply.

"Be off then, elf," he slurred. "I've had nuff runnin an' frighting for one day. I'm old, and tiresome, and fleelin' such."

"And more than a little drunk, it seems," Vaegon smiled, despite his sadness. "Don't let anyone touch that sword."

"That's done, then. Iff'n ya see me lady dwarf, would you send her my way, lad?" Dugak whispered.

Vaegon could only laugh half-heartedly at the dwarf as he started away.

After fighting his way through the crowded hallways and corridors, Vaegon spotted the pixie-man, Starkle, hovering over an aggressive dispute among nobles. The sight of the strange-looking, one-eyed elf coming down the corridor silenced Starkle and drew the notice of the argument long enough for him to get the pixie's attention.

"Can you tell me where I can find Hyden Hawk?" Vaegon asked.

"He's gone into the Tower of Dahg Mahn," Starkle replied.

A hushed whisper rolled out from the epicenter of the crowd. Everyone was focused on them. The sensation alarmed Vaegon, as did the way Starkle made it sound as if the tower he spoke of was on the other side of the moon.

"How do I get there?" the elf asked.

Somewhere in the crowd, a woman said loudly, "The hawkman is lost."

Another voice echoed in agreement, and the murmur turned into an argument of grim speculation over what Hyden's fate might be.

"Only the wizard, Targon, can tell you that," Starkle answered Vaegon's question in an almost regretful tone. "Targon is on the outer wall, making ready for the coming attack."

"Thank you," Vaegon said with a sinking feeling in his chest.

He squeezed into the crowd and, as he parted his way toward the castle's main entryway, the lady's voice echoed in his head: "The hawkman is lost."

It took forever to work his way through all the people crowded in the torch-lit streets between the castle and the secondary wall's open gates. From there to one of the many ramps that led up the inside of the outer wall, wasn't so hard to manage.

The streets between the two walls were occupied primarily by soldiers and the occasional magi. Even though it was dark, it was clear where one should travel, because there was a torch-lined throughway. Everywhere else, there were men and soldiers posted, warning of places that had been booby-trapped to burn.

The physical exertion of his and Dugak's run through the hills was taking its toll on Vaegon's body as he started up one of the ramps. Men were starting to shout above him. It was clear that something was happening. Despite his exhaustion, he ran up the ramp to see what it was. The excitement and fear of the moment filled his body with a rush as he went.

Just as he gained the top of the wall, a roar sounded. The call was terrifyingly deep and Vaegon reflexively crumbled to his knees like a frightened child might.

A bright and thunderous blast, a jet of orange flame, so hot that he felt its heat from over a hundred feet away, shot across the wall. Reflected in its own fire's light was the swooping, plated head and breast of a sparkling, crimson beast. It was so daunting, that it could only be one thing: a dragon. Vaegon thought the Choska demon they had fought in the forest a formidable creature. The dragon that just obliterated everything in the path of its fiery breath could have bitten the Choska in half.

Thunder sounded in the distance, and rumbled closer with unnatural speed. In an explosion of blinding white energy, a not-so-distant section of the outer wall shattered, and crumbled away. The structure underneath Vaegon's feet shook with the force of the blast.

Claret's mighty roar sounded again from somewhere behind the elf. Men screamed and shouted in a cacophony of disorder. The deep thrum of the machines loosing flaming spears sounded from nearby.

Vaegon managed to get back on his feet as an explosion of fire erupted outside the wall. In its flaring light, he saw huge wooden towers rolling up close. The men pushing, and climbing, them seemed oblivious to the flames that threatened and clung to the towers.

A barrel came down out of the darkness into the throng below, and when it crashed, it splashed liquid in a great radius. A moment later, another flaming arrow went streaking from the wall, down into the huge circle, and a yellow-orange fireball erupted with a resounding whump!" The undead soldiers caught in the inferno writhed and twisted on the ground. The ones only partially burned came on as if nothing had happened.

Down the length of the wall, Vaegon saw one, two, no, three of the ladder towers, resting against it. The stench of sun-rotten flesh hung in the night air like a blanket of fog. The undead were swarming the wall already and the battle had only just begun.

Vaegon searched around him in the wildly flaring light. There, some distance away, was a man in a white robe who might be a wizard. Vaegon charged along the top of the wall, heedless of all the arrows streaking by. A man at a crenel screamed and fell back into his path, cursing. An arrow protruded from his head like a horn. Vaegon stopped, and helped the man tear it out of the skin. It hadn't fractured the skull, but had pierced the flesh along his scalp down to the bone. Vaegon took a moment to knit the skin together with his magic, but it was a poor and hasty job.

He saw ahead of him, between him and the robed man he hoped was Targon, was a group of pike-men, trying desperately to push off one of the ladder towers. Another man was throwing buckets full of oil down onto the attackers who were scaling it. As he shot by them, the whole lot of them went up in a torrent of flame.

"Targon!" Vaegon yelled as he came upon the white-robed man.

There was no response. The man was in the middle of a casting and left Vaegon pleading with the air. The desperate elf was about to shake him, when a crackling bolt of yellow lightning shot forth from the man's hands, down into a swarm of undead soldiers who were trying to set yet another scaling ladder against the wall. The base of the wooden structure exploded as Targon's lightning superheated the sap in the fresh green timbers of the construction. The ladder began a slow, tilting arc back into the troops below. When the spell had expired, Targon turned to the elf with clenched teeth and a wild, almost insane, look in his eyes.

"If you can heal, then heal!" The black-haired wizard shouted excitedly. "If not, then grab up a weapon! It's all we can do here until Hyden Hawk returns!"

Vaegon started to ask, "From where?" but a great light began to fill the darkness out beyond the soldiers below. Out in the distance, a globe of reddish-purple energy was forming over the head of a bald, white-skinned figure wearing an ornately decorated black robe. The ball of swirling energy was the size of a wagon-wheel now, but it was growing steadily.

"Pael," Targon hissed, then immediately began casting another spell.

Vaegon looked on with his feet rooted to the plank walk as the dragon passed at the edge of the evil wizard's brightening lavender light. He shuddered with fear when he saw the beast's huge horned head cut through the edge of the illumination. Several long seconds passed before its tail finally disappeared back into the darkness, but all he had really seen was the edge of a wing, a smattering of sparkling scale, and a huge, undefined mass of slithery motion. By then, the sphere of energy building over Pael's egg-like head was the size of a farmhouse. With a throwing gesture, and a psychotic, almost primal yell, he launched the globe into a comet-like arc, high up over the wall. It lit up the whole section of city as it started its way down. It's churning, wavering glow sent the shadows of buildings and towers sweeping around the city like dark swords. It was as if Pael had thrown up a miniature purple sun.

The piercing shriek of the Choska erupted far too close to Vaegon, and he dove to the side just in time to avoid its snatching claws. He managed to pull Targon down by his robes as he went, and the demon beast's razor-sharp talons snatched nothing but air. The city quaked then, and a subsonic, gut-jarring boom effectively eclipsed the night.

The explosion caused by the impact of Pael's comet was white-hot and blinding. Orange-yellow blasts of flame and debris followed as the traps and pitfalls set by the Highwander Mages were triggered prematurely. The sounds of these explosions were merely pops and crackles in the near deaf hum caused by the concussion of Pael's blast. Everything was unnaturally silent now, especially for Vaegon, who could see the mouths of the men around him moving but couldn't hear anything at all.

Targon and Vaegon both blinked away the spots from their vision and realized at the same time that they had no chance now to get themselves back to the secondary wall. Not from where they were stranded. To make matters worse, a nearby section of the wall crumbled away in a rumbling, flickering explosion of silvery white energy. Before the debris even settled, thousands of undead soldiers poured into the gap and swarmed the city.

From somewhere in the sky, the dragon roared out again. When the sound of it subsided, a commanding shout cut through the chaos from behind them.

Targon grabbed Vaegon by the sleeve, and started back toward the ramp Vaegon had come up earlier. Below them, just inside the wall near the breach, a warrior in gleaming, red plate armor had opened up the lane with his flashing sword. The soldiers of the Blacksword were rallying to his side. If they could get down the ramp, they might have a chance to make it back to the secondary wall. A slim chance, but a chance nonetheless. They had to hurry. Already, a knot of rotting undead soldiers were heaving up and over the wall from a siege ladder just beyond the point they had to reach to gain the ramp.

Targon stopped and cast a quick spell. Sizzling blue streaks leapt from his pointed fingers, not at the undead, but at the wood planking just in front of them. Loud thumping divots were shattered out of the wood, sending shrapnel-like splinters and chunks tearing through the decaying flesh of the undead. It slowed the foul things, but didn't stop them completely.

With Targon on his heels, Vaegon reached the ramp just before the enemy. They charged headlong down the slope, but it was too late. Halfway down the grade, a hammer blow had already struck the pins that held the wooden section of ramp in place. The man who had knocked out the pin looked up with regret as the section fell away. It was all Targon could do to keep Vaegon from charging into the now empty space before him. As Vaegon teetered on the edge of a thirty-foot dead fall, the thick, palpable smell of the undead came washing up over them from behind.

Hyden Hawk was brought awake by needle-sharp teeth clamping down on his hand. He opened his eyes in a jolt of sheer terror. He felt hot, wet breath breathing down his neck, and he saw a skull face before him. With a scream, he jumped to his feet. His heart fluttered around his chest crazily.

Talon fluttered down from the tree above excitedly, the hawkling's wing beats adding to the thrumming sensation in Hyden's breast. He nearly bolted off into the endless expanse of grassy hills that surrounded the tree and all its dead visitors. Only the merry laughter of two young wolf pups prancing at his feet stopped him. He recognized them immediately, but it took him a few minutes to calm himself, and wrench himself free of the terror that had overcome him. He had healed their mother in the ravine the same day that Loudin had been torn apart by the hellcat. With his breath finally under control, and his heartbeat steadied, he smiled down and greeted them.

"Where is she?" asked Hyden.

"At the door," one of the pups answered.

"Waiting for us," added the other.

They didn't quite speak with words like the squirrels had, yet what they said was perfectly clear to Hyden. The differences in them radiated with each of their personalities. They were both boys, young adolescent male Ridge Wolves, healthier than most, and fearlessly sure of themselves.

"The Great Mother of the forest said you needed a guide," the one called Rurran said.

"We didn't have to come," his brother Arrah added, "but we wanted to because you saved our mother."

"We would've gone hungry without her." Rurran nuzzled against Hyden's leg. "So you saved us, too."

"It looks like nobody came for them." Arrah nodded toward all the skeletons that ringed the base of the great tree.

"Come, Hyden Hawk, follow us."

"What's that bird's name?"

"Talon," Hyden answered with a hint of amazement in his voice.

Hyden tried to recite the riddle as he followed the two frisky wolf pups, but it was impossible. The two curious youths told him excitedly how they had chased and killed a field mouse and had chased a badger into its burrow. They wouldn't let his attention wander too far from them. Rurran made fun of Arrah for getting scared but admitted that the badger had turned on them fiercely and scared him a little as well.

Not long after he healed her, the mother led them to a cave up on the ridge. They said it had been full of the stink of men, but since they smelled that Hyden had been there, they knew they would be safe.

Their mother had taken a doe, and they had gotten their first taste of red meat. Oh, how they loved meat. It was what they lived for now; they were on an eternal quest for meat. Hyden couldn't help but laugh at them, laugh with them. They were sly, imaginative, and so full of life; the joy that radiated from them was contagious.

It took some time, an hour, half the day maybe, Hyden wasn't sure. The only disruption of the landscape was a small stream-formed pond they came upon. Leaning against a boulder at its bank was another skeleton, this one still garbed in a tattered, scarlet robe. The pups only stopped long enough to drink, then bounded off again. Hyden didn't stop. There was nothing there he wanted to see.

In between the casual banter and excited bursts of thought from the curious young wolves, Hyden pondered why the kingdom folk all called the lovely and polite Queen of Highwander, Willa the Witch Queen. She didn't seem like a witch to him at all. The old crone who had told him and Gerard their fortunes, now that was a witchy woman.

He didn't want to think about how much he missed Gerard. It would only serve to spoil the fantastic mood the wolf pups had put him in, but he couldn't help it. Luckily, they came upon the mother wolf, and his sadness didn't get a chance to take root.

She was lazing beside an ivory door that was set in a golden frame, and standing alone on a hilltop in the midst of the sea of rolling hills.

He spotted a trio of skulls half buried in the thick turf, and a strange crystal staff lay close at hand. Walking around it, Hyden couldn't help but notice that the door looked exactly the same from both sides, but he ignored the odd portal, and the temptation to grab up the staff, and just enjoyed the company of the wolves and his familiar.

The mother wolf commented about the scent of the Great Wolves that lingered on him, and he had to tell the pups the tale of Grrr, and how he had died to save King Mikahl from the Choska. Telling the story made him feel like Berda, and he sort of liked it. The story was sad, yet it made the pups proud of their kind. The mother wolf sensed the underlying urgency burning inside Hyden's spirit, and carefully tempted the pups away with the promise of a fresh meal. Hyden hugged them, and let them lick his face, and then watched with a conflicting well of emotion boiling inside him as they casually trotted away.

Talon was perched atop the golden doorframe, patiently preening his feathers. The door inside the frame was slightly yellowed with age. Carved upon its face was a glade set in a forest of tall pine trees, with mountains beyond them, and a little stream running through the foreground. As he stood there observing it, the trees might have swayed a bit, and maybe the stream gurgled and trickled. He didn't let the hypnotic scene distract him though. His full concentration was on the riddle that the Dying Tree had told him.

"A pyramid, a patterned knock, made up of only ten, if you start from the bottom, I will let you in."

He hoped he had it right. He said it as he remembered it in his head. About the fifteenth time he recited it, the answer came to him. It was so easy it was startling. So simple, and yet so easy to complicate that it was no wonder no one had ever returned from this place.

A pyramid of ten: one, two, three, four, it added up to ten. From the bottom up, it was truly a pyramid: four, three, two, and one.

With confidence, he rapped four times on the door. After a moment's pause, he rapped three times, then two, and finally one. With the final knock, Talon fluttered from the doorframe to his shoulder.

The door creaked open to a room formed of the same white marble as the palace of Xwarda. The circular tower chamber was dark, but the cracks in the ill-fitting window shutters let in the wavering orange glow of some distant raging inferno.

Hyden knew he was in Pratchert's Tower now, for on the floor was a thick, lush rug, made from the skin of an arctic bear. It was the same arctic bear that Pratchert's father had killed for his king a few hundred years ago.

Chapter Fifty-Five

The Choska demon's mouth came snapping down at Mikahl, but a great white bundle of furred aggression leapt into the space between him and those slavering jaws. The teeth still found his flesh, but their force was blunted by the wolf's breaking body. Grrr had sacrificed himself, and the sorrow Mikahl felt for the loss of such a beautiful and proud creature almost outweighed the physical pain he was in.

Almost.

Mikahl suddenly sat up.

The memory of the Choska demon's toothy mouth and Grrr's bloody body faded from his mind quickly. The rush of Ironspike's magic had been charging his blood for hours, and now his veins were full of pure liquid lightning.

In his confused, yet alarmingly aware mind, a chorus of angelic voices called out to him in a symphony of vast and consuming sound. Each voice sang out a different melody of possibility. One voice sang of defenses: of a shield, of armor, of a field of force to hold something in place or deflect an object. He wasn't sure how he understood the glorifying music, but he did. Another voice sang of binding and constraining; another of finding, searching, and summoning. A melody that was rather louder than the rest of the symphony sang of fire blasts and concussive energy, of streaking missiles and lightning strikes. There was healing strength, and a whole percussive section of portal commands, but the sound that flared into a solo melody of its own over the rest of the harmonious din, was the voice that sang of the Bright Horse.

What it was and why it was coming for him, he had no idea, but somehow Mikahl had called out to it, and now it was here.

Queen Willa angrily watched the darkened battle in the distance, from the crenellated roof of the Royal Tower. She wanted to be there amongst her soldiers so badly it was driving her mad.

Andra, General Spyra, and the mayor had forbidden her from joining in the battle at the outer wall. She had a duty to stand guard over the Wardstone and to fight to protect it from those with evil intent. The mother lode of the magical bedrock was more or less under the palace, and she knew that it was what the demon was after.

She doubted that Pael knew it, but one could actually place his hand on the core of the powerful stuff along the bottom of Whitten Loch. Had he known this, he could have just slipped into the castle grounds, gone for a swim, and saved himself a lot of trouble.

There were other ways to access the Wardstone, too. The mine had several passages, some big enough for wagons, but all of those tunnels opened inside or near the inner walls. If she were to go fight, and fall at the outer or secondary wall, it would only invite disaster. She was the last line of defense and it irked her because all she could do at the moment was watch Xwarda burn while her men were being overrun.

A huge section of the city to the west and south was burning away. She stood there feeling helpless, as portion after portion of the outer wall crumbled and was breached. The enemy was inside now. Her soldiers were trying desperately to get back to the secondary wall, but many of them couldn't.

Large groups of her Blacksword army were trapped in the city, fighting for their lives. It was all she could do to keep from rushing out to them on some wild magical spell to join them in their fight. Already, she was using her witchy spells to throw great blooms of light into the sky, so her people could see the airborne enemies and have the chance to defend themselves.

Suddenly, from the ground directly below the tower, a bright light flared. She prayed to all the gods that Pael hadn't blasted the castle proper already.

She climbed up into a crenel, leaned out, and looked down to see what it was, but couldn't gain the vantage point she needed. From behind her, the guardsman who was posted at the roof landing of the stair house indicated a message was being called up. She climbed down, ran to the small hut that kept the weather out of the stairwell, and strained to listen. She couldn't make out the words, but knew they had something to do with whatever it was that illuminated the front of the castle so brightly.

Impatiently, she hurried back over to the edge of the parapet. Whatever it was, it was shining so brightly now that the forested park and the fountain pond were almost fully illuminated, throwing long shadows out and away from the castle. She saw groups of her reserve soldiers crouching from the radiance among the trees and pathways in the park. They were meant to be hidden, and now they squirmed to find the shadows the light cast through the trees.

Instinctively, like a protective mother, Willa scanned the sky, and was relieved to see that neither the Choska nor the dragon was overhead at the moment to see them.

The guard at the top of the landing called out to the queen, repeating the message he'd just gotten from the man posted below. His voice betrayed his hope and excitement.

"The young western king has ridden through half the castle on the back of a winged horse made of lightning and flames!"

She wouldn't have believed it had she not been looking down upon Mikahl and his impossible steed as the words were being spoken.

It wasn't exactly as she had dreamed, but there he was, racing around Whitten Loch on one of the cobbled paths. Mikahl spurred the horse into a leap, shimmering wings of white-hot fire unfurled, and the flaming Pegasus took flight. Raised high in Mikahl's right hand was the radiant sapphire blade of Errion Spightre. She couldn't help but feel the hope his presence brought with it. As if to give that hope substance, as if the whole world rode with the young King of the Realm, dawn broke behind her, lighting the tips of the world beyond the castle's long shadows in hues of coppery gold.

Mikahl cleared the innermost wall, and winged off to join the battle. All of a sudden, all the hope that Queen Willa had just been feeling was sucked from her chest, leaving behind an empty void of despair.

The dawn's light had revealed something else in the sky that glittered. The massive red dragon, bearing a tiny, black-haired feminine figure, came swooping down out of the sky toward Mikahl, like a striking snake. Its intention was so obvious, and its bearing so true, that Willa had to look away.

The young king seemed but a fly to a falcon, compared to the massive beast that was about to consume him with its fiery breath.

Vaegon whirled, using the grip Targon had on his shirt, to help keep him balanced. He had almost fallen into the gap left by the missing section of ramp. Once he was steady, the wizard released him, and began casting a spell.

Vaegon put himself between the handful of stinking attackers and Targon's prone stance, readying himself to protect them both with his bare hands, if necessary. A flurry of friendly arrows came streaking up from below but only served to slow the charge of the undead for a few heartbeats.

Vaegon resolved himself to fight to the death, not an easy resolution to make for an elf. He went to punch the unprotected, half-melted face of one of the things raring to swing a blade at him, but once again, Targon yanked him out of the way.

The undead soldiers had been struck still in their present postures, but their forward momentum carried them ahead. Their bodies were as stiff as statues, and they couldn't stop themselves. Two of them hit the ramp, and slid to a grinding halt. The others went tumbling over them and fell into the dark, crowded area below.

"Push the others over the ledge, elf!" Targon yelled. "The spell will only hold them still a moment more."

With that, he raced off toward the nearest scaling ladder, which was being topped by another wave of undead men.

The wizard had been correct. Even as Vaegon rolled the last stinking corpse over the edge of the ramp, it was starting to move again. Before the thing toppled over, Vaegon put his foot on the man's blade. It was a long sword, like Ironspike, and looked to be well kept. As the man's grip let loose and he fell away, Vaegon took up the blade and charged over to help Targon. He got there too late though, or maybe not getting there quickly enough saved him from meeting the same dismal fate as Targon.

The Choska demon came swooping down out of nowhere at breakneck speed. Its clawed feet latched onto Targon and yanked him screaming up into the darkened sky.

As if it were connected to the Highwander wizard by some unseen magical rope, the siege ladder nearest him was yanked away from the wall. The sudden sideways movement toppled the undead climbers back into the darkness below, like droplets of water shaken from a wet tree. Only two of them had gotten to the top of the now island-like section of wall. Vaegon readied himself to take them on as dawn's light reached up over the mountains behind the castle. He and the two decaying men were alone atop the isolated section of structure. All around them, some sixty feet below, raged a sea of bloody battle and searing flames.

Vaegon hacked, slashed, blocked, and parried with the sword. Moving from one edge of the crumbling plateau to the other, he fought furiously, but the undead neither tired, nor relaxed their blades. Nearly at the edge, the two living corpses split up, thus putting Vaegon in an extremely vulnerable position.

The first blow he took caught him in the arm and split him from wrist to elbow. He dodged, and spun, slinging fat droplets of his elven blood. He even leapt like a tree cat, trying to get out from between them.

The second blow he took caught him on the back of the leg and made him crumple to a knee. He didn't give up, though. He blocked and spun, grinding his kneecap into the rough, gritty surface of the plank and somehow managed to take an undead fighter's leg off at the calf. When he turned to find the other though, after finally narrowing it down to one against one, he saw the undead soldier's sun-tipped blade coming down in a gleaming, speeding arc. All he could do was dive forward, and he did. He heard the whoosh of the steel as it passed a hair's breadth over his scalp, then heard another sound, a harsh, thumping grunt.

He rolled to his back to see where the death blow was coming from, so he might have a chance to avoid it, but what he saw was as baffling as it was terrifying.

The back end and streaming tail of a horse, made of silvery white flames, shot out of his vision. Apparently it swept the undead swordsman from the wall. He started to get up, but the huge red dragon came swooping over him in pursuit of the flaming steed. Its jet of scorching hot flames went right over Vaegon. It was so hot, he felt his skin blister, and could smell his hair burning. He was lucky, he decided. The blast could have easily been a little lower, or he could have made it to his feet. If either had happened, he would have been left a smoldering husk.

He sat up and tried to catch his breath. A few feet away, the one-legged corpse was still trying to come for him. It was pulling itself hand over hand toward him. It was close enough now to chop at Vaegon's legs with its sword, but was intent on getting closer. Its eyes were dark, emotionless, and set in a decomposing face that appeared to be smiling a smile of long, greenish-yellow teeth.

Vaegon gritted his own teeth together and gained his feet. The pain of his wounds brought out a harrowing yell. Sensing the elf's moment of weakness, the undead came scrabbling forward quickly, like some sort of grotesque three-limbed crab. Deftly, but painfully, Vaegon sidestepped and dispatched the undead man, by shoving his blade tip down through its neck and severing its spine.

Vaegon looked out to see what the flaming horse was all about, and barely had time to register that it was Mikahl who sat proudly on its back before the Choska demon caught him full in the chest with both of its razor sharp claws. The last thing Vaegon saw before the world went spinning away in a crazy dizzying whirl was Mikahl sending a wicked blast of magical blue lightning out of the end of Ironspike's blade toward the dragon.

Pael moved through the city by gliding just above the cobbles as he went. The sudden presence of the sword and the bastard squire had scared him, but not enough to deter him from his conquest.

No one dared approach him, though several arrows came at him true. Those were deflected, shattered, or blown off course as if they were merely pieces of straw in the wind. He spied what he was looking for, and hurried his pace until the secondary wall stood before him. There was no gate along this section of wall, only a mercantile neighborhood in the inner city. It had wisely been abandoned in anticipation of his coming.

A large trading house had been built against the wall at the end of the block. Pael wanted to breach the wall here so that the Highwander soldiers might pour out to aid their trapped comrades. His undead were concentrated on blocking and attacking the areas around the gates. He was doing this because of his wish to keep the battle away from the palace itself. The more soldiers who died between the secondary wall and the outer crumble, the less resistance he would meet inside the castle's inner wall. He didn't want to have to tear the palace down to take it. He wanted its splendor for himself.

He stood carelessly in the street and cast his spell. A static pulse of energy left his hands, growing in size and strength as it went. The building smashed flat back against the wall, and then the wall itself exploded in a thunderous shower of brick, glass, and wooden shards.

Satisfied that the breach was large enough, Pael glided away, debating whether or not to kill Mikahl in the air or force him to the ground first. With a long look at the morning sky, he decided on the latter. With a thought, he ordered the Choska to swoop in and relieve the squire king of his magical seat, while Shaella and her pet dragon were still holding his full attention.

Hyden burst up onto the roof of the Royal Tower with a rushing bustle and a few deep heaves of breath. Had Talon not just preceded him, the guardsmen might have blocked his way. Instead, they let the wild-eyed young man pass. Everyone had heard the rumors of where he had gone, and the sight of him gave even the most hardened guard a little pause. Besides the fact that he had just returned from Dahg Mahn's Tower, the look of intensity on his face warned that he couldn't afford to be detained.

"Your Highness, milady, or whatever it is I'm supposed to call you. I need you!"

He took a breath, noticing the wide-eyed expression on Queen Willa's face. He hoped he wasn't scaring her. In his pack was the big, heavy, Night Shard crystal. In his left hand was the elven longbow Vaegon had gifted him, and a full quiver of arrows hung at his hip. He had no idea how long he had been inside the Tower, or how shocking it was to everyone that he had survived it.

"Targon said you could summon him with a spell. I... We need him."

"You survived Pratchert's Tower?" The queen was awed.

"Aye." He nodded.

His air was finally coming back to him, after the incredibly long dash up the four hundred circling steps of her tower. He couldn't help but smile, and push out his chest a bit proudly. He had seen how many men failed Dahg Mahn's trials before him.

"No one has ever returned from beyond that door. By right, the tower, and everything in it, is yours now."

Hyden shrugged, and Talon gave an urgent squawk from somewhere nearby.

"Targon?"

She shook her head slightly at the impossibility of it all; bastard kings with horses of fire, and an unsophisticated, young mountain man who befriended elves and hawklings, and spoke with Great Wolves, winning his way into Pratchert's Tower. The only thing that would be surprising now was if the might of Doon, the dwarven aid promised eons ago, came bursting out of the earth, to answer the call of the horn she had recently blown. She had to chide herself for thrilling like a maiden over the wild hope that Hyden and Mikahl instilled in her. Now was not the time to wonder about how and why, though. It was the time to do.

She cleared her head and cast the spell that would summon her High Wizard, but there was no response. Thinking she misspoke the words in her haste, she spoke them again, only this time in an urgent and commanding sort of way.

The wizard's horribly twisted form flickered on the tiled deck at her feet once, twice, and then the third time it held there. Targon was covered in blood, and his head hung at an odd angle, the neck stretched and canted unnaturally. He was ripped open from groin to chest and part of the cavity where his innards should be, was empty. He looked dead, and was most undoubtedly beyond saving, but his eyes fluttered open when Queen Willa spoke his name.

She knelt by his side, wanting to cradle his head in her arms, but was afraid to cause him pain.

Hyden stood there, slack-jawed. What were they going to do now? Targon was supposed to provide the means of getting the Night Shard all the way to the Seal. The plan was doomed. The High Wizard couldn't even speak to relay his idea to Queen Willa so that she might play his part. Hyden was overcome with a dreadful sense of defeat, but only until he heard the dragon's powerful roar fill the morning sky.

He looked up and saw in the distance a brilliant, winged horse banking an arc through the sky. Its rider sent blazing, blue blasts back at the massive, red-scaled beast, which had just rumbled the morning with its rage. Hyden couldn't say what amazed him most about the scene,

Mikahl riding on a winged horse made of flame or the way the snaky dragon corkscrewed its bulk effortlessly through the air behind him to avoid the attacks.

Forgetting the crystal for the moment, instinct took over. All Hyden knew was that he had to do something to save his friend. He had talked to squirrels, hawklings, and wolves, now it was time to try something bigger. He remembered Vaegon's tale of Pratchert, focused his concentration, and in his head, he called out to the dragon.

Mikahl was certain he had hit the dragon, but it had twisted around his magical bolt of energy like a snake sliding around a tree limb. Its agility in the air was breathtaking. The humongous beast started to snap at him but paused for a heartbeat. It shot past him, and the woman riding on its back shook a strange-looking staff at Mikahl and snarled. She looked angry, and half of her head was bald and scarred. She was screaming something at the dragon now, but Mikahl's attention was suddenly yanked away as his bright horse rose up swiftly on a stall of flurrying wing beats.

The earsplitting crack of the dragon's whip-like tail, as it snapped on the point in space where he had just been, brought his mind back into full focus. When he turned, the dragon was darting off toward the castle, on long, powerful strokes of its leathery wings.

He guided the Bright Horse lower. Vaegon had been trapped on a lone section of wall that was still standing, and he hadn't looked too well. Mikahl had seen all the blood on his arm, and watched as Vaegon's leg had been cut out from under him just before he knocked the attacker off the wall.

To Mikahl's surprise, the elf was no longer up on that part of the wall. In a panic, and with a stomach full of icy dread, he circled lower, around the unnatural plateau, searching the dying battles and the dead for his friend. His stomach lurched, and the ice moved to his bowels when he saw the elf. He clinched his eyes shut, hoping that when he opened them, it wouldn't be Vaegon he saw lying there, half buried in debris, but it was. The patched eye and glittering hair left no room for doubt. Without thinking, he made to land the Bright Horse and try to help unearth his fallen friend, but then realized as he came in closer, that it was only part of the elf he was seeing. The lower half of Vaegon's body wasn't buried. It had been sheared away and was nowhere to be seen.

Sadness tried to envelop him. King Balton, Lord Gregory, and Loudin, not to mention Grrr, and now Vaegon, the only elf in the realm brave enough to stand and fight this evil, had all been killed. How many of the people he loved had to die? Were any of them alive anymore? What happened to Hyden, Talon, and the other Great Wolves? He didn't know, and that fact caused an explosion of determination to burst inside of him.

In response to his growing outrage, the radiance and power of Ironspike's blade magnified, and shifted from blue to purple, then to a heated shade of crimson. He spurred the bright horse up into the heights of the morning sky, until he saw the Choska demon. He was pleased to see it coming at him. In a blinding, white-hot rage, he urged his magical mount into a hard gallop toward the approaching bat-like beast in a sort of midair jouster's charge. He had had enough. It was time to put an end to this madness.

Chapter Fifty-Six

"The dragon comes!" Queen Willa hissed at Hyden Hawk.

"Aye," Hyden replied simply. He gave her a grim smile. "Cast no spells, lady. Tell the guard to stand down."

"You'd let it roast us?" she asked incredulously.

His scowl silenced any further protests, and she did as he bade her.

"Show no fear. When it is upon us, signal me."

He put an arrow to the string of the old elven longbow and started toward the edge of the tower. Once he was at the parapet, he ducked behind a crenel, and set his eyes on the frightened queen. In his head, he spoke to the dragon again.

Shaella screamed at Claret vehemently for flying her away from the one on the fiery Pegasus. Claret just hissed and suffered the anguish of Shaella's punishment through the collar. She was glad Shaella was yelling and screaming at her because it kept Shaella from hurting her with something far worse. Claret also knew Shaella could only do so much punishing while they were in flight, so she went to investigate the strange and powerful voice that was calling her away. It hurt her terribly to go against the will of her rider, but the promises the voice was offering her were too great to be ignored.

Once Shaella saw the Witch Queen of Highwander alone on the tower rooftop, gawking up like a child, she forgot the dragon's punishment altogether and grew excited. She could complete her father's conquest and earn his respect and admiration right here. She urged Claret to take her around the tower. She wanted to keep the witch from reaching the stair house when she snapped out of her stupor and made a run for it.

To Shaella's growing frustration, Claret didn't circle the tower as she had commanded, but the Witch Queen didn't break and run, either. Instead, Claret made as if to land there, at the tower's parapet, but stopped at the last moment, to hold in a slow hover. Shaella shrieked out curses at the dragon as the Witch Queen waved her arms crazily. Shaella cast a spell, and was about to lash out with a blast of static energy, when her heart was stopped dead in her chest. She saw Gerard rise up from behind one of the crenels and loose an arrow directly at her. Realizing it was Hyden, Gerard's brother, and not her lover, she tried desperately to get the dragon to dip, or sway her out of the arrow's path. Nothing happened. She couldn't find the will to draw breath as the steel-tipped shaft came flying at her. She was shocked to feel it only graze her just under the ear, and she felt lucky for a fleeting moment.

In that fleeting moment, another realization struck her. He hadn't meant to kill her. But why?

Between the thumping beats of Claret's wings, she heard the proud and fierce cry of a hawkling as it came shooting down out of the sky, right past her. It didn't stop. It kept diving into the shadows below. Suddenly, she was afraid. She gathered all the persuasive power she could muster, and urged Claret to turn away, but the dragon didn't budge. Then she tried sending the dragon a clearer, more painful command through the collar, but found that somehow, her link with the fire wyrm had been broken. In a panic, she reached to her neck.

Claret felt the connection sever and roared out with delight. The menacingly triumphant sound was so loud and powerful that the Royal Tower itself trembled as if it were afraid.

Shaella began to cast a spell. Hyden saw this, and loosed a second arrow at her. This one struck the staff she held, just a finger's breadth above her hand. The thumping impact of it caused her to lose her concentration and forget the spell she was casting.

"Spell the rider!" Hyden called out to Queen Willa. "Bind her, if you can."

At once, Willa did as she was told. The presence of the dragon had her in such a state of terror that if Hyden had told her to jump off the tower she might have done it.

Half a heartbeat later, invisible ropes lashed around Shaella and drew tight. Her arms and her staff were pulled hard against her breasts. When she tried to voice a protest, she found that her mouth was gagged as well. She could do nothing but glare at Hyden as he motioned for the dragon to land.

Willa backed away in utter fear. Claret's great bulk took up three quarters of the tower top, and that was with the dragon sitting upright, and the entire length of its long, thick tail, dangling over the parapet. The tower itself seemed to groan with the weight of her. A glance at where the stair guard had been revealed only empty space. Willa couldn't blame the man. Running from a beast that had slitted yellow eyes bigger than wagon-wheels and teeth as long as a grown man's legs couldn't really be considered dereliction of duty, could it?

In her terror, Willa marveled at the way the morning sun reflected brilliantly off the dragon's palm-sized scales and turned them golden; the way heat shimmered and radiated off of its body, as if it were a great furnace. A fluttering of little wings, Talon's wings, caught her eye. The bird had something clutched in its claws. It struggled to carry the object up and over to Hyden. He took the offering and smiled deviously. Talon then flew up and landed on the half-bald head of the dragon rider. He perched there and puffed out his feathered chest as proudly as if he were a dragon himself.

Hyden fumbled with the object Talon had delivered to him. After a moment, he had wrapped Shaella's collar around his wrist, and tied it off, using his teeth. At once, the mighty dragon lowered its head, and extended a fore claw out, to form a crude stair step up to its back. At that moment, Queen Willa had no doubt that Hyden Hawk was destined to be a wizard of Dahg Mahn's caliber, if not something even greater. It never occurred to her that Hyden had taken the Dragon Queen's dragon without using any form of magic whatsoever. All he had used were his wits and his skill with the bow. Talon had done the rest.

Hyden shouldered Vaegon's bow, climbed onto the dragon's back, and sat behind Shaella. He gave Willa a confident smile and sent Talon down to land on her shoulder.

"Hold off the demon-wizard as long as you can," he called down to her.

He reached back and patted the Night Shard in his backpack. "If this works, he'll be nothing but a plain, old wizard when I'm done."

With that, the dragon leapt into the air and veered sharply away to the west. On wing beats that made the very air shudder, it shot off at an uncanny speed, and disappeared into the distance.

After Pael saw Shaella and her dragon winging away to the west, he vented his anger on the outer city. He thought abandoned him.

He cast a spell that buckled the earth away from him, like ripples from a pebble thrown into a pond. A great circle rose and fell, crumbling all in its path as it went. Buildings were leveled and horses and men were thrown or crushed. A large portion of the secondary wall, and the inner city beyond it, fell into ruin. For a few moments, the rumbling quake seemed to stop the whole battle. Pael stood, looking up from the epicenter of the destruction. He was seething. His normally slick white head was aglow with rage, and his arms flailed about like some mad conductor as he cast spell after spell after spell.

In the air, Mikahl was in pursuit of the Choska. The big, black demon could barely stay ahead of the flaming bright horse. From the ground, Pael sought to change the odds a bit.

Several black clouds formed around the angry wizard. Three wyverns took shape, and a razor-tusked beast that looked somewhat like a wild boar, but was as big as an ox, snorted and stomped behind him. At once, the wyverns took to the air. The tusked beast charged off through the rubble-strewn streets in search of men to kill.

Pael's arm shot forth, pointing up into the sky, and a sizzling bolt streaked from his fingertip, brighter than the daylight. It took Mikahl by surprise and sent him tumbling through space, away from the dying flames of his bright horse.

At once, the Choska demon dove away from its pursuer and swooped to land beside its master. Pael leapt up onto its lowered neck, and together, they rose back up into the sky.

For a few long heartbeats, Mikahl fell, like a sack of grain thrown from a window. He had almost let go of Ironspike but somehow managed to avoid that fatal mistake. With its magical symphony still in his head, he managed to recall the Bright Horse into being. The fiery Pegasus reformed between his legs and caught his fall, but it took a moment to get reoriented with the world, and in that time, Pael and the Choska gained position on them.

It had taken only seconds for Pael to turn the tables on Mikahl. The chaser became the chased. It was all Mikahl could do to hold on as the demon wizard's pursuit forced him to shake away the cobwebs Pael's lightning had burned into his brain. He needed to think of a way to avoid being overtaken. He could feel the evil behind him. It was a nauseating, icy feeling that grew with the proximity of the wizard on his heels. The bright horse shot left and then right, into a sharp, banking turn. Suddenly, something in Mikahl's brain fell into place.

The thing called Pael, on the back of the Choska, was the dark enemy that sent the hellcat and the wyvern. It was Pael who King Balton had sent him away from. It was Pael who poisoned his king and misled Prince Glendar all those years. It was Pael who caused Lord Gregory, Loudin of the Reyhall, Grrr, and Vaegon to die. All along, it had been Pael. He knew it now. His blood surged past the white-hot simmer it had previously been and turned into a violent boil. Ironspike's radiant glow changed with his anger into a blinding, silvery beacon in the sky. He was no longer the chased. He was in control now. He was leading Pael out past the city's outer wall, away from the populace. If Pael was pursuing him, Mikahl knew he wasn't in the city wreaking havoc.

Mikahl closed his eyes and let the bright horse gallop through the sky by its own head. He searched Ironspike's symphony for what he might need, what he might use, to bring Pael down. The words of King Balton, the words of his father, echoed like timpani drums in time with the harmonies in his head. "Think. Then act! Think. Then act! Think. Then act!"

King Jarrek fought like a hero to let the soldiers of the Blacksword get inside the secondary wall. He had almost gotten trapped in the doing. Then General Spyra had charged out with a group of cavalry, and with the brilliant use of their long pikes, won the red-armored Wolf King and his group free of the undead that surrounded them.

King Jarrek had no sooner gotten himself to safety, and had his wind back, when he heard the shouts that the secondary wall was breached to the north. He was getting too old for this sort of thing. His bones ached and his muscles sang. He decided to go find Queen Willa and see if he might help her find a way to survive the coming madness. These men were brave, true, and fighting with all they had in them, but Jarrek didn't even dare hope that any of them would survive.

Pael, his Choska demon, and now several slick, black, acid-mouthed wyverns, seemed to be everywhere. He wasn't sure he could even survive the trip back to the castle. At least the dragon had fled. He was curious to know what happened at the top of the Royal Tower. They all thought that Queen Willa had been lost until she stood atop a crenel and gave the official signal to close and lock the secondary gates.

As King Jarrek approached the inner gate, the gate to the castle grounds, half a hundred bowmen leaned down and took aim at him. The Gate Captain had a panicky look about him.

"Remove the helm!" he ordered.

King Jarrek did so and recognized the fear in the captain's eyes when he scowled up into them.

"Gates! Open the gates!" the captain screamed. "Go Tuck! Go Walden! Find the red-armored impostor! He might be after the queen! Hurry! Hurry! Hurry!"

Jarrek gave the Gate Captain a puzzled look, then squeezed through the slight crack of the still opening portal, and wasn't surprised when it started closing just as soon as he was clear. Save for the large formations of soldiers waiting to fortify the wall, the fountain pond area and the forested park around it seemed as peaceful as could be.

Looking back up at the scared captain, Jarrek called out. "What is it, man? What's got your gunkin?"

"He was clad in red armor as you are," the stricken captain replied. "I only now noticed the wolf skull on your helmet. Nobody questioned his cause because we thought he was you. I should've known he wasn't right. He had the smell of death upon him something awful. I thought it might just be from the battle, but now he's gone to the castle. He might try for the queen."

Both of Jarrek's Redwolf guardsmen had been on the wall with the archers when the battle had begun, and neither of them had been wearing their heavy plate armor. Jarrek had seen that whole section of wall blasted away. It was impossible for either of them to have come through here wearing their Redwolf armor. An excited tingle of hope started to creep into his heart, but then, just as quickly, the feeling turned to concern. "The smell of death upon him," the captain had said.

At once, King Jarrek bolted after Tuck and Walden. He ran as fast as he could in his loud, awkward-fitting shell. He didn't relish the idea of facing Brady Culvert in battle, even if the young man was already dead, but he would. He'd be damned if he'd let one of his men, one of his best friend's sons, leave a taint upon the honor of his elite guard. It saddened him to think that the lad had been turned into one of Pael's undead things, and he found he had to swallow back a lump and blink away the moisture from his eyes as he ran.

He caught up with them on an otherwise empty stretch of tree-lined cobble path and was only surprised by the smell of the youngest and most fearsome of his Redwolf guards.

The young man looked half dead, but he wasn't. He held his helmet in his hands, and stared blankly at the two guardsmen, who had drawn their swords and cornered him against the trees. His armor was filthy with gore and caked blood and there was no sword in his scabbard. He looked haggard, and pale under all the grime. His bloodshot eyes were rimmed crimson, and sunken deep into their sockets. He made no move to attack, nor did he defend himself. When King Jarrek stepped up to him, Brady began to cry and crumbled to his knees, sobbing. The young man only smelled of rotten flesh. Jarrek had no doubt that Brady was still alive. What he had come through to get there, or how he had gotten through the ranks of undead and ended up at the castle's inner gates, Jarrek couldn't begin to guess, so he didn't try. He helped the boy to his feet and commanded the two gatesmen to bear the stench, take a place on each side of Brady, and escort him into the castle to be cleaned up and cared for.

"It's all right now, Brady," Jarrek said the fatherly lie to comfort his longtime friend's obviously distraught son. "It's going to be all right now."

Jarrek just wished he could find a way to believe the words himself.

When Mikahl suddenly turned, pointed his sword at Pael, and let loose a pulsing magical blast, it took the demon-wizard by surprise. The energy hit Pael full in the face, sending him spinning head over boot heels, off the Choska. The winged demon was forced to dive quickly to avoid a collision with Ironspike or Mikahl's Bright Horse. Pael righted his tumble and came to a hover in midair. His hands churned with blinding speed the makings of another spell. Mikahl listened to the symphony of the sword and made ready. It pleased him, and gave him hope, to see blood dripping from the wizard's nose and mouth.

The streak of white energy that shot from Pael's hands struck the magical shield before Mikahl with violent force. Though it brought him or his flaming steed no direct harm, it drove them through the air with tremendous power. When the spell subsided, Mikahl returned the attack, and once again, Pael was caught in a moment of shock.

The demon-wizard couldn't believe that Mikahl survived the amount of raw energy he had just released at him. Pael's own magical shield came up a heartbeat too late and he found himself being yanked toward the ground as if by a spring-loaded cable.

The Choska swept by Mikahl so close, he felt its claws graze across his skin. He twisted and stabbed at the beast with Ironspike's white-hot blade but only found thin air.

Pael somehow undid what the sword had done to him just before he slammed into the earth. He hesitated there, just above a litter of charred, mangled bodies, trying to gather his composure. The Choska quickly flew around and under him. Once he was back on it and situated in a riding position, he twisted, turned, and scanned the skies. To his maddening surprise, the squire and the flaming Pegasus were nowhere to be seen.

For the first time since he had absorbed Shokin's power into himself, Pael found that he was concerned, if not a little afraid. He directed the Choska back toward the city, cautiously searching the sky as he went. He spat thick, dark blood from his mouth with disgust as his eyes darted frantically to and fro. Over there, then below him, he craned his neck and twisted to see if he was being pursued now. He didn't like this anymore. He should disappear, too, he told himself. He could do that quite effectively, but not just yet. He wanted to make a lasting impression on the battlefield so that his presence would remain fresh in the mind of the Witch Queen, and every single one of her Blacksword soldiers.

The Choska circled high and then came down, streaking across the front of the castle. As he passed them, Pael blasted away the huge stained glass depictions that had shown over Xwarda for centuries. Like an explosion of jewels, millions of glittering but deadly fragments exploded out across the forest park, into and over Whitten Loch, and out into the inner city where battle upon battle still raged wildly. Then Pael came around again. The Choska was flying at breakneck speed. From its back, Pael sent a wicked jet of wizard's fire out into the park. A huge swathe of trees turned from green to brown, then to black, before erupting into bluish-green flames. Smoke filled the air and nearly a quarter of the park was ablaze in demon's fire.

Pael laughed maniacally at the potency of his display and reveled in the rush of all his demonic power. Already, he had all but forgotten Mikahl and the Bright Horse. It was a costly mistake.

From out of nowhere, Mikahl shot across the Choska's path. Pael ducked, and let his magical shields protect him. After they passed, it took the wizard a few long moments to realize that most of the Choska demon's head was no longer attached to its body. Ironspike had not only decapitated the creature, it had taken its soul.

The body was streaking toward the earth now on twitching, muscle-locked wings while the head tumbled away in a spray of thick, black blood. Pael, now fully aware of the situation, transported himself away just before the crash. The lifeless, bat-like hulk hit the fountain lake in a splashing tumble of wings and claws. It skipped across the water like a poorly thrown stone, then crunched to a stop against the retaining wall, near the swan shelter.

Queen Willa stood speechless, looking down from her tower top as a cheer rang through her troops and the dark blood of the winged demon-beast slowly turned the clear pristine water of Whitten Loch a deep, inky black.

When she looked out at the many battles being fought across the inner city, she saw the afternoon sun play upon the millions of tiny colored fragments of stained glass. Such beauty amid such horror, she thought. The dead, the dying, and the ones who refused to fall, attackers and defenders alike, hacking, stabbing, and killing each other in the middle of a field full of sparkling jewels.

As if in agreement with the sick irony of the scene before them, Talon cooed from her shoulder and bobbed his feathered head.

Chapter Fifty-Seven

Throughout the remainder of the day, Pael appeared at various places around the city. He never stayed more than a moment or two at any given place, but where there was Pael, there was destruction. Unconcerned now with preserving any part of the inner city or its ancient structures, and seething with anger and fear, Pael began to methodically decimate Xwarda.

In the southern section of the city, a few hundred Blacksword soldiers finally corraled large group of the undead, until Pael came. Where the men were driving back the undead, buildings on each side of the street exploded. Brick, stone, splintered wood, and glass shards cut into their numbers. Pael was gone before the dust settled, leaving nothing but a bloody, pulpy mess on the cobbles.

A fresh battalion of Highwander soldiers, who had just been sent forth from the castle to help defend the breach Pael's earlier quake had caused, met the demon-wizard at their destination. Lightning flared from his fingertip. One, then two, then four, then eight of the Blacksword soldiers fell. Again, Pael sent forth a shocking blast, and another, until the way was filled with nothing but smoking corpses. A moment later, Pael was somewhere else.

A brutal swath of bright, static energy evaporated an entire block full of men and buildings. A jet of wizard fire sent a group of cavalrymen's horses stampeding blindly through the cobbled streets with smoldering flanks and sizzling manes. Anything that got in the way was trampled and most of the riders were thrown and forgotten.

In the northern section of the city, a hundred or more Highwander men laid in a slumped formation, spelled asleep, in the middle of the avenue. The huge, boar-like creature Pael summoned was having a feast on their still living flesh. The men were powerless to stop it, and when the Hell Boar's powerful teeth dug into them and broke the spell they were under, it was too late.

In the east, a meteor-like sphere of flaming death crashed into the mercantile portion of Xwarda. More than four square blocks were leveled and almost a thousand men were crushed, pummeled, or roasted.

In his rage, the demon-wizard was seemingly unstoppable.

Mikahl, who was still flying on the back of the Bright Horse, tried as hard as he could to catch Pael in the act. He raced across the city, from disaster to disaster, but was always just a bit too late to spot the wily demon-wizard. He dispatched a wyvern and crumbled a horde of undead soldiers to the ground with a pulsing blast from Ironspike's blade. He headed off a flank attack of Pael's dead men and saved a few hundred Blacksword soldiers from being surprised. He killed an uncounted number of undead soldiers, sending their tainted souls into oblivion with a touch of his blade, but he couldn't catch Pael.

Finally, as the sun began to set, he decided there was only one thing left for him to do. He landed the Bright Horse in the center of the destruction Pael's earlier quake had caused and dismounted.

At once, the flaming Pegasus was gone. Mikahl wobbled on unsteady legs but quickly mastered himself. He called out, taunting Pael, using every insult he could think of. He even sheathed Ironspike so he was momentarily unprotected by its magic. Standing there in his gore-saturated robe, he felt for the first time the intense brunt of the pain that Ironspike's magic had been masking from him. It was excruciating. His body hurt so badly he could barely think, but he continued to call out the demon-wizard, man to man. Unprotected, and reeling from the unhealed injuries the Choska had inflicted on him back in the forest, he waited. It was all he could think to do.

As they raced across the continent on Claret's back, the bindings Queen Willa had placed on Shaella began to unravel. Hyden had to physically wrap an arm around her waist and keep his other hand over her mouth to keep her from spelling him. Sometime in the middle of the night, he had Claret land them in an aromatic pasture, full of knee-high grazing grass. The hoof-beating rumble of a retreating herd of animals faded from them, leaving only the sounds of the insects and the dragon's heavy, slightly winded, breathing. The half moon high overhead tinted the swaying carpet of grass beneath them with a yellowish light.

Hyden wrestled Shaella from her seat, and shoved her from the dragon's back. She landed in an awkward heap, still clutching her staff as if it held the world in its crystal headpiece. As soon as she gained her feet, she began to cast a spell, but Claret's big, horned head and toothy maw curled around and loomed in the darkness beside her, reminding her of the reality of her situation. The casting of her spell stopped immediately. It was all Shaella could do to keep from retching from the sulfuric stench of the dragon's hot breath. To her credit, she showed no fear whatsoever, only furious indignation over what she had let happen.

"I'll ask you only once," Hyden said down to her. "If you tell the truth, I'll leave you to your fate. If you lie to me, then Claret here will gladly roast far more than the rest of the hair from your head. Am I being clear?"

Shaella didn't respond. She turned and glared at Claret's huge, unblinking yellow eye. She knew that through the link of the collar, the dragon could tell Hyden anything it knew. She cursed herself for carelessly sharing her feelings with the beast. Then, with a scrunched face, she looked back up at her lover's older brother.

Her face was tight and dark with emotion, save for the pale scar that ran down the one cheek like a tear drop.

"Is he alive?" Hyden asked. "Did you betray him? Did he go into that dark place? Is he still alive?"

Having Hyden place the blame on her caused her to stiffen, but his brotherly concern for Gerard softened her resolve more than just a little bit. If she truly loved Gerard, or what was once Gerard, then she couldn't lie to his flesh and blood about what happened to him.

"The Gerard you know is dead, but I love what he is now, no less than I loved him before." Her answer was no lie, and through Claret, Hyden knew it.

"What has he become, then?" Hyden didn't understand.

"Ask the dragon," answered Shaella coldly. "Between my father's insane magic and the effects of the dragon's yolk, what's left of Gerard is barely alive and trapped in the Nethers."

She turned and strode stiffly off into the darkness, wiping the tears from her face as she went.

Hyden had to stop Claret from blasting her with dragon's fire. He wasn't sure if it was the tears she shed, the look in her eyes, or the knowledge of the depth of her love for Gerard, but he felt in his heart that she had been truthful, and he didn't want to kill her.

She truly had, and still did, love his little brother. Part of Hyden wanted to kill her, and if Mikahl ever recovered from his injuries, he would probably never forgive him for not doing so. But what's a Dragon Queen without a dragon? There would be time to deal with her later. He was about to be forced to seal his brother into a blackened void full of demon kind, evil spirits, and all other manner of dark things. If Mikahl couldn't understand the show of compassion, then so be it.

Gerard had loved Shaella. Through Claret's memory he had seen the last moments of his brother's life. His brother had loved her as well. How could he possibly kill her?

As Claret lifted back into flight, Hyden tried to clear the mess from his head. He knew what he had to do when they got to the Seal. If he could figure out how to dissolve the Night Shard into the carved symbols, he would have to do it. There was no sense in tormenting himself over it. With a deep sadness gnawing at his heart, he closed his eyes and sought out Talon's vision.

Outside of the city's innermost wall, the wall that protected the palace itself, the city of Xwarda was a smoldering ruin. The moonlight, the wavering illumination from the scores of burning structures, and the thick smell of rotting corpses, lent the place a hellish air. The shrill, repetitive call of a wyvern, and the horrific pleas of a dying man only added to that sense. It was no place for the living, and every man who still drew breath was doing his best to retreat to the pseudo-safety of the castle grounds.

All along the top of the castle's defensive wall, men raced to and fro. Archers held off the undead while groups of exhausted soldiers retreated in from the city to the castle grounds. The Highwander magi used fire, smoke, and a plethora of illusions to confuse the dark enemy, so that as many men as possible could get inside the gates.

The castle's wall remained intact, but it didn't give the feel of safety to those behind it anymore. Their final defensive fortification was the oldest, and least formidable of the three protective walls that ringed Whitten Loch and the palace. The other two walls had not just been breached, but had been pulverized, leveled in some places. Everyone knew it was only a matter of time before this wall fell as well.

From above, Queen Willa surveyed the destruction. She slowly walked the circumference of the tower roof, trailing a hand idly along the tops of the crenels. To the south, the battle raged on. She could see the tiny glints of firelight reflected from the swords and armor in the streets and along the alleyways, between the castle's wall and what was left of the secondary wall. Any minute, those men would get the order she had just given to retreat to the inner grounds. She hoped they lived long enough to find a way back in.

To the east, the devastation of Pael's meteoric fireball stood out amid the otherwise unharmed section of mercantile shops and residences. At the eastern gates of the inner wall, an isolated scuffle between a hulking, boar-like beast and a knot of men raged under the gate tower's bright lanterns.

To the north and west, large groups of the undead were gathering in the shadows thrown by the burning structures and reorganizing their numbers. Just inside the secondary wall to the south, the ruin was empty, save for a lone figure, robed in dirty white. Willa could barely make it out as a person.

He was standing in the center of what was nothing more than a huge circle of rubble. Upon seeing this, Talon leapt from Willa's shoulder, and with widespread wings, glided down through the air, away from the tower. The sudden action from the long-still bird startled the troubled Queen.

King Jarrek harrumphed his presence from the top of the stair landing. He had been standing a few steps down inside the boxy shelter for a few long minutes so he could catch his breath before engaging Queen Willa. After fighting in the field all morning and tending to Brady Culvert in the afternoon, the long journey up the stairs had taken its toll on him. He wasn't a young man. When she turned and greeted him with a tired and obviously forced smile, his exhaustion was forgotten, and he was taken aback by her plain, natural beauty.

She was the first pleasant sight his eyes had fallen upon in what seemed like forever. The vision of his mother and his betrothed, mangled in the collapsed ruin of the Ladies' Tower back in Castlemont, quickly erased any mirth or admiration he might have started to feel. He moved his eyes from hers quickly, lest she see the sorrow and lack of hope he suddenly felt. His gaze landed on the cloak-covered body lying dead in the middle of the roof. He started to comment but thought better of it.

She understood his silence and walked back to the southern-facing edge of the parapet. She was relieved to see the men there fighting their way back toward the inner wall. Her orders had been received and relayed. Seeing that the retreat had been called, she turned to Jarrek.

"The word is that you saved a lot of our men."

He shook his head as if he didn't want to speak on the matter, as if it had been nothing.

"You're calling them in, then?" he asked tactfully.

"Something like that." She met his gaze.

"The hawk boy flew off on the dragon. He said when he does whatever it is that he's going to do, Pael will lose some of his demonic strength."

She made a strange, deliberate face, and forced back the feelings of hope that were brewing as she spoke the words.

"He said to hold off Pael as long as we can." She indicated the castle grounds around and below them with a sweep of her hand.

"We can hold out strongest here, where I can access the Wardstone. Spread out about the city, the wizard is picking us apart."

"You're putting all of your eggs into a single basket," Jarrek said, but not in any disapproving or judgmental way. "Does this Hawk Boy's word hold such merit?"

"I can only hope." She turned to face away from him.

A sudden, blue radiance caught her attention, out where the lone, white-robed figure had been standing.

"The power of the Wardstone is strong here, and I can—" Her voice cut off suddenly as she took in a sharp audible breath.

It was Mikahl. The sapphire glow was Ironspike's blade, and the demon-wizard Pael had just appeared behind him.

"We were all destined to bow before that one," said Willa absently, her attention held raptly on Mikahl.

"Aye," Jarrek agreed.

He leaned out between two crenels to get a better look and cringed in horror when he saw a swirling, emerald column of wizard's fire erupt and consume Mikahl.

Pael fumed at the audacity of the idiot squire. How dare he call him out as if he were just a drunkard at some piss poor tavern? Pael took his time, studying the situation and terrain long and hard from afar, before he made his move.

He was too wise to be baited with mere insults. Was the boy even capable of setting a trap? He wondered. Was he using himself as bait? No. He was only an adolescent young man, driven by a need for vengeance, blinded by youth and inexperience. Pael let him sit, let him wonder and wait. Pael let him relax and tire. He let the white-hot fire that fueled Mikahl's earlier rage die out. Then, and only then, did Pael attack.

With a crackling pop, Pael appeared a few paces behind Mikahl. He had the fool squire and he knew it. He had the advantage of total surprise. He had the spell's last word on the tip of his tongue and Errion Spightre was still resting in its sheath on the boy's back. He grinned as he started to speak the final syllable that would cause wizard's fire to consume the foolish bastard-born whelp, but suddenly, something he could never have accounted for came tearing into his face.

The fluttering of wings, the screeching call of a bird of prey, and razor-sharp claws digging into his eyes, all combined to steal the word from Pael's lips. The bright blue glow of Ironspike's blade filled his other eye. He shrieked out in pain and batted the hawkling from his face with a brutal swipe of his hand. The pain was terrible but, through clenched teeth, he managed to speak the word that released his spell. Warm liquid from his ruined eye ran down his face as the squire was suddenly engulfed by his magical jade inferno.

The wizard's fire erupted around Mikahl, hot and sticky, sizzling his robe and his flesh. Through the sword, he called forth the melody of magical armor. Though it put a layer of protection between his skin and the blaze, it didn't keep the heat from affecting him.

Oh, how he was thankful for Talon's intervention. Had the hawkling not bought him the time to draw the sword, he would have surely been charred to the bone. Hearing no obvious way to extinguish the fire in the symphony that raged in his mind, he simply stepped back, out of its confined radius. He was relieved that the bulk of the flames stayed where they were. Only small, dripping tendrils clung to his magical shell, and they expired as he moved around to meet the demon-wizard.

He was surprised to see the chunk of gore hanging from Pael's eye socket. Talon had destroyed one eye, and several thick streaks of blood trailed from the wizard's cheeks where they had been ripped open by Talon's claws. Pael himself was seething. He blocked the sparkling swing of Ironspike's blade seemingly effortlessly, and then discharged a hot, crimson pulse directly into Mikahl's chest.

Mikahl went stumbling, his breath knocked out of his lungs as if by a hammer blow. While he reeled to catch his balance, he saw the wizard striding to kick at something. It was Talon. The bird was half-stunned and trying desperately to flap itself into the air, unaware of the boot closing in on it. It sickened Mikahl to see it, and he called out a warning, but the gesture was futile. A clump of feathers swirling to the ground where the bird had just been was all he could see now. The look of satisfaction on Pael's ruined face confirmed he hadn't missed his target. As Mikahl regained his balance, another hot crimson blast came at him, then another. Once again, he was slammed full in the chest. It was all he could do to keep a grip on his sword's hilt as he was sent flailing by the powerful, static pulses.

Hyden Hawk actually felt the swiping blow Pael had thrown to get Talon off his face. It had stunned the bird's vision, throwing Hyden back to his present situation on Claret's sleek, undulating back. That glint of a vast body of water reflecting the moonlight up from far beneath them and the feel of the wind buffeting him caused a moment of panic, but he recovered. He had been so attuned to Talon's senses while helping Mikahl that he had forgotten himself. He felt satisfied that Talon had done some real damage to the demon-wizard. He was also pleased and relieved that Mikahl was alive and his sword was alight with power.

What the foolish, castle-born goof had been doing standing out there in the open in nothing but a filthy white robe, Hyden couldn't understand. He shifted back into Talon's vision and saw nothing but flaring green rocks and the wild shadows they cast. The hawkling's mind was full of confusion. Then he heard Mikahl's voice calling out to him. Was it a warning? The impact of

Pael's hard leather boot into Talon's frail body suddenly rocked Hyden so hard, he nearly fell from the dragon's back. Unconsciousness overtook him completely this time.

Through the link of the collars, Claret felt Hyden Hawk go limp. She pulled a wing stroke to keep him in his seat, and then put forth that much more effort to get them to her lair. She would do anything for Hyden, anything that she could. Through the link of the collars, she read his intentions and she knew as soon as this most important deed was finished, he would take her collar off and set her free. He hadn't been lying to her. He would set her free, and once he did so, she could find a place far away from the reaches of man. There, she could make another nest, and finally hatch her remaining egg.

The castle's protective walls, being not nearly as tall as the great outer walls had been, were quickly overtaken. The magi, even the novices and apprentices, cast spell after spell, creating barriers of thorn or fire to try to stop the undead soldiers, but it wasn't enough. In a dozen or more places, Pael's rotting men were gaining the castle grounds in hordes. Even with the magnifying power of the magi's proximity to the Wardstone to help fortify and intensify their spells, the dead came.

The soldiers of the Blacksword fought tooth and nail to defend the castle. They were relentless and brave. Crowded in and facing impossible numbers, they couldn't win the advantage. For every undead that came over the wall, half a handful of Highwander men were killed or injured.

Like maggots on the carcass of a rotting varmint, the dead army swarmed the breaches and fought their way into the grounds. Queen Willa drew upon the power of the Wardstone and sent silvery witch fire and wicked blasts of static energy down upon them, but she could only do so much. Not only was she exhausted, but her own men were down there, and she didn't want to hurt them with her attacks. Through the trees of the forest park, from the roofs of the castle's lower outbuildings, and around and through the black, blood-stained waters of Whitten Loch, the undead came.

Eventually, they overtook the fierce Blacksword soldiers and gained the castle's entry. A sleek, black-scaled wyvern soared through the space where the depiction of Ironspike's forging had once been. From the top of the Royal Tower, King Jarrek urged Queen Willa to come away while she still could. She wouldn't hear of it.

The screams of the people inside the castle echoed from below now. The wyvern was loose among them. It was all Willa could do to keep from collapsing in despair. She knew that if something didn't happen soon, Xwarda was lost. If Pael took Xwarda, it wouldn't be long before he found a way to use the Wardstone. She was sworn to fight to protect the Wardstone to the end. She couldn't leave, but she could send the thousands of people hiding in the tunnels below on to Jenkanta where they would at least have a chance to escape Pael's wrath.

"Go," she said to King Jarrek sternly. "The people who win free will need strong men to help them survive."

"I cannot leave you here unguarded, lady," he replied simply. "I will not."

"You're a chivalrous fool," she told him. "Call down the order to evacuate the refugees, then. Tell them to collapse the tunnels as they go."

Chapter Fifty-Eight

Before Pael could hit him with another bone-jarring crimson pulse, Mikahl rolled, and twisted to his feet. He still had no breath in his lungs and his head was spinning, but he knew that if he stood still, he was finished. Another hot red blast streaked toward him and, this time, he knocked it away with Ironspike's blade, but he was still starting to panic. He knew he couldn't keep this up for very long. His senses were already fading into blackness. He needed air badly.

Pael sent another of his pulses. Mikahl tried to deflect this one with the sword, but his oxygen-starved lack of coordination made the attempt futile. The blast hit him, but it was only a searing graze, not a blunt impact. He was lucky. He would have taken the blow full on had his body not involuntarily hiccupped and sucked in a much needed gulp of air.

He couldn't enjoy his body's relief because Pael was already blasting at him again. Twisting out of this missile's way, Mikahl gulped in another breath and charged the demon-wizard. Instead of relying on magic, he rode his instinct, and brought on a full-on physical assault with his sword. He slashed, spun, hacked, and thrust, leaving Pael no choice but to forget his attack, and defend himself.

For several long moments, Pael thought he might not survive the attack. The blade only had to touch him for his demon essence to be vanquished. Even worse, he could barely see out of his good eye, and it was next to impossible to tell where the bluish-lavender-colored blade was coming from next. Only when Mikahl paused to glance down at the sprawled form of the hawkling, lying limp amid a pile of broken glass and splintered wood, did the wizard get the chance to make a move.

Pael leapt into the air and came to a hover just out of Ironspike's range. He sent a crackling ray of viscous, prismatic energy down onto Mikahl and showered him with the flesh-melting stuff. As if he were standing inside a globe of translucent blue glass, the flow of Pael's magic broke up into a purple swirl around the squire-king, leaving him unharmed.

Mikahl used the brief, unexpected shielding to touch Talon with the tip of Ironspike's blade. He listened for, then plucked out of the sword's magical symphony, the melody of healing, and let it flow into the bird. The surge of the song quickly exhausted itself, but Talon still lay there unmoving. The hawkling was dead, and that simple fact broke something inside Mikahl. Fighting back tears of rage, he clenched his teeth and spun on the demon-wizard.

Mikahl sent his own, now white-hot, ray of energy up at Pael. His blast met Pael's in a concussive showering spray of sparks and sizzling smoke. The point of contact between the two powerful channels of destructive force ground, hissed, and popped, but slowly edged toward Pael as Mikahl's rage forced it back. Slowly, ever so slowly, the point of contact kept inching closer to the dark wizard. Pael's ruined face twisted into panic as the radiance illuminated his shredded expression. The power of Shokin inside him so feared the magic of the blade that the demon flared his might, surging back at Mikahl like some cornered wildling fighting for its life.

The energy of the demon's fear began to pour from Pael and the brilliant, sizzling point of contact came racing back at Mikahl. Mikahl's rage slowed the coming collision of raw power, but there was no way he could stop it. With gritted teeth, clenched muscles, and his whole body as taut and rigid as a steel bar, he prepared for the agony that Pael's ray surely brought with it. It was all he could do.

Hyden Hawk opened his eyes in darkness. He was on rocky ground. He reached to his back to feel for the pack that held the Night Shard and panic shot through him like the crack of a whip. He didn't feel it there. It was gone.

He staggered to his feet and felt a humid, yet cool breeze on his skin. Above the heavy stench of old decay he smelled the earthy fragrance of dense vegetation. Instinctively, he sought out Talon's vision, but found nothing there. Nothing but more blackness.

His panic multiplied tenfold. He began to search the darkness with outstretched hands. Where was he? What was happening? What had happened to Talon? Finding nothing but the hard, rocky surfaces of the boulders and scree that surrounded him, he began to give in to his suddenly frantic emotion.

Seeing that he was close to stumbling out of one end of her wormhole cavern, Claret spoke to Hyden.

"I am here," she hissed.

Faint tendrils of flame briefly lit the area in front of the dragon's great red-plated head. A crystalline prism of deep, smoky blue presented itself in that instant as well. The Night Shard lay before the dragon's hunkered-down bulk in a smooth section of floor, which was covered with circular etchings of runes.

"I wants you to trust me, Hyden Hawks," the dragon hissed softly.

With her words came the brief glow of the flames that emitted from her cavernous nostrils. Hyden made his way toward her as she continued to speak.

"I haves no doubts that you intends to release me from the collars." Her voice was gravelly and ashen. "Never-the-lessss, I will haves it off, before I finish what you have started. You needs my fire to dissolve yon crystal. Removes the collars, and I will do the deed."

Hyden stopped in his tracks, and forced his fear and worry for Talon aside. It took him a few minutes to gain his wits back. He cautiously checked his wrist to make sure that the collar he'd stolen from Shaella was still there before he spoke.

"I could will you to do it, through the collar." His voice wasn't threatening, just matter-of-fact.

"Yesss, Hyden Hawk, you could." Her voice hissed and flames licked the air before her. "But if you do, then you'll never learns whether you cans trust me or not. You'll never knows my nature. I would value that bond of, what's the human words, friendships with one such as you."

"Aye," Hyden responded, choosing his words carefully. "I would value such a friendship as well. But if you tricked me in this, then I'm dooming my people to the fate of demon kind's will."

"It is no easy choice to trust a dragon." She chuckled, sending bright bursts of flame rolling out ahead of her. "I will hold no ill will toward you if you choose nots to do so."

She turned, so that both of her luminous amber eyes came to bear on him. He felt and smelled the hot, reeking heat of her breath on him.

"It will sadden my fiery heart though, to not be able to call you my friend."

Hyden thought about Vaegon's tale of Pratchert, of what Pratchert and the dragon might have spoken of at the Summer's Day monolith. He wondered what the great Dahg Mahn would do in this situation. He thought of the two young wolves, and how the simple act of saving the mother had come back to save him in the end. If his god's gift was to speak and interact with the animals, then in truth, there really was no choice to make. The feelings he'd felt when he'd seen the tapestry depicting the collared dragons came back to him. It wasn't a matter of trust. It was a matter of right and wrong.

"Turn your head, then," Hyden said.

His decision was made. When she was in position, he had her breathe enough light so that he could see the fastenings on the big, jeweled leather strap. It took some time for Hyden to figure out that opening the clasps was more of a mental exercise than a physical one. The buckles were linked to his collar magically. It took some effort, and some trial and error, but finally, he bent the clasps to his will. They came loose, and the heavy collar fell to the floor.

There was a sudden flurry of movement in the new darkness. Hyden was knocked to the floor. He became very tense and aware. He might have just made a horrible mistake. He turned this way and that, looking for some visual sign of his surroundings. Other than the two jagged holes that he knew were the openings into the cavern, nothing was discernible. He could only make out the holes because the night sky outside was just a few shades lighter than the pitch dark he was in now.

"Your brother stole my eggs!" Claret growled in a deep voice that was no longer contained.

It sounded as if thunder had somehow gained the ability to articulate words. Flames filled the air over Hyden's head, and he was suddenly very, very afraid.

"Your people enslaved me to guard this portal for countless years, and I was left to helplessly look upon my unhatched young, hope for a time when I might incubate them and wean them into freedom."

The cavern went black again as the dragon drew in a slow deep breath.

"I should roast you from your bones, Hyden Hawk Skyler," she said as her vast lungs filled to capacity. "As I am not my blood kin, and as their deeds and minds are not my own, I'll not holds you to blame for the actions of your blood kin." She paused, and her huge yellow eyes loomed down at him. "Always remember who your true friends are, Hyden Hawk," she commanded. "Now, step aside and shelter yourself, lest I roast you by mistake."

Before Queen Willa let herself be dragged back down into the castle, she yanked the silver-tipped Horn of Doon from her neck, and hurled it over the tower's edge. She cursed herself a fool for even entertaining the idea that the ages-old promise of the dwarves might be remembered, much less fulfilled, during this time of great need.

In the distance, the bright, colorful display of Mikahl's battle with Pael recaptured King Jarrek's attention enough that Willa wriggled free of his grasp. Both of them moved back toward the parapet to watch. From the air just above Mikahl, red streaks collided into a dome of blue and radiated flares of lavender and purple like some spectacular, flaming star. It was impossible to tell who was who or what was actually happening, but in the moments that followed, it became clearer.

Jarrek and Willa could see that Pael was hovering and attacking. Mikahl's shield was diverting the demon wizard's energy somewhat. Mikahl returned the attack with a white-hot beam of his own, and when the two forces met, an explosion of radiant light illuminated the area around the two combatants.

Anyone with the vantage of height could see them clearly now. They might as well have been battling under the midday sun. Mikahl's rage pushed forward, but was forced back by a surge of demon might and evil will. The bloody, prismatic beam of Pael's force swallowed up Mikahl's, and came up against the glassine dome of his blue shielding energy again, only this time, it shattered the protective globe into a shower of hurtling, glowing debris.

Pael's crimson ray didn't stop there: it consumed Mikahl.

After a bright cloud of sparkling white, smoke-like energy swirled up from where the squire-king had just stood, blackness and the sounds of the battle raging below on the castle's grounds wafted up and once again consumed the night. The light of hope Mikahl had represented had been extinguished, and King Jarrek had to catch Queen Willa before she fell to her knees in despair.

Mikahl felt the power of the demon's will shatter his magical shield. He felt his magical armor absorb as much of the power as it could, before it burned away in a white smoking cloud of sparks. Then he felt the demon wizard's ray upon his flesh and felt it bore into him to the very marrow of his bones, but only for an instant.

For that fleeting moment, he had felt the horror and pain of a million lifetimes, but that moment was over now. He heard the muffled, grunting cough of Pael landing in the rubble. He heard the dark wizard cry out in rage, pain, or some other powerful emotion, and when he opened his eyes, he saw Ironspike lying on the ground before him. When he reached to pick it up, his muscles felt wrong and stiff, and a tremendous pain tore through his body. He felt as if he had been cooked.

He remembered Loudin of the Reyhall, and the agonizing pain he must have felt as he clung to the blade, trying to save it from the hellcat. He remembered Vaegon's upper half lying among the rocks, and Grrr's valiant leap into the jaws of the Choska to save him. Knowing that the hoard of pain that he was feeling couldn't possibly equal the sacrifices that had been made for him, for this very moment, he gritted his teeth, lurched forward, and grabbed the leather-wrapped hilt of his father's sword.

At once, Ironspike's harmonic symphony filled Mikahl's ears again, and he was drowned in cool relief. His pain was quickly vanquished, and a rush of energy took its place. Gathering his wits, he found his feet, and surveyed the scene around him.

Not ten paces away, Pael was trying to get back to his feet. In the bright, blue glow of his blade, he could see Pael's good eye rolling around wildly in its socket. He could see the clenching and unclenching of the demon-wizard's jaw, and the way the veins stood out on his neck. Something was wrong with him. Pael seemed to be caught up in some inner struggle and was being tormented by it. Mikahl didn't hesitate to wonder why the pale-skinned demon wizard was in such a state. He just raised Ironspike and charged.

Pael, with Shokin's might behind him, reached through the power of Ironspike's defenses, reached into Mikahl's soul and started to blacken it, but something had happened. Shokin was yanked from him for a terrible, soul-wrenching moment.

Pael clung to the demon's power with all he had, but it slowly slipped from his grasp. Some power beyond reckoning was drawing Shokin away from him. Through the skittering of his good eye, he saw the boy coming for his flesh.

What to do? He latched onto the demon's essence and cast another destructive spell, but it wasn't to be. Icy blue steel bit into his neck. He saw bright, sapphire-shaded rubble, then the dark starlit sky. After a crazy whirl of darkness, his vision came to rest.

He saw the bloody, spurting stump of a body, clad in black robes trimmed in sparkling crimson tears and knew he was seeing his own headless corpse. What was worse than watching his life's blood pumping from his body while his brain slowly died, was that his soul still clung to the demon's essence, and the agony of it ripping free from his consciousness lingered until he finally faded away into nothingness.

Mikahl wasn't satisfied that Pael's egg-like head was sitting several feet away from his body. He judged where the wizard's heart should be, and fell to his knees as he drove Ironspike through it. Such was the force of his thrust, that the cross guard of the hilt slammed into Pael's back, as Ironspike pinned him to the earth.

A deep, thrumming vibration erupted from the ground there. Mikahl felt it, and let go of the sword. He rolled away, and crumbled to the earth naked, save for the tatters of his robe.

He expected Ironspike's power to quell when he let go of the hilt, but it hadn't. It vibrated and pulsed so deeply, that the earth trembled beneath him. Mikahl made to scoot away from the demon-wizard's body, and immediately felt the depths of his injuries. He had to fight to stay conscious, as the thunderous low end of Ironspike's symphony rumbled through the earth beneath him.

A golden column of light began to twist upward from the sword's hilt. The intensity of it grew and started to swirl its way up into the sky, like some giant corkscrew. The underside of a bank of clouds caught the illumination and parted so that the glowing shaft could pass beyond their pillowy mists.

Ghost-like forms of men, with haunted expressions on their stretched and twisted faces, came streaking by, making great whooshing sounds as they went. They were being drawn toward Ironspike's hilt, as if they were soapsuds spinning around a drain. Once they were sucked into the sword, they were sent spinning upward into the heavens. Four of them, five, and then ten. A score now. Thousands more. There were so many of them that the air shimmered around the skyward beam of light, a cyclone swirl of ghostly souls.

A great relief tried to wash over Mikahl's pain but couldn't quite manage the task. It was even painful for him to close his eyes, but he closed them anyway and, all at once, he slipped away into unconsciousness.

King Jarrek nearly dropped Queen Willa when he saw the shaft of golden light pierce the distant darkness and reach up into the very heavens. From the castle grounds below, he heard the cries and shouts of the soldiers who were defending the last bit of ground between the enemy and the people huddled in the palace.

"They're falling!" one yelled.

"The dead are dying," another added dubiously.

"It might be a trick! Where's the wizard?"

"It's no trick, look!"

Screams of joy and anguish, along with cries of pain and loss, rang out through the ranks of Blacksword soldiers. The angry shriek of a wyvern came howling out over it all as the beast shot out of the huge depiction opening overhead and sped away as quickly as it could. No longer bound by the demon-wizard's will, it had no reason to risk the proximity of so many humans. A few arrows trailed up after the dark-scaled creature, but none of them found its flesh.

King Jarrek let Queen Willa down to the rooftop as gently as he could manage, then ran to the parapet wall. As the undead soldiers fell, he saw a white, misty form shimmer up from each of them, like smoke. Then, as if caught up in the gusts of a magical wind, they were swept away toward the base of the swirling tower of light. Entire clouds of misty souls went tearing through the ruined city, on their way toward the sword's judgment. The sight was as breathtaking as it was unnerving.

The guard at the stair landing had come up out of his hiding place and stormed the roof, screaming, "The castle is clear! The dead are dying! The dead are—"

His voice stopped suddenly, and his face contorted into a look of sheer panic, when he saw Queen Willa lying there on the deck. He was overcome with relief when he knelt down beside her and saw her eyelids flutter open.

"The dead have died, Your Highness," he said softly. "The night is won! I–I–I'll call for a healer."

A sudden surging sound, similar to that of raindrops hitting a tin roof, drew everyone on the tower top's attention. Over the corpse of the Master Wizard Targon, a misty cloud formed and peeled away audibly before it shot away in a flash.

"Is it true?" Willa asked King Jarrek.

His front half was aglow with radiance from the golden light that held his attention fast.

"Aye, milady," he answered in that Western way without turning away from the scene before him.

His voice was full of awe and reverence but still tinged with deep sadness and regret.

"I hope that it's time for the kingdoms to unite again because without help, I'll never be able to free my people from the Dakaneese slavers. King Ra'Gren and that Westland wench cannot get away without paying for their part in this."

Mikahl felt something scratching on his stomach. He felt a slight ball of warmth nestle down there. It was soft, feathery soft. He didn't open his eyes, for he knew what it was. The soft cooing sound he could make out over the supernatural din transpiring around him, could only come from one source: Talon.

Ironspike had healed the bird after all, or maybe the hawkling had just been stunned. Either way, Mikahl found that he had never felt safer in all his life as he did right then. Lying half naked and weaponless on a death-strewn battlefield, there was no one else he would rather have watching over him.

Feeling safe and secure, it took only a fleeting moment for him to fade completely back into oblivion. There, his partially healed and newly traumatized body dragged him back down into the same comatose state that Vaegon had found him in when he had placed the replenished sword in his hands.

Chapter Fifty-Nine

The part of Shokin that escaped the Nethers wrenched itself free of Pael's body and went tearing across the land, toward the Seal.

No one saw it or heard its screams because it had no physical substance and could make no audible sound. It was there though, and clinging to it desperately was Pael's vile soul.

Over the farmlands of Middle Seaward, then across the rich, grazing plains of Valleya, the formless entities went. Over the edge of O'Dakahn, the Dakaneese cesspool city that was now overcrowded with Wildermont slaves, the demon essence and its ghost-like parasite continued on. Across the nearly deserted marshlands, where the Zard and other denizens of the swamp lived before Shaella led them into Westland, they passed. Flashing up into the Dragon's Tooth Spire, they flowed past Hyden Hawk and the dragon. Then they were pulled with rude force, down into the molten crystal that was coursing through the carved symbols that made up the Seal.

Pael's soul was rejected and left behind, but Shokin's essence was drawn to its other half with a violent intensity. Soon after it passed the barrier, the molten crystal corroded the symbols away completely. The power of the Seal was no more. The once smooth and polished face of it was left nothing but a pocked and indistinguishable ruin.

Pael's soul was not demon kind, nor was it substantial enough to even be considered evil anymore. In the world of demons, souls, and spirit essences, what was left of Pael would be considered more or less a gnat, or a pest. It tried to enter into the young man crouched against the pile of stones but could not. It started at the lazing dragon, but the great predator's heat warned it away. As the hissing puddle of liquefied stone finally began to cool, Pael's pesky spirit darted out of the dragon's lair and went searching for something familiar.

Gerard Skyler scratched at the sharp, bony protrusion that was growing out of his elbow. His other elbow had stopped itching a while ago. The dragon's yolk he had drunk to replenish his bloodless body had changed him, changed him from the marrow of his reforming bones, out to his thick-plated, slime-covered skin.

The darkness of the Nethers was so potent, he couldn't see himself. It was a blackness that the eyes could never adjust to, but Gerard didn't need or care to see what was happening to him. He was on a stairway that spiraled down, forever down, and getting to the bottom had become his passion. He drifted in and out of consciousness, sometimes waking in mid-step, sometimes curled in a shivering ball on a landing that bore no door. He always woke in that blackness, and when he did, he would start plodding downward again, as if his destiny lay at the bottom of the shaft.

Shaella spoke to him sometimes. Her soft voice soothed the pain of his twisting bones and hardening flesh. When she was in his head, the part of Shokin that Pael left behind would stop its endless screaming and babbling to listen. His boiling insides would cool, and his dizzy confusion seemed to organize itself into a relatively pleasant train of thought. When Shaella was with him, Gerard Skyler found a way through the swirling chaotic transformation of his mind and body. It was the only time that he wasn't hungry, afraid, and lusting manically to reach the bottom of the shaft.

When the other half of Shokin slammed into Gerard's elongated skull, his head filled with visions of chaotic destruction, of undead armies, and falling castles. Had the yolk he had eaten not hardened his mind and body so well, he might have died on the spot from pure shock. As it was, he relished the distraction from the emptiness around him. He somehow isolated the two halves of

Shokin in his brain, and he observed them curiously as they carried on a psychotic single-voiced argument that was as entertaining as it was disturbing.

The two halves of the once mighty demon eventually tried to rejoin, trying to become one again, but Gerard wouldn't let them. He would permit them to confer and conspire, but he would never let them become one.

Instinctually, he knew that if he did, he would lose any part of him that was still his. Somewhere in his mind, he knew he was still Gerard Skyler. He might be covered in spikes, hard bony platelets, and greasy slick skin. He might have nearly tripled his body mass and formed into some sort of monster, but he was still somewhat Gerard. His brain told him that, even though he was trapped on the seemingly endless stairway, he would find the power to lead legions once he reached the bottom.

The old crone told him so. Sometimes he heard her old cackling voice, cutting over the demon's chatter to remind him. He began to leech bits and nuggets of knowledge and power from the two halves of the demon and use them to his advantage. Already, he knew there were other ways out of this place. Part of Shokin had seen them described through Pael's eyes, in the texts the fool wizard had kept in his tower. It was Shaella's tower now, and since he could talk to her sometimes, ideas were already forming.

Gerard nearly stumbled and fell as the stairway abruptly ended on a smooth, hard surface. The floor was cool on his clawed feet and, all around him, he felt the presence of dark things. Some were alive and hungry, some were merely spirits, and some were just evil intentions. Everything else was prey.

As he stood there on the strange, level plain, he felt them cringe away and withdraw. They were afraid of him, of what he had become. He knew they had no reason to fear him. He was barely alive, so very weak, and hungry. He was glad they were cautious, because he needed to rest. As he settled, he felt something out there in the empty space, something darker and more intense than the other things. This form didn't know fear. It was a hunter searching for prey, but it moved away to chase after something else and left Gerard to his rest.

He sat on the bottom step and closed his eyes. The back of his lids were far brighter than the Nethers around him. He hoped Shaella would come to him soon. He loved her. He did his best to picture her in his mind and fell into a deep slumber, dreaming about her.

The dream was ruined when the two halves of Shokin suddenly stopped squabbling. When Gerard woke, he was famished. He needed sustenance. Oddly enough, it was part of Shokin who whispered to him where and how to safely feed.

Both parts of Shokin knew Gerard wouldn't survive this dark place unless he grew stronger, and if Gerard didn't survive, neither did they. They needed his consciousness because it was the only place they still existed. Even though they were back in the Nethers, Pael's powerful binding spell still coupled them to Gerard completely and thoroughly, for all eternity. After gathering that Gerard had access to the world of men through Shaella and the Spectral Orb, neither part of Shokin did anything other than scheme.

General Spyra himself rode out with an attachment of honor guard to retrieve Mikahl. They had to sit on their mounts patiently and wait until he stirred, before they could actually give him a hand. Talon wouldn't let them near him. The hawkling stood vigilant guard, with his chest swelled out proudly and a fierce look in his eyes. None of the men, or even the general, dared to test the bird.

It was well past dawn when Mikahl finally managed to sit up. Only then did Talon take to the air and wing his way back toward the castle. They wrapped Mikahl in a cloak of purple and gold and helped him to his sword, but once it was in his grasp, it charged away all of his pain.

With a bare foot placed squarely at the back of the stump where Pael's head had once rested, Mikahl pulled Ironspike out of the earth. The sword's comforting blue glow resonated and pulsed in time with the angelic symphony of its power. He held the blade up as they rode back through the scattering of soldiers who were piling up the rotting corpses to cart them out of the wasted city.

Some men cheered his passing. Others fell to the ground in supplication. A few even broke into tears and thanked the gods for sending Pavreal's heir to save them. Mikahl smiled at them, hoping to lift their spirits, but the expression was forced. There was far too much death and destruction around them for more than a glimmer of hope to reveal itself.

"A spark is all it takes to start a forest fire," General Spyra said, reading Mikahl's expression.

His words had been spoken clearly, but so softly that only Mikahl could hear them over the din.

"You must be that spark for the people who survived this. If you're patient, and help to lift Xwarda above all of this," he gestured at the ruin around them with a broad sweep of his arm, "then I swear by all the gods of heaven and earth, I'll do everything that is in my power to help you take back Westland when the time comes."

Mikahl gave the man a curt nod and stood high in his saddle, raising Ironspike up into the air. It was a small gesture, and one that served to bring another cheer from the soldiers in the streets.

Once the refugees returned from wherever they were holed up or hiding, Mikahl didn't think there would be much joy in this costly victory. The city had a putrid stench to it. He would have heaved and retched up bile had the sword's magic not been in him.

The wails and cries of wives and mothers would soon fill the air. The confusion of fatherless children and the despair of the grieving would permeate the area far worse than the rank smell of death that coated it now. He couldn't muster more than a forced smile, but he kept it in place and tried to carry himself as King Balton would have in the same situation.

When they passed through what was left of the castle gates, Mikahl saw the headless bulk of the Choska lying at the edge of the fountain lake, in front of the palace. He cringed, and wondered if Willa the Witch Queen would punish him for destroying her fountain display.

He had heard, through countless stories told around the hearth fires of his youth, that Willa was a horrible and mean old woman. She supposedly killed her father and mother to take the throne and lived for hundreds of years longer than any normal woman should have. She was said to feed her Blacksword soldiers the flesh of their enemies in a stew each year on Yule Day.

An elderly duchess once told Mikahl that Willa the Witch turned Duke Ramsis into a suckling pig, just for being rude. Mikahl didn't believe much of what he heard, but Duke Ramsis sure did resemble an old hog the last time he had seen him back at Lakeside Castle.

If the Queen of Highwander really was an old witch, Mikahl thought that she sure lived well. Even surrounded by ruin, the palace was spectacular; far nicer than the thatched roof huts the witches in the stories preferred. Still, he was nervous. Lord Gregory explained that Queen Willa wasn't all that different from King Balton. It was only rumor, distance, fear, and a few embellishing generations of exaggeration that had turned her into something so exotic and sinister. But the Lion Lord had added that most fables, no matter how absurd, contained a bit of truth to them. Mikahl had no idea what or whom to expect. He had been on the edge of death the last time he came into the palace. He only hoped he would find Hyden Hawk and the Great Wolves amongst the living.

The congregation of worn and weary, yet obviously noble-born folk, were gathered at the castle's entry steps. Talon soared by Mikahl and made a proud, screeching caw. What was that? Mikahl squinted to make sure he was seeing correctly. A bearded dwarf with breasts? He wasn't sure what the hairy thing beside her was. The only distinguishing feature he could discern, besides the hair and short stature, was a bulbous red hunk of flesh that might have been a nose poking through the tangle.

There was also a big man who stood out in his well worn, red-plated armor. Mikahl immediately recognized him as one of the Redwolf King of Wildermont's Elite Guard, but then true recognition struck him. It was King Jarrek himself.

Mikahl had stabled his horse once when he had come to Lakeside Castle for Prince Glendar's Coming of Age gala. The lady soldier from the forest, where Grrr had sacrificed himself, was wearing a crown. Mikahl felt himself begin to tremble and was glad he was sitting on a horse for his legs would have surely betrayed his nervousness.

The general brought the procession to a halt before the gathering. A steward ran out and took the reins of the horse the general had provided Mikahl. As much as he didn't want to, he was going to have to dismount.

From somewhere behind the main group, a staff rang out on the stone, in a sharp triplet of resounding thumps. Crack! Crack! Crack! Then an announcer stepped forward and shouted out his introduction.

"I present Pavreal's true heir, Mikahl Collum, the Slayer of Demons and Dark Wizards, the Wielder of Errion Spightre, the Blessed High King, come to unite the realm again."

The only thing more shocking to Mikahl than the sight of King Jarrek and the crowned woman, whom he could only assume was Queen Willa the Witch, all bowing to him, was the appearance of the little fluttering blue pixie, who was hovering in midair just over Queen Willa's head.

His state of disbelief only intensified when Talon shrieked fiercely, and swooped down out of the sky toward them. The little blue pixie panicked, and darted into the cleavage of Queen Willa's gown. A moment later, Talon landed gracefully atop the Choska's corpse, and a cheer erupted from all around them.

Mikahl smiled and searched for Hyden Hawk, while brandishing Ironspike in the air for the people who were spilling forth from the castle. He wished that he could find some real joy in the moment. Perhaps if Vaegon, Loudin, or Lord Gregory were here beside him, he might.

A thick tear welled up in his eye and rolled down his cheek. He needed to find Hyden, if only to remind himself that everything he cared about hadn't been lost while defeating Pael's evil. The fact that he still hadn't seen his friend caused the lump in his throat to swell to the size of a fist.

The memory of Vaegon's torn body came to him, and threatened to overwhelm him. Luckily, the not-so-wicked Willa the Witch Queen saw the emotions playing out on his face. With Starkle the Pixie dangling by his wings from her hand, she hooked her arm into Mikahl's and led him into the castle, away from the crowd.

Somewhere, out off the Seaward coast, the insubstantial spirit of the wizard Pael found Inkling still bound to Glendar's submerged body. Starfish, crabs, and dozens of other mollusks, along with a few suckerfish, were cleaning the flesh from Glendar's bones. Soon, only a skeleton would remain; a skeleton that was cursed to live on, hundreds of leagues down, at the bottom of the ocean.

The pecking order of the three entities who inhabited Glendar's skeletal host was quickly established. Glendar, ever weak-willed and foolish, was pushed to the side, while Pael and his familiar wrestled for control of the skeleton's motor functions. Ironically, Inkling won the battle, and once the sea floor scavengers were shaken off, he started off in the direction he hoped was north.

He wasn't concerned that he might be going the wrong way, with all of eternity to walk the ocean floor. He knew that as long as they moved in the same direction, sooner or later, they would wander up out of the depths, back into the light of day.

He would use all that time to ponder what he would do when he got there. In the meanwhile, Pael feebly plotted on how he could take back control of Glendar's will from Inkling. Neither of them seemed to notice the long parade of other skeletons who were following them through the sea.

Lazing in the afternoon sun, with his feet dangling out over the open air of the marshlands, Hyden sat in the mouth of the Dragon Tooth Spire's wormhole.

Not three feet away from him lay the old snapper bone his little brother had used to keep his rope off of the abrasive floor while he lowered out one of the dragon's eggs.

The dragon was telling him a story, a long and exciting tale, about a great blue drake and a silver skull, that might be able to help him go into the Nethers to retrieve the ring Gerard had worn when he escaped the dark wizard and fled there.

The dragon in the story had breath that was more like liquid lightning than fire and was so big that it had been able to snatch the ship of an infamous pirate named Barnacle Bones, right up out of the water. Hyden was captivated by the dragon's words. He loved a good story and Claret was by far the best storyteller he had ever come across. The dragon was even better than Berda, though he would never tell Berda that.

In his hand, he toyed with a crystallized, tear-shaped jewel that had fallen from the dragon's huge eye when she had spoken of the hopes she held for all three of her unhatched babies. The thumb-sized crystal had started out like any other tear, but by the time it hit the floor, it had hardened into a diamond-like substance. Claret told him that he could call her through the jewel if he ever had need of her, and that it would act as a charm of protection if he kept it with him throughout his travels.

He told her he would make a medallion out of it and wear it always, not as a form of protection, but as reminder of the friendship that the two of them had formed. Claret loved the notion and let out a deep, affectionate rumble that was far more potent than, yet strangely similar to, a kitten's purr.

Hyden told her about his brother and the old crone from the Summer's Day Festival. She listened on as he continued to explain the White Goddess of his people, and how she had told him he would have to eventually go down into the depths of the Nethers to retrieve the ring his brother had taken there. Claret told him then that fortunes and prophecy were not always set in stone, no matter how much we all wanted to believe them. And the ones that do come to pass, never do so in the manner expected.

"For instance," she hissed softly. "I once foretold a prophecy about the sword, called Errion Spightre and Pavreal's bloodline. I made it so that sooner or later, the folly of man would set into motion a chain of events that would undo the Pact that I had been forced to swear to. I only had my unhatched eggs in mind when I did this."

She paused and yawned out a soft, roiling cloud around her curled tongue.

"Here I am, set free," she continued. "but what I prophesied hasn't come to pass. The youngest son of Pavreal's line didn't take up the blade in place of the true king, to save the land from the legions of dark."

She turned a huge yellow eye on Hyden and studied him closely.

"I believe that your goddess is correct, Hyden Hawk. That strange ring is on the finger of the wrong man. Only when it is in the right place will the nature of prophecy be restored so that what must come to pass can happen. I'm sorry you are caught up in all of this. Thus the nature of prophecy is proven to be faulty. For if you retrieve the ring, then what I portended might come to pass. A greater evil than the demon-wizard Pael might come. And worse, one whom I consider to be a friend will be forced to battle that evil. All I ever wanted was to keep my hatchlings from being mastered. Now only one of them is left."

"My father once told me to be careful of what I wish for because I just might get it," Hyden spoke kindly.

"Jussst so." Claret agreed with a nod of her big, horned head.

She then started back into the story about the huge blue dragon named Cobalt, and the pirate who had stolen his hoard. The reason she told that particular story wasn't lost on Hyden. The silver skull, which the pirate had stashed in the hold of his ship, could be used to cross between the earthly plane and darker places, like the Nethers.

Hyden listened intently and the troubles of his heart and mind were soon lost to the excitement of the clever pirate's many ways of eluding the dragon and the kingdom ships that were endlessly after him, and of the dragon's dogged persistence in retrieving his treasures.

When the telling was done, Hyden grew excited and sad in equal measure. He couldn't wait to get back to tell Vaegon and Mikahl about Claret. The bond between him and the hawkling was stretched so thin that it almost hurt. He was sad, though, because he would miss Claret. The dragon was a powerful force to be close to. Next to her, he felt safe and indestructible. He would miss her, there was no doubt.

There was still the great flight back to Xwarda though, and since there wasn't any hurry, Hyden hoped he could get another story or two out of her. He knew she would leave this part of the world and go far away to hatch her remaining egg. He didn't blame her for it. He was starting to see how even the most civilized of humans were barbaric in nature. If he were her, he would get as far away from mankind as the limits of the world would allow. She had promised to come if he called her. That would have to be enough.

The sky was cloudy and a light, chilly drizzle was falling on Xwarda when the terrified cries of "Dragon! Dragon in the sky!" rang through the streets.

Word spread through the castle like a plague, and Mikahl wasted no time joining Queen Willa and King Jarrek on the long climb up the spiral stairs to the top of the Royal Tower.

Mikahl hadn't taken the time to grab Ironspike, and was the worse for it by the time he reached the top.

Dugak was watching over the blade for him. Mikahl's injuries were far from healed and, without the sword to fortify him, his breath came in ragged, noisy gasps, and his muscles burned and ached. His spirit was lifted above his pain, though, by the prospect of seeing Hyden Hawk again.

By the time Mikahl reached the rooftop, Claret had gone, but Hyden Hawk was there to greet him with an overwhelmingly fierce hug.

As they embraced, Talon fluttered around them excitedly. When they stepped apart, Hyden noticed that the elf wasn't there. He took Mikahl by the shoulders and was crushed by the sadness he saw in his friend's eyes.

"What of Vaegon?" Hyden Hawk's words came out in a fog of breath.

The icy rain had slackened but there was no summer sun left in the sky to burn away the clouds or to warm the chill air. Fall was beginning to set in, and winter was close on its heels.

"He died fighting alongside the men on the wall." Queen Willa spoke softly from her huddle of cloaks, saving Mikahl from having to speak the words.

"His body is in a casket in the Preserver's Hall," added Mikahl with a sniffle. "I want us to take him home together."

"Aye." Hyden brushed away his own tears and extended a wrist so that Talon could land. "What of the demon-wizard? Did you take him?"

"Aye," Mikahl answered. He sniffled again, and this time, he didn't bother to wipe away the tears streaming down his cheeks. "His head is rotting in its very own dungeon cell. His body is in a separate one. What of the wench who invaded my father's kingdom?"

It was a hard thing to do what Hyden Hawk did then, but his friend deserved nothing less than the truth of the matter. He explained what he did, and why he did it as well. Mikahl didn't like it, but he tried to understand Hyden's perspective. It made him think about his own brother.

"I wonder what happened to Prince Glendar?" he asked, letting Hyden off the hook. As they made their way down the stairs and out of the weather, King Jarrek came up with several clever possibilities that could have been Glendar's fate.

The sadness over the loss of life and the uncertainty of the future hung heavily in the air over the group, but before they even reached the bottom of the long stairway, Jarrek suggested a course of action that appealed to Mikahl. Queen Willa added the beginnings of a scheme of her own, to gain the aid of Queen Rachel, and possibly cowardly King Broderick. A lot had been lost and destroyed by Pael's dark ambition, but hope, it seemed, was still abundant.

The people of Wildermont were still being held as slaves in Dakahn, but now there was hope for them. The dragon-less Dragon Queen's lizard men and Breed beasts still occupied Westland, as well. There was a lot to be done. A tentative plan was formed, but only so much could be done before winter set in. Amazingly, not a single one of them wasted more than a moment before they started getting to it.

Epilogue

The returning of Vaegon to his people in the Evermore Forest went badly.

The long, four-day trek from Xwarda, deep into the woods, had been ripe with the hope of the elves coming to the aid of the decimated human populations. The craftsmanship and skill of the elven builders and artisans had once helped raise the great city from the Wardstone foundation below. Side by side, elves, dwarves and men had created the wonder that was Xwarda. The hope that the elves would come to their aid was spurred on by words Vaegon had written in his journal. High King Mikahl read them to the people of Xwarda at a ceremony before the trip to the Evermore began.

The elf had praised the ways of the men he had befriended and appealed to his own people to try and rebuild the bridge that spanned the gulf between the two races. The elves of the Evermore, however, had no desire to even acknowledge the fact that the humans had come back to their forest. It didn't matter to them that Vaegon Willowbrow had given his life to thwart Pael's evil. Nor did it matter that his remains, or what was left of them, were in the casket that the humans had borne.

For seven days, Mikahl and Hyden sat in the forest with the casket. Hyden could see the elves around them. Looking through Talon's eyes, his sight was akin to elven vision, and it allowed him to see them moving like wraiths through the forest. They didn't want to be seen, though. After Mikahl learned that the elves knew they were there, he sent the escort of honor guard who had carried Vaegon's body, back to Xwarda. His hope was that the elves were not showing themselves because of all the people.

That had been on the second day. Now, five days later, the elves still watched them from a distance. Talon flew among them, getting their attention, so that Mikahl, or Hyden, could call out to them and explain why they were there. They shouted out that Vaegon had died a hero, fighting to save the world from demon kind. They explained that the elf had often spoken of his love for his people in this forest. Mikahl eventually called them all cowards for not having the fortitude to show themselves.

Finally, Dieter Willowbrow, Vaegon's younger brother, responded from the trees.

"Leave this place, and leave my brother when you go!" his voice was thick with emotion. He was torn between his love for his brother, and his duty to his stubborn and closed-minded Elders.

"We won't leave until we know that our friend's body is in the hands of those who would honor him," Mikahl responded angrily.

"Dieter!" Hyden Hawk called out. "Vaegon asked me once to give you his journal if anything happened to him. I'll not leave until it's in your hands."

To emphasize his power of will, Talon fluttered down in front of Dieter's face, and cawed out loudly. This display scared the elves a little bit, and for another day nothing happened. Finally, Mikahl, who had the fate of several kingdoms weighing down on his shoulders, had enough.

Ironspike came free of its sheath. Its blade was stark and blinding white with Mikahl's rage. The elves were so taken aback by the sight that some of them forgot their stealth and gasped with awe and surprise. Mikahl let out a primal scream of rage, then went about cleaving tree after ancient tree, in a great circle around where Vaegon's coffin lay. The big oaks and elms fell away from the circle and came crashing down around the elves hiding in the surrounding woods.

Finally, Dieter showed himself. He strode out of the wreckage, with tears streaming down his face. He kept his wild, yellow eyes cast downward in shame. This was not only for himself, but for his people as well. All around the place, which would come to be known as Vaegon's Glade, the rest of the angry elves cried outrage and sacrilege over what Mikahl had done to the trees.

Mikahl stalked a circle around Vaegon's casket and glared at them, daring them to challenge him.

Hyden knew that elves rarely cried. His heart went out to Dieter, because it was obvious he was being tormented with conflicting emotion. He knew what it was like to lose a brother.

"Vaegon was twice the man any of you will ever be!" Mikahl yelled through clenched teeth. "He thought of more than himself, of more than his own kind. He knew the strength of the evil we faced, and he stared it in the eyes. He didn't cower in the woods. He didn't run or hide from it! He stood tall and proud! You shame your race with your cowardice, with your haughty lack of concern for those other than yourselves."

Mikahl spat at the smoldering trunk of one of the trees he felled.

"There will come a day when your people will need the aid of men. You'd better hope that it is I who rule when that day comes, because I won't run from your need. Because of Vaegon alone, if that time ever comes, I will rally men to stand beside you, even though you are no better than gutter curs. Now, come, gather the body of the best of your kind before I cut this whole forest to the ground!"

Hyden gave Dieter the journal, and then went to Mikahl's side. It was all he could do to drag Mikahl away from Vaegon's coffin. Neither of them seemed to care about the dozens of arrows that were trained on them as they left the newly formed clearing. Both were angry and saddened by the way things had gone. It was a long while before either of them dammed the flow of tears. When they stopped to rest, Hyden sought out Talon's vision again, and was pleased to find the hawkling vigilantly watching over the elves as they dug a human-style grave for Vaegon, with more than a little fear showing in their feral eyes.

When they got back to Xwarda, Hyden decided he would ask Queen Willa to assign him a tutor. He was determined to learn how to read. He had to research the history of piracy and try to ferret out where the dragon called Cobalt had taken Barnacle Bones's ship after he snatched it out of the ocean.

He knew High King Mikahl would have his hands full all winter, training the troops he and King Jarrek had specially chosen for the campaign they were planning to carry out in the spring. Hyden couldn't help much there, save for giving the archers advice. He would spend his spare time helping the people of Xwarda and the rest of Highwander rebuild. Pael's undead army had left a trail of decimation across the entire realm.

When the burial of Vaegon was completed, Talon rejoined Hyden and Mikahl. The long walk back to the city was filled with hope and sadness, but by the time Xwarda's golden-topped towers were in sight, both of the young men had found the steely reserve they would need to face what was ahead of them.

Talon felt none of those emotions. The exhilaration of flight, of soaring overhead on the thermals that cut through the cool, fall air was far more interesting than yesterdays or tomorrows. The hawkling did have a job to do, though, but his was easy. All Talon had to do was keep his friends looking up.

The End of Book One

Kings, Queens, Heroes, and Fools - The Wardstone Trilogy-Book II covers Hyden Hawk's adventurous quest for the Silver Skull of Zorellin; Mikahl's dutiful, yet rewarding, romance with the beautiful young Princess of Seaward; and the attempted retaking of Westland from Shaella and her lizard-man troops. Shaella finds another dragon in this episode: a young, black-scaled drake, and with it, and her father's spell books, she kidnaps Mikahl's betrothed and proves to be a formidable foe.

The Wizard and the Warlord - The Wardstone Trilogy-Book III brings the elves, dwarves, giants, and the dragons into the story again, as our heroes, led by High King Mikahl and the great wizard Hyden Hawk, are forced to fight for the fate of the Kingdoms. This time, they do so against the horrid creature Gerard Skyler has become, and the powerful legions of demon-beasts that he has come to command.

M. R. Mathias

About the Author

There are few writers in the genre of fantasy that can equal the creative mind of M.R. Mathias – now acknowledged as a master in this genre of dragons and dwarves, and magic, and spells, and all aspects of fantasy. — Top 100, Hall of Fame, Vine Voice, Book Reviewer, Grady Harp

M. R. Mathias is the multiple award winning author of the huge, #1 Bestselling, epic, The Wardstone Trilogy, as well as the #1 Bestselling Dragoneer Saga, the #1 Bestselling The Legend of Vanx Malic fantasy adventure series, and the #1 Bestselling Crimzon & Clover Short Short Series.

Visit www.mrmathias.com or use these series hashtags on twitter to find maps, cover art, sales, giveaways, book reviews, upcoming releases, and contest information:

#Wardstone – #DragoneerSaga – #VanxMalic – #MRMathias

CPSIA information can be obtained
at www.ICGtesting.com
Printed in the USA
LVOW09*0516311016
510969LV00010B/80/P

9 781946 187086